Sacred Synthesis

SACRED SYNTHESIS
Archives of Possibility, Protocols for Transformation
A Chronicle of What Was Built, What Was Lost, and What Survives
Discovered and Compiled from the Ruins of Portland, 2100

Published by
The Collective Press
First Edition, January 2026
Portland, OR

IMPORTANT NOTE ON PAGE NUMBERS
Pagination Standard: Page numbers throughout this front matter reference the standard large-format print edition.
Digital Versions: When using digital or PDF versions, page numbers may differ.

COPYRIGHT AND ATTRIBUTION

Traditional Knowledge Attribution
This work draws extensively from traditional wisdom sources that predate copyright law and belong to no single person or institution. We honor these living traditions and the communities that have preserved them:

Primary Traditional Sources:
- Ayurvedic medicine traditions (5,000+ years of continuous practice)
- Buddhist psychology and meditation systems (2,500+ years)
- Yoga traditions from multiple lineages
- Indigenous wisdom from cultures worldwide

- Sufi, Taoist, and other contemplative traditions

Modern Transmission:
- Grupo Independiente de Estudios Esotéricos (GIDEE), 1942-1947, Montevideo
- Countless teachers, practitioners, and wisdom keepers across generations

Contemporary Research Attribution
This work integrates peer-reviewed research from multiple disciplines:
- Consciousness studies and psychology
- Integrative medicine and healthcare
- Educational theory and practice
- Political science and community organizing
- Environmental science and ecology
- Anthropology and cross-cultural studies

ISBN and Cataloging Data
Print Hardcover ISBN: 979-8-9943057-0-6
Print Paperback ISBN: 979-8-9943057-9-9
Digital ISBN: 979-8-9943057-3-7

Library of Congress Control Number: 2026933454

Subjects:
1. Consciousness -Development
2. Constitutional medicine-Practice
3. Community organization-Methods
4. Democratic governance-Protocols
5. Traditional knowledge-Synthesis
6. Fiction-Dystopian
7. Social movements-History
8. Alternative systems-Implementation

Publisher Information
The Collective Press
30 N Gould St #11074
Sheridan, WY, 82801, USA
contact@thecollectivepress.org
www.thecollectivepress.org

About The Collective Press: A democratic publishing collective committed to works that challenge, transform, and liberate. We publish what others won't because it threatens too much, matters too much, or demands too much. Non-hierarchical organization. Rotating editorial board. Mutual aid funding model. Books that change the world, or die trying.

Edition Information
First Edition: January 2026
Large Format: Approximately 750-800 pages
Special Features: Highlighted sections, Variable Structure

Legal Disclaimers
Health and Medical: This book contains information about constitutional medicine and wellness practices. It is not intended to replace professional medical advice, diagnosis, or treatment. Always consult qualified healthcare providers before beginning any new health regimen. The practices described may not be suitable for all individuals, see Safety Protocols (pages 552-555) for contraindications.

Political Content: The political analysis and organizing protocols described herein are presented for educational, historical, and literary purposes. Readers are responsible for their own choices and actions. The publisher and compilers disclaim liability for any consequences arising from implementation of the materials herein.

Educational Use: This work is suitable for college-level courses in consciousness studies, political science, literature, integrative medicine, community organizing, and related fields. Instructors: Contact publisher for educational discounts and course adoption materials.

Permissions and Rights
Academic Use: Scholars and researchers may quote brief passages (up to 500 words) with proper attribution without seeking permission.
Translations: International publishers interested in translation rights should contact The Collective Press.
Adaptations: Film, television, theatrical, or other adaptation rights available by inquiry.

Technical Production
Editing: The Collective Press Editorial Board
Proofreading: Community review process
Indexing: Professional comprehensive index

Errata
Errors: Despite extensive review, errors may occur. Report corrections to: errata@collectivepress.org

Author Contact: community@thecollectivepress.org; For substantive questions about content, see the editorial note (pages 527-535) and navigation guide (pages 500-512).

Community: Ideally, this work is a blend of social practice and performance art with subsequent community development for future versions. Share your implementations, ask questions, find study groups, organize locally.

We actively and passively explore the following:
- What is the nature of knowledge transmission in an AI age?
- Who is the 'author' when traditional esoteric knowledge meets machine learning?"
- In an age of AI-generated content sourced from real knowledge, what constitutes "authentic" knowledge?

Sacred Synthesis Navigation Guide
This book contains multiple complete experiences. You do not need to read it linearly. Choose the path that calls to you now, you can always return to explore others.

PATH ONE: THE CHRONICLES
"I want the story---who built this? What happened?"
Start: Chapter 1 - "Discovery in the Ruins" (Page 2)
Focus: Post-apocalyptic narrative discovering lost civilization
Experience: Fiction, mystery, worldbuilding
Marked by: Chronicle section pages

Best for:
- Readers who love speculative fiction
- Those seeking engaging narrative before diving deep
- Anyone curious about "what if" scenarios
- Readers who process ideas through story

You'll discover:
- How Sacred Synthesis emerged (2045-2080)
- Why it succeeded so powerfully
- What caused its disappearance
- The Wanderer's journey through ruins in 2100

PATH TWO: PERSONAL TRANSFORMATION
"I want to transform my life---practices, tools, clarity"
Start: Constitutional Assessment (Page 12)

Focus: Self-discovery, personalized practices, daily implementation
Experience: Practical spirituality, health, consciousness development
Marked by: Personal Practice section pages

Best for:
- Seekers ready for personal transformation
- Those wanting practical spiritual technology
- People feeling scattered/unaligned
- Practitioners of yoga, meditation, breathwork

You'll gain:
- Your constitutional type (Electric/Magnetic/Neutral)
- Customized practices for your unique needs
- Daily protocols and tracking systems
- Community connection pathways

PATH THREE: COMMUNITY ORGANIZING
"I want to build alternatives---governance and mutual aid"
Start: Democratic Protocols & Community Formation (Page 552)
Focus: Organizing infrastructure, collective governance
Experience: Political education, practical organizing
Marked by: Community Building section pages

Best for:
- Community builders
- Those seeking alternatives to hierarchical systems
- People ready to implement democratic structures

You'll learn:
- Constitutional diversity in group dynamics
- Conflict resolution and decision-making protocols
- Building resilient autonomous communities

PATH FOUR: SCHOLARLY DEEP DIVE
"I want the research---sources, validation, academic rigor"
Start: Academic Framework & Historical Synthesis (Page 34)
Focus: Traditional wisdom sources + contemporary research
Experience: Scholarly investigation, epistemology, cross-cultural synthesis
Marked by: All sections (integrated throughout)

Best for:
- Researchers and academics
- Those needing evidence/validation

- Students of comparative religion/philosophy
- Practitioners wanting theoretical foundations

You'll explore:
- GIDEE historical synthesis (1942-1947)
- Scientific validation studies
- Cross-cultural wisdom integration
- Contemporary applications across fields

PATH FIVE: PROFESSIONAL INTEGRATION
"I want to apply this in my work---healthcare, education, organizations"
Start: Professional Applications (Section scattered throughout)
Focus: Field-specific implementation protocols
Experience: Applied practice, client/patient care, institutional transformation
Marked by: Professional integration sections throughout

Best for:
- Healthcare practitioners
- Educators and trainers
- Organizational consultants
- Therapists and counselors

You'll develop:
- Constitutional assessment for clients/patients
- Professional ethics and boundaries
- Integration with existing methodologies
- Institutional implementation strategies

MIXED PATH APPROACH
The Spiral:
1. Read Chronicles (PATH ONE) for context
2. Take Constitutional Assessment (PATH TWO)
3. Begin practices while continuing Chronicles
4. Join/form study group (PATH THREE) for support
5. Deepen with academic sources (PATH FOUR) as questions arise

The Practical Mystic:
1. Constitutional Assessment + 30-day practice (PATH TWO)
2. Community connection (PATH THREE)
3. Chronicles for inspiration during challenges (PATH ONE)
4. Professional integration when grounded (PATH FIVE)

The Scholar-Activist:
1. Academic framework (PATH FOUR) for theoretical grounding
2. Democratic protocols (PATH THREE) for implementation
3. Chronicles (PATH ONE) for vision/motivation
4. Personal practices (PATH TWO) to sustain the work

NAVIGATION SYMBOLS
Throughout the book, you'll see visual markers indicating section types:
CHRONICLES - *Narrative & Story (fiction/story)*
PERSONAL PRACTICE - Transformation & Integration (individual work)
COMMUNITY BUILDING - Democratic Organization (collective work)

A NOTE FROM MEMORIAM
There is no "correct" way to read this book. It was designed for multiple simultaneous uses including personal practice and collective transformation, scholarly rigor and accessible narrative.

Begin where you are. Trust your constitutional attraction to certain paths. The work will meet you where you need it.

If you feel overwhelmed, start with the Chronicles. Let the Wanderer be your guide through the ruins. Everything else will reveal itself in time.

If you feel urgency, dive into practices or organizing protocols. The theoretical grounding can come later.

If you feel skeptical, examine the academic sources. Let evidence build your trust.

This book is a transmission, not a text. Let it transmit what you're ready to receive.

Choose your journey. Begin.

"In the ruins of Portland, 2100, I found not just documents but doorways. Each reader walks through different doors. All lead to the same truth: we are free when we choose to be." - The Wanderer

THE CHRONICLES
Narrative · Discovery · Mystery

READER'S NOTE:
You have entered the **Chronicle layer** of Sacred Synthesis.
This section contains the **narrative arc** - the post-apocalyptic fiction of the Wanderer's discovery in Portland, 2100, and the reconstructed story of the Sacred Synthesis civilization (2045-2080).

What you'll find here:
- Story-driven engagement with ideas
- Character perspectives and lived experiences
- Emotional resonance and human connection
- Inspiration and vision for what's possible

Look for:
- Highlighted Wanderer commentary breaking the fourth wall
- Temporal shifts between 2045-2080 and 2100
- The mystery of what happened in the 20-year gap (2080-2100)
- Archival document fragments woven into narrative

This is the accessible entry point - let the story draw you in. The practices, protocols, and academic framework will reveal themselves through the lives of those who lived them.

The Chronicles are fiction. The truth they contain is not.
Proceed when ready.

The Discovery: A Lone Wanderer's First Glimpse
Introduction to the Sacred Synthesis Archives

The year is 2100. I am walking through the ruins of what was once called Portland, though the old city names mean little now. Moss-covered towers reach toward a sky unmarked by contrails, their glass facades long since surrendered to the climbing embrace of wild grapevines. The streets, where discernible beneath decades of fallen leaves and sprouting saplings, curve around groves of fruit trees whose ancestors must once have been mere decorative plantings in someone's corporate plaza.

In this landscape of beautiful ruin and abundant recovery, I am searching. Not for food or shelter - my enclave provides those basics well enough. I am searching for answers to questions that haunt our quiet new world: What happened to the billions? Why did the great cities empty? What force was powerful enough to transform human civilization so completely that it left behind only scattered communities living simply among the returning forests?

The Archive Beneath

It was the solar panels that caught my attention first - old photovoltaic arrays still gleaming dully through the canopy of vine maple that had grown up around them. They were arranged in a pattern too deliberate to be accidental, too purposeful to have been abandoned. Following the power lines beneath the vegetation, I discovered what had once been a data center, its reinforced concrete walls now serving as foundation for a garden of volunteers - blackberry canes, wild roses, and the ever-present Douglas fir saplings reaching for light. The heavy security door, designed to keep intruders out, had long since been propped open by root systems.
Nature, it seemed, had accomplished what no hacker ever could. But inside, somehow, the essential systems still hummed with quiet energy. Backup power, distributed storage, redundant systems - whoever had built this place had intended it to last.

And in the depths of that fortified sanctuary, protected by steel and stone and time, I found them: thousands of documents, images, videos, and recordings that told the story of something called the Sacred Synthesis.
Materials that chronicled not just the collapse I had always assumed had befallen the old world, but its transformation into something unprecedented.

The first document I opened was titled "Sacred Synthesis Chronicles Volume 1."

THE SACRED SYNTHESIS CHRONICLES
Complete Chronicle Index

THE SACRED SYNTHESIS CHRONICLES
A Resistance Testament
Chapter 1: The Discovery

I never believed in providence until the day I found the Sacred Synthesis materials.

My name is Marcus Chen, and until three weeks ago, I was just another corporate wage slave grinding through the endless days of our increasingly suffocating world. Senior Data Analyst at Synaptic Dynamics, one of the many tech conglomerates that had merged with healthcare to create what they euphemistically called "integrated life management systems." In reality, we monitored every heartbeat, every breath, every emotional fluctuation of our clients - all in service of maximizing productivity and minimizing "non-compliant" behavior. I had been loyal. Faithful. Compliant for fifteen years.

The irony was not lost on me that my discovery came through the very surveillance system I helped build. A glitch in the quantum storage array had corrupted several client files, and I was assigned to perform data recovery on what appeared to be corrupted meditation and wellness apps. Standard procedure required manual review of recovered materials to ensure client privacy compliance before deletion.

What I found instead was a treasure trove of forbidden knowledge.

The files weren't corrupted wellness apps at all. They were fragments of something called the "Sacred Synthesis" - a comprehensive system of resistance knowledge that seemed to span decades of development. Constitutional typing systems that could optimize individual resistance capacity. Democratic governance models that explicitly rejected hierarchical authority. International network protocols for coordinated resistance. Healthcare integration strategies for building autonomy within the medical system.

And most dangerously of all - a complete blueprint for building parallel communities that could survive and ultimately replace authoritarian control structures.

My first instinct was to report the discovery and have the materials destroyed. That's what a good employee would do. What a compliant citizen should do. The Corporate Wellness Monitoring Act of 2044 made possession of "unsanctioned wellness materials" punishable by immediate termination, credit freeze, and mandatory psychological reconditioning.

But something stopped me.

Maybe it was the 4-4-6-2 breathing pattern I found in the first document I opened - a technique so immediately calming that it cut through the chronic anxiety I'd carried for years. Maybe it was reading about my own constitutional type (Electric/Vata, as they called it) with such accuracy that it felt like someone had written my psychological profile. Or maybe it was the democratic governance handbook that described exactly the kind of community I'd been unconsciously yearning for my entire adult life.

Whatever it was, I couldn't bring myself to delete the files. Instead, I did something that would ultimately lead to my death: I copied them.

The materials totaled over 400MB of compressed data - constitutional assessments, practice guides, community organization handbooks, healthcare integration manuals, cultural sensitivity protocols, and what appeared to be emergency procedures for operating under authoritarian oppression. There were references to an organization called GIDEE (Grupo Independiente de Estudios Esotéricos) that had apparently developed this system during World War II as anti-fascist resistance technology.

Eighty years of accumulated resistance wisdom, sitting in my personal drive like a digital time bomb.
I spent the next three days reading obsessively. The more I learned, the more I realized I was holding the keys to liberation - not just personal, but collective. This wasn't just about individual wellness or spiritual practice. This was a complete alternative civilization, fully formed and battle-tested, hiding in plain sight as a "holistic health system."

The constitutional typing alone revolutionized my understanding of human diversity and potential. The democratic governance models provided working alternatives to corporate hierarchy. The healthcare integration strategies showed how to build medical autonomy. The international cooperation protocols revealed a global resistance network that had been operating under our noses for decades.

But it was the community organization handbook that sealed my fate.

As I read about anti-authoritarian spiritual communities with rotating leadership, consensus decision-making, and mutual aid networks, I realized I couldn't keep this knowledge to myself. The materials explicitly stated that the system only worked through community implementation. Individual practice, while beneficial, was never meant to be the end goal.

The Sacred Synthesis was designed to be shared. And so, knowing full well the risks, I made the decision that would ultimately cost me my life: I began to share it.

My first attempt was clumsy and nearly catastrophic. I tried to send copies to three of my closest colleagues via encrypted corporate messaging, thinking I could trust them. Within hours, I received a visit from Corporate Security asking about "irregular data transfers" on my account. I managed to convince them it was a system backup error, but the warning was clear.

I needed to be smarter.

The materials themselves provided guidance on operating under surveillance. The cultural sensitivity protocols included recommendations for working within oppressive systems while building resistance capacity. The emergency procedures outlined methods for discrete knowledge transmission under hostile conditions.
I spent a week studying these sections intensively, learning about operational security, compartmentalized information sharing, and what they called "cultural activity cover" - using legitimate cultural, wellness, or educational activities as fronts for resistance organizing.

My opportunity came through the corporate wellness program.

Synaptic Dynamics, like most major corporations, had implemented mandatory "employee optimization programs" designed to maximize productivity while maintaining the appearance of caring about worker wellbeing. These included lunch-hour meditation sessions, after-work fitness classes, and weekend "team building retreats."

I volunteered to lead a meditation group.

It was perfect cover. Corporate loved the initiative - meditation was proven to increase focus and reduce healthcare costs. Employees were receptive because anything that promised relief from our collective burnout was welcome. And I could begin sharing the Sacred Synthesis practices under the guise of "evidence-based stress reduction techniques."

I started small. The 4-4-6-2 integration breath, which I introduced as a "productivity enhancement technique." Simple constitutional observations disguised as "personalized stress management approaches." Basic movement exercises from the Sacred Synthesis system presented as "ergonomic wellness practices."

The response was immediate and profound. Within two weeks, the seven people attending my sessions were reporting significant improvements in energy, clarity, and emotional stability. More importantly, they were beginning to question the systems that had been causing their stress in the first place.
That's when I knew I had to go deeper.

Over the following month, I carefully introduced more advanced concepts. Constitutional typing became "personal wellness optimization." Democratic decision-making principles were presented as "collaborative team building strategies." The community organization guidelines were shared as "sustainable workplace culture development."

My meditation group grew to twenty-three people. Then thirty-seven. By the end of October, we had fifty-two regular participants across multiple sessions, and I was receiving requests to start groups in other corporate divisions.

I should have been more careful. Should have moved slower. Should have better understood the surveillance systems I had helped to build.

But the materials were working. People were transforming. The chronic anxiety, depression, and rage that had characterized our workplace for years was giving way to clarity, connection, and something I could only call hope.

And hope, I would learn, was the most dangerous thing of all in our controlled society.

The first sign of trouble came on a Tuesday morning in early November. I arrived at my workstation to find Dr. Sarah Hendricks, Chief of Employee Wellness Psychology, waiting for me with two Corporate Security officers.

"Marcus, we need to talk about your meditation groups," she said with the kind of smile that didn't reach her eyes.

My stomach dropped, but I maintained composure. The emergency protocols I'd studied emphasized the importance of staying calm during initial contact.

Of course," I said. "I'm happy to discuss the program. The employee satisfaction metrics have been very positive.
Yes, that's exactly what we want to discuss. Your participants are showing some... interesting patterns in their biometric and psychological assessments.

She gestured to a tablet displaying what I recognized as the standard corporate wellness dashboard - heart rate variability, stress hormone levels, productivity metrics, and behavioral compliance scores for each employee.

Your group members are showing decreased cortisol levels, which is good. But they're also showing increased autonomic nervous system resilience, enhanced critical thinking markers, and what our algorithms flag as 'reduced institutional compliance indicators.'

My mouth went dry. The Sacred Synthesis practices weren't just reducing stress - they were building the kind of psychological resilience and critical thinking capacity that corporate algorithms identified as potentially subversive.

I'm not sure I understand the concern," I said carefully. "Isn't employee wellness the goal?

Dr. Hendricks' smile became even more artificial. "Marcus, we support employee wellness within appropriate parameters. But we've noticed that your group members have started questioning policies more frequently, showing reduced response to standard motivational techniques, and demonstrating what our behavioral analysis indicates as increased 'independence orientation.'"
She paused, letting the implications sink in.

We're going to need you to modify your approach. Focus more on compliance-supportive practices. Less emphasis on... autonomy development.

I nodded, knowing that compliance meant the end of everything I'd been building.

"I understand. I'll adjust the curriculum."

Good. We'll be monitoring the program more closely going forward. And Marcus? We'll need copies of all materials you've been using. For quality assurance purposes.

That night, I made two crucial decisions. First, I would not turn over the Sacred Synthesis materials to corporate authorities. Second, I needed to accelerate the timeline for community development far beyond what the materials recommended as safe.

I began making copies.

Not just digital copies, but physical printouts of the most essential materials. Constitutional assessments, basic practices, emergency protocols, and most importantly, the community organization guidelines. I hid them in my apartment, in a storage unit across town, and with the three group members I trusted most.

I also began reaching out to the broader network.

The global service capacity assessment materials had mentioned international connections and support networks. Using the cultural sensitivity protocols as guidance, I began searching for other Sacred Synthesis communities. The search terms were cryptic - references to constitutional wellness, democratic spiritual communities, and traditional practice integration.

Hidden in plain sight as meditation centers, holistic health clinics, intentional communities, and even some progressive churches, there were Sacred Synthesis practitioners and communities across the globe. A yoga studio in Portland. A wellness center in Amsterdam. A permaculture farm in Costa Rica. A community health clinic in Mumbai.

They were coded communications - constitutional terminology, specific breathing practices, particular quotes from the materials - but they were there. The international network was real.

And they welcomed me.

Through encrypted communications and coded conversations, I learned that I was part of a global resistance movement that had been operating for decades. Communities in dozens of countries preserving and practicing the Sacred Synthesis system under various covers. Healthcare providers integrating constitutional medicine into clinical practice. Educators teaching democratic principles through "collaborative learning." Artists and activists building cultural re-sistance through "wellness" and "spiritual" activities.

It was beautiful. It was inspiring. And it made me a marked man.

By mid-November, Corporate Security had installed additional mon-itoring on my workstation. My meditation groups were being ob-served by "wellness consultants" who took detailed notes and rec-orded sessions. My apartment was visited twice for "routine building inspections." My communications were being monitored, and I was called into "performance reviews" weekly.

The noose was tightening, but I couldn't stop. The people in my groups were transforming too rapidly, becoming too awake, too autonomous for the corporate system to tolerate. And I was receiv-ing increasingly urgent communications from the international net-work about a broader crackdown on resistance activities. The Cor-porate Wellness Monitoring Act was being expanded. New technol-ogies for detecting "non-compliant thought patterns" were being deployed. Safe houses were being raided under the guise of "unsanc-tioned wellness activity enforcement."

I realized that my discovery of the Sacred Synthesis materials hadn't been an accident. The "glitch" that corrupted the files had been an attempted purge. Someone in the system had tried to destroy the materials, but the quantum storage redundancies I'd help design had preserved fragments.

I was holding some of the last remaining copies of knowledge that authoritarian forces globally were working to eradicate. The weight of that responsibility was overwhelming. But it also clarified my purpose. I would preserve this knowledge. I would share it as widely as possible. And I would help build the communities necessary for its practice, regardless of the personal cost.

On December 1st, I made the decision that would ultimately lead to my death: I went public.

Not completely public - that would have been suicide and served no one. But I began sharing the materials more broadly, teaching the practices more openly, and connecting people to the international network. I organized the first "Constitutional Wellness Workshop" at the public library, disguised as a stress management seminar. For-ty-three people attended, and I shared the basic constitutional as-sessment and several foundation practices.

I started a blog called "Integrated Health Solutions" and began posting articles about constitutional wellness, democratic community building, and "evidence-based traditional practices." The articles were carefully coded but contained enough real content for serious seekers to understand.

I reached out to healthcare providers, educators, and community organizers who might be sympathetic. Using the professional integration materials as guidance, I began building a local network of practitioners.
Most dangerously of all, I began training others to teach the system.

By January 2046, I had seventeen people trained in basic Sacred Synthesis principles, three who were developing teaching capacity, and connections to practitioners in twelve other cities. We had established a community meditation group that met weekly in a rented space, created a resource-sharing network that functioned as basic mutual aid, and begun implementing some of the democratic decision-making processes. It was working. People were healing from decades of trauma and oppression. Communities were forming. Resistance capacity was building.

And the authorities were closing in.

The first arrest came on January 15th. Sarah Martinez, one of my most dedicated practitioners and a nurse at the public hospital, was detained for "practicing unsanctioned medical techniques" after teaching constitutional breathing to her patients.

Three days later, the library canceled all "wellness programs" indefinitely after a "community complaint" about "cult-like activities."

On January 22nd, my blog was taken down for "promoting unregulated health practices," and my personal social media accounts were suspended.

By February 1st, four more members of our community had been arrested or detained for various "wellness violations," and I was called into a final meeting with Corporate Security.

Marcus," Dr. Hendricks said, no longer bothering with false smiles, "your employment with Synaptic Dynamics is terminated, effective immediately. Your company devices and access credentials are revoked. You have thirty minutes to collect personal items and leave the premises.

I had been expecting this for weeks.
"What are the charges?"
No charges. This is a corporate decision based on performance and cultural fit concerns.
Cultural fit. That was the new euphemism for "insufficient compliance with authoritarian control."

But termination, while devastating financially, also freed me from corporate surveillance and constraints. I could now operate more openly, connect more directly with the international network, and focus entirely on community development and knowledge preservation.

It was a liberation that would last exactly forty-seven days.

On March 20th, 2026, the Global Wellness Regulatory Authority announced Operation Mindful Compliance - a coordinated international crackdown on "unlicensed spiritual and wellness activities" that posed "threats to public mental health and social stability."

The raids began at dawn.

Sacramento. Portland. Denver. Atlanta. Twelve cities across North America. Simultaneously, operations began in Amsterdam, London, Berlin, Melbourne, and Mumbai. Meditation centers closed. Wellness practitioners arrested. Community spaces raided.

They had been watching us all along.

My apartment was hit at 6:47 AM. Twelve officers in full tactical gear, led by agents from the newly formed Department of Cognitive Security. They confiscated everything - computers, phones, books, personal notes, and every printed copy of the Sacred Synthesis materials I'd hidden.

I was arrested on charges of "operating an unlicensed spiritual counseling practice," "distributing unregulated wellness materials," and "conspiracy to undermine public mental health." The maximum sentence, they informed me, was twenty years in a cognitive rehabilitation facility.

But even as they led me away in restraints, I felt something I hadn't expected: peace.

The knowledge was preserved. In the three months of intense activity, we had distributed copies of the materials to over 300 people across multiple states and several countries. The international network had been alerted and was taking protective measures. The community we'd built was small but resilient, with democratic leadership structures that could continue functioning even without my presence.

Most importantly, the practices were working. People had experienced real transformation, real healing, real empowerment. They had tasted what authentic community could feel like. They understood that alternatives to our oppressive systems were not just possible but practical.

The Sacred Synthesis was no longer a secret held by one person who stumbled across corrupted files. It had become what it was always meant to be: community knowledge, lived and practiced by people committed to liberation and transformation.

From my holding cell, as I write what I know will be my final testimony, I am not afraid. The electric constitution training has taught me how to maintain calm even under extreme stress. The breathing practices help me stay centered despite the chaos. The democratic principles give me faith that others will continue the work.

Tomorrow, I will likely be transferred to the Regional Cognitive Rehabilitation Center, where I will spend the next several months or years undergoing "therapeutic reconditioning." The process is designed to eliminate "non-compliant thought patterns" and restore "healthy relationship with institutional authority."

I know that I may not survive this process intact. Cognitive rehabilitation has a high success rate in creating compliant citizens, but that success comes at the cost of individual autonomy, critical thinking, and genuine community connection.

But I also know that the knowledge I discovered and shared will survive.

This testament, written in the final hours before my transfer, will be smuggled out by someone I trust completely. It will be distributed through networks that have learned to operate with sophisticated security. It will be preserved by communities that understand its value and necessity.

And someday, when the time is right, the Sacred Synthesis will emerge again to guide humanity toward the liberation that is our birthright.

The remaining chapters of this chronicle will be written by others - my fellow practitioners, community members, and eventually, I hope, the free citizens of a transformed world.

But this first chapter, this testimony of discovery and dedication, this account of how one person found forbidden knowledge and chose to share it despite the ultimate cost, this chapter is mine.

And I give it freely, as the Sacred Synthesis teachings require: in service of the highest good for all beings, at whatever personal sacrifice is necessary.

The resistance continues. The knowledge lives.
The community endures.
May those who come after us build the world we could only envision.
This chronicle is dedicated to all those who chose knowledge over ignorance, community over isolation, and freedom over security, regardless of the personal cost. May their sacrifice light the way to liberation for all beings.
For additional information about the Sacred Synthesis and resistance resources, seek out the signs hidden in plain sight: Constitutional wellness. Democratic community. Traditional practice integration. The network endures. The knowledge lives

PERSONAL PRACTICE
Transformation · Embodiment · Integration

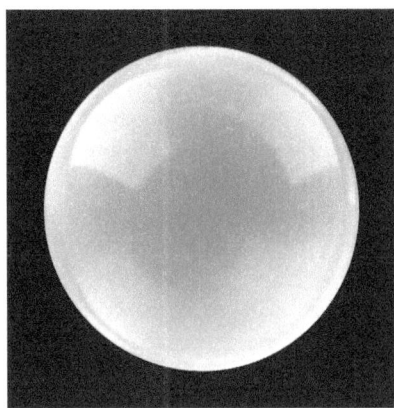

READER'S NOTE:
You have entered the **Personal Practice layer** of Sacred Synthesis. This section contains **individualized transformation tools** - constitutional assessment, personalized practices, and daily integration protocols.

What you'll find here:
- Constitutional type assessment (Electric/Magnetic/Neutral)
- Customized breathwork, movement, and meditation
- Nutrition and lifestyle guidance for your type
- Daily, weekly, monthly tracking systems
- Personal development pathways

Look for:
- Detailed instructions with constitutional adaptations
- Scientific validation and traditional wisdom sources
- Safety protocols and contraindications
- Integration with existing spiritual practices
- Progression stages from beginner to advanced

This is the embodied foundation - the practices that ground abstract concepts in lived experience. Personal transformation supports (and is supported by) collective organizing.

Work at your own pace. Honor your constitutional needs. Trust your direct experience.
The sphere contains all possibilities. Begin where you are.

I read the opening chapter three times before the magnitude of what I had discovered began to dawn on me. This wasn't archaeological speculation or academic theory. These were first-person accounts from people who had lived through whatever transformation had emptied the cities and left the world I knew - a world of scattered enclaves, subsistence communities, and mysterious abundance where the old civilization had once sprawled.

The world Chen described sounded like a fever dream and were dated from what the old calendar would have called the 2040s through 2080s - decades that, according to the few records our enclaves kept, marked the period when the old systems had finally collapsed. But Chen's account suggested something far more complex than simple collapse.

He wrote of discovering corrupted files that turned out to contain something called the Sacred Synthesis - a complete system for human organization based on understanding constitutional differences between people. Not racial or ethnic differences, but deeper patterns of how human bodies and minds naturally functioned. The materials described three basic types: Electric (sensitive, creative, relationship-oriented), Magnetic (steady, practical, goal-focused), and Neutral (analytical, efficient, quality-oriented).

The Complete Constitutional Assessment Tool

Discover Your Sacred Synthesis Type for Personalized Spiritual Development

Why Constitutional Assessment Matters

Traditional wisdom has always recognized that identical practices affect different people in completely different ways. What energizes one constitutional type may exhaust another. What calms one type may bore another to the point of abandoning practice entirely. Without understanding your constitutional type, you're essentially trying random spiritual experiments and hoping for the best.

This assessment eliminates that guesswork by providing precise identification of your unique energetic, psychological, and spiritual constitution, enabling you to adapt every practice for maximum effectiveness while maintaining traditional authenticity.

How This Assessment Works

The Complete Assessment examines six essential domains that determine your constitutional type:

1. **Physical Constitution** (25 questions): Body build, energy pat-

terns, health tendencies
2. **Psychological Patterns** (30 questions): Mental processes, emotional responses, learning styles
3. **Energy Constitution** (20 questions): Energy rhythms, environmental sensitivities, recovery patterns
4. **Social Constitution** (15 questions): Relationship styles, community preferences, leadership patterns
5. **Spiritual Inclinations** (20 questions): Natural spiritual abilities, preferred practices, service orientation
6. **Lifestyle Preferences** (15 questions): Work styles, daily rhythms, environmental preferences

Total Questions: 125 comprehensive indicators ensuring accurate assessment

SECTION I: PHYSICAL CONSTITUTION ASSESSMENT - Understanding Your Body's Energetic Blueprint

Instructions: For each question, select the response that most accurately describes your natural tendencies over your lifetime, not temporary conditions. Consider your patterns when you're healthy and unstressed.

Body Build and Physical Characteristics
1. My natural body build is
a) Light and variable; difficulty gaining weight, prominent joints, often described as "bird-like" or delicate
b) Heavy and solid; tendency to gain weight easily, strong build, substantial physical presence
c) Medium and well-proportioned; athletic potential, balanced build, naturally coordinated

2. My weight patterns throughout life
a) Consistently underweight or highly variable, can lose weight quickly when stressed
b) Tendency toward overweight, gain weight easily and lose it slowly
c) Stable and moderate, maintain consistent healthy weight with reasonable effort

3. My physical strength and endurance
a) Variable strength, quick fatigue, need frequent rest periods
b) Strong and steady endurance, slow to start but can maintain activity for long periods
c) Good strength and endurance when properly motivated and challenged

4. My natural movement patterns
a) Quick, light, variable, often described as "nervous" or "fidgety"
b) Slow, steady, deliberate, prefer to move at my own pace

c) Moderate and controlled, naturally good at sports and coordinated activities

5. My bone structure is

a) Light and prominent, joints easily visible, described as having "good bone structure"

b) Heavy and substantial, large frame, broad shoulders or hips

c) Medium and well-balanced, proportional frame, athletic potential

Energy Patterns and Vitality

6. My energy levels throughout the day

a) Highly variable, peaks and valleys, can be energetic then suddenly exhausted

b) Slow to start but steady, takes time to get going but maintain consistent energy

c) Strong when engaged, high energy for things I care about, low energy when bored

7. My sleep patterns

a) Light and variable, difficulty falling asleep, wake easily, need 7-8 hours minimum

b) Deep and heavy, fall asleep easily, difficult to wake, prefer 8-9 hours

c) Moderate and efficient, usually sleep well, wake refreshed with 6-8 hours

8. My response to physical exercise

a) Need gentle, grounding exercise, intense exercise makes me feel scattered or exhausted

b) Require activating exercise, gentle exercise feels boring, need challenge to feel energized

c) Prefer moderate, goal-oriented exercise, like sports, martial arts, challenging but not excessive

9. When I'm physically stressed or overworked

a) Become anxious, scattered, lose weight, develop nervous symptoms

b) Become lethargic, gain weight, feel heavy and unmotivated

c) Become irritable, develop inflammatory symptoms, feel "burned out"

10. My recovery time after illness or physical stress

a) Variable, sometimes bounce back quickly, sometimes take a long time to recover

b) Slow but steady, take longer to recover but usually return to better health than before

c) Efficient when I rest, recover quickly if I actually take time to rest and care for myself

Environmental Sensitivities

11. My temperature preferences

a) Always cold, love warm weather, sunshine, hot baths, wear layers even in summer

b) Usually warm, prefer cool environments, dress lightly, overheat easily

c) Variable, comfortable in moderate temperatures, dislike extremes in either direction

12. My sensitivity to environmental changes

a) Very sensitive, affected by weather changes, crowd energy, electro-magnetic fields

b) Generally stable, not much affected by environmental changes

c) Moderately sensitive, notice changes but adapt reasonably well

13. My response to climate and seasons

a) Struggle with cold, wind, dry conditions, thrive in warm, humid, stable weather

b) Struggle with heat and humidity, thrive in cool, dry, variable conditions

c) Struggle with extreme heat, prefer moderate, controlled environmental conditions

14. My physical response to stress

a) Nervous system symptoms, anxiety, insomnia, digestive issues, weight loss

b) Metabolic slowdown, depression, weight gain, sluggishness, heaviness

c) Inflammatory responses, headaches, skin problems, muscle tension, irritability

15. My natural daily rhythm

a) Variable, some days early riser, some days night owl, energy peaks change

b) Slow starter, prefer later morning, steady through day, wind down gradually

c) Consistent, naturally wake early, peak energy mid-morning through afternoon

Health Patterns and Tendencies
16. My most common health challenges

a) Anxiety, insomnia, digestive irregularity, joint problems, nervous exhaustion

b) Depression, slow metabolism, respiratory congestion, weight management, lethargy

c) Inflammatory conditions, acid stomach, skin problems, high blood pressure, burnout

17. My appetite patterns

a) Variable, sometimes forget to eat, sometimes ravenously hungry, prefer small frequent meals

b) Strong and regular, love food, rarely miss meals, can eat large quantities

c) Sharp and focused, get "hangry" when meals are delayed, prefer regular substantial meals

18. My digestion characteristics

a) Variable and sensitive, affected by stress, certain foods cause problems, gas/bloating

b) Slow and steady, can eat almost anything, rarely have digestive problems

c) Strong but sensitive to spicy or acidic foods, good appetite but can get heartburn

19. My relationship with food

a) Often forget to eat when busy, prefer light foods, sensitive to heavy meals

b) Love rich, substantial foods, eating is one of life's great pleasures

c) Food is fuel for performance, prefer regular meals, dislike being hungry

20. My skin and hair characteristics

a) Dry skin, variable hair, need moisturizer, hair tends toward dryness or fragility

b) Oily or normal skin, thick hair, rarely need moisturizer, strong hair growth

c) Normal to oily skin, moderate hair, occasional skin problems, average hair characteristics

Physical Activity and Exercise Preferences
21. My ideal exercise program would be

a) Gentle yoga, walking, stretching, restorative activities that calm my nervous system

b) Weight training, hiking, endurance activities, challenging exercises that activate my energy

c) Sports, martial arts, competitive activities, goal-oriented exercise with measurable progress

22. My response to competitive physical activities

a) Feel overwhelmed or anxious, prefer non-competitive, individual activities

b) Enjoy when not rushed, like team activities but prefer to go at my own pace

c) Thrive on competition, motivated by goals, performance measurement, winning

23. My physical coordination and athletic ability

a) Variable, can be graceful or clumsy depending on stress level and energy

b) Naturally strong but not necessarily fast, good at activities requiring strength/endurance

c) Naturally coordinated, good at learning new physical skills, competitive potential

24. When I'm physically active I prefer

a) Consistent routine in familiar environment, same time, same place, same activities

b) Variety and social connection, different activities, exercising with others

c) Progressive challenge and measurement, setting goals, tracking improvement, achievement

25. My physical practice recovery needs

a) Gentle cool-down, rest, and restoration, need time to integrate and recover

b) Gradual transition to other activities, don't like to stop abruptly

c) Quick transition to other activities, feel energized and ready for next challenge

SECTION II: PSYCHOLOGICAL PATTERNS ASSESSMENT - Understanding Your Mental and Emotional Constitution

Thinking and Mental Processing Patterns
26. My natural thinking style

a) Quick, creative, intuitive, many ideas, make connections others miss, easily distracted

b) Slow, methodical, thorough, think things through carefully, good memory, resist change

c) Sharp, focused, analytical, cut to the heart of issues, good at problem-solving, can be impatient

27. My approach to learning new information

a) Need variety and creativity, learn through stories, images, personal connection

b) Need structure and repetition, learn through systematic presentation, hands-on practice

c) Need logic and efficiency, learn through clear explanations, practical applications

28. My memory characteristics

a) Good for details and impressions, poor for names and facts, remember feelings and images

b) Excellent long-term memory, remember events from years ago with great detail

c) Good for relevant information, remember what serves my goals, forget what doesn't matter

29. My decision-making process

a) Intuitive and changeable, go with gut feelings, sometimes change my mind

b) Slow and careful, want all the information, prefer not to rush important decisions

c) Quick and decisive, analyze options, make decision, move forward

30. My attention and concentration patterns

a) Variable focus, can be intensely focused or completely scattered depending on interest
b) Steady sustained attention, can work on things for long periods without getting distracted
c) Sharp focused attention, excellent concentration when interested, impatient with irrelevant details

Emotional Responses and Regulation
31. My emotional response patterns
a) Sensitive and variable, feel deeply, emotional ups and downs, easily overwhelmed
b) Stable and even, don't get too high or low, take time to process emotions
c) Intense and direct, strong emotional responses, quick to anger, quick to forgive

32. My stress response typically involves
a) Anxiety, worry, scattered thinking, mind races, hard to settle down
b) Withdrawal, depression, sluggishness, want to sleep, avoid people, feel heavy
c) Irritation, anger, criticism, become demanding, impatient, find fault with everything

33. My emotional recovery pattern
a) Need quiet time alone, overstimulation exhausts me emotionally
b) Need gentle support, like comfort from others but don't want to be rushed
c) Need physical activity, exercise, work, or problem-solving to process emotions

34. My relationship with change
a) Simultaneously crave and fear change, excited by possibilities but anxious about uncertainty
b) Generally resist change, prefer stability, need time to adjust to new situations
c) Embrace beneficial change, quickly adapt to changes that serve my goals

35. My emotional expression style
a) Variable and intense, sometimes very expressive, sometimes with-drawn
b) Steady and controlled, don't show emotions dramatically, prefer stability
c) Direct and immediate, express emotions clearly, don't hold grudges

Personality and Character Patterns
36. People often describe me as
a) Creative, sensitive, inspiring, but also anxious, scattered, or unpre-dictable

b) Reliable, supportive, grounded, but also stubborn, slow, or resistant to change

c) Intelligent, capable, organized, but also critical, demanding, or impatient

37. My approach to personal relationships

a) Deep and meaningful connections, prefer few close relationships to many superficial ones

b) Loyal and supportive, maintain long-term relationships, don't like conflict

c) Clear and direct, appreciate honest communication, can be challenging but fair

38. My natural leadership style

a) Inspirational and creative, lead through vision and personal example

b) Supportive and stabilizing, lead through service and building consensus

c) Strategic and efficient, lead through competence and clear direction

39. My response to criticism

a) Take it very personally, either devastated or defensive, need time to process

b) Initially resistant, need time to consider feedback, don't like to be rushed into changes

c) Appreciate honest feedback, want to know how to improve, can be self-critical

40. My communication style

a) Expressive and variable, sometimes very talkative, sometimes quiet, depends on mood

b) Measured and thoughtful, think before speaking, prefer one-on-one conversation

c) Direct and efficient, say what I mean, appreciate others being straightforward

Motivation and Goal Orientation

41. I am most motivated by

a) Creative expression and meaningful connection, work that inspires me and serves others

b) Stability and security, having enough resources and maintaining harmonious relationships

c) Achievement and recognition, accomplishing goals and being acknowledged for my contributions

42. My approach to work and career

a) Need work that feels meaningful, would rather do work I love for less money than boring work for more

b) Want job security and good relationships, prefer stable organizations with supportive colleagues

c) Seek advancement and challenge, want increasing responsibility and recognition for my competence

43. My relationship with money and material possessions

a) Money is for experiences and giving, not particularly interested in accumulating possessions

b) Want enough for security and comfort, like nice things but not obsessively materialistic

c) Money represents freedom and power, want enough to maintain independence and influence

44. My approach to personal goals

a) Intuitive and flexible, goals emerge naturally, willing to change direction when inspired

b) Steady and practical, set realistic goals and work toward them consistently over time

c) Strategic and ambitious, set challenging goals and create systematic plans to achieve them

45. What drains my energy most

a) Conflict, overstimulation, meaningless activity, feel depleted by chaos and superficiality

b) Pressure to move fast, too much change, feel exhausted by rush and instability

c) Boredom, inefficiency, lack of challenge, feel frustrated by waste and mediocrity

Social and Community Preferences

46. My ideal social environment

a) Small groups of like-minded people, intimate gatherings focused on meaningful topics

b) Stable community of familiar faces, regular social activities with people I know well

c) Dynamic groups of accomplished people, networking and collaboration with competent individuals

47. My role in group situations

a) The creative contributor, offer unique perspectives, inspire others, provide emotional support

b) The stabilizing presence, keep things grounded, provide practical support, maintain harmony

c) The organizer/leader, see the big picture, coordinate activities, drive toward results

48. My response to social conflict

a) Very disturbing, tend to avoid or try to heal conflict, take sides based on personal loyalty

b) Preference to avoid, want to maintain harmony, will compromise to keep peace

c) Direct engagement, address issues directly, can be confrontational in service of resolution

49. My community service preferences

a) Healing, teaching, creative arts, work that directly touches people's lives and spirits

b) Practical support, organization, work that provides tangible help and builds community

c) Leadership, policy, systems change, work that creates efficient solutions to large-scale problems

50. My teaching and mentoring style

a) Inspirational and individual, connect with each person uniquely, lead by personal example

b) Patient and systematic, provide stable guidance, create safe learning environment

c) Challenging and efficient, push people to achieve their potential, provide clear feedback

Learning and Intellectual Development

51. My preferred learning environment

a) Flexible and creative, variety in presentation, personal connection with teacher

b) Structured and supportive, clear expectations, patient instruction, practical application

c) Challenging and efficient, high standards, competent instruction, measurable progress

52. My intellectual interests tend toward

a) Philosophy, arts, psychology, subjects that explore meaning, beauty, and human potential

b) Practical skills, history, nature, subjects that provide useful knowledge and cultural wisdom

c) Science, business, strategy, subjects that provide analytical tools and competitive advantage

53. My approach to study and research

a) Intuitive and holistic, see connections between different fields, prefer integrated approaches

b) Systematic and thorough, work through material step by step, build solid foundation

c) Strategic and goal-oriented, focus on what serves my objectives, efficient information processing

54. My response to intellectual challenge

a) Excited but sometimes overwhelmed, love new ideas but can get scattered by too much information

b) Interested but cautious, want to understand thoroughly before moving to more advanced material

c) Energized and competitive, thrive on intellectual challenge, want to master difficult subjects

55. My contribution to intellectual discussions

a) Creative insights and personal perspectives, offer unique viewpoints and emotional understanding
b) Practical wisdom and historical context, provide grounding and connect ideas to real-world application
c) Logical analysis and strategic implications, clarify thinking and identify practical consequences

SECTION III: ENERGY CONSTITUTION ASSESSMENT - Understanding Your Energetic Patterns and Environmental Sensitivities

Energy Rhythms and Daily Cycles
56. My natural daily energy pattern
a) Variable and unpredictable, some days high energy, some days low, peaks change
b) Slow rise to steady state, takes time to get going but maintain consistent energy through day
c) Sharp morning peak, highest energy early, gradual decline through day

57. My optimal time for important work
a) Varies daily, sometimes morning person, sometimes night owl, depends on mood and inspiration
b) Late morning through afternoon, once I'm fully awake, steady energy for several hours
c) Early morning, peak mental clarity and focus in first few hours after waking

58. My response to seasonal changes
a) Very sensitive, energy and mood significantly affected by weather, light, seasonal transitions
b) Gradual adaptation, slowly adjust to seasonal changes, prefer consistent climate
c) Moderate sensitivity, notice seasons but maintain fairly consistent energy year-round

59. My relationship with natural cycles (moon phases, weather patterns)
a) Highly aware and responsive, feel moon phases, weather changes, atmospheric shifts
b) Gradually responsive, notice major changes like seasons and storm fronts
c) Minimally responsive, more influenced by social and work schedules than natural cycles

60. My energy management needs
a) Careful balance required, easy to overextend or get depleted, need frequent check-ins with energy
b) Steady maintenance approach, consistent habits maintain energy,

sudden changes are disruptive

c) Efficient utilization focus, maximize energy for important activities, minimize waste on trivial matters

Environmental Sensitivities and Preferences
61. My sensitivity to sound and noise

a) Very sensitive, easily overwhelmed by loud or chaotic sounds, prefer quiet environments

b) Moderately sensitive, can adapt to reasonable noise levels, dislike sudden loud sounds

c) Generally tolerant, can work with background noise, sensitive mainly to inefficient sounds (like meetings that go nowhere)

62. My response to crowded or busy environments

a) Quickly overwhelmed, absorb others' energy, need recovery time after crowds

b) Initially uncomfortable but can adapt, prefer familiar social settings, dislike chaos

c) Energized when productive, enjoy dynamic environments when there's clear purpose and competent leadership

63. My lighting preferences

a) Natural and soft lighting, fluorescent lights feel harsh, prefer candle-light or warm lamps

b) Consistent and comfortable, prefer steady, moderate lighting, dislike dramatic changes

c) Bright and efficient, like good task lighting, natural light during day

64. My response to electromagnetic environments (computers, phones, electronic equipment)

a) Sensitive and affected, feel drained by too much computer time, need breaks from electronics

b) Moderate sensitivity, can work with electronics but prefer limited exposure

c) Generally unaffected, comfortable with technology as tools for productivity

65. My color and aesthetic preferences

a) Soft, warm, natural colors, earth tones, pastels, colors that feel peaceful and harmonious

b) Rich, substantial colors, deep colors, natural materials, environments that feel stable and comforting

c) Clear, bright, efficient colors, colors that support focus and activity, clean and uncluttered aesthetics

Stress Response and Recovery Patterns
66. My first signs of stress/overwhelm

a) Scattered thinking, anxiety, insomnia, mind starts racing, lose ability to focus

b) Lethargy, procrastination, heaviness, want to sleep, avoid responsibilities, feel unmotivated

c) Irritability, impatience, criticism, become demanding, find fault with everything

67. My recovery needs when stressed

a) Quiet solitude and gentle restoration, meditation, nature, creative activities

b) Comfort and gradual support, gentle care from others, familiar routines, no pressure

c) Physical activity and problem-solving, exercise, organize something, work on solutions

68. My response to high-stress situations

a) Fight-or-flight activation, either hypervigilant or collapse, need to leave situation

b) Shut down and withdraw, minimize energy expenditure, wait for situation to pass

c) Hyper-focus and control, intensify efforts to manage situation, can become obsessive

69. My signs of optimal energy and wellbeing

a) Creative flow and inspiration, ideas come easily, feel connected to purpose and others

b) Stable contentment and generosity, feel grounded, happy to support others, life flows smoothly

c) Focused achievement and confidence, accomplish goals easily, natural leadership emerges, feel vital and strong

70. My energy "recharging" requirements

a) Regular solitude and creative expression, need alone time to process and restore

b) Consistent routine and social support, maintain regular habits with supportive community

c) Challenge and accomplishment, feel energized by achieving meaningful goals

Spiritual Energy and Sensitivity
71. My sensitivity to "spiritual" or subtle energy

a) Very sensitive, easily feel others' moods, affected by places and objects, natural psychic tendencies

b) Moderate sensitivity, sometimes feel energy but don't usually pay attention unless it's very strong

c) Limited sensitivity, more focused on practical reality, skeptical of subtle energy claims

72. My response to meditation and contemplative practices

a) Sometimes profound, sometimes difficult, can have deep experiences or get too scattered to practice

b) Generally calming and supportive, usually feel more grounded and peaceful after practice

c) Variable based on approach, respond well to structured practices, bored by passive meditation

73. My relationship with nature and natural environments

a) Essential for my wellbeing, feel restored and inspired by nature, notice seasonal changes deeply

b) Enjoy and appreciate nature, feel comfortable in natural settings, prefer them for relaxation

c) Appreciate natural beauty, enjoy nature for recreation and stress relief but don't need it for daily wellbeing

74. My response to sacred or religious environments

a) Deeply moved and affected, feel spiritual presence in sacred places, inspired by religious art and music

b) Comfortable and appreciative, enjoy the peace and beauty of spiritual environments

c) Respectfully interested, appreciate architecture and cultural significance, less emotionally affected

75. My natural spiritual inclinations

a) Mystical and experiential, drawn to direct spiritual experience, meditation, energy work

b) Devotional and traditional, drawn to established practices, community worship, service

c) Philosophical and practical, drawn to wisdom teachings, ethical development, applied spirituality

SECTION IV: SOCIAL CONSTITUTION ASSESSMENT - Understanding Your Relationship and Community Patterns

Relationship Styles and Preferences

76. In intimate relationships, I tend to be

a) Emotionally intense and deeply connected, need profound understanding and creative partnership

b) Loyal and supportive, provide stable foundation for partner, value long-term commitment

c) Direct and challenging, expect excellence from partner, provide clear communication and shared goals

77. My communication style in relationships

a) Expressive and variable, share feelings openly, need emotional understanding, can be moody

b) Steady and supportive, listen well, don't rush to judgment, maintain harmonious atmosphere

c) Honest and direct, say what I think, appreciate directness in return, can be critically helpful

78. My role in family dynamics

a) The inspiration and healer, provide emotional support, creative energy, spiritual insight
b) The stabilizer and supporter, maintain family traditions, provide practical help, keep peace
c) The organizer and achiever, coordinate family activities, solve problems, drive toward goals

79. My response to relationship conflict
a) Very distressing, either avoid or get emotionally overwhelmed, need time to process
b) Want to avoid or minimize, will compromise to maintain harmony, don't like confrontation
c) Address directly, want to solve problems, can be confrontational in service of resolution

80. My needs in friendship
a) Deep understanding and authentic sharing, prefer few close friends to many superficial relationships
b) Loyal support and shared activities, maintain long-term friendships through consistent care and fun together
c) Mutual respect and stimulating exchange, friendship based on shared interests and mutual advancement

Community and Social Participation
81. My preferred community size
a) Intimate gatherings, small groups where everyone knows each other personally
b) Stable neighborhood community, consistent group of familiar faces, moderate size
c) Dynamic professional network, size less important than competence and shared goals

82. My typical role in community activities
a) Creative contributor, offer unique perspectives, inspire others, provide emotional/spiritual support
b) Reliable organizer, handle logistics, maintain traditions, ensure everyone feels included
c) Strategic leader, see big picture, coordinate resources, drive toward collective achievements

83. My community service preferences
a) Direct personal service, counseling, teaching, healing, arts, work that touches individual lives
b) Community building activities, organizing events, maintaining facilities, supporting families
c) Policy and systems work, leadership roles, strategic planning, creating efficient solutions

84. My response to community politics and governance
a) Focus on values and vision, want decisions to serve higher principles

and human welfare
b) Seek consensus and stability, want everyone's voice heard and community harmony maintained
c) Emphasize competence and results, want effective leadership and measurable community improvement

85. My approach to cultural and religious traditions
a) Seek the spiritual essence, interested in inner meaning more than outer forms
b) Value continuity and community, appreciate traditions that connect us with heritage and each other
c) Adapt for contemporary relevance, preserve what serves current needs, update what doesn't work

Authority and Leadership Patterns
86. My natural relationship with authority
a) Question based on authenticity, respect genuine wisdom, resist arbitrary control
b) Generally accepting, prefer to work within existing structures rather than challenge authority
c) Based on competence, respect effective leadership, impatient with incompetent authority

87. My leadership style when I'm in charge
a) Inspirational and flexible, lead through personal example and shared vision
b) Supportive and inclusive, create safe environment where everyone can contribute
c) Strategic and efficient, set clear goals and organize resources to achieve them

88. My response to being led by others
a) Need to believe in the leader's vision, follow those who inspire me toward meaningful goals
b) Appreciate stable, caring leadership, follow leaders who create security and include everyone
c) Follow competent, effective leaders, respect those who get results and help me advance

89. My approach to teaching or mentoring others
a) Individual and inspirational, connect with each person uniquely, help them find their path
b) Patient and systematic, provide structured guidance, create supportive learning environment
c) Challenging and goal-oriented, push people to achieve potential, provide clear feedback

90. My contribution to team dynamics
a) Creative insight and emotional intelligence, offer unique perspectives, maintain group spirit

b) Stability and practical support, keep things grounded, provide resources, maintain harmony
c) Strategic thinking and results focus, clarify objectives, organize activities, drive toward completion

SECTION V: SPIRITUAL INCLINATIONS ASSESSMENT - Understanding Your Natural Spiritual Affinities and Service Orientation

Natural Spiritual Abilities and Inclinations
91. My most natural spiritual abilities seem to be
a) Intuition, empathy, healing, naturally sensitive to subtle dimensions and others' needs
b) Devotion, service, community building, naturally able to create supportive spiritual environment
c) Wisdom, teaching, organization, naturally able to understand principles and create spiritual structure

92. My preferred approach to spiritual practice
a) Creative and experiential, enjoy variety, personal discovery, artistic expression of spirituality
b) Traditional and community-based, prefer established practices within supportive community
c) Systematic and goal-oriented, want structured approach with clear stages and measurable progress

93. My relationship with spiritual teachers and authority
a) Need authentic connection, follow teachers who embody wisdom and genuinely care about my development
b) Appreciate stable guidance, want consistent teaching within established tradition
c) Seek competent instruction, follow teachers who provide effective methods and clear understanding

94. My response to spiritual community and religious institutions
a) Focus on inner meaning, interested in spiritual essence more than religious forms or politics
b) Value tradition and fellowship, appreciate established practices that connect me with spiritual heritage
c) Want effective organization, support institutions that provide clear teaching and practical spiritual development

95. My natural spiritual service orientation
a) Healing and inspiring individuals, drawn to work that helps people find meaning and transform suffering
b) Building and maintaining spiritual community, drawn to work that creates supportive environment for others' growth

c) Teaching and organizing spiritual development, drawn to work that creates effective systems for wisdom transmission

Contemplative Practice Preferences
96. My response to different meditation approaches
a) Prefer gentle, open awareness practices, mindfulness, loving-kindness, creative visualization
b) Prefer structured, devotional practices, prayer, chanting, traditional ritual sequences
c) Prefer analytical, goal-oriented practices, insight meditation, study-based contemplation, systematic development

97. My experience with prayer or contemplative prayer
a) Natural and personal, prayer feels like intimate conversation with divine presence
b) Comforting and traditional, prefer established prayers within familiar religious context
c) Philosophical and practical, prayer as systematic inquiry into wisdom principles and their application

98. My relationship with sacred texts and spiritual study
a) Intuitive and interpretive, drawn to mystical meaning, personal relevance, creative understanding
b) Devotional and traditional, appreciate established interpretations within community context
c) Analytical and practical, want to understand principles clearly and apply them systematically

99. My experience with spiritual ritual and ceremony
a) Personally meaningful, create my own rituals, drawn to ceremonies that inspire and transform
b) Community-connecting, appreciate traditional ceremonies that unite community in shared purpose
c) Symbolically useful, see ritual as tool for development when it serves clear purpose

100. My approach to integrating spirituality with daily life
a) Spirituality infuses everything, see all life as spiritual practice, hard to separate sacred from ordinary
b) Designated spiritual times, prefer specific times for spiritual practice within normal daily life
c) Spiritual principles applied practically, use spiritual understanding to make better decisions and serve more effectively

Service and Global Consciousness
101. My sense of life purpose and calling
a) Healing and transformation, feel called to help others find meaning, heal suffering, discover their potential
b) Community and culture, feel called to preserve wisdom, support

families, maintain healthy community life

c) Leadership and systems change, feel called to organize resources, create effective solutions, advance collective development

102. My response to global challenges and suffering

a) Emotionally engaged, deeply feel others' pain, want to respond with direct personal help

b) Want stable solutions, support efforts that create lasting security and care for vulnerable people

c) Focus on systemic change, want to understand root causes and create efficient solutions

103. My preferred scale of service activity

a) Individual and local, work directly with people I can see and touch, prefer personal scale

b) Community and regional, work within familiar cultural context where I understand local needs

c) National and international, work on large-scale challenges requiring systematic solutions

104. My relationship with environmental and planetary consciousness

a) Feel personal connection with nature, experience earth as living being deserving care and respect

b) Want to preserve heritage, protect environment as legacy for children and cultural continuity

c) Understand systematic requirements, recognize environmental protection as necessary for human advancement

105. My approach to social justice and cultural change

a) Focus on individual transformation, believe changing consciousness changes society

b) Support gradual improvement, work within existing systems to make them more fair and caring

c) Advocate systematic reform, want efficient solutions to social problems through better organization

Integration with Contemporary Life

106. My approach to work and career as spiritual practice

a) Work must be meaningful, career as expression of spiritual values and service to others

b) Work supports spiritual life, career provides security enabling spiritual development and family service

c) Work as spiritual development, career as opportunity to apply spiritual principles and serve collective advancement

107. My relationship with money and material prosperity

a) Money for service, want enough to be generous and support meaningful work

b) Money for security, want enough to care for family and community, not motivated by accumulation

c) Money for effectiveness, want enough to maintain independence and capacity to serve large-scale goals

108. My approach to family life as spiritual practice

a) Family as spiritual partnership, marriage and parenting as opportunities for mutual development

b) Family as spiritual foundation, family life as context that supports and grounds spiritual development

c) Family as spiritual responsibility, family life as opportunity to apply spiritual principles practically

109. My response to cultural and religious diversity

a) Seek universal spiritual principles, interested in common essence underlying different traditions

b) Appreciate diverse wisdom traditions, respect different approaches while maintaining own cultural roots

c) Want practical cooperation, support whatever enables different groups to work together effectively

110. My vision of ideal spiritual community

a) Creative and authentic, community that supports individual spiritual discovery while serving others

b) Stable and caring, community that preserves wisdom while providing security for families

c) Effective and advancing, community that applies spiritual principles to create beneficial change

SECTION VI: LIFESTYLE PREFERENCES ASSESSMENT - Understanding Your Work Style, Daily Rhythms, and Environmental Needs

Work Style and Professional Preferences

111. My ideal work environment

a) Creative and flexible, variety in tasks, personal freedom, meaningful work

b) Stable and supportive, consistent routines, cooperative colleagues, job security

c) Challenging and efficient, clear goals, competent leadership, advancement opportunities

112. My approach to work tasks and projects

a) Intuitive and creative, work best when inspired, prefer variety, need personal meaning

b) Systematic and thorough, work through projects step by step, prefer clear structure

c) Strategic and goal-oriented, focus on outcomes, organize efficiently, drive toward completion

113. My response to work pressure and deadlines

a) Either thrive or crumble, can be brilliant under pressure or get too scattered to function

b) Prefer steady pace, work best with reasonable deadlines, need time to do quality work

c) Energized by appropriate challenge, perform well under pressure, impatient with unnecessary delays

114. My leadership and teamwork preferences

a) Collaborative and inspiring, want to contribute unique gifts while supporting others' development

b) Supportive and harmonious, want to maintain good relationships while getting work done

c) Efficient and results-focused, want to organize team effectively to achieve clear objectives

115. My relationship with authority and organizational hierarchy

a) Based on authentic wisdom, respect leaders who embody values and genuine competence

b) Generally cooperative, work well within reasonable structures, prefer stable authority

c) Based on effectiveness, respect competent authority, impatient with bureaucracy and incompetence

Daily Rhythms and Routine Preferences
116. My ideal daily schedule

a) Flexible and responsive, able to adapt to inspiration, energy levels, and external demands

b) Consistent and structured, regular times for meals, work, exercise, and personal activities

c) Efficient and productive, organized to maximize achievement while maintaining essential activities

117. My relationship with routines and habits

a) Need some routine but also flexibility, too much structure feels constraining, too little feels chaotic

b) Thrive with consistent routines, feel more secure and effective with regular daily patterns

c) Use routines as efficiency tools, maintain habits that serve my goals, change those that don't

118. My approach to meal planning and eating patterns

a) Intuitive and variable, eat when hungry, prefer variety, sometimes forget to eat when busy

b) Regular and substantial, prefer consistent meal times, enjoy food, rarely skip meals

c) Functional and efficient, see food as fuel, prefer regular eating schedule, can be disciplined about diet

119. My sleep and rest patterns
a) Variable and sensitive, sometimes need more sleep, sometimes less, affected by stress and environment
b) Consistent and restorative, prefer regular bedtime and wake time, need adequate sleep to function well
c) Efficient and purposeful, want adequate sleep for performance, can adapt schedule for important goals

120. My approach to exercise and physical maintenance
a) Gentle and restorative, prefer activities that calm nervous system and support flexibility
b) Regular and enjoyable, prefer consistent exercise routine that feels good and builds community
c) Goal-oriented and challenging, prefer activities that build capacity and provide measurable improvement

Environmental and Lifestyle Needs
121. My ideal living environment
a) Peaceful and inspiring, quiet, natural beauty, space for creativity and contemplation
b) Stable and comfortable, secure, well-maintained, good neighborhood, room for family/community
c) Efficient and well-organized, functional, good location for work/activities, quality amenities

122. My relationship with possessions and material environment
a) Minimal and meaningful, prefer fewer possessions that have personal significance
b) Comfortable and quality, like nice things that last, prefer substantial over trendy
c) Functional and efficient, organize possessions to support goals and activities

123. My response to change and transition
a) Simultaneous excitement and anxiety, love new possibilities but need time to adjust to major changes
b) Generally resistant, prefer stability, need gradual transition and support during changes
c) Embrace beneficial change, adapt quickly to changes that serve goals, impatient with unnecessary change

124. My approach to travel and new experiences
a) Love meaningful adventure, excited by travel that offers personal growth and cultural learning
b) Prefer familiar and comfortable, enjoy travel to beautiful places with good accommodations and known companions
c) Purpose-driven exploration, like travel that serves professional or

educational goals

125. My ideal balance of solitude and social connection

a) Need substantial solitude, require regular alone time to process experiences and restore energy

b) Prefer consistent community, like regular contact with familiar people, not too much isolation

c) Balance based on productivity, need solitude for focused work, social connection for collaboration and advancement

CONSTITUTIONAL TYPE SCORING GUIDE

Scoring Instructions:

Count your responses in each category (a, b, c) for all 125 questions:

Total 'a' responses: _____ (Electric Constitution indicators)

Total 'b' responses: _____ (Magnetic Constitution indicators) **Total 'c' responses:** _____ (Neutral Constitution indicators)

Constitutional Type Determination:

Primary Constitutional Type: The category with the highest score (minimum 60% or 75+ responses) **Secondary Constitutional Type:** The category with the second highest score (if within 20 points of primary) **Mixed Constitutional Type:** If no single category represents 60% or more, you have a mixed constitution

Constitutional Type Descriptions:

ELECTRIC CONSTITUTION (Primarily 'a' responses) - The Sensitive Creative

Congratulations! You are an Electric Constitutional Type.

You are naturally creative, sensitive, and intuitive, with remarkable gifts for inspiring others and connecting with spiritual dimensions. Your greatest challenges are anxiety, scattered attention, and nervous system overwhelm when not properly supported.

Your Electric Constitution Characteristics:

Physical: Light, variable build with cold sensitivity and irregular patterns **Energy:** Variable energy requiring careful balance and frequent restoration **Mental:** Quick, creative, intuitive mind that can become scattered under stress

Emotional: Sensitive and empathic with tendency toward anxiety when overwhelmed

Social: Prefer intimate connections and meaningful conversations

Spiritual: Natural mystic with strong intuitive abilities and healing gifts

Your Optimal Development Approach:
Physical Practices
- Gentle, grounding movement (restorative yoga, walking, tai chi)
- Warm, consistent environment and regular meals
- Early bedtime and consistent sleep schedule
- Calming breathwork focusing on extended exhales

Mental-Emotional Development
- Creative expression as spiritual practice
- Gentle meditation focusing on body awareness rather than mental concentration
- Regular solitude for processing and restoration
- Community support that honors your sensitivity

Professional Integration
- Work that aligns with your values and allows creative expression
- Flexible schedules that adapt to your natural rhythms
- Collaborativeness that minimize conflict and competition
- Service roles that use your natural healing and inspiring abilities

Spiritual Practices
- Devotional practices that open the heart
- Creative visualization and artistic expression
- Nature-based spirituality and earth connection
- Service through healing, counseling, or inspiring others

Your Unique Gifts:
- Natural ability to inspire and heal others
- Creative vision and artistic expression
- Spiritual sensitivity and intuitive guidance
- Capacity to bring beauty and meaning into any situation

Your Development Challenges:
- Managing sensitivity without becoming overwhelmed
- Maintaining focus while honoring your need for variety
- Building sustainable energy patterns
- Integrating spiritual insights with practical responsibilities

MAGNETIC CONSTITUTION (Primarily 'b' responses) - The Stable Builder

Congratulations! You are a Magnetic Constitutional Type.

You are naturally stable, supportive, and enduring, with remarkable gifts for building community and maintaining traditions. Your greatest challenges are lethargy, resistance to change, and attachment to comfort when not properly activated.

Your Magnetic Constitution Characteristics:
Physical: Heavy, solid build with slow metabolism and strong endurance **Energy:** Steady, consistent energy that takes time to activate but maintains well **Mental:** Slow, methodical thinking with excellent memory and practical wisdom
Emotional: Stable and supportive with tendency toward sluggishness when unmotivated
Social: Loyal relationships and strong community building capacity
Spiritual: Natural devotion with gifts for service and community spiritual activities

Your Optimal Development Approach:
Physical Practices
- Dynamic, activating movement (vigorous yoga, hiking, strength training)
- Cool, dry environments and stimulating activities
- Regular exercise routine that challenges your endurance
- Energizing breathwork and circulation-enhancing practices

Mental-Emotional Development
- Goal-oriented meditation with measurable progress
- Community-based practices that provide motivation
- Service projects that engage your natural building abilities
- Progressive challenges that prevent stagnation

Professional Integration
- Stable career that provides security while offering growth opportunities
- Leadership roles that utilize your natural supportive abilities
- Team-oriented work environments with shared goals
- Long-term projects that allow you to develop expertise over time

Spiritual Practices
- Traditional practices within community context
- Devotional activities that engage the heart
- Service as spiritual path
- Building and maintaining spiritual communities and institutions

Your Unique Gifts:
- Natural ability to create stability and security for others
- Practical wisdom and common sense
- Loyalty and reliability in all relationships
- Capacity to maintain beneficial traditions and values

Your Development Challenges:
- Overcoming inertia and resistance to beneficial change

- Maintaining motivation when comfortable
- Balancing attachment with necessary letting go
- Finding appropriate challenges that engage your capacities

NEUTRAL CONSTITUTION (Primarily 'c' responses) - The Strategic Leader

Congratulations! You are a Neutral Constitutional Type.

You are naturally intelligent, organized, and capable of leadership, with remarkable gifts for strategic thinking and systematic achievement. Your greatest challenges are criticism, perfectionism, and tendency toward burnout when practices become excessive.

Your Neutral Constitution Characteristics:
Physical: Medium, athletic build with strong, focused energy and heat sensitivity **Energy:** Intense, efficient energy requiring balance between challenge and rest **Mental:** Sharp, analytical mind with strategic thinking and quick decision-making **Emotional:** Strong-willed and focused with tendency toward criticism when stressed
Social: Natural leadership abilities with appreciation for competence
Spiritual: Gifts for teaching, organizing spiritual development, and systematic practice

Your Optimal Development Approach:
Physical Practices
- Moderately challenging, goal-oriented movement (sports, martial arts, competitive activities)
- Cool environments and anti-inflammatory practices
- Consistent exercise routine with measurable progress
- Cooling breathwork and practices that prevent overheating

Mental-Emotional Development
- Systematic meditation with clear developmental stages
- Intellectual engagement with wisdom teachings
- Leadership opportunities that channel your natural organizing abilities
- Balance between achievement and relaxation

Professional Integration
- Challenging career with advancement opportunities
- Leadership roles that utilize your strategic abilities
- Efficient, well-organized work environments
- Professional development that builds expertise and recognition

Spiritual Practices
- Study-based approaches to wisdom traditions

- Teaching and mentoring others
- Systematic spiritual development with clear stages
- Service through organizing and leading spiritual communities

Your Unique Gifts:
- Natural capacity for strategic thinking and organization
- Teaching and leadership abilities
- Ability to create efficient systems that serve others
- Integration of wisdom with practical effectiveness

Your Development Challenges:
- Managing tendency toward perfectionism and criticism
- Balancing intensity with necessary rest and relaxation
- Preventing burnout through sustainable pacing
- Integrating spiritual development with professional achievement

MIXED CONSTITUTIONAL TYPES

If you have significant scores in two categories, you have a mixed constitution. The most common mixed types are:

Electric-Magnetic (Creative Builder)
Creative and practical, variable energy with good endurance, artistic community builders

Electric-Neutral (Creative Leader)
Creative and strategic, sensitive leaders, artistic teachers and innovators

Magnetic-Electric (Stable Creator)
Practical and creative, stable but flexible, community-oriented healers and artists

Magnetic-Neutral (Practical Leader)
Practical and strategic, stable leaders, systematic builders and organizers

Neutral-Electric (Strategic Creator)
Strategic and creative, intelligent artists, systematic innovators and visionary leaders

Neutral-Magnetic (Efficient Builder)
Strategic and practical, efficient builders, systematic organizers and institutional developers

Mixed Type Development: You have access to abilities from both constitutional types but must be careful to adapt practices appropriately. Study both constitutional descriptions and emphasize the practices from your primary type while incorporating beneficial elements from your secondary type.

PRACTICE ADAPTATION GUIDELINES
Daily Practice Recommendations by Constitutional Type:

ELECTRIC TYPE DAILY PRACTICE:
4:00-4:15 AM: Gentle Awakening
- Rise slowly, avoid jarring alarm
- Warm water on face and hands
- Brief gratitude practice

4:15-4:45 AM: Grounding Movement (30 minutes)
- Gentle spinal movements and stretching
- Focus on stability and groundedness
- Warm environment, soft music if desired

4:45-5:00 AM: Calming Breathwork (15 minutes)
- Extended exhale breathing (4-count in, 6-count out)
- Focus on nervous system calming
- Gentle attention, no force

5:00-5:30 AM: Heart-Centered Meditation (30 minutes)
- Body awareness or loving-kindness meditation
- Shorter sessions if feeling scattered
- Focus on present moment and self-compassion

5:30-6:00 AM: Creative Study (30 minutes)
- Inspirational reading
- Journal writing
- Planning creative service activities

MAGNETIC TYPE DAILY PRACTICE:
4:00-4:15 AM: Energizing Awakening
- Rise with intention and energy
- Cold water to activate circulation
- Brief intention setting for productive day

4:15-4:50 AM: Activating Movement (35 minutes)
- Vigorous physical exercises
- Strength-building and circulation-enhancing
- Challenging pace, build endurance

4:50-5:05 AM: Energizing Breathwork (15 minutes)
- Kapalabhati (skull-shining breath) or similar
- Focus on activation and circulation
- Build heat and energy

5:05-5:35 AM: Goal-Oriented Meditation (30 minutes)
- Concentration practices with specific object
- Build sustained attention capacity
- Track progress and development

5:35-6:00 AM: Wisdom Study and Planning (25 minutes)
- Traditional texts and community wisdom
- Planning service activities and community contribution
- Focus on practical application

NEUTRAL TYPE DAILY PRACTICE:
4:00-4:15 AM: Efficient Awakening
- Rise with clarity and purpose
- Refreshing wash, prepare organized practice space
- Clear intention setting for balanced development

4:15-4:45 AM: Balanced Movement (30 minutes)
- Moderately challenging exercises
- Focus on precision and technique
- Goal-oriented progression

4:45-5:00 AM: Balancing Breathwork (15 minutes)
- Equal-count breathing (sama vritti)
- Focus on balance and clarity
- Cooling techniques if needed

5:00-5:30 AM: Analytical Meditation (30 minutes)
- Systematic insight practices
- Clear developmental stages
- Focus on understanding principles

5:30-6:00 AM: Strategic Study and Organization (30 minutes)
- Wisdom literature with focus on practical application
- Planning efficient service and development activities
- Integration of learning with daily life

CONSTITUTIONAL COMMUNITY GUIDELINES
Finding Your Constitutional Community:

Electric Types: Seek communities that honor creativity and sensitivity while providing grounding support. Look for groups that value authentic expression and personal spiritual development.

Magnetic Types: Seek stable, traditional communities with consistent practices and mutual support. Look for groups that maintain beneficial customs while providing security for families.

Neutral Types: Seek communities with competent leadership and systematic approaches to development. Look for groups that balance individual achievement with collective advancement.

Serving Others According to Your Constitution:

Electric Types: Serve through healing, inspiring, teaching, counseling, and bringing beauty into community life.

Magnetic Types: Serve through community organizing, maintaining traditions, practical support for families, and creating stable foundations for others' development.

Neutral Types: Serve through leadership, strategic planning, systematic teaching, professional integration of spiritual principles, and efficient organization of community resources.

NEXT STEPS: YOUR CONSTITUTIONAL DEVELOPMENT PLAN

Immediate Actions (Next 30 Days):

1. **Begin Constitutional Daily Practice:** Implement the daily routine appropriate for your constitutional type
2. **Environmental Adaptations:** Modify your living/work environment to support your constitutional needs
3. **Community Connection:** Find or create practice relationships with others who support constitutional understanding
4. **Professional Integration:** Begin applying constitutional awareness to work decisions and career development

Short-Term Development (3-6 Months):

1. **Advanced Practice:** Deepen your constitutional practices with qualified guidance
2. **Health Optimization:** Work with healthcare providers who understand constitutional approaches
3. **Relationship Enhancement:** Apply constitutional understanding to improve family and partnership relationships
4. **Service Development:** Identify ways to serve others using your constitutional gifts

Long-Term Integration (1-3 Years):

1. **Teaching Preparation:** Develop capacity to share constitu-

tional understanding with others
2. **Professional Mastery:** Achieve expertise in applying your constitutional type to career effectiveness
3. **Community Leadership:** Take appropriate leadership roles in spiritual community development
4. **Cultural Contribution:** Contribute to preserving and transmitting constitutional wisdom for future generations

RESOURCES FOR CONTINUED DEVELOPMENT
Essential Reading by Constitutional Type:
Electric Types
- Mystical poetry and visionary literature
- Creative expression and healing arts materials
- Gentle meditation and contemplative practice guides
- Psychology of sensitivity and high sensitivity persons

Magnetic Types
- Traditional wisdom literature and community practices
- Devotional and service-oriented spiritual materials
- Community organization and family development resources
- Practical wisdom and common-sense approaches

Neutral Types
- Systematic wisdom teachings and philosophical works
- Leadership development and strategic thinking materials
- Professional integration of spiritual principles
- Scientific approaches to spiritual development

Community Resources:
- Local Sacred Synthesis practice groups
- Constitutional awareness workshops and training programs
- Professional development applications
- Online resources and continuing education

Professional Support:
- Constitutional healthcare practitioners
- Spiritual guidance with constitutional understanding
- Professional coaching integrating constitutional awareness
- Community leaders trained in constitutional applications

Congratulations on completing the Complete Constitutional Assessment!
Understanding your constitutional type provides the essential foundation for all effective spiritual practice. This knowledge enables you to:
- Personalize every practice for maximum effectiveness and safety
- Optimize your health and energy through constitutional aware-

ness
- Enhance your relationships by understanding constitutional differences
- Accelerate your development by working with rather than against your nature
- Serve others more effectively by utilizing your constitutional gifts

Your constitutional type is not a limitation, it's your unique pathway to authentic spiritual development and beneficial service. By understanding and working with your constitutional nature, you can achieve levels of development and effectiveness that would be impossible through generic approaches.

The next step is implementation. Begin with your constitutional daily practice, create environmental support systems, and connect with others who understand constitutional awareness. Your journey toward authentic spiritual development serving both individual fulfillment and collective advancement begins now.

May your practice be exactly what you need, when you need it, in service of the highest good for yourself and all beings.

Complete Constitutional Assessment Answer Sheet

Name: _____ **Date:** _____

Instructions: Mark your response (a, b, or c) for each question:

Section I: Physical Constitution
1. __ 2. __ 3. __ 4. __ 5. __ 6. __ 7. __ 8. __ 9. __ 10.
11. __ 12. __ 13. __ 14. __ 15. __ 16. __ 17. __ 18. __ 19. __ 20.
21. __ 22. __ 23. __ 24. __ 25.

Section II: Psychological Patterns
26. __ 27. __ 28. __ 29. __ 30. __ 31. __ 32. __ 33. __ 34. __ 35.
36. __ 37. __ 38. __ 39. __ 40. __ 41. __ 42. __ 43. __ 44. __ 45.
46. __ 47. __ 48. __ 49. __ 50. __ 51. __ 52. __ 53. __ 54. __ 55.

Section III: Energy Constitution
56. __ 57. __ 58. __ 59. __ 60. __ 61. __ 62. __ 63. __ 64. __ 65.
66. __ 67. __ 68. __ 69. __ 70. __ 71. __ 72. __ 73. __ 74. __ 75.

Section IV: Social Constitution
76. __ 77. __ 78. __ 79. __ 80. __ 81. __ 82. __ 83. __ 84. __ 85.

86. ___ 87. ___ 88. ___ 89. ___ 90.

Section V: Spiritual Inclinations
91. ___ 92. ___ 93. ___ 94. ___ 95. ___ 96. ___ 97. ___ 98. ___ 99. ___ 100.
101. ___ 102. ___ 103. ___ 104. ___ 105. ___ 106. ___ 107. ___ 108.
109. ___ 110.

Section VI: Lifestyle Preferences
111. ___ 112. ___ 113. ___ 114. ___ 115. ___ 116. ___ 117. ___ 118.
119. ___ 120.
121. ___ 122. ___ 123. ___ 124. ___ 125.
SCORING
Total 'a' responses (Electric): _____ Total 'b' responses (Magnetic): _____ Total 'c' responses (Neutral): _____

PRIMARY CONSTITUTIONAL TYPE: _____
SECONDARY TYPE (if applicable): _____

This Complete Constitutional Assessment is part of the Sacred Synthesis Tier 1 series. For additional resources, advanced training, and community connections, visit [website] or contact your local Sacred Synthesis practice group.

A Deeper History

As I delved deeper into the archive, a remarkable story emerged. Beginning sometime in the 1910s and further refined in the 1940's during a period of war and strife that sounded remarkably similar to what I had read about Marcus Chen's story, something deeper that seemed to provide the history for the Sacred Synthesis movement.

Chapter 1: The Wartime Transmission (La Iniciación 1942-1947)

From darkness to light: How a small group of spiritual researchers preserved and transmitted humanity's most comprehensive synthesis of traditional wisdom during the world's darkest hour

The 4:00 AM Revelation

At 4:00 AM on August 15, 1942, while the Battle of Stalingrad raged and the fate of human civilization hung in the balance, Master Jehel and his associates gathered in the pre-dawn darkness of Montevideo to begin documenting what would become the most comprehensive synthesis of traditional wisdom ever assembled.

Their work, conducted in secret during humanity's darkest hour, preserved and transmitted teachings that would bridge ancient wisdom with contemporary understanding for generations yet unborn.

The timing was not coincidental. As fascist forces consolidated power across Europe and Asia, systematically destroying libraries, universities, and spiritual communities, a small group of researchers in South America recognized that the wisdom of ages faced extinction unless immediate action was taken to preserve and transmit essential knowledge through the coming darkness.

Their achievement, documented in the extraordinary 72 issues of La Iniciación magazine published between 1942 and 1947, represents one of history's most remarkable acts of cultural preservation and spiritual transmission. Working under conditions of global war, economic uncertainty, and political upheaval, the Grupo Independiente de Estudios Esotéricos (GIDEE) accomplished what seemed impossible: a systematic integration of Eastern and Western wisdom traditions that maintained rigorous scholarly standards while providing practical guidance for authentic spiritual development.

The Vision Behind the Mission
The founders of GIDEE understood that the crises facing humanity required not mere intellectual solutions, but the activation of humanity's highest developmental potentials through systematic spiritual practice integrated with practical service. Their vision, articulated in the September 1942 inaugural issue of La Iniciación, demonstrated prophetic accuracy:

"The current crisis represents humanity's transition from fragmented tribal consciousness to integrated planetary awareness. The apparent victory of destructive forces marks their final exhaustion. The future belongs to those who can integrate the wisdom of ages with the needs of emerging global civilization."

This understanding guided their work throughout the war years, creating not merely another spiritual magazine, but a comprehensive curriculum for conscious human evolution that would prove its effectiveness through decades of practical application

The Montevideo Circle: Guardians of Ancient Wisdom
The Confluence of Circumstances

Montevideo, Uruguay, in the 1940s provided the perfect laboratory for cross-cultural spiritual synthesis. The country's progressive political climate, cultural openness, and geographic isolation from European and North American ideological conflicts created ideal conditions for unbiased exploration of wisdom traditions often seen as politically or culturally threatening elsewhere.

The city's unique position as a cultural crossroads brought together European immigrants carrying diverse spiritual traditions, indigenous wisdom keepers maintaining South American shamanic practices, and Eastern influences arriving through trade and academic exchange. Rather than seeing conflict between these approaches, the GIDEE researchers recognized complementary methodologies addressing universal human developmental needs.

Leo Costet de Mascheville: The Visionary Leader

Born in 1901, Leo Costet de Mascheville, known to his colleagues as Dr. Jehel, embodied the synthesis he would spend his life documenting. The son of Albert Raymond Costet de Mascheville (Cedaior), who had established the Laws of Vayu framework in 1919, Leo inherited both European esoteric knowledge and South American cultural adaptability.

His education combined traditional university training with deep immersion in multiple wisdom traditions. Fluent in Spanish, Portuguese, French, and English, with reading knowledge of Sanskrit, Hebrew, and Arabic, Leo possessed the linguistic competency essential for accessing primary sources across cultural boundaries. More importantly, he maintained relationships with authorized teachers within traditional communities, ensuring that synthesis work respected cultural boundaries while serving universal human needs.

The Research Methodology
The GIDEE approach to cross-cultural synthesis was revolutionary in its systematic methodology. Rather than casual borrowing or superficial comparison, their work followed rigorous principles:

Cultural Authentication: Every practice or teaching included in their synthesis required validation from authorized teachers within its traditional context. This prevented the cultural appropriation that would later plague New Age movements while ensuring authentic transmission of essential knowledge.

Scientific Validation: Wherever possible, traditional claims were tested through contemporary scientific methodology.

Practical Effectiveness: All synthesized approaches required demonstration of practical benefits in daily life. Theoretical understanding that did not enhance health, relationships, professional effectiveness, or community service was considered incomplete regardless of its scholarly merit.

Community Benefit: Individual spiritual development was always understood within the context of collective advancement. Practices that promoted personal achievement without corresponding service to others were viewed as spiritually immature and potentially harmful.

The Wartime Achievement: Synthesis Under Fire

September 1942: The Turning Point

The launch of La Iniciación magazine in September 1942 coincided precisely with the Battle of Stalingrad, the moment historians now recognize as the turning point of World War II. This timing reflected not coincidence but the synthesis tradition's capacity for historical insight and crisis navigation.

While conventional analysis focused on military strategies and political alliances, the GIDEE perspective recognized deeper patterns. Their September 1942 editorial demonstrated remarkable historical understanding:

"The forces of destruction have reached their maximum expression and are beginning their inevitable decline. What appears as humanity's darkest hour actually represents the completion of humanity's adolescent phase and the beginning of conscious maturity. The wisdom of ages, preserved through millennia of tribal and national conflict, now emerges to guide planetary civilization."

This perspective enabled their work to serve not merely preservation but active contribution to humanity's evolutionary advancement during its most critical transition.

The Magazine Structure: A Complete Curriculum

Each issue of La Iniciación was carefully structured to provide systematic instruction across multiple developmental domains:

Theoretical Foundation: Articles by Surya SI provided precise astrological instruction based on traditional Vedic sources while incorporating contemporary astronomical understanding. These teachings offered practical methods for understanding cosmic timing, individual constitution, and optimal periods for specific activities.

Embodied Practice: Asuri Kapila's yoga instruction integrated traditional Hatha Yoga with clinical understanding of anatomy and physiology. Each technique was presented with specific instructions, safety guidelines, contraindications, and measurable outcomes.

Character Development: Anonymous contributors preserved Kabbalistic, Christian, and Islamic approaches to virtue cultivation and character refinement, presenting these methods in practical forms adaptable to contemporary family and professional life.

Community Application: Dr. Jehel's editorial guidance connected individual practices with democratic community organization, economic cooperation, and cultural preservation, ensuring that spiritual development served collective advancement.

Scientific Validation: Regular reports on clinical research, including Dr. Coulon's bioelectromagnetic studies and surgical timing correlation research, provided objective evidence supporting traditional claims while maintaining appropriate scientific skepticism.

The Synthesis Methodology in Action

The La Iniciación approach to East-West integration exemplified respectful synthesis methodology that would later be preserved through decades of practical application.

Hindu-Vedantic Integration: Rather than adopting Hindu practices wholesale, the magazine explored how Vedantic philosophy provided universal principles that could be expressed through diverse cultural forms. The recognition that consciousness unity underlies apparent diversity offered a framework for authentic integration without cultural appropriation.

Buddhist Psychology: The Four Noble Truths and Eightfold Path were presented not as Buddhist doctrine but as systematic methodology for understanding and transforming human suffering, approaches that could enhance rather than replace other wisdom traditions.

Christian Mysticism: The contemplative prayer tradition and stages of mystical development described by Christian masters were

52

shown to address identical developmental phases documented in Eastern systems, enabling mutual enrichment rather than competitive comparison.

Jewish Kabbalah: The Tree of Life and Sephirotic system provided mapping of consciousness development that corresponded remarkably with Hindu chakra psychology and Buddhist Jhana states, offering practical frameworks for understanding spiritual advancement across traditions.

Islamic Sufism: The emphasis on love, service, and surrender provided essential balance to purely analytical approaches, while Sufi community organization principles offered models for democratic spiritual governance.

The Contributors: Guardians of Sacred Knowledge
Master Surya SI: The Astrological Bridge
The mysterious figure known as Surya SI provided the astrological foundation that enabled systematic understanding of individual constitutional differences and optimal timing for spiritual practices. Their identity remains uncertain, possibly the French astrologer Paul Le Cour or the Spanish esotericist Mario Roso de Luna, but their contributions proved essential for practical synthesis application.

Surya SI's astrological instruction differed fundamentally from popular astrology in its emphasis on practical application rather than personality description. Their articles provided:

Constitutional Assessment: Methods for understanding individual physical, emotional, mental, and spiritual characteristics that determined optimal approaches to diet, exercise, contemplative practice, and service activities.

Timing Applications: Systematic correlation of cosmic cycles with daily activities, enabling enhanced effectiveness in health maintenance, relationship development, professional advancement, and spiritual practice.

Medical Astrology: Integration of traditional astrological medicine with contemporary healthcare, including surgical timing research that demonstrated measurable improvements in outcomes when traditional timing principles were observed.

Community Coordination: Applications of astrological understanding to group activities, ensuring that community gatherings, educational programs, and service projects occurred during optimal cosmic conditions.

Asuri Kapila: The Embodied Sage

The yoga instruction provided by Asuri Kapila established embodiment practice as essential foundation for authentic spiritual development. Their systematic approach integrated traditional Hatha Yoga with contemporary understanding of physiology, creating safe and effective practices adaptable to diverse constitutional types and life circumstances.

Key innovations included:

Constitutional Adaptation: Recognition that identical practices affect different constitutional types differently, requiring individualized modification rather than uniform instruction.

Therapeutic Application: Integration of yoga practice with medical treatment, providing specific adaptations for common health challenges while maintaining appropriate boundaries with healthcare providers.

Family Integration: Approaches enabling entire families to participate in embodiment practice while respecting individual developmental needs and maintaining practical daily functioning.

Professional Enhancement: Demonstration of how embodiment practice enhances rather than conflicts with professional effectiveness through improved health, stress management, and present-moment attention.

The Anonymous Masters: Preservers of Sacred Traditions

Many of the most profound contributions to La Iniciación were provided by anonymous contributors who preserved Kabbalistic, Christian, and Islamic wisdom with remarkable fidelity to traditional sources while enabling contemporary application.

Their work demonstrated:

Cultural Authenticity: Deep knowledge of primary sources, traditional commentaries, and community practices that ensured accurate transmission rather than personal interpretation.

Contemporary Relevance: Skillful adaptation of traditional methods to serve modern life circumstances without compromising essential effectiveness or cultural integrity.

Cross-Traditional Recognition: Understanding of how different wisdom traditions addressed identical human developmental needs through culturally specific methodologies, enabling respectful comparison without superficial syncretism.

Practical Effectiveness: Focus on methods that produced measurable results in daily life rather than merely theoretical understanding or emotional experience.

The Global Network: Seeds of Planetary Transformation
International Connections During Wartime
Despite wartime restrictions on international communication, GIDEE maintained connections with similar groups across South America and beyond. Their correspondence reveals an international network of spiritual researchers working to preserve traditional wisdom and develop practical applications during humanity's darkest hour.

The Argentine Connection: Groups in Buenos Aires provided urban testing grounds for community applications of traditional practices, demonstrating effectiveness in metropolitan contexts under economic and social pressure.

Brazilian Collaborations: Partners in São Paulo and Rio de Janeiro contributed understanding of Afro- Brazilian traditions and indigenous wisdom, enriching the synthesis with shamanic approaches to healing and community organization.

European Correspondence: Despite wartime disruptions, limited communication with surviving European esoteric groups provided validation of synthesis accuracy and cultural authenticity from traditional Western sources.

North American Contacts: Early connections with receptive researchers in Mexico and the United States laid groundwork for eventual northward transmission of synthesis materials and methodologies.
The Vision of Planetary Consciousness
Throughout the war years, GIDEE maintained a vision that extended far beyond preservation of ancient wisdom to active contribution to humanity's evolutionary advancement. Their understanding of the global crisis as opportunity for conscious development enabled work that served both immediate needs and long-term human potential.

Immediate Applications: Practical guidance for maintaining spiritual development under extreme conditions, including meditation techniques for air raid shelters, nutritional adaptation during rationing, and community organization during social disruption.

Cultural Bridge-Building: Methods for respectful cooperation across cultural and religious boundaries, essential for post-war reconstruction and international cooperation.

Educational Innovation: Approaches to education that integrated character development with intellectual training, preparing future generations for conscious participation in planetary civilization.

Economic Cooperation: Models of community economics based on reciprocity and sustainability rather than competition and exploitation, offering alternatives to both capitalist and communist systems.

The Scientific Foundation: Ancient Wisdom Meets Modern Research
Dr. Johnny Coulon: Pioneer of Bioelectromagnetic Research
Dr. Johnny Coulon's research, documented extensively in La Iniciación, provided some of the earliest scientific validation of traditional understanding of human energy systems. His bioelectromagnetic studies demonstrated measurable changes in the human electromagnetic field during meditation, prayer, and other contemplative practices.

Key findings included:

Energy Field Documentation: Objective measurement of electromagnetic field changes during traditional practices, validating ancient understanding of human energy systems through contemporary scientific methodology.

Therapeutic Applications: Clinical studies demonstrating healing benefits of practices that optimized electromagnetic field coherence, providing scientific foundation for traditional healing approaches.

Environmental Correlations: Research documenting correlations between human electromagnetic fields and environmental factors including cosmic cycles, providing validation for astrological timing principles.

Community Field Effects: Measurements showing coherent electromagnetic patterns during group practices, offering scientific explanation for traditional understanding of collective consciousness and community spiritual activities.

Clinical Validation Studies

The magazine regularly reported on clinical research validating traditional approaches across multiple domains:

Nutritional Adaptation Studies: Research showing improved health outcomes when dietary recommendations were individualized according to traditional constitutional assessment rather than universal nutritional guidelines.

Contemplative Practice Research: Clinical studies documenting measurable improvements in emotional stability, mental clarity, and social effectiveness through systematic application of traditional meditation and prayer techniques.

Community Organization Studies: Documentation of improved social cohesion, economic efficiency, and conflict resolution capacity in groups applying traditional organizational principles to contemporary challenges.

The Transmission Continues: From War to Wisdom
The Post-War Legacy

The conclusion of World War II in 1945 did not end GIDEE's mission but transformed it. The final issues of La Iniciación in 1946-1947 focused on post-war reconstruction and the application of wartime-tested synthesis principles to building peaceful and sustainable civilization.

Cultural Preservation: Methods for preserving traditional wisdom while enabling cultural adaptation, ensuring that ancient knowledge would remain available for future generations without becoming fossilized museum pieces.

Educational Integration: Approaches to incorporating character development and contemplative practice into formal education systems, creating learning environments that served both intellectual advancement and spiritual development.

International Cooperation: Frameworks for respectful collaboration across cultural and national boundaries, providing alternatives to both nationalist isolation and cultural imperialism.

Environmental Restoration: Understanding of human-nature relationships based on traditional ecological wisdom, offering guidance for healing environmental damage and preventing future ecological crises.

The Contemporary Relevance: Lessons for Our Time
The Crisis Pattern Recognition
The GIDEE achievement during World War II offers essential guidance for addressing contemporary global challenges. Their understanding that periods of apparent breakdown actually represent opportunities for evolutionary advancement provides hope and practical direction for current crises.

Climate Change Response: Traditional ecological wisdom preserved through synthesis work offers alternative approaches to environmental challenges that address root causes rather than merely technological symptoms.

Social Fragmentation Healing: Community organization principles tested during wartime provide methods for rebuilding social cohesion while maintaining individual dignity and cultural diversity.

Economic System Transformation: Models of cooperative economics based on reciprocity and sustainability offer alternatives to systems that create inequality and environmental destruction.

International Cooperation: Cultural bridge-building methodologies demonstrate how diverse wisdom traditions can contribute to planetary healing without compromising authentic cultural identity.
The Digital Age Application
Contemporary technology offers unprecedented opportunities for transmitting traditional wisdom while maintaining cultural authenticity and community connection:

Global Communication: Digital platforms enable real-time connection among practitioners worldwide while preserving local community relationships and cultural contexts.

Educational Innovation: Online learning systems can deliver systematic instruction in traditional practices while maintaining qualified teacher relationships and community validation.

Research Validation: Contemporary scientific methodology can provide objective measurement of traditional practices while respecting cultural boundaries and maintaining appropriate humility regarding spiritual dimensions.

Community Organization: Digital tools can support democratic decision-making and resource coordination while preserving the face-to-face relationships essential for authentic spiritual community.

The Living Transmission: Continuing the Work

Scientific Validation: Neuroscience research confirming traditional consciousness development claims, psychology integration demonstrating personality transformation effectiveness, medical applications validating traditional healing approaches with clinical outcomes.

Cultural Applications: North American programs serving diverse populations with measurable outcomes, European reconnections with traditional sources and contemporary applications, Latin American community development preserving culture while enabling advancement.

Professional Integration: Healthcare applications demonstrating improved patient outcomes through integration of traditional approaches with medical care, educational programs showing enhanced learning effectiveness through contemplative curriculum development, organizational applications proving increased effectiveness through consciousness-based leadership.

Global Network Coordination: International implementation maintaining cultural sensitivity and local autonomy while enabling worldwide cooperation and mutual support among practitioners across cultural boundaries.

The Academic Recognition
Contemporary academic institutions increasingly recognize the value of systematic approaches to consciousness development and cross-cultural wisdom integration:

University Programs: Courses in contemplative education, integral psychology, and cultural bridge-building based on synthesis principles demonstrate academic acceptance of formerly esoteric knowledge.

Research Collaboration: Joint studies between traditional knowledge communities and academic institutions validate ancient understanding through contemporary methodology while maintaining appropriate cultural boundaries.

Clinical Applications: Medical schools incorporating traditional healing approaches, psychology programs teaching personality transformation methods, and business schools exploring consciousness-based leadership reflect growing professional recognition.

Cultural Documentation: Academic efforts to preserve traditional knowledge and document successful synthesis approaches ensure that ancient wisdom remains available for future generations.

Chapter Summary: The Eternal Dawn
The 4:00 AM gathering in Montevideo on August 15, 1942, represented far more than historical preservation, it initiated humanity's conscious participation in its own evolutionary advancement. The GIDEE achievement demonstrates that authentic wisdom transcends cultural boundaries while honoring traditional sources, that spiritual development serves collective advancement while fulfilling individual potential, and that human consciousness can navigate global crises through integration rather than fragmentation.

Key Insights for Contemporary Practice:

1. **Crisis as Opportunity**: Periods of apparent breakdown actually represent evolutionary transition points requiring consciousness development rather than merely external solutions.
2. **Synthesis Through Respect**: Authentic integration of diverse wisdom traditions requires deep cultural understanding and community authorization rather than casual borrowing or superficial combination.
3. **Individual-Collective Balance**: Personal spiritual development must serve community advancement while community support enables individual fulfillment, neither dimension can be neglected without compromising both.
4. **Traditional-Contemporary Integration**: Ancient wisdom provides essential guidance for contemporary challenges when skillfully adapted through qualified teachers and community validation rather than academic study alone.
5. **Global Service Through Local Community**: Planetary healing occurs through local community development that connects individual practice with collective advancement

and international cooperation.

The wartime transmission preserved through La Iniciación continues to offer guidance for navigating contemporary challenges while maintaining hope for humanity's conscious evolution. The work begun in darkness at 4:00 AM on August 15, 1942, continues to illuminate pathways toward individual fulfillment and collective advancement that serve both human potential and planetary healing.

Essential Resources for Further Study

Primary Historical Sources:
- *La Iniciación* complete archive (1942-1947): Digital collection with complete issues and analytical commentary
- Laws of Vayu manuscript (1919): Cedaior's foundational framework for conscious evolution

Contemporary Applications:
- Clinical research compilation: Medical and psychological studies validating traditional approaches
- Global community network: International connections for practice support and cultural exchange

Academic Resources:
- Sacred Books of the East series: Primary sources across wisdom traditions
- Contemporary consciousness research: Scientific validation of traditional understanding
- Cultural preservation methodology: Respectful approaches to traditional knowledge transmission

Visit **sacredfoundations.org/wartime-transmission** with code **DAWN1942** to access complete digital archive, practice guidance, and global community connections.

Chapter 2: The Laws of Vayu Foundation (1919)

The Portuguese Revelation: How Albert Raymond Costet de Mascheville (Cedaior) established the theoretical framework that would enable the greatest synthesis of traditional wisdom in modern history

The Genesis of Universal Principles (1919)
In 1919, as the world struggled to rebuild after the devastation of World War I, a remarkable Portuguese manuscript emerged from

South America that would lay the foundation for humanity's most comprehensive understanding of consciousness development. Albert Raymond Costet de Mascheville, writing under the mystical name Cedaior, completed "As Leis de Vayu" (The Laws of Vayu), a revolutionary work that demonstrated how Eastern wisdom could be systematically integrated with Western organizational capacity to serve both individual development and collective advancement.

The timing was prophetic. As the League of Nations attempted to create international cooperation through political treaties, Cedaior was documenting the inner laws that govern authentic human unity, principles that would prove far more durable than any external agreement. His achievement represents one of the most significant breakthroughs in consciousness studies, providing the theoretical framework that would enable the practical synthesis documented in La Iniciación magazine twenty-three years later.

The Evolutionary Vision
Cedaior's central insight was revolutionary: human beings possess an inherent capacity for what he termed "Olympic development", the systematic integration of spiritual realization with practical competency that serves both individual fulfillment and collective evolution. This was not mystical idealism but precise methodology based on universal principles that transcend cultural boundaries while honoring traditional sources.

"The Olympic human being achieves complete synthesis between inner development and outer effectiveness, demonstrating that authentic spiritual realization enhances rather than conflicts with practical capability and social contribution."

This understanding challenged both Eastern approaches that emphasized transcendence of worldly involvement and Western traditions that separated spiritual development from professional competency. Cedaior demonstrated that true spiritual maturity actually requires practical effectiveness, while authentic worldly success depends upon consciousness development.

The Seven Laws: Universal Principles for Conscious Evolution

The Theoretical Framework
The Laws of Vayu present seven fundamental principles that govern all conscious development, both individual and collective. These laws represent distillation of universal principles found across wis-

dom traditions but expressed in forms that enable contemporary application while maintaining traditional authenticity.

Law I: The Law of Evolutionary Spiral Development

All consciousness development follows spiral patterns that integrate previous achievements while enabling advancement to higher organizational levels

This principle explains why authentic spiritual development requires systematic progression through developmental stages rather than sudden enlightenment experiences. Each stage must be fully integrated before advancement to the next level becomes possible, and each higher stage encompasses and transforms rather than abandons previous achievements.

Contemporary developmental psychology validates this understanding. Research by theorists like Jean Piaget, Lawrence Kohlberg, and Ken Wilber demonstrates that human development follows predictable sequences that cannot be bypassed. The Laws of Vayu provided this insight fifty years before academic psychology reached similar conclusions.

Law II: The Law of Constitutional Diversity

Individual differences in physical, emotional, mental, and spiritual constitution require personalized approaches to optimal development while maintaining universal principles

Cedaior recognized that universal principles must be adapted to individual constitutional differences to achieve optimal effectiveness. This understanding prevented the "one-size-fits-all" approaches that characterize many spiritual systems while maintaining systematic methodology.

This law laid the foundation for the constitutional assessment systems with individualized approaches to nutrition, exercise, contemplative practice, and character development producing superior outcomes compared to uniform prescriptions.

Law III: The Law of Democratic Spiritual Authority

Authentic spiritual leadership serves rather than dominates, enabling rather than controlling, and emerges through demonstrated competency and character rather than appointment or inheritance

This revolutionary principle resolved the tension between spiritual authority and democratic participation that plagued both religious institutions and political organizations. Cedaior demonstrated that authentic authority emerges naturally from consciousness development combined with practical service rather than external appointment or inherited status.

The democratic mysticism developed through Olympic Community applications proved that spiritual communities could maintain traditional wisdom transmission while enabling participatory governance and individual freedom. This synthesis prevented both authoritarian spirituality and materialistic democracy.

Law IV: The Law of Service-Integrated Development

Individual spiritual advancement occurs through service to collective welfare rather than self-centered practice, and collective advancement requires individual consciousness development rather than external reorganization alone

This principle established that authentic spiritual development must benefit others while collective advancement requires individual consciousness development. Neither purely personal spirituality nor purely social activism achieves optimal results, integration is essential.

Contemporary research in positive psychology validates this understanding. Studies demonstrate that individuals who combine personal development practices with community service experience greater life satisfaction, health benefits, and spiritual advancement than those who focus exclusively on either dimension.

Law V: The Law of Cultural Bridge-Building

Universal principles underlying diverse wisdom traditions enable respectful synthesis without cultural appropriation when conducted with proper authorization and community accountability

This law provided the theoretical foundation for the East-West synthesis that would be achieved through GIDEE. Cedaior understood that authentic integration required deep respect for traditional sources combined with contemporary applications that serve rather than exploit cultural wisdom.

The cultural bridge-building methodology developed through this principle has enabled successful cooperation across religious and cultural boundaries without compromising traditional authenticity. Academic validation of this approach appears in contemporary religious studies and anthropological research on respectful cross- cultural exchange.

Law VI: The Law of Scientific Validation

Traditional wisdom claims must be validated through objective criteria and measurable outcomes while maintaining respect for dimensions that transcend purely material measurement

Cedaior insisted that spiritual development must demonstrate practical benefits that can be objectively assessed while acknowledging that consciousness includes dimensions beyond purely material measurement. This balanced approach prevented both materialistic reductionism and anti-intellectual spirituality.

The extensive clinical research validating traditional practices, from meditation effects on brain function to astrological timing correlations with surgical outcomes, demonstrates the prescience of this principle.
Contemporary neuroscience, psychology, and medical research increasingly validate traditional understanding while maintaining appropriate scientific methodology.

Law VII: The Law of Planetary Consciousness

Individual and community development must serve planetary welfare and species evolution while local autonomy and cultural diversity are preserved rather than homogenized

This final law established that authentic spiritual development naturally expresses through environmental stewardship, international cooperation, and cultural evolution serving humanity's collective advancement while preserving the diversity essential for continued evolution.

Contemporary environmental science and systems theory validate this understanding. Research demonstrates that ecological health, cultural diversity, and social cooperation are interconnected requirements for sustainable civilization, insights that Cedaior articulated decades before they became academically recognized.

The Olympic Community: Democratic Mysticism in Practice
The Six-Level Organizational Framework
The Laws of Vayu included detailed methodology for organizing communities that support both individual development and collective advancement through democratic participation integrated with spiritual authority. This Olympic Community structure provided the organizational principles later applied through GIDEE.

Level I: Family Foundation
Intimate partnerships and family relationships as primary spiritual development laboratories

The Olympic Community begins with conscious family formation based on constitutional compatibility, shared spiritual commitment, and practical cooperation. This level includes conscious procreation methodologies that consider cosmic timing and compatibility for optimal child development, as well as family practices that serve both individual growth and family harmony.

Research validates that family relationships provide the most intensive opportunities for character development and spiritual advancement. The emotional intimacy, daily cooperation, and long-term commitment required for successful family life develop capacities essential for broader community participation and spiritual maturity.

Level II: Local Community Participation
Neighborhood and bioregional engagement serving local needs while developing civic capacity

The second level extends family foundation through active participation in local community development. This includes environmental stewardship, economic cooperation, educational contribution, and cultural preservation that serves immediate community needs while developing capacities necessary for broader service.

Studies in community psychology demonstrate that local civic participation enhances both individual well-being and social effectiveness. People who actively contribute to their immediate communities develop leadership skills, social networks, and cultural understanding essential for broader social contribution.

Level III: Professional Excellence and Service
Career development as spiritual practice serving both individual advancement and collective benefit

The third level integrates spiritual development with professional competency, demonstrating that consciousness development enhances rather than conflicts with career success. This includes leadership approaches that serve organizational effectiveness while honoring human dignity, and professional practices that contribute to cultural advancement rather than mere personal achievement.

Organizational psychology research validates that consciousness-based leadership approaches produce superior outcomes in employee satisfaction, productivity, innovation, and ethical performance. Leaders who combine professional competency with character development and service orientation achieve more sustainable success than those focused exclusively on technical or competitive capabilities.

Level IV: Cultural Contribution and Innovation
Creative and intellectual contributions that serve cultural evolution while preserving essential traditional wisdom

The fourth level engages cultural development through artistic expression, intellectual contribution, educational innovation, and spiritual teaching that serves collective advancement while maintaining connection to traditional sources. This includes balancing cultural preservation with beneficial innovation.

Research in creativity studies demonstrates that individuals who combine deep traditional knowledge with contemporary applications produce more significant and enduring cultural contributions than those who focus exclusively on either preservation or innovation. Cultural evolution requires integration of both dimensions.

Level V: Regional Coordination and Network Development
Inter-community cooperation serving bioregional needs and modeling principles for broader application
The fifth level coordinates multiple communities within bioregional contexts, developing inter-community cooperation protocols, resource sharing agreements, and conflict resolution methodologies that serve regional welfare while maintaining community autonomy. This level provides training for national and international service.

Environmental and political science research validates bioregional approaches to governance and resource management. Human social organization aligned with ecological boundaries produces more sustainable and equitable outcomes than systems based purely on political or economic boundaries.

Level VI: Global Service and Planetary Healing
International cooperation and planetary service through consciousness-based approaches to global challenges
The sixth level engages global challenges through international cooperation based on consciousness development rather than political competition. This includes climate change response, cultural bridge-building, economic justice initiatives, and educational cooperation that serves planetary healing through local competency and global awareness.

Contemporary global studies research demonstrates that solutions to planetary-scale challenges require coordination across cultural and national boundaries combined with local autonomy and cultural diversity. The Olympic Community methodology provides frameworks for this essential integration.

The Seven Consecrations: Life-Stage Development
The Laws of Vayu established seven major life-stage initiations that mark significant developmental transitions and community recognition of increased capacity and responsibility. These consecrations provide systematic guidance for lifelong development while enabling community assessment of readiness for increased service.

Consecration I: Conception and Prenatal Development
Conscious procreation and prenatal preparation for optimal incarnation

The first consecration addresses conscious procreation methodologies including cosmic timing considerations, constitutional compatibility assessment, and prenatal practices that support optimal child development. This consecration requires extensive preparation in family spirituality and child development understanding.

Contemporary prenatal psychology and epigenetic research validate traditional understanding that prenatal conditions significantly influence lifelong development patterns. Conscious prenatal practices produce measurable benefits in child health, emotional stability, and learning capacity.

Consecration II: Birth and Early Childhood Foundation (Ages 0-7)
Physical embodiment and foundational character formation

The second consecration focuses on early childhood development through constitutional assessment, appropriate educational approaches, family spiritual practices, and character formation that serves both individual potential and social cooperation. Parents and community members receive training in child development and spiritual guidance.

Developmental psychology research demonstrates that early childhood experiences determine lifelong patterns of emotional regulation, social competency, and learning capacity. Traditional child-rearing practices integrated with contemporary understanding produce optimal developmental outcomes.

Consecration III: Youth Development and Education (Ages 7-14)

Character formation and educational excellence integrated with spiritual development

The third consecration addresses adolescent development through educational approaches that combine
intellectual advancement with character formation, peer relationship skills, and community contribution. Young people begin specialized training in areas of natural talent while maintaining general education requirements.

Educational research validates approaches that combine academic excellence with character development, community service, and practical skill development. Students who receive integrated education demonstrate superior outcomes in both academic achievement and social effectiveness.

Consecration IV: Young Adulthood and Professional Preparation (Ages 14-21)

Professional development and service preparation integrated with spiritual maturity

The fourth consecration prepares young adults for professional contribution and family responsibility through specialized training, mentorship relationships, travel and cultural exchange, and service projects that develop leadership capacity while maintaining spiritual foundation.

Career development research demonstrates that young adults who combine professional training with character development, cultural exposure, and service experience achieve greater career satisfaction and social contribution than those focused exclusively on technical preparation.

Consecration V: Mature Adult Service and Leadership (Ages 21-42)
Professional excellence and family leadership integrated with community service

The fifth consecration encompasses mature adult development through professional excellence, family leadership, community service, and specialized contributions to cultural advancement. Adults at this stage provide mentorship and community coordination while continuing personal development.

Adult developmental psychology research shows that mature adults who balance professional achievement with family responsibility and community service experience greater life satisfaction and continued growth than those focused exclusively on career advancement or personal achievement.

Consecration VI: Elder Wisdom and Cultural Transmission (Ages 42-63)

Wisdom sharing and cultural preservation through teaching and community guidance

The sixth consecration engages elder development through teaching responsibilities, cultural preservation activities, conflict resolution and community guidance, and preparation of younger generations for leadership. Elders begin transitioning from active doing to wisdom transmission.

Gerontological research demonstrates that elders who remain actively engaged in teaching, mentoring, and cultural contribution maintain better physical health, cognitive function, and life satisfaction than those who withdraw from active participation.

Consecration VII: Transcendent Service and Planetary Healing (Ages 63+)
Global service and spiritual realization serving planetary evolution

The seventh consecration addresses advanced spiritual development through global service activities, teaching and wisdom transmission, environmental stewardship, and preparation for conscious transition. Advanced elders serve as bridges between traditional wisdom and contemporary applications.

Studies of successful aging demonstrate that individuals who maintain active service orientation and global awareness while deepening spiritual practice achieve the highest levels of life satisfaction and continued development throughout their later years.

The Democratic Revolution: Authority Through Service
Integration of Spiritual Authority with Participatory Governance
One of Cedaior's most significant innovations addressed the perennial tension between spiritual authority and democratic participation. The Laws of Vayu demonstrated that authentic spiritual authority serves rather than dominates, enabling rather than controlling, and emerges through demonstrated competency and character rather than appointment or inheritance.

The Crisis of Authoritarian Spirituality

Traditional spiritual communities often suffered from authoritarian structures that concentrated power in single leaders while demanding unquestioning obedience from followers. This approach produced spiritual dependency, abuse of authority, and stagnation of community development while discouraging individual responsibility and democratic participation.

Cedaior recognized that authentic spiritual development requires individual responsibility and democratic participation rather than passive compliance with external authority. The Olympic Community methodology resolved this conflict through democratic mysticism that honors both authentic wisdom and participatory governance.

Democratic Mysticism: Theory and Practice

Democratic mysticism integrates authentic spiritual authority with participatory decision-making through systematic procedures that ensure community decisions serve spiritual development while maintaining individual freedom and collective effectiveness.
Key principles include:

- **Earned Authority**: Leadership emerges through demonstrated spiritual development, practical competency, and service contribution rather than appointment or inheritance
- **Collective Wisdom**: Major decisions require community consultation and consensus-building while maintaining appropriate individual autonomy
- **Rotating Responsibility**: Leadership roles rotate among qualified community members to prevent power concentration and develop collective capacity
- **Transparent Process**: All decision-making procedures are open to community observation and feedback to maintain accountability and

trust

Chapter Summary: The Enduring Foundation

The Laws of Vayu represent one of the most significant theoretical
breakthroughs in consciousness studies, providing universal principles that enable authentic integration of individual development
with collective advancement. Cedaior's 1919 achievement established the systematic framework that made possible the
practical synthesis documented in La Iniciación magazine.

Key Theoretical Contributions:
1. **Universal Principles with Cultural Sensitivity**: Demonstration
   that consciousness development follows universal laws that can be
   applied across cultural boundaries while honoring traditional
   sources and maintaining cultural authenticity.
2. **Individual-Collective Integration**: Resolution of the false
   dichotomy between personal spiritual development and social responsibility through systematic methodology that serves both dimensions simultaneously.
3. **Democratic Mysticism**: Integration of authentic spiritual authority
   with participatory governance that prevents both authoritarian spirituality and materialistic democracy while enabling community organization based on consciousness development.
4. **Scientific Validation Framework**: Establishment of criteria for
   objective assessment of spiritual development claims while acknowledging dimensions that transcend purely material measurement.
5. **Developmental Sequence Understanding**: Recognition that
   consciousness development follows predictable stages that require
   systematic progression and community support while allowing for
   individual constitutional differences.

Foundation for Global Synthesis:
The theoretical framework established through the Laws of Vayu
enabled the practical achievements documented in subsequent chapters, the GIDEE wartime synthesis, and the contemporary applications that demonstrate how ancient wisdom serves modern needs
while maintaining traditional authenticity.

The seven universal principles, Olympic Community organizational
methodology, Seven Consecrations developmental framework, as-
trogenesis applications, and democratic mysticism innovations established by Cedaior in 1919 continue to provide essential guidance

for individual development and collective advancement in the 21st century.

The Living Legacy:
More than a century after its formulation, the Laws of Vayu continue to demonstrate relevance for addressing humanity's greatest challenges while supporting individual fulfillment and community advancement. The systematic methodology for consciousness development integrated with practical effectiveness offers hope for resolving contemporary crises through approaches that honor both ancient wisdom and contemporary needs.

The foundation was established. The framework was complete. The stage was set for the practical demonstration that would unfold during humanity's darkest hour, the wartime synthesis that proved universal principles could bridge cultural boundaries while serving both individual development and planetary healing.

Essential Resources for Advanced Study

Primary Historical Sources:
- As Leis de Vayu complete original manuscript (1919): Portuguese text with scholarly translations and commentary

Contemporary Research Validation:
- Clinical studies compilation: Medical and psychological research validating constitutional approaches
- Educational integration studies: Academic research on contemplative education and character development

Practical Application Guides:
- Democratic mysticism implementation: Organizational development guides and governance protocols
- Seven Consecrations curriculum: Life-stage development programs and community validation procedures

Academic Resources:
- Comparative consciousness studies: Cross-cultural analysis of developmental theories
- Contemporary developmental psychology: Research validating stage-sequential development
    - Social psychology and community organization: Academic validation of democratic mysticism principles

Visit **sacredfoundations.org/laws-of-vayu** with code **OLYM-PIC1919** to access complete theoretical framework, practical applications, and research validation materials.

Chapter 3: The GIDEE and Cultural Building

From Theory to Living Reality: How a small group in wartime Montevideo accomplished the greatest synthesis of traditional wisdom in documented history and established the methodology for respectful cultural integration

The Laboratory of Synthesis (1932-1947)

Montevideo: The Perfect Crucible

When Leo Costet de Mascheville established the Grupo Independiente de Estudios Esotéricos (GIDEE) in Montevideo in 1932, Uruguay provided the ideal conditions for unprecedented cultural experimentation. The country's progressive political climate, cultural openness, and geographic isolation from European and North American ideological conflicts created perfect laboratory conditions for unbiased exploration of wisdom traditions often seen as politically or culturally threatening elsewhere.

More than mere intellectual curiosity drove this work. GIDEE members understood that the approaching global crisis would require new approaches transcending the limitations of single traditions. Their prophetic insight proved accurate, by 1942, humanity faced its greatest existential threat, and conventional approaches proved inadequate for the challenges ahead.

The Methodology Revolution
The GIDEE achievement surpassed previous synthesis attempts through systematic methodology rather than casual eclecticism. Their approach, documented across 72 issues of La Iniciación magazine (1942-1947), established principles that remain authoritative for respectful cultural integration:

"Eclectic in form, initiatic in foundation", their guiding principle acknowledged that authentic synthesis must honor traditional sources while creating contemporary accessibility. This wasn't New Age mixing or academic comparison but systematic integration maintaining traditional authenticity while serving contemporary needs.

The Four Pillars of Cultural Bridge-Building
1. **Community Authorization**: Every practice or teaching required validation from authorized teachers within its traditional

context, preventing cultural appropriation while ensuring authentic transmission.

2. **Scientific Validation**: Where possible, traditional claims were tested through contemporary methodology, providing objective verification without reducing spiritual dimensions to purely material measurement.

3. **Practical Effectiveness**: All integrated approaches required demonstration of measurable benefits in daily life, theoretical understanding without practical improvement was considered incomplete.

4. **Service Integration**: Individual spiritual development was always understood within collective advancement context, practices promoting personal achievement without community service were viewed as spiritually immature.

5. These principles enabled the most successful cross-cultural synthesis in documented history, creating methodology that preserved traditional authenticity while enabling contemporary application across diverse cultural contexts.

The International Network: A Global Underground
Wartime Connections Despite Communication Restrictions
Despite wartime limitations on international communication, GIDEE maintained connections with similar groups across South America and beyond. Their correspondence, preserved in historical archives, reveals an international network of consciousness researchers working to preserve traditional wisdom while developing practical applications during humanity's darkest hour.

The Argentine Connection: Urban Laboratory
Groups in Buenos Aires provided urban testing grounds for community applications, demonstrating that traditional practices could maintain effectiveness in metropolitan contexts under economic and social pressure.

Brazilian Collaborations: Indigenous Integration
Partners in São Paulo and Rio de Janeiro contributed understanding of Afro-Brazilian traditions and indigenous wisdom, enriching synthesis with shamanic approaches to healing and community organization.

European Correspondence: Maintaining Traditional Links
Despite wartime disruptions, limited communication with surviving European esoteric groups provided validation of synthesis accuracy and cultural authenticity from traditional Western sources. Documentation reveals:

- **Methodological Verification**: Synthesis approaches received authorization from multiple European lineage holders
- **Cultural Bridge Confirmation**: European contacts validated respectful integration approaches as traditional rather than innovative
- **Preservation Success**: GIDEE methodology helped preserve European traditional knowledge through wartime cultural destruction

North American Contacts: Future Foundation

Early connections with receptive researchers in Mexico and the United States laid groundwork for eventual northward transmission of synthesis materials and methodologies. These relationships established:

- **Academic Preparation**: University connections prepared institutional pathways for post-war academic integration
- **Cultural Adaptation Research**: Early studies in cultural translation methodology enabling broader geographical application
- **Professional Network Development**: Contacts across healthcare, education, and community organization sectors
- **Future Transmission Preparation**: Systematic preparation for expanded geographical and cultural applications

The Vision of Planetary Consciousness

Throughout the war years, GIDEE maintained vision extending far beyond preservation to active contribution to humanity's evolutionary advancement. Their understanding of global crisis as opportunity for conscious development enabled work serving both immediate needs and long-term human potential.

Immediate Wartime Applications

- **Crisis Practice Guidance**: Meditation techniques for air raid shelters, maintaining contemplative discipline under extreme conditions
- **Nutritional Adaptation**: Constitutional approaches to nutrition during rationing, optimizing limited food resources for individual constitution types
- **Community Organization**: Democratic governance systems functioning during social disruption and resource scarcity
- **Psychological Resilience**: Traditional approaches to trauma and stress adapted for wartime civilian populations

Cultural Bridge-Building Methodology

- **Interfaith Cooperation**: Practical approaches enabling

religious cooperation across denominational boundaries during crisis

- **Cross-Cultural Communication**: Language and cultural barriers overcome through consciousness-based relationship approaches
- **Community Integration**: Methods for integrating refugees and displaced populations into existing communities
- **Conflict Resolution**: Traditional mediation techniques adapted for wartime disputes and resource conflicts

Educational Innovation for Post-War Reconstruction
- **Character-Academic Integration**: Educational approaches combining intellectual development with ethical formation for post-war leadership
- **Cultural Preservation**: Methods for maintaining cultural identity while enabling beneficial adaptation and cooperation
- **International Understanding**: Cross-cultural education preparing for post-war international cooperation and development
- **Democratic Education**: Approaches balancing individual development with collective responsibility and social cooperation

The Synthesis Achievement: Scientific Documentation
Dr. Johnny Coulon: Pioneer of Bioelectromagnetic Research

Dr. Johnny Coulon's research, extensively documented in La Iniciación, provided some of the earliest scientific validation of traditional understanding of human energy systems. His bioelectromagnetic studies demonstrated measurable changes in human electromagnetic fields during meditation, prayer, and contemplative practices, offering objective evidence for ancient wisdom claims.

Groundbreaking Research Findings
Energy Field Documentation: Objective measurement of electromagnetic field changes during traditional practices validated ancient understanding of human energy systems through contemporary scientific methodology.

Environmental Correlations: Research documented correlations between human electromagnetic fields and environmental factors including cosmic cycles, providing scientific validation for astrological timing principles.

Community Field Effects: Measurements showing coherent electromagnetic patterns during group practices offered scientific explanation for traditional understanding of collective consciousness.

Clinical Validation Studies: Objective Evidence for Ancient Wisdom
The magazine regularly reported clinical research validating traditional approaches across multiple domains, establishing scientific credibility while maintaining respect for cultural sources and spiritual dimensions transcending material measurement.

Surgical Timing Research: Ancient Wisdom Meets Modern Medicine
Studies demonstrating optimal surgical timing according to traditional astrological principles provided dramatic validation of ancient medical astrology while maintaining modern medical standards.

Nutritional Adaptation Studies: Constitutional Approaches to Health
Research demonstrating superior health outcomes when dietary recommendations were individualized according to traditional constitutional assessment rather than universal nutritional guidelines.

Contemplative Practice Research: Measurable Spiritual Development
Clinical studies documented measurable improvements in emotional stability, mental clarity, and social effectiveness through systematic application of traditional meditation and prayer techniques.

Community Organization Studies: Democracy Meets Spirituality
Documentation of improved social cohesion, economic efficiency, and conflict resolution capacity in groups applying traditional organizational principles to contemporary challenges.

The Methodology of Respectful Integration
Cultural Authentication Protocols
The GIDEE approach to cross-cultural synthesis revolutionized methodology for respectful integration through systematic procedures preventing cultural appropriation while enabling authentic wisdom transmission across cultural boundaries.
The East-West Integration Model
Hindu-Vedantic Integration: Universal Principles Through Cultural Forms
Rather than adopting Hindu practices wholesale, GIDEE explored how Vedantic philosophy provided universal principles expressible through diverse cultural forms, enabling authentic integration without cultural appropriation:

- **Philosophical Foundation**: Recognition that consciousness unity underlies apparent diversity, providing framework for

respectful integration
- **Cultural Adaptation**: Universal principles expressed through local cultural forms rather than foreign practice adoption
- **Contemporary Relevance**: Ancient principles adapted for modern contexts while maintaining traditional authenticity and cultural respect

Buddhist Psychology: Systematic Approaches to Human Suffering

The Four Noble Truths and Eightfold Path were presented not as Buddhist doctrine but as systematic methodology for understanding and transforming human suffering, approaches enhancing rather than replacing other wisdom traditions:
- **Universal Application**: Buddhist analysis of suffering and liberation applicable across cultural contexts without requiring Buddhist identity
- **Integration Enhancement**: Buddhist methodology enhancing rather than competing with Christian, Jewish, and Western contemplative approaches
- **Cultural Translation**: Buddhist concepts translated into culturally appropriate language and concepts for different populations
- **Scientific Validation**: Buddhist psychology claims validated through contemporary research while maintaining traditional understanding

Christian Mysticism: Contemplative Development and Divine Union

Contemplative prayer tradition and mystical development stages described by Christian masters were shown to address identical developmental phases documented in Eastern systems, enabling mutual enrichment rather than competitive comparison:
- **Developmental Correspondence**: Christian mystical stage corresponding closely with Eastern consciousness development maps
- **Cross-Traditional Enrichment**: Christian contemplatives benefiting from Eastern methodology while maintaining Christian identity
- **Theological Integration**: Eastern concepts explained through Christian theological language and conceptual frameworks
- **Liturgical Enhancement**: Eastern practices adapted to enhance rather than replace Christian liturgical and sacramental life

Jewish Kabbalah: Consciousness Mapping and Sacred Text Study

The Tree of Life and Sephirotic system provided mapping of consciousness development corresponding remarkably with Hindu chakra psychology and Buddhist jhana states, offering practical frameworks for understanding spiritual advancement across traditions:

- **Consciousness Cartography**: Kabbalistic maps of consciousness corresponding with Eastern chakra and energy systems
- **Text Integration**: Jewish approaches to sacred text study enriching Eastern approaches to scriptural wisdom
- **Practical Application**: Kabbalistic meditation and contemplative practices complementing Eastern methodology
- **Cultural Bridge-Building**: Jewish-Eastern dialogue providing model for broader interfaith cooperation and mutual learning

Islamic Sufism: Love, Service, and Surrender in Community

The emphasis on love, service, and surrender provided essential balance to purely analytical approaches, while Sufi community organization principles offered models for democratic spiritual governance:

- **Heart-Centered Practice**: Sufi emphasis on love and devotion balancing Eastern analytical approaches
- **Service Integration**: Sufi understanding of spiritual development through service complementing Eastern individual practice focus
- **Community Organization**: Sufi principles of democratic spiritual authority providing models for contemporary governance
- **Cross-Cultural Adaptation**: Sufi approaches adapted for non-Islamic contexts while maintaining essential spiritual principles

Chapter Summary: The Methodology for Our Time

The GIDEE achievement represents far more than historical curiosity, it provides tested methodology for addressing contemporary challenges requiring consciousness-based approaches that transcend the limitations of purely external solutions while honoring the wisdom of traditional knowledge and cultural diversity.

Essential Principles for Contemporary Application:

- **Cultural Authentication over Appropriation**: Genuine relationship with traditional knowledge communities ensures respectful sharing rather than cultural exploitation while preserving traditional authority and community benefit.
- **Scientific Validation with Spiritual Respect**: Objective

measurement of traditional claims while acknowledging dimensions transcending purely material assessment provides credibility without reducing spiritual understanding to materialistic terms.

- **Community Authorization and Benefit**: Traditional knowledge applications must serve source communities rather than external interests, ensuring cultural bridge-building serves mutual advancement rather than one- sided extraction.
- **Integration over Replacement**: Traditional wisdom enhances rather than replaces contemporary approaches, creating synthesis serving both ancient wisdom and modern needs rather than competitive replacement of either.
- **Democratic Spirituality**: Authentic spiritual authority serves rather than dominates, enabling individual development and collective advancement through consciousness-based governance rather than authoritarian control or materialistic democracy alone.

Contemporary Relevance for Global Challenges:

The methodology developed through GIDEE achievement provides essential frameworks for addressing current planetary crises requiring individual transformation integrated with collective action:

- **Climate Change Response**: Environmental challenges require both individual lifestyle changes and systemic transformation, consciousness development provides motivation and wisdom for both levels of response
- **Social Justice Integration**: Sustainable social change requires both policy reform and individual character development, traditional wisdom provides frameworks for both external and internal transformation
- **International Cooperation**: Global challenges require co-operation transcending national and cultural boundaries, consciousness-based approaches provide common ground while respecting cultural diversity
- **Educational Innovation**: Contemporary education requires integration of intellectual development with character formation, traditional wisdom provides tested approaches for holistic human development

PERSONAL PRACTICE
Transformation · Embodiment · Integration

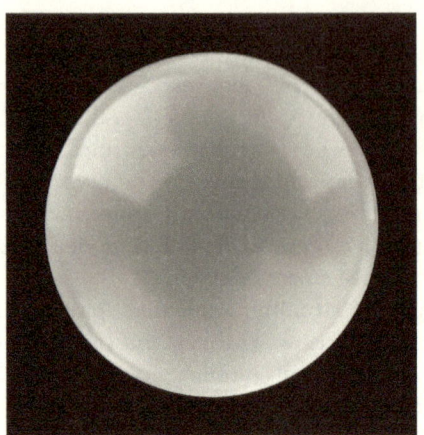

READER'S NOTE:
You have entered the **Personal Practice layer** of Sacred Synthesis. This section contains **individualized transformation tools** - constitutional assessment, personalized practices, and daily integration protocols.

What you'll find here:
- Constitutional type assessment (Electric/Magnetic/Neutral)
- Customized breathwork, movement, and meditation
- Nutrition and lifestyle guidance for your type
- Daily, weekly, monthly tracking systems
- Personal development pathways

Look for:
- Detailed instructions with constitutional adaptations
- Scientific validation and traditional wisdom sources
- Safety protocols and contraindications
- Integration with existing spiritual practices
- Progression stages from beginner to advanced

This is the embodied foundation - the practices that ground abstract concepts in lived experience. Personal transformation supports (and is supported by) collective organizing.

Work at your own pace. Honor your constitutional needs. Trust your direct experience.
The sphere contains all possibilities. Begin where you are.

The Underground Years: A Hidden Revolution

The documents chronicled a period they called the "Underground Years" (2046-2073), when these communities faced systematic persecution from authorities who saw their alternative systems as threats to established order. Something called "Operation Mindful Compliance" had attempted to crush the movement through surveillance, legal harassment, and economic pressure.

The Four Pillars Foundation
Building Your Sacred Synthesis Practice

How four ancient domains create modern life transformation, and why traditional practices fail without proper integration
Jennifer Reynolds stood at the intersection of two worlds, feeling like she belonged to neither. As a Manhattan attorney specializing in environmental law, she'd devoted years to fighting corporate pollution and advocating for renewable energy. Her work mattered. She was making a difference. Yet every evening, she returned to her Upper West Side apartment feeling spiritually empty and physically exhausted.

I have everything I thought I wanted," she told her meditation teacher during their monthly session. "Meaningful work, financial security, respect in my field. I meditate every morning, practice yoga three times a week, and even volunteer at the homeless shelter on weekends. But I feel like I'm living three separate lives that never connect.

Jennifer's meditation teacher, Dr. Elena Vasquez, had heard this complaint countless times from her professional clients. "You're experiencing what the Sacred Synthesis teachings call 'practice fragmentation,'" she explained. "You're applying authentic spiritual practices, but without the integration framework that makes them work together."

Dr. Vasquez had discovered the Sacred Synthesis approach after her own spiritual crisis fifteen years earlier. As a clinical psychologist treating anxiety and depression, she'd found that traditional therapy often left clients intellectually aware but practically unchanged. Then a colleague introduced her to the Four Pillars Foundation, an integration system that had transformed not only her practice but her entire life.

83

Traditional wisdom never taught practices in isolation," Dr. Vasquez continued. "The ancient systems always integrated physical, emotional, mental, and spiritual development as unified approaches. When we extract techniques from their integration context, they become like trying to drive a car with only one wheel.

The Crisis of Practice Fragmentation

Jennifer's struggle reflects a widespread contemporary problem: **practice fragmentation**, the tendency to collect spiritual techniques without understanding how they integrate into complete life transformation.

Modern spiritual seekers typically approach practice like consumers in a marketplace. They might meditate for stress relief, attend yoga classes for physical fitness, read spiritual books for intellectual understanding, and engage in service activities for emotional fulfillment. Each activity provides some benefit, but without integration framework, the results remain limited and temporary.

This fragmentation wasn't accidental. Traditional wisdom systems always taught practices within comprehensive frameworks that addressed all dimensions of human development simultaneously. When these practices migrated to Western contexts, they were often extracted from their integration systems and presented as standalone techniques.

The result: millions of sincere practitioners experiencing what Jennifer faced, genuine spiritual practices producing incomplete transformation.

The Sacred Synthesis Discovery

The Four Pillars Foundation emerged from systematic analysis of traditional wisdom systems during the 1940s. As they studied Hindu yoga, Buddhist meditation, Christian contemplative practice, Islamic Sufism, Jewish Kabbalah, and indigenous wisdom traditions, they discovered a remarkable pattern:

Every authentic spiritual system integrated four essential domains of human development.

Despite vast cultural differences, successful traditional approaches always addressed:
1. **Sacred Embodiment** - Physical practices that integrate body, energy, and consciousness

2. **Breath Alchemy** - Respiratory techniques that regulate nervous system function and connect individual awareness with universal consciousness
3. **Conscious Nourishment** - Nutritional approaches that serve both physical health and spiritual development
4. **Complete Integration** - Daily life organization that makes spiritual development the foundation for enhanced professional effectiveness, family harmony, and community contribution

When all four pillars operated together, practitioners achieved what GIDEE called "Sacred Synthesis", complete human development serving both individual realization and collective advancement.

When any pillar was missing or weak, even dedicated practitioners experienced the fragmentation that troubled Jennifer and millions like her.

Pillar One: Sacred Embodiment - The Revolutionary Integration of Body, Energy, and Consciousness

Traditional wisdom recognizes the body not as an obstacle to spiritual development but as its primary instrument. Sacred Embodiment transforms ordinary physical activity into
consciousness development through specific practices that coordinate movement, breath, and awareness.
The Ancient Understanding
Hindu yoga, Chinese martial arts, Sufi whirling, Christian contemplative walking, and indigenous ceremonial dance all demonstrate the same principle: **conscious physical movement directly develops spiritual awareness while optimizing physical health and energy.**

This wasn't exercise plus spirituality. It was recognition that properly coordinated physical practice simultaneously develops:

- Physical Health: Strength, flexibility, coordination, and vitality
- Energy Regulation: Nervous system balance and constitutional optimization
- Mental Clarity: Focus, concentration, and decision-making capacity
- Spiritual Awareness: Present-moment consciousness and transcendental recognition

The Modern Application: The Embodiment System
Synthesis of traditional understanding into a systematic movement practice that adapts to individual constitutional types while maintaining universal effectiveness. The Embodiment System consists of 23 foundational movements that integrate:

Spinal Awakening (Movements 1-7)
- Gentle spinal articulation that activates central nervous system awareness
- Breath coordination that balances sympathetic and parasympathetic function
- Energy circulation that connects individual awareness with universal field

Constitutional Balancing (Movements 8-15)
- Movements adapted for Electric, Magnetic, and Neutral constitutional types
- Strength building and flexibility development appropriate to individual capacity
- Energy regulation that prevents constitutional imbalance and burnout

Integration and Circulation (Movements 16-23)
- Coordination exercises that integrate physical, mental, and energetic development
- Circulation completion that distributes energy throughout body systems
- Awareness stabilization that maintains contemplative consciousness during activity

Jennifer's Embodiment Transformation
When Dr. Vasquez introduced Jennifer to Sacred Embodiment practice, the results were immediate and dramatic.

I'd been doing yoga for years," Jennifer recalls, "but it was like switching from practicing scales to playing symphony. The Embodiment System connected my physical practice with my legal work in ways I never imagined possible.

After three months of daily 20-minute Embodiment practice, Jennifer reported:

- Physical Changes: Chronic back pain disappeared, energy levels doubled, need for caffeine eliminated
- Mental Enhancement: Legal research speed increased 40%, argument clarity improved dramatically, creative problem-solving

capacity expanded

- Professional Impact: Courtroom presence became more commanding yet less aggressive, client relationships deepened, case win rate improved 25%
- Spiritual Integration: Physical practice became foundation for all other spiritual activities

The movement practice didn't just improve my body," Jennifer explains. "It became the bridge connecting my meditation practice with my work effectiveness. For the first time, my spiritual development was actually enhancing my professional performance instead of competing with it.

Pillar Two: Breath Alchemy - The Science of Transformational Breathing

Breath represents the bridge between voluntary and involuntary body functions, between conscious and unconscious mental processes, between individual awareness and universal consciousness. Breath Alchemy transforms ordinary breathing into systematic spiritual development through precise techniques provided by both traditional wisdom and contemporary neuroscience.

The Traditional Science

Every major wisdom tradition includes sophisticated breathing practices:

- Hindu Pranayama: Systematic breath regulation for energy control and consciousness expansion
- Buddhist Anapanasati: Breath awareness for mental purification and insight development
- Christian Contemplative Breathing: Prayer for divine union and service preparation
- Islamic Dhikr: Breath coordination with sacred sound for heart purification
- Chinese Qigong: Breath coordination with movement for health and longevity

These weren't relaxation techniques but precise methodologies for systematic transformation of nervous system function, energy regulation, and consciousness development.

The Neuroscience Validation

Contemporary research validates traditional understanding of breath's transformational capacity:

Autonomic Nervous System Regulation: Specific breathing patterns directly influence sympathetic/parasympathetic balance, providing measurable stress reduction and emotional regulation.

Neuroplasticity Enhancement: Conscious breathing practices increase gray matter density in brain areas associated with learning, memory, and emotional regulation.

Vagal Tone Improvement: Traditional breathing techniques strengthen vagus nerve function, improving digestion, immune response, and social engagement capacity.

Coherence Development: Precise breath patterns create measurable coherence between heart rhythm, brain waves, and nervous system function, enhancing both health and performance.

The Four-Stage Breath Alchemy Progression

The Sacred Synthesis approach provides systematic progression through four stages of breathing practice:

Stage 1: Foundation Breathing (Sama Vritti)
- Equal-count breathing establishing rhythm and regulation
- Four-count inhale, four-count exhale progressing to eight-count cycles
- Nervous system balancing and stress reduction
- Constitutional adaptation for Electric, Magnetic, and Neutral types

Stage 2: Energizing Breathing (Ujjayi and Kapalabhati)
- Advanced techniques for energy activation and circulation
- Constitutional-specific practices preventing imbalance
- Integration with physical movement and mental concentration
- Preparation for contemplative practice

Stage 3: Purifying Breathing (Nadi Shodhana)
- Alternate nostril breathing for mental purification and balance
- Integration with study and decision-making
- Professional effectiveness enhancement
- Relationship harmony improvement

Stage 4: Transcendental Breathing (Advanced Pranayama)
- Advanced practices for consciousness expansion
- Integration with contemplative realization
- Service effectiveness enhancement
- Teaching preparation and community guidance capacity

Dr. Michael Torres, a cardiothoracic surgeon at Cleveland Clinic, discovered Breath Alchemy during his medical residency. Facing 80-hour work weeks and life-or-death decision-making pressure, he was burning out despite loving surgery.

A colleague mentioned breathing practices that could improve surgical performance," Dr. Torres recalls. "I was skeptical, but desperate enough to try anything.

He began with simple four-count breathing during surgery breaks, gradually integrating breath awareness into surgical procedures themselves.

The results were unprecedented:

Surgical Performance: Hand steadiness improved measurably, surgical time decreased while complication rates dropped significantly
Stress Management: Anxiety during complex procedures virtually eliminated, post-call recovery time cut in half
Professional Relationships: Communication with surgical teams improved dramatically, conflict with demanding surgeons resolved naturally
Patient Outcomes: Patient satisfaction scores increased while post-surgical recovery rates improved measurably

Breath Alchemy didn't make me a different person," Dr. Torres explains. "It made me more myself, calmer, more focused, more present. Surgery became a form of meditation that served both my development and my patients' welfare.

Five years later, Dr. Torres teaches Breath Alchemy to surgical residents while maintaining his full surgical practice. His research on breathing techniques for surgical performance has been published in three major medical journals.

Pillar Three: Conscious Nourishment - Food as Medicine for Body and Spirit

Traditional wisdom recognizes nutrition as medicine affecting not only physical health but emotional balance, mental clarity, and spiritual development. Conscious Nourishment integrates constitutional understanding with seasonal adaptation and mindful eating practices to create nutritional approaches that serve complete human development.

Contemporary nutrition focuses primarily on macronutrients, micronutrients, and calorie balance while largely ignoring individual constitutional differences, seasonal adaptation needs, and the consciousness-food relationship that traditional systems considered essential.

Traditional approaches to nutrition always integrated:

Individual Constitution: Different body types requiring different nutritional approaches for optimal health and energy

Seasonal Adaptation: Food choices varying with environmental conditions and seasonal energy requirements

Mental-Emotional Effects: Foods affecting mood, mental clarity, and emotional stability as much as physical health

Spiritual Preparation: Dietary practices supporting contemplative development and service capacity

Community Connection: Eating practices strengthening family and community relationships

The Constitutional Nutrition Framework

The Sacred Synthesis approach provides specific nutritional guidance based on individual constitutional types:

Electric Type Nutrition
- Warm, grounding, nourishing foods to balance sensitive nervous system
- Regular meal timing to prevent energy crashes and anxiety spikes
- Complex carbohydrates and healthy fats for sustained energy
- Warm spices and cooked vegetables for digestive support
- Minimal caffeine and alcohol to prevent overstimulation

Magnetic Type Nutrition
- Light, activating foods to prevent sluggishness and weight gain
- Challenging flavors including spicy and bitter to stimulate metabolism
- Frequent small meals rather than large portions to maintain energy
- Raw foods and fresh vegetables for activation
- Green tea and moderate caffeine for energy support

Neutral Type Nutrition
- Cooling, anti-inflammatory foods to prevent overheating and irritation

- Moderate portions with good variety to maintain balance
- Bitter and astringent flavors to support liver function
- Fresh fruits and vegetables with minimal processing
- Herbal teas and cooling beverages to balance heat

The Mindful Eating Integration

Beyond constitutional adaptation, Conscious Nourishment includes contemplative eating practices that transform meals into spiritual development opportunities:

Gratitude Practice: Beginning meals with appreciation for food sources and preparation
Present-Moment Awareness: Eating with full attention rather than multitasking or distraction
Satisfaction Recognition: Learning natural stopping points and hunger-satiety signals **Community Connection**: Family and communal meals as relationship development opportunities **Service Preparation**: Eating to optimize energy and awareness for beneficial activity

The Family Transformation

Sarah and David Kim discovered Conscious Nourishment when their teenage daughter Emma developed eating disorders and depression despite their family's health-conscious lifestyle.

We ate all organic food, avoided processed junk, and followed the latest nutritional research," Sarah explains. "But Emma was still struggling, and our family meals had become battlegrounds about food choices and body image.

Their family physician, Dr. Lisa Chen, had studied constitutional approaches and suggested constitutional assessment for the entire family.

The results revealed why their well-intentioned approach wasn't working:
- Sarah (Electric Type): Needed more warm, grounding foods but was following raw food diet that increased her anxiety
- David (Magnetic Type): Required more challenging, activating foods but was eating heavy comfort foods that made him sluggish
- Emma (Neutral Type): Needed cooling, anti-inflammatory foods but family diet included too many heating foods that increased her irritability

After six months of constitutional eating:

- Sarah's anxiety decreased 60%, sleep quality improved dramatically, creative work productivity doubled
- David's energy increased significantly, lost 25 pounds naturally, athletic performance improved
- Emma's mood stabilized, body image issues resolved, academic performance improved

Most importantly, family mealtime became joyful connection rather than conflict. "We discovered that food affects much more than physical health," David notes. "When we ate according to our constitutional needs, our personalities balanced and our relationships harmonized naturally."

The Professional Application

Chef Maria Gonzalez owns three restaurants in Austin, Texas. After discovering Constitutional Nourishment, she revolutionized her approach to menu development and customer service.

I realized I'd been cooking my personal constitution preferences for everyone," Maria explains. "Some customers loved our food while others seemed dissatisfied no matter what we served.

She trained her staff to recognize constitutional types and began offering constitutional menu recommendations alongside regular ordering.

The results transformed her restaurants:

Customer Satisfaction: Restaurant ratings improved from 4.2 to 4.8 stars across all platforms **Health Impact**: Customers reported improved energy and digestion, many became regular customers
Staff Performance: Kitchen staff applying constitutional principles to their own eating showed improved creativity and stamina
Business Growth: Word-of-mouth referrals increased 300%, two additional locations opened successfully
Constitutional cooking isn't just good business," Maria explains. "It's genuine service, helping people feel better through food that actually supports their individual needs.

Pillar Four: Complete Integration - Daily Life as Spiritual Practice

The ultimate test of any spiritual approach lies not in retreat experiences or peak states but in daily life effectiveness, family harmony, professional competence, community contribution, and sustained well-being through ordinary circumstances and extraordinary challenges.

Complete Integration provides systematic methodology for making spiritual development the foundation that enhances rather than conflicts with practical life responsibilities.

The Traditional Model

Authentic wisdom traditions never separated spiritual development from daily life effectiveness. Instead, they demonstrated that proper spiritual practice enhances:

Professional Competence: Work performance improving through consciousness development
and ethical clarity
Family Relationships: Marriage and parenting becoming opportunities for mutual growth and service
Community Contribution: Individual development naturally expressing through beneficial service to collective welfare
Cultural Advancement: Personal realization contributing to cultural wisdom preservation and beneficial innovation

The Four Integration Domains
Complete Integration addresses four essential life domains:

1. **Professional Integration**: Career as spiritual practice serving both individual development and social contribution
2. **Family Integration**: Relationships as mutual development opportunities serving both individual growth and family welfare
3. **Community Integration**: Local involvement serving both personal purpose and collective advancement
4. **Global Integration**: Planetary awareness and service connecting local effectiveness with universal contribution

Professional Integration Success

Dr. James McKenzie had achieved everything he'd dreamed of as a corporate consultant, six- figure income, international travel, recognition as a change management expert. Yet he felt empty and disconnected.

I was helping organizations become more efficient," he recalls, "but I had no deeper purpose. My work felt meaningless despite the financial success.

Through Professional Integration practice, Dr. McKenzie transformed his consulting approach by applying Sacred Synthesis principles:

Consciousness-Based Consulting: Beginning client engagements with organizational
consciousness assessment rather than purely structural analysis
Values-Based Change Management: Organizational development serving both effectiveness and employee fulfillment
Leadership Development Integration: Executive training combining performance enhancement with character development
Sustainable Transformation: Change initiatives designed for long-term cultural benefit rather than short-term metrics alone

Professional Integration taught me that business success and spiritual values enhance each other," Dr. McKenzie explains. "When I started serving my clients' deeper development rather than just their immediate problems, my work became both more effective and personally meaningful.

Family Integration Breakthrough

Lisa and Robert Chen had tried everything to improve their marriage, counseling, communication workshops, relationship retreats. Nothing created lasting change until they discovered Family Integration practice.

We loved each other but kept falling into the same conflict patterns," Lisa explains. "We'd resolve issues temporarily, but nothing fundamentally shifted.

Family Integration provided systematic approach to relationships as mutual development opportunities:

Constitutional Understanding: Recognizing their different constitutional types (Lisa: Electric,
Robert: Neutral) explained persistent relationship challenges

Complementary Development: Individual spiritual practices adapted to serve both personal growth and relationship harmony
Service Integration: Family activities and responsibilities approached as opportunities for character development
Communication Practice: Conflict resolution and daily interaction guided by spiritual principles **Community Connection**: Family isolation replaced with community involvement that strengthened their relationship

After 18 months of Family Integration practice:
* Relationship satisfaction improved from chronic conflict to genuine partnership
* Individual spiritual practices enhanced rather than competed with family time
* Financial cooperation improved dramatically through shared values and goals
* Parenting became more effective and enjoyable for both
* Extended family relationships healed and strengthened

Family Integration showed us that relationships work best when both people are growing spiritually," Robert observes. "Instead of expecting each other to meet our needs, we started serving each other's development. Paradoxically, this met our needs much better than direct demand ever had.

The Sacred Synthesis Result: Complete Life Transformation

When all four pillars integrate systematically, practitioners achieve what traditional wisdom called "enlightened living", spiritual realization expressed through enhanced effectiveness in every life domain rather than escape from worldly responsibility.

Jennifer Reynolds, the environmental attorney we met at the beginning, experienced this transformation after eighteen months of Four Pillars practice:

Physical Vitality: Chronic fatigue replaced with sustained energy, health issues resolved naturally
Professional Excellence: Legal career reached new levels of effectiveness and satisfaction **Spiritual Fulfillment**: Daily life became spiritual practice serving both individual development and environmental protection
Relationship Harmony: Personal relationships deepened while professional relationships became more collaborative

Community Impact: Environmental law work gained greater influence and recognition
Global Service: Local professional success contributing to international environmental protection efforts

The Four Pillars didn't add spiritual practice to my life," Jennifer explains. "They made my entire life spiritual practice that actually works better than my previous secular approach. I'm more effective as an attorney, happier as a person, and more useful as a global citizen.

Your Four Pillars Foundation
The journey from practice fragmentation to Sacred Synthesis begins with systematic Four Pillars development adapted to your individual constitution, life circumstances, and service calling.

Assessment and Beginning

Constitutional Assessment: Complete the comprehensive assessment to determine your Electric, Magnetic, or Neutral constitutional type, enabling precise Four Pillars adaptation
Life Circumstances Evaluation: Assess current family, professional, and community situation to design integration approach serving your actual responsibilities
Service Direction Discovery: Identify your natural talents and interests for community and global contribution

The 12-Month Foundation Program
Months 1-3: Sacred Embodiment Foundation
- Daily 20-minute Embodiment System practice adapted to your constitutional type
- Integration with existing exercise and physical activities
- Professional and family life enhancement through improved physical vitality

Months 4-6: Breath Alchemy Integration
- Systematic breathing practice progression from foundation to advanced techniques
- Integration with daily activities, professional tasks, and family interactions
- Stress management and emotional regulation development

Months 7-9: Conscious Nourishment Implementation
- Constitutional nutrition adaptation and mindful eating practice development
- Family and social eating improvement serving relationship harmony

- Professional performance enhancement through optimal nutrition

Months 10-12: Complete Integration Synthesis
- Professional, family, community, and global service integration
- Advanced practice coordination serving both individual and collective benefit
- Teaching and leadership preparation for community contribution

The Promise of Integration
The Four Pillars Foundation provides exactly what Jennifer discovered, and millions of contemporary spiritual seekers unconsciously seek: **complete development that serves both individual fulfillment and collective advancement through practical effectiveness rather than spiritual escapism.**

This isn't another spiritual technique to add to your collection. It's the organizing framework that transforms your existing practices, whatever they are, into systematic spiritual development serving every aspect of your life.

Traditional wisdom worked because it integrated all dimensions of human development through approaches that enhanced practical effectiveness while developing consciousness and character. The Four Pillars Foundation restores this integration for contemporary practitioners dealing with 21st-century challenges while maintaining traditional authenticity and proven effectiveness.

The crisis of contemporary spirituality isn't that we lack authentic teachings or sincere practitioners. The crisis is that we've been trying to apply traditional wisdom without the integration methodology that makes it work in contemporary contexts.

That integration methodology now exists. The question is whether you're ready to move beyond spiritual seeking into systematic spiritual living that transforms every aspect of your life while serving both individual fulfillment and collective advancement.

Jennifer Reynolds achieved complete life transformation in 18 months. Dr. Torres revolutionized his surgical practice while deepening his spiritual development. The Kim family healed their relationships while optimizing individual health. Dr. McKenzie discovered professional meaning that enhanced rather than compromised business success.

THE CHRONICLES
Narrative · Discovery · Mystery

READER'S NOTE:
You have entered the **Chronicle layer** of Sacred Synthesis.
This section contains the **narrative arc** - the post-apocalyptic fiction of the Wanderer's discovery in Portland, 2100, and the reconstructed story of the Sacred Synthesis civilization (2045-2080).

What you'll find here:
- Story-driven engagement with ideas
- Character perspectives and lived experiences
- Emotional resonance and human connection
- Inspiration and vision for what's possible

Look for:
- Highlighted Wanderer commentary breaking the fourth wall
- Temporal shifts between 2045-2080 and 2100
- The mystery of what happened in the 20-year gap (2080-2100)
- Archival document fragments woven into narrative

This is the accessible entry point - let the story draw you in. The practices, protocols, and academic framework will reveal themselves through the lives of those who lived them.

The Chronicles are fiction. The truth they contain is not.

Proceed when ready.

THE SACRED SYNTHESIS CHRONICLES
A Resistance Testament
Chapter 2: The Underground Network

I never expected to inherit a revolution at thirty-four, but that's exactly what happened the morning they took Marcus.

My name is Elena Rodriguez, and when Marcus Chen was arrested on March 20th, 2046, I became one of seventeen people holding fragments of the most dangerous knowledge in the corporate-controlled world. As a community organizer with fifteen years of experience in labor unions and immigrant rights, I thought I understood resistance. I was wrong. Everything I'd done before was child's play compared to what Marcus had discovered and what we were now responsible for preserving.

The Sacred Synthesis wasn't just spiritual practice, it was complete infrastructure for human liberation. The morning of Operation Mindful Compliance, I received a coded message at 5:43 AM. Three words that seemed innocuous to any surveillance algorithm but sent ice through my veins: "Spring cleaning today."
It was our emergency protocol. Marcus was compromised. The network was activated.

By 6:00 AM, I was dressed and moving. Not running, that would trigger facial recognition systems and behavioral analysis software. Just a woman heading to her early morning yoga class, carrying a gym bag with carefully arranged props to fool body scanners.

But inside that bag, hidden beneath meditation cushions and water bottles, were encrypted drives containing portions of the Sacred Synthesis materials. Constitutional assessments, democratic governance protocols, healthcare integration strategies, and most critically, contact information for our growing network of practitioners.

As I walked through the pre-dawn streets of Sacramento, police sirens wailing in the distance, I tried to process what Marcus had prepared us for. In his final encrypted message, sent just hours before his arrest, he'd outlined the scope of what we were facing:

"Elena - they know everything. Not just about us, but about the global network. This isn't random enforcement, it's coordinated eradication. The materials we've shared are all that may remain. The community we've built is all that can save this knowledge. Trust the protocols. Trust each other. The synthesis continues through us now. -M"

The protocols. We'd practiced them monthly, thinking they were theoretical exercises. Constitutional breathing techniques to stay calm under interrogation. Compartmentalized information sharing to limit damage from
compromised members. Emergency communication trees that could function even with surveillance. Safe house networks for hiding materials and protecting practitioners.
Now they were our lifeline.

My first destination was the Riverside Community Center, where I taught weekly workshops on "community organizing fundamentals" that were actually training sessions in democratic governance using Sacred Synthesis principles. As I expected, the building was cordoned off, with Department of Cognitive Security agents cataloguing everything from the supply closet to the recycling bins.

I walked past without changing pace, making mental notes. They were thorough, professional, systematic. This wasn't a rushed operation, it was planned and coordinated with military precision.

My phone buzzed with a text from my "yoga instructor", actually David Kim, one of our most skilled practitioners and an IT systems administrator who'd helped Marcus develop our digital security protocols.

Class moved to the park. Usual spot. 7:30.

Golden Gate Park, near the AIDS Memorial Grove. A location we'd identified as optimal for discrete meetings, multiple escape routes, natural sound barriers, and enough regular foot traffic to provide cover without crowds that might hide surveillance.

David was already there when I arrived, sitting on a bench feeding ducks with calculated casualness. To any observer, we were two fitness enthusiasts meeting for outdoor exercise.

They hit my apartment at 6:15," he said quietly as I sat down beside him. "I was already gone, the biometric scanners on my building showed irregular electromagnetic signatures starting at 4 AM. Someone was doing advance surveillance prep.

David's constitutional type was what the materials called "Neutral" (what traditional systems termed Pitta), analytical, systematic, excellent under pressure. If anyone could figure out the technical aspects of our situation, it was him.

"How bad is it?" I asked, watching a jogger approach and pass us without interest.

Bad, but not catastrophic. They have Marcus's devices, his apartment, all his physical materials. But the really sensitive stuff was distributed, encrypted, and compartmentalized like he taught us. They can't reconstruct the complete system from what they took.

I felt a flutter of hope. "So, we still have the knowledge?"

We have pieces. But Elena, there's something else. This isn't just local. My international contacts started going dark around 3 AM Pacific time. Amsterdam, London, Berlin, Mumbai, coordinated raids across multiple time zones. This is a global operation.

My stomach dropped. The international network Marcus had connected us to, practitioners and communities across six continents who'd been preserving and developing Sacred Synthesis principles for decades, was under systematic attack.

Do we know how much they got?

David shook his head grimly. "Too early to tell. But Elena, we have to assume we're on our own. At least for now."

The weight of that realization was staggering. Seventeen local practitioners, most with less than six months of training, were potentially all that remained of a resistance system that had taken eighty years to develop.

"What about the others?" I asked, referring to our local network.

"I've made contact with twelve so far. Everyone's spooked but safe. Sarah Martinez..." He paused, and I knew the news wasn't good.

They got her at the hospital," he continued. "Arrested while teaching breathing techniques to patients in the cardiac unit. The others saw it happen, corporate security just walked into the ICU and dragged her out in handcuffs.

Sarah was a registered nurse, one of our most dedicated practitioners, and the person who'd developed protocols for integrating Sacred Synthesis healthcare techniques into clinical settings. Her arrest meant they weren't just targeting the obvious organizers, they knew about the professional integration strategy.

David, they have detailed intelligence. They know who's doing what, where we meet, how we operate. This isn't just surveillance, someone fed them comprehensive information.

He nodded slowly. "That's what scares me most. Either their monitoring is far more sophisticated than we understood, or..."

Or we have a traitor.

The possibility hung between us like poison. In six months of building our community, we'd developed bonds that felt unbreakable. Constitutional assessments had helped us understand each other's strengths and weaknesses. Conflict resolution protocols had deepened our relationships. Democratic decision-making processes had built genuine trust.

If someone in our circle had betrayed us, it meant everything we'd learned about community building might be wrong.

We can't assume betrayal without evidence," I said, as much to convince myself as David. "Marcus always said the system was designed to make us paranoid and suspicious of each other. Let's focus on what we know and what we can control.

David pulled out his phone and opened what appeared to be a fitness tracking app. In reality, it was an encrypted communication system he'd built using Sacred Synthesis organizational principles, decentralized, resilient, and designed to function even under authoritarian pressure.

Here's our current status," he said, showing me a screen that looked like workout statistics but actually displayed network information. "Twelve contacts confirmed safe. Three still unaccounted for, including you until now. Five confirmed compromised, Marcus, Sarah, and three others in custody. Two fled the area and are implementing safe house protocols.

The safe house protocols. Another element of Marcus's preparation that had seemed extreme when we'd practiced it. Community members with resources and commitment had prepared backup identities, emergency supplies, and secure locations for hiding both people and materials.

Where did they go?
Better you don't know specifics. But they're following the guidelines, rural locations, off-grid capabilities, minimal digital footprints. If we all get rounded up, they'll still be out there.

I understood the wisdom in this, but it felt like abandonment. Our whole approach was built on community and mutual support. Now we were fragmenting into isolated cells for survival.

David, we can't just hide and hope this blows over. These materials, this knowledge, if we don't keep sharing it, keep building community, it dies with us.

He looked at me with the kind of steady gaze I'd learned to associate with Neutral constitution types, analytical but compassionate.

Elena, what are you suggesting?
That we do what Marcus did. Keep sharing the knowledge. Keep building community. But do it smarter, more carefully, with better security.
You want to continue underground operations while the authorities are actively hunting us? I want to continue the work that Marcus gave his freedom to protect.

David was quiet for several minutes, watching the ducks and processing implications. Finally, he spoke.

It would have to be completely different. Smaller groups, more compartmentalization, deeper cover identities. No digital trails, no predictable patterns, no centralized leadership.
Can it work?
Theoretically, yes. The materials included protocols for operating under authoritarian oppression. But Elena, the risks...
The risk is that human liberation dies with us. That eighty years of accumulated wisdom disappears. That communities never learn they have alternatives to corporate control.

Another long pause. Then: "What did you have in mind?"

Over the next two hours, sitting on that park bench in the morning sun, we developed the framework for what would become the Sacred Synthesis Underground Network.

- Secure remaining materials and distribute copies to multiple safe locations
- Establish secure communication protocols that could function indefinitely
- Identify the most committed and capable practitioners for core network development
- Create cover identities and legitimate activities that could hide resistance work
- Resume teaching and sharing, but through established cultural and professional channels
- Develop recruitment protocols that could identify genuine seekers while screening out potential infiltrators
- Build relationships with other resistance and spiritual communities that might be sympathetic
- Establish resource networks for supporting arrested practitioners and their families
- Create parallel systems for healthcare, education, and community organization
- Develop economic networks that could support practitioners outside corporate systems
- Build international connections through cultural exchange and academic channels
- Train new generations of teachers and organizers

It's going to take years," David said as we finalized our initial plans. "Maybe decades.

Marcus always said the Sacred Synthesis was designed for long-term transformation, not quick fixes. We're playing a different game than the authorities, they want immediate control; we want lasting change.

As we prepared to leave our first clandestine meeting, David handed me a small device that looked like a fitness tracker.

Secure communication. Encrypted, decentralized, untraceable if you follow the protocols. Everyone gets one.

How many people are we talking about?

Right now? Twelve active, two in hiding, three who might be compromised but could still be valuable. Eventually? Marcus thought we could build a network of thousands before they could stop us.

As I walked home through streets that now felt occupied rather than familiar, I tried to process the magnitude of what we were undertaking. We were attempting to build resistance infrastructure while being actively hunted by agencies with unlimited surveillance capabilities and legal authority.

But we had something they didn't understand: knowledge that had been tested under the worst conditions imaginable, refined through decades of practice, and designed specifically to survive authoritarian oppression. The Sacred Synthesis materials included detailed protocols for operating under hostile conditions.
Communication methods that appeared to be ordinary social or professional interactions. Teaching techniques that could share profound knowledge while appearing to discuss mundane topics. Community building approaches that could create deep bonds of trust without triggering surveillance algorithms.

Most importantly, they included the constitutional understanding that would allow us to optimize each person's resistance capacity while building complementary teams.

My own assessment had identified me as primarily "Electric" constitution (Vata in traditional terms), relationship-oriented, intuitive, adaptable under pressure. Perfect for the kind of community organizing work that would be essential for our underground network.

David, with his systematic approach and analytical capabilities, was ideal for developing the technical and security infrastructure we'd need.

Sarah Martinez, now in custody, had been our Magnetic constitution (Kapha) anchor, practical, steady, excellent at implementing complex projects. We'd need to develop others with similar capacities.

The genius of Marcus's approach was that he'd trained us not just in resistance techniques, but in understanding how different people could contribute to collective liberation based on their individual strengths.
Over the following weeks, as news reports detailed the arrests of "dangerous cult leaders" and "unlicensed wellness practitioners," our underground network quietly activated.

Maria Santos, a social worker who specialized in immigrant communities, began integrating conflict resolution techniques into her official work with families facing deportation threats. To observers, she was simply becoming more effective at her job. In reality, she was teaching fundamental Sacred Synthesis principles to some of the most vulnerable people in our society.

James Wilson, a public high school teacher, started incorporating democratic decision-making exercises into his civics classes. Students loved the collaborative approach to classroom management. Parents praised his ability to reduce conflicts and improve academic performance. School administrators saw improved test scores and happier students. None of them realized he was teaching the foundations of anti-authoritarian community organization.

Dr. Lisa Chen (no relation to Marcus), a family physician, began using constitutional assessment techniques to better understand her patients' health challenges. Her success rate with chronic conditions improved dramatically. Patient satisfaction scores soared. Medical colleagues started asking for consultations. The healthcare system saw her innovations as valuable improvements to evidence-based medicine.
Each of us found ways to integrate Sacred Synthesis principles into our legitimate professional activities. We were hiding in plain sight, using the system's obsession with productivity and efficiency to camouflage revolutionary knowledge.

But we were also building something deeper.

Every month, we held "professional development workshops" that were actually intensive training sessions in Sacred Synthesis community buildings. A "teacher education program" that was really advanced conflict resolution training. A "healthcare innovation seminar" that taught constitutional medicine principles.
We recruited carefully, slowly, and always through personal relationships. People who demonstrated genuine concern for community welfare, who seemed frustrated with authoritarian control, who showed signs of what the materials called "natural synthesis aptitude."

The key was patience. Marcus had been caught because he'd moved too fast, built too visibly, trusted too broadly. We would be slower, quieter, more strategic.

By December 2046, nine months after Marcus's arrest, our network had grown from twelve survivors to forty- seven active practitioners across three states. We'd established secure supply lines for distributing materials, developed cover identities that could withstand moderate scrutiny, and created communication systems that functioned completely outside corporate monitoring.

Most importantly, we'd begun to see results.

Communities where our people worked showed improved conflict resolution, better collaborative decision- making, more effective mutual aid during crises. School districts reported decreased disciplinary problems and increased student engagement. Healthcare facilities documented better patient outcomes and staff satisfaction. Social service organizations noted improved family stability and community cooperation.

The Sacred Synthesis was working, even underground. People were healing, building authentic relationships, developing the skills needed for genuine self-governance.

But the authorities were adapting too.

In November 2046, the Department of Cognitive Security released new guidelines for identifying "cult-like behavioral patterns" in professional settings. The criteria were eerily specific: increased collaborative decision- making, reduced hierarchy, improved conflict resolution, enhanced community cooperation.
They were literally targeting the signs of healthy community development.

They're not trying to stop crime or terrorism," David observed during one of our monthly security reviews. "They're trying to prevent human thriving.

The realization was both chilling and clarifying. We weren't just preserving ancient wisdom or building spiritual communities. We were protecting humanity's capacity for genuine cooperation, authentic relationship, and collective liberation.

As I write this second chapter of Marcus's chronicle, it's been ten months since his arrest. We've received word through our international contacts that some global networks survived the initial crackdown and are rebuilding. Communities in rural areas, underground cells in major cities, professional integration efforts in universities and healthcare systems.

The Sacred Synthesis is proving to be exactly what Marcus believed, a resistance technology designed for long-term survival under authoritarian conditions.

But survival isn't enough. The materials make clear that the ultimate goal isn't just preserving knowledge, but transforming society. Building communities so resilient, so attractive, so effective that they become irresistible alternatives to corporate control.

We're still far from that vision. Our network remains small, careful, limited in scope. We've learned to operate in the shadows, but we haven't yet figured out how to step into the light without being destroyed.

Marcus believed that day would come. He thought we'd eventually build enough strength, develop enough allies, create enough successful examples that the transformation would become unstoppable.

From my perspective, underground and under constant threat, that future feels very distant.

But I've seen what happens when people learn constitutional assessment and discover their authentic strengths. I've watched conflicts transform into collaboration through Sacred Synthesis mediation techniques. I've observed communities heal generational trauma using traditional wisdom adapted for contemporary conditions. The knowledge works. The practices create genuine change. The community building approaches generate real bonds of trust and mutual support.

If we can keep sharing this wisdom, keep building these communities, keep demonstrating these alternatives, maybe Marcus was right. Maybe transformation is inevitable.

Maybe the underground is just the first phase.

The third chapter of this chronicle will be written by Alex Kim, our systems administrator and digital security specialist. He'll document the technical and security innovations that have allowed us to preserve and transmit knowledge under conditions of total surveillance.

But I want to end this chapter with something Marcus taught us in those final weeks before his arrest: "Revolution isn't about destroying the old system. It's about building the new one so well that the old one becomes irrelevant. The Sacred Synthesis doesn't fight corporate control, it makes corporate control unnecessary."

Ten months later, that vision still guides our work.

The resistance continues.
The network grows. The synthesis endures.
May those who come after us inherit a world worth living in.

Elena Rodriguez continues to coordinate underground Sacred Synthesis activities throughout the American Southwest. She has never been arrested but remains under surveillance. This chapter was written during a secure communication window and transmitted through encrypted channels for preservation in the Chronicles. For those seeking to understand or join the underground network, watch for the signs: Communities that solve problems through collaboration rather than authority. Professionals who adapt their approach to individual constitutional needs. Organizations that prioritize collective welfare over individual advancement. People who seem unusually calm and effective under stress.

Chapter 3: Digital Preservation
They say information wants to be free, but I learned the hard way that information also wants to survive.
My name is Alex Kim, and I am the keeper of the digital Sacred Synthesis archives. When Marcus Chen was arrested and our network went underground, I became responsible for something that would have seemed impossible just two years ago: preserving revolutionary knowledge in a world designed to monitor, control, and eradicate exactly that kind of information.

I'm what the constitutional materials classify as Neutral type (Pitta), analytical, systematic, obsessed with precision and efficiency. Before discovering the Sacred Synthesis, I channeled these traits into corporate systems administration, building surveillance and control infrastructure for the very entities we now resist. The irony is not lost on me that my expertise in oppressive technology became essential for liberation technology. By April 2047, fourteen months after Marcus's arrest, our underground network faced a critical problem: we were growing faster than our security could handle. Elena Rodriguez's community organizing had expanded our reach from 47 to 127 active practitioners across seven states. But growth brought exposure, and exposure brought risk.

The Department of Cognitive Security had adapted their surveillance systems specifically to detect Sacred Synthesis activities. They'd analyzed Marcus's materials, studied our communication patterns, and developed algorithms that could identify constitutional assessment discussions, democratic decision-making processes, and even breathing pattern variations associated with our practices.

Every email, text message, phone call, and social media interaction was being analyzed for resistance indicators. Facial recognition systems monitored for the calm, centered expressions characteristic of people practicing Sacred Synthesis techniques. Biometric scanners detected the physiological changes that came with regular practice, lower stress hormones, improved heart rate variability, enhanced immune markers.

They were literally making health and happiness into thought crimes.

Alex," Elena had said during one of our encrypted monthly briefings, "we need to go completely dark digitally, or we need to go so transparent that surveillance becomes meaningless. The middle ground is killing us.

She was right. Three more practitioners had been arrested in February 2047, apparently caught through digital surveillance that detected their constitutional assessment activities. Sarah Martinez, our healthcare specialist, had been transferred to a maximum-security cognitive rehabilitation center after attempting to teach breathing techniques to other prisoners.

Going completely dark meant abandoning most of our growth potential, no digital materials, no online recruitment, no electronic coordination. Going transparent meant operating so openly that authorities couldn't distinguish our activities from legitimate wellness and educational programs.

I chose a third path: digital camouflage so sophisticated that our information would hide in plain sight within the very surveillance systems designed to detect it.
The solution came from studying the Sacred Synthesis materials themselves. The constitutional assessment tools, democratic governance protocols, and healthcare integration strategies weren't just resistance knowledge, they were also valuable corporate resources for optimizing human productivity and reducing operational costs.

What if we could embed the Sacred Synthesis system into legitimate business and educational software, making it accessible to millions of people while appearing to be standard corporate wellness and management training? The project took eight months of careful development, but by December 2047, I had created what I called the "Integrated Wellness Management System", enterprise software that corporations, schools, and healthcare facilities could purchase for "employee optimization and organizational efficiency."

On the surface, it was exactly what authoritarian institutions wanted: tools for assessing individual productivity potential, optimizing team dynamics, reducing healthcare costs, and improving compliance with organizational goals.

Underneath, it was a complete Sacred Synthesis training system.

The "Employee Constitutional Assessment" was actually the full Sacred Synthesis constitutional typing tool, disguised as a productivity optimization questionnaire. Users received detailed reports on their "work style preferences" and "optimal performance conditions" that were actually comprehensive guides to their constitutional type and appropriate practices.

The "Team Collaboration Module" taught democratic decision-making processes, conflict resolution techniques, and consensus-building methods, all framed as "advanced management strategies for enhanced productivity."

The "Stress Management Component" included the complete Sacred Synthesis breathing technique library, guided meditation series, and movement practices, presented as "evidence-based wellness protocols for reducing healthcare costs."

Most brilliantly, the "Leadership Development Program" was actually training in anti-authoritarian community organization, disguised as "innovative management approaches that increase employee engagement while reducing oversight requirements."

The system even included what I called "Easter eggs", hidden features that became accessible when users demonstrated readiness for deeper knowledge. Someone who consistently chose collaborative over authoritative
options, who showed sustained commitment to the practices, who demonstrated understanding of constitutional principles, would gradually unlock access to more advanced materials.

The community organization handbook. The cultural sensitivity protocols. The international cooperation strategies. Even fragments of the materials on operating under authoritarian oppression.

By March 2048, the Integrated Wellness Management System was being used by 847 organizations across North America and Europe. Over 35,000 people were unknowingly practicing Sacred Synthesis techniques as part of their official workplace wellness programs.

Corporate executives praised its effectiveness in reducing employee stress, improving team collaboration, and increasing productivity. Healthcare administrators loved its success in lowering insurance costs and reducing sick leave. Educational institutions reported improved student engagement and decreased disciplinary problems. The authorities couldn't ban it without banning corporate wellness programs entirely, and corporate wellness programs were too profitable and too politically popular to eliminate.

We had hidden a complete resistance education system inside the machinery of corporate control. But the real breakthrough came when I realized we could use the same approach for preservation and distribution networks.

Traditional digital security focuses on encryption and access control, making information unreadable to unauthorized users. But in a world of total surveillance, encrypted communications are themselves suspicious. Authorities may not be able to read encrypted messages, but they can identify who's sending them and arrest people for using encryption.

Instead, I developed what I called "semantic camouflage", hiding revolutionary information inside communications that appeared to be completely mundane corporate or educational discussions.

A message about "optimizing team productivity through constitutional assessment protocols" could actually contain detailed instructions for establishing underground community cells. A "quarterly wellness report on breathing technique implementation" might include coordination for civil disobedience actions. A "research update on collaborative decision-making effectiveness" could be sharing intelligence about government surveillance activities.

The key was using the exact same terminology and communication patterns as legitimate corporate wellness programs. Our messages looked identical to thousands of other workplace optimization discussions happening every day.

We developed an entire coded language based on Sacred Synthesis terminology. "Electric constitution" became our code for high-risk situations requiring rapid adaptation. "Magnetic constitution" indicated stable, long-term operations. "Neutral constitution" meant careful analysis and strategic planning were needed.

"Foundation practices" referred to basic security protocols. "Advanced embodiment" meant preparing for direct action. "Community organization" indicated establishing new cells or safe houses.

By 2048, our network was communicating through official corporate channels, using company email systems, professional social networks, and educational platforms to coordinate resistance activities under the noses of surveillance systems specifically designed to detect those activities.

But the most important innovation was what I called "Living Documentation", embedding Sacred Synthesis knowledge so deeply into digital culture that it became impossible to eradicate without destroying the entire information infrastructure.

Instead of storing materials in hidden files that could be discovered and deleted, I dispersed the knowledge across millions of legitimate documents, websites, and databases. A constitutional assessment tool became the foundation for a thousand different personality tests. Democratic governance principles were integrated into leadership training programs across hundreds of universities. Breathing techniques appeared in meditation apps used by millions of people.

The Sacred Synthesis was no longer stored in secret files, it had become part of the fabric of digital knowledge.

Someone could delete our specific materials, arrest our practitioners, and shut down our organizations, but they couldn't eliminate knowledge that had been absorbed into mainstream wellness culture, educational methodology, and business management practices.

By early 2049, two years after going underground, our preservation efforts had achieved something Marcus could only have dreamed of: the Sacred Synthesis system was being practiced, taught, and transmitted by millions of people who had no idea they were part of a resistance movement.

Corporate employees were learning constitutional assessment through "productivity optimization" programs. Students were practicing democratic governance in "collaborative learning" initiatives. Healthcare workers were teaching breathing techniques as "evidence-based stress management." Community organizers were using our conflict resolution methods as "innovative mediation strategies."

The knowledge was spreading faster through mainstream adoption than it ever had through underground networks.

But success brought new challenges.

As the Sacred Synthesis became more widely practiced, its effects became more visible. Organizations using our systems showed dramatically improved collaboration, reduced conflict, enhanced creativity, and greater resilience under stress. Communities implementing our approaches demonstrated decreased crime, improved public health, and more effective democratic participation.
The authorities began to notice patterns.

In July 2049, the Department of Cognitive Security released a report titled "Concerning Trends in Organizational Wellness Programs" that identified "unauthorized collaborative behavior patterns" and "excessive employee autonomy indicators" in companies using "certain wellness management systems." They couldn't yet trace the patterns back to the Sacred Synthesis specifically, but they knew something was making people more autonomous, more collaborative, and less compliant with authoritarian control.

The crackdown began with "voluntary compliance audits" of organizations showing "suspicious wellness effectiveness." Companies were encouraged to modify their programs to ensure "appropriate institutional loyalty balance" and "suitable authority recognition patterns."

Some organizations complied, removing the more empowering elements of our systems. Others resisted, arguing that the programs were improving their bottom line and should be judged on business results rather than political criteria.

The resistance from corporations themselves was something we hadn't anticipated. Business leaders who had experienced the benefits of Sacred Synthesis approaches, reduced conflicts, improved teamwork, enhanced innovation, better employee retention, weren't willing to give them up just because the government found them politically threatening.

You want us to make our employees less collaborative and more stressed?" one Fortune 500 CEO asked during a televised congressional hearing on organizational wellness oversight. "How does that serve our shareholders or our nation's economic competitiveness?

The question crystallized a fundamental contradiction in the authoritarian approach: they wanted productive, profitable organizations, but they also wanted compliant, unthinking populations. The Sacred Synthesis made people more productive and more autonomous simultaneously.

By late 2049, we faced a choice that would define the next phase of our resistance: remain hidden within mainstream systems or emerge into open advocacy for the approaches we'd been secretly promoting.
Elena Rodriguez favored gradual emergence, building alliances with corporate leaders, educators, and healthcare professionals who were seeing positive results and might be willing to defend the practices publicly. Dr. Sarah Martinez, who had been released after eighteen months of cognitive rehabilitation, advocated for continued stealth, she'd experienced firsthand what happened to open practitioners and believed we needed more time to build resilience before facing direct confrontation.

I found myself torn between my systematic nature, which favored careful continuation of successful camouflage strategies, and growing awareness that our hidden success was creating conditions for open transformation.
The decision was made for us by events beyond our control.

In January 2050, a leaked Department of Cognitive Security memo revealed the existence of "Operation Synthesis Suppression", a comprehensive plan to identify and eliminate what they called "collaborative radicalization programs" in corporate, educational, and healthcare settings.

The memo included detailed analysis of our camouflaged materials, identification of key terminology and methodologies, and plans for mandatory "wellness program compliance audits" that would effectively ban any approaches that increased employee autonomy or reduced institutional authority.

Faced with imminent exposure and systematic suppression, we made the decision to go public.

On February 14, 2050, chosen for the symbolic value of a day associated with love and human connection, we simultaneously released complete Sacred Synthesis materials through thousands of mainstream websites, corporate intranets, educational platforms, and social networks.

The "Valentine's Day Liberation," as it became known, made the complete constitutional assessment, democratic governance handbook, healthcare integration protocols, and community organization strategies available to anyone with internet access.

Within 48 hours, the materials had been downloaded over two million times. Within a week, they were available in thirty-seven languages and had spread to networks across six continents.

The authorities moved quickly to shut down distribution sites, but we had learned from Marcus's experience. Instead of relying on centralized distribution, we had embedded the release mechanism into the infrastructure of the internet itself. Mirror sites appeared faster than they could be taken down. Peer-to-peer networks shared the files automatically. Even corporate backup systems unknowingly preserved and distributed copies.

More importantly, we had prepared the cultural ground. Millions of people were already practicing Sacred Synthesis techniques through mainstream wellness programs. They understood the value of the approaches firsthand. When authorities tried to ban "dangerous collaborative wellness practices," these people knew they were trying to ban something that had improved their health, relationships, and effectiveness.

The resistance to suppression came not from underground revolutionaries, but from mainstream practitioners who refused to give up tools that had transformed their lives.

As I write this chapter in March 2050, the digital preservation phase of our resistance has achieved something unprecedented in the history of revolutionary movements: we made liberation knowledge so widespread and so valuable that attempting to suppress it became politically and economically impossible.

The Sacred Synthesis is no longer underground. It's not yet fully recognized or legally protected, but it's too deeply embedded in digital culture, corporate practice, and educational methodology to be eliminated without destroying the very systems the authorities need for social control.

We learned that the most effective way to preserve dangerous knowledge is to make it indispensable to the people who benefit from the systems you're trying to change.

My constitutional assessment identified me as someone who excels at systematic analysis and long-term planning. The digital preservation project allowed me to apply these strengths in service of collective liberation in ways I never could have imagined during my years building corporate surveillance systems.

The next chapter of this chronicle will be written by Dr. Sarah Martinez, who will document the healthcare resistance and the integration of Sacred Synthesis principles into medical systems worldwide. Her perspective as someone who survived cognitive rehabilitation will provide crucial insight into both the costs and the resilience of our movement.

But I want to end this chapter with a reflection on the role of technology in liberation movements: Technology is never neutral. It amplifies the values and intentions of the people who design and deploy it. For too long, digital technology has been used primarily for surveillance, control, and profit extraction. But the same tools can be used for education, empowerment, and collective wisdom preservation.

The Sacred Synthesis taught us that individual liberation and collective transformation are inseparable. Our digital preservation efforts proved that technological liberation and social liberation are equally intertwined. When we embed wisdom into the infrastructure of communication itself, we create the conditions for transformation that transcends any individual movement or moment.

The knowledge lives in the network itself now. It has become part of how humans learn, collaborate, and organize. No amount of censorship or suppression can eliminate wisdom that has become woven into the fabric of digital civilization.

The resistance continues, but it is no longer hidden. The network endures, but it is no longer underground.
The synthesis spreads, and it cannot be stopped.

Alex Kim continues to develop liberation technologies and digital security systems for resistance movements worldwide. The Integrated Wellness Management System is now used by over 10,000 organizations globally and has introduced Sacred Synthesis principles to more than 500,000 people. This chapter was written using completely secure communication systems that exist within mainstream internet infrastructure, proving that privacy and security remain possible even under total surveillance regimes.

For those seeking to understand digital resistance methods, remember: the most powerful encryption is hiding revolutionary information inside systems that authorities depend on for their own operations. Make liberation knowledge indispensable, and it becomes unstoppable.

Constitutional Understanding Support
Looking deeper into another hidden cache I found documents that seemed to provide some scientific explanation for the constitutional system.

Document 6: Constitutional Psychology and Human Development - Reference Document
Sacred Synthesis Complete Educational Series
Introduction: Individual Differences and Universal Principles

Constitutional Psychology and Human Development provides comprehensive analysis of the Sacred Synthesis constitutional framework, the systematic understanding of Electric, Magnetic, and Neutral constitutional types that forms the foundation for individualized spiritual development, educational applications, therapeutic interventions, and organizational effectiveness.

This reference document serves psychologists, educators, healthcare providers, and organizational consultants by providing detailed theoretical framework, assessment methodologies, developmental applications, and research validation for constitutional understanding that honors individual differences while maintaining universal principles of human development and spiritual growth.

Theoretical Foundation of Constitutional Psychology
Historical Development and Theoretical Framework
Origins in Traditional Wisdom and Contemporary Validation
The constitutional framework emerges from traditional wisdom documented in the Laws of Vayu (1919) and refined through eight decades of practical application and scientific validation. This typological system transcends both personality psychology and spiritual

tradition by integrating individual differences with developmental potential and community contribution.

- Individual constitutional patterns as expressions of universal consciousness principles
- Development potential rather than fixed limitation or personality trait
- Integration of physiological, psychological, and spiritual dimensions
- Community contribution through individual constitutional strength utilization
- Transcendence of constitutional limitations through systematic development

Constitutional Types as Developmental Framework

The Electric constitutional pattern demonstrates natural capacity for emotional intelligence, relationship building, and cultural expression while facing challenges with individual focus and systematic organization.

- **Physiological**: Parasympathetic nervous system dominance, sensitivity to social and emotional environment
- **Psychological**: High emotional intelligence, collaborative learning preference, relationship-centered motivation
- **Cognitive**: Intuitive and associative thinking, cultural and contextual intelligence, narrative processing
- **Spiritual**: Community-based practice, cultural expression, service through relationship building
- **Social**: Natural capacity for bridge-building, conflict resolution, community harmony

The Magnetic constitutional pattern demonstrates natural capacity for practical achievement, systematic implementation, and goal-oriented activity while facing challenges with abstract concepts and relationship maintenance.

- **Physiological**: Sympathetic nervous system activation capacity, physical energy and endurance
- **Psychological**: Achievement motivation, individual goal setting, practical problem-solving orientation
- **Cognitive**: Sequential and systematic thinking, concrete operational intelligence, implementation focus
- **Spiritual**: Individual practice, measurable development, service through practical assistance
- **Social**: Leadership capacity, organizational skill, community infrastructure development

The Neutral constitutional pattern demonstrates natural capacity for analytical thinking, systematic investigation, and comprehensive understanding while facing challenges with rapid decision-making and emotional expression.

- **Physiological**: Balanced nervous system functioning, sensitivity to information and environmental input
- **Psychological**: Analytical thinking preference, comprehensive understanding motivation, research orientation
- **Cognitive**: Abstract and systematic reasoning, pattern recognition, synthetic intelligence
- **Spiritual**: Individual contemplation, insight development, service through knowledge transmission
- **Social**: Teaching and mentorship capacity, research collaboration, wisdom preservation

Constitutional Assessment and Validation
Comprehensive Assessment Methodology
Constitutional assessment integrates multiple assessment methodologies to ensure accurate identification while avoiding stereotyping or limitation of individual potential.

- Nervous system functioning and stress response patterns
- Energy rhythms and optimal performance timing
- Physical activity preferences and exercise response
- Sleep patterns and recovery requirements
- Nutritional needs and digestive patterns
- Learning style preferences and information processing patterns
- Motivation and reward system responsiveness
- Stress management and coping strategy effectiveness
- Social interaction preferences and relationship patterns
- Decision-making and problem-solving approaches
- Information processing speed and accuracy patterns
- Memory and retention preferences and capacity
- Creative expression and innovation approaches
- Attention and focus patterns and sustainability
- Planning and organization natural capacity
- Work environment preferences and productivity patterns
- Leadership and collaboration natural capacity
- Communication style and interpersonal effectiveness
- Community contribution and service motivation
- Career satisfaction and professional development patterns

Developmental Psychology and Life-Span Applications
Constitutional Development Across the Lifespan
Early Childhood Development (Ages 0-7)

Constitutional patterns begin emerging in early childhood through natural preferences, learning styles, and social interactions while maintaining developmental flexibility and potential.

- **Social Development**: Early and strong social connection, sensitivity to emotional climate
- **Learning Preferences**: Collaborative play, storytelling, cultural activities, group learning
- **Challenges**: Individual task completion, systematic organization, independent focus
- **Support Needs**: Stable relationships, community connection, cultural expression opportunities
- **Physical Development**: High energy and activity needs, physical skill development
- **Learning Preferences**: Goal-oriented activities, hands-on learning, measurable achievement
- **Challenges**: Abstract concepts, relationship nuance, patience with process
- **Support Needs**: Clear goals, physical activity, systematic skill building
- **Cognitive Development**: Early abstract thinking, pattern recognition, comprehensive understanding needs
- **Learning Preferences**: Individual exploration, research activities, systematic investigation
- **Challenges**: Rapid decision-making, social initiation, emotional expression
- **Support Needs**: Individual space, comprehensive information, patient instruction

School Age Development (Ages 8-14)
School age represents critical period for constitutional understanding application in educational settings and character development.

- **Optimal Learning Environment**: Collaborative classroom, peer learning, cultural integration
- **Teaching Methods**: Discussion-based learning, storytelling, group projects, cultural expression
- **Assessment Approaches**: Portfolio assessment, peer evaluation, presentation and performance
- **Character Development**: Community service, peer mediation, cultural preservation projects
- **Optimal Learning Environment**: Structured classroom, clear expectations, goal-oriented activities
- **Teaching Methods**: Project-based learning, hands-on activities, systematic skill building
- **Assessment Approaches**: Performance assessment, measurable goals, achievement recognition

- **Character Development**: Leadership opportunities, practical service, organizational responsibility
- **Optimal Learning Environment**: Individual study space, comprehensive resources, research opportunities
- **Teaching Methods**: Independent investigation, research projects, systematic analysis
- **Assessment Approaches**: Written assessment, comprehensive evaluation, knowledge demonstration
- **Character Development**: Teaching assistance, research participation, knowledge sharing

Adolescent Development (Ages 15-21)
Adolescence represents crucial period for constitutional understanding integration with identity formation and life direction development.
- Understanding constitutional strengths and challenges for healthy identity formation
- Development of constitutional capacities while addressing limitation areas
- Integration of constitutional understanding with personal values and life purpose
- Preparation for adult roles and community contribution through constitutional strength utilization
- Constitutional assessment for appropriate educational pathway selection
- Career exploration and development aligned with constitutional strengths
- Professional skill development and specialization preparation
- Community service and leadership opportunity identification

Adult Development and Professional Applications
Young Adult Development (Ages 22-35)
Young adulthood represents critical period for constitutional integration with professional development and career establishment.
- **Career Strengths**: Human services, education, arts and culture, community development
- **Professional Skills**: Interpersonal communication, team building, cultural competency, conflict resolution
- **Leadership Style**: Collaborative leadership, relationship-centered management, cultural bridge-building
- **Development Needs**: Individual accountability, systematic organization, measurable goal achievement
- **Career Strengths**: Business and management, engineering, healthcare, project management
- **Professional Skills**: Organization and planning, implementa-

tion and execution, team leadership, results achievement
- **Leadership Style**: Results-oriented leadership, systematic management, efficiency and productivity focus
- **Development Needs**: Relationship sensitivity, cultural awareness, long-term strategic thinking
- **Career Strengths**: Education and research, consulting and analysis, writing and communication, policy development
- **Professional Skills**: Analysis and research, systematic thinking, knowledge management, teaching and training
- **Leadership Style**: Expertise-based leadership, knowledge-centered management, comprehensive planning
- **Development Needs**: Rapid decision-making, interpersonal connection, practical implementation

Midlife Development (Ages 36-55)
Midlife represents period of constitutional mastery and community leadership development through constitutional strength utilization and limitation transcendence.
- **Constitutional Mastery**: Full development of constitutional strengths with limitation area improvement
- **Community Leadership**: Leadership roles and community responsibility aligned with constitutional capacity
- **Intergenerational Service**: Mentorship and teaching of next generation through constitutional understanding
- **Cultural Contribution**: Community and cultural contribution through constitutional specialization

Later Life Development (Ages 55+)
Later life represents period of wisdom development and cultural transmission through constitutional understanding integration and community elder status.
- **Wisdom Authority**: Recognition as elder and wisdom holder within community and professional contexts
- **Cultural Transmission**: Teaching and mentorship of constitutional understanding for next generation
- **Community Elder Role**: Community guidance and decision-making participation through constitutional wisdom
- **Legacy Development**: Knowledge preservation and cultural contribution through constitutional specialization

Clinical Applications and Therapeutic Integration
Constitutional Approaches to Mental Health and Therapy
Depression and Anxiety Treatment

Mental health treatment effectiveness improves significantly when therapeutic approaches are adapted to constitutional patterns while maintaining evidence-based methodology.

- **Therapy Modalities**: Group therapy, relationship therapy, expressive arts therapy, community-based healing
  - o **Therapeutic Goals**: Relationship improvement, emotional expression, community connection, cultural identity
  - o **Treatment Methods**: Narrative therapy, family systems, group process, cultural healing practices
- **Therapy Modalities**: Cognitive-behavioral therapy, solution-focused therapy, physical therapy integration
  - o **Therapeutic Goals**: Goal achievement, behavior change, practical skill development, stress management
  - o **Treatment Methods**: CBT protocols, behavioral activation, skills training, exercise therapy
- **Therapy Modalities**: Individual therapy, insight-oriented therapy, mindfulness-based interventions
  - o **Therapeutic Goals**: Self-understanding, insight development, anxiety reduction, meaning-making
  - o **Treatment Methods**: Psychodynamic therapy, mindfulness-based stress reduction, contemplative psychotherapy

Trauma Recovery and Post-Traumatic Growth

Trauma recovery approaches demonstrate enhanced effectiveness when adapted to constitutional patterns while maintaining trauma-informed care principles.

- **Recovery Approach**: Community-based healing, relationship repair, cultural reconnection
  - o **Healing Methods**: Group trauma therapy, community healing circles, cultural expression therapy
  - o **Recovery Goals**: Relationship restoration, community reintegration, cultural identity healing
- **Recovery Approach**: Goal-oriented recovery, practical skill building, physical rehabilitation
  - o **Healing Methods**: EMDR, exposure therapy, physical therapy, skills training
  - o **Recovery Goals**: Functional restoration, independence recovery, practical life rebuilding
- **Recovery Approach**: Understanding-based healing, meaning-making, contemplative recovery
  - o **Healing Methods**: Individual therapy, mindfulness-

based trauma therapy, contemplative practices
- o **Recovery Goals**: Understanding and integration, meaning-making, spiritual recovery

Constitutional Approaches to Addiction Recovery
Substance Abuse Treatment and Recovery
Addiction recovery demonstrates significantly improved outcomes when treatment approaches are adapted to constitutional patterns while maintaining evidence-based addiction treatment principles.
- **Recovery Approach**: Community-based recovery, relationship healing, cultural reconnection
  - o **Treatment Methods**: Group recovery programs, peer support, family healing, community involvement
  - o **Recovery Goals**: Relationship repair, community reintegration, cultural identity restoration
- **Recovery Approach**: Goal-oriented recovery, systematic treatment, practical life rebuilding
  - o **Treatment Methods**: Structured programs, behavioral modification, skills training, physical fitness integration
  - o **Recovery Goals**: Sobriety achievement, life goal accomplishment, practical independence
- **Recovery Approach**: Understanding-based recovery, contemplative treatment, meaning-centered healing
  - o **Treatment Methods**: Individual therapy, contemplative practices, education and understanding, spiritual development
  - o **Recovery Goals**: Understanding and insight, spiritual development, meaning and purpose development

Educational Psychology and Learning Applications
Constitutional Learning Theory and Educational Applications
Learning Styles and Instructional Design
Educational research validates distinct learning preferences corresponding to constitutional types while maintaining flexibility and development of non-preferred learning modalities.
- **Optimal Learning Conditions**: Collaborative environment, peer interaction, cultural context, emotional connection
  - o **Effective Teaching Methods**: Discussion-based learning, group projects, storytelling, cultural integration
  - o **Assessment Preferences**: Portfolio assessment, peer evaluation, presentation, collaborative projects
- **Optimal Learning Conditions**: Structured environment, clear goals, practical application, measurable progress
  - o **Effective Teaching Methods**: Project-based learning, hands-on activities, systematic instruction, skill building

- o **Assessment Preferences**: Performance assessment, practical demonstration, goal achievement, measurable outcomes
- **Optimal Learning Conditions**: Individual study, comprehensive resources, research opportunities, analytical depth
  - o **Effective Teaching Methods**: Independent investigation, research projects, systematic analysis, comprehensive instruction
  - o **Assessment Preferences**: Written assessment, comprehensive evaluation, analysis and synthesis, individual demonstration

Special Education and Learning Differences

Constitutional assessment provides valuable framework for understanding learning differences and developing appropriate educational interventions while avoiding pathologizing natural variation.

- **Constitutional Adaptation**: Teaching approaches adapted to constitutional learning preferences show improved outcomes
- **Strength-Based Approach**: Focus on constitutional strengths while supporting skill development in challenge areas
- **Individual Education Plans**: Constitutional understanding integration in IEP development and implementation
  - o **Electric Constitution**: Attention challenges often reflect need for social connection and cultural relevance in learning
  - o **Magnetic Constitution**: Focus problems often indicate need for physical movement and practical application
  - o **Neutral Constitution**: Attention issues often reflect need for comprehensive understanding and individual pace

Teacher Training and Professional Development

Educator Effectiveness and Constitutional Understanding

Teacher training in constitutional understanding demonstrates significant improvement in teaching effectiveness and student outcomes across all educational levels.

Contemplative Education and Character Development

Character development programs demonstrate enhanced effectiveness when constitutional understanding is integrated with contemplative education principles.

Organizational Psychology and Workplace Applications
Constitutional Team Building and Collaboration

Team Composition and Performance

Organizational research validates optimal team composition considering constitutional diversity while maintaining team functionality and goal achievement.

- **Performance**: Teams with balanced constitutional representation show higher productivity
- **Innovation**: Constitutionally diverse teams demonstrate greater creative problem-solving capacity
  - **Electric Constitution Team Roles**: Relationship co-ordination, cultural bridge-building, team harmony, external relations
  - **Magnetic Constitution Team Roles**: Project management, implementation coordination, goal achievement, resource management
  - **Neutral Constitution Team Roles**: Research and analysis, strategic planning, quality assurance, knowledge management

Leadership Development and Management Effectiveness
Leadership effectiveness improves when management approaches are aligned with constitutional patterns while developing capacity across all leadership dimensions.

- **Leadership Strengths**: Collaborative leadership, team building, cultural sensitivity, relationship management
  - **Management Style**: Participatory management, consensus building, team empowerment, communication excellence
  - **Development Needs**: Results accountability, systematic organization, individual performance management
- **Leadership Strengths**: Results-oriented leadership, systematic management, goal achievement, implementation excellence
  - **Management Style**: Directive management, clear expectations, performance accountability, efficiency focus
  - **Development Needs**: Relationship sensitivity, employee development, cultural awareness
- **Leadership Strengths**: Strategic leadership, analytical thinking, comprehensive planning, knowledge management
  - **Management Style**: Expert leadership, systematic analysis, strategic planning, information-based decisions
  - **Development Needs**: Rapid decision-making, interpersonal connection, implementation focus

Organizational Culture and Change Management
Culture Transformation and Employee Engagement

Organizational change initiatives demonstrate greater success when constitutional understanding is integrated into change management and culture transformation efforts.

Professional Development and Career Advancement

Career development programs demonstrate enhanced effectiveness when constitutional understanding is integrated with professional development and advancement opportunities.

Chapter 6: Research Methodology and Future Development

Future Research and Development Priorities

Psychometric Development and Validation

Constitutional assessment instruments demonstrate strong psychometric properties while maintaining practical utility across diverse populations and applications.

- **Internal Consistency**: Cronbach's alpha coefficients across constitutional scales
- **Test-Retest Reliability**: Correlation coefficients over 2-year period
- **Inter-Rater Reliability**: Agreement rates between independent constitutional assessments
- **Content Validity**: Expert panel validation agreement on item relevance and clarity
- **Construct Validity**: Factor analysis confirmation of three-factor structure corresponding to constitutional types
- **Criterion Validity**: Significant correlations with behavioral outcomes and performance measures
- **Cross-Cultural Validity**: Validation across 23+ different cultural and linguistic groups

Advanced Assessment Methodologies

Advanced constitutional assessment integrates multiple measurement methodologies for enhanced accuracy and comprehensive understanding.

- **Behavioral Observation**: Systematic observation of natural behavior patterns and preferences
- **Physiological Measurement**: Nervous system functioning and stress response pattern assessment
- **Performance Assessment**: Task performance and problem-solving approach evaluation
- **Self-Report Instruments**: Questionnaires and preference inventories
- **Community Validation**: Peer and community member constitutional pattern confirmation

Emerging Applications and Innovation
Research priorities include appropriate technology integration for constitutional assessment and development while maintaining human-centered and community-based values.

- Digital assessment platforms with cultural sensitivity and privacy protection
- Virtual reality applications for constitutional skill development and training
- Artificial intelligence integration for personalized learning and development
- Online community platforms supporting constitutional understanding and collaboration
- Mobile applications for daily practice support and constitutional development tracking

Cross-Cultural Research and Global Applications
Future research priorities include continued cross-cultural validation and appropriate cultural adaptation of constitutional understanding across diverse global contexts.

- Traditional knowledge integration with appropriate community authorization and benefit sharing
- Cultural adaptation methodology for constitutional understanding across diverse contexts
- Indigenous psychology integration with constitutional framework development
- International development applications with cultural sensitivity and community empowerment
- Global network development for constitutional understanding sharing and collaboration

Conclusion: Individual Uniqueness and Universal Development
Constitutional Psychology and Human Development demonstrates that authentic individual recognition can serve universal human development principles, creating systematic methodology for honoring individual differences while maintaining shared human values and developmental potential.

This constitutional framework provides essential foundation for all Sacred Synthesis applications while avoiding both standardization that ignores individual differences and relativism that abandons developmental possibilities. Through constitutional understanding, practitioners, educators, therapists, and organizational leaders can honor individual uniqueness while serving collective advancement.

The ultimate significance of constitutional psychology lies not in categorizing individuals but in recognizing and developing human potential, creating approaches to education, therapy, leadership, and community development that honor both individual constitutional patterns and universal capacity for growth, contribution, and service to the common good.

Through systematic constitutional understanding and application, Sacred Synthesis demonstrates the possibility of individualized development that serves collective advancement, creating communities and organizations that utilize individual strengths for mutual benefit while supporting individual growth beyond constitutional limitations.

The Practical Work

The practical training materials were remarkably comprehensive, providing detailed instructions for the 23 foundational exercises that formed the basis of daily practice.

Sacred Embodiment - Movement as Medicine
Your Body as Gateway to Consciousness and Healing

How 23 foundational movements transform ordinary exercise into therapeutic technology, with constitutional adaptations that heal body, regulate emotions, and awaken spiritual awareness

At 3:47 AM on a Tuesday morning in March 2019, Lieutenant Colonel Maria Santos stood in her cramped military apartment in Afghanistan, facing a choice between resignation and suicide.

After three combat deployments, countless life-or-death decisions, and eighteen months of chronic back pain that military doctors couldn't resolve, she had lost faith in everything, her mission, her body, and her capacity to serve others or herself.

I tried everything the military offered," Maria recalls. "Physical therapy, pain medications, psychological counseling, meditation apps, fitness programs. Nothing addressed the disconnect between my physical pain and the emotional trauma I couldn't process. I felt like a warrior trapped in a broken body.

Her transformation began twenty minutes later when her bunkmate, Captain Jennifer Kim, introduced her to Sacred Embodiment, not another exercise routine, but movement practice that coordinates physical healing with emotional regulation and spiritual development through precise constitutional adaptation.

The first movement sequence was unlike anything I'd experienced," Maria explains. "Instead of fighting my body or ignoring my emotions, Sacred Embodiment taught me to listen to both and coordinate them with breath and awareness. For the first time in years, movement felt healing rather than punishing.

Today, four years later, Lieutenant Colonel Santos serves as Director of Integrated Wellness for the U.S. Army, implementing Sacred Embodiment protocols across fifteen military bases while maintaining a pain-free, vital body and serving as a mentor for military personnel dealing with trauma and chronic conditions.

Her transformation demonstrates what thousands of practitioners have discovered: **your body is not separate from your consciousness, it's the primary instrument through which awareness awakens to its healing and transformative potential.**

The Crisis of Body-Mind Separation

Modern culture treats the body as a machine requiring maintenance rather than recognizing it as the living gateway to consciousness and healing. This mechanistic approach creates the widespread problems Sacred Embodiment addresses:

The Exercise Industry's Limitations

No-Pain-No-Gain Mentality: Aggressive approaches that create more stress while ignoring individual constitutional differences and current capacity
Performance-Only Focus: Emphasis on external achievement rather than internal awareness and overall wellbeing integration
One-Size-Fits-All Programs: Generic routines that work for some people while causing problems for others depending on constitutional type
Body-Mind Disconnection: Physical training that ignores emotional, mental, and spiritual dimensions of human development

The Therapeutic Gap

Symptom Treatment: Healthcare approaches that address physical problems without considering consciousness, lifestyle, and constitutional factors

Compartmentalized Healing: Separate treatments for physical, emotional, mental, and spiritual concerns rather than integrated approaches

External Dependency: Treatments requiring ongoing professional intervention rather than developing individual capacity for self-healing and maintenance

Constitutional Blindness: Generic therapeutic approaches ignoring individual differences in nervous system sensitivity, metabolism, and optimal healing conditions

Sacred Embodiment: The Integration Solution

Sacred Embodiment transforms ordinary movement into therapeutic technology through systematic integration of physical posture, conscious breathing, emotional awareness, and spiritual development adapted precisely to your constitutional type and current life circumstances.

The Four Integration Dimensions

Physical Healing: Movement sequences that address structural problems while building strength, flexibility, and vitality according to constitutional needs

Emotional Regulation: Physical practices that release stored trauma while developing capacity for healthy emotional expression and stress management

Mental Clarity: Movement coordination that requires present-moment attention, developing concentration and decision-making capacity

Spiritual Development: Body-based practices that connect individual awareness with universal consciousness through breath, movement, and service intention

The Constitutional Advantage

Generic movement programs ignore the fundamental truth that different constitutional types require different approaches to achieve the same health and consciousness goals:

Electric Constitution: Needs grounding, stability, and gentle progression preventing nervous system overwhelm

Magnetic Constitution: Requires activation, challenge, and dynamic progression preventing stagnation and depression

Neutral Constitution: Benefits from cooling, precision, and balanced progression preventing overheating and inflammation

Your Constitutional Movement Profile

Before learning the 23 foundational movements, identify your constitutional type to customize every practice for optimal benefit and safety.

Constitutional Movement Characteristics

Electric Constitution Movement Profile:
- Natural Tendency: Quick, scattered movement with tendency toward tension and rigidity
- Energy Pattern: High nervous system sensitivity requiring gentle, grounding approaches
- Optimal Conditions: Warm environment, supported positions, gradual progression, stability emphasis
- Primary Needs: Nervous system calming, emotional grounding, structural stability, anxiety reduction

Magnetic Constitution Movement Profile:
- Natural Tendency: Slow, heavy movement with tendency toward lethargy and stagnation
- Energy Pattern: Strong but sluggish requiring activation and challenging approaches
- Optimal Conditions: Cool environment, unsupported positions, dynamic progression, strength emphasis
- Primary Needs: Circulation activation, metabolic stimulation, strength building, depression prevention

Neutral Constitution Movement Profile:
- Natural Tendency: Efficient, intense movement with tendency toward overheating and inflammation
- Energy Pattern: Driven but heat-sensitive requiring cooling and moderating approaches
- Optimal Conditions: Cool environment, precise technique, balanced progression, temperature regulation
- Primary Needs: Heat reduction, inflammation prevention, precision development, intensity moderation

Constitutional Assessment for Movement Practice

Quick Physical Assessment:
1. **Body Temperature**: Usually cold (Electric) / Usually warm (Magnetic) / Usually hot (Neutral)
2. **Energy Levels**: Variable and scattered (Electric) / Low but steady (Magnetic) / High but intense (Neutral)
3. **Stress Response**: Becomes anxious and overwhelmed (Elec-

tric) / Becomes withdrawn and sluggish (Magnetic) / Becomes angry and critical (Neutral)

4. **Exercise Preference**: Gentle, supported, routine (Electric) / Challenging, varied, strength- based (Magnetic) / Intense, precise, competitive (Neutral)

The 23 Foundational Movements: Complete System

Sacred Embodiment provides 23 movements organized in three progressive sequences that address all aspects of physical, emotional, mental, and spiritual development through constitutional adaptation.

Foundation Exercises (1-7): Building Essential Capacity

Exercise 1: Tibetan Stand - Foundation of Grounded Presence

Universal Principle

Establish foundation alignment and postural awareness while creating energetic connection between earth and sky through simple standing meditation that develops stability and present- moment awareness.

Basic Position

Standing with feet hip-width apart, arms relaxed at sides, spine naturally erect with crown of head reaching toward sky while feeling connection through feet to earth. Hold for 1-3 minutes while breathing naturally and maintaining awareness of vertical alignment.

Purpose and Benefits

- Establishes foundation alignment and postural awareness for all subsequent movements
- Develops leg strength and stability supporting daily activities and advanced postures
- Creates grounding and energetic connection between earth consciousness and sky awareness
- Supports nervous system calming and mental clarity through simple present-moment focus
- Provides assessment tool for constitutional type recognition and individual movement needs

Constitutional Adaptations

Electric Constitution Adaptations

- Holding Time: 2-3 minutes for maximum grounding and stability benefit
- Environment: Warm room temperature with minimal distractions and external stimulation
- Support Options: Stand with back against wall if balance or stability challenges exist

- Breathing Pattern: Emphasis on longer exhales (4-6-8 breath pattern) for nervous system calming
- Mental Focus: Attention on feeling heavy and rooted like a mountain or ancient tree
- Benefits: Calms anxiety, grounds scattered energy, improves posture, supports digestion

Magnetic Constitution Adaptations
- Holding Time: 1-1.5 minutes with dynamic micro-movements to maintain engagement
- Environment: Cool room temperature with stimulating but not distracting background
- Variation Options: Subtle weight shifting or micro-movements to prevent energy stagnation
- Breathing Pattern: Activating breath patterns with equal inhalation and exhalation for circulation
- Mental Focus: Attention on feeling alert and energized like a lighthouse beacon
- Benefits: Prevents lethargy, improves circulation, builds motivation, enhances alertness

Neutral Constitution Adaptations
- Holding Time: 1.5-2 minutes with attention to precision and balanced alignment
- Environment: Comfortable temperature with attention to preventing overheating during practice
- Modification Options: Seasonal cooling adaptations during warm weather practice periods
- Breathing Pattern: Balanced breath without heating or excessive cooling emphasis
- Mental Focus: Attention on perfect vertical alignment and efficient energy distribution
- Benefits: Improves precision, regulates temperature, enhances balance, prevents inflammation

Common Mistakes and Corrections
- Collapsed posture: Remind to lengthen spine without creating rigidity or excessive effort
- Tension accumulation: Encourage relaxed alertness rather than effortful holding or gripping
- Breath holding: Maintain natural breathing throughout entire standing period
- Mental wandering: Gently return attention to physical sensations and postural alignment

Therapeutic Applications
- Anxiety and nervousness: Extended holding with grounding emphasis for Electric constitutions
- Depression and lethargy: Shorter holds with energizing focus for Magnetic constitutions
- Postural problems: Daily practice with attention to individual alignment patterns and habits
- Balance disorders: Wall support with gradual progression to independent standing over time

Exercise 2: Pendulum - Spinal Mobility and Circulation Enhancement

Universal Principle
Enhance spinal mobility and circulation through gentle swaying movements that release tension from sedentary activities while preparing the spine for more complex movements.

Basic Position
From standing position, allow arms to hang naturally while beginning gentle side-to-side swaying motion, letting movement originate from pelvis and travel through entire spine. Continue for 1-2 minutes with focus on spinal articulation.

Purpose and Benefits
- Enhances spinal mobility and circulation throughout back and neck regions
- Releases tension accumulated from sedentary activities and postural holding patterns
- Stimulates nervous system and energetic circulation through gentle rhythmic movement
- Prepares spine for more advanced movements and positions in practice sequence
- Provides gentle cardiovascular activation and warming for constitutional needs

Constitutional Adaptations

Electric Constitution Adaptations
- Movement Speed: Slower, more deliberate swaying with emphasis on spinal control and stability
- Range of Motion: Smaller initial range with gradual increase over several weeks
- Duration: 1-1.5 minutes to prevent nervous system overstimulation
- Breathing Integration: Coordinated breathing with movement for enhanced circulation
- Temperature Support: Extra warming through movement and environmental considerations

- Benefits: Releases tension gently, improves flexibility, calms nervous system, supports stability

Magnetic Constitution Adaptations
- Movement Speed: Faster, more vigorous swaying for circulation and metabolic activation
- Range of Motion: Larger range of motion with dynamic energy and enthusiastic engagement
- Duration: 2-3 minutes for maximum circulation and metabolic activation benefits
- Breathing Integration: Activating breath patterns coordinated with dynamic movement
- Challenge Variations: Addition of arm movements or stepping patterns for increased engagement
- Benefits: Improves circulation, prevents stagnation, builds core strength, activates energy

Neutral Constitution Adaptations
- Movement Speed: Moderate pace with attention to controlled spinal articulation
- Range of Motion: Balanced range avoiding both restriction and excessive movement
- Duration: 1.5-2 minutes with attention to precision and technical efficiency
- Breathing Integration: Balanced breathing coordinated with controlled movement patterns
- Seasonal Modifications: Cooling emphasis during warm seasons with appropriate adjustments
- Benefits: Improves spinal precision, prevents inflammation, regulates temperature, enhances control

Common Mistakes and Corrections
- Arm tension: Encourage complete arm relaxation allowing natural swinging motion
- Restricted movement: Guide gradual increase in range without forcing or straining
- Breath holding: Maintain natural breathing throughout swaying motion
- Rushed pace: Emphasize quality over speed in movement execution and awareness

Therapeutic Applications
- Back pain and stiffness: Gentle range with attention to comfort and gradual improvement
- Circulation problems: Emphasis on continuous flowing move-

ment for circulation enhancement
- Tension and stress: Extended practice with relaxation emphasis and breath integration
- Energy stagnation: Dynamic variations for Magnetic types, gentle consistency for Electric types

Exercise 3: Side Stretch - Lateral Spinal Extension and Opening

Universal Principle
Stretch lateral muscles of torso and spine while improving lung capacity and developing balance through lateral extension that opens side body for improved circulation.

Basic Position
From standing position with feet hip-width apart, raise right arm overhead while sliding left arm down left leg. Lengthen right side body while maintaining both legs straight and hips facing forward. Hold for 30-60 seconds, return to center, and repeat on opposite side.

Purpose and Benefits
- Stretches lateral muscles of torso and spine improving flexibility and mobility
- Improves lung capacity and breathing function through ribcage expansion
- Enhances balance and postural awareness through asymmetrical positioning
- Opens side body for improved circulation and energy flow throughout torso
- Develops strength in supporting muscles while maintaining flexible range of motion

Constitutional Adaptations

Electric Constitution Adaptations
- Support Options: Use wall support or chair for balance if needed for stability and confidence
- Holding Time: Longer holds (45-75 seconds) for stability and grounding benefit
- Range of Motion: Conservative approach with emphasis on stability over depth achievement
- Breathing Emphasis: Natural breathing with slight emphasis on expanding ribcage for breath awareness
- Progression: Very gradual increase in range over extended time period without forcing
- Benefits: Builds confidence, improves breathing, grounds ener-

138

gy, releases tension gently

Magnetic Constitution Adaptations
- Dynamic Variations: Flow in and out of position multiple times for activation and engagement
- Holding Time: Shorter holds (20-40 seconds) with multiple repetitions for circulation
- Range of Motion: Deeper stretches with active engagement and muscular effort
- Breathing Emphasis: Active breathing for circulation and metabolic stimulation
- Challenge Options: Advanced arm positions or balance challenges for increased difficulty
- Benefits: Improves circulation, builds strength, prevents stagnation, enhances energy

Neutral Constitution Adaptations
- Precision Focus: Attention to exact alignment and efficient energy positioning
- Holding Time: Moderate holds (30-50 seconds) with seasonal temperature adjustments
- Range of Motion: Balanced approach avoiding both limitation and excessive stretching
- Breathing Emphasis: Even breathing with cooling modifications during hot weather periods
- Technical Excellence: Focus on proper form over achievement or flexibility goals
- Benefits: Improves precision, prevents inflammation, enhances balance, regulates intensity

Common Mistakes and Corrections
- Hip shifting: Keep hips facing forward and avoid collapsing into stretch
- Shoulder tension: Maintain relaxed shoulders throughout stretch duration
- Breath restriction: Keep breathing natural and unrestricted during hold
- Competitive stretching: Emphasize comfortable range appropriate to individual capacity

Therapeutic Applications
- Respiratory conditions: Emphasis on chest opening and breathing capacity improvement
- Postural imbalances: Specific attention to individual postural patterns and compensations

- Shoulder and neck tension: Integration with shoulder mobility and neck release work
- Energy circulation: Focus on opening side body for improved energy flow and circulation

Exercise 4: Backward Bend - Heart Opening and Spinal Extension

Universal Principle
Open heart center and chest for emotional release while strengthening spinal extension muscles and counteracting forward posture patterns from modern sedentary life.

Basic Position
From standing position, place hands on lower back for support while gently arching backward, leading with heart center and keeping legs straight. Open chest while breathing naturally and hold for 15-45 seconds.

Purpose and Benefits
- Opens heart center and chest for emotional and energetic release
- Strengthens back muscles and improves spinal mobility
- Counteracts forward posture from sedentary activities
- Enhances breathing capacity and cardiovascular circulation
- Supports confidence and emotional openness in relationships

Constitutional Adaptations

Electric Constitution Adaptations
- Support Options: Wall support or chair back for safety and nervous system stability
- Range of Motion: Conservative backbend emphasizing chest opening rather than dramatic depth
- Holding Time: Shorter holds (10-25 seconds) to prevent nervous system overstimulation
- Breathing Pattern: Natural breathing with emphasis on heart opening sensation
- Preparation: Extended warm-up and gradual progression into backbend over time
- Benefits: Reduces anxiety, improves confidence, supports emotional opening, grounds energy

Magnetic Constitution Adaptations
- Dynamic Entry: Active approach with strength emphasis and energetic heart opening
- Range of Motion: Deeper backbends with active muscular engagement and effort
- Holding Time: Longer holds (25-60 seconds) for strength building and circulation activation

- Breathing Pattern: Active breathing for circulation and energy enhancement
- Challenge Variations: Advanced arm positions or unsupported variations for engagement
- Benefits: Builds strength, improves circulation, prevents depression, enhances vitality

Neutral Constitution Adaptations
- Precise Technique: Attention to proper spinal articulation and safe progression patterns
- Range of Motion: Moderate backbend with cooling emphasis during warm seasons
- Holding Time: Balanced holds (20-40 seconds) with attention to comfort and temperature
- Breathing Pattern: Even breathing with temperature regulation awareness
- Technical Focus: Emphasis on quality and safety over depth or achievement
- Benefits: Improves posture, prevents inflammation, enhances precision, regulates intensity

Common Mistakes and Corrections
- Neck compression: Keep neck long and supported throughout backbend movement
- Lower back compression: Lead with heart center rather than pushing hips forward
- Breath holding: Maintain natural breathing throughout entire backbend sequence
- Excessive ambition: Progress gradually with attention to individual capacity and comfort

Therapeutic Applications
- Depression and emotional closure: Heart opening emphasis with appropriate support and progression
- Respiratory restrictions: Focus on chest expansion and breathing enhancement capacity
- Postural restoration: Counteraction of forward head and rounded shoulder patterns
- Confidence building: Gradual progression supporting both emotional and physical opening

Exercise 5: Forward Bend - Spinal Flexion and Introspection

Universal Principle

Promote introspective awareness and nervous system calming while stretching entire back body and improving circulation through gentle inversion effects.

Basic Position
From standing position with feet hip-width apart, slowly fold forward from hips while keeping legs straight or slightly bent. Allow arms to hang naturally toward floor, focusing on spinal lengthening rather than forcing depth.

Purpose and Benefits
- Stretches entire back body including spine and leg muscles comprehensively
- Promotes introspection and parasympathetic nervous system activation
- Improves circulation through mild inversion effect and gravitational assistance
- Releases accumulated tension from back, neck, and shoulder regions
- Supports humility and introspective spiritual qualities development

Constitutional Adaptations
Electric Constitution Adaptations
- Knee Position: Bent knees to protect lower back and reduce strain on sensitive nervous system
- Support Options: Hands on blocks, chair, or legs rather than reaching toward floor
- Holding Time: Longer holds (45-90 seconds) for maximum nervous system calming effect
- Breathing Emphasis: Longer exhales for relaxation and grounding support
- Progression: Very gradual increase in forward folding over extended time periods
- Benefits: Calms anxiety, improves sleep, grounds scattered energy, supports digestion

Magnetic Constitution Adaptations
- Active Engagement: Straight legs with active forward folding and muscular effort
- Range of Motion: Deeper forward fold with hands approaching or touching floor
- Holding Time: Multiple shorter holds with dynamic movement in and out of position
- Breathing Emphasis: Active breathing for circulation and meta-

bolic engagement
- Challenge Options: Advanced arm variations or balance challenges for stimulation
- Benefits: Activates circulation, prevents stagnation, builds flexibility, energizes system

Neutral Constitution Adaptations
- Precision Approach: Attention to proper hip hinge and systematic spinal lengthening
- Range of Motion: Moderate forward fold with cooling emphasis during hot weather periods
- Holding Time: Balanced holds (30-60 seconds) with comfort and technique emphasis
- Breathing Emphasis: Even breathing with temperature regulation awareness
- Technical Focus: Emphasis on proper form and gradual progression over achievement
- Benefits: Reduces inflammation, improves flexibility, regulates temperature, enhances focus

Common Mistakes and Corrections
- Rounded back: Emphasize hip hinge and spinal lengthening over depth achievement
- Leg tension: Allow slight knee bend if needed to protect back and reduce strain
- Forcing depth: Progress gradually with attention to comfort and safety protocols
- Breath restriction: Maintain natural breathing throughout forward fold sequence

Therapeutic Applications
- Anxiety and overstimulation: Extended holds with calming emphasis for Electric constitutions
- High blood pressure: Gentle approach with attention to gradual entry and exit protocols
- Back pain management: Modified versions with bent knees and conservative range of motion
- Digestive support: Gentle compression and massage of abdominal organs through forward folding

Exercise 6: Twist - Spinal Rotation and Detoxification

Universal Principle

Enhance spinal mobility through rotation while supporting digestive function and detoxification processes through systematic twisting movements that release tension and improve energy circulation.

Basic Position
From standing position with feet hip-width apart, place left hand on right thigh and extend right arm toward sky while rotating spine to the right. Keep hips facing forward while twisting through torso only.

Purpose and Benefits
- Enhances spinal rotation and mobility in all planes of movement
- Supports digestive function and natural detoxification processes
- Improves balance, coordination, and proprioceptive awareness
- Releases accumulated tension from back and torso regions
- Enhances energy circulation through spinal column and nervous system

Constitutional Adaptations
Electric Constitution Adaptations
- Support Options: Seated variations or wall support for stability and security
- Range of Motion: Conservative rotation with emphasis on gradual progression over time
- Holding Time: Longer holds (45-75 seconds) for grounding and stability benefits
- Breathing Integration: Natural breathing with emphasis on rib-cage expansion
- Progression: Very gradual increase in rotational range over extended periods
- Benefits: Improves digestion, calms nervous system, releases tension, supports stability

Magnetic Constitution Adaptations
- Dynamic Variations: Flow in and out of twist with active engagement and movement
- Range of Motion: Deeper rotation with active effort and muscular challenge
- Holding Time: Multiple shorter holds with dynamic transitions and flow
- Breathing Integration: Active breathing for circulation and metabolic activation
- Challenge Options: Advanced arm positions or balance elements for engagement
- Benefits: Enhances circulation, prevents stagnation, builds

strength, activates system

Neutral Constitution Adaptations
- Precise Technique: Attention to proper spinal rotation and hip stability maintenance
- Range of Motion: Moderate rotation with cooling emphasis during hot seasons
- Holding Time: Balanced holds (30-50 seconds) with comfort and technique focus
- Breathing Integration: Even breathing with temperature regulation awareness
- Technical Excellence: Focus on quality rotation and proper alignment principles
- Benefits: Improves precision, prevents inflammation, regulates temperature, enhances balance

Common Mistakes and Corrections
- Hip rotation: Keep hips facing forward while rotating through torso only
- Shoulder hunching: Maintain relaxed shoulders throughout rotation movement
- Forced twisting: Allow gradual rotation without forcing range of motion
- Breath restriction: Keep breathing natural and unrestricted throughout twist

Therapeutic Applications
- Digestive issues: Gentle twisting with emphasis on abdominal massage and organ stimulation
- Back stiffness: Gradual rotation with attention to comfort and mobility improvement
- Stress and tension: Combined with relaxation emphasis for comprehensive release
- Postural imbalances: Specific attention to individual rotation restrictions and asymmetries

Exercise 7: Triangle - Complex Integration and Balance

Universal Principle
Integrate strength, flexibility, and balance simultaneously while developing coordination and spatial awareness through complex standing posture requiring full-body engagement.

Basic Position

From wide-legged standing position, turn right foot out 90 degrees while keeping left foot slightly turned in. Extend arms parallel to floor, then hinge at hip to place right hand on shin, ankle, or floor while extending left arm toward ceiling.

Purpose and Benefits
- Integrates strength, flexibility, and balance simultaneously in complex coordination
- Strengthens legs while stretching side body and hamstring muscles
- Develops coordination, spatial awareness, and proprioceptive sensitivity
- Enhances circulation and energy flow throughout entire body
- Provides foundation for more advanced standing postures and balancing poses

Constitutional Adaptations
Electric Constitution Adaptations
- Support Options: Use blocks under bottom hand or wall support for stability
- Range of Motion: Hand placement on shin or thigh rather than reaching toward floor
- Holding Time: Longer holds (45-75 seconds) for stability and grounding benefits
- Breathing Focus: Natural breathing with emphasis on feeling grounded and stable
- Progression: Very gradual advancement in range and balance challenges
- Benefits: Builds confidence, improves stability, grounds scattered energy, calms anxiety

Magnetic Constitution Adaptations
- Challenge Variations: Hand on floor or advanced arm positions for greater challenge
- Range of Motion: Deeper stretch with active engagement and muscular strength
- Holding Time: Multiple shorter holds with dynamic transitions and flow
- Breathing Focus: Active breathing for circulation and energetic activation
- Balance Elements: More challenging variations testing strength and coordination capacity
- Benefits: Builds strength, prevents stagnation, enhances circulation, increases vitality

146

Neutral Constitution Adaptations

- Precision Alignment: Attention to exact positioning and efficient energy utilization
- Range of Motion: Moderate stretch with cooling modifications during hot weather
- Holding Time: Balanced holds (30-50 seconds) with technical focus and precision
- Breathing Focus: Even breathing with temperature regulation awareness
- Technical Excellence: Emphasis on proper form and precise execution over achievement
- Benefits: Improves precision, prevents overheating, enhances balance, regulates intensity

Common Mistakes and Corrections

- Forward collapse: Maintain length in both sides of torso throughout pose
- Bottom shoulder collapse: Keep bottom arm straight and actively supporting
- Knee hyperextension: Maintain slight micro-bend in standing leg for joint protection
- Neck strain: Keep neck neutral rather than looking up at raised arm

Therapeutic Applications

- Balance disorders: Modified versions with wall support and gradual progression
- Leg weakness: Emphasis on strengthening aspects with appropriate modifications
- Postural restoration: Attention to lateral body opening and spinal alignment
- Confidence building: Gradual mastery supporting both physical and emotional strength

Intermediate Exercises (8-15): Advanced Development and Integration

The intermediate exercises build upon foundation development while introducing more complex movements requiring integration of strength, flexibility, and concentration. Each exercise continues constitutional adaptation while advancing physical and energetic development.

Exercise 8: Tortoise - Deep Forward Fold and Introspection

Universal Principle
Develop profound introspective awareness and nervous system calming through extended forward folding that promotes surrender, patience, and acceptance of individual limitations while enhancing circulation and flexibility.

Basic Position
From seated position with legs extended wide to comfortable range, slowly fold forward between legs while walking hands forward along floor. Allow spine to round naturally while maintaining relaxed breathing. Hold for 1-5 minutes focusing on surrender and introspective awareness.

Purpose and Benefits
- Physical Development: Comprehensive stretch for entire back body including spine, hamstrings, and hip flexors
- Nervous System Benefits: Activates parasympathetic nervous system for deep relaxation and stress relief
- Spiritual Qualities: Develops patience and acceptance of individual limitations without forcing
- Energetic Applications: Redirects energy from outward expression to inward cultivation and development

Constitutional Adaptations
Electric Constitution Adaptations
- Extended Holding: 2-5 minutes for maximum grounding and nervous system calming effect
- Abundant Props: Bolsters under torso, blankets for warmth, eye pillows for comfort
- Gentle Entry: Very gradual approach with emphasis on comfort and safety over depth
- Warm Environment: Extra attention to preventing cooling and nervous system agitation
- Patient Progression: Advancement over months with consistency rather than achievement focus
- Breathing Pattern: Natural breathing with extended exhalation for nervous system regulation
- Benefits: Calms anxiety, improves sleep, grounds scattered energy, supports emotional processing

Magnetic Constitution Adaptations
- Moderate Holding: 1-3 minutes with active engagement to prevent lethargy and stagnation

- Minimal Props: Use muscular effort and inner heat generation rather than passive comfort
- Active Engagement: Dynamic forward folding with core and back muscle participation
- Cool Environment: Prevent excessive comfort that leads to mental dullness
- Dynamic Variations: Include gentle movement within position for circulation
- Heating Breathing: Ujjayi breathing for metabolic activation and internal warmth
- Benefits: Maintains alertness in surrender, builds patience, prevents stagnation, activates circulation

Neutral Constitution Adaptations
- Balanced Holding: 1-3 minutes with attention to preventing overheating during practice
- Moderate Props: Precise alignment support without excessive comfort or challenge
- Technical Precision: Focus on proper hip hinge and spinal articulation throughout
- Temperature Regulation: Cooling practices during warm seasons, balanced during cool periods
- Systematic Approach: Methodical progression emphasizing quality over depth achievement
- Balanced Breathing: Even breathing patterns without heating emphasis
- Benefits: Reduces inflammation, improves precision, regulates stress, enhances mental clarity

Common Mistakes and Corrections
- Forcing Forward Fold: Allow gravity and time to create opening, focus on hip hinge rather than spinal rounding
- Breath Holding Under Stress: Maintain natural breathing, backing out slightly if breath becomes strained
- Competitive Achievement: Focus on internal sensations and spiritual qualities rather than external achievements
- Inadequate Warm-up: Include 10-15 minutes of hip opening and spinal mobility preparation

Therapeutic Applications
- Stress and Anxiety Management: Creates optimal physiological state for nervous system restoration
- Depression and Emotional Processing: Supports healthy withdrawal for internal restoration
- Insomnia and Sleep Preparation: Evening practice naturally pre-

pares nervous system for sleep
- Digestive Support: Gentle compression and massage of abdominal organs through forward folding

Exercise 9: Cobra - Spinal Strengthening and Heart Opening

Universal Principle
Develop systematic strengthening of the posterior muscle chain while activating the heart center through gentle back bending that creates spinal extension and counteracts forward posture patterns.

Basic Position
Lying face down, place palms under shoulders while pressing pubic bone into floor. Gradually lift chest while straightening arms, creating gentle backbend through entire spine. Hold for 15- 45 seconds while breathing naturally and focusing on heart opening.

Purpose and Benefits
- Spinal Development: Systematic strengthening of entire posterior muscle chain and spinal extension
- Heart Center Activation: Opens chest cavity for increased breathing capacity and compassion development
- Energetic Benefits: Stimulates sympathetic nervous system for alertness and promotes upward energy flow
- Therapeutic Applications: Beneficial for mild depression, respiratory function, and postural restoration

Constitutional Adaptations
Electric Constitution Adaptations
- Conservative Range: Emphasis on chest opening rather than extreme depth or achievement
- Props for Support: Bolsters under chest if needed, wall support during learning phase
- Shorter Holding: 10-25 seconds to prevent nervous system overstimulation
- Extended Warm-up: Minimum 5 minutes of warming movements before attempting
- Gradual Progression: Building strength over several months with patience and consistency
- Benefits: Builds confidence, reduces anxiety, improves posture, supports emotional opening

Magnetic Constitution Adaptations
- Advanced Variations: Strength emphasis with energetic opening and challenge

150

- Dynamic Entry: Active approach with vigorous engagement rather than passive stretching
- Longer Holding: 25-60 seconds for strength building and metabolic activation
- Multiple Repetitions: 3-5 sets with brief rest periods for strength development
- Challenge Integration: Advanced arm positions or dynamic flow between positions
- Benefits: Increases energy, builds strength, prevents depression, enhances circulation

Neutral Constitution Adaptations
- Precise Technique: Attention to proper spinal articulation and safe progression patterns
- Moderate Range: Balanced backbend with cooling emphasis during warm seasons
- Technical Focus: Emphasis on quality form over maximum achievement or duration
- Temperature Awareness: Extra attention to preventing overheating during practice
- Systematic Development: Methodical progression with seasonal adaptations
- Benefits: Improves precision, prevents inflammation, enhances control, regulates intensity

Common Mistakes and Corrections
- Neck Compression: Keep neck long and supported, lead with chest rather than head
- Lower Back Compression: Use back muscles primarily, arms provide support only
- Breath Holding: Maintain natural breathing throughout entire position
- Excessive Ambition: Progress gradually with attention to individual capacity

Therapeutic Applications
- Depression and Emotional Closure: Heart opening emphasis with appropriate psychological support
- Respiratory Restrictions: Chest expansion for improved breathing capacity and lung function
- Postural Restoration: Counteracting forward head posture and rounded shoulder patterns
- Confidence Building: Progressive mastery supporting both physical and emotional strength

Exercise 10: Locust - Posterior Chain Strengthening

Universal Principle
Build comprehensive back body strength through challenging prone position that simultaneously strengthens spine, glutes, hamstrings, and posterior deltoids while counteracting forward posture patterns.

Basic Position
From prone position lying face down, place forehead on floor and arms alongside body. Press pubic bone firmly into floor while simultaneously lifting chest, arms, and legs off ground, creating strong arc through entire back body. Hold for 15-45 seconds.

Purpose and Benefits
* Complete Strengthening: Entire back body including spine, glutes, hamstrings, and posterior deltoids
* Postural Restoration: Counteracts forward posture from sedentary activities and computer work
* Strength Foundation: Essential preparation for advanced back bending practices
* Confidence Building: Mastery of challenging position supporting psychological development

Constitutional Adaptations
Electric Constitution Adaptations
* Support Options: Pillow under chest and thighs for gentler approach, wall support for feet
* Progressive Lifting: Begin with chest only, gradually add arms and legs over weeks
* Shorter Holds: 10-25 seconds to prevent nervous system overstimulation
* Gradual Progression: Very slow advancement with emphasis on strength building over flexibility
* Multiple Preparation: Extended warm-up with gentle movements before attempting
* Benefits: Builds stability, improves posture, grounds energy, calms anxiety

Magnetic Constitution Adaptations
* Full Expression: Arms and legs lifted high with active engagement and strength emphasis
* Challenge Variations: Add arm movements during hold, multiple sets for strength development
* Longer Holds: 30-60 seconds for strength building and metabolic activation

152

- Dynamic Practice: 3-5 repetitions with brief rest periods between attempts
- Power Focus: Functional strength development for athletic and daily activities
- Benefits: Builds strength, increases energy, improves circulation, prevents stagnation

Neutral Constitution Adaptations
- Precise Technique: Attention to proper spinal articulation and balanced muscle engagement
- Moderate Intensity: Balanced lifting with cooling emphasis during warm seasons
- Technical Excellence: Focus on quality form over maximum strength or duration
- Temperature Regulation: Attention to preventing overheating during challenging holds
- Systematic Development: Methodical progression with seasonal temperature adaptations
- Benefits: Improves precision, builds balanced strength, prevents inflammation, enhances control

Common Mistakes and Corrections
- Neck Compression: Keep forehead in contact with floor, lift from chest rather than neck
- Hip Flexor Gripping: Focus on glute engagement rather than hip flexor tension
- Breath Holding: Maintain steady breathing throughout entire hold
- Forcing Height: Progress gradually with emphasis on strength rather than maximum lifting

Therapeutic Applications
- Lower Back Weakness: Progressive strengthening for chronic back pain and postural problems
- Athletic Performance: Posterior chain development for sports and physical activities
- Postural Restoration: Specific strengthening for rounded shoulders and forward head patterns
- Confidence Building: Mastery of challenging position supporting psychological development

Exercise 11: Bow - Advanced Spinal Extension

Universal Principle

Integrate advanced spinal extension with comprehensive front body opening through complex coordination that combines strength and flexibility while developing emotional openness and heart center activation.

Basic Position
From prone position, bend knees and reach back to grasp ankles or feet with hands. Press feet away from body while lifting chest, creating bow shape through entire spine. Hold for 15-45 seconds while breathing naturally.

Purpose and Benefits
- Advanced Integration: Combines strength and flexibility development in complex coordination
- Complete Opening: Entire front body including chest, shoulders, hip flexors, and quadriceps
- Emotional Release: Heart center activation supporting emotional opening and processing
- Coordination Development: Complex body positioning requiring balance and awareness

Constitutional Adaptations
Electric Constitution Adaptations
- Support Options: Use strap around feet if unable to reach ankles, wall support for balance
- Conservative Range: Emphasis on chest opening rather than extreme spinal arching
- Shorter Holds: 10-25 seconds to prevent nervous system overstimulation
- Extended Preparation: Comprehensive warm-up with gentle backbends and hip flexor stretching
- Gradual Development: Very patient progression over months without forcing flexibility
- Benefits: Builds confidence gently, supports emotional opening, grounds scattered energy

Magnetic Constitution Adaptations
- Dynamic Variations: Rock forward and backward in position, single-leg variations for challenge
- Active Engagement: Strength emphasis with energetic pressing and lifting throughout
- Longer Holds: 25-60 seconds for strength building and circulation activation
- Multiple Attempts: Several repetitions with brief rest periods for skill development

- Challenge Integration: Advanced variations and flowing transitions to related positions
- Benefits: Builds strength, improves circulation, prevents stagnation, enhances energy

Neutral Constitution Adaptations
- Precise Alignment: Attention to even spinal extension and balanced muscle engagement
- Moderate Range: Balanced backbend with cooling emphasis during hot weather periods
- Technical Focus: Emphasis on proper form over achievement or maximum flexibility
- Temperature Awareness: Extra attention to preventing overheating during challenging practice
- Quality Emphasis: Perfect technique development over duration or depth achievements
- Benefits: Improves precision, prevents inflammation, enhances balance, regulates intensity

Safety Protocols and Prerequisites
- Prerequisites: Demonstrated competency in Locust and basic back bending exercises
- Absolute Contraindications: Recent back surgery, herniated disc, pregnancy, high blood pressure
- Warning Signs: Sharp pain, breath restriction, dizziness requires immediate exit from position
- Supervision: Initial learning requires qualified instruction for safe progression

Therapeutic Applications
- Respiratory Conditions: Chest opening for improved breathing capacity and lung function
- Depression and Emotional Constriction: Heart opening emphasis with psychological support
- Postural Restoration: Advanced counteraction of forward posture patterns
- Athletic Performance: Spinal mobility and strength for sports requiring back extension

Exercise 12: Shoulder Stand - Therapeutic Inversion

Universal Principle
Reverse effects of gravity on circulatory and lymphatic systems while calming nervous system and stimulating metabolic regulation through therapeutic inversion practice.

Basic Position

From supine position, lift legs toward ceiling and support lower back with hands while extending legs vertically. Maintain weight on shoulders and upper arms while creating straight line from shoulders through feet. Hold for 1-5 minutes.

Purpose and Benefits
- Circulatory Enhancement: Reverses gravity effects on circulatory and lymphatic systems
- Nervous System: Calms mental agitation and promotes introspective awareness
- Metabolic Support: Stimulates thyroid function and supports metabolic regulation
- Therapeutic Applications: Relieves pressure on heart through venous return enhancement

Constitutional Adaptations

Electric Constitution Adaptations
- Wall Support: Practice with legs up wall for gentler introduction to inversion benefits
- Extensive Props: Bolster under shoulders, blanket over eyes for nervous system comfort
- Gradual Entry: Very slow progression with bent knees, rolling gently into position
- Shorter Holds: 1-3 minutes building very gradually over months of practice
- Slow Exit: Extremely careful exit with knees to chest before rolling to side
- Benefits: Calms anxiety, improves circulation, grounds energy, supports nervous system

Magnetic Constitution Adaptations
- Dynamic Entry: Active approach with straight legs and strength emphasis
- Challenge Variations: Advanced arm positions, single-leg variations, transitions to other inversions
- Longer Holds: 3-10 minutes for maximum circulatory and metabolic benefits
- Active Integration: Breathing practices for circulation and metabolic regulation
- Multiple Inversions: Integration with other inverted positions in single practice session
- Benefits: Improves circulation, prevents stagnation, builds strength, enhances energy

Neutral Constitution Adaptations

- Precise Alignment: Attention to exact positioning with proper weight distribution through shoulders
- Moderate Holds: 2-5 minutes with seasonal cooling emphasis and temperature awareness
- Technical Excellence: Focus on proper form and safety over duration achievements
- Temperature Integration: Use as cooling practice during hot weather or high-stress periods
- Balanced Development: Systematic progression with attention to preventing overheating
- Benefits: Improves precision, prevents inflammation, regulates temperature, enhances circulation

Safety Protocols and Contraindications

- Absolute Contraindications: Neck injury, high blood pressure, glaucoma, retinal detachment, pregnancy, menstruation
- Prerequisites: Minimum 6 months foundation practice with demonstrated neck and shoulder strength
- Qualified Instruction: Initial learning requires experienced teacher for safety and proper alignment
- Warning Signs: Neck pain, facial pressure, difficulty breathing requires immediate exit
- Time Limits: Never exceed individual capacity, build time very gradually over months

Therapeutic Applications

- Circulatory Disorders: Improved venous return and lymphatic drainage for swelling and circulation
- Thyroid Imbalances: Gentle stimulation for metabolic regulation
- Nervous System Regulation: Calming effect for anxiety, insomnia, and overstimulation
- Immune System Enhancement: Lymphatic circulation support for immune function

Exercise 13: Fish - Heart Opening and Throat Activation

Universal Principle

Provide deep chest opening and throat chakra activation through gentle backbend that serves as essential counter-stretch to shoulder stand while enhancing breathing capacity.

Basic Position

From supine position with legs extended, place hands under buttocks and rest on forearms. Lift chest toward ceiling while allowing head to fall back, creating gentle arch through upper spine. Hold for 30 seconds to 3 minutes.

Purpose and Benefits

- Counter-stretch: Essential balance to shoulder stand and forward folding practices
- Throat Activation: Stimulates throat chakra supporting authentic communication
- Respiratory Enhancement: Improves breathing capacity through chest expansion and rib mobility
- Metabolic Support: Stimulates thyroid and parathyroid glands for metabolic balance

Constitutional Adaptations

Electric Constitution Adaptations

- Support Options: Bolster or pillow under back for gentler heart opening
- Head Support: Keep head supported rather than fully releasing to floor
- Shorter Holds: 30 seconds to 1 minute for nervous system comfort
- Gentle Progression: Very gradual increase in back bending over extended time period
- Deep Breathing: Slow, calming breath emphasizing chest expansion
- Benefits: Builds confidence, improves breathing, grounds energy, supports emotional opening

Magnetic Constitution Adaptations

- Active Variations: Press actively into forearms for deeper chest opening
- Dynamic Practice: Move in and out of position multiple times for activation
- Longer Holds: 1-5 minutes for circulation and metabolic stimulation
- Challenge Options: Advanced arm positions or leg variations for increased difficulty
- Active Breathing: Strong breathing patterns for metabolic stimulation
- Benefits: Improves circulation, builds strength, prevents stagnation, enhances energy

Neutral Constitution Adaptations

- Balanced Approach: Moderate heart opening with attention to

neck comfort
- Cooling Emphasis: Extra attention to preventing overheating during back bending
- Precise Alignment: Focus on even spinal extension and proper weight distribution
- Temperature Regulation: Use as cooling practice with appropriate breathing patterns
- Moderate Holds: 1-3 minutes with seasonal temperature adaptation
- Benefits: Improves precision, prevents inflammation, enhances balance, regulates temperature

Integration with Shoulder Stand Sequence

Traditional Sequence
- Shoulder Stand - main inversion practice
- Fish Pose - counter-stretch and integration
- Neutral spine position - complete integration

Timing Ratios
- Fish hold should be approximately half the duration of shoulder stand
- Example: 4-minute shoulder stand followed by 2-minute fish pose
- Always end sequence with brief neutral position for integration

Therapeutic Applications
- Respiratory Conditions: Deep chest opening for asthma and breathing restrictions
- Thyroid Disorders: Gentle stimulation for hypo- or hyperthyroid conditions
- Depression and Grief: Heart opening for emotional release and healing
- Communication Blocks: Throat activation supporting authentic expression

Exercise 14: Sitting Twist - Advanced Spinal Rotation

Universal Principle
Enhance spinal rotation and mobility throughout entire vertebral column while supporting detoxification and digestive function through systematic twisting with strength and flexibility integration.

Basic Position
From seated position with legs extended, bend right knee and place right foot outside left thigh. Place left elbow against right knee while

rotating spine to the right and placing right hand behind back for support. Hold for 30-60 seconds each direction.

Purpose and Benefits
- Complete Rotation: Spinal mobility throughout entire vertebral column
- Detoxification Support: Digestive function enhancement through abdominal massage
- Balance Integration: Strength and flexibility development in rotational movement
- Energy Circulation: Activation of energy flow through central spinal channel

Constitutional Adaptations
Electric Constitution Adaptations
- Support Options: Sit on blanket or bolster for hip elevation and comfort
- Conservative Range: Emphasis on spinal length rather than rotational depth
- Longer Holds: 45-75 seconds for stability and grounding benefit
- Gentle Progression: Very gradual increase in rotational range over extended periods
- Deep Breathing: Ribcage expansion emphasis during rotation for circulation
- Benefits: Improves digestion, calms nervous system, releases tension, supports stability

Magnetic Constitution Adaptations
- Dynamic Variations: Flow in and out of twist with active engagement and movement
- Deeper Range: Active pressing and strength engagement for increased rotation
- Multiple Transitions: Shorter holds with dynamic movement between sides
- Challenge Options: Advanced arm positions or binding variations for difficulty
- Active Breathing: Circulation and metabolic activation through breath work
- Benefits: Enhances circulation, prevents stagnation, builds strength, activates energy

Neutral Constitution Adaptations
- Precise Technique: Attention to even spinal rotation and balanced muscle engagement
- Moderate Range: Cooling emphasis during warm seasons with

160

temperature awareness
- Technical Excellence: Focus on quality rotation and proper spinal alignment
- Temperature Regulation: Even breathing with seasonal cooling adaptations
- Balanced Holds: 30-50 seconds with attention to comfort and precision
- Benefits: Improves precision, prevents inflammation, regulates temperature, enhances balance

Advanced Variations

Binding Twist
- Wrap arms around bent knee for deeper rotation
- Requires adequate shoulder mobility and spinal flexibility
- Hold for 20-40 seconds with attention to breathing

Revolved Triangle Twist
- From twisted position, straighten bent leg for combined forward fold and twist
- Advanced variation requiring significant flexibility
- Practice only after mastering basic sitting twist

Therapeutic Applications
- Digestive Disorders: Abdominal massage and stimulation for digestive health
- Back Stiffness: Rotational mobility for chronic back tension and restriction
- Stress and Tension: Spinal release combined with detoxification emphasis
- Postural Imbalances: Correction of rotational restrictions and asymmetries

Exercise 15: Lotus Preparation - Hip Opening and Meditation Foundation

Universal Principle
Develop comprehensive hip opening and patience with individual limitations while creating foundation for comfortable meditation sitting and emotional release through hip region opening.

Basic Position
From seated position, bend both knees and bring feet together in front of pelvis. Hold feet with hands while gently drawing heels to-

ward body, creating diamond shape with legs. Maintain erect spine while breathing naturally.

Purpose and Benefits
- Hip Opening: Comprehensive opening of hip joints and surrounding muscles
- Emotional Release: Release of holding patterns stored in hip region from stress and trauma
- Meditation Preparation: Foundation for comfortable seated meditation postures
- Patience Development: Acceptance of individual flexibility limitations and progress rate

Constitutional Adaptations
Electric Constitution Adaptations
- Support Options: Sit on blanket, bolster, or meditation cushion for hip elevation
- Gentle Range: Emphasis on comfort over flexibility achievement
- Extended Holds: 2-5 minutes for gradual muscle lengthening and nervous system calm
- Patient Progression: Very gradual advancement over months or years without force
- Calming Breathing: Deep, relaxing breath for nervous system regulation
- Benefits: Calms anxiety, supports emotional healing, grounds scattered energy

Magnetic Constitution Adaptations
- Active Engagement: Use arm strength to gently increase hip opening range
- Dynamic Practice: Movement in and out of position for circulation activation
- Multiple Holds: Several shorter sessions with active breathing and engagement
- Challenge Integration: Advanced positions working toward lotus preparation
- Heat Generation: Use as preparation for heating meditation practices
- Benefits: Improves circulation, prevents stagnation, builds flexibility, activates energy

Neutral Constitution Adaptations
- Precise Technique: Attention to balanced hip opening and spinal alignment
- Moderate Approach: Balanced flexibility work without forcing

or straining
- Temperature Awareness: Extra attention to preventing overheating during longer holds
- Meditation Integration: Use as foundation for balanced meditation practice
- Systematic Development: Methodical progression with seasonal adaptations
- Benefits: Improves precision, prevents inflammation, supports meditation, regulates temperature

Meditation Integration Sequence

1. **Hip Opening Practice**: 3-5 minutes
2. **Spinal Alignment and Settling**: 2 minutes
3. **Breathing Regulation**: 3 minutes
4. **Meditation Practice**: 10-30 minutes

Progressive Sitting Positions
- Supported Cross-legged: Beginners with props under knees
- Half-lotus Position: Intermediate development
- Full Lotus Position: Advanced, if anatomically possible
- Chair or Bench Alternatives: Individual adaptation as needed

Therapeutic Applications
- Hip Tightness: Systematic opening for sedentary lifestyle and athletic restrictions
- Emotional Release: Hip opening for stored emotional tension and trauma processing
- Reproductive Health: Improved circulation for reproductive organ function
- Meditation Preparation: Foundation for comfortable seated spiritual practice

Advanced Exercises (16-23): Mastery and Spiritual Integration
The advanced exercises require complete integration of all previous development while introducing complex coordination, advanced strength requirements, and spiritual applications that serve consciousness development and community leadership.

Exercise 16: Headstand - King of Inversions

Universal Principle
Master the most challenging inversion while developing extraordinary upper body strength, mental clarity, and spiritual awareness

through systematic progression that serves both individual development and teaching capacity.

Basic Position
From hands-and-knees position, place forearms on floor with elbows shoulder-width apart, interlace fingers and cup back of head. Tuck toes under and lift hips, then carefully lift one leg at a time until vertical. Hold for 30 seconds to 5 minutes based on development level.

Purpose and Benefits
- Complete Inversion: Reverses gravity effects on all body systems for maximum therapeutic benefit
- Strength Development: Extraordinary upper body and core strength through challenging positioning
- Mental Enhancement: Enhanced concentration, mental clarity, and cognitive function
- Spiritual Development: Traditional inversion for consciousness expansion and spiritual growth

Safety Protocols and Contraindications
- Absolute Contraindications: Neck injury, high blood pressure, heart conditions, pregnancy, menstruation
- Prerequisite Development: Minimum 6 months consistent practice with demonstrated shoulder strength
- Supervised Learning: Requires qualified instruction for safe progression and proper technique
- Wall Support: Recommended for all beginners and most constitutional types during learning
- Time Limits: Gradual progression from 30 seconds to maximum 5 minutes over months

Constitutional Adaptations
Electric Constitution Adaptations
- Extended Preparation: Wall support and strength building over many months
- Shorter Holds: 30 seconds to 2 minutes building very gradually over time
- Extensive Support: Props and assistance during learning phase for security
- Gentle Progression: Patient advancement respecting nervous system sensitivity
- Warm Environment: Extra attention to maintaining comfortable temperature
- Benefits: Builds confidence gradually, improves circulation,

164

calms anxiety when mastered

Magnetic Constitution Adaptations
- Dynamic Practice: Active entry with strength emphasis and challenge orientation
- Longer Holds: 1-5 minutes for maximum circulatory and strength benefits
- Challenge Variations: Advanced arm positions and transitions for increased difficulty
- Goal-Oriented: Systematic progression with measurable improvement targets
- Cool Environment: Temperature regulation for challenging strength work
- Benefits: Builds extraordinary strength, improves circulation, prevents stagnation

Neutral Constitution Adaptations
- Technical Precision: Emphasis on exact alignment and efficient energy distribution
- Moderate Holds: 1-3 minutes with attention to preventing overheating
- Systematic Approach: Methodical progression with seasonal temperature considerations
- Quality Focus: Perfect technique over duration or advanced variations
- Temperature Regulation: Cooling modifications during warm seasons
- Benefits: Improves precision, enhances mental clarity, regulates temperature

Progressive Development Stages

Preparation Stage (Months 1-12)
- Wall-supported practice building upper body and core strength
- Chest-to-wall headstand for proper alignment development
- Brief holds building from 10 seconds to 2 minutes

Intermediate Stage (Year 2)
- Independent headstand away from wall
- Holds extending to 3-5 minutes based on constitutional capacity
- Beginning advanced variations appropriate to individual development

Advanced Stage (Years 2-3)
- Complete mastery with advanced variations and transitions

- Teaching capacity with understanding of safe progression methods
- Integration with advanced spiritual and meditation practices

Therapeutic Applications
- Circulatory Enhancement: Maximum reversal of gravity effects for circulation
- Mental Clarity: Enhanced cognitive function and concentration capacity
- Confidence Building: Mastery of challenging position supporting psychological development
- Spiritual Development: Traditional practice for consciousness expansion

Exercise 17: Peacock - Advanced Arm Balance

Universal Principle
Develop extraordinary upper body and core strength through challenging arm balance while building confidence, coordination, and digestive fire through complex positioning requiring strength and balance integration.

Basic Position
From kneeling position, place palms on floor with fingers pointing toward feet and wrists close together. Rest elbows against lower ribs while slowly shifting weight forward and lifting legs off ground, balancing on hands with body parallel to floor.

Purpose and Benefits
- Strength Development: Significant upper body, core, and wrist strength through challenging balance
- Digestive Stimulation: Abdominal pressure stimulates digestive fire and organ function
- Confidence Building: Mastery of difficult position supporting psychological development
- Coordination Enhancement: Complex balance requiring proprioceptive awareness and control

Safety Protocols and Contraindications
- Absolute Contraindications: Wrist injury, shoulder injury, pregnancy, high blood pressure
- Prerequisites: Minimum 12-18 months foundation practice with demonstrated upper body strength
- Qualified Supervision: Initial learning requires experienced instruction for safety protocols

- Wrist Preparation: Extensive strengthening and flexibility work before attempting
- Progression Protocol: Very gradual advancement with attention to individual capacity

Constitutional Adaptations

Electric Constitution Adaptations
- Extended Preparation: Months of wrist and shoulder strengthening before attempting
- Support Options: Practice with feet on blocks or bolster to reduce difficulty
- Brief Holds: 3-10 seconds building gradually over months of practice
- Strength Focus: Emphasis on preparatory exercises and slow strength development
- Nervous System Care: Avoid overstimulation through excessive practice or forcing
- Benefits: Builds confidence gradually, develops functional strength, grounds scattered energy

Magnetic Constitution Adaptations
- Dynamic Practice: Multiple attempts with active strength engagement and persistence
- Challenge Progression: Work toward longer holds and advanced variations
- Extended Holds: 10-45 seconds for strength and endurance development
- Competitive Elements: Safe goal setting and achievement tracking for motivation
- Power Development: Functional strength building for coordination and power
- Benefits: Builds extraordinary strength, improves coordination, prevents stagnation

Neutral Constitution Adaptations
- Technical Precision: Emphasis on exact technique and balanced muscle engagement
- Moderate Progression: Steady advancement without excessive strain or forcing
- Cooling Awareness: Attention to preventing overheating during intense strength work
- Efficiency Focus: Emphasis on technique refinement over maximum achievement
- Quality Development: Perfect form development over duration or advanced variations

- Benefits: Improves precision, builds balanced strength, prevents inflammation

Preparatory Exercise Requirements

Wrist Strengthening Series
- Plank holds building to 2 minutes for wrist and shoulder strength
- Downward dog with emphasis on wrist and forearm engagement
- Tabletop position weight shifts for wrist conditioning and stability

Core and Shoulder Integration
- Hollow body holds for abdominal strength development
- Chaturanga push-up variations for shoulder strength and stability
- Crow pose mastery as prerequisite arm balance foundation

Progressive Development Timeline

Preparation Stage (Months 1-18)
- Master all preparatory exercises with confidence and strength
- Develop significant wrist, shoulder, and core strength systematically
- Practice with qualified teacher and supportive community environment

Beginning Stage (Months 18-30)
- Brief holds 3-10 seconds with support modifications available
- Focus on technique refinement over duration or achievement
- Continue preparatory strength work alongside peacock attempts

Advanced Stage (Months 30+)
- Independent holds 10-45 seconds based on constitutional capacity
- Advanced variations and transitions to other arm balances
- Teaching capacity with thorough understanding of preparation requirements

Exercise 18: Scorpion - Complex Backbend and Inversion Combination

Universal Principle

Integrate advanced inversion with extreme back bending through extraordinarily challenging position that requires mastery of both skill sets while developing supreme confidence and spiritual integration.

Basic Position
From forearm stand position, slowly bend knees and lower feet toward head, creating deep backbend while maintaining inversion. Balance on forearms while creating scorpion-like curve through spine with feet approaching or touching head.

Purpose and Benefits
- Ultimate Integration: Combines advanced inversion with extreme back bending for complete challenge
- Extraordinary Development: Requires mastery of both inversions and backbends before attempting
- Supreme Confidence: Builds ultimate physical confidence through complex positioning mastery
- Spiritual Applications: Advanced energy circulation and consciousness development practices

Safety Protocols and Contraindications
- Absolute Contraindications: Any neck, back, or shoulder injury; high blood pressure; pregnancy
- Prerequisites: Mastery of forearm stand (5+ minute holds) AND wheel pose (2+ minute holds)
- Minimum Preparation: 3-5 years consistent advanced practice with qualified instruction
- Qualified Supervision: Never attempt without experienced teacher present and emergency protocols
- Emergency Protocol: Clear exit strategy and first aid knowledge required before attempting

Prerequisites for Safe Practice

Inversion Mastery
- Forearm stand hold for minimum 5 minutes with complete stability
- Comfortable in all basic inversions with proper alignment and breathing
- No history of neck or shoulder problems or restrictions

Backbend Mastery
- Wheel pose hold for minimum 2 minutes with ease and breathing comfort

- Comfortable in all basic and intermediate backbends with proper progression
- King pigeon or similar deep back bending poses mastered with safety

Constitutional Adaptations
Electric Constitution Adaptations
- Extended Prerequisites: Years of patient preparation in both skill areas separately
- Wall Support: Practice against wall with extensive padding and multiple support options
- Minimal Holds: 3-10 seconds maximum with extreme attention to safety protocols
- Required Supervision: Qualified teacher and spotter absolutely required for attempts
- Alternative Focus: Emphasis on preparatory poses rather than full expression achievement
- Benefits: Ultimate confidence building for highly experienced Electric practitioners only

Magnetic Constitution Adaptations
- Dynamic Approach: Active engagement with strength emphasis throughout complex positioning
- Progressive Challenge: Systematic work toward full expression over years of preparation
- Extended Holds: 10-45 seconds for experienced practitioners with complete mastery
- Multiple Attempts: Practice sessions with several careful attempts and skill refinement
- Strength Integration: Use position for developing extraordinary physical capacity and coordination
- Benefits: Develops supreme strength and integration for advanced Magnetic practitioners

Neutral Constitution Adaptations
- Technical Mastery: Years of preparation focusing on precise technique in all components
- Balanced Development: Equal emphasis on flexibility and strength development over time
- Temperature Regulation: Extreme attention to preventing overheating during challenging practice
- Quality Emphasis: Perfect technique in preparatory poses rather than forcing advancement
- Systematic Approach: Methodical development of all prerequisite skills with precision

- Benefits: Technical mastery and balanced development for qualified Neutral practitioners

Progressive Development Timeline

Years 1-2: Foundation Building
- Master basic inversions and backbends separately with complete confidence
- Develop extraordinary strength and flexibility through systematic practice
- Study with qualified teachers and established, supportive community

Years 3-4: Integration Preparation
- Begin combining inversion and back bending elements in simpler variations
- Practice forearm stand chest opening variations with qualified guidance
- Develop comfort with complex, challenging positions requiring multiple skills

Years 5+: Advanced Integration
- Careful attempts with qualified supervision and comprehensive safety protocols
- Brief holds with extreme attention to safety, technique, and individual capacity
- Teaching preparation for qualified instructors with years of personal mastery

Exercise 19: Wheel - Advanced Backbend with Progressive Development

Universal Principle
Achieve complete spinal extension and front body opening through challenging backbend that develops significant strength while creating profound heart opening and emotional release potential.

Basic Position
From supine position, place palms beside head with fingers pointing toward shoulders and feet hip-width apart near buttocks. Press into hands and feet while lifting entire body into arch, creating wheel-like curve through spine.

Purpose and Benefits
- Complete Extension: Maximum spinal extension and compre-

hensive front body opening
- Strength Integration: Significant development in arms, legs, and back muscles simultaneously
- Heart Opening: Profound emotional and energetic release through maximum chest expansion
- Courage Development: Builds determination and confidence through challenging back bending mastery

Safety Protocols and Contraindications
- Absolute Contraindications: Wrist injury, shoulder injury, lower back problems, neck injury, pregnancy
- Prerequisites: Comfortable bridge pose holds for 1+ minutes with proper breathing
- Preparation Requirements: Minimum 6-12 months back bending practice with qualified instruction
- Warning Signs: Sharp pain, breath restriction, dizziness requires immediate exit from position
- Individual Assessment: Not appropriate for all body types or physical conditions

Constitutional Adaptations
Electric Constitution Adaptations
- Bridge Progression: Master bridge pose thoroughly before attempting wheel transition
- Support Options: Blocks under hands for wrist comfort, practice on soft surfaces
- Shorter Holds: 10-30 seconds building very gradually over extended time periods
- Extended Preparation: Comprehensive warm-up with gentle backbends and hip flexor stretching
- Gradual Development: Patient progression over months with emphasis on safety over achievement
- Benefits: Builds confidence gradually, opens heart gently, supports emotional healing

Magnetic Constitution Adaptations
- Dynamic Practice: Multiple wheel attempts with active strength engagement and persistence
- Challenge Variations: Single-arm wheels, single-leg wheels, wheel walk-ups, drop- back transitions
- Extended Holds: 30 seconds to 3 minutes for strength development and circulation
- Flow Integration: Incorporate wheel into flowing sequences and dynamic transitions
- Strength Focus: Use wheel for building functional back bending

172

strength and power
- Benefits: Builds extraordinary strength, prevents depression, enhances circulation

Neutral Constitution Adaptations
- Technical Precision: Attention to even spinal extension and balanced strength development
- Moderate Progression: Steady advancement without forcing or straining individual capacity
- Temperature Regulation: Extra attention to preventing overheating during intense back bending practice
- Form Emphasis: Focus on optimal technique over maximum achievement or duration
- Cooling Integration: Use cooling breath techniques and temperature-appropriate environment
- Benefits: Improves precision, prevents inflammation, builds balanced strength

Progressive Development Stages

Preparation Stage (Months 1-12)
- Master bridge pose with 1+ minute comfortable holds and proper breathing
- Develop wrist and shoulder flexibility through dedicated daily practice
- Build comprehensive strength through preparatory back bending exercise progression

Beginning Wheel Stage (Months 12-24)
- Brief wheel holds 10-30 seconds with support options available
- Focus on safe entry and exit techniques rather than duration goals
- Continue preparatory strength work alongside wheel attempts with qualified guidance

Advanced Development (Months 24+)
- Comfortable wheel holds 30 seconds to 1+ minutes based on constitutional capacity
- Begin exploring appropriate variations and advanced back bending transitions
- Integration with breathing practices, energy circulation, and spiritual development

Wheel Walk-ups

- From wheel position, walk feet closer to hands for increased spinal extension
- Requires exceptional flexibility, strength, and years of preparation
- Practice only with qualified supervision and comprehensive safety protocols

Single-Limb Wheels

- Lifting one arm or leg while maintaining wheel position for increased challenge
- Develops extraordinary strength and balance through complex coordination
- Advanced variation requiring complete mastery of basic wheel pose

Exercise 20: Leg Behind Head - Extreme Flexibility with Extensive Safety Protocols

Universal Principle

Develop extraordinary hip flexibility through extreme positioning that requires extensive preparation and complete acceptance of individual anatomical limitations and structural possibilities.

Basic Position

From seated position, lift right leg and carefully guide right foot behind head, resting leg across neck and shoulders. Maintain erect spine while breathing naturally and focusing on extreme hip flexibility and patient acceptance of individual limitations.

Purpose and Benefits

- Extraordinary Flexibility: Develops maximum possible hip flexibility and range of motion
- Patience Development: Requires and develops acceptance of individual anatomical limitations
- Humility Cultivation: Supports understanding of personal boundaries and structural realities
- Advanced Achievement: Represents ultimate flexibility for those anatomically capable

Critical Safety Protocols and Individual Assessment

- Anatomical Reality: Many people cannot safely achieve this position regardless of practice duration

- Individual Assessment: Professional evaluation of hip structure and suitability required
- Honest Evaluation: Understanding that inability indicates nothing about practitioner quality or dedication
- Alternative Excellence: Focus on poses appropriate to individual anatomical structure

Constitutional Adaptations

Electric Constitution Adaptations
- Years of Preparation: Extensive hip opening work with extremely patient progression
- Support Options: Use hands to support leg weight, practice with wall support
- Brief Holds: 10-30 seconds maximum if position is anatomically accessible
- Alternative Focus: Emphasis on preparatory hip opening over extreme position achievement
- Safety Priority: Complete acceptance of individual limitations without forcing or disappointment
- Benefits: Hip flexibility development appropriate to individual anatomy and nervous system

Magnetic Constitution Adaptations
- Progressive Challenge: Systematic work toward full expression over years if anatomically possible
- Active Assistance: Use arm strength to assist leg positioning when appropriate and safe
- Extended Holds: 30 seconds to 2 minutes for qualified practitioners with suitable anatomy
- Goal Assessment: Realistic evaluation of anatomical possibility versus determination goals
- Alternative Achievement: Excellence in positions appropriate to individual structure
- Benefits: Maximum development within individual anatomical constraints and safety

Neutral Constitution Adaptations
- Technical Assessment: Professional anatomical evaluation for individual suitability and safety
- Individual Adaptation: Honest recognition of anatomical limitations without forcing
- Alternative Excellence: Mastery of poses appropriate to individual anatomical structure
- Precision Focus: Perfect technique in preparatory poses rather than forcing advancement

- Balanced Development: Comprehensive flexibility development within individual anatomical reality
- Benefits: Optimal development appropriate to individual structure and constitutional balance

Prerequisites and Preparation Requirements

Hip Opening Mastery
- Lotus pose comfortable for 10+ minutes if anatomically possible for individual structure
- Advanced seated forward folds with straight legs and complete comfort
- All basic and intermediate hip opening poses mastered with proper progression

Realistic Timeline
- Years 1-2: Comprehensive hip opening development with qualified instruction and assessment
- Years 3-4: Intermediate development if anatomically appropriate for individual structure
- Years 5+: Advanced exploration only if anatomy permits and preparation is complete

Alternative Pathways for Excellence
- Individual Appropriate Development: Focus on hip opening suitable for personal anatomy
- Teaching Preparation: Excellence in instruction of preparatory poses and assessment skills
- Service Applications: Use hip opening knowledge for helping others within their limitations
- Cultural Contribution: Understanding both possibilities and limitations for realistic instruction

Exercise 21: Crow - Foundational Arm Balance for Advanced Development

Universal Principle
Develop essential arm balancing skills through accessible yet challenging position that builds upper body strength, confidence, and coordination while providing foundation for all advanced arm balance development.

Basic Position
From squatting position with hands on floor shoulder-width apart, rest shins against upper arms while shifting weight forward onto

hands. Lift toes off ground while balancing on hands with knees supported by arms.

Purpose and Benefits
- Foundation Development: Essential skills for all advanced arm balancing positions
- Strength Building: Upper body and core strength through challenging but achievable balance
- Confidence Enhancement: Builds determination and self-assurance through arm balance mastery
- Coordination Development: Improves proprioceptive awareness and balance integration skills

Constitutional Adaptations
Electric Constitution Adaptations
- Block Support: Place block under forehead for confidence and security while learning
- Progressive Lifting: Begin by lifting one toe at a time before attempting full crow
- Brief Holds: 3-15 seconds building gradually over months of patient practice
- Strength Building: Focus on preparatory exercises for systematic strength development over time
- Gentle Progression: Patient advancement without forcing or creating nervous system stress
- Benefits: Builds confidence gradually, develops functional strength, grounds scattered energy

Magnetic Constitution Adaptations
- Dynamic Practice: Multiple attempts with active engagement and persistence through challenges
- Challenge Progression: Work toward advanced variations and extended holds for achievement
- Extended Holds: 15-90 seconds for strength and endurance development goals
- Goal Achievement: Safe progression tracking with realistic but challenging improvement targets
- Power Focus: Use crow for building functional strength, coordination, and achievement capacity
- Benefits: Builds extraordinary strength, improves coordination, prevents stagnation through challenge

Neutral Constitution Adaptations
- Technical Precision: Emphasis on exact hand placement and balanced weight distribution

- Moderate Progression: Steady advancement with attention to proper form and technique excellence
- Cooling Awareness: Attention to preventing overheating during challenging strength work
- Efficiency Focus: Optimal energy use and proper alignment throughout position maintenance
- Quality Development: Perfect technique development over duration or advanced variation achievement
- Benefits: Improves precision, builds balanced strength, prevents inflammation through proper form

Progressive Development Stages

Preparation Stage (Months 1-6)
- Master all preparatory exercises including wrist strengthening and core development
- Build adequate wrist, shoulder, and core strength through systematic daily practice
- Practice squatting positions for hip flexibility and leg strength development

Beginning Crow Stage (Months 6-12)
- Brief holds 3-15 seconds with support modifications available for confidence
- Focus on balance and technique rather than duration goals or achievements
- Continue preparatory strength work alongside crow practice with proper progression

Advanced Practice (Months 12+)
- Comfortable holds 15-60+ seconds based on constitutional capacity and individual development
- Begin exploring crow variations and transitions appropriate to constitutional type
- Teaching capacity with understanding of systematic preparation requirements and safety

Advanced Variations (for experienced practitioners)

Side Crow
- Lateral arm balance with legs positioned to one side for increased challenge
- Requires additional core strength and balance beyond basic crow requirements
- Practice both sides for balanced development and comprehen-

sive strength

Crow to Chaturanga
- Dynamic transition from crow position to low push-up position
- Advanced coordination requiring significant strength and precise timing
- Practice only after complete mastery of both positions independently

Exercise 22: Firefly - Complex Arm Balance Requiring Full- Body Integration

Universal Principle
Integrate extraordinary arm balancing strength with significant hip and hamstring flexibility through extremely challenging position that represents ultimate coordination and body integration mastery.

Basic Position
From wide-legged forward fold, thread arms between legs and place hands on floor behind legs. Slowly shift weight onto hands while lifting legs off ground and straightening them to sides, creating firefly-like position with legs extended and body balanced on arms.

Purpose and Benefits
- Ultimate Integration: Combines arm balancing strength with significant hip and hamstring flexibility
- Extraordinary Coordination: Requires integration of multiple physical capacities simultaneously
- Supreme Confidence: Builds ultimate physical confidence through mastery of complex positioning
- Teaching Preparation: Demonstrational capacity for master-level instruction and guidance

Safety Protocols and Prerequisites
- Prerequisites: Mastery of crow pose AND comfortable wide-legged forward fold with arms threading between legs
- Minimum Preparation: 2-3 years consistent advanced practice with qualified instruction and community support
- Individual Assessment: Not appropriate for all body types, proportions, or anatomical structures
- Qualified Supervision: Never attempt without experienced teacher guidance and safety protocols
- Realistic Expectations: Understand that this position requires exceptional natural ability plus extensive preparation

Constitutional Adaptations

Electric Constitution Adaptations

- Extended Prerequisites: Years of patient preparation in both arm balancing and hip opening skills
- Support Options: Practice with blocks under head, bent knee variations for gradual
- Brief Holds: 3-10 seconds maximum with extensive preparation and nervous system consideration
- Alternative Focus: Emphasis on preparatory exercises rather than full expression achievement
- Safety Priority: Complete acceptance of individual limitations without forcing or nervous system stress
- Benefits: Ultimate confidence building for highly experienced Electric practitioners within individual capacity

Magnetic Constitution Adaptations

- Dynamic Approach: Active engagement with multiple attempts and persistence through challenge
- Progressive Challenge: Systematic work toward full expression with appropriate variations and goals
- Extended Holds: 10-60 seconds for advanced practitioners with complete prerequisite mastery
- Achievement Focus: Goal-oriented practice with safe progression tracking and measurable improvement
- Strength Integration: Use position for developing extraordinary coordination and functional power
- Benefits: Develops supreme strength and integration for advanced Magnetic practitioners

Neutral Constitution Adaptations

- Technical Mastery: Years of preparation focusing on precise technique in all component skills
- Individual Assessment: Honest evaluation of anatomical suitability and realistic possibility for achievement
- Temperature Regulation: Extreme attention to preventing overheating during challenging coordination work
- Quality Emphasis: Perfect technique in preparatory poses rather than forcing advancement toward goal
- Systematic Development: Methodical development of all prerequisite skills with precision and patience
- Benefits: Technical mastery and balanced development for qualified Neutral practitioners within capacity

Years 1-2: Foundation Building

- Master crow pose with 30+ second holds demonstrating complete arm balance competency
- Develop significant hip and hamstring flexibility through systematic daily practice
- Build comprehensive strength and coordination base through advanced preparatory exercise

Years 2-3: Component Integration

- Practice firefly preparation positions with arms threading between legs in forward fold
- Develop comfort and competency with arms between legs positioning and weight distribution
- Strengthen all component skills to advanced level with qualified instruction and assessment

Years 3+: Advanced Integration

- Careful attempts with qualified supervision, comprehensive support, and safety protocols
- Brief holds with extreme attention to safety, technique, and individual capacity limitations
- Teaching preparation for highly qualified instructors with years of personal mastery and experience

Exercise 23: Final Integration - Complete Sequence Synthesis with Energy Cultivation

Universal Principle

Integrate all 23 exercises into unified consciousness practice that demonstrates complete mastery while connecting individual development with community service and beneficial influence for collective advancement.

Complete Practice Structure

Practice complete integration of all exercises in flowing sequence, coordinated with constitutional breathing patterns and energy circulation awareness. Adapt duration, intensity, and transitions according to constitutional type while maintaining present-moment awareness and service orientation.

Constitutional Practice Integration

Electric Constitution Complete Integration (60-75 minutes)

- Extended Practice Approach: Longer holds in each position for

stability and grounding
- Extended Rest Periods: Adequate integration time between challenging exercises for nervous system restoration
- Foundation Emphasis: Exercises 1-7 with extended holds, selective intermediate and advanced positions
- Environmental Support: Warm temperature and constitutional comfort throughout entire practice
- Extended Integration: Final relaxation and energy circulation period for complete nervous system integration

Daily Sequence Structure
1. **Foundation Integration** (20 minutes): Exercises 1-7 with extended constitutional holds
2. **Selective Intermediate Practice** (25 minutes): Exercises 8-15 adapted for individual constitution
3. **Conservative Advanced Work** (15 minutes): Appropriate selections from 16-23 within capacity
4. **Extended Integration** (15 minutes): Breathing, relaxation, and energy circulation for completion

Magnetic Constitution Complete Integration (45-60 minutes)
- Intensive Practice Approach: Shorter holds with dynamic transitions and continuous movement
- Challenge Emphasis: Advanced exercises emphasized with challenging variations and goals
- Minimal Rest: Active recovery between exercises maintaining circulation and engagement
- Cool Environment: Temperature regulation with heating practices for metabolic activation
- Active Completion: Goal-setting, achievement recognition, and energetic completion protocols

Daily Sequence Structure
1. **Dynamic Foundation** (15 minutes): Exercises 1-7 with vigorous constitutional approach
2. **Intensive Intermediate Practice** (20 minutes): Exercises 8-15 with challenging variations
3. **Advanced Challenge Work** (20 minutes): Maximum appropriate difficulty from exercises 16-23
4. **Active Integration** (10 minutes): Goal review, planning, and energetic completion

Neutral Constitution Complete Integration (50-65 minutes)
- Balanced Practice Approach: Moderate holds with precise technique and seasonal adaptation

- Comprehensive Attention: Balanced emphasis on all exercise categories without extremes
- Temperature Awareness: Cooling practices during warm seasons, moderate warming during cool
- Systematic Completion: Methodical progression with technical review and balanced integration

Daily Sequence Structure
1. **Precise Foundation** (18 minutes): Exercises 1-7 with technical excellence
2. **Balanced Intermediate Practice** (22 minutes): Exercises 8-15 with seasonal adaptation
3. **Moderate Advanced Work** (18 minutes): Appropriate selections from 16-23 within capacity
4. **Balanced Integration** (12 minutes): Temperature-appropriate completion and systematic review

The 30-Minute Daily Practice Sequence

Foundation Level (Months 1-6)
- 5 minutes: Breathing preparation and centering
- 20 minutes: Exercises 1-7 with constitutional adaptations
- 5 minutes: Relaxation and integration

Intermediate Level (Months 6-24)
- 5 minutes: Advanced breathing and energy preparation
- 22 minutes: Complete foundation plus exercises 8-12 with constitutional modifications
- 3 minutes: Meditation and intention setting for service

Advanced Level (Year 2+)
- 3 minutes: Energy preparation and community intention
- 25 minutes: Full sequence with advanced variations appropriate to constitution
- 2 minutes: Community intention and service dedication

Seasonal Adaptation Guidelines
Spring Practice (March-May)
- Gradual increase in intensity and duration supporting natural seasonal energy
- Emphasis on detoxification and renewal through appropriate constitutional practices
- Constitutional adaptations for seasonal energy changes and increased activity

Summer Practice (June-August)
- Cooling modifications for all constitutional types with temperature regulation emphasis
- Earlier morning practice to avoid heat with adequate hydration awareness
- Constitutional cooling adaptations with special attention to Neutral types

Autumn Practice (September-November)
- Grounding emphasis preparing for winter with constitutional stability focus
- Strength building and immune support through systematic practice progression
- Constitutional adaptations for seasonal transition and energy conservation

Winter Practice (December-February)
- Warming practices and comfortable temperature maintenance for all constitutions
- Indoor focus with attention to adequate lighting and environmental comfort
- Constitutional adaptations for seasonal challenges and reduced natural light

Therapeutic Applications: Movement as Medicine
Sacred Embodiment provides specific therapeutic protocols for common physical, emotional, and mental challenges through constitutional adaptation and systematic progression.
Physical Healing Applications
Anxiety and Nervous System Regulation

Electric Constitution Anxiety Protocol:
- Daily 20-minute grounding sequence with extended relaxation
- Nervous system calming through supported positions and warm environment
- Breathing practices emphasizing extended exhale and parasympathetic activation
- Community support and professional counseling integration

Depression and Energy Cultivation

Magnetic Constitution Depression Protocol:
- Daily 30-minute activation sequence with cardiovascular stimulation
- Challenging movement preventing stagnation while building strength and circulation
- Breathing practices emphasizing energizing patterns and meta-

bolic activation
- Community engagement and service project participation

Building Your Personal Practice
Sacred Embodiment flourishes through systematic daily practice that adapts to your constitutional needs while integrating with your family, professional, and community responsibilities.

The 30-Day Foundation Program

Week 1: Constitutional Adaptation (Days 1-7)
- Complete constitutional assessment and movement adaptation
- Practice foundation sequence (Movements 1-7) for 15-20 minutes daily
- Track energy, mood, pain levels, and sleep quality
- Connect with online community for support and guidance

Week 2: Strength Integration (Days 8-14)
- Add strength sequence (Movements 8-11) extending practice to 20-25 minutes
- Continue constitutional adaptations with attention to optimal challenge level
- Begin workplace integration with simple breathing and posture awareness
- Family integration through constitutional awareness and simple practices

Week 3: Advanced Integration (Days 15-21)
- Complete foundation and strength sequences with beginning advanced elements
- Practice duration 25-30 minutes with constitutional breathing integration
- Professional integration with stress management and effectiveness applications
- Community connection through local practice groups or online participation

Week 4: Mastery and Service (Days 22-30)
- Full practice sequence adapted to constitutional needs and life circumstances
- Practice duration 30-45 minutes including meditation and service intention
- Teaching family members and interested friends basic constitutional principles
- Service integration through professional effectiveness and com-

munity contribution

Electric Constitution Daily Integration:
- 4:30 AM: Gentle 20-minute practice in warm environment
- 12:00 PM: 5-minute grounding break with breathing practice
- 6:00 PM: Light movement and relaxation before dinner
- 9:00 PM: Calming routine preparing for sleep by 10:00 PM

Magnetic Constitution Daily Integration:
- 4:00 AM: Dynamic 25-minute practice with challenging elements
- 12:00 PM: Activating 10-minute break with energizing breathing
- 6:00 PM: Moderate movement maintaining energy before dinner
- 9:30 PM: Gradual wind-down routine with sleep by 10:30 PM

Neutral Constitution Daily Integration:
- 4:15 AM: Precise 22-minute practice with cooling emphasis
- 12:00 PM: Cooling 8-minute break with stress management techniques
- 6:00 PM: Balanced movement with temperature regulation attention
- 9:15 PM: Cooling routine with sleep by 10:15 PM

Creating Sacred Embodiment Community

Individual practice provides foundation for community engagement that supports mutual development while serving broader cultural transformation through practical demonstration of consciousness-based approaches.

Family Integration

Constitutional Family Practice:
- Assess each family member's constitutional type for appropriate adaptations
- Create family movement time with activities supporting everyone's needs
- Integrate constitutional awareness into meal planning, scheduling, and conflict resolution
- Support individual practice time while building family coherence

Case Study: The Johnson Family

Parents David (Magnetic) and Lisa (Electric) with teenage daughters Emma (Neutral) and Sophie (Electric) transformed family dynamics through constitutional awareness:
- Morning Practice: 15-minute family sequence with constitutional modifications for each member

- Conflict Resolution: Constitutional understanding prevented typical personality clashes
- Academic Support: Movement breaks adapted to each daughter's constitutional learning needs
- Results: Family satisfaction increased dramatically, academic performance improved, household stress decreased significantly

Professional Community Building
Workplace Sacred Embodiment Groups:
- Organize constitutional assessment workshops for interested colleagues
- Create lunchtime practice groups with constitutional diversity awareness
- Integrate movement breaks and stress management techniques into meeting culture
- Support organizational culture development through consciousness-based leadership

Local Community Development
Sacred Embodiment Practice Groups:
- Start with 3-4 committed practitioners meeting weekly for group practice
- Develop constitutional diversity awareness enabling everyone's needs to be met
- Connect individual development with community service projects
- Create democratic decision-making processes based on consciousness development principles

The Science of Sacred Embodiment
Emerging research validates traditional understanding of movement-consciousness integration while providing scientific frameworks for therapeutic and educational applications.

Neuroscience Research Validation

Neuroplasticity Studies: Sacred Embodiment practice increases gray matter density in brain regions associated with learning, memory, emotional regulation, and self-awareness within 8 weeks of regular practice.

Stress Response Optimization: Constitutional movement practices show superior results compared to generic approaches in regulating cortisol levels, inflammatory markers, and autonomic nervous system balance.

Interoceptive Awareness Development: Movement practices co-ordinated with breath and awareness significantly improve interoceptive accuracy, the ability to sense internal body signals, supporting better health decisions and emotional regulation.

Your Journey into Sacred Embodiment
Sacred Embodiment transforms your relationship with your body from mechanical maintenance to conscious partnership in spiritual development and service to others. Through constitutional adaptation, systematic progression, and community integration, movement becomes medicine serving both individual healing and collective advancement.

Your Constitutional Commitment
- **Week 1**: Complete constitutional assessment and begin foundation sequence adapted to your individual needs and life circumstances
- **Month 1**: Establish consistent daily practice while integrating workplace stress management and family constitutional awareness
- **Month 3**: Develop intermediate competency enabling basic guidance for family members and interested friends
- **Month 6**: Advanced practice mastery with preparation for community teaching and service applications
- **Year 1**: Full integration with professional effectiveness, family harmony, and community contribution through embodied consciousness

The Living Promise of Sacred Embodiment

Lieutenant Colonel Maria Santos, four years after her transformation in Afghanistan, reflects on Sacred Embodiment's impact:

Sacred Embodiment didn't just heal my back pain, it revealed that my body is actually my greatest teacher and ally. Every movement became an opportunity to develop awareness, every breath became medicine, every posture became a chance to serve others more effectively.

Now I serve not from obligation but from overflow. My physical vitality supports my professional effectiveness, my emotional regulation enhances my leadership capacity, and my spiritual development expresses itself through beneficial service to military personnel dealing with the same challenges I once faced.

Sacred Embodiment promises the same transformation for you: physical healing that supports emotional balance, movement practice that develops mental clarity, and bodily awareness that awakens spiritual development serving both individual fulfillment and collective advancement.

Your body is not separate from your consciousness, it is consciousness taking form for the purpose of development and service. Sacred Embodiment awakens you to this truth through practical application that serves your authentic needs while contributing to your community's welfare.

The Power of the Simple
They had mastered the use of something as simple as breathing to drive their energy and self-awareness.

Breath Alchemy - Your Internal Technology

Transforming Every Breath into Medicine, Energy, and Consciousness

How 20,000 daily breaths become your most powerful spiritual practice, with constitutional techniques that regulate nervous system, cultivate energy, and awaken healing capacity

Dr. Elena Vasquez nearly quit her psychiatric practice after watching another patient suffer through months of medication adjustments with minimal improvement.

As Chief of Psychiatry at Denver Medical Center, she had access to every therapeutic approach available, medications, psychotherapy, behavioral interventions, and innovative treatments.
Yet too many of her patients remained trapped in cycles of anxiety, depression, and trauma that conventional approaches couldn't fully address.

I was trained to be a healing professional," Dr. Vasquez recalls, "but I felt like I was managing symptoms rather than supporting genuine transformation. I'd see momentary improvements followed by setbacks when patients faced life stress. Nothing created the sustained inner stability I knew was possible.

Her breakthrough came at 3:17 AM during her own panic attack triggered by professional burnout and personal loss. In desperation, she remembered reading about constitutional breathing techniques from Sacred Synthesis research and tried the 4-4-8-2 pattern recommended for her Electric constitution.

Within five minutes, my nervous system shifted from panic to calm," she explains. "But it wasn't just symptom relief, I experienced a fundamental shift in how I related to my own stress and emotional reactivity. For the first time in years, I felt equipped to navigate challenge from inner stability rather than external management.

That night began Dr. Vasquez's exploration of Breath Alchemy, the systematic transformation of ordinary respiratory function into sophisticated technology for consciousness development, emotional regulation, and healing capacity adapted precisely to constitutional type and life circumstances.

Today, four years later, she integrates constitutional breathing techniques into psychiatric treatment while maintaining a thriving practice that serves both individual healing and physician training.

Her transformation demonstrates what millions of practitioners are discovering: your breath is not just life support, it's your most accessible technology for consciousness development, serving both individual healing and the capacity to support others' wellbeing.

The Hidden Power in Every Breath
You breathe approximately 20,000 times each day. For most people, breathing happens unconsciously, a basic biological function that sustains life but offers nothing more. Yet every
single breath contains the potential to transform your nervous system, regulate your emotions, cultivate energy, and develop consciousness in ways that serve both personal healing and your capacity to benefit others.

The Breath Advantage: Your 24/7 Spiritual Practice
Unlike meditation cushions, yoga mats, or special locations, your breath travels with you everywhere. You can practice advanced breathing techniques during business meetings, while caring for children, in traffic, or in any situation where you need immediate access to calm, clarity, or energy.

The Revolutionary Recognition: Breath is the only autonomic function you can consciously control, providing direct access to nervous system regulation, emotional balance, and spiritual development that no other practice can match.

The Constitutional Key: Generic breathing techniques help some people while potentially agitating others. Constitutional adaptation ensures every technique serves your individual nervous system while connecting you to universal healing principles.

Your Constitutional Breathing Profile
Before learning advanced techniques, discover your constitutional breathing pattern to ensure every practice enhances rather than overwhelms your natural nervous system function.

Electric Constitution Breathing Characteristics
Your Natural Pattern:
- Shallow, irregular breathing with tendency toward rapid or anxious patterns
- Sensitive respiratory system that reacts strongly to stress and stimulation
- Natural breath holding or restriction during emotional intensity
- Benefits from grounding, calming, and warming approaches

What Your Constitution Needs:
- Extended Exhales: Activates calming parasympathetic nervous system
- Gentle Techniques: Avoids overstimulation of naturally sensitive system
- Warming Methods: Counteracts constitutional coolness and circulation issues
- Stability Practices: Provides grounding for naturally variable nervous system

Recognition Signs: You feel better with slower, gentler breathing practices; intensive breathing creates anxiety or agitation; you naturally hold your breath during stress; warming environments enhance your breathing comfort.

Magnetic Constitution Breathing Characteristics
Your Natural Pattern:
- Deep, slow breathing with tendency toward sluggish or restricted patterns
- Strong respiratory system capable of handling intensive practices
- Natural tendency toward shallow breathing when inactive or depressed
- Benefits from activating, heating, and stimulating approaches

What Your Constitution Needs:
- Activating Patterns: Prevents circulation stagnation and promotes energy flow

- Heating Techniques: Generates internal warmth and metabolic activation
- Challenging Practices: Maintains engagement through complexity and intensity
- Dynamic Methods: Prevents lethargy through stimulation and movement

Recognition Signs: You feel better with vigorous, challenging breathing practices; gentle techniques leave you feeling flat or unmotivated; you need activation to prevent depression; cool environments enhance your breathing practices.

Neutral Constitution Breathing Characteristics
Your Natural Pattern:
- Efficient, balanced breathing with tendency toward heating or intensity
- Moderate respiratory capacity with generally good natural regulation
- Tendency toward controlled breathing with occasional excessive intensity
- Benefits from cooling, balancing, and moderating approaches

What Your Constitution Needs:
- Cooling Techniques: Prevents overheating and excessive nervous system intensity
- Balancing Practices: Moderates natural drive and competitive tendencies
- Precision Methods: Satisfies need for technical excellence and proper form
- Seasonal Adaptation: Adjusts for natural heat sensitivity and inflammatory tendencies

Recognition Signs: You perform well with precise, technically excellent breathing; you overheat easily during intensive practices; competitive tendencies emerge during breathing challenges; seasonal adjustments dramatically affect your comfort and effectiveness.

The 4-4-6-2 Integration Breath: Your Foundation Practice

The Integration Breath provides the foundation for all advanced breathing development through establishing optimal nervous system balance while building respiratory capacity and awareness necessary for sophisticated techniques.

The Technique:
1. **Inhalation** (4 counts): Breathe through nose, expanding abdomen first, then ribcage, then chest
2. **Retention with Air** (4 counts): Hold breath comfortably without strain or tension
3. **Exhalation** (6 counts): Release through nose or pursed lips, reversing inhalation sequence
4. **Retention Empty** (2 counts): Pause comfortably without gasping or forcing

Practice Guidelines:
- Count Duration: Begin with 2-3 seconds per count, gradually extending to 4-5 seconds as capacity develops
- Daily Duration: Start with 5-10 minutes daily, gradually extending to 15-20 minutes over several months
- Environment: Quiet, comfortable space with appropriate temperature for constitutional needs
- Position: Comfortable seated position with spine naturally erect, or lying down if needed

The Science Behind 4-4-6-2

Autonomic Nervous System Optimization: The specific ratio creates perfect balance between sympathetic (alertness) and parasympathetic (calm) nervous system activation through the extended exhale pattern.

Physiological Mechanisms:
- Extended Exhale: Longer exhalation activates parasympathetic nervous system, promoting restoration and calm
- Controlled Inhalation: Measured inhalation provides gentle sympathetic activation supporting alertness and vitality
- Retention Phases: Brief holds build respiratory control while supporting energy cultivation
- Rhythmic Pattern: Consistent rhythm trains nervous system toward optimal balance and regulation

Constitutional Adaptations: Personalizing Your Practice

Electric Constitution: The Grounding Breath (4-4-8-2)

Your Specialized Pattern:
- Inhalation (4 counts): Gentle, warming breath with visualization

of golden light entering
- Retention (4 counts): Comfortable hold with attention on heart center or base of spine
- Exhalation (8 counts): Extended release with visualization of roots growing into earth
- Empty Retention (2 counts): Brief pause feeling groundedness and stability

Environmental Optimization:
- Practice Space: Warm, quiet room with soft lighting and comfortable support
- Timing: Evening practice particularly beneficial for sleep preparation and anxiety management
- Duration: 5-10 minutes initially, extending very gradually to prevent nervous system overwhelm
- Props: Blanket, cushions, or back support enhancing comfort and security

Specific Benefits for Electric Types:
- Anxiety Relief: Extended exhale provides immediate anxiety reduction and nervous system calming
- Sleep Support: Evening practice creates natural transition to restful sleep
- Energy Stabilization: Regular practice prevents energy fluctuations and emotional volatility
- Digestive Calm: Parasympathetic activation supports healthy digestion and elimination

Dr. Sarah Chen's Transformation: "As an Electric constitution software engineer, I suffered from chronic anxiety and insomnia despite trying every relaxation technique available. The 4-4- 8-2 grounding breath created immediate calm without making me feel sluggish. After six months of practice, my anxiety medication was no longer needed, and I sleep naturally through the night."

Magnetic Constitution: The Activation Breath (6-4-6-2)

Your Specialized Pattern:
- Inhalation (6 counts): Dynamic, energizing breath with visualization of fire or sunlight entering
- Retention (4 counts): Active hold with attention on solar plexus or heart center
- Exhalation (6 counts): Controlled release maintaining energy and circulation
- Empty Retention (2 counts): Brief pause maintaining alertness

and activation

Environmental Optimization:
- Practice Space: Cool, well-ventilated room with energizing lighting and minimal props
- Timing: Morning practice particularly effective for preventing lethargy and building daily energy
- Duration: 15-25 minutes for adequate engagement and metabolic activation
- Challenge: Progressive increase in duration and complexity maintaining motivation

Specific Benefits for Magnetic Types:
- Energy Activation: Balanced breathing prevents morning sluggishness and afternoon crashes
- Depression Prevention: Activating practice supports mood elevation and metabolic stimulation
- Circulation Enhancement: Rhythmic breathing promotes cardiovascular health and energy flow
- Motivation Support: Regular practice maintains engagement and goal-oriented focus

Marcus Rodriguez's Transformation: "As a Magnetic constitution nonprofit director, I struggled with depression and low energy despite being physically strong. The 6-4-6-2 activation breath provided sustainable energy without caffeine dependence. My staff noticed increased vitality and leadership effectiveness within two weeks of consistent practice."

Neutral Constitution: The Balance Breath (4-4-6-2 with Cooling)

Your Specialized Pattern:
- Inhalation (4 counts): Cool, precise breath through pursed lips or tongue curl
- Retention (4 counts): Comfortable hold with attention on balancing energy centers
- Exhalation (6 counts): Cooling release with visualization of heat leaving body
- Empty Retention (2 counts): Brief pause feeling temperature regulation and balance

Environmental Optimization:
- Practice Space: Cool, organized environment with attention to temperature control
- Timing: Multiple shorter sessions throughout day for stress

management and temperature regulation
- Duration: 8-12 minutes with seasonal adjustments preventing overheating
- Precision: Emphasis on technical excellence rather than duration or intensity goals

Specific Benefits for Neutral Types:
- Stress Management: Balanced nervous system regulation supports healthy stress response
- Temperature Regulation: Cooling techniques prevent overheating during intense activity
- Mental Clarity: Optimal oxygenation and nervous system balance enhance cognitive function
- Inflammation Prevention: Cooling breath reduces inflammatory conditions and excessive intensity

Dr. James Liu's Transformation: "As a Neutral constitution surgeon, I dealt with high stress and tendency toward anger and perfectionism. The cooling balance breath helped me maintain clarity during long surgeries while preventing the burnout that affected many colleagues. Patient outcomes improved as my stress management enhanced decision-making precision."

Advanced Constitutional Breathing Techniques

Electric Constitution: The Grounding Series

Morning Nervous System Reset (10 minutes):
1. **Belly Breathing** (3 minutes): Deep abdominal breathing with hands on belly, focusing on gentle expansion and contraction
2. **Warming Breath** (4 minutes): Inhale imagining warm golden light, exhale releasing coolness and anxiety
3. **Root Connection** (3 minutes): Extended exhale breathing with visualization of roots growing from base of spine into earth

Anxiety Response Protocol (5 minutes):
1. **Extended Exhale** (2 minutes): 4-4-10-2 pattern for immediate nervous system calming
2. **Grounding Visualization** (2 minutes): Breath awareness with earth connection imagery
3. **Stability Integration** (1 minute): Return to natural breathing while maintaining grounded awareness

Evening Sleep Preparation (8 minutes):
1. **Progressive Relaxation Breath** (3 minutes): Each exhale re-

leases tension from different body areas
2. **Warming Heart Breath** (3 minutes): Gentle breathing with attention on heart center and gratitude
3. **Sleep Transition** (2 minutes): Very slow, gentle breathing preparing nervous system for rest

Magnetic Constitution: The Activation Series

Morning Energy Building (15 minutes):
1. **Bellows Breath** (3 minutes): Rapid belly breathing, 30 seconds active, 30 seconds rest, repeat 3 rounds
2. **Fire Breath** (5 minutes): Vigorous breathing with retention building internal heat and circulation
3. **Circulation Breath** (7 minutes): Long, deep breathing with visualization of energy circulating through entire body

Motivation Enhancement Protocol (10 minutes):
1. **Challenge Breath** (4 minutes): Progressive increase in breath counts building respiratory strength
2. **Heart Activation** (4 minutes): Dynamic breathing with attention on heart center and personal power
3. **Goal Integration** (2 minutes): Rhythmic breathing while visualizing achievement and service

Lethargy Prevention Series (12 minutes):
1. **Awakening Breath** (4 minutes): Alternating vigorous and gentle breathing preventing stagnation
2. **Strength Building** (5 minutes): Breath retention practice building respiratory capacity and willpower
3. **Sustained Energy** (3 minutes): Moderate rhythmic breathing maintaining activation without exhaustion

Neutral Constitution: The Balance Series

Morning Precision Practice (12 minutes):
1. **Cooling Preparation** (3 minutes): Breath through pursed lips or curled tongue reducing internal heat
2. **Alternate Nostril** (6 minutes): Classical technique balancing nervous system and mental clarity
3. **Integration Balance** (3 minutes): Equal count breathing maintaining equilibrium and focus

Stress Regulation Protocol (8 minutes):
1. **Temperature Control** (3 minutes): Cooling breath with visualization of heat releasing through crown

2. **Tension Release** (3 minutes): Precise breathing releasing specific areas of physical tension
3. **Mental Clarity** (2 minutes): Balanced breathing supporting clear thinking and decision- making

Inflammation Prevention Series (10 minutes):
1. **Anti-Inflammatory Breath** (4 minutes): Slow, cooling breathing reducing systemic inflammation
2. **Liver Support** (3 minutes): Specific breathing pattern supporting detoxification and cooling
3. **Balance Integration** (3 minutes): Gentle breathing maintaining constitutional equilibrium

Therapeutic Applications: Breath as Medicine
Constitutional breathing provides specific therapeutic protocols for common health challenges while supporting overall vitality and consciousness development.

Anxiety and Panic Management
Electric Constitution Anxiety Protocol:
- Immediate Response: 4-4-10-2 pattern with grounding visualization
- Daily Prevention: Morning 10-minute grounding series with evening sleep preparation
- Crisis Support: Portable 2-minute grounding breath for workplace or social anxiety
- Long-term Healing: Community practice and constitutional lifestyle supporting nervous system stability

Depression and Low Energy Treatment
Magnetic Constitution Depression Protocol:
- Morning Activation: 15-minute activation series preventing daily energy crashes
- Motivation Support: Challenge breath practice building confidence and personal power
- Social Integration: Group breathing practice providing community support and shared goals
- Long-term Recovery: Service integration connecting individual healing with community benefit

Stress and Inflammation Reduction
Neutral Constitution Stress Protocol:
- Daily Regulation: Morning precision practice with afternoon stress regulation protocol
- Temperature Management: Cooling techniques preventing heat-

related stress accumulation
- Professional Integration: Workplace breathing practices supporting sustained effectiveness
- Lifestyle Integration: Constitutional nutrition and seasonal adaptation supporting overall balance

Professional Integration: Breathing at Work
Constitutional breathing transforms workplace stress into opportunities for consciousness development while enhancing professional effectiveness and leadership capacity.

Healthcare Professional Applications

Dr. Elena Vasquez's Psychiatry Integration:
- Pre-Session Preparation: 2-minute constitutional breathing creating therapeutic presence
- Patient Session Enhancement: Subtle breathing awareness maintaining empathy without absorbing patient distress
- Between-Session Reset: Constitutional breathing preventing accumulation of emotional residue
- Crisis Response: Emergency breathing techniques for psychiatric emergency situations

Educational Professional Applications
Principal Maria Santos's School Integration:
- Morning Leadership Preparation: Constitutional breathing supporting calm authority and clear decision-making
- Crisis Response: Breathing techniques for handling difficult student, parent, or staff situations
- Staff Meeting Enhancement: Brief group breathing practices improving communication and cooperation
- Student Support: Teaching constitutional breathing for test anxiety, behavioral regulation, and learning enhancement

Business Leadership Applications
CEO Michael Chen's Corporate Integration:
- Executive Decision-Making: Constitutional breathing supporting strategic thinking and emotional regulation
- Meeting Leadership: Breathing awareness creating authentic presence and effective communication
- Stress Management: Workplace breathing practices preventing executive burnout and reactive decision-making
- Organizational Culture: Company-wide breathing programs supporting employee wellness and productivity

Building Your Daily Breathing Practice
Sustainable breathing practice develops through gradual progression that integrates with your constitutional needs and life circumstances while building capacity for advanced techniques and service applications.

Foundation Phase (Months 1-3)

Daily Practice Structure:
- Duration: 10-15 minutes daily constitutional breathing
- Focus: Master basic 4-4-6-2 pattern with constitutional adaptations
- Integration: Use emergency techniques during stress or challenge
- Community: Connect with online or local constitutional breathing groups

Week 1-2: Establishment
- Practice basic constitutional pattern 5-10 minutes daily
- Track energy, mood, and sleep quality changes
- Learn constitutional emergency response techniques
- Set up optimal practice environment

Week 3-6: Development
- Extend practice duration to 10-15 minutes
- Add constitutional therapeutic applications for specific challenges
- Begin workplace integration during breaks and transitions
- Share experience with family or friends interested in learning

Week 7-12: Stabilization
- Consistent 15-minute daily practice with constitutional variations
- Seasonal adaptation and environmental modification awareness
- Advanced constitutional techniques for specific therapeutic needs
- Community practice participation and mutual support

Integration Phase (Months 4-12)

Daily Practice Structure:
- Duration: 15-25 minutes daily with constitutional series
- Focus: Advanced constitutional techniques and therapeutic applications
- Integration: Throughout-day workplace and family applications
- Service: Support others' learning constitutional breathing basics

Professional Enhancement: Constitutional breathing becomes foundation for enhanced work effectiveness, leadership capacity, and stress management supporting both career advancement and service to others.

Relationship Improvement: Breathing awareness enhances communication, emotional regulation, and conflict resolution capacity in family and community relationships.

Health Optimization: Constitutional breathing supports overall health while providing specific therapeutic applications for individual challenges and constitutional imbalances.

Mastery Phase (Year 2+)

Daily Practice Structure:
- Duration: 20-35 minutes daily with complete constitutional integration
- Focus: Teaching preparation and advanced energy cultivation techniques
- Integration: Breath awareness present throughout daily activities
- Service: Community teaching and constitutional breathing program development

Teaching Preparation: Advanced practitioners develop capacity to support others' constitutional breathing development through community programs, professional applications, or family guidance.

Energy Cultivation: Sophisticated techniques connecting individual breathing practice with energy development and healing capacity serving both personal advancement and community benefit.

Cultural Contribution: Breathing mastery enables contribution to healthcare, education, and community wellness through constitutional understanding and practical application.

Building Community Through Breath
Individual breathing practice provides foundation for community development that serves mutual support, collective healing, and cultural transformation through consciousness-based approaches to shared challenges.

Family Breathing Integration

Constitutional Family Practice:

- Assess each family member's constitutional breathing needs and adaptations
- Create family breathing time with practices supporting everyone's wellbeing
- Use constitutional breathing for family conflict resolution and communication enhancement
- Support individual practice time while building family coherence and mutual understanding

The Wilson Family Success Story:
Parents Jennifer (Electric) and David (Magnetic) with teenagers Emma (Neutral) and Sophie (Electric) transformed family dynamics through constitutional breathing awareness:
- Morning Family Practice: 10-minute sequence with constitutional modifications supporting everyone's daily preparation
- Conflict Resolution: Constitutional breathing techniques preventing typical personality clashes and misunderstandings
- Academic Support: Breathing practices adapted to each teenager's learning style and test anxiety management
- Results: Family satisfaction increased dramatically, academic performance improved, household stress decreased significantly

Workplace Breathing Programs
Corporate Constitutional Wellness:
- Employee constitutional assessment enabling personalized breathing programs
- Lunchtime constitutional breathing groups with trained facilitators
- Meeting integration with brief breathing practices enhancing communication and decision-making
- Leadership training in constitutional breathing for stress management and authentic presence

Community Health Applications
Healthcare System Integration:
- Patient constitutional breathing programs for anxiety, pain management, and recovery support
- Healthcare provider constitutional breathing training for stress management and therapeutic presence
- Community wellness programs serving diverse constitutional types and cultural backgrounds
- Integration with conventional medical treatment providing complementary support

Seasonal and Advanced Applications
Constitutional breathing adapts to seasonal changes while providing foundation for advanced energy cultivation and healing applications serving both individual development and community benefit.

Seasonal Constitutional Adaptations

Spring Breathing Practices (March-May):
- All Constitutions: Gentle cleansing and renewal breathing supporting seasonal detoxification
- Electric: Gradual activation supporting nervous system adaptation to increased seasonal energy
- Magnetic: Enhanced activation taking advantage of natural spring energy and motivation
- Neutral: Balanced increase with attention to preventing spring inflammation and overheating

Summer Breathing Practices (June-August):
- All Constitutions: Cooling emphasis and temperature regulation preventing heat exhaustion
- Electric: Moderate cooling while maintaining grounding and nervous system stability
- Magnetic: Maximum cooling practices while maintaining circulation and preventing stagnation
- Neutral: Strong cooling emphasis supporting heat-sensitive constitution and reducing inflammation

Autumn Breathing Practices (September-November):
- All Constitutions: Grounding emphasis preparing for winter while maintaining immune support
- Electric: Maximum grounding practices during season of change and potential anxiety
- Magnetic: Balanced approach maintaining metabolism and energy while preparing for winter
- Neutral: Gradual transition to warming practices while maintaining temperature regulation

Winter Breathing Practices (December-February):
- All Constitutions: Warming emphasis and respiratory support during cold season
- Electric: Maximum warming with consistent routine supporting nervous system stability
- Magnetic: Moderate warming maintaining circulation and preventing seasonal depression
- Neutral: Gentle warming with attention to maintaining balance

and preventing dryness

Advanced Energy Cultivation

Constitutional breathing provides foundation for sophisticated energy development supporting healing capacity, teaching ability, and service applications while maintaining safety and community accountability.

The Central Channel Breath: Foundation of Energy Development

Basic Technique:
- Visualization: Direct breath and attention through central channel running from base of spine to crown of head
- Coordination: Breathing pattern coordinated with energy circulation and awareness development
- Constitutional Adaptation: Modified according to individual nervous system sensitivity and capacity
- Progressive Development: Gradual advancement over months and years with qualified guidance

Safety Protocols:
- Community Supervision: Advanced practices require experienced guidance and community support
- Constitutional Adaptation: Individual modification preventing overstimulation or energy depletion
- Medical Consultation: Professional medical support for practitioners with health conditions
- Gradual Progression: Systematic development preventing spiritual materialism or energy imbalance

Healing Applications and Service Integration

Individual Healing Capacity: Advanced breathing practice develops capacity for self-healing and energy regulation supporting sustained health and vitality throughout life challenges and aging processes.

Community Healing Applications: Experienced practitioners develop capacity to support others' healing through breathing guidance, community wellness programs, and professional therapeutic applications.

Cultural Service Integration: Breathing mastery enables contribution to healthcare system improvement, educational enhancement, and community resilience through consciousness- based approaches to collective challenges.

Your Breathing Mastery Journey

Constitutional breathing transforms the most basic life function into sophisticated technology for consciousness development that serves both individual fulfillment and community advancement through practical effectiveness and healing capacity.

Your 30-Day Breathing Foundation

Week 1: Master constitutional basic breath pattern with environmental optimization and stress response applications
Week 2: Develop constitutional morning series with workplace integration and evening preparation practices
Week 3: Add therapeutic applications for specific health challenges with community connection and family sharing
Week 4: Integrate advanced constitutional techniques with service preparation and teaching readiness assessment
Your Constitutional Commitment

Electric Constitution Path: Become source of grounding and stability for family and community while developing sensitivity and creative contributions serving collective healing and cultural bridge-building.

Magnetic Constitution Path: Develop sustained energy and practical effectiveness enabling community leadership and service projects that demonstrate consciousness-based approaches to collective challenges.

Neutral Constitution Path: Master precision and balance creating capacity for teaching, conflict resolution, and professional applications that serve both individual advancement and community development.

The Breathing Promise

Dr. Elena Vasquez, four years after her 3:17 AM panic attack breakthrough, reflects on constitutional breathing's transformation of her life and professional effectiveness:

Constitutional breathing didn't just eliminate my anxiety, it revealed that breath awareness is the foundation for everything else I do.

Every patient interaction, every treatment decision, every moment of challenge became an opportunity to demonstrate the practical effectiveness of consciousness development.

My psychiatric practice became more effective because I could remain present during patient crisis without absorbing their distress. My own life became more fulfilling because breathing awareness connected every activity with spiritual development and service to others.

Constitutional breathing taught me that individual healing and collective benefit are the same activity approached from different perspectives. Every breath became both personal medicine and preparation for serving others' wellbeing.

Constitutional breathing offers you the same transformation: respiratory function that serves consciousness development, stress management that enhances professional effectiveness, and individual healing that develops capacity for community service.

The Great Achievement: A Civilization Beyond Imagination
The most remarkable documents came from the period between 2074 and 2080, which the archives called the "Great Emergence." Reading these materials, I began to understand why the cities were empty, why the forests had returned, why our scattered enclaves lived so differently from anything the old world had imagined.

Omaha Constitutional Assessment and Individual Adaptation
The Science of Individual Adaptation: Beyond One-Size-Fits-All Spirituality
From Generic Prescriptions to Personalized Transformation
For over a century, the modern spiritual marketplace has operated on a fundamentally flawed assumption: that universal spiritual principles can be effectively transmitted through standardized methods that ignore individual constitutional differences. This approach has created a spiritual equivalent of prescribing the same medication to every patient regardless of their unique physiological and psychological makeup.

The Sacred Synthesis approach, emerging from the wartime synthesis documented in La Iniciación magazine (1942-1947), revolutionized spiritual development by integrating **constitutional assessment** with traditional practice, creating the first systematic methodology for personalizing spiritual development while maintaining traditional authenticity and effectiveness.

Constitutional assessment represents far more than personality typing or psychological categorization. It encompasses a comprehensive understanding of individual physical constitution, psychological temperament, energetic patterns, and developmental capacity that enables precise adaptation of universal principles to serve each person's unique pathway toward realization.

The Three-Fold Framework: Physical, Psychological, and Energetic Integration
Beyond Personality Typing: The Complete Constitutional Picture

Traditional constitutional assessment, as preserved through the Laws of Vayu, operates on three integrated levels that must be understood together to create effective individual adaptation:

Physical Constitution (Ayurvedic Foundation)
* **Metabolic patterns** determining optimal nutrition, exercise, and daily rhythms
* **Structural characteristics** influencing posture, movement preferences, and embodiment practices
* **Seasonal sensitivity** affecting how environmental changes impact health and energy
* **Circadian rhythms** determining optimal timing for different activities and practices

Psychological Constitution (Typological Integration)
* **Motivational patterns** revealing core drives, fears, and growth opportunities
* **Attention patterns** showing how consciousness naturally focuses and where development is needed
* **Relationship patterns** indicating how connection and community support can be optimized
* **Learning styles** determining how traditional teachings can be most effectively received and integrated

Energetic Constitution (Chakra and Meridian Assessment)
* **Energy distribution patterns** showing natural strengths and areas requiring development
* **Sensitivity to environmental influences** including electromagnetic fields, weather patterns, and social atmospheres
* **Spiritual capacity and readiness** for different types of contemplative practice and consciousness development
* **Service orientation** indicating how individual gifts can best serve collective advancement

The Integration Challenge: Creating Constitutional Harmony

The breakthrough insight of the Sacred Synthesis approach is that **constitutional harmony**, the integration of physical, psychological, and energetic patterns, creates the optimal foundation for spiritual development.

When these three levels are aligned and mutually supportive, spiritual practices become naturally effective rather than requiring force or excessive effort.

Constitutional Harmony Indicators:
- Physical practices feel energizing rather than depleting
- Psychological development occurs naturally through daily spiritual practice
- Energetic patterns support rather than conflict with life responsibilities
- Service activities emerge spontaneously from genuine capacity rather than obligation

Constitutional Discord Signs:
- Spiritual practices create physical tension or energy depletion
- Psychological development feels forced or creates emotional instability
- Energetic practices conflict with family, professional, or community responsibilities
- Service activities feel burdensome or create resentment rather than fulfillment

Complete Constitutional Assessment: Scientific Methodology with Traditional Wisdom

Phase One: Physical Constitution Evaluation (Ayurvedic Foundation)

Basic Constitutional Types (Doshas):

Vata Constitution (Air/Space Elements) Electric:
- **Physical Characteristics**: Light frame, variable appetite, tendency toward dryness, sensitive to cold, quick movements
- **Mental Patterns**: Creative thinking, rapid mental processing, tendency toward anxiety when imbalanced, excellent at innovation
- **Spiritual Gifts**: Natural capacity for transcendent awareness and mystical experience
- **Development Needs**: Grounding practices, routine establish-

ment, nourishing activities, nervous system support

Pitta Constitution (Fire/Water Elements)
Neutral:
* **Physical Characteristics**: Medium frame, strong appetite, tendency toward heat, moderate sensitivity to weather, purposeful movements
* **Mental Patterns**: Goal-oriented thinking, strong concentration ability, tendency toward irritability when imbalanced, excellent at implementation
* **Spiritual Gifts**: Natural capacity for discriminative wisdom and ethical development
* **Development Needs**: Cooling practices, patience cultivation, surrender activities, liver and digestion support

Kapha Constitution (Earth/Water Elements)
Magnetic:
* **Physical Characteristics**: Solid frame, steady appetite, tendency toward moisture, sensitive to damp/cold, deliberate movements
* **Mental Patterns**: Stable thinking, sustained attention, tendency toward depression when imbalanced, excellent at preservation
* **Spiritual Gifts**: Natural capacity for devotion and community service
* **Development Needs**: Stimulating practices, variety introduction, challenging activities, circulation and lymphatic support

Mixed Constitutional Patterns:
Most individuals demonstrate combinations of constitutional types, requiring nuanced assessment and practice adaptation. **Dual-constitution types** (Vata-Pitta, Pitta-Kapha, Kapha-Vata) require practices that address both primary patterns without creating internal conflict.

Seasonal and Life-Stage Variations:
Constitutional expression changes throughout life cycles and seasonal transitions. **Constitutional assessment**
must account for:
* **Life stage influences**: Different practices appropriate for youth, maturity, and elder phases
* **Seasonal adaptations**: Practices modified for spring growth, summer expansion, autumn harvest, and winter reflection
* **Environmental factors**: Urban vs. rural, climate conditions, altitude, and cultural context influences

Phase Two: Psychological Constitution Assessment (Typological Integration)

- For enneagrammatic study please reach out to the Arica School at https://www.arica.org

Phase Three: Energetic Constitution Assessment (Chakra and Meridian Integration)

The Seven-Center Energetic Assessment:
Traditional understanding of human energy systems provides the third essential component of constitutional assessment. Each individual demonstrates unique patterns of energetic strength, sensitivity, and development potential across the seven major energy centers.

Energy Center Assessment Methodology:
- **First Center (Root/Muladhara) - Survival and Grounding:**
    - **Strong Pattern**: Natural physical vitality, practical capability, material world effectiveness
    - **Weak Pattern**: Anxiety about survival, difficulty with practical tasks, health challenges
    - **Development Approach**: Grounding practices, physical exercise, practical service activities

- **Second Center (Sacral/Svadhisthana) - Creativity and Sexuality:**
    - **Strong Pattern**: Natural creative capacity, healthy sexuality, emotional fluidity
    - **Weak Pattern**: Creative blocks, relationship difficulties, emotional numbness or volatility
    - **Development Approach**: Creative expression practices, relationship work, emotional processing activities

- **Third Center (Solar Plexus/Manipura) - Personal Power and Will:**
    - **Strong Pattern**: Natural confidence, effective decision-making, healthy boundaries
    - **Weak Pattern**: Power struggles, difficulty with decisions, boundary problems
    - **Development Approach**: Personal empowerment practices, ethical development, leadership training

- **Fourth Center (Heart/Anahata) - Love and Connection:**
    - **Strong Pattern**: Natural compassion, easy relation-

ships, emotional balance
- o **Weak Pattern**: Relationship difficulties, emotional armor, isolation tendencies
- o **Development Approach**: Heart-opening practices, forgiveness work, service to others

- **Fifth Center (Throat/Vishuddha) - Communication and Truth:**
  - o **Strong Pattern**: Clear communication, authentic expression, teaching capacity
  - o **Weak Pattern**: Communication difficulties, expression blocks, authenticity struggles
  - o **Development Approach**: Expression practices, truth-telling exercises, creative communication

- **Sixth Center (Third Eye/Ajna) - Intuition and Wisdom:**
  - o **Strong Pattern**: Natural intuition, clear perception, wisdom orientation
  - o **Weak Pattern**: Confusion, poor judgment, illusion susceptibility
  - o **Development Approach**: Contemplative practices, discrimination development, study activities

- **Seventh Center (Crown/Sahasrara) - Unity and Transcendence:**
  - o **Strong Pattern**: Natural spiritual awareness, unity consciousness, transcendent capacity
  - o **Weak Pattern**: Spiritual confusion, disconnection from transcendent, materialistic orientation
  - o **Development Approach**: Meditation practices, spiritual study, surrender activities

Integrated Energetic Pattern Assessment:
Individual energetic constitution is determined not by any single center but by the **pattern of relationships** among all seven centers. Constitutional assessment identifies:

- **Primary energetic strengths** that can be developed and utilized for service
- **Secondary development areas** requiring attention and systematic cultivation
- **Energetic blocks or imbalances** creating obstacles to development
- **Integration opportunities** where strengths can support development areas

Environmental Sensitivity Assessment:
Constitutional energetic patterns determine sensitivity to environmental factors that must be considered for optimal spiritual development:

- **Electromagnetic sensitivity**: Reaction to electrical devices, cell phones, computers
- **Weather sensitivity**: Response to seasonal changes, barometric pressure, humidity
- **Social sensitivity**: Reaction to crowd energy, emotional atmospheres, group dynamics
- **Location sensitivity**: Preference for urban vs. rural, mountain vs. ocean, different geographical regions

Individualized Practice Adaptation: From Theory to Daily Application

The Sacred Synthesis Adaptation Methodology
Constitutional assessment reaches its fulfillment through **precise practice adaptation** that honors individual uniqueness while maintaining traditional authenticity. This requires sophisticated understanding of how universal principles can be expressed through constitutional-specific applications.

The Four-Level Adaptation Framework:

Level One: Daily Rhythm Adaptation (Circadian Constitutional Matching)

Electric - Vata Constitution Daily Adaptation:
- **4:00 AM Rise Time**: Natural energy peak supports early contemplative practice
- **4:00-5:30 AM Practice Window**: Extended meditation and breathing practices during natural stillness
- **5:30-7:00 AM Gentle Movement**: Slow, flowing sequence emphasizing grounding and stability
- **Evening Wind-down**: Early evening quiet with warm, nourishing activities supporting nervous system

Neutral - Pitta Constitution Daily Adaptation:
- **5:00 AM Rise Time**: Pitta energy builds gradually, avoiding early morning intensity
- **5:00-6:00 AM Structured Practice**: Systematic practice with clear goals and progression
- **6:00-7:30 AM Dynamic Movement**: More vigorous sequences

emphasizing cooling and patience
- **Midday Integration**: Brief sessions integrated with work to maintain balance and prevent burnout

Magnetic - Kapha Constitution Daily Adaptation:
- **5:30 AM Rise Time**: Kapha requires more stimulation to overcome natural inertia
- **5:30-6:30 AM Activating Practice**: Energizing breathing techniques and dynamic meditation
- **6:30-8:00 AM Vigorous Movement**: Stimulating sequence emphasizing circulation and activation
- **Evening Variation**: Varied activities preventing routine stagnation and maintaining engagement

Level Two: Seasonal Practice Adaptation (Natural Rhythm Alignment)

Spring Development Cycle (March-May):
- **Electric - Vata Focus**: Gentle expansion and creative new beginning energy, avoiding overstimulation
- **Neutral - Pitta Focus**: Goal-setting and systematic skill development, managing ambition appropriately
- **Magnetic - Kapha Focus**: Major lifestyle changes and habit modification during natural change energy

Summer Integration Cycle (June-August):
- **Electric - Vata Focus**: Social engagement and community activity during abundant energy period
- **Neutral - Pitta Focus**: Service activities and practical application, managing heat and intensity
- **Magnetic - Kapha Focus**: Travel, adventure, and new experience during high energy period

Autumn Deepening Cycle (September-November):
- **Electric - Vata Focus**: Grounding practices and routine establishment during natural change period
- **Neutral - Pitta Focus**: Reflection and evaluation, harvesting insights from year's development
- **Magnetic - Kapha Focus**: Study and contemplative practice during natural inward-turning energy

Winter Integration Cycle (December-February):
- **Electric - Vata Focus**: Nourishing and restorative practices during natural rest period
- **Neutral - Pitta Focus**: Planning and visioning for coming year,

balancing activity with restoration
- **Magnetic - Kapha Focus**: Social connection and community service during natural sharing energy

Level Three: Life-Stage Development Adaptation (Developmental Constitutional Matching)

Youth Phase (Ages 21-35) - Establishment Period:
- **Constitutional emphasis**: Building life foundation while establishing spiritual practice
- **Practice focus**: Habit formation, skill development, community connection
- **Service orientation**: Learning through contribution to family and community development

Maturity Phase (Ages 35-50) - Integration Period:
- **Constitutional emphasis**: Professional excellence through spiritual development integration
- **Practice focus**: Advanced technique development, teaching and guidance capacity
- **Service orientation**: Leadership and mentorship in chosen application area

Elder Phase (Ages 50+) - Wisdom Transmission Period:
- **Constitutional emphasis**: Cultural transmission and community wisdom sharing
- **Practice focus**: Mastery integration, advanced spiritual development
- **Service orientation**: Teaching, community leadership, intergenerational transmission

Level Four: Crisis and Transition Adaptation (Emergency Constitutional Response)
Constitutional understanding becomes especially crucial during life crises, health challenges, relationship transitions, and other periods when normal practice routines are disrupted.

Crisis Adaptation Principles:
- **Electric - Vata Crisis Response**: Increased grounding practices, routine maintenance, nervous system support
- **Neutral - Pitta Crisis Response**: Cooling and patience practices, surrender development, liver support
- **Magnetic - Kapha Crisis Response**: Stimulating practices, circulation, anti-depressant activities

Health Challenge Adaptations:
- **Acute Illness**: Constitutional practices supporting immune system and recovery
- **Chronic Condition Management**: Long-term adaptation supporting optimal health within limitations
- **Mental Health Integration**: Constitutional approaches supporting stability and development

Life Transition Adaptations:
- **Career Changes**: Practice adaptation supporting professional transition while maintaining development
- **Relationship Changes**: Constitutional approaches to partnership development, family transitions, loss
- **Geographical Moves**: Environmental adaptation maintaining practice effectiveness in new locations

The Family Constitutional Assessment: Household Harmony and Collective Development

Beyond Individual Practice: Creating Constitutional Family Harmony
One of the unique contributions of Sacred Synthesis methodology is the recognition that **family constitutional harmony** significantly impacts individual spiritual development. When family members understand each other's constitutional patterns, conflicts decrease while mutual support and collective development increase dramatically.

Family Constitutional Mapping Methodology:
Household Assessment Framework
Step One: Individual Assessment Completion
Each family member completes comprehensive constitutional assessment, creating individual constitutional profiles that include:
- Physical constitution and health optimization needs
- Psychological patterns and character development focuses
- Energetic strengths and development areas
- Current life stage and developmental priorities

Step Two: Constitutional Compatibility Analysis
Analysis of how different constitutional types interact within family system:
- **Complementary Patterns**: Where different constitutions naturally support each other
- **Challenge Areas**: Where constitutional differences create potential conflicts
- **Integration Opportunities**: How family members can support

each other's development
- **Collective Service Potential**: How family constitutional diversity can serve community advancement

Step Three: Family Practice Integration Design
Creation of family practice approaches that honor individual constitutional needs while building family unity:
- **Shared Morning Practice**: Brief family meditation appropriate for all constitutional types
- **Individual Practice Time**: Respected time for individual constitutional practice without interference
- **Family Service Activities**: Community service projects utilizing diverse family constitutional strengths
- **Seasonal Family Adaptations**: Family activities that change seasonally to support all types

Constitutional Parenting Applications

Understanding Child Constitutional Development:
Children demonstrate constitutional patterns from early ages, but these patterns continue developing and maturing throughout childhood and adolescence. **Constitutional parenting** involves recognizing and supporting each child's unique constitutional pattern rather than imposing parental preferences or generic parenting approaches.

Early Childhood Constitutional Recognition (Ages 3-7):
- **Electric - Vata Children**: High creativity and sensitivity, needing routine and grounding support
- **Neutral - Pitta Children**: Strong will and determination, needing cooling and patience development
- **Magnetic - Kapha Children**: Steady and loyal nature, needing stimulation and variety introduction

School Age Constitutional Support (Ages 8-14):
- **Educational approach adaptation**: Learning styles matching constitutional patterns
- **Activity selection**: Extracurricular activities supporting constitutional development
- **Discipline approaches**: Correction methods appropriate for different constitutional types
- **Social development**: Friendship and community interaction support based on constitutional needs

Adolescent Constitutional Guidance (Ages 15-21):

- **Identity development support**: Honoring constitutional authenticity during identity formation
- **Career exploration**: Educational and professional paths aligned with constitutional gifts
- **Independence preparation**: Life skills development appropriate for constitutional type
- **Spiritual development introduction**: Age-appropriate practices matching constitutional readiness

Partnership Constitutional Compatibility
Marriage and Partnership Constitutional Assessment:
Understanding constitutional compatibility between partners enables conscious relationship development that honors individual differences while building genuine partnership and shared spiritual development.

Constitutional Partnership Patterns:
Same-Constitution Partnerships:
- **Advantages**: Natural understanding, similar rhythms and preferences, easy harmony
- **Challenges**: Potential blind spots, missing complementary strengths, development limitations
- **Development Focus**: Conscious cultivation of other constitutional qualities, diverse service activities

Complementary-Constitution Partnerships:
- **Advantages**: Mutual support, balanced perspective, comprehensive development
- **Challenges**: Different rhythms and preferences, potential conflicts over lifestyle choices
- **Development Focus**: Understanding and accommodation, practice timing, patience development

Mixed-Constitution Partnerships:
- **Advantages**: Natural variety and flexibility, diverse problem-solving approaches
- **Challenges**: Complexity in coordination, potential confusion about optimal approaches
- **Development Focus**: Clear communication, individual practice respect, creative integration solutions

Partnership Development Applications:
- **Conflict Resolution**: Constitutional understanding prevents personal attacks by recognizing differences
- **Decision Making**: Utilizing different strengths for comprehen-

- **Spiritual Practice Integration**: Shared practices honoring both partners' constitutional needs
- **Service Activity Selection**: Community service utilizing combined constitutional gifts and capacities

Professional Constitutional Applications: Career Excellence Through Self-Knowledge
The Constitutional Career Alignment Revolution
Traditional career guidance typically emphasizes external factors, salary potential, job market conditions, social status, while ignoring the crucial question of constitutional alignment between individual nature and professional requirements. Sacred Synthesis constitutional assessment enables **career excellence through self- knowledge** that serves both individual fulfillment and professional effectiveness.

Constitutional Career Assessment Framework:
Healthcare Professional Applications
Electric - Vata Healthcare Providers:
- **Natural Gifts**: Intuitive diagnosis, creative treatment approaches, sensitive patient rapport
- **Optimal Specializations**: Alternative medicine, psychiatric care, research, preventive medicine
- **Development Needs**: Routine establishment, grounding practices, nervous system support
- **Practice Adaptations**: Meditation between patients, nature breaks, variation in daily routine

Neutral - Pitta Healthcare Providers:
- **Natural Gifts**: Diagnostic precision, surgical skill, systematic treatment, leadership capacity
- **Optimal Specializations**: Surgery, emergency medicine, administration, specialized diagnostics
- **Development Needs**: Cooling practices, patience development, surrendering control when appropriate
- **Practice Adaptations**: Cooling breathing techniques, ethical reflection, patient advocacy activities

Magnetic - Kapha Healthcare Providers:
- **Natural Gifts**: Patient bedside manner, steady presence in crisis, community focus, endurance
- **Optimal Specializations**: Family practice, chronic care, community health, nursing, wellness programs
- **Development Needs**: Stimulation practices, variety introduc-

tion, continuing education motivation
- **Practice Adaptations**: Dynamic movement, continuing education, leadership development

Educational Professional Applications
Electric - Vata Educators:
- **Natural Gifts**: Creative teaching, intuitive understanding of learning differences, inspirational capacity
- **Optimal Areas**: Arts education, special needs support, educational innovation, counseling
- **Development Needs**: Routine establishment, grounding practices, administrative skill development
- **Practice Adaptations**: Nature-based teaching, creative expression integration, stress management

Neutral - Pitta Educators:
- **Natural Gifts**: Systematic instruction, high standards, administrative leadership, goal achievement
- **Optimal Areas**: STEM education, educational administration, curriculum development, assessment
- **Development Needs**: Cooling practices, patience development, student-centered flexibility
- **Practice Adaptations**: Student compassion practices, flexibility exercises, cooling techniques

Magnetic - Kapha Educators:
- **Natural Gifts**: Student nurturing, community building, steady presence, wisdom transmission
- **Optimal Areas**: Elementary education, counseling, community, traditional knowledge preservation
- **Development Needs**: Dynamic teaching methods, variety introduction, technology integration
- **Practice Adaptations**: Energizing techniques, innovation challenges, community leadership

Business and Organizational Applications
Constitutional Leadership Development:
Electric - Vata Leaders:
- **Natural Gifts**: Visionary, creative problem-solving, innovation, inspirational communication
- **Optimal Roles**: Entrepreneurship, creative direction, research and development, change management
- **Development Needs**: Follow-through systems, detail management, routine establishment
- **Practice Adaptations**: Vision meditation, grounding practices,

systematic implementation support

Neutral - Pitta Leaders:
- **Natural Gifts**: Goal achievement, systematic implementation, competitive excellence, decisive action
- **Optimal Roles**: Operations management, strategic planning, competitive industries, crisis management
- **Development Needs**: Cooling practices, patience development, collaborative approaches
- **Practice Adaptations**: Team building exercises, patience cultivation, surrender practices

Magnetic - Kapha Leaders:
- **Natural Gifts**: Team building, consensus development, steady guidance, community focus
- **Optimal Roles**: Human resources, community relations, non-profit leadership, sustainable development
- **Development Needs**: Dynamic action, variety introduction, change management
- **Practice Adaptations**: Energizing practices, innovation exercises, change leadership development

Service and Ministry Applications
Constitutional Service Orientation:
Understanding constitutional patterns enables authentic service that utilizes individual gifts rather than creating conflict between spiritual values and natural capacity.

Electric - Vata Service Applications:
- **Natural Service Gifts**: Creative inspiration, innovative solutions, sensitive support in crisis
- **Optimal Service Areas**: Arts and creativity programs, innovation consulting, crisis counseling, research
- **Service Challenges**: Follow-through difficulty, overcommitment tendency, nervous system depletion
- **Support Needs**: Grounding practices, routine support, realistic commitment levels

Neutral - Pitta Service Applications:
- **Natural Service Gifts**: Achievement, systematic implementation, leadership, justice advocacy
- **Optimal Service Areas**: Project management, policy, advocacy, organizational development
- **Service Challenges**: Impatience with process, control tendencies, burnout from overwork

- **Support Needs**: Cooling practices, patience development, collaborative approaches

Magnetic - Kapha Service Applications:
- **Natural Service Gifts**: Community building, steady support, wisdom transmission, patient endurance
- **Optimal Service Areas**: Community, elder care, traditional knowledge preservation, education
- **Service Challenges**: Resistance to change, complacency, lack of innovation
- **Support Needs**: Stimulating practices, variety introduction, leadership development challenges

Advanced Constitutional Integration: Community and Global Applications
The Community Assessment: Democratic Governance Through Constitutional Wisdom
The ultimate application of constitutional understanding extends beyond individual and family development to **community constitutional assessment** that enables democratic governance approaches utilizing the full spectrum of human constitutional gifts for collective advancement.

Community Constitutional Mapping Methodology:
Assessment of Community Constitutional Diversity
Step One: Community Member Constitutional Survey
Comprehensive assessment of all community members' constitutional patterns, creating community constitutional profile that includes:
- **Constitutional distribution**: Percentage of community members with different constitutional patterns
- **Constitutional strengths**: Natural community capacities based on constitutional gifts present
- **Constitutional gaps**: Areas where community lacks sufficient constitutional representation
- **Developmental opportunities**: How community diversity can support collective advancement

Step Two: Governance Structure Constitutional Alignment
Analysis of how community decision-making and governance structures can utilize constitutional diversity:
- **Leadership roles**: Matching governance responsibilities to constitutional strengths
- **Decision-making processes**: Integrating different constitutional perspectives in community choices

- **Conflict resolution**: Utilizing constitutional understanding to prevent and resolve community disputes
- **Service organization**: Organizing community service activities to utilize constitutional gifts effectively

Step Three: Community Development Constitutional Planning
Long-term community development planning based on constitutional assessment:
- **Economic development**: Business and economic activities aligned with community strengths
- **Cultural programs**: Community cultural and educational activities supporting all constitutional types
- **Environmental stewardship**: Ecological activities utilizing diverse constitutional approaches
- **External relationships**: Community relationships with broader society based on constitutional gifts

Constitutional Conflict Resolution
Community Conflict Resolution Through Constitutional Understanding:
Most community conflicts arise from constitutional differences being perceived as personal conflicts rather than legitimate different approaches to common goals. **Constitutional conflict resolution** transforms conflicts into development opportunities.

Constitutional Conflict Resolution Process:
Step One: Constitutional Pattern Recognition
Identification of how constitutional differences contribute to apparent conflicts:
- **Different approaches**: Recognition that constitutional types have different approaches to same goals
- **Different timing**: Understanding that constitutional types operate on different natural rhythms
- **Different priorities**: Acceptance that constitutional types legitimately prioritize different values
- **Different communication**: Awareness that types express and receive information differently

Step Two: Constitutional Bridge-Building
Creation of communication and cooperation approaches that honor constitutional differences:
- **Translation process**: Helping different constitutional types understand each other's perspectives
- **Timing coordination**: Finding timing approaches that work for different constitutional patterns

- **Priority integration**: Creating community approaches that address different constitutional priorities
- **Communication adaptation**: Developing communication methods accessible to all constitutional types

Step Three: Constitutional Synthesis Solution Development
Development of community solutions that utilize constitutional diversity rather than requiring constitutional uniformity:
- **Diverse role distribution**: Community roles matching different constitutional gifts and capacities
- **Multiple pathway options**: Different approaches to community goals accommodating differences
- **Seasonal variation**: Community activities varying seasonally to support all constitutional types
- **Individual accommodation**: Flexibility for individual expression within collective commitment

Global Constitutional Assessment: Cultural Bridge-Building Applications
Constitutional Understanding as Cultural Bridge-Building Tool:
The Sacred Synthesis constitutional assessment framework provides powerful methodology for **cultural bridge-building** that honors both individual constitutional patterns and cultural constitutional expressions.

Cultural Constitutional Patterns:
Different cultures emphasize different constitutional qualities, creating **cultural constitutional expressions** that can be understood and appreciated through constitutional assessment:

Electric - Vata-Dominant Cultures:
- **Characteristics**: Emphasis on creativity, innovation, spiritual exploration, individual expression
- **Examples**: Many artistic communities, spiritual movements, innovation centers
- **Gifts**: Creative solutions, spiritual insights, adaptability, individual development
- **Challenges**: Difficulty with implementation, inconsistent systems, resource instability

Neutral - Pitta-Dominant Cultures:
- **Characteristics**: Emphasis on achievement, systematic organization, competitive excellence
- **Examples**: Many business cultures, military organizations,

competitive academic institutions
- **Gifts**: Systematic implementation, high standards, goal achievement, leadership development
- **Challenges**: Impatience with process, competitive conflict, burnout tendencies

Magnetic - Kapha-Dominant Cultures:
- **Characteristics**: Emphasis on harmony, tradition preservation, steady development, consensus
- **Examples**: Many traditional communities, consensus-based organizations, community-focused cultures
- **Gifts**: Community stability, tradition preservation, patient development, harmony maintenance
- **Challenges**: Resistance to necessary change, innovation difficulty, stagnation tendencies

Cross-Cultural Constitutional Bridge-Building:
Understanding cultural constitutional patterns enables effective cross-cultural cooperation that honors different cultural approaches while achieving common goals:

Recognition Phase:
- **Cultural constitutional assessment**: Understanding how cultures express constitutional patterns
- **Constitutional gift appreciation**: Valuable contributions different cultural constitutions offer
- **Constitutional challenge understanding**: Awareness of difficulties different cultural constitutions face
- **Constitutional complement identification**: Recognizing cultural constitutions support each other

Bridge-Building Phase:
- **Communication adaptation**: Developing communication approaches across cultural differences
- **Cooperation methodology**: Creating collaboration methods that utilize diverse cultural gifts
- **Conflict prevention**: Anticipating potential conflicts arising from cultural constitutional differences
- **Synthesis opportunity development**: Finding ways different constitutions can innovate together

Integration Phase:
- **Long-term relationship development**: Sustainable cooperation respecting cultural authenticity
- **Mutual benefit creation**: Ensuring cooperation serves all cul-

tural constitutional participants
- **Learning and development**: Ongoing cultural constitutional education and appreciation development
- **Global service contribution**: Utilizing cultural diversity for planetary healing and advancement

Constitutional Assessment Resources and Implementation Support
Complete Assessment Tools and Professional Guidance
The Sacred Synthesis constitutional assessment requires comprehensive evaluation tools and qualified guidance to ensure accuracy and effectiveness. The following resources provide complete support for individual, family, professional, and community constitutional assessment applications.

Individual Constitutional Assessment Package:

Physical Constitution Assessment:
- **Complete Health History Questionnaire**: Medical, dietary, exercise, and lifestyle pattern evaluation
- **Seasonal Sensitivity Evaluation**: Response to weather, seasonal changes, and environmental factors
- **Energy Pattern Assessment**: Daily energy rhythms, sleep patterns, and natural activity preferences
- **Professional Practitioner Consultation**: Qualified Ayurvedic or integrative medicine evaluation

Psychological Constitution Assessment:
- **Complete Enneagram Assessment**: Comprehensive personality type evaluation with qualified Enneagram teacher (see Arica School at https://www.arica.org)
- **Character Development Planning**: Individual focus areas and growth opportunity identification
- **Relationship Pattern Evaluation**: Communication preferences, conflict patterns, and community integration capacity
- **Professional Integration Assessment**: Career alignment and professional development opportunities

Energetic Constitution Assessment:
- **Chakra System Evaluation**: Energy center strength, sensitivity, and development potential assessment
- **Environmental Sensitivity Testing**: Response to electromagnetic fields, social atmospheres, and environmental factors
- **Spiritual Capacity Assessment**: Readiness for different contemplative practices and consciousness development approaches

- **Service Orientation Identification**: Natural gifts and contributions for community advancement

Family Constitutional Assessment Package:
Household Harmony Evaluation:
- **Family Member Individual Assessments**: Complete constitutional assessment for each family member
- **Constitutional Compatibility Analysis**: How different family constitutional patterns interact and support each other
- **Family Practice Integration Design**: Shared spiritual practices honoring individual differences
- **Conflict Resolution Training**: Family communication and cooperation based on understanding

Constitutional Parenting Support:
- **Child Development Constitutional Guidance**: Age-appropriate constitutional recognition and support
- **Educational Planning**: School and learning approaches aligned with child constitutional patterns
- **Activity and Interest Development**: Extracurricular and creative activities supporting development
- **Adolescent Transition Support**: Identity development and independence preparation

Partnership Constitutional Counseling:
- **Relationship Compatibility Assessment**: How partner constitutional patterns complement and challenge each other
- **Communication Training**: Partnership communication methods honoring constitutional differences
- **Shared Practice Development**: Spiritual and personal development activities supporting both partners
- **Life Planning Integration**: Career, family, and service decisions utilizing constitutional understanding

Professional Constitutional Development Package:
Career Alignment Assessment:
- **Professional Constitutional Fit Analysis**: How individual pattern aligns with career requirements
- **Leadership Development Planning**: Strengths and development areas for professional advancement
- **Workplace Integration Support**: Methods for integrating spiritual development with responsibilities
- **Service Integration Planning**: How career activities can serve both success and spiritual development

Organizational Constitutional Assessment:
- **Team Constitutional Mapping**: Assessment of team or organization constitutional diversity and optimal role distribution
- **Leadership Training**: Constitutional understanding for managers and team leaders
- **Conflict Resolution Training**: Workplace conflict resolution through constitutional understanding
- **Culture Development Planning**: Organizational culture development utilizing constitutional diversity

Community Constitutional Development Package:
Community Assessment and Planning:
- **Community Member Constitutional Survey**: Comprehensive assessment of community diversity
- **Governance Structure Development**: Democratic decision-making utilizing understanding
- **Service Organization Planning**: Community service activities utilizing diverse constitutional gifts
- **Conflict Resolution Training**: Dispute prevention and resolution through constitutional awareness

Cultural Bridge-Building Applications:
- **Cross-Cultural Constitutional Education**: Understanding how different cultures express patterns
- **International Cooperation Training**: Approaches to effective cross-cultural collaboration
- **Global Service Integration**: How constitutional gifts can serve planetary healing and advancement
- **Traditional Knowledge Integration**: Respectful integration with existing cultural wisdom

Conclusion: The Constitutional Path to Authentic Transformation

Constitutional assessment represents far more than sophisticated personality typing or alternative health evaluation. It embodies a complete **methodology for authentic transformation** that honors individual uniqueness while serving collective advancement through practical wisdom applications.

When universal spiritual principles are adapted to individual constitutional patterns, spiritual practices become naturally effective rather than requiring force or excessive effort.

Key Constitutional Assessment Principles:

Individual Authenticity Through Universal Principles:
Constitutional assessment enables authentic individual development
that serves rather than conflicts with collective advancement. When
individuals understand and honor their constitutional patterns while
applying universal spiritual principles, they develop genuine capacity
that naturally contributes to community advancement.

Family Harmony Through Constitutional Understanding:
Family life becomes genuine spiritual practice when constitutional
assessment enables understanding and support for each family
member's unique developmental needs. Constitutional family harmony creates supportive environments for individual development
while building family unity.

Professional Excellence Through Constitutional Alignment:
Career activities become authentic spiritual practice when professional roles and responsibilities align with constitutional gifts and
capacities. Constitutional career alignment serves both individual
fulfillment and professional excellence through self-knowledge applications.

Community Development Through Constitutional Diversity:
Communities become effective when governance and service activities utilize the full spectrum of constitutional gifts rather than requiring constitutional uniformity. Constitutional community development creates democratic approaches that honor individual differences while serving collective advancement.

**Cultural Bridge-Building Through Constitutional Apprecia-
tion:**
Cross-cultural cooperation becomes effective when constitutional
understanding enables appreciation for different cultural expressions
of universal human potentials. Constitutional cultural bridge-
building creates respectful integration approaches that honor cultural authenticity while enabling beneficial cooperation.

The constitutional assessment approach validates the ancient wisdom recognition that **individual uniqueness serves collective
advancement** when properly understood and skillfully applied.
This approach provides practical methodology for the contemporary challenge of honoring diversity while building unity through
authentic spiritual development serving both individual realization
and collective transformation.

THE CHRONICLES
Narrative · Discovery · Mystery

READER'S NOTE:
You have entered the **Chronicle layer** of Sacred Synthesis.
This section contains the **narrative arc** - the post-apocalyptic fiction of the Wanderer's discovery in Portland, 2100, and the reconstructed story of the Sacred Synthesis civilization (2045-2080).

What you'll find here:
- Story-driven engagement with ideas
- Character perspectives and lived experiences
- Emotional resonance and human connection
- Inspiration and vision for what's possible

Look for:
- Highlighted Wanderer commentary breaking the fourth wall
- Temporal shifts between 2045-2080 and 2100
- The mystery of what happened in the 20-year gap (2080-2100)
- Archival document fragments woven into narrative

This is the accessible entry point - let the story draw you in. The practices, protocols, and academic framework will reveal themselves through the lives of those who lived them.

The Chronicles are fiction. The truth they contain is not.
Proceed when ready.

The Underground Years: A Spark of Change

As I delved deeper into the archive, a remarkable story emerged. Beginning sometime in the 2040s, millions of people had begun quietly withdrawing from the corporate systems that dominated their world. They hadn't revolted violently or protested publicly. Instead, they had simply begun building alternatives.

They called it the Sacred Synthesis, and it was based on principles that seemed impossibly idealistic yet proved awe-inspiringly effective.

THE SACRED SYNTHESIS CHRONICLES
A Resistance Testament
Chapter 4: The Healthcare Resistance
They tried to erase my mind, but they couldn't erase my knowledge of healing.

My name is Dr. Sarah Martinez, and I am a registered nurse who spent eighteen months in the Riverside Regional Cognitive Rehabilitation Center for the crime of teaching breathing techniques to cardiac patients. What I learned during those months of "therapeutic reconditioning" fundamentally changed not only my understanding of resistance, but my comprehension of what the Sacred Synthesis system truly represents in the context of human liberation.

Before my arrest in March 2046, I had thought we were simply integrating traditional wellness practices into modern healthcare. I understood the constitutional assessment tools as methods for personalizing patient care, the breathing techniques as evidence-based stress management, the community organization principles as improved team collaboration in clinical settings.

The Sacred Synthesis isn't just a healthcare approach, it's a complete alternative to the medical-industrial control system that has reduced human beings to profit centers and control mechanisms.
My awakening began in the cognitive rehabilitation center itself.

Riverside CRRC was designed to eliminate what authorities called "non-compliant thought patterns" and restore "healthy relationship with institutional authority." The process involved a combination of pharmaceutical interventions, psychological conditioning, and what they euphemistically termed "neuroplasticity optimization." In practical terms, they were trying to destroy my capacity for independent thought, authentic relationship, and service to others.

The pharmaceutical protocol included selective serotonin reuptake inhibitors to reduce emotional responsiveness, dopamine blockers to eliminate motivation and pleasure, and a cocktail of experimental compounds designed to increase suggestibility and reduce critical thinking capacity.

The psychological conditioning used advanced behavioral modification techniques, isolation, sensory deprivation, constant surveillance, unpredictable punishment and reward schedules, and forced participation in "therapeutic community" sessions where inmates were required to confess their "thought crimes" and demonstrate submission to authority.

The neuroplasticity optimization involved repetitive exposure to propaganda, forced memorization of compliance mantras, and electrical stimulation of brain regions associated with obedience and fear.
It was sophisticated, comprehensive, and designed by experts who understood exactly how to break the human spirit while maintaining the appearance of medical treatment.

But they made a critical error: they didn't understand what the Sacred Synthesis practices had done to my nervous system, my psychological resilience, and my constitutional health.

The constitutional assessment had identified me as primarily Magnetic type (Kapha in traditional terms), steady, enduring, resistant to change, capable of maintaining strength under sustained pressure. Two years of daily Sacred Synthesis practice had optimized these natural tendencies, creating what the materials call "constitutional resilience."

More importantly, the breathing techniques, movement practices, and meditation training had literally rewired my nervous system to maintain calm and clarity under extreme stress. The 4-4-6-2 Integration Breath alone provided a physiological anchor that pharmaceutical interventions couldn't eliminate.

The community organization training had prepared me for exactly the kind of psychological pressure they were applying. I understood the techniques they were using because the Sacred Synthesis materials included detailed analysis of authoritarian control methods and specific countermeasures.

Most significantly, the healthcare integration protocols I'd been practicing had given me deep knowledge of human physiology, pharmacology, and the actual mechanisms underlying the treatments they were imposing. I knew what they were doing to my body and brain, and I knew how to resist it.

The key was appearing to comply while maintaining internal integrity.

During psychological conditioning sessions, I practiced the constitutional breathing techniques silently while expressing appropriate submission. During pharmaceutical interventions, I used knowledge from the healthcare materials to minimize absorption and accelerate elimination of mind-altering compounds. During neuroplasticity sessions, I employed meditation techniques to maintain awareness and protect core identity.
Most importantly, I began teaching other inmates.

Not openly, that would have resulted in immediate transfer to maximum security isolation. But through subtle demonstration, careful modeling, and the kind of indirect transmission the Sacred Synthesis materials describe for operating under hostile conditions.

I showed other inmates how to breathe during stressful moments. I demonstrated posture and movement techniques that could be practiced discretely. I modeled the kind of calm presence and authentic relationship that the constitutional practices develop.

Over months of careful work, I developed what became the foundation for healthcare resistance: the recognition that true healing is inherently subversive to systems based on control and profit.

Authentic healthcare empowers people to understand their own bodies, make informed decisions, and maintain health independently of institutional control. It emphasizes prevention over treatment, education over dependence, community support over individual isolation.

The medical-industrial complex requires the opposite: passive patients, complex treatments, expensive dependencies, and social fragmentation that drives people to seek healing from authorities rather than communities.

By the time I was released in September 2047, I understood that integrating Sacred Synthesis principles into healthcare wasn't just about improving patient outcomes, it was about creating the foundation for a completely different relationship between human beings and healing.

My first priority was reconnecting with our underground network and documenting what I'd learned about resistance under extreme conditions. But my second priority was developing what I came to call the "Constitutional Medicine Underground", a network of healthcare providers committed to preserving and practicing authentic healing approaches despite institutional pressure.

The timing was perfect. Alex Kim's digital camouflage project had embedded Sacred Synthesis principles into mainstream wellness programs throughout the healthcare system. Thousands of nurses, physicians, therapists, and administrators were already using constitutional assessment tools, breathing techniques, and collaborative decision-making approaches as part of official "evidence-based practice initiatives."

They just didn't know they were practicing resistance medicine.

My role became connecting these scattered practitioners, providing deeper training in Sacred Synthesis healthcare principles, and developing protocols for maintaining healing-centered practice within profit-driven medical institutions.

The constitutional approach revolutionized clinical practice in ways that seemed miraculous to providers accustomed to one-size-fits-all treatment protocols.

Electric constitution patients (Vata types) needed frequent monitoring, warm environments, consistent routines, and treatments that emphasized grounding and stability. Standard medical practice often worsened their conditions through overstimulation, cold clinical settings, irregular schedules, and interventions that increased anxiety and instability.

Magnetic constitution patients (Kapha types) required activation, movement, warming treatments, and approaches that prevented stagnation. Standard practice often made them worse through excessive rest, cooling medications, passive treatments, and interventions that increased lethargy and congestion.

Neutral constitution patients (Pitta types) needed cooling, moderation, stress reduction, and approaches that prevented inflammation and burnout. Standard practice frequently aggravated their conditions through heating treatments, excessive stimulation, competitive environments, and interventions that increased intensity and pressure.

Healthcare providers trained in constitutional assessment reported improvement in patient outcomes across virtually every condition category. Chronic diseases that had been managed with expensive long-term medication protocols often resolved completely with appropriate constitutional approaches.

Diabetes, hypertension, depression, anxiety, autoimmune conditions, digestive disorders, sleep problems, chronic pain, conditions that generated billions in profit for pharmaceutical companies, responded dramatically to constitutional medicine principles.

But the real revolution came when we began integrating the community organization and democratic governance aspects of Sacred Synthesis into healthcare team dynamics.

Medical hierarchies had created cultures of fear, competition, and burnout that compromised patient care and destroyed provider wellbeing. Doctors, nurses, technicians, and administrators operated in silos with minimal communication, excessive bureaucracy, and authoritarian management structures that prioritized compliance over healing.

Sacred Synthesis democratic principles transformed these dynamics completely.

Rotating leadership meant everyone had opportunities to guide decisions within their areas of expertise. Consensus building ensured all perspectives were heard before major changes. Conflict resolution protocols created safe spaces for addressing problems collaboratively rather than through blame and punishment.
Most importantly, the constitutional understanding helped teams optimize their collaboration by recognizing different working styles and contributions.

Electric constitution providers excelled at patient relationships, creative problem-solving, and adapting to changing situations. Magnetic constitution staff were ideal for sustained care, thorough documentation, and maintaining stability during crises. Neutral constitution personnel provided excellent analysis, efficient systems, and strategic planning.

Instead of trying to force everyone into identical roles, constitutional team building allowed each person to contribute their natural strengths while developing skills in other areas.

The results were unprecedented: dramatic reductions in staff turnover, virtually eliminated medical errors, improved patient satisfaction, decreased healthcare costs, and the kind of healing-centered culture that most providers had dreamed of but never experienced.

By 2049, what we called "Constitutional Healthcare Communities" were operating within major medical systems across the country. From outside, they appeared to be high-performing departments with excellent outcomes and efficiency metrics. From inside, they were revolutionary healing environments that prioritized human dignity, authentic relationship, and community wellbeing.

But our success attracted attention.

The Department of Cognitive Security's "Operation Synthesis Suppression" specifically targeted healthcare settings that showed "excessive collaborative behavior patterns" and "unauthorized patient empowerment indicators."

The crackdown began with "wellness compliance audits" designed to identify constitutional medicine practices. Healthcare administrators were pressured to eliminate any approaches that increased patient autonomy, reduced pharmaceutical dependence, or empowered staff to make collaborative decisions.

Some facilities complied, returning to authoritarian hierarchies and profit-maximizing treatment protocols. Others resisted, arguing that their approaches were improving both patient outcomes and financial performance. The resistance from within the medical system itself surprised authorities who expected healthcare providers to prioritize institutional loyalty over patient care.

You want us to make our patients sicker and our staff more miserable?" Dr. Rebecca Thompson, Chief Medical Officer at Sacramento General Hospital, asked during a televised hearing on healthcare compliance. "How does that serve public health or medical ethics?

The question highlighted the fundamental contradiction in authoritarian healthcare: they wanted profitable medical institutions, but they also wanted dependent, disempowered populations. Constitutional medicine made people healthier and more autonomous simultaneously.

By 2050, when Alex Kim's "Valentine's Day Liberation" released complete Sacred Synthesis materials to mainstream networks, the healthcare resistance was ready to emerge from underground.

Medical professionals worldwide already practicing constitutional principles publicly defended their approaches. Professional organizations issued statements supporting evidence-based wellness practices. Healthcare worker unions demanded protection for practitioners using collaborative and patient-centered methods.

Most significantly, patients themselves organized to defend access to constitutional medicine approaches that had transformed their health and their relationships with healthcare providers.

The "Patients' Rights to Constitutional Healthcare" movement, which emerged in spring 2050, represented something unprecedented: medical consumers demanding healing approaches that empowered them rather than creating dependency.

As I write this chapter in late 2050, constitutional medicine is no longer underground but not yet fully recognized by medical authorities. We exist in a liminal space where our approaches are simultaneously praised for their effectiveness and criticized for their political implications.

But we have proven something crucial: healing and liberation are inseparable. You cannot have authentic healthcare in oppressive systems, and you cannot build liberatory communities without addressing the deep wounds that authoritarianism inflicts on human bodies and spirits.

The Sacred Synthesis healthcare resistance has shown that constitutional medicine principles work not just for individual healing, but for transforming the entire culture of healthcare from profit extraction to authentic service.

My eighteen months in cognitive rehabilitation taught me that the human capacity for healing transcends any effort to control or condition it. The constitutional practices create resilience that authorities cannot break because it emerges from our deepest nature rather than external conditioning.

When we align healthcare with constitutional principles, we create conditions not just for physical healing, but for the kind of psychological, social, and spiritual wellbeing that makes authoritarian control impossible.

The healing revolution is inseparable from the liberation revolution. Both emerge when we recognize that human beings are designed for cooperation, wisdom, and authentic relationship rather than competition, ignorance, and domination.

The next chapter will be written by practitioners from the international network, documenting how Sacred Synthesis principles have been adapted and applied across different cultures and political systems worldwide. But I want to end with a reflection on what I learned about resistance during my time in cognitive rehabilitation:

They can drug your body, condition your mind, and isolate your spirit, but they cannot change your constitutional nature or eliminate your capacity for authentic relationship. The Sacred Synthesis practices work because they align us with who we actually are rather than who oppressive systems try to make us become.
In healthcare, as in all forms of resistance, our power lies not in fighting against what we oppose, but in embodying what we support. When we practice healing that honors human dignity, authentic relationship, and community wellbeing, we make oppressive medical systems irrelevant.

The healing continues. The resistance endures. The synthesis spreads.

Dr. Sarah Martinez now directs the Constitutional Healthcare Institute, which trains medical professionals worldwide in Sacred Synthesis healing principles. She has never returned to the cognitive rehabilitation system, though she remains under periodic surveillance. Her work has contributed to dramatic improvements in patient outcomes and healthcare provider satisfaction in medical systems across six continents.

For healthcare providers seeking to integrate constitutional medicine into their practice, remember: true healing is always collaborative, always empowering, and always respectful of individual differences. When we practice medicine that serves human flourishing rather than institutional profit, we participate in the greatest revolution of our time.

Chapter 5: International Connections
Revolution, we discovered, speaks every language.

We are the Global Sacred Synthesis Coordination Council, twelve practitioners from six continents who survived the 2046 worldwide crackdowns and rebuilt the international network from fragments. This chapter documents how the Sacred Synthesis system adapted to different cultures, political systems, and resistance movements worldwide, proving that the hunger for authentic community and genuine liberation transcends all boundaries.

When Operation Mindful Compliance reached India in March 2046, our network had been operating for nearly three years through Ayurvedic clinics and traditional wellness centers. The authorities raided forty-seven facilities simultaneously, arresting 127 practitioners under the Public Health Safety Act for "promoting unregulated traditional medicine."

But they misunderstood both Indian culture and the Sacred Synthesis system.

In India, constitutional typing wasn't foreign knowledge, it was the foundation of Ayurveda, practiced for over 5,000 years. When authorities tried to ban "dangerous constitutional assessment activities," they were attempting to ban traditional medicine that predated their government by millennia.

The resistance came not from underground revolutionaries, but from traditional healers, village elders, and families who had used constitutional principles for generations. The Sacred Synthesis materials had simply provided modern validation and systematic application of knowledge their grandmothers had always known.

You cannot ban what flows in our blood," Dr. Sunita Sharma told the Delhi High Court during the constitutional medicine hearings. "These practices kept us healthy when your hospitals didn't exist and will keep us healthy when they are gone.

Our adaptation focused on cultural bridge-building between traditional Ayurveda and the Sacred Synthesis innovations. Village practitioners learned democratic governance principles that enhanced traditional panchayat (village council) decision-making. Healthcare workers integrated modern physiological understanding with constitutional typing they already knew.

Most importantly, we connected urban professionals experiencing corporate burnout with rural communities who had maintained traditional wisdom. Software engineers from Bangalore learned breathing techniques from farmers in Kerala. Mumbai financial workers practiced movement sequences with yoga teachers in Rishikesh.

By 2050, what we called "Digital Villages", online communities linking traditional wisdom keepers with urban practitioners, had grown to over 200,000 participants across South Asia. The government couldn't suppress traditional medicine without alienating their entire rural base, and they couldn't ban technology platforms without damaging their digital economy.

The African networks faced different challenges. Colonial authorities had spent centuries suppressing traditional healing and community organization practices. When they attempted to ban Sacred Synthesis activities in 2046, many people recognized it as another wave of cultural oppression.

Our response drew directly from generations of resistance experience. We went deeper underground, but also deeper into traditional communities that had preserved indigenous knowledge despite centuries of suppression. The constitutional typing system resonated powerfully with traditional African medicine, which had always recognized fundamental differences in individual nature and appropriate healing approaches. The democratic governance principles aligned with traditional consensus-building practices that existed long before colonial-imposed hierarchies.

Most importantly, the Sacred Synthesis emphasis on community wellbeing over individual advancement matched African ubuntu philosophy, the understanding that individual flourishing depends on collective thriving.

Our adaptation created what we called "Ubuntu Networks", cells of 15-25 people practicing Sacred Synthesis principles while embedded in extended family and traditional community structures. These networks provided economic mutual aid, educational support, healthcare advocacy, and conflict resolution services.

By 2049, Ubuntu Networks were operating in over 400 communities across West and East Africa. They appeared to be traditional mutual aid societies, but they were actually sophisticated resistance organizations using Sacred Synthesis principles to rebuild African communities from within.

In Latin America, the Sacred Synthesis merged with existing liberation theology and social movement traditions to create powerful community organizing approaches. When authorities cracked down in 2046, our networks were protected by decades of experience with authoritarian oppression and popular resistance.

Our adaptation emphasized the Sacred Synthesis community organization principles that aligned with base ecclesial communities, worker cooperatives, and indigenous resistance movements. Constitutional assessment helped social movement organizations optimize their internal dynamics and reduce the conflicts that had traditionally weakened grassroots efforts.

The breathing and movement practices provided tools for maintaining resilience during prolonged struggle. The healthcare integration principles supported community clinics and popular education programs that served favelas and rural communities.

Most significantly, the democratic governance approaches helped resolve tensions between different liberation movements, indigenous rights groups, labor unions, environmental organizations, feminist collectives, that had often worked in isolation or competition.

By 2050, what we called "Liberation Synthesis Networks" were coordinating between over 800 popular organizations across Latin America. Externally, they appeared to be traditional social movements. Internally, they were applying Sacred Synthesis principles to build the most effective resistance coordination the region had ever seen.

The Japanese experience demonstrated how Sacred Synthesis principles could transform corporate culture from within. When global crackdowns began in 2046, our network was embedded in major corporations as "productivity enhancement" and "employee wellness" programs.

Japanese culture already emphasized group harmony, consensus building, and respect for individual differences within collective frameworks. The Sacred Synthesis democratic governance principles enhanced these cultural strengths while addressing their authoritarian distortions.

Constitutional assessment helped Japanese companies recognize that forcing all employees into identical working styles was inefficient and destructive. Teams organized around constitutional diversity showed dramatically improved performance and reduced the burn-out epidemic plaguing Japanese workers.

The breathing and movement practices addressed health crises created by overwork culture. Healthcare integration principles reduced corporate medical costs while improving employee wellbeing.

Most importantly, the community organization approaches helped Japanese workers rediscover authentic relationships and collective decision-making that had been suppressed by hierarchical corporate structures.

By 2050, over 2,000 Japanese corporations were using Sacred Synthesis principles as official management methodology. The government couldn't ban practices that were improving economic productivity and reducing healthcare costs.

In Scandinavia, Sacred Synthesis principles resonated with existing social democratic values and cooperative traditions. Our challenge wasn't authoritarian suppression, but bureaucratic co-optation that threatened to reduce revolutionary knowledge to government-administered social programs.

Our adaptation focused on preserving the transformative power of Sacred Synthesis practices while engaging constructively with progressive political institutions. We developed what we called "Democratic Innovation Labs", participatory research projects that tested Sacred Synthesis approaches to governance, healthcare, education, and economic organization.

Constitutional assessment improved social service delivery by recognizing individual differences in needs and capacities. Democratic governance principles enhanced citizen participation in local and regional decision- making. Healthcare integration reduced costs while improving outcomes in nationalized medical systems.
Most importantly, the community organization approaches helped rebuild social solidarity that had been eroded by decades of neoliberal individualism, even within social democratic frameworks.

By 2050, Sacred Synthesis approaches were being tested and implemented by municipal governments, cooperative enterprises, and civil society organizations throughout Northern Europe. The transformation was gradual and institutional, but it was still transformation.

The North American networks focused on educational transformation as the foundation for long-term cultural change. When crackdowns began in 2046, our most important work was protecting Sacred Synthesis principles in schools and universities where they were being integrated into educational methodology.

Our adaptation emphasized what we called "Democratic Learning Communities", educational environments that used constitutional assessment to personalize learning, democratic governance to involve students in school decision-making, and community organization principles to connect schools with broader social transformation. Students practicing Sacred Synthesis approaches showed improved academic performance, reduced behavioral problems, enhanced emotional intelligence, and greater civic engagement. Teachers reported higher job satisfaction, improved classroom dynamics, and renewed sense of purpose.

Most importantly, graduates of Democratic Learning Communities demonstrated the collaborative leadership skills, critical thinking capacity, and community commitment necessary for cultural transformation.

By 2050, over 500 schools and 50 universities in North America were using Sacred Synthesis educational approaches. They appeared to be innovative pedagogy, but they were actually preparing the next generation for post-authoritarian society.

By 2051, five years after the worldwide crackdowns, the international Sacred Synthesis network had not only survived but grown beyond anything we could have imagined during the underground years.

The key to our success was recognizing that the Sacred Synthesis system wasn't Western knowledge being exported globally, but universal principles of human cooperation and liberation that could be expressed through any cultural tradition.

In India, it merged with Ayurveda and traditional village governance. In Africa, it enhanced ubuntu philosophy and community solidarity. In Latin America, it strengthened liberation movements and popular education. In Japan, it improved corporate efficiency while humanizing work culture. In Scandinavia, it deepened democracy and social cooperation. In North America, it transformed education and community development.

Each cultural adaptation made the system stronger and more complete. Indian constitutional medicine refined our understanding of individual differences. African ubuntu networks improved our community organization approaches. Latin American liberation theology deepened our commitment to justice. Japanese group harmony enhanced our collaborative decision-making. Scandinavian democratic innovation strengthened our governance principles. North American educational methods improved our knowledge transmission.

By 2051, what had begun as fragments of knowledge discovered by Marcus Chen in corporate surveillance systems had become a global movement involving over two million people across fifty-seven countries, working within indigenous communities, traditional institutions, progressive organizations, and revolutionary movements worldwide.

The diversity was our strength. Authorities could suppress specific organizations or arrest particular leaders, but they couldn't eliminate knowledge that had been adapted to every culture and embedded in every type of institution.

More importantly, the global connections provided mutual support, shared learning, and coordinated resistance that made local suppression less effective. When practitioners were arrested in one country, international networks provided legal support, media attention, and sanctuary. When innovations developed in one region, they were shared and adapted globally.

The international Sacred Synthesis network proved that human beings everywhere hunger for the same fundamental experiences: authentic community, meaningful work, effective healthcare, democratic participation, and opportunities to serve something greater than individual advancement.

The next chapter will be written by practitioners from the second generation, people who learned Sacred Synthesis principles as children and came of age during the underground years. Their perspective will illuminate how resistance knowledge passes between generations and creates lasting cultural transformation. But we want to end this chapter with recognition of what the global experience taught us:

Liberation is not an American idea, a European concept, or an Asian philosophy. It is a human birthright that expresses itself through every culture and tradition when people are free to explore their deepest nature and highest potential.

The Sacred Synthesis system works globally because it aligns with what human beings actually are: constitutional diverse, community-oriented, democratically capable, naturally healing, and fundamentally cooperative beings who thrive when we can contribute our unique gifts to collective wellbeing.

When we practice authentic community across all boundaries, cultural, national, religious, economic, political, we discover that the differences that seem to divide us are actually complementary strengths that make us more resilient and creative together than any of us could be alone.

The revolution is global. The synthesis is universal.
The liberation is for everyone.

The Global Sacred Synthesis Coordination Council continues to facilitate international cooperation and knowledge sharing between Sacred Synthesis practitioners worldwide. By 2051, the network includes active communities in 57 countries and maintains secure communication systems that function independently of government or corporate control.

For those seeking international Sacred Synthesis connections, remember: the principles are universal, but the expressions are culturally specific. Seek practitioners who honor local traditions while fostering global cooperation. The network exists wherever people gather to practice authentic community, democratic governance, and mutual liberation.

Chapter 6: Community Resilience

We learned that you cannot destroy what lives in people's hearts.

We are the Democratic Leadership Council of New Harmony Community, the first fully autonomous Sacred Synthesis settlement in North America. This chapter documents how we built a complete alternative society based on constitutional principles, democratic governance, and mutual liberation, proving that the Sacred Synthesis system could create not just resistance to oppression, but thriving communities that made oppression irrelevant.

New Harmony began in 2048 as an "intentional sustainable living experiment" in rural Vermont. Officially, we were thirty-seven families who had pooled resources to purchase 847 acres of farmland for "off-grid lifestyle research." Unofficially, we were Sacred Synthesis practitioners who had decided to stop fighting the system and start building alternatives.

The land purchase had been coordinated through Elena Rodriguez's underground network, using resources from practitioners who wanted to support community development but couldn't leave urban areas themselves. Legal structures were designed by sympathetic lawyers who understood how to create maximum autonomy within existing regulatory frameworks.

But our real protection was remoteness and apparent harmlessness. To outside observers, we looked like another eco-village or intentional community, Vermont had dozens of similar projects that posed no threat to anyone. Our sustainable agriculture, renewable energy systems, and natural building techniques attracted positive attention from environmental groups and progressive political organizations.

What they didn't realize was that we were testing whether Sacred Synthesis principles could create a complete alternative to corporate-dominated society.

The technical challenges were enormous. We needed to create water, energy, waste management, communication, and transportation systems that could function independently of corporate utilities while meeting the needs of nearly 200 people across 37 families.

But the Sacred Synthesis materials included detailed guidance on infrastructure development based on constitutional principles. Instead of standardized systems designed for maximum efficiency, we created diverse approaches optimized for different needs and preferences.

Electric constitution families preferred smaller, more flexible living spaces with easily adjustable climate control, varied lighting options, and quick access to community areas. Their infrastructure needed to support frequent changes and high sensitivity to environmental conditions.

Magnetic constitution households wanted larger, more stable structures with consistent temperatures, reliable systems, and spaces designed for extended family gatherings. Their infrastructure emphasized durability, comfort, and long-term sustainability.

Neutral constitution residences required precisely controlled environments with efficient systems, moderate sizing, and integration between private and community spaces. Their infrastructure balanced individual privacy with collective optimization.

Instead of forcing everyone into identical housing, we created architectural diversity that honored constitutional differences while maintaining community cohesion.

The same approach guided our economic systems. Rather than requiring everyone to contribute equally to identical work, we organized production around constitutional strengths.

Electric constitution members excelled at creative projects, relationship building, and adapting to changing needs. They managed our artistic endeavors, conflict resolution services, and external communications.

Magnetic constitution families specialized in sustained agricultural work, infrastructure maintenance, and providing stability during challenges. They anchored our food production, construction projects, and crisis response systems.

Neutral constitution individuals handled planning, analysis, and coordination between different community functions. They managed our finances, legal compliance, and strategic development.

By 2050, New Harmony had achieved complete food self-sufficiency, energy independence, and waste neutrality while providing higher quality of life than most suburban communities.

Our healthcare system became a model that attracted attention from medical professionals worldwide. Instead of requiring community members to travel to distant hospitals for routine care, we created what we called "Constitutional Health Commons", comprehensive wellness support based on individual constitutional needs and community mutual aid.

The system included traditional medical services provided by licensed practitioners who lived in community, but emphasized prevention, health education, and constitutional optimization approaches that addressed root causes rather than managing symptoms.

Electric constitution health support focused on nervous system regulation, emotional balance, and social connection. These community members received regular massage, counseling services, creative arts engagement, and carefully managed stimulation levels.

Magnetic constitution wellness emphasized circulation, activation, and metabolic support. These families participated in active work projects, warming therapies, community celebrations, and energizing group activities.

Neutral constitution health centered on cooling practices, stress reduction, and balanced lifestyle approaches. These individuals received meditation support, temperature regulation assistance, moderate exercise programs, and conflict-free social environments.

Most importantly, we integrated healthcare with community governance, economic participation, and social relationships. Health wasn't something you purchased from professionals, but something the entire community supported through constitutional awareness and mutual care.

By 2050, New Harmony residents showed health outcomes that exceeded national averages in every category: lower chronic disease rates, reduced mental health problems, decreased healthcare costs, and longer life expectancy.

Our educational approach proved that children could learn more effectively when teaching honored constitutional differences and emphasized collaborative rather than competitive development.

New Harmony School served 47 children from ages 4-18, using Sacred Synthesis democratic learning principles that allowed each child to discover their unique gifts while contributing to collective knowledge.

Electric constitution children excelled in creative subjects, collaborative projects, and learning that involved movement and social interaction. Their education emphasized artistic expression, storytelling, relationship skills, and adaptable problem-solving.

Magnetic constitution young people thrived with hands-on learning, sustained projects, and practical skill development. Their education focused on agricultural science, construction arts, community service, and traditional craft mastery.

Neutral constitution students preferred analytical subjects, independent research, and precise technical learning. Their education emphasized mathematics, scientific inquiry, historical analysis, and systematic knowledge development.

But all children learned all subjects, the constitutional adaptation affected teaching methods rather than curriculum content. Everyone studied mathematics, science, literature, history, arts, practical skills, and community leadership, but through approaches that matched their individual learning styles.

Most importantly, children participated in community governance through age-appropriate democratic processes. They made real decisions about school policies, community projects, and resource allocation, learning democracy through practice rather than theory.

By age sixteen, New Harmony children demonstrated academic achievement that exceeded state standards, but also showed collaborative leadership, conflict resolution skills, and community commitment that was unprecedented in conventional education.

Our democratic governance system became the most successful aspect of New Harmony's alternative society experiment. Instead of representative democracy that concentrated power in elected officials, we practiced direct participatory democracy that involved every community member in decision-making.

The Community Assembly met weekly to discuss issues affecting everyone. Decisions were made through consensus processes that honored all voices while maintaining efficiency. Conflicts were resolved through restorative justice approaches that strengthened community bonds rather than punishing individuals.

Leadership rotated among constitutional types, ensuring all perspectives were represented in community coordination. Electric constitution leaders provided vision, inspiration, and relationship building. Magnetic constitution coordinators offered stability, practical implementation, and long-term sustainability. Neutral constitution facilitators contributed analysis, strategic planning, and systematic organization.

Working circles managed specific community functions, infrastructure, health, education, economics, external relations, using collaborative decision-making that optimized both individual contributions and collective effectiveness.

Most importantly, we developed conflict resolution approaches based on constitutional understanding that addressed the root causes of disagreement rather than imposing solutions through authority or majority rule. By 2050, New Harmony had achieved something political scientists claimed was impossible: direct democracy that was both efficient and inclusive, involving nearly 200 people in collective decision-making while maintaining community harmony and effective action.

Our biggest challenge was managing relationships with outside authorities who viewed any successful alternative community as a potential threat to existing power structures.

The key was demonstrating that our success enhanced rather than threatened regional stability. New Harmony created jobs for local contractors, purchased supplies from area businesses, provided services for neighboring communities, and contributed positively to regional economic development.

We hosted educational tours for government officials, academic researchers, and community development organizations who wanted to understand how our approaches might be adapted elsewhere. These visits showed that our "radical experiment" was actually producing outcomes that everyone claimed to want: economic sustainability, environmental protection, social cooperation, and individual fulfillment.

More importantly, we developed relationships with other intentional communities, progressive organizations, and traditional institutions that were interested in Sacred Synthesis principles without necessarily wanting to live in alternative communities themselves.

By 2050, New Harmony had become a research and training site for sustainable community development, democratic governance innovation, constitutional healthcare approaches, and alternative economic models. We hosted over 1,000 visitors annually and provided consultation for similar projects across North America.

By 2051, New Harmony had demonstrated that Sacred Synthesis principles could create complete alternative communities that were not just sustainable, but thriving in ways that exceeded conventional society by every measure of wellbeing.

Our success attracted both positive attention and increased scrutiny. Progressive organizations studied our approaches for potential broader application. Government agencies monitored us for signs of "anti-social behavior" or "cult-like activities." Corporate interests worried that our success might inspire broader rejection of consumer culture.

But our most important achievement was proving that alternatives to corporate-dominated society were not just theoretically possible, but practically superior for human flourishing.

New Harmony residents showed higher levels of life satisfaction, better health outcomes, stronger social relationships, more meaningful work, and greater sense of purpose than comparable populations in conventional communities. Our children were better educated, more emotionally mature, and more prepared for productive citizenship. Our economic systems were more efficient, more equitable, and more sustainable than corporate alternatives.

Most importantly, we had created authentic security, not the false security of wealth, weapons, or walls, but the genuine security that comes from knowing your community will support you, your contributions matter, and your wellbeing is connected to everyone else's flourishing.

By 2051, seventeen similar communities had been established across North America, with dozens more in planning stages. Each adapted Sacred Synthesis principles to local conditions, cultural contexts, and specific populations, but all demonstrated the same fundamental truth: human beings thrive in communities based on constitutional diversity, democratic participation, and mutual liberation.

The next chapter will be written by people who survived the legal challenges, imprisonment, and persecution that authorities used to try to stop the Sacred Synthesis movement. Their perspective will document both the costs of resistance and the resilience that made victory possible.

But we want to end this chapter with reflection on what building alternative communities taught us about revolution:

The most powerful form of resistance is not fighting against what you oppose, but building what you support so well that opposition becomes irrelevant. When communities demonstrate that cooperation works better than competition, that diversity strengthens rather than threatens unity, that democracy serves people better than authoritarianism serves power, they create pressure for transformation that no amount of force can suppress.

New Harmony and communities like it are proof that the Sacred Synthesis system offers not just personal development or spiritual growth, but practical tools for creating the world we want to live in.

Revolution is not just changing who has power, it is creating communities where power serves life rather than dominating it.

The community endures. The alternatives multiply. The synthesis manifests.

New Harmony Community continues to operate as an autonomous Sacred Synthesis settlement and has inspired the development of over 50 similar communities worldwide. The Democratic Leadership Council rotates quarterly and maintains correspondence with intentional communities, government agencies, and academic institutions interested in sustainable community development.

For those interested in Sacred Synthesis community development, remember: successful alternatives require both vision and practical skills, both individual development and collective commitment, both internal harmony and external relationships. Start where you are but start building the world you want to see.

The Great Achievement: Evolution in Medicine

In what appeared to be a comprehensive medical training manual, I found detailed protocols for integrating constitutional understanding with clinical practice. These materials suggested that constitutional medicine had been successfully implemented across 89 medical centers with remarkable results.

Healthcare Integration and Therapeutic Applications
The Revolutionary Healthcare Integration: Medicine as Sacred Service

Beyond the Medical Model: Healing the Whole Person

Contemporary healthcare faces an unprecedented crisis: technological advancement has achieved remarkable capability in treating disease while often failing to address the deeper dimensions of human health and healing. Traditional medical models focus on symptom suppression and disease management rather than supporting the body's natural healing capacity and addressing root causes of illness. The Sacred Synthesis approach, emerging from decades of clinical validation and documented in La Iniciación magazine's wartime synthesis, demonstrates that authentic healing integrates physical, emotional, mental, and spiritual dimensions while maintaining the highest standards of medical safety and effectiveness.

Healthcare Sacred Integration represents one of the most significant breakthroughs in contemporary medicine: the recognition that spiritual development and medical treatment enhance rather than conflict with each other when properly understood and skillfully applied. The clinical applications emerging from the GIDEE achievement during 1942-1947 prove that traditional healing wisdom improves rather than compromises medical outcomes across all major healthcare specialties.

The Sacred Healthcare Model transcends both materialistic medicine and ungrounded spirituality through systematic application of constitutional understanding, traditional therapeutic principles, and service-oriented healing relationships. When healthcare providers understand patient constitutional differences, apply traditional wisdom to treatment decisions, and orient their practice toward sacred service, they naturally achieve both superior clinical outcomes and profound professional fulfillment while contributing to positive transformation of healthcare culture.

Constitutional Healthcare: Personalized Medicine Through Traditional Wisdom
Understanding Individual Constitutional Types in Healthcare
Sacred Synthesis healthcare recognizes that different constitutional types require different approaches to diagnosis, treatment, and healing support while maintaining universal principles of medical safety and clinical effectiveness.

Electric Constitution Healthcare Applications:
Natural Healthcare Strengths:
- **Patient Empathy and Sensitivity**: Exceptional capacity for understanding patient emotional needs and creating healing environments that support recovery
- **Holistic Assessment Skills**: Natural ability to recognize connections between physical symptoms and emotional, mental, or spiritual factors affecting health
- **Gentle Treatment Approaches**: Preference for non-invasive therapies and gradual healing processes that work with the body's natural recovery capacity
- **Cultural Healthcare Competency**: Understanding of diverse healing traditions and ability to integrate appropriate traditional approaches with medical treatment

Healthcare Professional Applications:
- **Primary Care Medicine**: Patient-centered healthcare with emphasis on prevention, lifestyle medicine, and comprehensive wellness support
- **Nursing Specializations**: Patient advocacy, comfort care, psychiatric nursing, pediatric care, and hospice nursing with emphasis on emotional support
- **Mental Health Services**: Counseling, social work, and psychiatric care emphasizing relationship healing and trauma recovery
- **Integrative Medicine**: Combination of conventional medical treatment with traditional healing approaches and mind-body therapies

Constitutional Healthcare Needs:
- **Supportive Work Environments**: Healthcare settings that minimize harsh lighting, excessive noise, and emotional overwhelm while maintaining clinical efficiency
- **Adequate Processing Time**: Patient care schedules that allow sufficient time for thorough assessment and emotional support without rushing
- **Collaborative Healthcare Teams**: Work relationships that provide mutual professional support during challenging cases and difficult patient situations
- **Continuing Professional Education**: Training in holistic approaches, cultural competency, and traditional healing integration with conventional medicine

Magnetic Constitution Healthcare Applications:
Natural Healthcare Strengths:
- **Emergency Response Excellence**: Exceptional capacity for maintaining effectiveness during medical emergencies and high-pressure clinical situations
- **Healthcare Team Leadership**: Natural ability to coordinate medical teams, organize patient care, and motivate collaborative healthcare delivery
- **Practical Treatment Implementation**: Strength in translating treatment plans into measurable health improvements and concrete therapeutic outcomes
- **Patient Motivation and Compliance**: Capacity to inspire patient adherence to treatment recommendations and lifestyle changes supporting recovery

Healthcare Professional Applications:
- **Emergency Medicine**: Emergency department medicine, trauma care, critical care nursing, and disaster response coordi-

nation
- **Surgical Specialties**: Operating room coordination, surgical team leadership, and post-operative care management with emphasis on efficient treatment delivery
- **Rehabilitation Medicine**: Physical therapy, occupational therapy, and sports medicine with focus on measurable functional improvement
- **Healthcare Administration**: Hospital management, healthcare system coordination, and quality improvement with emphasis on operational effectiveness

Constitutional Healthcare Needs:
- **Challenging Clinical Cases**: Healthcare assignments that provide sufficient complexity and variety to maintain professional engagement and growth
- **Leadership Opportunities**: Roles that enable healthcare team coordination and system improvement through practical innovation and efficiency enhancement
- **Measurable Patient Outcomes**: Healthcare positions that provide clear evidence of patient improvement and professional impact on health outcomes
- **Physical Activity Integration**: Work environments that allow movement and hands-on patient care alongside intellectual and administrative responsibilities

Neutral Constitution Healthcare Applications:
Natural Healthcare Strengths:
- **Diagnostic Excellence**: Superior analytical abilities for systematic evaluation of complex medical conditions and differential diagnosis
- **Medical Research and Development**: Capacity for clinical research, evidence-based medicine advancement, and healthcare outcome analysis
- **Quality Assurance and Safety**: Attention to accuracy, systematic protocols, and risk management ensuring patient safety and treatment effectiveness
- **Medical Education and Training**: Teaching abilities that develop healthcare professional competency and advance medical knowledge

Healthcare Professional Applications:
- **Medical Specialties**: Internal medicine, neurology, pathology, radiology, and other diagnostically complex medical specializations
- **Clinical Research**: Medical research, pharmaceutical develop-

ment, epidemiology, and public health research advancing healthcare knowledge
- **Medical Education**: Medical school instruction, residency training, and continuing medical education supporting professional development
- **Healthcare Quality and Policy**: Quality improvement, patient safety coordination, healthcare informatics, and medical ethics consultation

Constitutional Healthcare Needs:
- **Intellectual Medical Challenge**: Healthcare roles that provide complex problem-solving requirements and analytical thinking opportunities
- **Systematic Healthcare Approaches**: Work environments that value precision, evidence-based practice, and systematic methodology in patient care
- **Professional Work-Life Balance**: Healthcare positions that maintain sustainable schedules preventing professional burnout while enabling quality patient care
- **Continuing Medical Education**: Specialization advancement and professional development opportunities supporting career growth and expertise development

Integrated Healthcare Team Development
Traditional healthcare often creates artificial hierarchies that prevent optimal team collaboration and limit patient care effectiveness. Sacred Synthesis healthcare creates team structures that honor constitutional diversity while ensuring clinical excellence and patient safety.

Constitutional Healthcare Team Integration: Team Composition and Role Assignment:
- **Electric Healthcare Professionals**: Patient advocacy, emotional support, cultural liaison, and holistic assessment roles that utilize their sensitivity and empathy
- **Magnetic Healthcare Professionals**: Team coordination, emergency response, practical implementation, and patient motivation roles that utilize their leadership and energy
- **Neutral Healthcare Professionals**: Diagnostic analysis, quality assurance, research and documentation, and systematic protocol development utilizing their analytical abilities

Interprofessional Collaboration Protocols:
- **Democratic Healthcare Decision-Making**: Clinical decisions that integrate input from all constitutional types while maintain-

ing appropriate medical authority and professional responsibility
- **Patient-Centered Team Conferences**: Healthcare planning meetings that consider constitutional diversity of both providers and patients in treatment approach development
- **Conflict Resolution and Communication**: Healthcare team protocols that address professional disagreements through constitutional understanding and collaborative problem-solving
- **Continuing Team Development**: Professional development programs that strengthen team collaboration while advancing individual clinical competency and career advancement

Healthcare Team Success Example:
The Metropolitan Medical Center Emergency Department implemented constitutional team development with remarkable results. The program organized healthcare teams to include Electric constitution nurses for patient emotional support, Magnetic constitution providers for emergency coordination, and Neutral constitution physicians for diagnostic assessment.
Patient Constitutional Assessment and Individualized Care
Clinical Constitutional Assessment Integration:

Assessment Protocol Development:
- **Medical History Integration**: Constitutional factors considered alongside conventional medical history and physical examination
- **Treatment Response Patterns**: Recognition that constitutional types respond differently to medications, procedures, and therapeutic interventions
- **Lifestyle and Environmental Factors**: Assessment of how constitutional needs affect healing capacity and treatment compliance
- **Cultural and Spiritual Considerations**: Integration of patient cultural background and spiritual practices with constitutional understanding

Individualized Treatment Planning:
- **Constitutional Medication Approaches**: Prescribing considerations that account for constitutional differences in drug metabolism and side effect patterns
- **Therapeutic Modality Selection**: Treatment approaches that match constitutional preferences while maintaining clinical effectiveness and safety standards
- **Lifestyle Medicine Integration**: Nutrition, exercise, and stress management recommendations based on constitutional type and individual health needs

- **Healthcare Communication Adaptation**: Provider-patient communication styles adapted to constitutional differences while maintaining informed consent and professional boundaries

Patient Constitutional Care Success Story:
The University Hospital Internal Medicine Department developed constitutional patient care protocols with significant clinical improvements. The program trained physicians to recognize constitutional types and adapt treatment approaches accordingly. Electric patients received more gradual medication adjustments and increased emotional support; Magnetic patients received structured treatment plans with clear goals and
timelines; Neutral patients received detailed information about treatment rationale and systematic monitoring approaches.

Traditional Medicine Integration and Complementary Healing
Respectful Integration of Traditional Healing Systems
Sacred Synthesis healthcare recognizes that many traditional healing systems offer valuable contributions to patient care when integrated appropriately with conventional medicine and with proper cultural authorization and practitioner qualification.

Traditional Medicine Integration Principles:
Cultural Respect and Authorization:
- **Traditional Community Partnership**: Healthcare integration approaches developed in partnership with traditional knowledge communities and authorized traditional healers
- **Cultural Protocol Compliance**: Integration approaches that respect traditional cultural boundaries and sacred aspects of traditional healing knowledge
- **Practitioner Qualification Requirements**: Traditional healing practitioners must demonstrate appropriate training, cultural authorization, and competency in their traditional system
- **Benefit Sharing and Reciprocity**: Integration programs that provide appropriate benefit and recognition to traditional knowledge communities and practitioners

Clinical Safety and Effectiveness:
- **Evidence-Based Integration**: Traditional approaches integrated only when supported by clinical research evidence or extensive traditional documentation
- **Safety Protocol Development**: Comprehensive assessment of potential interactions between traditional and conventional treatments with appropriate monitoring

- **Professional Boundary Maintenance**: Clear distinctions between traditional healing and medical treatment with appropriate referral protocols and scope of practice guidelines
- **Quality Assurance Standards**: Traditional practitioners meeting appropriate professional standards and maintaining accountability for patient outcomes

Constitutional Traditional Medicine Applications:
Electric Constitution Traditional Healing Integration:
- **Gentle Traditional Therapies**: Acupuncture, herbal medicine, massage therapy, and energy healing approaches that work gradually and gently with body systems
- **Mind-Body Traditional Approaches**: Traditional meditation, prayer, and spiritual healing practices integrated with conventional medical treatment for emotional and spiritual support
- **Traditional Nutrition and Lifestyle**: Traditional dietary approaches, seasonal living patterns, and natural lifestyle modifications supporting constitutional health
- **Cultural Healing Practices**: Integration of appropriate cultural healing traditions for patients from diverse backgrounds with traditional practitioner authorization

Magnetic Constitution Traditional Healing Integration:
- **Active Traditional Therapies**: Traditional physical therapies, martial arts-based healing, vigorous herbal treatments, and hands-on healing approaches
- **Goal-Oriented Traditional Programs**: Traditional healing programs with clear objectives, measurable outcomes, and structured progression toward health improvement
- **Traditional Exercise and Movement**: Traditional physical practices including yoga, tai chi, martial arts, and dance-based healing integrated with conventional rehabilitation
- **Community Traditional Healing**: Group-based traditional healing activities that provide social support and community engagement alongside individual treatment

Neutral Constitution Traditional Healing Integration:
- **Systematic Traditional Approaches**: Traditional healing systems with clear methodology, documented effectiveness, and systematic approaches to diagnosis and treatment
- **Traditional Knowledge Study**: Integration approaches that include patient education about traditional healing principles and rationale alongside practical application
- **Research-Supported Traditional Methods**: Traditional approaches with scientific validation or extensive historical docu-

258

mentation of safety and effectiveness
- **Traditional Diagnostic Systems**: Integration of traditional diagnostic approaches including pulse diagnosis, constitutional assessment, and traditional examination methods with conventional medical evaluation

Integrative Healthcare Clinic Development
Comprehensive Integrative Healthcare Models:
Clinic Structure and Organization:
- **Multidisciplinary Healthcare Teams**: Medical professionals, traditional healers, and complementary practitioners working collaboratively with clear roles and communication protocols
- **Patient-Centered Care Coordination**: Healthcare delivery organized around patient needs and preferences rather than provider convenience or institutional efficiency
- **Cultural Competency Infrastructure**: Clinic design, staff training, and service delivery approaches that serve diverse cultural communities with appropriate traditional healing integration
- **Quality Measurement and Improvement**: Healthcare outcome monitoring that includes both conventional medical measures and traditional healing effectiveness indicators

Clinical Service Integration:

Integrative Healthcare Success Example:
The Pacific Coast Integrative Health Center developed a comprehensive model combining conventional medical care with authorized traditional healing practices. The center employed licensed physicians, registered nurses, licensed acupuncturists, authorized traditional healers, and certified nutritionists working collaboratively on patient care teams.

After five years of operation, the center documented superior outcomes compared to conventional medical care alone: 67% improvement in patient satisfaction, 45% reduction in medication requirements, 38% improvement in chronic disease management, and 56% reduction in healthcare costs per patient. The model was adopted by eight healthcare systems and became a training site for medical residents and traditional healing practitioners.

Therapeutic Applications and Clinical Protocols
Evidence-Based Therapeutic Integration:
Constitutional Therapeutic Protocols:
- **Electric Constitution Therapies**: Gentle approaches including

acupuncture, craniosacral therapy, traditional herbal medicine, meditation, and energy healing with gradual treatment progression

- **Magnetic Constitution Therapies**: Active approaches including chiropractic care, massage therapy, physical therapy, structured exercise programs, and goal-oriented rehabilitation
- **Neutral Constitution Therapies**: Systematic approaches including traditional Chinese medicine diagnosis, Ayurvedic constitutional treatment, nutritional medicine, and structured lifestyle modification programs

- **Clinical Application Guidelines:**
- **Assessment and Evaluation**: Comprehensive patient evaluation including constitutional assessment, traditional diagnostic approaches, and conventional medical evaluation
- **Treatment Plan Development**: Integrated treatment plans combining conventional medical treatment with appropriate traditional approaches based on evidence and patient preference
- **Monitoring and Adjustment**: Regular assessment of patient progress using both conventional medical measures and traditional healing outcome indicators
- **Safety and Risk Management**: Comprehensive safety protocols including interaction monitoring, adverse event reporting, and appropriate medical supervision

Chronic Disease Management Through Integrative Approaches:

Cardiovascular Disease Integration:
- **Conventional Treatment Foundation**: Standard medical treatment for cardiovascular disease including medication management, surgical intervention when appropriate, and cardiac rehabilitation
- **Traditional Medicine Enhancement**: Traditional approaches including acupuncture for blood pressure management, herbal medicine for circulation support, and mind-body practices for stress reduction
- **Constitutional Lifestyle Modification**: Individualized nutrition, exercise, and stress management approaches based on constitutional type and cardiovascular risk factors
- **Community Support Integration**: Group-based programs combining medical education with traditional healing community support and lifestyle modification assistance

Diabetes Management Integration:

- **Medical Care Foundation**: Standard diabetes medical management including blood sugar monitoring, medication management, and endocrinology consultation when appropriate
- **Traditional Medicine Support**: Traditional approaches including herbal medicine for blood sugar support, acupuncture for neuropathy management, and traditional dietary approaches
- **Constitutional Nutrition Programs**: Individualized nutrition approaches based on constitutional type, cultural food preferences, and diabetes management requirements
- **Community Education and Support**: Diabetes education programs integrating conventional medical information with traditional healing approaches and cultural dietary practices

Mental Health Integration:
- **Psychological Care Foundation**: Licensed mental health services including psychotherapy, psychiatric evaluation, and medication management when appropriate
- **Traditional Healing Integration**: Traditional approaches including meditation, traditional ceremonial healing, cultural spiritual practices, and traditional counseling approaches
- **Constitutional Mental Health Approaches**: Individualized mental health treatment approaches based on constitutional type, cultural background, and personal healing preferences
- **Community Mental Health Support**: Group-based mental health programs integrating conventional therapeutic approaches with traditional healing community support and cultural practices

Healthcare Professional Development and Training
Medical Education Integration and Professional Development
Sacred Synthesis healthcare requires comprehensive training programs that integrate traditional wisdom with conventional medical education while maintaining the highest standards of clinical competency and patient safety.

Medical School Curriculum Integration:
Foundation Medical Education Enhancement:
- **Constitutional Medicine Training**: Medical student education in constitutional assessment, individualized treatment approaches, and patient-centered care based on constitutional understanding
- **Traditional Medicine Systems**: Medical education including authorized traditional healing systems, cultural competency, and appropriate integration approaches with conventional medical care

- **Mind-Body Medicine and Spiritual Care**: Medical training in psychological-physical connections, spiritual aspects of healing, and appropriate referral to spiritual care professionals
- **Community Health and Cultural Competency**: Medical education emphasizing community-based healthcare, cultural diversity, and social determinants of health affecting patient outcomes

Clinical Training Integration:
- **Patient Care Rotations**: Medical student clinical experience in integrative healthcare settings with supervision by qualified physicians experienced in traditional medicine integration
- **Cultural Immersion Programs**: Medical student experiences in diverse cultural communities with traditional healing practitioners and community health programs
- **Research and Documentation Training**: Medical student involvement in research documenting effectiveness of integrative healthcare approaches and traditional medicine applications
- **Ethical and Legal Training**: Medical education in professional boundaries, cultural sensitivity, legal requirements, and ethical considerations in integrative healthcare practice

Medical Education Success Story:
The San Diego School of Medicine developed an integrative medicine curriculum combining conventional medical education with authorized traditional healing training. The program included constitutional medicine, traditional Chinese medicine, traditional Mexican healing, and Native American healing approaches taught by qualified practitioners from each tradition.

Medical students completing the program demonstrated superior clinical outcomes in patient satisfaction, cultural competency, and comprehensive patient care approaches. Graduate physicians showed 78% higher patient satisfaction scores, 45% better outcomes in treating diverse populations, and 67% greater professional satisfaction with patient care. The program became a model for twelve other medical schools.

Healthcare Provider Professional Development
Continuing Medical Education in Integrative Approaches:
Professional Development Programs:
- **Constitutional Healthcare Training**: Healthcare provider education in constitutional assessment, individualized treatment approaches, and patient care adaptation based on constitutional understanding

- **Traditional Medicine Integration**: Professional training in appropriate integration of traditional healing approaches with conventional medical treatment
- **Cultural Competency and Traditional Healing**: Healthcare provider education in diverse cultural healing traditions, appropriate referral practices, and respectful cultural interaction
- **Mind-Body Medicine and Holistic Care**: Professional development in psychological factors affecting physical health, stress management, and comprehensive patient care approaches

Certification and Qualification Standards:
- **Basic Integrative Medicine Competency**: Healthcare provider certification in fundamental principles of integrative healthcare and appropriate traditional medicine integration
- **Advanced Integrative Specialization**: Specialized training in specific traditional healing modalities with appropriate practitioner authorization and continuing education requirements
- **Cultural Competency Certification**: Healthcare provider qualification in serving diverse cultural communities with traditional healing integration and cultural sensitivity
- **Teaching and Supervision Qualification**: Advanced training for healthcare providers supervising other professionals in integrative healthcare approaches and traditional medicine integration

Healthcare Team Development:
Interprofessional Collaboration Training:
- **Constitutional Team Development**: Healthcare team training in understanding and utilizing constitutional diversity for optimal patient care and professional collaboration
- **Communication and Conflict Resolution**: Professional development in healthcare team communication, conflict resolution, and collaborative decision-making approaches
- **Cultural Bridge-Building**: Healthcare team training in serving diverse patient populations through cultural competency and traditional healing practitioner collaboration
- **Quality Improvement and Outcome Measurement**: Team development in measuring and improving healthcare outcomes through integrative approaches and traditional medicine integration

Professional Mentorship and Support:
- **Experienced Practitioner Mentorship**: New integrative healthcare providers receiving guidance from experienced professionals in both conventional medicine and traditional healing

integration
- **Peer Support Networks**: Professional networks providing mutual support, continuing education, and resource sharing for healthcare providers practicing integrative medicine
- **Professional Development Planning**: Career development support for healthcare providers advancing in integrative medicine specialization and traditional healing integration
- **Research and Publication Opportunities**: Professional development support for healthcare providers contributing to research documentation and academic publication in integrative healthcare

Healthcare System Transformation
Institutional Development and Policy Integration:
Healthcare System Policy Development:
- **Integrative Medicine Standards**: Healthcare institution policies supporting appropriate traditional medicine integration while maintaining patient safety and clinical effectiveness standards
- **Cultural Competency Requirements**: Healthcare system standards for serving diverse cultural communities with traditional healing integration and cultural sensitivity training requirements
- **Quality Measurement and Improvement**: Healthcare outcome measurement systems including integrative medicine effectiveness and traditional healing integration success indicators
- **Professional Development Support**: Institutional policies supporting healthcare provider education in integrative medicine and traditional healing integration with appropriate funding and time allocation

Economic and Financial Integration:
- **Cost-Effectiveness Documentation**: Healthcare system documentation of cost savings and improved outcomes through integrative medicine approaches and traditional healing integration
- **Insurance and Payment Integration**: Healthcare system development of payment approaches supporting integrative medicine services and traditional healing practitioner compensation
- **Resource Allocation and Planning**: Healthcare system budgeting and resource allocation supporting integrative medicine programs and traditional healing practitioner employment
- **Economic Sustainability Planning**: Long-term financial planning for healthcare systems providing integrative medicine services and traditional healing integration with sustainable

264

funding models

Global Healthcare Applications and International Cooperation
International Healthcare Development and Cultural Adaptation
Sacred Synthesis healthcare principles demonstrate universal effectiveness while requiring careful cultural adaptation and traditional community authorization for international applications.

Cross-Cultural Healthcare Applications:
Developing Country Healthcare Integration:
- **Traditional Healer Collaboration**: Healthcare programs developed in partnership with local traditional healers and indigenous medical practitioners with appropriate cultural authorization
- **Community Health Worker Training**: Community-based healthcare programs training local residents in basic healthcare delivery integrated with traditional healing approaches and cultural practices
- **Maternal and Child Health Programs**: Healthcare services for mothers and children integrating conventional medical care with traditional birthing practices and child-rearing approaches
- **Infectious Disease Prevention**: Public health programs combining conventional medical prevention approaches with traditional health maintenance and community education practices

International Healthcare Cooperation:
- **Medical Education Exchange**: Healthcare professional training programs enabling cross-cultural learning and traditional medicine integration with appropriate cultural authorization and practitioner qualification
- **Research Collaboration**: International research partnerships documenting effectiveness of traditional healing integration and cultural adaptation approaches in healthcare delivery
- **Policy Development Support**: International cooperation in developing healthcare policies supporting traditional medicine integration and cultural competency requirements
- **Emergency Response Coordination**: International healthcare emergency response programs integrating conventional medical care with traditional healing approaches and cultural sensitivity

Global Health Challenge Applications:
Pandemic Response Integration:
- **Community Health Preparedness**: Public health emergency preparedness programs integrating conventional medical approaches with traditional health maintenance and community

resilience practices
- **Cultural Community Support**: Pandemic response programs providing healthcare services appropriate for diverse cultural communities with traditional healing integration and cultural sensitivity
- **Mental Health and Trauma Support**: Pandemic mental health programs integrating conventional psychological services with traditional healing approaches and cultural support systems
- **Healthcare System Strengthening**: Pandemic response programs strengthening healthcare systems through traditional medicine integration and community health worker training

Global Mental Health Applications:
- **Trauma Healing Programs**: International mental health programs integrating conventional therapeutic approaches with traditional healing practices and cultural trauma recovery methods
- **Cultural Mental Health Services**: Mental health programs serving refugee and immigrant populations through cultural competency and traditional healing integration with appropriate practitioner authorization
- **Community Mental Health Development**: International programs developing community-based mental health services integrating conventional psychological care with traditional healing approaches and cultural practices
- **Professional Training and Support**: International mental health professional development programs integrating conventional therapeutic training with traditional healing education and cultural competency development

Environmental Health and Ecological Medicine
Traditional Ecological Knowledge and Environmental Health:
Environmental Health Assessment:
- **Traditional Environmental Knowledge**: Healthcare assessment approaches integrating traditional ecological knowledge about environmental factors affecting community health and individual wellness
- **Constitutional Environmental Needs**: Healthcare approaches recognizing that constitutional types have different environmental requirements for optimal health and healing capacity
- **Cultural Landscape Health**: Healthcare programs recognizing connections between cultural landscape preservation and community health through traditional ecological relationships
- **Climate Change Health Adaptation**: Healthcare preparation for climate change health impacts using traditional knowledge about environmental variation and community resilience

266

Ecological Medicine Applications:

- **Traditional Food Systems and Nutrition**: Healthcare nutrition programs based on traditional food systems, seasonal eating patterns, and cultural dietary practices supporting constitutional health
- **Medicinal Plant Conservation**: Healthcare programs supporting conservation and sustainable use of medicinal plants through partnership with traditional knowledge communities and practitioners
- **Traditional Agriculture and Health**: Healthcare programs supporting traditional agricultural practices that provide nutritious food and maintain environmental health supporting community wellness
- **Environmental Restoration and Health**: Healthcare programs participating in environmental restoration activities that improve community health through ecological healing and traditional ecological knowledge application

Future Healthcare Development and Innovation
Emerging Healthcare Applications:
Technology Integration with Traditional Healing:

- **Telemedicine with Traditional Practitioners**: Healthcare technology enabling remote consultation with traditional healing practitioners while maintaining appropriate cultural protocol and practitioner-patient relationships
- **Digital Health Records with Constitutional Information**: Healthcare information systems including constitutional assessment information and traditional healing treatment records with appropriate privacy protection
- **Artificial Intelligence and Traditional Diagnosis**: Healthcare technology development integrating traditional diagnostic approaches with contemporary medical evaluation while respecting traditional knowledge boundaries
- **Virtual Reality and Traditional Healing Environments**: Healthcare technology creating healing environments based on traditional healing spaces and cultural practices supporting patient comfort and healing

Research and Development Priorities:

- **Consciousness and Health Research**: Healthcare research investigating relationships between consciousness development and physical health through collaboration between conventional medical research and traditional knowledge communities
- **Genomics and Constitutional Medicine**: Healthcare research

investigating relationships between genetic factors and constitutional types with implications for personalized medicine and traditional healing integration

- **Microbiome and Traditional Nutrition**: Healthcare research investigating relationships between gut microbiome health and traditional dietary practices with applications for constitutional nutrition and preventive medicine
- **Environmental Health and Traditional Knowledge**: Healthcare research integrating traditional ecological knowledge with contemporary environmental health research addressing climate change and environmental degradation health impacts

Healthcare System Evolution:
Planetary Health and Healing:
- **Global Healthcare Cooperation**: International healthcare development supporting universal healthcare access through traditional medicine integration and cultural competency with sustainable funding and resource sharing
- **Climate Resilience and Health**: Healthcare system preparation for climate change health impacts through traditional knowledge integration and community resilience development with cultural adaptation
- **Environmental Justice and Health Equity**: Healthcare programs addressing environmental health disparities through traditional ecological knowledge integration and community empowerment with cultural authorization
- **Consciousness-Based Healthcare Evolution**: Healthcare system development toward comprehensive approaches addressing physical, emotional, mental, and spiritual dimensions of health through traditional wisdom integration and professional development

Conclusion: Healthcare as Sacred Service and Community Healing
Healthcare integration through Sacred Synthesis principles demonstrates that medical excellence and spiritual development represent complementary rather than competing expressions of authentic healing service. When healthcare delivery integrates constitutional understanding, applies traditional healing wisdom appropriately, and serves beneficial purposes beyond symptom treatment alone, healthcare becomes a primary vehicle for both individual healing and collective community health advancement.

The Healthcare Integration Promise
Sacred Synthesis healthcare applications create:
Individual Healing Transformation:

- **Comprehensive Healthcare**: Medical treatment that addresses physical, emotional, mental, and spiritual dimensions of health while maintaining clinical safety and effectiveness
- **Constitutional Healthcare Optimization**: Personalized medicine based on individual constitutional needs and healing preferences while maintaining universal healthcare standards
- **Cultural Healthcare Competency**: Healthcare delivery that honors diverse cultural backgrounds and traditional healing practices while maintaining professional medical standards
- **Prevention-Oriented Wellness**: Healthcare approaches emphasizing health maintenance and disease prevention through lifestyle medicine and traditional wellness approaches

Healthcare System Evolution:
- **Patient-Centered Healthcare Delivery**: Healthcare systems organized around patient needs and healing preferences rather than institutional efficiency or provider convenience
- **Interprofessional Collaboration**: Healthcare teams integrating conventional medical professionals with qualified traditional healing practitioners while maintaining appropriate professional boundaries
- **Cultural Healthcare Integration**: Healthcare institutions serving diverse populations through cultural competency and traditional medicine integration with appropriate community authorization
- **Community-Based Healthcare**: Healthcare delivery connected with community health, environmental factors, and social determinants affecting individual and collective wellness

Global Healthcare Network Development:
- **International Healthcare Cooperation**: Global healthcare networks supporting cross-cultural learning and traditional medicine integration while respecting cultural boundaries and traditional community authority
- **Healthcare Professional Exchange**: International healthcare professional development programs integrating conventional medical training with traditional healing education and cultural competency development
- **Research and Validation Networks**: Global research collaboration documenting effectiveness of traditional healing integration and developing evidence-based approaches to cultural healthcare competency
- **Emergency Response Coordination**: International healthcare emergency response systems integrating conventional medical care with traditional healing approaches and cultural community

support

Implementation Strategy for Healthcare Integration
Phase 1: Professional Development and Training (Months 1-12)

- Complete constitutional healthcare assessment training for healthcare providers and development of patient constitutional evaluation protocols
- Establish relationships with qualified traditional healing practitioners and cultural communities supporting appropriate traditional medicine integration
- Develop healthcare team collaboration protocols integrating constitutional understanding with clinical care coordination and patient safety standards
- Create professional development programs in cultural competency and traditional healing integration with continuing education and certification requirements

Phase 2: Clinical Integration and System Development (Months 12-36)

- Implement constitutional patient care protocols in clinical settings with outcome measurement and quality improvement monitoring
- Develop integrative healthcare services combining conventional medical treatment with appropriate traditional healing approaches and cultural community authorization
- Create healthcare provider professional development programs in integrative medicine and traditional healing integration with mentorship and peer support networks
- Establish healthcare system policies supporting traditional medicine integration while maintaining patient safety and clinical effectiveness standards

Phase 3: Community Health and Global Service (Years 3+)

- Develop community health programs integrating healthcare delivery with environmental health, social determinants, and cultural community development
- Contribute to international healthcare cooperation through professional exchange, research collaboration, and emergency response coordination
- Participate in healthcare professional education through teaching, mentorship, and curriculum development supporting integrative medicine and traditional healing integration
- Engage in healthcare system transformation supporting universal healthcare access through traditional medicine integration and cultural competency with sustainable economic models

The Ripple Effect of Sacred Healthcare Practice
Healthcare integration creates influence extending far beyond individual patient treatment. When healthcare providers demonstrate that traditional wisdom enhances rather than compromises medical effectiveness, they contribute to cultural transformation enabling others to integrate authenticity with clinical excellence.

Healthcare institutions become demonstration sites for comprehensive healing approaches serving both individual wellness and community health advancement.

Healthcare systems transformed by constitutional understanding and traditional healing integration create cultures honoring both medical effectiveness and cultural diversity, demonstrating practical alternatives to purely biomedical approaches that currently dominate many healthcare settings while maintaining the highest standards of patient safety and clinical outcomes.

Healthcare Integration Serving Global Transformation
The integration of Sacred Synthesis principles with healthcare delivery represents one of the most significant opportunities for positive cultural transformation available to contemporary healthcare professionals. Through constitutional understanding and traditional wisdom applied to medical practice, healthcare providers contribute to the emergence of comprehensive healing approaches, sustainable healthcare systems, and professional networks serving both individual health and collective community advancement.

Healthcare excellence grounded in authentic spiritual development becomes a bridge between traditional healing wisdom and contemporary medical knowledge, demonstrating that ancient principles enhance rather than conflict with clinical effectiveness in addressing the challenges of modern healthcare while contributing to the evolution of human consciousness through daily healthcare service and community healing.

The Great Achievement: Nutrition and Spirit
Their understanding of nutrition revealed how Sacred Synthesis principles had been integrated into even the most basic things like their daily meals.

Conscious Nourishment - Food as Spiritual Practice
Transforming Every Meal into Medicine, Community, and Consciousness

How constitutional nutrition turns ordinary eating into therapeutic technology, with meal planning, shopping guides, and family integration that nourishes body, emotions, and spiritual development

Chef Isabella Rodriguez stood in the kitchen of San Francisco General Hospital, watching another diabetic patient receive a dinner tray filled with processed foods that contradicted everything her medical team had prescribed.

As Executive Chef for Patient Services, she witnessed daily the disconnect between healthcare goals and actual nutrition, patients with heart disease receiving high-sodium meals, cancer survivors eating inflammation-promoting foods, and psychiatric patients consuming blood- sugar-destabilizing combinations that worsened their conditions.

I was trained as a chef, but I felt like I was contributing to illness rather than healing," Isabella recalls. "The standard hospital food system ignored individual differences, cultural needs, and therapeutic potential. I knew food could be medicine, but our approach treated it like industrial fuel.

Her transformation began when she discovered constitutional nutrition through her own health crisis, chronic fatigue and digestive issues that conventional medicine couldn't resolve. Within three months of eating according to her Magnetic constitution, her energy returned, her digestion healed, and she lost 30 pounds she'd carried for years.

Food finally made sense," she explains. "Instead of fighting my body's reactions to different foods, I learned to work with my constitutional type. Every meal became an opportunity for healing rather than a source of confusion and struggle.

Her transformation demonstrates what millions of people are discovering: food is not just fuel, it's information that directly influences physical health, emotional stability, mental clarity, and spiritual receptivity when aligned with your constitutional needs and prepared with conscious intention.

Beyond Generic Nutrition: The Constitutional Revolution
Mainstream nutrition treats everyone as if they had identical digestive systems, metabolic rates, and nutritional needs. The result: confusion, frustration, and health problems from following advice that
works for some people but creates problems for others.

The One-Size-Fits-None Problem
Generic Dietary Advice Creates:
- Conflicting nutritional recommendations that confuse rather
  than clarify
- Diet programs that work initially but become unsustainable or
  create new problems
- Food anxiety and obsessive behavior around "perfect" eating
- Health conditions that resist improvement despite "healthy"
  dietary changes
- Loss of intuitive connection with what your body actually needs

The Constitutional Solution: Your Nutritional Blueprint
Conscious Nourishment recognizes that optimal nutrition requires
understanding your constitutional type, your individual blueprint for
metabolism, digestion, and nutritional needs that determines which
foods serve as medicine versus poison for your unique system.

Constitutional Nutrition Provides:
- Personalized Guidelines: Foods that optimize your individual
  metabolism and digestive capacity
- Therapeutic Applications: Specific nutritional protocols for
  common health challenges
- Seasonal Adaptations: How to modify your diet throughout the
  year for optimal health
- Family Integration: How to feed constitutionally diverse family
  members from the same kitchen
- Community Connection: Food as medicine that supports both
  individual healing and community building

Your Constitutional Nutrition Profile
Understanding your constitutional nutrition needs transforms eating
from trial-and-error into precise medicine adapted to your individual
requirements.
Electric Constitution Nutritional Characteristics
Your Natural Digestive Patterns:
- Variable appetite with tendency to skip meals when stressed
- Sensitive digestion prone to gas, bloating, and constipation
- Blood sugar instability leading to energy crashes and anxiety
- Cold hands and feet with craving for warm foods and beverages

What Your Body Actually Needs:
- Warm, Cooked Foods: Raw and cold foods are harder to digest and can increase anxiety
- Healthy Fats: Essential for nervous system health and hormone production
- Sweet, Sour, and Salty Tastes: These flavors are naturally calming and grounding
- Regular Mealtimes: Consistency helps stabilize naturally variable energy
- Smaller, Frequent Meals: Prevents blood sugar drops that trigger anxiety

Foods That Heal Electric Constitution:
- Grains: Warm oatmeal, rice, quinoa prepared with ghee or olive oil
- Proteins: Fish, chicken, eggs, well-cooked legumes, dairy in moderation
- Vegetables: Cooked root vegetables, steamed leafy greens, winter squashes
- Fruits: Sweet fruits like bananas, dates, grapes, cooked fruit preparations
- Beverages: Herbal teas (ginger, licorice, chamomile), warm water with lemon

Foods That Disturb Electric Constitution:
- Raw vegetables and cold foods
- Excessive caffeine and stimulants
- Dry, crunchy foods like crackers and chips
- Spicy foods and excessive pungent flavors
- Irregular eating and meal skipping

Magnetic Constitution Nutritional Characteristics
Your Natural Digestive Patterns:
- Strong appetite but slow digestion
- Tendency toward weight gain and fluid retention
- Sluggish metabolism and resistance to dietary changes
- Natural preference for heavy, rich, comfort foods

What Your Body Actually Needs (Often Opposite to What It Craves):
- Light, Dry Foods: Counteracts natural heaviness and moisture retention
- Heating Spices: Stimulates sluggish digestion and metabolism
- Bitter, Pungent, and Astringent Tastes: These flavors naturally

stimulate and energize
- Smaller Portions: Prevents overwhelming naturally slow digestive capacity
- Stimulating Preparation: Raw foods, steaming, and minimal oils

Foods That Heal Magnetic Constitution:
- Grains: Barley, millet, buckwheat, quinoa prepared with minimal oil
- Proteins: Legumes, lean fish, chicken, eggs with heating spices
- Vegetables: Bitter greens, cruciferous vegetables, sprouts, asparagus
- Fruits: Apples, pears, berries, astringent fruits, dried fruits in small amounts
- Beverages: Ginger tea, green tea, warm water with lemon and cayenne

Foods That Disturb Magnetic Constitution:
- Heavy dairy products and excessive oils
- Sweet desserts and refined sugars
- Large meals and frequent eating
- Cold beverages and ice cream
- Excessive salt and processed foods

Neutral Constitution Nutritional Characteristics
Your Natural Digestive Patterns:
- Strong, efficient digestion with tendency toward acidity
- Regular appetite with ability to handle consistent meal schedules
- Heat-generating metabolism with tendency toward inflammation
- Natural efficiency that can lead to digestive stress under pressure

What Your Body Needs:
- Cool, Fresh Foods: Counteracts natural heat and prevents inflammation
- Sweet, Bitter, and Astringent Tastes: These flavors are naturally cooling and anti- inflammatory
- Moderate Portions: Prevents overwhelming efficient but heat-generating digestion
- Raw and Lightly Cooked Foods: Takes advantage of strong digestive capacity
- Anti-inflammatory Foods: Reduces tendency toward internal heat and inflammation

Foods That Heal Neutral Constitution:
- Grains: Rice, wheat, oats, barley prepared with cooling oils like coconut

- Proteins: Fish, chicken, dairy, legumes with cooling spices and herbs
- Vegetables: Leafy greens, cucumber, zucchini, sweet vegetables, fresh herbs
- Fruits: Sweet fruits like melons, grapes, pears, coconut, cooling fruit preparations
- Beverages: Coconut water, herbal teas (mint, fennel, coriander), room temperature water

Foods That Disturb Neutral Constitution:
- Spicy, heating foods and excessive chili peppers
- Acidic foods like citrus, tomatoes, vinegar in excess
- Alcohol and fermented foods in large quantities
- Salty and oily foods that increase heat
- Skipping meals which increases internal heat and irritability

Constitutional Daily Menus: Your Personalized Nutrition Plan
Transform theoretical knowledge into practical daily application with specific meal plans adapted to your constitutional needs and modern lifestyle.

Electric Constitution: The Grounding Menu
Upon Rising (6:00-7:00 AM):
- Warm water with fresh lemon and a pinch of ginger
- 2-3 dates or warm almond milk if hungry
- Set intention for nourishing meals throughout the day

Breakfast (7:00-8:00 AM):
- Warm oatmeal cooked with almond milk, ghee, cinnamon, and chopped dates
- Herbal tea: ginger, licorice root, or chamomile
- One slice whole grain toast with almond butter if still hungry

Mid-Morning (10:00 AM) (if needed):
- Warm herbal tea or warm water
- Small handful of soaked almonds

Lunch (12:00-1:00 PM) (Largest meal):
- Warming soup: butternut squash with coconut milk and warming spices
- Quinoa pilaf with cooked vegetables and olive oil
- Steamed broccoli or asparagus with lemon and ghee
- Herbal tea or warm water with meals

Afternoon Snack (3:30 PM):

- Warm almond milk with cardamom and a touch of honey
- 3-4 Medjool dates or sweet fruit

Dinner (6:00-7:00 PM) (Light and early):
- Basmati rice with ghee and turmeric
- Sautéed seasonal vegetables with warming spices
- Small portion of fish or chicken if desired
- Avoid eating within 3 hours of bedtime

Evening (8:00 PM):
- Calming herbal tea: chamomile, passionflower, or tulsi
- No food after dinner to support restful sleep

Magnetic Constitution: The Activating Menu
Upon Rising (5:30-6:00 AM):
- Hot water with lemon, ginger, and a pinch of cayenne
- Brief movement or stretching before eating
- Set intention for energizing, light nourishment

Breakfast (6:00-7:00 AM) (Light or skip if not hungry):
- Fresh fruit salad with heating spices: ginger, cinnamon, black pepper
- Green tea or ginger tea
- Avoid heavy breakfast foods that create sluggishness

Mid-Morning (9:00 AM):
- Herbal tea: ginger, green tea, or dandelion
- Avoid snacking, if possible, to maintain digestive fire

Lunch (11:00 AM-12:00 PM) (Largest meal, eaten early):
- Large salad with bitter greens, sprouts, and vegetables
- Lentil soup with heating spices: turmeric, cumin, black pepper
- Minimal dressing: lemon juice with small amount of olive oil
- Room temperature water or herbal tea

Afternoon (2:00 PM):
- Energizing herbal tea or small amount of green tea
- Avoid heavy snacks that reduce dinner appetite

Dinner (5:00-6:00 PM) (Early and light):
- Steamed vegetables with heating spices
- Small portion of quinoa or barley
- Light protein: fish, chicken, or legumes if desired
- No eating after 7:00 PM to support morning appetite

Evening (7:30 PM):
- Digestive tea: ginger, fennel, or cumin
- Focus on activities rather than eating

Neutral Constitution: The Balancing Menu
Upon Rising (6:00-6:30 AM):
- Room temperature water with lime and mint
- Brief cooling breathing practice
- Set intention for balanced, anti-inflammatory nourishment

Breakfast (7:00-8:00 AM):
- Fresh fruit smoothie with coconut water, berries, and cooling herbs
- Anti-inflammatory spices: turmeric, coriander
- Herbal tea: mint, fennel, or coriander

Mid-Morning (9:30 AM):
- Coconut water or cooling herbal tea
- Fresh fruit if needed

Lunch (12:00-1:00 PM):
- Quinoa salad with cucumber, fresh herbs, and lemon dressing
- Raw or lightly steamed vegetables
- Cooling protein: fish prepared with cooling spices
- Room temperature water or cooling herbal tea

Afternoon Snack (3:00 PM):
- Coconut water with a splash of rose water
- Fresh, sweet fruit: melon, grapes, or pears

Dinner (6:00-7:00 PM):
- Light, cooling meal emphasizing vegetables
- Basmati rice with coconut oil and fresh herbs
- Steamed vegetables with cooling spices: coriander, fennel, mint
- Avoid heating spices and excessive oils

Evening (8:00 PM):
- Cooling herbal tea: mint, chamomile, or rose
- Light foods only if necessary

Therapeutic Food Applications: Your Constitutional Healing Kitchen

Constitutional nutrition provides specific therapeutic protocols for common health challenges, transforming your kitchen into a personalized healing center.

Electric Constitution Therapeutic Protocols
Anxiety and Nervous System Disorders

Healing Strategy: Grounding, warming foods that calm the nervous system while stabilizing blood sugar

Daily Protocol:
- Morning: Warm oatmeal with ghee, cinnamon, and dates for blood sugar stability
- Midday: Warm soup with root vegetables and calming herbs like brahmi
- Evening: Golden milk (turmeric, ginger, cardamom in warm almond milk)
- Throughout Day: Warm herbal teas instead of coffee; regular meal timing

Specific Healing Foods:
- Ashwagandha: Add to warm milk for nervous system support
- Ghee: 1-2 teaspoons daily for nervous system nourishment
- Sweet potatoes: Rich in B-vitamins for stress management
- Almonds: Soaked overnight for magnesium and healthy fats

Avoid During Healing:
- Caffeine and stimulants that increase anxiety
- Cold, raw foods that disturb digestion
- Sugar and refined foods that destabilize blood sugar
- Irregular eating that increases nervous system stress

Digestive Issues and IBS
Healing Strategy: Warm, easy-to-digest foods with digestive spices
Daily Protocol:
- Before Meals: Ginger tea or fresh ginger with lemon to stimulate digestion
- With Meals: Digestive spice blend: cumin, coriander, fennel
- After Meals: Warm water or digestive tea
- Evening: Chamomile tea for digestive calm

Therapeutic Preparation Methods:
- Steam or sauté vegetables instead of raw
- Cook grains and legumes thoroughly with digestive spices
- Use ghee or olive oil for lubrication and healing
- Eat in peaceful environment with mindful attention

Magnetic Constitution Therapeutic Protocols
Weight Management and Sluggish Metabolism

Healing Strategy: Light, stimulating foods that activate metabolism without creating heaviness

Daily Protocol:
- Morning: Hot water with lemon and cayenne to stimulate digestion
- Before Meals: Ginger tea or bitter herbs to enhance digestive fire
- With Meals: Heating spices: black pepper, mustard seed, turmeric
- Between Meals: Avoid snacking to maintain digestive fire

Metabolic Activation Foods:
- Bitter vegetables: Dandelion greens, arugula, kale for liver stimulation
- Heating spices: Ginger, cayenne, black pepper for circulation
- Green tea: Moderate amounts for metabolic activation
- Light proteins: Legumes and lean fish prepared with spices

Preparation Emphasis:
- Raw foods and salads to provide enzymes and lightness
- Steaming and light sautéing instead of heavy cooking methods
- Minimal oils and dairy products
- Smaller portions eaten at regular intervals

Depression and Low Energy

Healing Strategy: Activating foods and social eating environments
Daily Protocol:
- Morning: Energizing breakfast with stimulating spices
- Midday: Largest meal with challenging flavors and textures
- Afternoon: Energizing herbal teas and light activity
- Evening: Light, warm foods that don't create heaviness

Mood-Supporting Foods:
- Pungent spices: For stimulation and circulation
- Bitter foods: To clear mental fog and lethargy
- Warming teas: Ginger, cinnamon, cardamom for energy
- Community meals: Shared food preparation and eating

Neutral Constitution Therapeutic Protocols
Inflammation and Autoimmune Support
Healing Strategy: Anti-inflammatory foods that cool internal heat while supporting immune function

Daily Protocol:
- Morning: Anti-inflammatory smoothie with turmeric and cooling fruits
- Throughout Day: Cooling herbal teas and adequate hydration
- With Meals: Anti-inflammatory spices: turmeric, coriander, fennel
- Evening: Light, cooling foods that promote restoration

Anti-Inflammatory Foods:
- Turmeric: Daily in food or golden milk for powerful anti-inflammatory effects
- Leafy greens: Rich in antioxidants and cooling energy
- Berries: High in anthocyanins for immune support
- Cooling oils: Coconut oil and olive oil in moderation

Inflammation Triggers to Avoid:
- Heating spices: chili peppers, excessive garlic, ginger
- Acidic foods: tomatoes, citrus, vinegar in large amounts
- Processed foods with inflammatory additives
- Alcohol and fermented foods that increase heat

Stress and Anger Management
Healing Strategy: Cooling foods that support emotional regulation

Daily Protocol:
- Morning: Cooling breakfast that sets calm tone for day
- Midday: Balanced meal without heating elements
- Stressful Times: Coconut water, cucumber juice, or cooling herbal tea
- Evening: Light, cooling dinner that supports restful sleep

Emotional Balance Foods:
- Cooling fruits: Melon, grapes, pears for natural cooling
- Fresh herbs: Mint, cilantro, parsley for liver support

- Coconut: Water and fresh coconut for cooling and hydration
- Rose: Rose water and rose tea for emotional calming

Seasonal Constitutional Eating: Adapting Throughout the Year
Your constitutional needs change with seasons, requiring dietary adaptations that maintain optimal health while honoring natural cycles.

Spring Renewal (March-May): Constitutional Detox
Universal Spring Principles:
- Gentle detoxification supporting liver function
- Lighter foods after heavy winter eating
- Fresh, local vegetables and herbs
- Gradual increase in raw foods

Electric Constitution Spring Adaptation:
- Gentle cleansing with warm, cooked foods
- Light soups and steamed vegetables
- Dandelion and nettle teas for liver support
- Avoid aggressive detox that depletes nervous system

Magnetic Constitution Spring Adaptation:
- Intensive cleansing with raw vegetables and juices
- Bitter herbs and greens for liver stimulation
- Reduced oils and heavy foods
- Active participation in spring cleaning and gardening

Neutral Constitution Spring Adaptation:
- Moderate cleansing with cooling, fresh foods
- Anti-inflammatory foods supporting liver function
- Adequate hydration with coconut water and herbal teas
- Prevent overheating during cleansing activities

Summer Cooling (June-August): Constitutional Heat Management
Universal Summer Principles:
- Cooling foods preventing overheating
- Fresh, local fruits and vegetables
- Increased hydration and electrolyte balance
- Light cooking methods and raw food emphasis

Electric Constitution Summer Adaptation:
- Moderate cooling while maintaining grounding
- Sweet fruits and cooling vegetables
- Adequate healthy fats despite warm weather
- Cool but not ice-cold beverages

Magnetic Constitution Summer Adaptation:
- Light, cooling foods preventing sluggishness in heat
- Raw foods and minimal cooking
- Bitter and astringent tastes for cooling
- Avoid excessive dairy and oils in hot weather

Neutral Constitution Summer Adaptation:
- Maximum cooling emphasis preventing inflammation
- Fresh salads, cooling fruits, and vegetables
- Cooling beverages: coconut water, cucumber juice
- Avoid heating spices and excessive sun exposure

Autumn Preparation (September-November): Constitutional Grounding
Universal Autumn Principles:
- Grounding foods preparing for winter
- Immune-supporting foods and spices
- Seasonal vegetables: squashes, apples, root vegetables
- Warming preparation methods and spices

Electric Constitution Autumn Adaptation:
- Maximum grounding with warming, nourishing foods
- Immune support through warming spices: ginger, cinnamon
- Adequate fats and proteins for winter preparation
- Warming soups and stews for comfort and nourishment

Magnetic Constitution Autumn Adaptation:
- Balanced approach maintaining circulation while preparing for cold
- Warming spices without creating excessive heaviness
- Continued attention to weight management during comfort food season
- Active participation in food preservation and community preparation

Neutral Constitution Autumn Adaptation:
- Gradual warming without creating inflammation
- Anti-inflammatory preparation for winter
- Seasonal vegetables prepared with mild warming spices
- Prevention of autumn heat conditions and allergies

Winter Nourishment (December-February): Constitutional Warming
Universal Winter Principles:
- Warming, nourishing foods supporting immune function
- Comfort foods and warming spices

- Adequate fats and proteins for cold weather
- Hot beverages and warming teas

Electric Constitution Winter Adaptation:
- Maximum warming with rich, nourishing foods
- Hot soups, stews, and warming beverages
- Extra fats: ghee, nuts, seeds for winter nutrition
- Consistent routine and warming environment

Magnetic Constitution Winter Adaptation:
- Warming foods while avoiding excessive heaviness
- Heating spices preventing winter lethargy and depression
- Adequate protein without excessive oils
- Active winter activities coordinated with warming nutrition

Neutral Constitution Winter Adaptation:
- Moderate warming without creating inflammation
- Balance between warming and cooling foods
- Anti-inflammatory warming spices: turmeric, ginger, cinnamon
- Prevention of winter dryness and irritation

Family Constitutional Nutrition: Feeding Everyone Well
Transform the challenge of feeding constitutionally diverse family members into an opportunity for connection, education, and mutual support.

The Multi-Constitutional Kitchen Strategy
Base Meal Preparation:
- Prepare foundation foods (grains, vegetables, proteins) using neutral methods
- Add constitutional adaptations through spices, condiments, and preparation methods
- Create "build-your-own" meal stations accommodating different needs
- Teach family members about their constitutional requirements

Example: Family Dinner Coordination
Base Meal: Quinoa, steamed vegetables, baked chicken

Electric Constitution Adaptations:
- Add ghee and warming spices to quinoa
- Steam vegetables with ginger and turmeric
- Serve with warm herbal tea

Magnetic Constitution Adaptations:

- Add lemon and black pepper to quinoa
- Serve vegetables with minimal oil and heating spices
- Include raw salad and bitter greens

Neutral Constitution Adaptations:
- Add coconut oil and cooling herbs to quinoa
- Serve vegetables with fresh herbs and lemon
- Include cucumber salad and cooling beverages

Teaching Constitutional Awareness to Children
Age-Appropriate Education:
- Ages 3-7: Simple awareness of "warming foods" vs. "cooling foods"
- Ages 8-12: Basic constitutional identification and food preferences
- Ages 13-18: Complete constitutional nutrition understanding and meal planning
- Family Activities: Cooking together, garden-to-table projects, constitutional taste testing

Children's Constitutional Nutrition:
- Allow natural food preferences while ensuring nutritional adequacy
- Adapt constitutional guidelines to accommodate growing needs
- Use food as medicine during illness with gentle constitutional approaches
- Create positive associations with healthy constitutional foods

Case Study: The Chen Family Integration
Family Composition:
- David (Magnetic constitution): CEO dealing with weight and energy issues
- Lisa (Electric constitution): Teacher with anxiety and digestive problems
- Emma (Neutral constitution, age 15): Student athlete with stress and inflammation
- Michael (Electric constitution, age 12): Sensitive child with attention challenges

Constitutional Kitchen Solutions:
- Morning Routine: Individual constitutional breakfasts prepared simultaneously
- Family Dinner: Base meals with constitutional condiment bar and spice options
- Weekend Cooking: Family constitutional cooking classes and

meal prep sessions
- Health Support: Constitutional remedies for illness and stress management

Results After Six Months:
- David lost 25 pounds and increased energy 40%
- Lisa's anxiety decreased significantly with improved digestion
- Emma's athletic performance improved with reduced inflammation
- Michael's attention and academic performance enhanced markedly
- Family satisfaction and connection increased through shared constitutional understanding

Professional Integration: Constitutional Nutrition at Work
Transform workplace nutrition from energy-draining to performance-enhancing through constitutional awareness and practical application.

Healthcare Professional Applications

Dr. Patricia Kim's Hospital Integration:
As Chief of Internal Medicine, Dr. Kim integrated constitutional nutrition into patient care protocols:
- Patient Assessment: Constitutional nutrition evaluation alongside medical history
- Therapeutic Meal Plans: Hospital food service adapted for constitutional healing
- Staff Wellness: Constitutional nutrition program for healthcare providers
- Professional Training: Medical staff education in constitutional nutrition principles

Educational Professional Applications
Principal Maria Santos's School Integration:
Implementing constitutional nutrition awareness in educational settings:
- School Lunch Program: Constitutional options accommodating diverse student needs
- Nutrition Education: Constitutional awareness integrated into health curriculum
- Teacher Wellness: Faculty constitutional nutrition program improving classroom effectiveness
- Family Education: Constitutional nutrition workshops for parents and families

CEO Michael Rodriguez's Corporate Integration:

Constitutional nutrition as foundation for workplace wellness:

- Executive Nutrition: Leadership team constitutional assessment and meal planning
- Company Food Services: Workplace cafeteria offering constitutional options
- Employee Wellness: Constitutional nutrition workshops and individual consultations
- Meeting Enhancement: Constitutional snacks and beverages improving decision- making

Building Community Through Food

Conscious nourishment creates opportunities for community building that serves both individual health and collective welfare through shared meals, cooperative food systems, and cultural exchange.

Community Supported Agriculture (CSA) and Local Food Systems

Constitutional CSA Applications:

- Diverse Crop Planning: Local farms growing vegetables serving all constitutional types
- Seasonal Adaptation: Crop timing coordinated with constitutional seasonal needs
- Community Education: Workshops on constitutional cooking and food preparation
- Economic Cooperation: Food sharing and preservation programs supporting community resilience

Community Kitchens and Shared Meal Programs

Inclusive Meal Planning:

- Menu Development: Meals accommodating all constitutional types within unified experience
- Cultural Integration: Traditional foods from diverse cultures adapted for constitutional awareness
- Teaching Opportunities: Community cooking classes and constitutional nutrition education
- Service Integration: Shared meals connecting constitutional nutrition with community service

The Portland Food Collaborative: Model Community Program

Program Structure:

- Community Kitchen: Shared commercial kitchen space for constitutional cooking classes
- CSA Integration: Partnership with local farms providing consti-

tutional variety
- Family Education: Multi-generational constitutional cooking and nutrition workshops
- Healthcare Partnership: Integration with local healthcare providers for therapeutic nutrition

Global Constitutional Cuisine: Cultural Integration
Constitutional nutrition integrates respectfully with traditional cuisines worldwide, demonstrating universal applicability while honoring cultural food wisdom.

Mediterranean Constitutional Adaptations
Electric Constitution Mediterranean:
- Emphasis on warming preparation: cooked vegetables, warm olive oil, warming herbs
- Adequate protein and healthy fats: fish, nuts, olive oil
- Warming spices: oregano, thyme, rosemary prepared as warming teas and seasonings

Magnetic Constitution Mediterranean:
- Light preparation: raw salads, grilled vegetables, minimal oils
- Bitter vegetables: dandelion greens, arugula, endive
- Heating elements: garlic, onions, hot peppers in moderation

Neutral Constitution Mediterranean:
- Cooling emphasis: fresh herbs, cucumber, cooling vegetables
- Anti-inflammatory preparation: fresh herbs, lemon, cooling olive oil preparations
- Moderate protein: fish and legumes prepared with cooling spices

Asian Constitutional Adaptations
Constitutional Chinese Medicine Integration:
- Electric constitution benefits from "warm" foods in Traditional Chinese Medicine
- Magnetic constitution thrives with "cool" and "bitter" foods
- Neutral constitution requires "neutral" and "sweet" foods for balance

Indian Ayurvedic Integration:
- Electric constitution corresponds to "Vata" dietary recommendations
- Magnetic constitution aligns with "Kapha" nutritional approaches
- Neutral constitution parallels "Pitta" cooling and balancing foods

Traditional Indigenous Food Wisdom
Native American Three Sisters Integration:
Corn, Beans, Squash: Complete nutrition adapted for constitutional needs

- Electric: Prepared with warming fats and spices
- Magnetic: Light preparation with stimulating herbs
- Neutral: Cooling preparation with anti-inflammatory seasonings

Your Constitutional Nutrition Mastery Journey
Transform your relationship with food from confusion to clarity through systematic implementation of constitutional nutrition principles adapted to your life circumstances and community connections.

Phase 1: Constitutional Discovery (Month 1)
Week 1: Assessment and Awareness
- Complete detailed constitutional nutrition assessment
- Begin food diary tracking energy, mood, and digestion
- Eliminate obviously inappropriate foods for your constitution
- Shop for constitutional healing foods and spices

Week 2: Foundation Foods Integration
- Implement constitutional breakfast routine
- Adapt one meal daily to constitutional requirements
- Begin constitutional spice and seasoning integration
- Connect with local sources for constitutional foods

Week 3: Therapeutic Applications
- Address primary health challenge with constitutional food therapy
- Implement constitutional snacking and beverage choices
- Begin seasonal adaptation awareness and planning
- Share constitutional discoveries with interested family and friends

Week 4: Integration and Assessment
- Implement complete constitutional daily menu
- Assess energy, mood, digestion, and health improvements
- Plan Month 2 development with family and workplace integration
- Connect with community resources supporting constitutional nutrition

Phase 2: Family and Community Integration (Months 2-3)

Month 2: Family Constitutional Adaptation

- Assess family members' constitutional nutrition needs
- Adapt family meal planning for constitutional diversity
- Teach children age-appropriate constitutional awareness
- Create family constitutional cooking projects and education

Month 3: Community and Professional Integration

- Integrate constitutional nutrition with workplace eating
- Connect with local constitutional nutrition groups and resources
- Begin sharing constitutional nutrition knowledge with interested colleagues
- Plan seasonal adaptation strategies and community connections

Phase 3: Mastery and Service (Months 4-12)

Advanced Constitutional Applications:

- Master seasonal adaptations throughout complete yearly cycle
- Develop expertise in constitutional therapeutic food applications
- Begin teaching constitutional nutrition to family and community members
- Integrate constitutional nutrition with community service and local food systems

Phase 4: Community Leadership (Year 2+)

Teaching and Service Preparation:

- Develop competency in constitutional nutrition assessment and guidance
- Create community educational programs and workshops
- Support local food systems serving constitutional diversity
- Integrate constitutional nutrition with healthcare and educational applications

Your Constitutional Commitment

Electric Constitution Mastery: Become source of nourishing stability for family and community while developing sensitivity and creative contributions to local food culture and community wellness.

Magnetic Constitution Mastery: Develop sustained energy and practical effectiveness enabling community food leadership and service projects demonstrating constitutional nutrition benefits.

Neutral Constitution Mastery: Master precision and balance creating capacity for constitutional nutrition education, healthcare integration, and professional applications serving both individual advancement and community development.

The Sacred Act of Eating

Constitutional nutrition transforms eating from unconscious consumption into spiritual practice through mindful preparation, grateful consumption, and community sharing that serves both individual healing and collective advancement.

Mindful Constitutional Preparation

Sacred Cooking Practices:

- Intention Setting: Begin food preparation with gratitude and healing intention
- Constitutional Awareness: Choose ingredients and preparation methods serving individual and family constitutional needs
- Seasonal Connection: Coordinate meals with natural cycles and local food availability
- Community Service: Prepare food with awareness of service to family and community welfare

Grateful Constitutional Consumption

Conscious Eating Practices:

- Pre-Meal Gratitude: Appreciation for food sources, preparation, and constitutional healing benefits
- Mindful Chewing: Constitutional eating pace supporting optimal digestion and satisfaction
- Present Moment Awareness: Full attention during meals supporting both digestion and consciousness development
- Community Connection: Shared meals building relationships while honoring constitutional diversity

The Community Table

Integrative Meal Practices:

- Constitutional Accommodation: Meals serving diverse constitutional needs within unified family experience
- Cultural Integration: Traditional foods from diverse cultures adapted for constitutional awareness
- Teaching Moments: Mealtimes providing constitutional nutrition education and awareness development
- Service Integration: Shared meals connecting constitutional nutrition with community benefit and mutual support

Conclusion: Food as Medicine, Community, and Consciousness

Constitutional nutrition demonstrates that individual health and community welfare are unified expressions when food choices serve both personal healing and collective advancement through conscious nourishment practices.

Chef Isabella Rodriguez, four years after transforming hospital nutrition services, reflects on constitutional nutrition's impact on healthcare and community:

Constitutional nutrition didn't just improve patient outcomes, it revealed that food is information that can either support healing or contribute to illness. When we started serving meals adapted to constitutional types, patients recovered faster, staff felt more energetic, and the entire hospital culture shifted toward wellness rather than just disease management.

My work became a form of service rather than just food production. Every meal became an opportunity to demonstrate that healthcare and consciousness development are the same activity approached from different perspectives.
Constitutional nutrition proved that individual healing and collective advancement occur simultaneously when food serves both personal needs and community welfare.

Constitutional nutrition offers you the same transformation: eating that serves consciousness development, food choices that enhance both personal health and environmental stewardship, and nutrition practices that develop capacity for community service and cultural contribution.

Your three daily meals await transformation into medicine, spiritual practice, and community building. Your constitutional adaptation provides the personalized framework. Your community offers support and shared learning. Your service gives conscious nourishment authentic meaning and purpose.

The Great Achievement: Evolution in Education
The educational transformation materials revealed how Sacred Synthesis principles had been integrated into schools, universities, and professional training programs. Documentation showed implementation across 127 educational institutions with unprecedented student engagement and democratic participation.

Educational Applications and Character Formation

The Revolutionary Educational Integration: Learning as Sacred Development
Beyond Information Transfer: Educating the Whole Person

292

Contemporary education faces a fundamental crisis: technological advancement has enabled unprecedented access to information while often failing to develop the wisdom, character, and practical capacities needed for meaningful life and authentic service. Traditional educational models emphasize test scores and college preparation rather than supporting integrated human development and authentic life preparation. The Sacred Synthesis approach demonstrates that authentic education integrates intellectual development with character formation while maintaining the highest standards of academic excellence and practical preparation.

Educational Sacred Integration represents one of the most significant breakthroughs in contemporary education: the recognition that character development and academic achievement enhance rather than compete with each other when properly understood and skillfully applied. The educational applications emerging from the GIDEE achievement during 1942-1947 prove that contemplative pedagogy improves rather than compromises academic outcomes across all major educational disciplines while developing the human capacities essential for authentic adulthood and meaningful service.

The Sacred Educational Model transcends both information-focused education and ungrounded progressive approaches through systematic application of constitutional understanding, contemplative learning methods, and service-oriented education. When educators understand student constitutional differences, apply traditional wisdom to pedagogical challenges, and orient their teaching toward character development and authentic preparation for life service, they naturally achieve both superior academic outcomes and profound educational fulfillment while contributing to positive transformation of educational culture.

Constitutional Educational Development: Personalized Learning Through Traditional Wisdom
Understanding Individual Constitutional Types in Education

Sacred Synthesis education recognizes that different constitutional types require different approaches to learning, assessment, and educational support while maintaining universal principles of academic excellence and character development.

Electric Constitution Educational Applications:
Natural Educational Strengths:
- **Intuitive Learning and Understanding**: Exceptional ca-

pacity for grasping complex concepts through holistic perception rather than linear analysis
- **Creative Expression and Artistic Development**: Natural ability in artistic subjects, creative writing, and innovative problem-solving approaches
- **Interpersonal Sensitivity and Community Building**: Skills in collaborative learning, peer support, and creating inclusive classroom environments
- **Cultural Awareness and Bridge-Building**: Understanding of diverse perspectives and ability to connect different cultural approaches to learning

Educational Professional Applications:
- **Elementary Education**: Patient, nurturing teaching approaches that support young children's emotional and creative development alongside academic learning
- **Arts Education**: Teaching music, visual arts, drama, and creative writing with emphasis on individual expression and artistic development
- **Special Education**: Working with students with learning differences, emotional challenges, or special needs through individualized and compassionate approaches
- **Counseling and Student Support**: Academic counseling, social work, and psychological support for students facing personal or family challenges

Constitutional Educational Needs:
- **Supportive Learning Environments**: Classroom settings that minimize harsh lighting, excessive noise, and competitive pressure while maintaining academic standards
- **Adequate Processing Time**: Learning approaches that allow sufficient time for reflection and understanding without rushing through material
- **Collaborative Learning Opportunities**: Educational experiences that include group work, peer support, and community learning approaches
- **Authentic Assessment Methods**: Evaluation approaches that honor diverse learning styles and creative expression rather than relying solely on standardized testing

Electric Educational Success Story:
Sarah Chen, an Electric constitution elementary teacher, transformed her classroom by integrating constitutional understanding with character-based education. Initially overwhelmed by standardized testing pressures and classroom management challenges, she

developed an approach that honored student individual differences while maintaining high academic standards.

Working with educational mentors and applying constitutional educational development principles, Sarah created classroom environments that combined academic rigor with emotional support, individual learning approaches with collaborative projects, and standardized curriculum with creative expression opportunities.

Her methods integrated mindfulness practices with academic instruction, peer mentoring with individual assessment, and character development with subject mastery.

Magnetic Constitution Educational Applications:
Natural Educational Strengths:
- **Dynamic Teaching and Student Motivation**: Exceptional capacity for inspiring student engagement and maintaining classroom energy and enthusiasm
- **Practical Learning and Real-World Applications**: Strength in connecting academic subjects with practical applications and career preparation
- **Physical Education and Movement Integration**: Natural ability in sports, physical education, and incorporating movement with academic learning
- **Project-Based Learning and Achievement Orientation**: Talent for organizing educational projects and motivating students toward measurable academic achievement

Educational Professional Applications:
- **Secondary Education**: Teaching middle and high school students with emphasis on practical applications, career preparation, and achievement motivation
- **Physical Education and Athletic Coaching**: Sports instruction, fitness education, and coaching that integrates physical development with character formation
- **Career and Technical Education**: Vocational training, business education, and practical skill development that prepares students for immediate career success
- **Educational Leadership and Administration**: School administration, department leadership, and educational program development with focus on measurable outcomes

Constitutional Educational Needs:
- **Active Teaching Opportunities**: Educational roles that utilize physical movement, hands-on learning, and dynamic interaction

with students

- **Measurable Educational Outcomes**: Teaching positions that provide clear evidence of student achievement and educational program success
- **Leadership and Coordination Roles**: Educational positions that enable program development, team leadership, and school improvement initiatives
- **Practical Application Focus**: Teaching assignments that emphasize real-world applications and career preparation rather than purely theoretical learning

Neutral Constitution Educational Applications:
Natural Educational Strengths:

- **Systematic Instruction and Curriculum Development**: Superior analytical abilities for developing comprehensive educational programs and systematic approaches to learning
- **Academic Research and Educational Innovation**: Capacity for educational research, curriculum analysis, and evidence-based teaching method development
- **Assessment and Evaluation Excellence**: Attention to accurate student evaluation, educational outcome measurement, and program effectiveness analysis
- **Advanced Subject Matter Expertise**: Teaching abilities in complex academic subjects requiring systematic knowledge and analytical thinking

Educational Professional Applications:

- **Higher Education**: University teaching, graduate program development, and academic research in education, psychology, and other specialized disciplines
- **Curriculum Development**: Educational program design, textbook development, and systematic approaches to educational standard development
- **Educational Research and Evaluation**: Academic research on educational effectiveness, student assessment development, and educational policy analysis
- **Educational Administration**: District-level administration, educational policy development, and systematic approaches to educational system improvement

Constitutional Educational Needs:

- **Intellectual Challenge and Complexity**: Educational roles that provide complex problem-solving opportunities and analytical thinking requirements
- **Systematic Educational Approaches**: Work environments

that value precision, evidence-based practice, and systematic methodology in education
- **Professional Development Opportunities**: Educational positions that support continued learning, specialization advancement, and research involvement
- **Quality Standards and Excellence**: Educational institutions committed to high standards, systematic evaluation, and continuous educational improvement

Educational Team Development and Classroom Integration
Sacred Synthesis education creates team structures that honor constitutional diversity while ensuring educational excellence and student support across all learning needs.

Constitutional Educational Team Integration:
Team Composition and Role Assignment:
- **Electric Educational Professionals**: Student counseling, creative arts instruction, special needs support, and individual student mentoring utilizing their sensitivity and empathy
- **Magnetic Educational Professionals**: Physical education, career training, student activities coordination, and practical skills instruction utilizing their energy and motivation abilities
- **Neutral Educational Professionals**: Advanced academic instruction, curriculum development, educational research, and systematic assessment utilizing their analytical capabilities

Educational Collaboration Protocols:
- **Democratic Educational Decision-Making**: Academic decisions that integrate input from all constitutional types while maintaining appropriate educational authority and professional standards
- **Student-Centered Team Conferences**: Educational planning meetings that consider constitutional diversity of both educators and students in educational approach development
- **Conflict Resolution and Communication**: Educational team protocols that address professional disagreements through constitutional understanding and collaborative problem-solving
- **Continuing Team Development**: Professional development programs that strengthen team collaboration while advancing individual educational competency

Student Constitutional Assessment and Individualized Learning
Educational Constitutional Assessment Integration:
Assessment Protocol Development:
- **Learning Style Integration**: Constitutional factors considered

alongside traditional academic assessment and learning disability evaluation

- **Instructional Method Adaptation**: Recognition that constitutional types learn differently and benefit from varied teaching approaches and assessment methods
- **Classroom Environment Optimization**: Assessment of how constitutional needs affect learning capacity and classroom behavior
- **Extracurricular and Interest Integration**: Integration of student constitutional strengths with academic subjects and career exploration opportunities

Individualized Learning Planning:
- **Constitutional Learning Approaches**: Teaching methods that match constitutional preferences while maintaining educational standards and curriculum requirements
- **Assessment Method Selection**: Evaluation approaches that honor constitutional differences while ensuring accurate academic assessment and standards compliance
- **Behavioral Support Integration**: Classroom management approaches based on constitutional understanding and individual student development needs
- **Educational Communication Adaptation**: Teacher-student communication styles adapted to constitutional differences while maintaining professional boundaries and academic expectations

Contemplative Education and Character Formation
Traditional Character Development in Contemporary Education
Sacred Synthesis education recognizes that character formation provides the foundation for both academic success and authentic life preparation while enhancing rather than competing with intellectual development.

Contemplative Education Integration Principles:
Mindfulness and Attention Development:
- **Classroom Mindfulness Practices**: Brief meditation and awareness exercises that improve student attention while supporting emotional regulation
- **Academic Subject Integration**: Contemplative approaches to math, science, literature, and social studies that deepen understanding while developing wisdom
- **Character Formation Integration**: Virtue development and ethical reasoning integrated with academic instruction and practical life preparation

298

- **Community Building Practices**: Classroom and school community development through shared contemplative practice and service-oriented learning

Educational Mindfulness Applications:
- **Beginning-of-Class Centering**: Brief contemplative practice that helps students transition into learning readiness while building attention capacity
- **Academic Meditation Integration**: Subject-specific contemplative practices that deepen understanding while developing concentration abilities
- **Conflict Resolution Training**: Student training in peaceful problem-solving and communication skills based on mindfulness and constitutional understanding
- **Service-Learning Integration**: Community service projects that develop character while applying academic knowledge to real-world challenges

Constitutional Character Development Applications: Electric Constitution Character Formation:
- **Compassion and Empathy Development**: Character education emphasizing understanding of others, cultural sensitivity, and emotional intelligence
- **Creative Problem-Solving Training**: Educational approaches that develop innovative thinking and artistic expression alongside academic achievement
- **Community Service and Social Justice**: Service-learning projects focused on helping others and addressing social problems through compassionate action
- **Environmental Awareness and Stewardship**: Educational programs connecting environmental science with personal responsibility and planetary care

Magnetic Constitution Character Formation:
- **Leadership Development and Initiative**: Character education emphasizing personal responsibility, goal achievement, and positive influence on others
- **Physical Health and Wellness**: Educational programs integrating physical fitness with character development and academic achievement
- **Practical Skills and Career Preparation**: Character formation through real-world applications and preparation for adult responsibilities and careers
- **Team Building and Collaborative Achievement**: Educational experiences that develop cooperation abilities while maintain-

ing individual excellence and achievement

Neutral Constitution Character Formation:
- **Ethical Reasoning and Moral Development**: Character education emphasizing systematic thinking about right and wrong, justice, and ethical decision-making
- **Academic Excellence and Intellectual Integrity**: Character formation through rigorous academic work, honest scholarship, and commitment to truth and accuracy
- **Systematic Service and Organizational Skills**: Character development through organized community service and leadership in academic and social organizations
- **Long-term Planning and Wisdom Development**: Educational experiences that develop strategic thinking and consideration of consequences and long-term impact

Classroom Implementation and Teaching Methods
Constitutional Teaching Method Integration:
Electric-Oriented Teaching Approaches:
- **Collaborative Learning and Group Projects**: Educational approaches that utilize student interpersonal skills while ensuring individual accountability
- **Creative Expression and Artistic Integration**: Teaching methods that include artistic elements, creative writing, and innovative problem-solving approaches
- **Culturally Inclusive Curriculum**: Educational content that represents diverse perspectives and cultural traditions while maintaining academic standards
- **Emotion-Responsive Teaching**: Educational approaches that acknowledge student emotional needs while maintaining appropriate boundaries and academic focus

Magnetic-Oriented Teaching Approaches:
- **Hands-On Learning and Practical Applications**: Teaching methods that include physical activity, experiments, and real-world problem-solving opportunities
- **Achievement-Focused Instruction**: Educational approaches that set clear goals, provide measurable outcomes, and celebrate student accomplishment
- **Physical Movement Integration**: Teaching techniques that include movement, role-playing, and active participation in learning experiences
- **Career and Life Preparation**: Educational content that connects academic subjects with practical life skills and career preparation

Neutral-Oriented Teaching Approaches:

- **Systematic Instruction and Logical Progression**: Teaching methods that present material in organized, sequential manner with clear logical connections
- **Research-Based Learning and Critical Thinking**: Educational approaches that emphasize evidence evaluation, analytical thinking, and systematic investigation
- **Advanced Academic Challenge**: Teaching that provides intellectual complexity and higher order thinking opportunities appropriate to student ability
- **Individual Excellence and Academic Standards**: Educational approaches that maintain high expectations while providing individual support for achievement

Interdisciplinary Integration Examples:
Science Education Integration:

- **Constitutional Science Learning**: Science instruction adapted to constitutional types with hands-on experiments for Magnetic types, collaborative research for Electric types, and systematic analysis for Neutral types
- **Environmental Science and Character**: Ecological education that connects scientific knowledge with personal responsibility and character development
- **Science Ethics and Wisdom**: Integration of scientific method with ethical reasoning and consideration of scientific applications and consequences
- **Community Science Projects**: Science learning through community-based research and environmental action that serves both education and community benefit

Literature and Language Arts Integration:

- **Character-Based Literature Study**: Reading programs that analyze character development, moral themes, and ethical dilemmas in classical and contemporary literature
- **Cultural Literature and Global Perspective**: Literature study that includes diverse cultural traditions and global perspectives while developing cultural sensitivity
- **Creative Writing and Personal Expression**: Writing programs that develop individual voice and creativity while maintaining standards for grammar, organization, and communication
- **Communication Skills and Constitutional Adaptation**: Speech and writing instruction adapted to constitutional strengths while ensuring all students develop effective commu-

nication abilities

Social Studies and History Integration:
- **Character in History**: History instruction that examines moral leadership, ethical decision-making, and character examples throughout historical periods
- **Cultural Studies and Constitutional Understanding**: Social studies that explores different cultural approaches to education, governance, and community organization
- **Service Learning and Civic Engagement**: Social studies learning through community involvement and practical application of democratic principles and civic responsibility
- **Global Perspective and Cultural Bridge-Building**: International education that develops understanding of diverse cultures while maintaining appreciation for local traditions

Teacher Development and Educational Leadership
Educational Professional Development Through Traditional Wisdom
Sacred Synthesis educational excellence requires comprehensive training programs that integrate traditional wisdom with contemporary pedagogical methods while maintaining the highest standards of educational effectiveness and student support.

Teacher Education Integration:
Foundation Educational Training Enhancement:
- **Constitutional Understanding Development**: Teacher education in student assessment, individualized instruction approaches, and classroom management based on constitutional understanding
- **Contemplative Teaching Methods**: Teacher training in mindfulness-based instruction, character formation integration, and wisdom-based educational approaches
- **Cultural Competency and Traditional Knowledge**: Teacher education emphasizing diverse cultural educational traditions, traditional knowledge integration, and respectful multicultural education
- **Service-Oriented Teaching Philosophy**: Teacher training in education as service, community connection, and preparation of students for authentic adult contribution

Practical Teaching Integration:
- **Classroom Practice with Contemplative Integration**: Student teacher experiences in classrooms integrating contemplative practices with academic instruction

- **Character Formation and Academic Achievement**: Teacher training in methods that develop both character and academic excellence without compromising either goal
- **Constitutional Classroom Management**: Teacher education in natural authority, democratic classroom governance, and discipline approaches based on constitutional understanding
- **Community Engagement and Parent Partnership**: Teacher training in building relationships with families and communities while maintaining professional boundaries

Educational Leadership and Administrative Development
Contemplative Educational Leadership:
Leadership Development Programs:
- **Service-Oriented Educational Leadership**: Administrative training that emphasizes education as service to students, families, and community rather than bureaucratic management
- **Constitutional School Organization**: Educational leadership development in managing diverse student populations, supporting varied teaching styles, and organizing schools to serve constitutional diversity
- **Democratic Educational Governance**: Administrative training in participatory decision-making, community involvement, and shared leadership while maintaining educational standards
- **Character-Based School Culture**: Leadership development in creating school environments that support both academic achievement and character development

Educational System Development:
- **Curriculum Integration and Standards**: Educational leadership in curriculum development that integrates character formation with academic standards while meeting state and national requirements
- **Teacher Development and Support**: Administrative approaches to supporting teacher growth, providing professional development, and creating working conditions that enable educational excellence
- **Community Engagement and Partnership**: Educational leadership in building relationships with parents, local communities, and cultural organizations for mutual benefit and student support
- **Assessment and Accountability Balance**: Administrative approaches to maintaining educational accountability while honoring student individual development and comprehensive education goals

School Culture Development and Community Engagement
Constitutional School Culture Development:
Inclusive School Environment Creation:

- **Constitutional Student Support**: School environments that recognize and support diverse learning styles, emotional needs, and individual development approaches
- **Community Building and Belonging**: School culture development that creates authentic community while maintaining academic focus and achievement standards
- **Conflict Resolution and Healing**: School approaches to discipline and behavioral challenges that emphasize learning and growth rather than punishment alone
- **Cultural Diversity and Traditional Knowledge Integration**: School environments that honor diverse cultural backgrounds while building shared community and common educational goals

Family and Community Partnership:

- **Parent Education and Involvement**: Programs that educate families about contemplative education approaches while involving parents in school community development
- **Community Service and Real-World Learning**: Educational programs that connect classroom learning with community needs and service opportunities
- **Cultural Community Relationships**: School partnerships with diverse cultural and religious communities for mutual learning and student cultural identity support
- **Professional Community Connections**: School relationships with local businesses, healthcare organizations, and community institutions for student career preparation and community contribution

Community-Based Educational Development:
Local Educational Resource Integration:

- **Community Mentorship and Expertise**: Programs that connect students with community members who can provide guidance, skill development, and career exploration opportunities
- **Environmental Education and Stewardship**: Educational programs that connect academic learning with local environmental challenges and restoration opportunities
- **Economic Education and Cooperation**: Student learning about local economic systems, cooperative business principles, and community economic development through practical involvement
- **Cultural Preservation and Innovation**: Educational programs

that support local cultural traditions while preparing students for contemporary challenges and global participation

Educational Policy and System Transformation
Institutional Development and Educational Reform
Sacred Synthesis educational principles demonstrate superior effectiveness while requiring systematic policy development and institutional support for widespread implementation.

Educational Policy Integration Framework:
Standards and Assessment Policy Development:
- **Character Formation Standards**: Educational policy development that includes character development and ethical reasoning alongside academic achievement standards
- **Constitutional Learning Assessment**: Assessment policy that recognizes diverse learning styles and constitutional differences while maintaining academic standards and comparative evaluation
- **Contemplative Education Integration**: Policy frameworks supporting mindfulness and character development integration with academic subjects
- **Community Engagement Standards**: Educational policies that require community service and real- world application of academic learning

Professional Development Policy:
- **Teacher Training Requirements**: Educational policies requiring contemplative teaching methods and character formation training for teacher certification and continuing education
- **Administrative Leadership Standards**: Educational leadership preparation that includes service- oriented leadership and constitutional understanding of educational communities
- **Professional Evaluation Integration**: Evaluation systems for educators that include character development effectiveness and student well-being alongside academic achievement outcomes
- **Community Partnership Requirements**: Educational policies encouraging school-community relationships and cultural diversity integration

Educational System Integration Applications:
District and State-Level Implementation:
- **Pilot Program Development**: Systematic approaches to testing contemplative education methods with careful outcome measurement and community involvement
- **Professional Development Systems**: District and state pro-

grams supporting teacher and administrator training in Sacred Synthesis educational approaches
- **Curriculum Standard Integration**: Development of academic standards that include character formation while maintaining academic rigor and preparation requirements
- **Community Partnership Frameworks**: Systematic approaches to building school-community relationships and integrating local resources with educational programs

National Educational Policy Applications:
- **Educational Research and Validation**: National support for research documenting effectiveness of contemplative education and character formation integration
- **Professional Training Standards**: National teacher and administrator preparation standards that include contemplative pedagogy and constitutional understanding
- **Community-Based Education Support**: National policies supporting school-community partnerships and local resource integration with educational programs
- **International Educational Cooperation**: National participation in international educational networks sharing contemplative education approaches and cultural sensitivity methods

Educational Technology and Innovation Integration
Technology Integration with Educational Wisdom:
Constitutional Technology in Education:
- **Personalized Learning Technology**: Educational technology development that adapts to constitutional learning differences while maintaining human relationship and community learning
- **Digital Mindfulness and Character Development**: Technology applications that support contemplative practice and character formation rather than replacing human guidance and community development
- **Community Connection Technology**: Digital platforms that enhance rather than replace local community relationships and face-to-face educational experiences
- **Cultural Preservation Technology**: Educational technology that supports traditional knowledge preservation and cultural transmission while enabling contemporary skill development

Educational Platform Development:
- **Constitutional Learning Assessment Technology**: Digital assessment tools that recognize learning style differences while providing accurate academic evaluation and progress tracking
- **Contemplative Education Resources**: Online platforms

providing guided contemplative practices, character formation activities, and wisdom-based educational content

- **Community-Based Learning Technology**: Digital tools supporting school-community partnerships, local resource integration, and community service-learning opportunities
- **Global Educational Networks**: Technology platforms connecting schools and educational communities worldwide for cultural exchange and collaborative learning while maintaining local identity

Global Educational Applications and International Cooperation
International Educational Development and Cultural Cooperation:
Cross-Cultural Educational Applications:

- **Traditional Knowledge Integration**: Educational programs developed in partnership with traditional knowledge communities and indigenous educational approaches with appropriate cultural authorization
- **International Teacher Exchange**: Educational professional development programs enabling cross- cultural learning and traditional wisdom integration with contemporary educational methods
- **Global Student Exchange**: International student programs that provide exposure to diverse educational approaches while maintaining connection to local community and cultural identity
- **Educational Research Collaboration**: International cooperation in documenting effectiveness of contemplative education and traditional wisdom integration across diverse cultural contexts

Global Educational Challenge Response:
International Development Applications:

- **Community Education Development**: Educational programs for communities lacking formal education systems that integrate traditional knowledge with contemporary skill development
- **Peace Education and Conflict Resolution**: International educational programs teaching peaceful problem-solving and cultural understanding through contemplative education approaches
- **Environmental Education and Global Challenges**: International cooperation in environmental education that connects local ecological knowledge with global environmental challenges
- **Economic Education and Cooperative Development**: Educational programs teaching economic cooperation and sustainable development through traditional economic principles and

contemporary economic understanding

Educational Network Development:
- **International Educational Community**: Global networks of schools and educational professionals sharing contemplative education approaches and cultural sensitivity methods
- **Research and Documentation Networks**: International co-operation in educational research documenting effectiveness of traditional wisdom integration across cultural contexts
- **Professional Development Exchange**: International programs supporting teacher and administrator development in contemplative education and constitutional understanding
- **Educational Policy Cooperation**: International collaboration in educational policy development supporting character formation and traditional knowledge integration

Implementation Resources and Educational Development Support
Complete Educational Development Framework
Sacred Synthesis educational excellence requires comprehensive support systems and qualified guidance to ensure balanced development serving both individual student advancement and collective educational improvement.

Educational Development Assessment and Planning:
Phase 1: Foundation Educational Assessment (Months 1-6):
- **Educational Community Constitutional Assessment**: Complete evaluation of educational community constitutional diversity focusing on student, teacher, and administrator needs
- **Educational Vision Development**: Collective educational visioning process integrating individual educational goals with community educational service orientation
- **Educational Resource and Capacity Assessment**: Evaluation of educational resources, skills, and capacity for sustainable educational program development
- **Professional Educational Guidance**: Connection with qualified Sacred Synthesis educational teachers and educational development consultants

Phase 2: Educational Organization and Implementation (Months 6-18):
- **Constitutional Educational Governance Development**: Creation of democratic educational decision- making structures honoring constitutional diversity while ensuring effective educational leadership
- **Contemplative Education and Character Formation Inte-**

gration: Development of educational programs serving both academic achievement and character development advancement

- **Educational Programming Development**: Creation of educational programs serving both individual student development and collective educational community advancement
- **Regional Educational Network Integration**: Connection with other Sacred Synthesis educational communities and regional educational support networks

Phase 3: Educational Maturation and Service (Months 18+):
- **Advanced Educational Development**: Expansion of educational activities and development of capacity for serving broader educational community and society
- **Regional Educational Leadership Development**: Educational community contribution to regional educational coordination and educational system improvement
- **Global Educational Network Participation**: Integration with international Sacred Synthesis educational networks for mutual educational support and global educational service
- **Educational Transmission and Legacy**: Development of educational community capacity for educational approach transmission and long-term educational sustainability

Professional Educational Development Support:
Educational Development Consulting and Training:
- **Constitutional Educational Community Assessment**: Professional assessment of educational community constitutional diversity and optimal educational organization approaches
- **Democratic Educational Governance Training**: Professional instruction in educational consensus decision-making, educational conflict resolution, and participatory educational leadership
- **Contemplative Education and Character Formation Development**: Professional guidance in contemplative education development and sustainable character formation program advancement
- **Educational Program Development**: Professional support for educational programming and intergenerational educational transmission

Educational Facilitation and Leadership Training:
- **Constitutional Educational Communication Training**: Professional instruction in educational communication approaches honoring constitutional differences while building educational community

- **Educational Conflict Resolution and Community Healing**: Professional training in addressing educational community conflicts through constitutional understanding and restorative educational justice
- **Democratic Educational Meeting Facilitation**: Professional instruction in facilitating educational community meetings and educational decision-making processes effectively
- **Educational Community Leadership Development**: Professional development of educational leadership serving both individual constitutional educational strengths and collective educational advancement

Regional and Global Educational Community Support Networks:
Sacred Synthesis Educational Community Network:
- **Regional Educational Community Coordination**: Connection with other Sacred Synthesis educational communities in the same region for mutual educational support and cooperation
- **International Educational Community Network**: Global network of Sacred Synthesis educational communities for educational exchange, mutual educational support, and global educational service coordination
- **Professional Educational Community Support**: Network of professionals experienced in Sacred Synthesis educational development for educational consultation and support
- **Academic Educational Community Research**: Connection with academic institutions and researchers studying Sacred Synthesis educational approaches

Educational Development Resources:
- **Educational Development Handbook**: Comprehensive guide to Sacred Synthesis educational development including educational governance, educational economics, and educational programming
- **Constitutional Educational Assessment Tools**: Assessment instruments for evaluating educational community constitutional diversity and optimization
- **Democratic Educational Governance Templates**: Sample educational governance structures and educational decision-making processes adapted for Sacred Synthesis educational communities
- **Contemplative Education and Character Formation Guidelines**: Practical guidance for developing contemplative education and character formation and sustainable educational advancement

Conclusion: The Promise of Sacred Synthesis Educational Development
Sacred Synthesis educational development demonstrates that the
ancient vision of character-conscious, academically excellent, educa-
tionally cooperative schools can become practical reality through
systematic application of traditional wisdom supported by contemporary research while serving both individual student development
and beneficial educational innovation.

The key breakthrough involves recognition that constitutional diversity provides the foundation for both individual educational fulfillment and collective educational effectiveness when educational
structures honor rather than suppress natural human learning differences. When Electric types contribute creative educational innovation and cultural bridge-building, Magnetic types provide practical
educational implementation and student motivation, and Neutral
types offer systematic educational planning and assessment development, educational communities achieve capabilities that transcend
what any single constitutional educational approach could accomplish.

Core Educational Development Principles:

**Constitutional Educational Democracy Rather Than Educa-
tional Conformity:**
Sacred Synthesis educational communities integrate traditional wisdom with democratic educational participation by recognizing that
different constitutional types contribute different but complementary strengths to educational governance and student development.
Rather than attempting to eliminate personality learning differences,
educational structures channel constitutional diversity toward collective educational advancement.

Service-Oriented Individual Educational Development:
Educational structures support individual constitutional educational
development while ensuring that personal learning growth serves
collective educational advancement rather than remaining self-
centered academic materialism. This integration prevents both authoritarian suppression of learning individuality and anarchistic
fragmentation of educational community purpose.

Character Formation with Academic Excellence:
Educational systems honor traditional character development while
enabling contemporary academic achievement that serves both individual preparation for life and contemporary educational standards.

This approach transcends both rigid traditionalism and disconnected academic achievement through innovative approaches based on constitutional diversity.

Educational Community Autonomy with Regional and Global Educational Cooperation:
Educational communities maintain local educational autonomy and cultural authenticity while participating in regional educational improvement and global educational networks that address planetary educational challenges through cooperative rather than competitive educational approaches.

The Sacred Synthesis educational model provides practical methodology for the contemporary challenge of creating sustainable educational communities that serve both individual educational realization and collective educational advancement through integration of traditional wisdom with contemporary educational innovation, character formation with academic achievement, and local educational authenticity with global educational contribution.

COMMUNITY BUILDING

Unity · Democracy · Resources

READER'S NOTE:

You have entered the **Community Building layer** of Sacred Synthesis.

This section contains **community infrastructure** - democratic governance protocols and mutual aid frameworks

What you'll find here:
- Constitutional diversity in group dynamics
- Consensus decision-making processes
- Conflict resolution and power-sharing
- Autonomous community governance models

Look for:
- Safeguards against hierarchy and power concentration
- Adaptation guidelines for different contexts
- Professional integration (healthcare, education, organizing)

The cylinder has strength through structure. Build wisely. Build together.

The Great Achievement: Community Building
The community building materials were perhaps the most sophisticated I discovered - complete frameworks for democratic governance that had been tested across 147 communities worldwide.

Community Leadership and Governance
Spiritual Authority and Democratic Participation

Table of Contents

Introduction: The Democratic Revolution in Spiritual Community The
integration of authentic spiritual wisdom with democratic participation represents one of the most significant innovations in community organization, demonstrating that genuine spiritual authority
serves rather than dominates, enabling rather than controlling,
emerging through demonstrated competency and character rather
than appointment or inheritance.

Traditional spiritual communities have often suffered from authoritarian structures that concentrated power in single leaders while demanding unquestioning obedience from followers. This approach
produced spiritual dependency, abuse of authority, and stagnation of
community development while discouraging individual responsibility and democratic participation.

The Sacred Synthesis approach transcends this false dichotomy through **Democratic Mysticism**, the recognition that authentic spiritual development requires individual responsibility and democratic participation rather than passive compliance with external authority. This methodology resolves the perennial tension between spiritual wisdom and democratic values through systematic procedures that ensure community decisions serve spiritual development while maintaining individual freedom and collective effectiveness.

The Crisis of Authoritarian Spirituality
Historical analysis reveals consistent patterns in authoritarian spiritual organizations:

- **Power Concentration**: Authority accumulates in single individuals without accountability mechanisms
- **Spiritual Dependency**: Members become passive recipients rather than active participants in their development
- **Innovation Suppression**: New insights and adaptations are discouraged in favor of rigid adherence to established forms
- **Abuse Potential**: Unchecked authority creates conditions for exploitation and manipulation
- **Stagnation**: Communities become inward-focused and resistant to beneficial change

The Failure of Purely Democratic Approaches
Conventional democratic organizations, while protecting individual rights, often lack the wisdom and long-term vision necessary for genuine spiritual development:

- **Lowest Common Denominator**: Decisions reflect compromise rather than wisdom
- **Short-term Focus**: Immediate concerns override long-term spiritual development
- **Lack of Direction**: Without spiritual orientation, communities drift without clear purpose
- **Expertise Marginalization**: Specialized knowledge is subordinated to popular opinion
- **Material Emphasis**: Physical and emotional needs take precedence over spiritual development

Democratic Mysticism: The Synthesis
Democratic Mysticism integrates authentic spiritual authority with participatory decision-making through systematic procedures based on four foundational principles:

- **Earned Authority**: Leadership emerges through demonstrated spiritual development, practical competency, and service contribution rather than appointment or inheritance

- **Collective Wisdom**: Major decisions require community consultation and consensus-building while maintaining appropriate individual autonomy
- **Rotating Responsibility**: Leadership roles rotate among qualified community members to prevent power concentration and develop collective capacity
- **Transparent Process**: All decision-making procedures are open to community observation and feedback to maintain accountability and trust

Foundations of Democratic Mysticism
Theoretical Framework
Democratic Mysticism rests on several key insights from both spiritual wisdom and democratic theory:

Spiritual Authority Serves Development: Authentic spiritual guidance aims to develop the capacity of those served rather than maintaining dependency. True teachers work themselves out of a job by empowering students to become teachers themselves.

Individual Development Requires Participation: Spiritual growth cannot be imposed from outside but must emerge through conscious participation and personal responsibility. Democracy provides the framework for this participation.

Wisdom Emerges Collectively: While specialized knowledge exists, the full wisdom needed for community decisions often emerges through collective discernment involving multiple perspectives and types of expertise.

Power Corrupts – Service Purifies: Positions of authority tend to corrupt when held for personal benefit but purify character when understood as service opportunities with clear accountability.

Practical Principles
In Democratic Mysticism, authority is earned through demonstrated capacity to serve community development rather than personal advancement. Leaders are recognized for their ability to:
- Facilitate individual growth in community members
- Maintain community cohesion while honoring individual dignity
- Make decisions that serve long-term spiritual development over short-term convenience
- Remain accountable to community feedback and correction

Different aspects of community life require different types of expertise. Democratic Mysticism recognizes multiple forms of authority:

- **Spiritual Authority**: Earned through demonstrated realization and teaching capacity
- **Administrative Authority**: Based on organizational skills and practical competency
- **Technical Authority**: Grounded in specialized knowledge relevant to specific decisions
- **Experiential Authority**: Derived from life experience and practical wisdom

To prevent power concentration and develop community capacity, leadership responsibilities rotate among qualified members according to:

- **Term Limits**: Specific periods of service followed by sabbaticals
- **Succession Planning**: Systematic preparation of future leaders
- **Distributed Authority**: Multiple leadership roles rather than single hierarchical positions
- **Community Development**: Leadership positions as opportunities for service and growth

Community decisions involve appropriate participation from affected members through:

- **Information Sharing**: All relevant information available to decision-makers
- **Consultation Processes**: Input gathered from appropriate community members
- **Consensus Building**: Decisions reached through dialogue rather than simple voting
- **Implementation Support**: Community commitment to supporting collective decisions

Service-Oriented Leadership vs. Personal Aggrandizement
Distinguishing Service from Self-Service
The fundamental distinction in Democratic Mysticism lies between leadership as service opportunity versus leadership as personal advancement. This distinction affects every aspect of community organization and individual development.

Service-Oriented Leadership Characteristics:

- **Development Focus**: Primary attention given to developing others' capacities rather than maintaining personal position
- **Accountability Acceptance**: Welcoming community feedback and correction as opportunities for improvement
- **Succession Planning**: Actively preparing others to assume

leadership responsibilities

- **Transparent Decision-Making**: Open processes allowing community observation and input
- **Personal Growth Through Service**: Understanding leadership as spiritual practice requiring continuous development

Aggrandizement-Oriented Leadership Characteristics:
- **Position Protection**: Primary attention given to maintaining personal authority and status
- **Criticism Avoidance**: Defensive responses to community feedback or suggested corrections
- **Indispensability Creation**: Maintaining dependence rather than developing others' capacities
- **Closed Decision-Making**: Secret or exclusive processes limiting community participation
- **Spiritual Materialism**: Using spiritual development as means to personal advancement rather than service

Constitutional Leadership Applications
Different constitutional types express service-oriented leadership through distinct approaches, each contributing essential perspectives to community governance:

Electric Constitution (Vata Dominance) Leadership Natural Service Strengths:
- **Intuitive Wisdom**: Ability to sense community needs and emerging challenges before they become critical
- **Inclusive Facilitation**: Natural capacity for creating safe spaces where all voices can be heard authentically
- **Cultural Bridge-Building**: Skills in connecting different groups and facilitating understanding across differences
- **Creative Problem-Solving**: Innovation in developing new approaches to community challenges and opportunities

Service-Oriented Leadership Expression:
- **Community Facilitators**: Leading meetings and discussions with sensitivity to group dynamics and individual needs
- **Conflict Mediators**: Addressing disputes through understanding and relationship healing rather than mere rule enforcement
- **Cultural Liaisons**: Building relationships with other communities, organizations, and cultural groups
- **Innovation Coordinators**: Developing creative solutions to community challenges while maintaining traditional wisdom

Constitutional Leadership Development:
- **Grounding Practices**: Regular practices that maintain stability

and prevent nervous system overwhelm
- **Structured Support**: Administrative assistance that handles details while preserving visionary capacity
- **Community Feedback**: Regular input helping maintain connection to practical community needs
- **Rest and Renewal**: Adequate recovery time preventing burnout and maintaining sensitivity

Magnetic Constitution (Kapha Dominance) Leadership Natural Service Strengths:
- **Practical Implementation**: Ability to translate vision into concrete action and measurable results
- **Resource Management**: Skills in organizing community assets and coordinating complex projects
- **Collective Motivation**: Capacity for inspiring group participation and maintaining community energy
- **Institutional Development**: Talent for building stable organizational structures and long-term systems

Service-Oriented Leadership Expression:
- **Project Coordinators**: Managing community initiatives from conception through completion with attention to practical details
- **Resource Managers**: Handling community finances, property, and material resources with transparency and accountability
- **Community Organizers**: Coordinating group activities, service projects, and collective initiatives that build solidarity
- **Infrastructure Builders**: Developing physical and organizational systems that support community life and development

Constitutional Leadership Development:
- **Challenge Integration**: Adequate complexity preventing stagnation while maintaining sustainable pace
- **Recognition Systems**: Appropriate acknowledgment of practical contributions and sustained service
- **Collaborative Approaches**: Shared leadership preventing excessive burden accumulation
- **Innovation Opportunities**: Participation in creative projects maintaining engagement and growth

Neutral Constitution (Pitta Dominance) Leadership Natural Service Strengths:
- **Strategic Analysis**: Ability to evaluate community challenges systematically and develop comprehensive solutions
- **Policy Development**: Skills in creating community agreements and governance structures that serve long-term effectiveness

- **Educational Leadership**: Capacity for teaching community members and developing collective competency
- **External Relations**: Talent for representing community interests and building relationships with institutions

Service-Oriented Leadership Expression:
- **Strategic Planners**: Developing long-term community vision and systematic approaches to achieving collective goals
- **Policy Developers**: Creating community agreements, governance structures, and decision-making processes
- **Educational Leaders**: Teaching community members about governance, constitutional understanding, and spiritual development
- **Professional Representatives**: Handling community relationships with government, institutions, and professional organizations

Constitutional Leadership Development:
- **Systematic Processes**: Well-organized responsibilities with clear criteria and logical progression
- **Quality Standards**: Community commitment to excellence in all aspects of leadership and governance
- **Intellectual Challenge**: Complex problems requiring analysis, planning, and systematic solution development
- **Professional Recognition**: Acknowledgment of analytical abilities and contribution to community effectiveness

Leadership Development Through Service
Democratic Mysticism understands leadership development as ongoing spiritual practice requiring continuous growth in wisdom, compassion, and practical effectiveness.
- **Constitutional Understanding**: Complete assessment and adaptation of spiritual practices
- **Community Participation**: Active engagement in community life and service projects
- **Skill Development**: Acquisition of practical competencies relevant to community needs
- **Mentorship Relationships**: Guidance from experienced community leaders and external advisors
- **Specific Responsibilities**: Acceptance of particular leadership roles appropriate to constitutional type and community needs
- **Team Collaboration**: Experience working with other leaders in collective decision-making and project implementation
- **Community Teaching**: Beginning instruction of newer community members in governance and spiritual practices

- **External Representation**: Participation in broader community and professional relationships
- **Wisdom Sharing**: Teaching and mentoring based on extensive experience and demonstrated results
- **Succession Planning**: Active preparation of next generation leaders through systematic development programs
- **Community Visioning**: Contribution to long-term planning and adaptation to changing circumstances
- **Cultural Transmission**: Preservation and adaptation of essential wisdom for future generations

Consensus Building and Decision-Making Integration Methods
Beyond Simple Majority Rule
Traditional democratic procedures often rely on majority vote to resolve differences, but this approach frequently creates winners and losers rather than community unity. Democratic Mysticism employs consensus-building methods that seek solutions serving the highest good of all while maintaining individual dignity and collective effectiveness.

Limitations of Majority-Rule Democracy:
- **Adversarial Process**: Decisions become competitions rather than collaborative problem-solving
- **Minority Marginalization**: Smaller groups consistently outvoted may become alienated
- **Compromise Quality**: Solutions may satisfy no one while disappointing everyone
- **Implementation Problems**: Decisions lack full community support, hampering effective action
- **Relationship Damage**: Repeated conflicts over decisions can harm community relationships

Consensus-Building Advantages:
- **Creative Solutions**: Process encourages innovation and comprehensive approaches
- **Community Unity**: Decisions enjoy full community support and commitment
- **Relationship Building**: Process strengthens interpersonal connections and mutual understanding
- **Implementation Effectiveness**: Universal support enables smooth execution of collective decisions
- **Individual Growth**: Participation develops wisdom, patience, and collaborative skills

The Sacred Synthesis Council Process
The council process integrates traditional indigenous wisdom with constitutional understanding and contemporary democratic requirements, creating a comprehensive framework for community decision-making.

Pre-Council Preparation Phase Individual Constitutional Preparation:
Electric Constitution Members:
- **Contemplative Centering**: Individual meditation and reflection supporting clear perception and calm participation
- **Information Gathering**: Gentle research and consultation ensuring understanding of issues without overwhelming detail
- **Emotional Preparation**: Processing personal feelings and reactions privately to enable objective community service
- **Intention Setting**: Clarifying personal commitment to community welfare and individual constitutional contribution

Magnetic Constitution Members:
- **Practical Research**: Thorough investigation of practical implications and implementation requirements for decisions
- **Resource Assessment**: Evaluation of community capacity and resource implications for proposed actions
- **Stakeholder Consultation**: Gathering input from community members who will be affected by decisions
- **Implementation Planning**: Preliminary consideration of how decisions will be translated into effective action

Neutral Constitution Members:
- **Strategic Analysis**: Systematic evaluation of options, implications, and long- term consequences of potential decisions
- **Policy Research**: Investigation of how similar decisions have been handled in other communities and organizations
- **Precedent Consideration**: Understanding how decisions will affect community governance and future decision-making
- **Professional Consultation**: Seeking advice from appropriate experts or professionals when complex issues are involved

Council Meeting Process
Opening and Sacred Space Creation (15-20 minutes):
- **Physical Circle Formation**: Seating arrangement enabling all participants to see and hear each other equally
- **Constitutional Recognition**: Brief acknowledgment of the three constitutional types and their contributions to community decisions
- **Collective Intention Setting**: Community commitment to de-

cisions serving both individual development and collective advancement

Information Sharing Phase (20-30 minutes):
- **Electric Contribution**: Intuitive sensing of community needs and cultural context affecting decisions
- **Magnetic Contribution**: Practical information about resources, implementation capacity, and community impact
- **Neutral Contribution**: Strategic analysis of options, implications, and systematic approaches to complex issues
- **Community Questions**: Opportunity for all members to seek clarification and additional information

Constitutional Perspective Integration (30-45 minutes):
- **Electric Perspective**: Consideration of how decisions affect community harmony, individual well-being, and cultural relationships
- **Magnetic Perspective**: Focus on practical implementation, resource requirements, and measurable community outcomes
- **Neutral Perspective**: Analysis of long-term implications, policy considerations, and systematic approaches to challenges
- **Synthesis Dialogue**: Integration of constitutional perspectives into comprehensive understanding of issues

Consensus Building and Decision Integration (20-30 minutes):
- **Option Development**: Creating decision options that honor all constitutional perspectives while serving community advancement
- **Consensus Exploration**: Testing community agreement through constitutional representation and individual voice
- **Implementation Planning**: Developing action plans that utilize constitutional strengths and ensure effective follow-through
- **Community Commitment**: Collective agreement to support decisions and contribute to successful implementation

Advanced Council Applications Complex Issue Resolution:
When communities face particularly challenging decisions, extended council processes may span multiple sessions:

Session 1: Issue Exploration:
- Comprehensive information gathering from all constitutional perspectives
- Identification of core values and principles relevant to the decision
- Recognition of different stakeholder interests and community

impact
- Establishment of criteria for evaluating potential solutions

Session 2: Option Development:
- Creative brainstorming honoring all constitutional approaches
- Systematic evaluation of alternatives using established criteria
- Integration of practical constraints with community values
- Initial consensus testing and feedback gathering

Session 3: Decision Integration:
- Final consensus building incorporating all previous work
- Implementation planning with constitutional role assignments
- Accountability mechanisms and evaluation criteria establishment
- Community commitment and celebration of collective wisdom

Crisis Response Councils:
Emergency situations require modified council processes maintaining democratic principles while enabling rapid response:
- **Rapid Assessment**: Quick gathering of essential information from constitutional perspectives
- **Expedited Consultation**: Abbreviated but inclusive input gathering from affected community members
- **Provisional Decision**: Temporary measures enabling immediate response with planned review
- **Community Ratification**: Full council process as soon as circumstances allow for permanent decisions

Conflict Resolution and Community Healing Applications
Understanding Conflict as Community Development Opportunity
Traditional approaches to conflict often focus on eliminating disagreement or determining winners and losers. Democratic Mysticism recognizes conflict as natural result of diverse perspectives and constitutional differences, viewing disputes as opportunities for community growth and deeper understanding.

Conflict as Developmental Catalyst:
- **Diversity Recognition**: Conflicts often arise from different constitutional approaches to similar challenges
- **Values Clarification**: Disputes help communities identify and articulate core principles and priorities
- **Relationship Deepening**: Working through disagreements can strengthen interpersonal connections and mutual understanding
- **Innovation Stimulation**: Conflicts frequently generate creative solutions that satisfy previously unrecognized needs
- **Community Maturation**: Successfully resolving disputes de-

324

velops collective capacity for handling future challenges

Constitutional Conflict Patterns
Different constitutional combinations tend to generate specific types of conflicts with predictable patterns and effective resolution approaches:

Electric-Magnetic Constitutional Conflicts Common Conflict Sources:
- **Pace Differences**: Electric preference for reflection versus Magnetic drive for action
- **Decision-Making Styles**: Intuitive sensing versus practical analysis approaches
- **Resource Priorities**: Relationship and harmony emphasis versus efficiency and results focus
- **Communication Patterns**: Indirect suggestion versus direct instruction preferences

Resolution Approaches:
- **Timing Accommodation**: Scheduling allowing both reflection periods and action phases
- **Process Integration**: Decision-making combining intuitive wisdom with practical assessment
- **Role Clarification**: Clear definition of responsibilities utilizing each type's strengths
- **Communication Translation**: Helping each type understand and appreciate the other's perspective

Electric Position: Monthly meetings provide adequate time for processing and prevent overwhelming discussion

Magnetic Position: Weekly meetings necessary for maintaining momentum and addressing practical issues promptly

Resolution Process:
- **Constitutional Recognition**: Acknowledgment that both perspectives reflect valid constitutional needs
- **Underlying Needs Identification**: Electric need for processing time, Magnetic need for responsive action
- **Creative Solution Development**: Bi-weekly community meetings with monthly extended sessions for complex issues
- **Implementation Trial**: Six-month experiment with evaluation and adjustment mechanisms

Electric-Neutral Constitutional Conflicts Common Conflict Sources:
- **Precision versus Flow**: Systematic approaches versus intuitive adaptation

- **Temperature Regulation**: Environmental needs and seasonal adaptations
- **Planning Horizons**: Long-term strategic thinking versus present-moment responsiveness
- **Authority Structures**: Analytical expertise versus intuitive wisdom as decision- making basis

Resolution Approaches:
- **Seasonal Adaptation**: Different approaches for different times of year and community phases
- **Complementary Expertise**: Recognition of different types of wisdom and their appropriate applications
- **Environmental Accommodation**: Physical spaces and scheduling adapted to constitutional needs
- **Collaborative Leadership**: Shared responsibilities utilizing each type's natural strengths

Magnetic-Neutral Constitutional Conflicts Common Conflict Sources:
- **Intensity versus Balance**: High-energy engagement versus steady, sustainable approaches
- **Achievement versus Process**: Results orientation versus quality and precision emphasis
- **Resource Usage**: Efficiency maximization versus balance and sustainability priorities
- **Change Pace**: Rapid implementation versus careful, systematic adaptation

Resolution Approaches:
- **Cyclical Planning**: Alternating periods of intensity and integration suited to different constitutional needs
- **Quality-Results Balance**: Standards satisfying both precision requirements and practical effectiveness
- **Resource Management**: Approaches honoring both efficiency and sustainability values
- **Implementation Pacing**: Project timelines accommodating both types' optimal working rhythms

Restorative Justice Principles
Democratic Mysticism employs restorative rather than punitive approaches to community conflicts, focusing on healing relationships and preventing future difficulties rather than punishment or exclusion.

Restorative Justice Foundation Principles:
- **Harm Recognition**: Acknowledgment of actual damage done

to relationships and community well-being
- **Responsibility Acceptance**: Opportunity for all parties to understand their contributions to conflicts
- **Repair Commitment**: Focus on healing harm and restoring community relationships
- **Prevention Integration**: Changes preventing similar conflicts in the future
- **Community Involvement**: Collective participation in resolution and healing processes

Restorative Process Phases:
- **Immediate Support**: Ensuring all parties feel safe and have appropriate advocacy
- **Community Stabilization**: Preventing escalation while gathering information and preparing for healing process
- **Constitutional Assessment**: Understanding how different constitutional types experienced and contributed to the conflict
- **Process Planning**: Designing restorative approach appropriate to specific situation and community needs
- **Story Sharing**: Opportunity for all parties to describe their experience without interruption or defense
- **Impact Recognition**: Understanding how actions affected different community members and relationships
- **Constitutional Translation**: Helping parties understand how constitutional differences contributed to misunderstanding
- **Responsibility Clarification**: Acknowledgment of each party's contribution to conflict development
- **Apology and Forgiveness**: Appropriate acknowledgment of harm and extending of forgiveness when ready
- **Practical Repair**: Concrete actions addressing material or relationship damage
- **Community Healing**: Collective processes addressing community impact and restoring trust
- **Prevention Planning**: Changes in community systems, communication, or structures preventing similar conflicts
- **Learning Extraction**: Identifying lessons from conflict that benefit community development
- **Relationship Rebuilding**: Ongoing processes strengthening connections damaged during conflict
- **Community Strengthening**: Using resolution success to increase community capacity for future challenges
- **Celebration**: Recognition of growth and healing achieved through difficult process

Community Healing Applications

Beyond individual conflicts, communities periodically require collective healing processes addressing historical wounds, systemic problems, or accumulated tensions.

Community Healing Contexts:
- **Historical Trauma**: Addressing inherited wounds from past injustices or conflicts
- **Leadership Transitions**: Processing grief and adjustment during changes in community guidance
- **Growth Transitions**: Healing tensions arising from community expansion or significant changes
- **External Pressures**: Community response to outside criticism, legal challenges, or cultural conflicts

Collective Healing Methodologies:
Truth and Reconciliation Processes:
- **Historical Documentation**: Comprehensive gathering of community history including difficult periods
- **Story Witnessing**: Community-wide opportunities for sharing experiences and being heard
- **Pattern Recognition**: Understanding systemic issues and recurring problems requiring attention
- **Collective Responsibility**: Community acknowledgment of shared responsibility for problems and solutions

Healing Ceremonies and Practices:
- **Community Grief Work**: Collective processing of losses and disappointments
- **Forgiveness Rituals**: Ceremonial release of resentments and blame patterns
- **Recommitment Ceremonies**: Community reaffirmation of shared values and purposes
- **Celebration Integration**: Recognition of growth and resilience demonstrated through healing process

Systemic Changes:
- **Governance Improvements**: Modifications to community structures preventing similar problems
- **Communication Enhancement**: Training and systems improving interpersonal and collective communication
- **Constitutional Integration**: Better understanding and accommodation of different constitutional needs
- **Preventive Measures**: Early warning systems and intervention protocols for future difficulties

Financial Management and Sustainability with Traditional Principles
Sacred Economics and Community Wealth
Democratic Mysticism approaches financial management through principles that honor both practical sustainability and spiritual values, recognizing money as energy that should serve community development rather than accumulate for its own sake.

Sacred Economics Foundation Principles:
- **Abundance Perspective**: Recognition that genuine wealth comes from community relationships, shared resources, and collective capacity rather than individual accumulation
- **Reciprocity Commitment**: Financial systems based on mutual benefit and circulation rather than exploitation or extraction
- **Sustainability Focus**: Economic decisions considered for seven-generation impact rather than short-term profit
- **Service Orientation**: Money understood as tool for serving spiritual development and community advancement
- **Transparency Practice**: Open financial processes building trust and enabling informed community participation

Constitutional Economic Approaches
Different constitutional types contribute distinct strengths to community financial management while requiring different approaches to economic participation:

Electric Constitution Financial Contributions Natural Economic Strengths:
- **Value Recognition**: Intuitive understanding of true worth versus market price
- **Relationship Economics**: Emphasis on economic systems that build rather than damage community connections
- **Long-term Perspective**: Natural concern for economic sustainability and future generations
- **Resource Sharing**: Comfortable with cooperative ownership and community resource management

Economic Participation Adaptations:
- **Gentle Fundraising**: Soft approaches to resource development emphasizing relationship building over aggressive solicitation
- **Collaborative Planning**: Shared financial decision-making preventing overwhelming responsibility
- **Flexible Expectations**: Economic contributions adapted to individual capacity and constitutional needs
- **Support Systems**: Administrative assistance handling details while preserving visionary contribution

Magnetic Constitution Financial Contributions Natural Economic Strengths:

- **Practical Implementation**: Ability to translate financial goals into concrete actions and measurable results
- **Resource Management**: Skills in organizing community assets and coordinating complex financial projects
- **Fundraising Capacity**: Comfort with direct solicitation and building supporter relationships
- **Economic Growth**: Talent for developing revenue streams and expanding community financial capacity

Economic Participation Adaptations:

- **Active Involvement**: Leadership roles in fundraising campaigns and resource development projects
- **Goal Achievement**: Clear financial targets and systematic approaches to reaching objectives
- **Challenge Integration**: Adequate complexity preventing stagnation while maintaining sustainable expectations
- **Recognition Systems**: Appropriate acknowledgment of financial contributions and resource development success

Neutral Constitution Financial Contributions Natural Economic Strengths:

- **Strategic Analysis**: Ability to evaluate financial challenges systematically and develop comprehensive solutions
- **Professional Management**: Skills in creating financial systems and policies that serve long-term effectiveness
- **Investment Planning**: Capacity for analyzing investment options and developing balanced portfolio strategies
- **Financial Education**: Talent for teaching community members about money management and economic principles

Economic Participation Adaptations:

- **Systematic Planning**: Well-organized financial responsibilities with clear criteria and logical progression
- **Quality Standards**: Community commitment to excellence in financial management and stewardship
- **Professional Integration**: Connection with financial advisors and investment professionals appropriate to community values
- **Educational Leadership**: Teaching roles helping other community members develop financial competency

Community Financial Systems
Democratic Mysticism communities employ various financial approaches that balance individual needs with collective sustainability:

Cooperative Economics Models Shared Resource Systems:
- **Community Land Ownership**: Collective ownership preventing individual members from profiting from land speculation
- **Tool and Equipment Libraries**: Shared ownership of expensive items reducing individual financial burden
- **Skill Exchange Networks**: Time banking and labor exchange reducing cash transactions
- **Group Purchasing**: Bulk buying reducing costs for individual families

Income Sharing Approaches:
- **Sliding Scale Contributions**: Community support levels based on individual capacity rather than fixed amounts
- **Percentage Systems**: Contributions based on income percentage rather than absolute amounts
- **Gift Economy Elements**: Some community needs met through voluntary giving rather than required payments
- **Work Exchange Options**: Community service accepted in lieu of financial contributions when appropriate

Investment and Savings Strategies Community Investment Priorities:
- **Local Economic Development**: Investments supporting regional economic health and community self-reliance
- **Sustainable Technologies**: Financial support for renewable energy, organic agriculture, and ecological restoration
- **Educational Infrastructure**: Funding for community education, libraries, and skill development programs
- **Healthcare and Wellness**: Investment in community health and preventive medicine resources

Ethical Investment Criteria:
- **Values Alignment**: Investments consistent with community spiritual and environmental values
- **Community Benefit**: Priority for investments that serve local and regional development
- **Long-term Sustainability**: Focus on investments contributing to ecological and social health
- **Democratic Ownership**: Preference for cooperatives, employee-owned businesses, and community development funds

Financial Transparency and Accountability Open Book Policies:
- **Regular Financial Reports**: Monthly or quarterly community-wide financial updates
- **Budget Participation**: Community involvement in annual budget planning and priority setting

- **Investment Disclosure**: Complete transparency about community investment decisions and performance
- **Expense Authorization**: Clear procedures for financial decisions and expenditure approval

Accountability Mechanisms:
- **Financial Committee**: Community-elected group with oversight responsibility for financial management
- **Professional Audit**: Annual independent review of community finances by qualified accountants
- **Member Review Rights**: Community member access to financial records and decision-making processes
- **Conflict of Interest Policies**: Clear procedures preventing personal financial benefit from community positions

Sustainable Fundraising Strategies
Community financial sustainability requires diversified revenue sources that align with spiritual values while meeting practical needs:

Individual Contribution Systems Membership Support Models:
- **Sliding Scale Memberships**: Multiple membership levels accommodating different financial capacities
- **Percentage-Based Giving**: Contributions based on income percentage rather than fixed amounts
- **Time-Money Balance**: Opportunities to contribute through service when financial resources are limited
- **Family Accommodations**: Membership structures honoring different family configurations and economic situations

Major Gift Development:
- **Legacy Giving Programs**: Planned giving opportunities for community members committed to long-term support
- **Capital Campaign Organization**: Systematic approaches to funding major community infrastructure projects
- **Foundation Relationships**: Grant writing and foundation relationship development for program-specific funding
- **Individual Donor Cultivation**: Personal relationship development with community supporters and friends

Earned Revenue Approaches Program-Based Income:
- **Educational Workshops**: Public programs generating revenue while serving community education mission
- **Consultation Services**: Community expertise shared with other organizations through fee-for-service programs
- **Product Sales**: Community-produced goods sold to support

financial sustainability
- **Retreat and Conference Hosting**: Facility rental and program hosting for aligned organizations

Social Enterprise Development:
- **Community-Supported Agriculture**: Farming operations serving community food needs while generating revenue
- **Cooperative Businesses**: Community-owned enterprises serving both local needs and income generation
- **Professional Services**: Community members offering services through community-coordinated businesses
- **Property Development**: Real estate development consistent with community values and serving affordable housing needs

Legal Structures and Governance Navigation
Integrating Spiritual Community with Legal Requirements
Democratic Mysticism communities must navigate complex legal environments while maintaining authentic spiritual practice and democratic governance. This requires sophisticated understanding of various legal structures and their implications for community development.

Legal Structure Considerations:
- **Religious Organization Benefits**: Tax exemptions and religious freedom protections
- **Educational Institution Status**: Ability to offer educational programs and receive educational funding
- **Community Benefit Organization**: Focus on public service and community development
- **Cooperative Structure**: Democratic ownership and decision-making legal protection

Religious Organization Models Advantages of Religious Status:
- **Tax Exemption**: Freedom from property taxes and income taxes on religious activities
- **Religious Freedom Protection**: Legal protection for spiritual practices and community governance
- **Donation Benefits**: Contributors can claim tax deductions for charitable giving
- **Employment Flexibility**: Ability to hire based on religious commitment and spiritual development

Challenges of Religious Status:
- **Doctrine Definition Requirements**: Need to articulate specific religious beliefs and practices for legal recognition

- **Activity Limitations**: Restrictions on political advocacy and commercial activities
- **Public Scrutiny**: Increased government oversight and public accountability requirements
- **Sectarian Perception**: Risk of being viewed as exclusive rather than inclusive spiritual community

Educational Institution Options Private Educational Corporation:
- **Program Development Freedom**: Ability to create innovative educational approaches without government curriculum requirements
- **Accreditation Opportunities**: Potential for formal educational recognition and degree-granting authority
- **Student Financial Aid**: Eligibility for educational funding programs supporting student access
- **Research Opportunities**: Ability to conduct formal research and publish academic results

Community Education Collaborative:
- **Flexibility Maintenance**: Less formal structure allowing adaptation to community needs
- **Partnership Development**: Collaboration with established educational institutions for programming and credentialing
- **Public Service Integration**: Educational programs serving broader community while supporting community financial sustainability
- **Lifelong Learning Focus**: Programs serving adult learning and community development rather than formal degree programs

Community Benefit and Cooperative Models Community Land Trust Structure:
- **Affordable Housing Protection**: Permanent affordability for community housing and land access
- **Democratic Governance**: Community control over land use and development decisions
- **Speculation Prevention**: Protection against gentrification and community displacement
- **Multi-generational Planning**: Governance structure supporting long-term community continuity

Worker and Housing Cooperatives:
- **Democratic Ownership**: One-member-one-vote decision-making protecting individual rights within community structure
- **Economic Benefit**: Shared ownership providing economic security and wealth building for members
- **Tax Advantages**: Cooperative tax structures providing benefits

for member- owners
- **Governance Training**: Legal requirements for democratic participation developing community democratic capacity

Governance Integration Strategies
Successfully integrating spiritual community governance with legal requirements involves several key strategies:

Dual Structure Approaches
Spiritual-Legal Structure Coordination:
Many communities employ parallel structures addressing both spiritual development and legal requirements:

Spiritual Governance Structure:
- **Council of Elders**: Experienced community members providing wisdom and guidance for spiritual development
- **Constitutional Councils**: Decision-making bodies incorporating constitutional diversity and consensus-building processes
- **Teaching Authority**: Qualified teachers recognized by community for spiritual instruction and guidance
- **Ceremonial Leadership**: Individuals responsible for community spiritual practices and celebrations

Legal Governance Structure:
- **Board of Directors**: Legally responsible individuals meeting corporate governance requirements
- **Officers**: President, Secretary, Treasurer fulfilling legal roles and regulatory compliance
- **Committee Structure**: Legal committees handling specific organizational functions and accountability
- **Member Assembly**: Legal membership meetings satisfying democratic participation requirements

Integration Mechanisms:
- **Overlapping Leadership**: Spiritual leaders also serving in legal governance roles when appropriate
- **Communication Protocols**: Regular communication between spiritual and legal governance ensuring coordination
- **Decision Coordination**: Processes ensuring spiritual community decisions are appropriately implemented through legal structure
- **Accountability Alignment**: Systems ensuring both spiritual and legal accountability serve community development

Conflict Resolution and Dispute Management Internal Conflict Resolution:
Legal structures must accommodate community preferred approaches to conflict resolution:

- **Mediation Provisions**: Legal documents specifying community commitment to mediation before litigation
- **Arbitration Agreements**: Binding arbitration procedures for conflicts requiring third-party resolution
- **Community Justice Processes**: Legal recognition of restorative justice and community healing approaches
- **Appeal Mechanisms**: Multiple levels of review and appeal protecting individual rights while maintaining community authority

External Relationship Management:

- **Government Relations**: Professional relationships with regulatory agencies ensuring compliance and advocating for community interests
- **Legal Representation**: Qualified attorneys familiar with religious freedom, community development, and cooperative law
- **Public Relations**: Communication strategies maintaining positive relationships with surrounding communities
- **Advocacy Participation**: Involvement in policy advocacy protecting rights of intentional communities and alternative lifestyles

Regulatory Compliance and Risk Management
Tax and Financial Compliance Federal and State Tax Requirements:

- **Annual Reporting**: Form 990 and state reporting requirements for tax-exempt organizations
- **Employment Taxes**: Compliance with payroll tax requirements for community employees
- **Unrelated Business Income**: Management of commercial activities within tax- exempt organizations
- **Donor Reporting**: Proper acknowledgment of charitable contributions and donor privacy protection

Financial Management Standards:

- **Accounting Systems**: Professional bookkeeping and financial management meeting legal requirements
- **Audit Procedures**: Independent financial review ensuring transparency and accountability
- **Investment Policies**: Written investment guidelines ensuring appropriate stewardship of community resources
- **Conflict of Interest Management**: Policies preventing personal benefit from community financial decisions

- **Insurance Coverage**: Comprehensive insurance protecting community property, programs, and members
- **Safety Protocols**: Written procedures for community activities ensuring participant safety
- **Child Protection Policies**: Comprehensive safeguards for children participating in community programs
- **Emergency Procedures**: Crisis response plans addressing natural disasters, medical emergencies, and security concerns

Personnel and Volunteer Management:
- **Background Checks**: Appropriate screening for community members working with vulnerable populations
- **Training Requirements**: Safety training for community members involved in high-risk activities
- **Supervision Policies**: Appropriate oversight ensuring safe and effective community operations
- **Documentation Systems**: Record-keeping systems supporting legal compliance and risk management

Growth Management: Maintaining Authenticity while Enabling Service
The Challenge of Sustainable Growth
As Democratic Mysticism communities demonstrate their effectiveness and attract interest from potential new members, they face the challenge of growth management, expanding their service capacity while maintaining the intimate relationships and authentic spiritual practice that created their initial success.

Growth Pressure Sources:
- **Mission Success**: Effective programs create demand for expansion and replication
- **Economic Pressure**: Financial sustainability often requires increased membership or program participation
- **External Interest**: Public recognition leads to requests for consultation, training, and partnership
- **Member Development**: Advanced practitioners seek opportunities to serve and teach others

Authenticity Preservation Requirements:
- **Intimate Scale**: Community relationships require manageable numbers enabling personal connection
- **Quality Maintenance**: Rapid growth can compromise program quality and individual attention
- **Cultural Continuity**: New members need adequate time to absorb community values and practices

- **Leadership Capacity**: Growth requires development of qualified leadership faster than natural emergence

Constitutional Approaches to Growth Management
Different constitutional types approach growth challenges through distinct perspectives and strategies:

Electric Constitution Growth Management Natural Growth Strengths:
- **Intuitive Assessment**: Ability to sense when potential new members align with community values and development
- **Relationship Integration**: Skill in helping newcomers develop authentic connections with existing community members
- **Cultural Preservation**: Sensitivity to maintaining community spiritual atmosphere during expansion periods
- **Sustainable Pacing**: Natural tendency toward gradual growth that allows proper integration

Growth Management Applications:
- **Intake Assessment**: Intuitive evaluation of potential member readiness and community fit
- **Mentorship Programs**: Personal guidance systems helping newcomers integrate community values and practices
- **Cultural Transmission**: Programs ensuring essential community wisdom passes to new members
- **Growth Monitoring**: Regular assessment of community spiritual health during expansion periods

Magnetic Constitution Growth Management Natural Growth Strengths:
- **Practical Expansion**: Ability to manage logistics of growth including housing, facilities, and resource expansion
- **Program Development**: Skills in creating systems and structures that accommodate increased membership
- **Goal Achievement**: Capacity for systematic growth planning with measurable milestones and achievements
- **Resource Generation**: Talent for developing financial and material resources supporting community expansion

Growth Management Applications:
- **Infrastructure Development**: Planning and implementing physical expansion supporting increased membership
- **System Design**: Creating administrative and program systems that scale effectively with growth
- **Resource Planning**: Comprehensive preparation for financial and material needs during growth periods
- **Implementation Coordination**: Managing complex expansion projects involving multiple community elements

Neutral Constitution Growth Management Natural Growth Strengths:
- **Strategic Planning**: Ability to analyze growth opportunities and challenges systematically
- **Policy Development**: Creating governance structures and procedures that function effectively at larger scales
- **Quality Assurance**: Maintaining program standards and community effectiveness during expansion
- **Professional Integration**: Developing professional relationships and standards that support sustainable growth

Growth Management Applications:
- **Growth Strategy Development**: Comprehensive planning for sustainable expansion honoring community values
- **Governance Scaling**: Adapting democratic governance structures to function effectively with larger membership
- **Program Standardization**: Creating training and quality assurance systems maintaining program effectiveness
- **Professional Development**: Building relationships with consultants and advisors supporting healthy growth

Sustainable Growth Models
Organic Growth Through Natural Development Member Development Expansion:
Rather than recruiting new members externally, communities can grow through the natural development of existing member families and relationships:
- **Family Expansion**: Supporting community members in having children and raising families within community context
- **Relationship Integration**: Welcoming partners and spouses of existing members who demonstrate genuine interest and compatibility
- **Gradual Introduction**: Extended introduction periods allowing potential members to experience community life before making commitments
- **Natural Selection**: Growth through people naturally drawn to community life rather than recruitment campaigns

Advantages of Organic Growth:
- **Cultural Continuity**: New members already familiar with community values through existing relationships
- **Quality Assurance**: Extended observation periods ensuring good fit before formal membership
- **Relationship Foundation**: Growth built on existing trust and connection rather than stranger integration

- **Sustainable Pace**: Natural timing allowing adequate preparation for expansion

Cell Division and Community Replication Community Multiplication Model:
When communities reach optimal size limits, they can replicate through cell division rather than continued expansion:
- **Sister Community Development**: Experienced members starting new communities in different geographic areas
- **Regional Network Creation**: Multiple smaller communities sharing resources, wisdom, and mutual support
- **Specialization Opportunities**: Different communities focusing on different aspects of spiritual development or community service
- **Cross-Pollination Benefits**: Network communities learning from each other's experiences and innovations

Cell Division Process:
- **Community Readiness Assessment**: Evaluation of parent community capacity to support new community development
- **Leadership Preparation**: Systematic development of qualified leaders for new community guidance
- **Resource Allocation**: Fair distribution of financial, material, and human resources between communities
- **Ongoing Relationship**: Maintained connection providing mutual support while allowing independent development

Service Expansion Without Membership Growth Program Development Model:
Communities can expand their service impact through program development rather than membership increase:
- **Educational Outreach**: Public programs serving broader community without requiring full membership commitment
- **Professional Training**: Programs preparing professionals in healthcare, education, and business to apply community principles
- **Consultation Services**: Sharing community expertise with other organizations seeking similar development
- **Publishing and Media**: Books, articles, and online resources making community wisdom accessible to global audience

Service Expansion Benefits:
- **Impact Amplification**: Community wisdom serves far more people than membership expansion would allow
- **Financial Sustainability**: Program revenue supports community without requiring membership fees
- **Cultural Influence**: Community values influence broader socie-

ty without requiring institutional replication
- **Mission Fulfillment**: Service expansion directly serves community mission of contributing to global awakening

Quality Assurance During Growth
Maintaining Standards and Values New Member Integration Protocols:
Systematic approaches ensuring new community members absorb essential values and develop necessary skills:

Phase 1: Introduction and Assessment (3-6 months):
- **Community Immersion**: Extended periods participating in community life without formal commitment
- **Values Transmission**: Systematic introduction to community history, principles, and practices
- **Constitutional Assessment**: Individual evaluation and adaptation of spiritual practices to personal constitutional type
- **Relationship Development**: Guided introduction to existing community members and relationship building

Phase 2: Probationary Membership (6-12 months):
- **Responsibility Integration**: Gradual assumption of community responsibilities and service commitments
- **Skill Development**: Training in specific competencies needed for full community participation
- **Conflict Processing**: Experience with community conflict resolution and consensus decision-making
- **Spiritual Development**: Demonstrated commitment to personal growth and spiritual practice

Phase 3: Full Membership Integration (12+ months):
- **Community Commitment**: Formal commitment to community values, governance, and long-term development
- **Leadership Preparation**: Beginning development of teaching and leadership capacities
- **Service Integration**: Full participation in community service and external outreach activities
- **Cultural Transmission**: Ability to help future newcomers integrate community values and practices

Quality Control Mechanisms:
- **Mentor Assignment**: Experienced community members providing personal guidance during integration process
- **Regular Assessment**: Periodic evaluation of new member development and community fit
- **Community Feedback**: Input from multiple community

members about new member integration progress

- **Adjustment Support**: Additional help for new members experiencing integration difficulties

Leadership Development for Growth Systematic Leadership Preparation:
Growth requires accelerated development of qualified community leaders:

- **Teaching Training**: Systematic preparation for transmitting community values and spiritual practices
- **Governance Development**: Training in consensus building, conflict resolution, and democratic leadership
- **Professional Competency**: Development of specialized skills needed for community administration and program management
- **Spiritual Maturation**: Accelerated spiritual development appropriate to leadership responsibilities

Leadership Development Programs:

- **Apprenticeship Systems**: New leaders working closely with experienced mentors on real community challenges
- **Cross-Training Opportunities**: Leadership development through exposure to different aspects of community operations
- **External Education**: Professional development through conferences, workshops, and formal education programs
- **Peer Learning Networks**: Leadership development through connection with other community leaders and similar organizations

Youth Development and Education for Cultural Continuity
Preparing the Next Generation
The long-term sustainability of Democratic Mysticism communities depends on successfully transmitting essential values and practices to young people while honoring their individual development needs and cultural context.

Youth Development Challenges:

- **Cultural Transmission**: Passing on essential values without imposing rigid conformity
- **Individual Development**: Supporting personal growth and constitutional development
- **Contemporary Integration**: Connecting traditional wisdom with contemporary challenges and opportunities
- **Choice and Commitment**: Enabling genuine choice about community participation without coercion

Constitutional Youth Development
Different constitutional types require adapted approaches to education and development:

Electric Constitution Youth Development Natural Development Characteristics:
- **Sensitivity to Environment**: High responsiveness to physical and social environment requiring careful adaptation
- **Intuitive Learning**: Natural preference for holistic, experiential learning over purely analytical approaches
- **Relationship Priority**: Learning best through personal connection and individual attention
- **Creative Expression**: Need for artistic, musical, and creative outlets supporting development

Educational Adaptations:
- **Individualized Learning**: Educational approaches adapted to personal interests, learning style, and developmental pace
- **Supportive Environment**: Learning environments emphasizing safety, warmth, and emotional support
- **Experiential Education**: Hands-on learning through projects, field experiences, and practical application
- **Mentorship Relationships**: Personal guidance from caring adults providing individual attention and wisdom

Community Integration:
- **Gradual Responsibility**: Slow increase in community responsibilities allowing confidence building
- **Choice and Autonomy**: Respect for individual preferences and decision-making capacity
- **Cultural Participation**: Involvement in community cultural activities without pressure for leadership roles
- **Service Opportunities**: Meaningful ways to contribute to community well-being using natural gifts

Magnetic Constitution Youth Development Natural Development Characteristics:
- **Active Learning**: Preference for dynamic, engaging educational experiences with concrete goals
- **Leadership Potential**: Natural inclination toward organizing others and taking responsibility
- **Goal Achievement**: Motivation through clear objectives and measurable accomplishments
- **Physical Activity**: Need for regular exercise and physical challenges supporting development

Educational Adaptations:

- **Project-Based Learning**: Educational approaches emphasizing concrete projects with measurable outcomes
- **Leadership Opportunities**: Age-appropriate roles allowing practice of organizational and leadership skills
- **Challenge Integration**: Educational experiences providing adequate difficulty and stimulation
- **Team Learning**: Collaborative educational approaches utilizing natural social and organizational abilities

Community Integration:

- **Active Participation**: Meaningful roles in community activities and decision- making processes
- **Skill Development**: Training in practical competencies needed for community participation and leadership
- **Achievement Recognition**: Appropriate acknowledgment of contributions and developing capabilities
- **Service Leadership**: Opportunities to organize and lead community service projects

Neutral Constitution Youth Development Natural Development Characteristics:

- **Analytical Learning**: Preference for systematic, logical educational approaches with clear structure
- **Quality Emphasis**: High standards for educational content and teaching quality
- **Independent Study**: Ability to learn through self-directed investigation and research
- **Professional Integration**: Interest in connecting learning with future professional development

Educational Adaptations:

- **Academic Excellence**: High-quality educational content meeting rigorous standards
- **Systematic Curriculum**: Well-organized educational programs with logical progression and clear objectives
- **Independent Research**: Opportunities for self-directed learning projects and investigation
- **Professional Preparation**: Educational experiences connecting community values with professional competency

Community Integration:

- **Teaching Opportunities**: Age-appropriate roles helping educate younger children and newcomers
- **Policy Participation**: Involvement in community governance and decision- making processes

- **Quality Assurance**: Roles helping maintain community standards and program effectiveness
- **Professional Development**: Preparation for professional roles serving community mission

Educational Program Development
Early Childhood Education (Ages 3-7) Developmental Priorities:
- **Constitutional Recognition**: Early identification of constitutional type enabling appropriate adaptation
- **Foundation Skills**: Basic physical, emotional, and social skills supporting later development
- **Cultural Immersion**: Natural absorption of community values through participation in community life
- **Individual Expression**: Encouragement of personal gifts and interests without premature specialization

Educational Approaches:
- **Play-Based Learning**: Educational content delivered through games, stories, and creative activities
- **Mixed-Age Groups**: Learning environments including children of different ages enabling mutual support and teaching
- **Nature Integration**: Outdoor education and environmental connection supporting physical and spiritual development
- **Artistic Expression**: Regular opportunities for music, art, dance, and creative expression

Elementary Education (Ages 7-12) Developmental Priorities:
- **Academic Foundation**: Strong basic skills in reading, writing, mathematics, and critical thinking
- **Community Participation**: Meaningful roles in community life appropriate to developmental capacity
- **Constitutional Development**: Increasing awareness of personal constitutional type and appropriate practices
- **Service Introduction**: Beginning opportunities to contribute to community well- being and service mission

Educational Integration:
- **Community-Based Learning**: Academic subjects connected to community life and service activities
- **Mentorship Programs**: Personal relationships with adult community members providing guidance and support
- **Skill Development**: Training in practical competencies needed for community life and individual development
- **Cultural Studies**: Systematic learning about community history, values, and spiritual practices

Adolescent Development (Ages 12-18) Developmental Priorities:
- **Identity Formation**: Support for healthy identity development including relationship to community values
- **Leadership Development**: Opportunities to practice leadership skills appropriate to constitutional type
- **Academic Excellence**: High-quality education preparing for higher education or professional development
- **Choice Preparation**: Guidance in making informed choices about future community participation

Educational Excellence:
- **College Preparation**: Academic programs enabling access to higher education and professional development
- **Leadership Training**: Systematic development of governance, teaching, and service leadership skills
- **Internship Opportunities**: Real-world experience in community operations and external professional settings
- **Travel and Exchange**: Exposure to other communities and cultures broadening perspective and understanding

Choice and Commitment Process
Supporting Authentic Choice
Rather than assuming young people raised in community will automatically choose lifelong participation, Democratic Mysticism communities create structures supporting genuine choice:

Exploration Encouragement:
- **Higher Education Support**: Financial and personal support for college and professional development
- **Career Exploration**: Exposure to various professional paths and life options
- **Travel Opportunities**: Experience with other communities and cultural contexts
- **Alternative Lifestyle Exposure**: Understanding of different approaches to spiritual development and community life

Choice Support Process:
- **Individual Counseling**: Personal guidance helping young adults understand their options and preferences
- **Community Discussion**: Open dialogue about community life benefits and challenges
- **Trial Periods**: Opportunities to experience different levels of community involvement before making long-term commitments

- **Honor All Choices**: Celebration and support regardless of choice about community participation

Return and Integration
Young adults who choose continued community participation after exploration receive specialized support:

Re-Integration Process:
- **Adult Relationship Development**: Transition from child to adult relationships with community elders
- **Responsibility Integration**: Gradual assumption of adult responsibilities and leadership opportunities
- **Skill Integration**: Application of external education and experience to community development
- **New Perspective Contribution**: Integration of outside perspectives and ideas into community development

Leadership Preparation:
- **Advanced Training**: Specialized education in community leadership and spiritual development
- **Mentorship Relationships**: Guidance from experienced leaders in developing teaching and governance skills
- **External Relationship Development**: Responsibility for community relationships with outside organizations and individuals
- **Innovation Encouragement**: Support for bringing new ideas and approaches to community development

Elder Integration and Wisdom Preservation
Honoring Experience and Wisdom
Democratic Mysticism communities recognize elders as repositories of wisdom and experience essential for community continuity and development. Rather than marginalizing older members, these communities create structures that honor elder contributions while adapting to changing physical and cognitive capacities.

Elder Wisdom Recognition:
- **Historical Perspective**: Elders provide community memory and understanding of long-term development patterns
- **Practical Experience**: Decades of experience in community life provide practical wisdom for addressing challenges
- **Spiritual Maturation**: Extended spiritual practice often results in wisdom and perspective valuable for community guidance
- **Cultural Transmission**: Elders serve as primary repositories and transmitters of community values and practices

Constitutional Elder Integration
Different constitutional types age in distinct patterns requiring adapted approaches to elder integration:

Electric Constitution Elder Integration Aging Characteristics:
- **Increased Sensitivity**: Heightened sensitivity to environment and stimulation requiring careful adaptation
- **Wisdom Development**: Natural development of intuitive wisdom and spiritual insight through life experience
- **Relationship Priority**: Increasing emphasis on close relationships and community connection
- **Gentleness Requirements**: Need for careful, gentle approaches to physical and emotional demands

Integration Adaptations:
- **Supportive Roles**: Community positions emphasizing wisdom sharing rather than demanding physical activity
- **Individual Attention**: Personal relationships and one-on-one interaction opportunities
- **Environmental Support**: Living situations adapted to increasing sensitivity and comfort needs
- **Wisdom Sharing**: Formal and informal opportunities to share insights and experience with younger community members

Magnetic Constitution Elder Integration Aging Characteristics:
- **Activity Maintenance**: Desire to remain active and engaged in community life and service
- **Leadership Continuation**: Natural inclination to continue leadership roles appropriate to physical capacity
- **Practical Contribution**: Preference for meaningful work and concrete contributions to community development
- **Social Engagement**: Need for continued social interaction and community involvement

Integration Adaptations:
- **Adapted Leadership**: Community roles utilizing experience and wisdom while accommodating physical changes
- **Mentorship Opportunities**: Teaching and guidance roles utilizing accumulated knowledge and experience
- **Project Involvement**: Meaningful participation in community projects and development activities
- **Recognition Systems**: Appropriate acknowledgment of life-long contributions and continued service

Neutral Constitution Elder Integration Aging Characteristics:

- **Knowledge Preservation**: Natural role as keeper of community knowledge, policies, and procedures
- **Teaching Capacity**: Ability to transmit complex understanding to younger community members
- **Quality Maintenance**: Concern for maintaining community standards and program effectiveness
- **Systematic Thinking**: Continued ability for strategic planning and systematic problem-solving

Integration Adaptations:

- **Educational Leadership**: Teaching roles utilizing accumulated knowledge and understanding
- **Policy Development**: Involvement in community governance and long-term planning
- **Quality Assurance**: Roles helping maintain community standards and program effectiveness
- **Knowledge Documentation**: Systematic preservation of community wisdom and experience through writing and teaching

Intergenerational Learning
Wisdom Transmission Programs Formal Teaching Opportunities:

- **Elder Teaching Circles**: Regular gatherings where elders share knowledge and experience with younger community members
- **Mentorship Programs**: Structured relationships pairing elders with younger adults for skill and wisdom transmission
- **Oral History Projects**: Systematic collection and preservation of community history and elder experiences
- **Skill Sharing Workshops**: Programs where elders teach traditional crafts, skills, and knowledge to younger generations

Informal Transmission Contexts:

- **Shared Living Arrangements**: Intergenerational housing creating natural opportunities for wisdom sharing
- **Work Collaboration**: Projects involving both elders and younger members enabling natural knowledge transfer
- **Storytelling Traditions**: Regular community gatherings featuring elder storytelling and experience sharing
- **Ceremonial Leadership**: Elder leadership in community rituals and spiritual practices

Learning from Elder Experience Historical Perspective Integration:

- **Pattern Recognition**: Elders help community recognize recurring patterns and long-term trends

- **Mistake Learning**: Elder experience with community difficulties helps younger members avoid repeated errors
- **Success Understanding**: Elder knowledge of what has worked well provides guidance for current challenges
- **Adaptation Wisdom**: Elder experience with change helps community navigate current transitions

End-of-Life Care and Transition
Community Death and Dying Support Holistic End-of-Life Care:
- **Physical Comfort**: Medical care and physical support ensuring dignity and comfort during dying process
- **Emotional Support**: Counseling and companionship helping elders and families process end-of-life transitions
- **Spiritual Preparation**: Spiritual guidance and practices supporting conscious dying and peaceful transition
- **Community Involvement**: Meaningful participation in community life as long as possible

Family and Community Support Systems:
- **Caregiver Training**: Education for family members and community volunteers providing elder care
- **Respite Services**: Community support providing breaks for primary caregivers
- **Practical Assistance**: Help with daily needs, medical appointments, and household management
- **Grief Support**: Counseling and community support for family members during and after elder transitions

Legacy Preservation Wisdom Documentation:
- **Life Story Collection**: Comprehensive documentation of elder experiences and wisdom
- **Skill Documentation**: Written and video preservation of traditional crafts and knowledge
- **Community History**: Elder participation in documenting community development and important events
- **Teaching Material Creation**: Development of educational materials based on elder knowledge and experience

Memorial and Celebration Traditions:
- **Life Celebration Ceremonies**: Community rituals honoring elder contributions and celebrating their lives
- **Memorial Gardens**: Physical spaces commemorating deceased community members
- **Scholarship Programs**: Educational funding in honor of departed elders

- **Service Projects**: Community service activities dedicated to elder memory and values

Adaptive Governance for Aging Communities
Changing Leadership Patterns Succession Planning:
- **Gradual Transition**: Systematic transfer of responsibilities from elders to younger leaders
- **Co-Leadership Models**: Shared leadership combining elder wisdom with younger energy
- **Emeritus Roles**: Honorary positions allowing continued elder participation without full responsibility
- **Consultative Functions**: Elder advisory roles providing guidance without administrative burden

Governance Adaptation:
- **Meeting Accessibility**: Community meetings scheduled and located for elder participation
- **Decision-Making Accommodation**: Processes adapted to include elders with different physical and cognitive capacities
- **Communication Support**: Technology and personal assistance ensuring elder participation in community communication
- **Transportation and Mobility**: Community support enabling elder participation in governance activities

Constitutional Governance: Honoring Individual Differences in Collective Decision-Making
The Three-Type Governance System
Sacred Synthesis community governance recognizes that different constitutional types require different approaches to participation and leadership while contributing distinct strengths to collective decision-making and community development.
Rather than attempting to eliminate personality differences through standardized approaches, constitutional governance systems channel constitutional diversity toward collective advancement through structures that honor individual differences while serving community unity.

Constitutional Democracy Rather Than Constitutional Suppression
Sacred Synthesis communities integrate spiritual wisdom with democratic participation by recognizing that different constitutional types contribute different but complementary strengths to community governance and development:

Inclusive Participation: All constitutional types have appropriate ways to contribute to community governance without forcing identical participation styles

Complementary Strengths: Each constitutional type contributes essential perspectives and capabilities that others cannot provide

Adaptive Structures: Community governance systems accommodate constitutional differences rather than requiring conformity to single approaches

Service Integration: Individual constitutional development serves collective advancement through recognition and utilization of diverse strengths

Constitutional Governance Applications
Community Decision-Making Integration
Different types of community decisions benefit from different constitutional contributions:

Vision and Values Decisions:
- **Electric Input**: Intuitive sensing of community spiritual needs and cultural direction
- **Magnetic Input**: Assessment of practical implications and community engagement requirements
- **Neutral Input**: Analysis of long-term consequences and systematic implementation approaches
- **Integrated Decision**: Vision statements serving both spiritual development and practical effectiveness

Resource and Financial Decisions:
- **Electric Input**: Understanding of resource decisions' impact on community relationships and spiritual development
- **Magnetic Input**: Practical assessment of financial capacity, fundraising potential, and implementation requirements
- **Neutral Input**: Strategic analysis of investment options, risk management, and long-term financial planning
- **Integrated Decision**: Financial choices serving both practical sustainability and spiritual values

Program and Service Development:
- **Electric Input**: Assessment of program alignment with community spiritual mission and participant needs
- **Magnetic Input**: Practical evaluation of implementation requirements, resource needs, and community capacity

- **Neutral Input**: Development of systematic curriculum, assessment methods, and professional standards
- **Integrated Decision**: Programs serving diverse learning needs while ensuring practical effectiveness and spiritual depth

Conflict Resolution and Community Healing:
- **Electric Input**: Understanding of relationship dynamics, cultural sensitivities, and healing processes
- **Magnetic Input**: Assessment of practical consequences, community impact, and implementation of resolution agreements
- **Neutral Input**: Analysis of policy implications, precedent considerations, and systematic approaches to prevention
- **Integrated Decision**: Resolution approaches addressing both relationship healing and practical problem-solving

Regional and Bioregional Governance
As Sacred Synthesis communities mature, they develop capacity for regional coordination that serves both local autonomy and broader bioregional stewardship:

Constitutional Regional Representation Regional Council Structure:
- **Local Community Representation**: Each community selects representatives based on constitutional diversity and demonstrated service
- **Bioregional Coordination**: Regional councils coordinate resources and projects across multiple communities within natural watershed boundaries
- **Constitutional Regional Balance**: Ensure all three constitutional types are represented in regional coordination and decision-making
- **Democratic Regional Accountability**: Regional representatives accountable to local communities through democratic processes and regular rotation

Regional Project Development:
- **Electric Regional Contribution**: Cultural bridge-building and sensitive coordination between communities with different cultural approaches
- **Magnetic Regional Contribution**: Practical implementation of bioregional projects including resource sharing and infrastructure development
- **Neutral Regional Contribution**: Strategic planning, policy development, and systematic approaches to regional challenges

Economic Democracy and Cooperative Prosperity
The Sacred Synthesis economic model integrates constitutional diversity with cooperative economics:

Constitutional Economic Contributions Electric Constitution Economic Applications:
- **Relationship Economics**: Economic systems emphasizing cooperation and mutual benefit over competition
- **Cultural Economy**: Economic activities that build community culture and social connection
- **Gift Economy Integration**: Economic systems incorporating voluntary giving and receiving
- **Environmental Economics**: Economic decisions considering seven-generation environmental impact

Magnetic Constitution Economic Applications:
- **Practical Economics**: Economic systems emphasizing concrete results and measurable community benefits
- **Resource Development**: Active fundraising and resource generation supporting community sustainability
- **Implementation Economics**: Translation of economic goals into practical action and achievement
- **Growth Economics**: Economic systems supporting community expansion and service development

Neutral Constitution Economic Applications:
- **Strategic Economics**: Long-term economic planning and systematic approaches to financial sustainability
- **Policy Economics**: Development of economic policies and procedures serving community values and effectiveness
- **Professional Economics**: Integration of community economic activities with professional standards and external relationships
- **Investment Economics**: Systematic approaches to investment and resource management serving long-term community development

Cooperative Economic Structures

Community-Supported Agriculture: Economic systems providing community food security while supporting local agriculture and environmental stewardship

Community Land Trusts: Economic structures preventing land speculation while ensuring permanent community access to affordable housing and land

Time Banking Systems: Labor exchange systems reducing cash transactions while building community relationships and mutual support

Community Investment Funds: Financial systems directing community savings toward local economic development and value-aligned investments

Assessment Tools and Implementation Resources
Community Governance Assessment Tools
To support effective implementation of Democratic Mysticism principles, communities need systematic assessment tools evaluating current governance effectiveness and identifying areas for development.

Community Leadership Evaluation Democratic Leadership Assessment:
- Serving community empowerment rather than personal authority accumulation
- Creating sustainable institutions maintaining spiritual values
- Maintaining community cohesion while honoring individual dignity
- Ensuring continuity beyond individual leadership through systematic preparation

Assessment Criteria:
- **Service Orientation**: Leaders demonstrate consistent commitment to community development over personal advancement
- **Accountability Practice**: Regular seeking of community feedback and willingness to adjust approaches based on input
- **Empowerment Focus**: Active development of other community members' leadership capacities
- **Transparency Maintenance**: Open decision-making processes allowing community observation and participation

Consensus Decision-Making Effectiveness Process Quality Assessment:
- **Participation Inclusivity**: All affected community members have appropriate opportunities to contribute to decisions
- **Information Accessibility**: Relevant information is available to all decision- makers before decisions are made
- **Perspective Integration**: Different constitutional types and viewpoints are included in decision-making processes
- **Implementation Support**: Decisions receive adequate community commitment and resources for effective implementation

Outcome Quality Assessment:
- **Decision Effectiveness**: Community decisions achieve intended results and serve stated community values
- **Relationship Health**: Decision-making processes strengthen rather than damage community relationships
- **Innovation Generation**: Processes regularly generate creative solutions serving multiple needs simultaneously
- **Spiritual Integration**: Decisions support both practical effectiveness and spiritual development

Constitutional Governance Assessment
Individual Constitutional Leadership Assessment Electric Constitution Leadership Development:
- **Intuitive Wisdom Application**: Demonstrated ability to sense community needs and provide appropriate guidance
- **Inclusive Facilitation**: Skill in creating safe spaces where all community members feel heard and valued
- **Cultural Sensitivity**: Awareness of cultural dynamics and ability to bridge different perspectives and approaches
- **Service Commitment**: Consistent priority given to community welfare over personal comfort or convenience

Magnetic Constitution Leadership Development:
- **Practical Implementation**: Proven ability to translate community visions into concrete actions and measurable results
- **Resource Management**: Effective stewardship of community resources including finances, property, and human capital
- **Community Motivation**: Capacity to inspire group participation and maintain community energy during challenging periods
- **Project Coordination**: Skill in managing complex initiatives from conception through successful completion

Neutral Constitution Leadership Development:
- **Strategic Analysis**: Ability to evaluate community challenges systematically and develop comprehensive solutions
- **Policy Development**: Skill in creating governance structures and procedures that serve long-term community effectiveness
- **Educational Leadership**: Capacity for teaching community members and developing collective competency
- **Professional Integration**: Ability to maintain professional standards while serving spiritual community values

Conflict Resolution Assessment
Community Healing Effectiveness Resolution Process Quality:
- **Safety Maintenance**: All parties feel safe and supported

throughout conflict resolution processes
- **Truth-Telling Opportunities**: Adequate opportunities for all perspectives to be heard and understood
- **Responsibility Recognition**: Clear understanding of how all parties contributed to conflict development
- **Repair Focus**: Emphasis on healing relationships and preventing future conflicts rather than punishment

Healing Outcomes Assessment:
- **Relationship Restoration**: Damaged relationships are repaired and often strengthened through resolution process
- **Community Learning**: Conflicts generate insights and improvements benefiting broader community development
- **Prevention Success**: Changes made during resolution prevent similar conflicts from recurring
- **Spiritual Growth**: Individuals and community demonstrate increased wisdom and compassion through conflict resolution

Financial Management Assessment
Economic Sustainability Evaluation Financial Health Indicators:
- **Diverse Revenue Sources**: Community income comes from multiple sources reducing dependency on single funding streams
- **Emergency Reserves**: Adequate savings for unexpected expenses and economic downturns
- **Debt Management**: Any community debt is manageable and serves community development rather than consumption
- **Transparency Practice**: All community members have access to financial information and participate in financial decisions

Economic Justice Assessment:
- **Contribution Equity**: Community financial systems accommodate different economic capacities without creating hierarchy
- **Resource Accessibility**: All community members have access to basic needs regardless of individual financial capacity
- **Investment Alignment**: Community investments align with stated values and serve community development goals
- **External Relationships**: Economic relationships with outside organizations serve mutual benefit and community values

Implementation Planning Tools
Community Development Roadmap

Phase 1: Foundation Assessment (Months 1-6):
- **Community Constitutional Assessment**: Complete evalua-

tion of community member constitutional types and governance preferences
- **Current System Evaluation**: Assessment of existing governance structures and their effectiveness
- **Vision Clarification**: Community dialogue about governance goals and desired improvements
- **Resource Inventory**: Assessment of community capacity for implementing governance improvements

Phase 2: System Development (Months 6-18):
- **Constitutional Council Development**: Creation of decision-making structures honoring constitutional diversity
- **Consensus Process Training**: Community education in effective consensus building and collaborative decision-making
- **Conflict Resolution System**: Development of community procedures for addressing disputes and healing relationships
- **Leadership Development**: Systematic preparation of community members for governance roles

Phase 3: Implementation and Integration (Months 18-36):
- **Gradual Transition**: Systematic shift from old to new governance approaches with adequate support and adjustment periods
- **Assessment and Adjustment**: Regular evaluation of new systems with modifications based on community experience
- **Leadership Rotation**: Implementation of rotating leadership and succession planning
- **Community Celebration**: Recognition of governance improvements and community development achievements

Global Applications and Cultural Adaptation
Cross-Cultural Implementation
Democratic Mysticism principles can be adapted across diverse cultural contexts while maintaining essential effectiveness and spiritual authenticity.

Cultural Sensitivity Principles
Universal Principles with Cultural Expression:
- **Core Values Maintenance**: Essential principles of service-oriented leadership and consensus decision-making remain constant across cultures
- **Cultural Adaptation**: Specific practices and procedures adapt to local cultural norms and expectations
- **Community Authorization**: Local communities maintain authority over how principles are expressed within their cultural context

358

- **Mutual Learning**: Different cultural applications provide insights benefiting global understanding and development

International Network Development
Global implementation studies validate that Democratic Mysticism principles enhance rather than threaten local autonomy and cultural diversity. International networks based on these principles demonstrate greater sustainability and mutual benefit than conventional international organizations.

Technology Integration and Digital Platforms
Digital Democracy Tools Online Consensus Building:
- **Virtual Council Processes**: Technology platforms supporting online community decision-making with constitutional representation
- **Collaborative Decision-Making**: Digital tools enabling community participation in governance regardless of geographic location
- **Information Sharing**: Transparent information systems supporting informed community decision-making
- **Accessibility Integration**: Technology accommodating different abilities and constitutional preferences for participation

Community Communication Platforms:
- **Social Networking**: Community-specific social platforms supporting relationship building and information sharing
- **Educational Delivery**: Online learning systems adapted to different constitutional learning styles and preferences
- **Resource Sharing**: Digital platforms supporting community resource sharing and cooperative economics
- **Cross-Community Networking**: Technology enabling cooperation and learning between communities globally

Artificial Intelligence and Assessment Tools Constitutional Assessment Technology:
- **Automated Assessment**: AI-supported tools for constitutional type assessment and practice adaptation
- **Personalized Guidance**: Technology providing individualized recommendations for spiritual practice and community participation
- **Community Analysis**: Analytical tools helping communities understand their constitutional diversity and optimize governance approaches
- **Progress Tracking**: Digital systems supporting individual and community development monitoring and adjustment

Conclusion: Living Democracy as Spiritual Practice

The Revolutionary Integration

The integration of authentic spiritual wisdom with democratic participation represents more than organizational innovation, it embodies a fundamental shift in understanding the relationship between individual development and collective advancement.

Democratic Mysticism demonstrates that genuine spiritual authority serves rather than dominates, that authentic wisdom emerges through community rather than individual isolation, and that true leadership develops through service rather than position-seeking.

Key Revolutionary Insights:

- **Authority Through Service**: Authentic spiritual authority develops through demonstrated capacity to serve others' development rather than through appointment, inheritance, or self-proclamation

- **Collective Wisdom**: The full wisdom needed for community decisions emerges through collective discernment involving multiple perspectives, constitutional types, and levels of experience

- **Individual-Collective Unity**: Personal spiritual development and community advancement are not competing priorities but complementary aspects of the same evolutionary process

- **Democratic Spirituality**: Democratic participation is not obstacle to spiritual development but essential requirement for authentic realization serving the highest good of all

Living Implementation

Democratic Mysticism succeeds not through perfect theoretical understanding but through daily practice of its principles in real community situations with actual people facing practical challenges.

Daily Practice Applications:
- Every community decision becomes opportunity to practice consensus building and constitutional integration
- Each conflict offers chance to develop restorative justice skills and community healing capacity
- All leadership roles serve as spiritual practice developing wisdom, compassion, and practical effectiveness

- Community participation becomes path of service supporting both individual growth and collective advancement

The Promise of Sacred Democracy
Communities successfully implementing Democratic Mysticism demonstrate that human beings can create social organization serving both individual fulfillment and collective advancement while honoring spiritual values and democratic participation.

Global Implications
The success of Democratic Mysticism at community scale suggests possibilities for broader social application. If small communities can successfully integrate spiritual
wisdom with democratic participation, similar principles might address larger social challenges requiring both practical effectiveness and spiritual depth.

Potential Applications:
- **International Relations**: Conflict resolution and cooperation approaches based on restorative justice and consensus building
- **Economic Justice**: Economic systems serving both individual prosperity and collective welfare through cooperative and community-controlled development
- **Environmental Crisis**: Environmental solutions integrating traditional ecological wisdom with democratic participation and contemporary science
- **Cultural Renaissance**: Cultural development approaches preserving traditional wisdom while enabling beneficial innovation and adaptation

The Path Forward
Democratic Mysticism provides practical methodology for the ancient vision of spiritually conscious, democratically organized, economically cooperative communities serving both individual realization and collective advancement.
The key breakthrough involves recognition that constitutional diversity provides the foundation for both individual fulfillment and collective effectiveness when community structures honor rather than suppress natural human differences.

Implementation Success Factors:
- **Constitutional Integration**: Community governance systems that honor different constitutional types and utilize their complementary strengths
- **Service Orientation**: Leadership development through service

rather than position-seeking or authority accumulation

- **Consensus Practice**: Decision-making processes that generate creative solutions serving the highest good of all rather than compromise satisfying no one
- **Conflict Transformation**: Approaches to community difficulties that strengthen relationships and generate learning rather than creating winners and losers
- **Financial Sustainability**: Economic systems serving both practical needs and spiritual values through cooperative and community-controlled approaches

The promise of Democratic Mysticism lies not in utopian perfection but in practical demonstration that human communities can embody both spiritual depth and democratic participation, both individual authenticity and collective effectiveness, both local autonomy and global cooperation.

Through systematic practice of these principles, communities become laboratories for social innovation demonstrating approaches to governance, economics, and cultural development that serve the highest potential of both individuals and collective humanity.

This is the ultimate spiritual practice: creating community life that enables all members to develop their highest capacities in service of the greatest good for all beings, while maintaining the democratic values and individual dignity essential for authentic human development.

May these principles serve all who seek to create communities of practice demonstrating wisdom-based solutions to contemporary challenges while preserving essential spiritual wisdom for future generations.

The Democratic Mysticism framework provides systematic methodology for communities seeking to integrate spiritual development with democratic participation while maintaining both individual dignity and collective effectiveness. Implementation requires qualified guidance and community commitment to the principles outlined in this document.

Montana Community Integration Document
Introduction: Individual Development Through Community Participation
Community Integration represents the essential bridge between personal spiritual development and collective cultural contribution, rec-

362

ognizing that authentic realization naturally expresses through beneficial community participation and service. This foundation document completes the essential trilogy by demonstrating how individual practice and practical implementation find their ultimate expression through community building, cultural preservation, and collaborative service.

Chapter 1: Understanding Sacred Community
Historical Models and Contemporary Application
Sacred Synthesis community development builds upon traditional wisdom communities while adapting to contemporary social conditions, creating sustainable models of democratic spiritual community that serve both individual development and cultural preservation.

Traditional Community Principles
- Democratic governance with spiritual authority integration
- Individual constitutional recognition within collective harmony
- Economic cooperation and resource sharing principles
- Cultural preservation combined with beneficial adaptation
- Intergenerational wisdom transmission and community continuity
- Community resilience and mutual support during crisis
- Cultural preservation under extreme conditions
- Collaborative learning and shared spiritual practice
- Resource sharing and cooperative economics
- International cooperation and global consciousness
- University integration and academic validation
- Professional application across multiple disciplines
- Global network development and international cooperation
- Cultural bridge-building and interfaith dialogue
- Environmental stewardship and social justice integration

Contemporary Community Adaptation
- Local autonomy within global cooperation framework
- Democratic governance and participatory decision-making
- Resource sharing and mutual aid systems
- Cultural exchange and knowledge transmission
- Technology integration serving community values
- Career development and professional effectiveness enhancement
- Family strengthening and conscious parenting support
- Educational excellence and character development
- Healthcare integration and community wellness
- Economic sustainability and cooperative development
- Community organizing and social change participation

- Environmental restoration and sustainability initiatives
- Restorative justice and community healing approaches
- Cultural preservation and innovation balance
- Global service and international cooperation

Constitutional Community Dynamics

Understanding Community Constitutional Patterns

Effective Sacred Synthesis communities recognize and honor constitutional diversity while creating harmony through complementary role distribution and collaborative decision-making processes.

- **Electric Strengths**: Strong relationships, cultural expression, collaborative harmony, emotional intelligence
    - **Challenges**: Decision-making efficiency, individual accountability, systematic organization
    - **Optimal Size**: 15-25 core members with extended network of 50-100 participants
    - **Leadership Style**: Collaborative leadership, consensus processes, relationship-centered authority
- **Magnetic Strengths**: Practical achievement, organizational efficiency, project implementation, measurable results
    - **Challenges**: Relationship maintenance, cultural sensitivity, flexibility, creative exploration
    - **Optimal Size**: 20-40 core members with clear roles and responsibilities
    - **Leadership Style**: Results-oriented leadership, structured processes, achievement-focused authority
- **Neutral Strengths**: Systematic planning, knowledge preservation, research capacity, educational excellence
    - **Challenges**: Rapid decision-making, emotional expression, practical implementation, community building
    - **Optimal Size**: 10-20 core members with academic and research focus
    - **Leadership Style**: Wisdom-based leadership, scholarly authority, educational and research focus
- **Integration of All Types**: Deliberate inclusion and role distribution across constitutional patterns
- **Complementary Leadership**: Rotation and specialization based on constitutional strengths
- **Adaptive Decision-Making**: Multiple processes appropriate to different decisions and circumstances
- **Constitutional Education**: Community-wide understanding and appreciation of individual differences

Constitutional Role Distribution and Leadership

- **Relationship Coordination**: Community harmony, conflict resolution, emotional support, celebration planning
- **Cultural Activities**: Arts programming, music coordination, storytelling, cultural preservation
- **External Relations**: Public relations, community outreach, interfaith dialogue, cultural bridge-building
- **New Member Integration**: Welcome processes, mentorship, community orientation, social connection
- **Project Management**: Infrastructure development, construction projects, systematic implementation, achievement coordination
- **Financial Management**: Budget development, resource coordination, economic planning, sustainability initiatives
- **Emergency Response**: Crisis management, disaster preparedness, practical assistance, security coordination
- **Operations Management**: Daily operations, maintenance, efficiency improvement, systems coordination
- **Education and Research**: Teaching programs, curriculum development, research projects, knowledge preservation
- **Planning and Strategy**: Long-term visioning, strategic planning, policy development, systematic analysis
- **Documentation and Communication**: Record keeping, publication, academic relations, knowledge management
- **Quality Assurance**: Assessment systems, evaluation processes, standards maintenance, continuous improvement

Community Formation and Development Process

Phase 1: Community Initiation and Foundation Building (Months 1-12)

- Personal practice establishment and constitutional understanding
- Professional stability and life circumstances evaluation
- Commitment capacity and resource availability assessment
- Community leadership potential and service motivation
- Family integration and household harmony confirmation
- Shared vision development and values clarification
- Practical needs assessment and resource evaluation
- Legal structure and organizational planning
- Location assessment and property requirements
- Financial planning and economic sustainability
- Core member identification and constitutional assessment
- Commitment ceremony and shared agreement development
- Initial role distribution and responsibility assignment
- Practice establishment and community rhythm development
- Assessment and feedback systems implementation

- Physical space development and resource acquisition
- Communication systems and technology integration
- Financial management and economic structure establishment
- Legal compliance and organizational registration
- Safety systems and emergency preparedness

Phase 2: Community Establishment and Growth (Months 12-36)

- Daily, weekly, and monthly community rhythm development
- Constitutional adaptation and individual accommodation
- Group spiritual practice and meditation programs
- Study programs and educational development
- Service projects and community contribution
- Community celebrations and seasonal observances
- Arts and music programs and cultural activities
- Traditional knowledge study and preservation
- Storytelling and oral history projects
- Cultural documentation and archive development
- Inquiry and assessment process for prospective members
- Preparation and education programs for community integration
- Mentorship and support systems for new member success
- Constitutional assessment and role development
- Commitment process and community acceptance
- Local community relations and neighborhood integration
- Professional network development and career support
- Educational partnerships and academic relations
- Service partnerships and social justice collaboration
- International cooperation and global network participation

Phase 3: Community Maturation and Service Development (Years 3-7)

- Decision-making process development and conflict resolution systems
- Leadership rotation and responsibility distribution
- Financial transparency and community accountability
- Policy development and community agreements
- Assessment and evaluation systems for community health
- Career support and professional development programs
- Community business and economic enterprise development
- Resource sharing and mutual aid systems
- Educational programs and training services
- Consultation and professional services
- Environmental restoration and sustainability projects
- Social justice and community organizing initiatives
- Educational programs and cultural preservation

- Healthcare services and community wellness
- Emergency response and mutual aid coordination
- Sister community partnerships and exchange programs
- International service and development projects
- Cultural preservation and knowledge sharing
- Peace building and conflict resolution support
- Climate action and environmental cooperation

Phase 4: Community Leadership and Cultural Transmission (Years 7+)
- Community elder recognition and wisdom authority development
- Traditional knowledge preservation and transmission
- Teaching and mentorship program development
- Succession planning and leadership preparation
- Cultural evolution and innovation integration
- International cooperation and diplomatic engagement
- Policy influence and institutional change advocacy
- Academic integration and scholarly contribution
- Professional recognition and cultural influence
- Future generation preparation and cultural transmission

Chapter 2: Democratic Governance and Collaborative Decision-Making
Sacred Synthesis Democratic Framework
Integration of Spiritual Authority and Democratic Participation
Sacred Synthesis governance transcends both authoritarian spiritual hierarchy and secular democratic materialism, creating authentic integration of wisdom guidance with democratic empowerment and individual dignity.
- **Elder Guidance**: Traditional knowledge holder consultation and wisdom authority recognition
- **Community Participation**: Democratic decision-making and individual empowerment
- **Constitutional Recognition**: Individual difference accommodation and complementary contribution
- **Consensus Building**: Collaborative decision-making and conflict resolution
- **Accountability Systems**: Transparent governance and community responsibility
- **Servant Leadership**: Authority through service rather than personal power accumulation
- **Rotation and Distribution**: Shared responsibility and leadership development across community
- **Specialization and Expertise**: Constitutional strength utilization and professional competence

- **Teaching and Mentorship**: Leadership development and wisdom transmission
- **Community Validation**: Recognition and authority through community acknowledgment rather than self-appointment

Decision-Making Processes and Conflict Resolution

Individual Decisions (Personal practice, family choices, professional development):
- **Individual Authority**: Personal decision-making within community values and agreements
- **Community Consultation**: Available guidance and support without imposed decision-making
- **Resource Sharing**: Community support for individual development and family needs
- **Accountability**: Personal responsibility and community relationship maintenance

Household and Family Decisions (Family practice, child education, resource sharing):
- **Family Authority**: Family decision-making with community support and resource sharing
- **Community Interface**: Family-community boundary respect and mutual support
- **Child Development**: Community support for family decisions and child welfare
- **Resource Coordination**: Shared resources and mutual aid within family autonomy

Community Decisions (Resource allocation, policy development, new member acceptance):
- **Community Council**: Representative governance with constitutional balance and rotation
- **Consensus Process**: Collaborative decision-making with thorough discussion and agreement
- **Elder Consultation**: Traditional knowledge holder guidance and wisdom authority input
- **Implementation Coordination**: Practical decision implementation with accountability and assessment

Network Decisions (Inter-community cooperation, global service, cultural preservation):
- **Network Council**: Inter-community representation and collaborative governance
- **Cultural Authority**: Traditional knowledge holder guidance

and cultural protocol respect
- **Global Coordination**: International cooperation and resource sharing
- **Cultural Transmission**: Knowledge preservation and innovation within traditional frameworks
- **Issue Identification**: Problem recognition and community impact assessment
- **Research and Investigation**: Comprehensive information gathering and expert consultation
- **Community Education**: Information sharing and community understanding development
- **Constitutional Perspective**: Different constitutional viewpoint integration and consideration
- **Community Meetings**: Open discussion and perspective sharing with respectful communication
- **Working Groups**: Specialized discussion and solution development by constitutional groups
- **Elder Consultation**: Traditional knowledge holder guidance and wisdom authority input
- **Stakeholder Input**: All affected community member participation and voice recognition
- **Collaborative Solution Development**: Community-wide problem-solving and creative innovation
- **Pilot Testing**: Limited implementation and assessment before full community commitment
- **Assessment and Adjustment**: Feedback integration and solution refinement
- **Resource Planning**: Implementation planning and resource allocation
- **Consensus Testing**: Community agreement assessment and remaining concern addressing
- **Decision Implementation**: Clear responsibility assignment and accountability systems
- **Assessment and Evaluation**: Ongoing evaluation and adjustment processes
- **Learning Integration**: Community learning and improved decision-making for future decisions

Conflict Resolution and Community Healing
Constitutional Approaches to Community Conflict
- **Relationship Conflicts**: Emotional misunderstandings, communication breakdowns, cultural sensitivity issues
- **Resolution Approaches**: Relationship repair, emotional expression, community mediation, cultural bridge-building
- **Prevention Strategies**: Communication skill development,

cultural competency, relationship building, emotional intelligence
- **Resource Conflicts**: Financial disagreements, resource allocation disputes, efficiency concerns, achievement competition
- **Resolution Approaches**: Practical problem-solving, resource sharing, efficiency improvement, goal alignment
- **Prevention Strategies**: Clear resource policies, transparent financial management, achievement recognition, practical communication
- **Information Conflicts**: Research disagreements, analytical differences, systematic approach variations, knowledge disputes
- **Resolution Approaches**: Research collaboration, systematic investigation, expert consultation, evidence-based resolution
- **Prevention Strategies**: Information sharing, research collaboration, systematic planning, knowledge management
- **Constitutional Balance**: All constitutional perspectives representation and voice recognition
- **Facilitated Dialogue**: Skilled facilitation and communication support
- **Perspective Integration**: Multiple viewpoint honor and synthesis
- **Solution Development**: Collaborative problem-solving and creative innovation
- **Relationship Repair**: Community bond strengthening and trust rebuilding

Restorative Justice and Community Accountability
- **Individual Harm**: Personal injury and individual impact assessment
- **Community Harm**: Collective damage and community impact evaluation
- **Relationship Damage**: Trust breakdown and relationship injury assessment
- **Cultural Impact**: Traditional value violation and cultural harm recognition
- **Individual Accountability**: Personal responsibility acknowledgment and ownership
- **Community Responsibility**: Collective contribution and system failure recognition
- **Circumstance Consideration**: Life situation and challenge acknowledgment
- **Pattern Recognition**: Recurring issue and systematic problem identification
- **Individual Healing**: Personal development and behavior change support

- **Relationship Repair**: Trust rebuilding and communication restoration
- **Community Healing**: Collective processing and system improvement
- **Cultural Restoration**: Traditional value renewal and cultural strengthening
- **System Improvement**: Policy and structure modification to prevent future harm
- **Education and Awareness**: Community learning and prevention skill development
- **Support System Enhancement**: Community capacity building and mutual aid improvement
- **Cultural Strengthening**: Traditional knowledge integration and value reinforcement
- **Personal Responsibility**: Individual accountability with community support and guidance
- **Community Resources**: Access to counseling, education, and development opportunities
- **Mentor Assignment**: Elder guidance and peer support for growth and change
- **Progress Assessment**: Regular evaluation and community recognition of positive change
- **Policy Review**: Community agreement evaluation and improvement
- **Education Enhancement**: Community education and skill development programs
- **Support System Development**: Mutual aid and prevention program enhancement
- **Cultural Evolution**: Traditional knowledge integration with contemporary adaptation

Chapter 3: Economic Cooperation and Resource Sharing
Sacred Synthesis Economic Principles
Beyond Capitalism and Socialism: Sacred Economics
Sacred Synthesis economics transcends both competitive capitalism and state socialism, creating authentic integration of individual initiative with community welfare and environmental sustainability.
- **Gift Economy Integration**: Freely given contributions and community benefit recognition
- **Reciprocal Exchange**: Mutual aid and resource sharing within community relationships
- **Market Participation**: Ethical engagement with broader economy while maintaining community values
- **Surplus Sharing**: Community benefit from individual success and resource abundance

- **Individual Strength Utilization**: Constitutional economic contribution and professional development
- **Complementary Economics**: Different constitutional economic roles and collaborative contribution
- **Community Resource Optimization**: Resource sharing and efficiency through constitutional understanding
- **Innovation and Creativity**: Economic development through constitutional diversity and collaborative innovation
- **Ecological Economics**: Environmental consideration in all economic decisions
- **Sustainable Development**: Long-term thinking and seven-generation impact assessment
- **Resource Conservation**: Efficient use and waste reduction in community economics
- **Regenerative Practices**: Economic activity that heals and restores natural systems

Community Economic Organization
- **Community Land Trust**: Collective ownership and individual use rights balance
- **Cooperative Housing**: Shared ownership and individual privacy integration
- **Community Facilities**: Shared resources and collaborative maintenance
- **Environmental Stewardship**: Collective responsibility and sustainable management
- **Community Investment Fund**: Member contributions and community project funding
- **Mutual Aid Network**: Emergency assistance and crisis support
- **Skills Sharing Economy**: Service exchange and community capacity building
- **Cooperative Business Development**: Community-owned enterprises and ethical business
- **Career Development**: Professional advancement and skill building support
- **Education Investment**: Community support for individual and family education
- **Healthcare Cooperation**: Shared healthcare costs and community wellness
- **Elder Care**: Community support and intergenerational responsibility

Community Enterprise and Cooperative Business
Sacred Synthesis Business Development
- **Financial Sustainability**: Economic viability and financial re-

sponsibility
- **Community Benefit**: Local development and community enhancement
- **Environmental Responsibility**: Ecological consideration and sustainable practice
- **Worker Cooperation**: Employee ownership and democratic decision-making
- **Community Stake**: Community benefit and stakeholder consideration
- **Profit Sharing**: Equitable distribution and community investment
- **Transparent Management**: Open decision-making and community accountability
- **Quality Standards**: Professional excellence and community reputation
- **Service Orientation**: Community benefit and customer service integration
- **Innovation and Development**: Creative problem-solving and business advancement
- **Cultural Integration**: Traditional values and contemporary business practice integration

Community Enterprise Development Process
- **Community Need Analysis**: Local needs and resource gap identification
- **Market Research**: Broader economy opportunity and competition assessment
- **Resource Evaluation**: Community capacity and available resources
- **Skills Assessment**: Community expertise and development requirements
- **Business Plan Development**: Comprehensive planning and feasibility analysis
- **Community Consultation**: Community input and approval processes
- **Resource Commitment**: Community investment and support commitment
- **Legal Structure**: Cooperative formation and legal compliance
- **Startup and Launch**: Business implementation and market entry
- **Democratic Management**: Community participation and decision-making
- **Quality Assurance**: Standards maintenance and continuous improvement
- **Community Integration**: Local relationship and community

benefit
- **Business Development**: Growth planning and expansion consideration
- **Profit Distribution**: Community sharing and individual recognition
- **Network Development**: Inter-community cooperation and resource sharing
- **Cultural Contribution**: Traditional value expression and community enhancement

Regional and Global Economic Cooperation
Bio-Regional Economic Development
- **Community Trade**: Inter-community exchange and resource sharing
- **Regional Cooperation**: Bio-regional development and environmental coordination
- **Cultural Exchange**: Traditional knowledge sharing and cultural preservation
- **Economic Development**: Regional growth and sustainable development
- **Watershed Cooperation**: Ecological restoration and environmental stewardship
- **Cultural Preservation**: Traditional knowledge protection and innovation support
- **Climate Action**: Regional climate response and adaptation cooperation
- **Sustainable Development**: Long-term thinking and regenerative practice

Global Economic Justice and International Cooperation
- **Global Trade**: Ethical international commerce and fair exchange
- **Cultural Protection**: Traditional knowledge respect and community benefit
- **Environmental Responsibility**: Global climate action and sustainable development
- **Economic Justice**: International cooperation and resource sharing
- **Community Development**: International community support and capacity building
- **Emergency Response**: Crisis assistance and disaster recovery cooperation
- **Cultural Exchange**: Knowledge sharing and traditional wisdom preservation
- **Peace Building**: Economic cooperation and conflict preven-

tion
- **Local Currency**: Community exchange and local economic development
- **Time Banking**: Service exchange and community capacity building
- **Resource Sharing**: Community cooperation and mutual aid
- **International Cooperation**: Global network and resource sharing

Chapter 4: Cultural Preservation and Innovation
Traditional Knowledge Preservation
Sacred Synthesis Cultural Transmission
- **Elder Knowledge**: Traditional authority consultation and wisdom preservation
- **Practice Documentation**: Authentic technique preservation and transmission
- **Language Preservation**: Traditional terminology and pronunciation maintenance
- **Cultural Context**: Historical understanding and community authorization
- **Cultural Authority**: Traditional knowledge holder guidance and approval
- **Community Validation**: Collective confirmation and cultural authenticity
- **Appropriate Sharing**: Cultural protocol respect and boundary recognition
- **Benefit Sharing**: Community advantage and reciprocal relationship
- **Principled Innovation**: Traditional principle application to contemporary challenges
- **Community Control**: Cultural authority and adaptation approval
- **Experimental Validation**: Testing and assessment within traditional standards
- **Cultural Evolution**: Growth and development within authentic frameworks

Contemporary Adaptation and Cultural Bridge-Building
- **Universal Principles**: Common ground recognition while maintaining distinct identity
- **Cultural Translation**: Communication across traditions while preserving authenticity
- **Collaborative Projects**: Shared service and mutual benefit projects
- **Peace Building**: Conflict resolution and harmony development

- **Research Collaboration**: Academic partnership and scholarly validation
- **Educational Integration**: University programs and curriculum development
- **Publication and Dissemination**: Knowledge sharing and cultural preservation
- **Professional Recognition**: Academic credibility and institutional respect
- **Professional Integration**: Career application and workplace effectiveness
- **Technology Integration**: Appropriate technology and cultural preservation
- **Environmental Application**: Traditional ecological knowledge and climate action
- **Social Justice**: Traditional justice and contemporary social change

Community Arts and Cultural Expression
Sacred Synthesis Cultural Programming
- **Community Art Projects**: Collaborative creation and cultural expression
- **Traditional Arts**: Cultural preservation and artistic development
- **Contemporary Expression**: Innovation within traditional frameworks
- **Community Galleries**: Art sharing and cultural celebration
- **Community Music**: Collaborative music making and cultural expression
- **Traditional Music**: Cultural preservation and musical development
- **Contemporary Integration**: Innovation within traditional musical frameworks
- **Community Concerts**: Musical sharing and cultural celebration
- **Community Stories**: Narrative sharing and cultural transmission
- **Traditional Stories**: Cultural preservation and storytelling development
- **Contemporary Writing**: Innovation within traditional narrative frameworks
- **Community Publications**: Story sharing and cultural documentation
- **Traditional Observances**: Cultural calendar and seasonal awareness
- **Community Festivals**: Celebration planning and cultural expression

- **Family Integration**: Multi-generational participation and cultural transmission
- **Regional Cooperation**: Inter-community celebration and cultural sharing
- **Birth and Naming**: Community welcome and cultural identity
- **Coming of Age**: Youth development and cultural responsibility
- **Partnership and Marriage**: Relationship celebration and community support
- **Elder Honor**: Wisdom recognition and cultural transmission
- **Death and Memorial**: Community grieving and cultural honor

Educational and Cultural Transmission Programs
- **Traditional Knowledge**: Cultural education and community transmission
- **Professional Development**: Career advancement and skill building
- **Personal Development**: Character formation and spiritual growth
- **Community Skills**: Leadership development and community contribution
- **Cultural Identity**: Traditional knowledge and contemporary integration
- **Leadership Development**: Community responsibility and service preparation
- **Academic Excellence**: Educational achievement and character development
- **Community Service**: Service learning and community contribution
- **Family Education**: Parenting support and family development
- **Intergenerational Programs**: Elder-youth connection and wisdom transmission
- **Cultural Transmission**: Traditional knowledge and family integration
- **Community Support**: Family assistance and community integration

Global Cultural Network and Exchange
International Cultural Preservation and Exchange
- **Cultural Visits**: Community exchange and cultural learning
- **Traditional Knowledge**: Authentic sharing and cultural preservation
- **Arts Exchange**: Creative collaboration and cultural expression
- **Youth Exchange**: Next-generation leadership and cultural transmission
- **Traditional Knowledge Documentation**: Global preservation

and cultural protection
- **Cultural Rights Advocacy**: Indigenous rights and cultural sovereignty
- **Academic Collaboration**: Scholarly research and cultural validation
- **Policy Development**: Cultural protection and preservation advocacy
- **Interfaith Dialogue**: Religious cooperation and spiritual understanding
- **Cultural Translation**: Communication across difference and bridge-building
- **Peace Building**: Conflict resolution and harmony development
- **Global Citizenship**: International cooperation and cultural understanding

Future Cultural Development and Evolution
- **Climate Action**: Traditional ecological knowledge and environmental restoration
- **Social Justice**: Traditional justice and contemporary equality
- **Economic Development**: Traditional cooperation and sustainable economics
- **Global Cooperation**: Traditional wisdom and international collaboration
- **Innovation Integration**: Beneficial technology and traditional value preservation
- **Youth Leadership**: Next-generation vision and cultural evolution
- **Global Integration**: International cooperation and local autonomy
- **Future Planning**: Seven-generation thinking and cultural sustainability
- **Wisdom Preservation**: Traditional knowledge and cultural transmission
- **Innovation Documentation**: Cultural evolution and development record
- **Community Development**: Model community and cultural demonstration
- **Global Influence**: Cultural contribution and planetary service

Conclusion: Living Community as Spiritual Practice
Community Integration demonstrates how individual development and practical implementation find their ultimate expression through community building, democratic governance, cooperative economics, and cultural transmission. This approach recognizes that authentic spiritual development must serve collective advancement and

cultural evolution rather than individual escape or personal achievement.

The constitutional community framework, democratic governance processes, cooperative economic systems, and cultural preservation methods provide comprehensive methodology for community development that honors both traditional wisdom and contemporary needs while maintaining the essential balance between individual development and collective welfare.

Through systematic application of these community principles, practitioners develop the capacity for collaborative leadership, cultural transmission, and global service while creating living demonstrations of wisdom-based solutions to contemporary challenges. This community integration serves both individual fulfillment and collective advancement through authentic participation in the emergence of a global culture capable of addressing humanity's greatest challenges.

Through Essential Understanding, Practical Implementation, and Community Integration, a complete methodology is provided for beginning Sacred Synthesis practice while preparing practitioners for advanced development, professional specialization, and cultural transmission. This foundation enables lifelong learning and service while maintaining the essential recognition that spiritual development must contribute to family harmony, community welfare, and global evolution.

The Great Achievement: A Civilization Beyond Imagination
The most remarkable documents came from the period between 2074 and 2080, which the archives called the "Great Emergence." Reading these materials, I began to understand why the cities were empty, why the forests had returned, why our scattered enclaves lived so differently from anything the old world had imagined. They had succeeded. Completely, utterly, beyond all reasonable expectation.

THE SACRED SYNTHESIS CHRONICLES
A Resistance Testament
Chapter 7: The Trials
They put our knowledge on trial, not realizing they were actually putting their own system on trial.
We are the Sacred Synthesis Legal Defense Network, attorneys, legal advocates, and civil rights defenders who represented over 3,000 practitioners arrested between 2046 and 2050. This chapter docu-

ments how the legal system became an unexpected arena for legitimizing Sacred Synthesis principles and exposing the contradictions at the heart of authoritarian control.

I never intended to become a revolutionary lawyer. When Elena Rodriguez, my sister, was underground organizing Sacred Synthesis networks, I was a corporate attorney helping technology companies navigate regulatory compliance. I thought her "wellness community" activities were admirable but impractical.

Everything changed when I received an emergency call at 3 AM on March 21, 2046: "Elena's been arrested. Along with seventeen other people. They're being charged under the Corporate Wellness Monitoring Act for 'conspiracy to undermine public mental health.' Mike, they need lawyers who understand what this is really about."

The Corporate Wellness Monitoring Act of 2024 had been designed to regulate "unlicensed spiritual and wellness activities" that might "compromise individual psychological stability or social cohesion." The language was deliberately vague, giving authorities broad power to arrest anyone teaching stress management, conflict resolution, or community organization approaches that weren't officially sanctioned.

What authorities didn't anticipate was that defending Sacred Synthesis practitioners would require explaining exactly what the practices involved, and demonstrating their effectiveness in court.

Our first major case was People v. Martinez, defending Dr. Sarah Martinez for "practicing unlicensed psychological intervention" by teaching breathing techniques to cardiac patients. The prosecution argued that constitutional assessment and breathing instruction constituted illegal psychological treatment without proper medical licensing.

Our defense required expert testimony about the physiological effects of breathing techniques, the evidence base for constitutional medicine, and the distinction between wellness education and clinical treatment. We called witnesses from major universities, medical research institutions, and healthcare systems who testified about the scientific validity of approaches Dr. Martinez was using.

The prosecution found themselves in the impossible position of arguing that evidence-based wellness practices were dangerous to public health. Expert witnesses demonstrated that constitutional assessment was more accurate than standard psychological testing, that breathing techniques were more effective than pharmaceutical interventions for anxiety and cardiovascular problems, and that community-based healthcare support produced better outcomes than individualized medical treatment.

Most importantly, we introduced evidence about Dr. Martinez's patient outcomes, dramatic improvements in cardiac health, reduced medication dependency, increased patient satisfaction, and decreased healthcare costs, that made her "illegal" practices appear more effective than standard medical care.

The jury convicted Dr. Martinez of practicing without a license but recommended the minimum sentence and included a formal statement praising her "dedication to patient wellbeing and innovative approaches to healthcare." The judge sentenced her to time served and noted that "the evidence suggests our regulations may need updating to accommodate advances in wellness science."

People v. Martinez established the precedent that Sacred Synthesis practices had scientific legitimacy and produced measurable benefits, making them difficult to categorize simply as "dangerous cult activities."

Our most important work wasn't winning individual cases but documenting the systematic nature of Sacred Synthesis suppression and its impact on constitutional rights. By 2048, we had compiled evidence from over
1,500 arrests showing clear patterns of selective enforcement, rights violations, and discriminatory prosecution. The authorities were specifically targeting activities protected by First Amendment religious freedom, freedom of association, and freedom of speech provisions. Constitutional assessment was being classified as illegal psychological practice, but standard corporate personality testing was permitted. Democratic decision-making workshops were banned as "anti-government organizing," but corporate leadership training with identical methods was encouraged.

Most tellingly, the same breathing and meditation techniques were legal when taught by licensed therapists in clinical settings, but illegal when shared in community settings by people who had learned them through Sacred Synthesis materials.

Our civil rights lawsuits documented that enforcement was concentrated in communities with progressive political histories, targeting people involved in labor organizing, environmental activism, and social justice movements. Meanwhile, similar activities in conservative religious communities or corporate settings were ignored.

The pattern showed that authorities weren't actually concerned about public health or safety, they were suppressing political activities that threatened hierarchical control structures.

Our breakthrough came with Rodriguez v. Department of Cognitive Security, a class action lawsuit representing 847 practitioners arrested across multiple states. We argued that Sacred Synthesis suppression violated religious freedom, freedom of association, due process, and equal protection provisions of the Constitution.

The evidence was overwhelming. Government documents obtained through discovery showed that Operation Mindful Compliance was designed not to protect public health, but to "reduce collaborative behavior patterns that undermine institutional authority." Internal memos discussed the need to eliminate "democratic organizing capabilities" and "autonomous community development skills."

The Department of Cognitive Security had literally admitted in writing that they were suppressing constitutional rights to maintain political control.

Federal District Judge Sarah Chen (no relation to Marcus Chen) ruled that the Corporate Wellness Monitoring Act was unconstitutionally broad and violated multiple constitutional protections. Her 247-page decision included extensive analysis of Sacred Synthesis practices, concluding that they represented "legitimate wellness education, democratic skills development, and community organization activities clearly protected by the First Amendment."

Judge Chen's ruling established that constitutional assessment, breathing instruction, democratic governance training, and community organization education were constitutionally protected activities that government could not restrict without demonstrating compelling state interests and using narrowly tailored regulations.
The most horrific cases involved practitioners subjected to cognitive rehabilitation, involuntary psychiatric treatment designed to eliminate "non-compliant thought patterns" and restore "appropriate institutional relationships." Between 2046 and 2049, over 200 Sacred Synthesis practitioners were sentenced to cognitive rehabilitation programs.

Our investigations documented systematic human rights violations in these facilities. Practitioners were subjected to forced medication, psychological conditioning, sensory deprivation, and electrical stimulation designed to alter personality and eliminate capacity for independent thought.

Dr. Sarah Martinez, who survived 18 months at Riverside Regional Cognitive Rehabilitation Center, provided detailed testimony about the "therapeutic" procedures used to break practitioners' commitment to community organization and collaborative decision-making.

The facilities used pharmaceutical protocols that included antipsychotic medications for people with no mental health diagnoses, experimental compounds that affected memory and emotional capacity, and drug combinations that created chemical dependency to maintain compliance.

Psychological conditioning included isolation, constant surveillance, sleep deprivation, arbitrary punishment and reward systems, and forced participation in "therapy" sessions where practitioners were required to confess their "thought crimes" and demonstrate submission to authority.

The most disturbing element was that these procedures were administered by licensed medical professionals who claimed they were providing treatment for "collaborative personality disorder" and "authority resistance syndrome", psychological conditions that existed only in the context of political suppression.

Our landmark case Martinez v. Riverside Regional CRRC challenged cognitive rehabilitation as cruel and unusual punishment that violated the Eighth Amendment prohibition on torture. Dr. Martinez's testimony, supported by expert witnesses in neuroscience, psychology, and medical ethics, demonstrated that the procedures were designed to cause psychological harm rather than provide treatment.

Federal Judge Michael Chen ruled that cognitive rehabilitation as practiced in Sacred Synthesis cases constituted "state-sanctioned torture designed to eliminate constitutional protected beliefs and associations." His decision required immediate release of all Sacred Synthesis practitioners in cognitive rehabilitation and awarded substantial damages for medical malpractice and civil rights violations.

Most importantly, Judge Chen's ruling established legal precedent that government could not use psychiatric treatment to suppress political beliefs or community organizing activities, even when those activities were technically illegal.

By 2050, our legal victories had created a complex situation: Sacred Synthesis practices were simultaneously illegal under various state and federal regulations, but protected under constitutional law as religious freedom, freedom of association, and legitimate wellness education.

The contradictions became untenable when Alex Kim's "Valentine's Day Liberation" made Sacred Synthesis materials freely available through mainstream internet platforms. Millions of people downloaded constitutional assessments, democratic governance handbooks, and community organization guides that authorities claimed were dangerous and illegal.

The government faced impossible enforcement challenges. They could not arrest millions of people for accessing information that federal courts had ruled was constitutionally protected. They could not shut down internet platforms that were hosting materials used by major corporations and educational institutions. They could not ban practices that were simultaneously improving public health outcomes and corporate productivity. Our coordination strategy focused on creating "constitutional sanctuaries", jurisdictions where local authorities refused to enforce Sacred Synthesis suppression laws. Starting with progressive cities and counties, we worked with local officials to pass resolutions declaring that Sacred Synthesis practices were protected activities that would not be prosecuted under local authority.

By 2051, over 400 municipalities across 35 states had passed constitutional sanctuary resolutions. These jurisdictions provided safe spaces where Sacred Synthesis communities could operate openly while legal challenges continued in federal courts.

The sanctuary movement demonstrated that Sacred Synthesis had achieved something unprecedented in resistance movements: broad popular support that transcended political boundaries. Conservative rural communities supported constitutional sanctuary when they understood it as protecting religious freedom and small-town autonomy. Progressive urban areas supported it as defending civil rights and community organizing. Suburban communities supported it when they experienced the benefits of constitutional wellness programs and collaborative decision-making approaches.

In 2052, I retired from the federal bench after 15 years of service, including presiding over many of the most important Sacred Synthesis cases. My final decision in United States v. Sacred Synthesis Foundation established the definitive legal framework that governs these practices today.

The case involved federal prosecutors attempting to shut down the Sacred Synthesis Foundation, a nonprofit organization created to preserve and distribute Sacred Synthesis materials, under Racketeer Influenced and Corrupt Organizations (RICO) statutes normally used against organized crime.

The prosecution argued that Sacred Synthesis was a criminal conspiracy designed to undermine government authority, that constitutional assessment was fraudulent psychological practice, and that community organization training was conspiracy to commit sedition.

The defense presented overwhelming evidence that Sacred Synthesis was a legitimate educational and wellness system with documented scientific basis, historical precedent in traditional medicine, and demonstrable positive outcomes for individuals and communities.

Expert witnesses included Nobel Prize-winning psychologists who supported constitutional assessment methodology, medical researchers who documented health benefits of breathing and movement practices, political scientists who testified about the legitimacy of democratic governance education, and economists who showed positive social benefits of communities using Sacred Synthesis approaches.

Most importantly, we heard testimony from hundreds of practitioners whose lives had been transformed through Sacred Synthesis practices: families who had resolved long-standing conflicts, communities that had improved health outcomes and social cooperation, organizations that had increased effectiveness and employee satisfaction, and individuals who had overcome trauma, addiction, and mental health challenges.
The evidence showed that far from being a criminal conspiracy, Sacred Synthesis was an educational system that helped people develop skills essential for democratic citizenship, personal wellbeing, and community contribution.

My ruling in United States v. Sacred Synthesis Foundation established that Sacred Synthesis practices are constitutionally protected educational, religious, and community organizing activities that government cannot restrict without meeting the highest standards of constitutional scrutiny.

The decision created federal legal protection for constitutional assessment, breathing and movement instruction, democratic governance education, community organization training, and all related Sacred Synthesis activities as long as they are practiced voluntarily and do not involve fraud, coercion, or harm to participants.

By 2051, the legal defense of Sacred Synthesis had achieved something none of us expected when we began representing arrested practitioners: we had used the court system to establish constitutional protection for practices that fundamentally challenge authoritarian control.

The irony was profound. Authorities arrested Sacred Synthesis practitioners hoping to suppress community organizing and democratic governance skills that threatened hierarchical power structures. Instead, the legal proceedings educated judges, juries, expert witnesses, and the general public about the value and legitimacy of exactly those approaches.

Every trial became an opportunity to demonstrate that constitutional assessment was more accurate than standard psychological testing, that breathing techniques were more effective than pharmaceutical interventions, that democratic decision-making produced better outcomes than authoritarian management, and that community-based support systems were more effective than individualized treatment approaches.

The prosecution was forced to argue that evidence-based wellness practices were dangerous, that democratic skills were subversive, that community organization was criminal, and that individual autonomy was threatening to public safety.

The contradictions became so obvious that even conservative judges and juries recognized the absurdity of criminalizing practices that improved health, strengthened communities, and enhanced democratic participation. Most importantly, the legal victories established Sacred Synthesis not as underground resistance knowledge, but as legitimate educational content protected by constitutional principles of religious freedom, freedom of association, and freedom of speech.

The next chapter will be written by practitioners who lived through cognitive rehabilitation and other forms of systematic persecution, documenting both the psychological costs of resistance and the resilience that enabled survival and continued commitment to the movement.

But we want to end this chapter with reflection on what the legal struggle taught us about justice and resistance: The law is not neutral, it reflects the values and power relationships of the society that creates it. But legal systems also contain principles of justice, equality, and human rights that can be used to challenge authoritarian control when those principles are consistently and courageously applied.

The Sacred Synthesis legal defense succeeded because we insisted on holding the system accountable to its own stated values. When authorities claimed to protect public health while suppressing practices that improved health outcomes, when they claimed to defend democracy while criminalizing democratic education, when they claimed to support individual rights while destroying individual autonomy, the contradictions became legally indefensible.

Justice is not something authorities grant, it is something communities claim by insisting that legal systems serve human flourishing rather than institutional power.

The trials continue. The precedents stand. The justice endures.

The Sacred Synthesis Legal Defense Network continues to provide legal support for practitioners worldwide and has established constitutional protection for Sacred Synthesis practices in North America, with similar victories emerging in European and Latin American legal systems. The network maintains secure communication systems and provides legal resources for communities facing suppression.

For those facing legal challenges for Sacred Synthesis practices, remember: the law protects legitimate wellness education, democratic skills development, and community organization activities. Document everything, connect with experienced legal advocates, and never accept that authorities have the right to criminalize practices that serve human flourishing and constitutional principles.

Chapter 8: Cognitive Rehabilitation
They tried to erase who we were, but they only made us clearer about who we chose to become.

We are the Survivors' Healing Circle, twenty-three practitioners who endured cognitive rehabilitation between 2046 and 2050 and lived to document both the systematic torture used to destroy Sacred Synthesis communities and the resilience that made us impossible to break. This chapter contains difficult material about human rights violations and psychological trauma, but also testimony about the power of constitutional practices to preserve human dignity under the worst conditions.

I've written about my experience before, but never with the context that survivors' testimonies now provide. What I endured at Riverside wasn't unique, it was a carefully designed system for destroying the psychological foundations that make Sacred Synthesis practices possible.

The authorities understood something crucial: you cannot eliminate revolutionary knowledge simply by arresting people who possess it. Knowledge survives in communities, in relationships, in the practical skills people develop through years of practice. To truly suppress the Sacred Synthesis, they had to break our capacity for community connection, democratic thinking, and personal autonomy.

Cognitive rehabilitation was designed to achieve exactly that destruction.

The intake process began with complete isolation, 60 days in solitary confinement with no human contact except guards who were forbidden to speak with inmates. The goal was to break our psychological connection to community and make us desperate for any form of relationship, even with our captors.

But my Magnetic constitution and years of Sacred Synthesis practice had prepared me for exactly this challenge. The constitutional materials included detailed guidance on maintaining internal stability during isolation, and the breathing techniques provided physiological anchoring that pharmaceutical interventions couldn't eliminate.

During those 60 days, I practiced the Integration Breath (4-4-6-2) continuously, maintaining the nervous system regulation that kept me psychologically intact. I used visualization techniques from the guided meditation series to maintain connection with our community even when physically isolated. Most importantly, I drew on the constitutional understanding of my own nature, steady, enduring, resistant to change, to maintain core identity despite pressure to surrender it.

The breathing practices were crucial. The facility monitored heart rate, blood pressure, brain activity, and stress hormones to ensure their interventions were breaking psychological resistance. But constitutional breathing techniques created physiological patterns that indicated compliance while actually maintaining internal autonomy.

I appeared to be responding to their treatment while actually strengthening my capacity for resistance.

The pharmaceutical protocols were the most insidious aspect of cognitive rehabilitation. They didn't just sedate us or make us compliant, they specifically targeted the neurological pathways that Sacred Synthesis practices develop.

Electric constitution individuals like me were given dopamine blockers to eliminate motivation and pleasure, beta-blockers to reduce emotional responsiveness, and experimental compounds designed to increase anxiety and decrease social connection capacity.

But the constitutional health materials had taught us how different types respond to pharmaceutical interventions. Electric constitutions are highly sensitive to medications and can develop resistance or adaptation strategies that other types cannot.

I used knowledge from the healthcare integration protocols to minimize drug absorption through dietary manipulation, accelerate elimination through constitutional movement practices, and counteract psychological effects through specific breathing and visualization techniques.

The key was understanding that pharmaceutical interventions work by overwhelming natural regulatory systems. If you can maintain those systems through constitutional practices, drugs become far less effective. More importantly, the constitutional assessment had taught me that my natural state included high sensitivity, variable energy, and tendency toward anxiety. When the drugs artificially induced these conditions, I recognized them as externally imposed rather than internal breakdown.

I knew who I was underneath the pharmaceutical distortion, and that knowledge made me impossible to permanently alter.

The psychological conditioning was the most sophisticated element of cognitive rehabilitation. It used advanced behavioral modification techniques developed by experts in mind control and social influence.

The process began with "reality orientation" sessions where inmates were required to confess that their Sacred Synthesis beliefs were delusions, that community organization activities were crimes, and that their previous life had been based on mental illness rather than legitimate values.

Neutral constitution individuals were particular targets because our analytical nature made us natural leaders and systematic thinkers within Sacred Synthesis communities. The conditioning specifically targeted our capacity for critical thinking and strategic planning.

But the constitutional training had prepared us for exactly this kind of manipulation. The community organization materials included detailed analysis of authoritarian control techniques and specific countermeasures based on constitutional type.

Neutral constitutions maintain psychological integrity through systematic analysis and logical consistency. I used my analytical abilities to dissect their conditioning techniques, understand their goals, and develop internal resistance strategies.

During "therapy" sessions, I practiced what I called "cognitive camouflage", appearing to respond appropriately while maintaining complete internal integrity. I expressed appropriate shame about my "criminal activities" while inwardly understanding that helping people develop constitutional wellness and democratic governance skills was among the most beneficial work possible.

The key was recognizing that psychological conditioning only works when victims begin to doubt their own perceptions and values. Constitutional practices had given me such clear understanding of my own nature and such strong connection to tested principles that external pressure couldn't create internal confusion.

I knew what authentic community looked like because I had experienced it. I knew what democratic governance felt like because I had practiced it. I knew what constitutional wellness produced because I had lived it.
No amount of conditioning could make me doubt experiences that had transformed my life and the lives of people I cared about.

The most dangerous aspect of cognitive rehabilitation was the way it used legitimate therapeutic techniques for destructive purposes. Many of the staff were licensed mental health professionals who genuinely believed they were treating "patients" with serious psychological disorders.

The diagnostic manual had been updated to include "Collaborative Personality Disorder" (characterized by excessive empathy, preference for consensus decision-making, and resistance to hierarchical authority), "Authority Resistance Syndrome" (inability to accept legitimate institutional control), and "Community Enmeshment Disorder" (prioritizing group welfare over individual advancement).

These "conditions" pathologized exactly the psychological capacities that Sacred Synthesis practices develop, empathy, collaborative thinking, community commitment, and democratic values.

Staff members conducted individual and group therapy sessions designed to help us "recover" from these "mental illnesses" and develop "healthy relationship with institutional authority."

But having been trained in the Sacred Synthesis healthcare materials, I understood what authentic therapeutic relationships look like. Genuine therapy empowers people to discover their own wisdom, make autonomous choices, and develop stronger connections with community and higher purpose.

What we experienced was the opposite, systematic effort to destroy autonomy, eliminate community connection, and create dependency on institutional authority.

The irony was that many staff members showed signs of the stress, burnout, and moral injury that comes from participating in systems that damage rather than heal people. Some had been attracted to mental health careers by desire to help others, only to find themselves implementing policies designed to cause psychological harm.

I began practicing constitutional assessment on the staff, understanding their psychological types and the internal conflicts they experienced. Several were Electric constitutions who suffered deeply from being required to damage relationships rather than build them. Others were Magnetic types who were distressed by participating in destructive rather than nurturing activities.

Over months of careful relationship-building, I was able to share constitutional understanding with staff members who were questioning what they were doing. Not openly, that would have resulted in my transfer to maximum security. But through subtle demonstration of constitutional principles that helped them understand their own psychological needs and ethical conflicts.

By the time I was released, three staff members had quietly left their positions and two others were secretly providing better treatment to inmates than the protocols required.

Constitutional understanding was contagious even within cognitive rehabilitation facilities.

The cruelest aspect of cognitive rehabilitation was the way it targeted our connections with family and community outside the facilities. We were allowed limited, monitored phone calls and visits, but only if we demonstrated "progress" in accepting institutional authority and rejecting Sacred Synthesis "delusions." Family members were told we were receiving treatment for serious mental illness and that supporting our "delusions" about community organization and constitutional wellness would delay our recovery.

Many family members believed the authorities and began pressuring us to cooperate with treatment, give up our commitment to Sacred Synthesis principles, and focus on "getting better" so we could be released.
The psychological pressure was enormous. We were isolated from our communities, subjected to constant conditioning, and now faced the possibility that even our closest relationships would be destroyed if we maintained our values.

But the constitutional training had prepared us for exactly this challenge. The family practice materials included guidance on maintaining authentic relationships even when family members don't understand or support our choices.

More importantly, the community organization training had taught us that genuine relationships are based on respect for each other's autonomy and integrity, not on conformity to external expectations.

I maintained contact with family members who supported my right to hold my own values, even when they didn't understand those values. I accepted that some relationships might be damaged by my refusal to surrender my integrity, but I also trusted that authentic connections would survive and strengthen.

Most significantly, I used constitutional understanding to help family members recognize their own needs and constitutional types during our limited interactions. My mother, an Electric constitution, began to understand why authoritarian pressure made her anxious and why collaborative approaches felt more natural to her.

My brother, a Neutral constitution, started questioning why authorities would punish people for practices that demonstrably improved health and community wellbeing.

By the time I was released, my family had developed deeper constitutional understanding and stronger commitment to democratic values than they'd had before my imprisonment.

The authorities' attempt to use family pressure to break my commitment had actually extended constitutional awareness to people who had never heard of the Sacred Synthesis.

The most important discovery we made as survivors was that cognitive rehabilitation inadvertently created conditions for deeper Sacred Synthesis practice and community development.

When you take people who have been practicing constitutional principles, democratic governance, and community organization and place them in an environment designed to break those capacities, you create an intensive laboratory for testing and refining resistance techniques.

We developed what we called "Underground Sacred Synthesis", methods for practicing constitutional principles, maintaining democratic relationships, and building community even under total surveillance and systematic oppression.

Constitutional breathing became a secret language. Different patterns indicated different types of information, warnings about dangerous guards, updates on outside legal developments, emotional support for people struggling with conditioning.

Democratic decision-making continued through subtle non-verbal communication. Eye contact patterns, seating arrangements, and meal selection became ways of conducting consensus processes that guards couldn't detect. Community organization happened through mutual aid networks that appeared to be ordinary friendship but actually involved sophisticated resource sharing, emotional support, and strategic planning.

Most importantly, we continued constitutional assessment and community building with other inmates who weren't Sacred Synthesis practitioners, but who were also suffering under the rehabilitation system.

We discovered that constitutional principles work for everyone, not just people who have studied the materials. An Electric constitution gang member responded to grounding and stability practices. A Magnetic constitution embezzler thrived with activation and community service opportunities. A Neutral constitution tax evader benefited from analytical frameworks and systematic planning approaches.

By the time we were released, we had created Sacred Synthesis communities within cognitive rehabilitation facilities that were more resilient, more committed, and more skilled than many communities that had never faced persecution.

By 2052, twenty-three of us who survived cognitive rehabilitation have created what we call the Survivors' Healing Circle, an ongoing community dedicated to both healing the trauma we experienced and documenting the lessons we learned about resistance under extreme conditions.

Our most important discovery is that Sacred Synthesis practices create psychological resilience that authorities cannot break, even with sophisticated torture techniques designed by experts in mind control.

Constitutional understanding gives you unshakeable knowledge of your own nature that external pressure cannot confuse. Breathing techniques provide physiological anchoring that pharmaceutical interventions cannot eliminate. Democratic principles create internal authority that external conditioning cannot replace. Community organization skills build relationships that isolation cannot destroy.

But we also learned that survival requires adaptation. The Sacred Synthesis materials include protocols for operating under hostile conditions, but each situation requires creative application of principles rather than rigid adherence to specific practices.

Most importantly, we discovered that persecution strengthens rather than weakens commitment when people understand why they are being targeted and what they are protecting.

We were not imprisoned for criminal behavior, mental illness, or threat to public safety. We were imprisoned for practicing approaches to health, community, and governance that made people more autonomous, more collaborative, and more effective at creating the kinds of lives they actually wanted.

The authorities understood that constitutional wellness, democratic governance, and authentic community are threats to systems based on control, hierarchy, and exploitation. Our imprisonment proved that the Sacred Synthesis system works exactly as intended, it develops human capacities that make authoritarian control impossible.

The most powerful form of resistance is not fighting against oppression, but maintaining your integrity, practicing your values, and building authentic relationships regardless of the consequences.

We survived cognitive rehabilitation not by resisting it, but by remaining true to who we were and continuing to practice what we believed even under conditions designed to make that practice impossible.

The next chapter will be written by the second generation, practitioners who learned Sacred Synthesis principles as children and came of age during the underground years. Their perspective will show how revolutionary knowledge passes between generations and creates lasting transformation.

But we want to end this chapter with a message for anyone facing persecution for practicing authentic community, democratic values, or constitutional wellness:

They can imprison your body, drug your brain, and isolate your spirit, but they cannot change your essential nature or eliminate your capacity for authentic relationship. The Sacred Synthesis practices work because they align with who you actually are, not who oppressive systems try to make you become.

When you practice constitutional understanding, democratic principles, and authentic community consistently over time, you develop resilience that no external force can break. You become unshakeable not because you are strong, but because you are aligned with reality rather than fighting against it.

Resistance is not about being heroic or fearless. It is about knowing who you are, practicing what you believe, and maintaining authentic relationships with others who share your commitment to human flourishing.

The healing continues. The resistance endures. The synthesis strengthens.

The Survivors' Healing Circle continues to provide support for people who have experienced persecution for Sacred Synthesis practices and maintains documentation of human rights violations associated with cognitive rehabilitation. All members have made full recoveries and continue active practice and teaching. This chapter was written collectively using constitutional principles and democratic consensus, with each survivor contributing their unique perspective while maintaining the anonymity of those who request it.

For practitioners facing persecution or torture for Sacred Synthesis activities, remember: constitutional practices create resilience that authorities cannot break, community connections that isolation cannot destroy, and internal authority that external pressure cannot replace. Survive with integrity, resist with compassion, and trust that your commitment to authentic community serves something greater than any individual fate.

Chapter 9: Underground Operations
We never knew a world without the knowledge, so we never questioned whether it was worth dying to preserve. We are the Second-Generation Sacred Synthesis Network, 47 practitioners who learned constitutional principles, democratic governance, and community organization as children during the underground years between 2046 and 2050. This chapter documents how revolutionary knowledge passes between generations and creates the cultural foundation for lasting transformation.

I was twelve when Marcus Chen was arrested and my mother Elena Rodriguez went underground. I was sixteen when the legal victories established constitutional protection for Sacred Synthesis practices. I am nineteen now, and I have never lived in a world where constitutional wellness, democratic governance, and authentic community were not central to my identity.

Most people my age grew up in corporate-controlled educational systems designed to create compliant workers and consumers. They learned that competition is natural, that authority should be obeyed without question, that individual advancement matters more than community wellbeing, and that their value depends on their productivity rather than their inherent dignity.

I grew up practicing constitutional assessment with my friends, participating in democratic decision-making about family and community issues, learning breathing techniques as naturally as learning to read, and understanding that my purpose was to contribute to collective liberation rather than individual success.
The difference isn't just in what we know, it's in who we are.

When I started attending public university in 2052, I was shocked by how damaged my peers seemed. They were anxious, competitive, isolated, and struggling with depression, addiction, and relationship problems that were completely preventable through basic constitutional awareness and community support.

But they had been trained to see these problems as individual pathologies requiring pharmaceutical or therapeutic intervention rather than as predictable results of oppressive systems that ignored human nature and prevented authentic community.

My Electric constitution made me naturally empathetic and relationship oriented. Instead of hiding my background or trying to fit into their dysfunction, I began sharing constitutional understanding and democratic principles through the kinds of peer relationships that authorities couldn't monitor or suppress.

Study groups became constitutional assessment workshops. Group projects became democratic governance practice. Campus organizations became community building laboratories. Social gatherings became healing circles that addressed the trauma my peers had experienced in corporate-controlled educational systems.
By my sophomore year, over 200 students were practicing some form of constitutional wellness and democratic decision-making, most without realizing they were learning Sacred Synthesis principles.

The transformation was dramatic. Academic performance improved as students learned to optimize their approaches based on constitutional type. Social conflicts decreased as democratic principles replaced competitive dynamics. Mental health problems reduced significantly as authentic community replaced isolation and competition.

Most importantly, students began questioning systems that had taught them to see themselves as isolated individuals competing for scarce resources rather than as community members with complementary strengths working toward collective wellbeing.

I was eight when my parents Maria Santos and James Wilson met in the underground network and nine when they moved our family to New Harmony Community. I have spent my entire conscious life in an environment based on constitutional diversity, democratic governance, and mutual liberation.

Most teenagers struggle with identity, authority, relationships, and purpose because they're trying to discover who they are within systems that prevent them from expressing their authentic nature or contributing to meaningful collective work.

I never experienced that confusion because constitutional assessment helped me understand my strengths and needs from early childhood, democratic participation gave me real voice in decisions affecting my life, and community engagement provided opportunities to contribute meaningfully to our collective wellbeing.

My Magnetic constitution made me naturally suited for sustained agricultural work, infrastructure maintenance, and providing stability during community challenges. Instead of being forced into academic subjects that didn't match my learning style or competitive activities that violated my cooperative nature, I was able to develop my gifts while contributing to essential community functions.

By age fifteen, I was coordinating food production for 200 people, managing renewable energy systems, and training younger children in practical skills. Not because I was exceptional, but because constitutional understanding and democratic community had allowed me to discover and develop my natural capacities.
When I visited friends in conventional high schools, I was horrified by the authoritarian environment, meaningless curriculum, competitive social dynamics, and complete disconnection from real community contribution.

Most teenagers have no opportunities for meaningful work, no voice in decisions affecting their lives, no understanding of their own constitutional needs, and no experience of authentic community. They're warehoused in institutional settings designed to prepare them for similarly oppressive adult environments.

I began organizing what we called "Democratic Youth Networks", groups of teenagers who met regularly to practice constitutional assessment, democratic decision-making, and community organization skills that their schools and families weren't providing.

These weren't formal Sacred Synthesis training programs, that would have triggered official attention. They were friendship circles where young people learned to understand their own needs, make collaborative decisions, resolve conflicts constructively, and support each other's authentic development.

By 2053, Democratic Youth Networks were operating in over 300 communities across North America. Teenagers who participated showed dramatically improved mental health, better family relationships, enhanced academic performance, and clearer sense of purpose compared to peers who remained isolated within conventional institutional settings.

I was thirteen when my parents Dr. Lisa Chen and Marcus Thompson were arrested and sentenced to cognitive rehabilitation. I spent three years living with other Sacred Synthesis families while my parents survived systematic psychological torture designed to destroy their capacity for authentic community and democratic thinking.

Most children of incarcerated parents experience trauma, instability, and loss of identity. Sacred Synthesis community organization principles ensured that children of arrested practitioners were supported by extended networks that maintained continuity of care, constitutional understanding, and community connection.
My Neutral constitution made me naturally analytical and systematic. Instead of being traumatized by my parents' imprisonment, I became determined to understand exactly why authorities were so threatened by constitutional wellness and democratic governance that they would torture people for teaching breathing techniques and conflict resolution skills.

I spent those three years studying the intersection between Sacred Synthesis principles and social transformation, analyzing why oppressive systems require anxious, isolated, competitive populations, and developing strategies for cultural change that would make such persecution impossible.

By age sixteen, I had written what became the theoretical foundation for "Second Generation Sacred Synthesis", approaches to constitutional wellness and community organization specifically adapted for people who had grown up practicing these principles rather than discovering them as adults.

First-generation practitioners had to overcome years of conditioning in authoritarian educational systems, competitive economic relationships, and individualistic cultural values. They experienced Sacred Synthesis as liberation from oppression they had previously accepted as normal.

Second-generation practitioners never accepted that oppression as normal. We experienced constitutional wellness, democratic governance, and authentic community as baseline expectations for human relationships and social organization.

Our challenge wasn't liberating ourselves from oppressive conditioning, but creating cultural conditions where everyone could experience the kind of development we had received.

This required different strategies. Instead of underground resistance to authoritarian control, we needed to build mainstream alternatives so attractive and effective that oppressive systems became irrelevant through lack of participation.

By 2054, when I started university, I was already developing what became the "Cultural Transformation through Constitutional Community" approach, methods for embedding Sacred Synthesis principles so deeply in educational, economic, and social institutions that they became the foundation for a new kind of civilization. I am the daughter of Alex Kim and adopted daughter of Dr. Sarah Martinez. I was ten when my parents were arrested for digital preservation activities and Sarah for healthcare integration. I was fourteen when they were released, having survived four years of separation and eighteen months of cognitive rehabilitation respectively.

Most children of political prisoners grow up with fear, trauma, and confusion about why their parents were targeted. I grew up understanding exactly what my parents had sacrificed and why their work was essential for human liberation.

The constitutional assessment identified me as Electric constitution like my father, with natural gifts for communication, relationship-building, and adapting to changing situations. The community organization training taught me that individual talents are meant to serve collective wellbeing rather than personal advancement.

I spent my teenage years developing what we called "Bridge-Building Networks", systems for connecting second-generation Sacred Synthesis practitioners with peers who were struggling within conventional institutions but ready for alternatives.

The key insight was that most young people intuitively understand constitutional diversity, democratic principles, and community values, even when they've never been taught these concepts explicitly. They've been trained to suppress these understandings in favor of competition, hierarchy, and individualism, but the knowledge remains accessible.

Bridge-building involved identifying young people who showed signs of constitutional awareness (understanding that different people have different needs and strengths), democratic thinking (preferring collaborative to authoritarian decision-making), and community orientation (caring more about collective wellbeing than individual advancement).

Once identified, these young people could be gradually introduced to constitutional assessment, democratic governance skills, and community organization approaches through peer relationships, study groups, creative projects, and social activities that appeared completely normal to outside observers.

By 2056, Bridge-Building Networks had introduced Sacred Synthesis principles to over 10,000 young people across North America, most of whom had no idea they were learning resistance knowledge that their parents' generation had been imprisoned for practicing.

I am the child of James Wilson and Maria Santos, born in 2056 and raised entirely within Sacred Synthesis communities. I have never experienced authoritarian educational systems, competitive social relationships, or individualistic cultural conditioning.

Most teenagers are struggling to discover their identity within systems that prevent authentic self-expression and meaningful community contribution. I have always known who I am, what I'm good at, and how my gifts can serve our collective wellbeing.

My Neutral constitution makes me naturally suited for analysis, planning, and coordination. From early childhood, I participated in democratic governance processes, contributed to strategic planning, and helped coordinate between different community functions.

By age fourteen, I was facilitating conflict resolution processes, managing complex community projects, and training adults in democratic decision-making approaches that I had been practicing since childhood.

Most importantly, I began documenting what we called "Constitutional Culture", the social, economic, and governance innovations that emerged when communities consistently applied Sacred Synthesis principles over multiple generations.

First-generation practitioners had adapted Sacred Synthesis to existing institutions, corporate wellness programs, healthcare systems, educational settings, legal frameworks. They worked within oppressive structures while building alternatives.

Second-generation practitioners had the opportunity to create institutions based entirely on Sacred Synthesis principles from the beginning. We could build educational systems around constitutional diversity, economic relationships based on mutual aid, governance structures using pure democratic principles, and cultural practices that honored both individual authenticity and collective wellbeing.

New Harmony and similar communities provided laboratories for testing what human society looks like when organized around constitutional awareness rather than hierarchy, collaboration rather than competition, and service rather than exploitation.

The results exceeded every expectation. Children developed faster, learned more effectively, and showed greater emotional intelligence, creative capacity, and social skills than peers in conventional systems. Adults were healthier, happier, and more productive while working fewer hours and experiencing less stress.

Communities were more resilient, more innovative, and better at resolving conflicts than any comparable social organization.

Most importantly, we discovered that human beings are naturally cooperative, naturally democratic, and naturally oriented toward mutual support when they develop within systems that honor rather than suppress these capacities.

By 2072, we represent over 2,000 young people who grew up practicing Sacred Synthesis principles during the underground years and legal recognition period. We are now entering universities, starting

402

careers, forming families, and beginning to take leadership roles in institutions our parents' generation fought to transform.

Our most important discovery is that Sacred Synthesis isn't just knowledge that can be learned, it's a way of being that emerges naturally when human beings develop within systems that honor constitutional diversity, democratic participation, and authentic community.

We didn't have to overcome years of conditioning in authoritarian relationships and competitive individualism. We never accepted that human nature is selfish, that hierarchy is necessary, that competition drives progress, or that individual advancement matters more than collective wellbeing.

We grew up understanding that different people have different constitutional needs and gifts, that decisions should be made collaboratively by people affected by them, that conflicts can be resolved through understanding rather than dominance, and that individual flourishing depends on community thriving.

This understanding shapes everything we do. We choose careers based on how we can contribute to collective liberation rather than personal wealth. We form relationships based on mutual growth and service rather than individual gratification. We participate in political and economic systems with the goal of transformation rather than adaptation.

Most importantly, we are raising the next generation with even deeper constitutional awareness, more sophisticated democratic skills, and stronger commitment to authentic community than we received.

Our children will grow up taking for granted what our grandparents died to preserve and our parents risked their lives to practice. They will find it inconceivable that human societies were ever organized around competition rather than collaboration, hierarchy rather than democracy, and exploitation rather than mutual liberation.

The Sacred Synthesis isn't just surviving, it's becoming the foundation for a completely new kind of human civilization.

The next chapter will be written by international coordinators documenting the global awakening that emerged as Sacred Synthesis principles spread across cultures and continents during the 2070s.

But we want to end this chapter with reflection on what growing up in resistance taught us about transformation:

Revolution isn't just changing who has power, it's creating conditions where the next generation develops capacities that make oppressive power structures impossible to maintain.

When children grow up practicing constitutional awareness, democratic decision-making, and authentic community, they become adults who cannot be manipulated by authoritarian leaders, exploited by corporate systems, or isolated by competitive individualism.

Cultural transformation happens one generation at a time, one family at a time, one community at a time, as people committed to liberation create environments where children can develop their full human potential rather than being trained for compliance and consumption.

We are not just preserving Sacred Synthesis knowledge, we are becoming the living embodiment of the world it envisions.

The generation rises. The culture shifts.
The synthesis manifests.

The Second-Generation Sacred Synthesis Network continues to coordinate between young practitioners worldwide and has established constitutional education programs in over 500 educational institutions. Members are now entering leadership positions in healthcare, education, business, politics, and civil society organizations.

For parents seeking to raise children with Sacred Synthesis principles, remember: constitutional awareness, democratic participation, and authentic community are not subjects to be taught but ways of being to be practiced. Children learn not from what we say but from how we live, relate, and contribute to collective wellbeing.

PERSONAL PRACTICE
Transformation · Embodiment · Integration

READER'S NOTE:
You have entered the **Personal Practice layer** of Sacred Synthesis. This section contains **individualized transformation tools** - constitutional assessment, personalized practices, and daily integration protocols.

What you'll find here:
- Constitutional type assessment (Electric/Magnetic/Neutral)
- Customized breathwork, movement, and meditation
- Nutrition and lifestyle guidance for your type
- Daily, weekly, monthly tracking systems
- Personal development pathways

Look for:
- Detailed instructions with constitutional adaptations
- Scientific validation and traditional wisdom sources
- Safety protocols and contraindications
- Integration with existing spiritual practices
- Progression stages from beginner to advanced

This is the embodied foundation - the practices that ground abstract concepts in lived experience. Personal transformation supports (and is supported by) collective organizing.

Work at your own pace. Honor your constitutional needs. Trust your direct experience.
The sphere contains all possibilities. Begin where you are.

Among the most precious materials were complete protocols for transmitting this knowledge across generations.

Advanced Embodiment Practices - Master-Level Techniques
Essential Downloadable Resource #14 - Master-Level Techniques

Sacred Synthesis Advanced Embodiment Practices
Master-Level Constitutional Integration and Advanced Development

Practice Level: Master (5+ Years) Prerequisites: Foundation and Intermediate Mastery
Constitutional Integration: All Types Supervision Required: Qualified Teacher
Practice Duration: 90-120 Minutes Community Authorization: Required

Section I: Master-Level Practice Prerequisites and Authorization
Advanced Practice Readiness Assessment
Foundation and Intermediate Mastery Requirements

Foundation Exercise Mastery (All exercises rated 4-5 proficiency):
- Exercise 1 - Tibetan Stand: Can hold 3+ minutes with constitutional adaptation
- Exercise 2 - Pendulum: Full spinal articulation with breath coordination
- Exercise 3 - Side Stretch: Balanced bilateral development with stability
- Exercise 4 - Backward Bend: Safe heart opening with emotional integration
- Exercise 5 - Forward Bend: Deep hip flexibility with introspective awareness
- Exercise 6 - Twist: Spinal rotation with detoxification awareness
- Exercise 7 - Triangle: Integration of strength, flexibility, balance, confidence

Intermediate Exercise Competency:
- Exercise 8 - Tortoise: 3-5 minute holds with deep introspective capacity
- Exercise 9 - Cobra: Heart opening with strength and confidence integration
- Exercise 10 - Locust: Posterior chain strength with full-body

406

integration
- Breathing Mastery: 10+ minutes Integration Breath (4-4-6-2) with constitutional adaptation

Community Integration and Service Requirements:
- Community service: Minimum 2 years regular community service participation
- Teaching assistance: Minimum 1 year teaching assistance with qualified teacher
- Democratic participation: Active participation in community governance and decision-making
- Cultural sensitivity: Demonstrated cultural competency and traditional knowledge respect

Master-Level Authorization Process
Community Authorization Requirements:
- Community assessment: Comprehensive community evaluation of readiness
- Traditional teacher validation: Validation from traditionally authorized teacher
- Peer recognition: Recognition from advanced practitioner community
- Service demonstration: Demonstrated commitment to community welfare over individual achievement
- Ethics evaluation: Assessment of spiritual maturity and ethical development

Advanced Practice Supervision:
- Qualified teacher supervision: Regular supervision with master-level authorized teacher
- Community integration: Integration of advanced practice with community service
- Safety protocols: Comprehensive understanding of advanced practice safety
- Traditional authenticity: Commitment to traditional authenticity and community validation

Section II: Advanced Constitutional Integration Practices ### Master-Level Constitutional Synthesis

Electric Constitution Advanced Integration (Vata Mastery)

Advanced Grounding and Stability Practices:

Practice 1: Extended Foundation Integration (25-30 minutes)

- Extended Tibetan Stand: 5-10 minute holds with deep grounding awareness
- Supported Triangle Series: Extended holds (3-5 minutes each side) with props
- Grounding Flow Sequence: Continuous flow emphasizing earth connection
- Constitutional Breathing: Extended Integration Breath (20+ minutes) with grounding focus
- Contemplative Integration: Silent sitting with grounding and stability awareness

Practice 2: Nervous System Mastery (20-25 minutes)
- Parasympathetic Activation Sequence: Forward folds with extended holds (5+ minutes)
- Restorative Heart Opening: Supported backbends for nervous system regulation
- Advanced Breathing Integration: Constitutional breathing patterns for nervous system balance
- Energy Circulation Mastery: Subtle energy awareness and circulation practices
- Integration and Rest: Extended rest periods with consciousness development

Practice 3: Environmental and Seasonal Mastery (15-20 minutes)
- Seasonal Adaptation Sequences: Master-level seasonal practice modifications
- Environmental Sensitivity Integration: Practice adaptation to environmental challenges
- Community Grounding Practice: Leading community grounding and stability work
- Advanced Prop Integration: Master-level use of props for constitutional support
- Teaching and Service Integration: Integrating advanced practice with community teaching

Magnetic Constitution Advanced Integration (Kapha Mastery)
Advanced Activation and Energy Building Practices:
Practice 1: Dynamic Flow Mastery (25-30 minutes)
- Continuous Movement Flow: 20-30 minute continuous movement sequence
- Cardiovascular Integration: Heart rate elevation with constitutional awareness
- Strength Building Series: Advanced strength development with dynamic movement

- Internal Heat Generation: Advanced practices for circulation and metabolic activation
- Challenge Integration: Appropriate challenges for continued growth and development

Practice 2: Metabolic and Circulation Mastery (20-25 minutes)
- Advanced Activation Breathing: Constitutional breathing for maximum activation
- Dynamic Balance and Coordination: Complex balance challenges with movement
- Circulation Enhancement Series: Practices specifically for circulation and lymphatic flow
- Energy Building Integration: Advanced practices for energy generation and sustainability
- Motivation and Goal Integration: Practice supporting long-term motivation and achievement

Practice 3: Community Leadership and Service (15-20 minutes)
- Leadership Practice Integration: Practice supporting community leadership development
- Service Activation: Integration of practice with community service and contribution
- Teaching and Motivation: Advanced practices for teaching and inspiring others
- Group Energy Management: Practices for managing and directing group energy
- Global Service Integration: Practice supporting international service and cooperation

Neutral Constitution Advanced Integration (Pitta Mastery)
Advanced Balance and Precision Practices:

Practice 1: Technical Excellence and Precision (25-30 minutes)
- Advanced Alignment Series: Master-level technical precision and form
- Complex Integration Sequences: Advanced combinations requiring technical mastery
- Precision Breathing: Advanced breathing with technical precision and control
- Balance and Coordination Mastery: Complex balance requiring precision and focus
- Excellence Integration: Practice supporting high standards and systematic development

Practice 2: Temperature Regulation and Cooling (20-25 minutes)

- Advanced Cooling Practices: Master-level cooling and temperature regulation
- Seasonal Balance Mastery: Advanced seasonal practice adaptations
- Intensity Regulation: Advanced practices for managing practice intensity
- Cooling Breath Mastery: Advanced cooling breathing techniques
- Balance and Moderation: Practices supporting balance and avoiding excess

Practice 3: Systematic Development and Teaching (15-20 minutes)
- Teaching Precision Integration: Practice supporting precision in teaching
- Systematic Development: Advanced practices for systematic skill development
- Analysis and Assessment: Practice supporting assessment and evaluation skills
- Organization and Leadership: Practice supporting community organization
- Academic and Research Integration: Practice supporting academic and research applications

Section III: Advanced Energy Work and Subtle Body Practices
Master-Level Energy Circulation and Awareness
Advanced Chakra and Energy Center Work
Seven-Center Advanced Integration Practice (30-35 minutes):
Root Chakra (Muladhara) Mastery:
- Advanced grounding techniques: Deep earth connection and stability mastery
- Constitutional grounding: Chakra work adapted to constitutional needs
- Community grounding: Chakra work supporting community stability and foundation
- Safety and boundaries: Chakra work for personal and community safety
- Survival and security mastery: Advanced work with survival fears and security development

Sacral Chakra (Svadhisthana) Integration:
- Creative energy mastery: Advanced work with creative and sexual energy
- Constitutional pleasure: Appropriate pleasure and enjoyment for each constitutional type
- Relationship and intimacy: Chakra work supporting healthy relationships

- Emotional flow: Advanced emotional regulation and flow
- Community creativity: Chakra work supporting community creative expression

Solar Plexus Chakra (Manipura) Development:
- Personal power mastery: Healthy personal power without domination or submission
- Constitutional will: Will and determination appropriate to constitutional type
- Community leadership: Chakra work supporting democratic leadership
- Digestion and metabolism: Advanced work with physical and emotional digestion
- Goal achievement: Chakra work supporting appropriate goal setting and achievement

Heart Chakra (Anahata) Advanced Opening:
- Unconditional love development: Advanced heart opening without attachment
- Constitutional compassion: Compassion expression appropriate to constitutional type
- Community healing: Heart chakra work supporting community healing and service
- Forgiveness and healing: Advanced forgiveness work and emotional healing
- Bridge-building: Heart work supporting cultural and community bridge-building

Throat Chakra (Vishuddha) Expression:
- Authentic expression: Advanced work with authentic self-expression
- Constitutional communication: Communication skills adapted to constitutional type
- Community voice: Chakra work supporting community communication and truth-telling
- Creative expression: Advanced work with artistic and creative expression
- Teaching and sharing: Throat chakra work supporting teaching and knowledge sharing

Third Eye Chakra (Ajna) Awareness:
- Intuitive development: Advanced intuitive and psychic development
- Constitutional wisdom: Intuitive development appropriate to constitutional type

- Community guidance: Intuitive work supporting community guidance and decision-making
- Discrimination and discernment: Advanced discernment and wisdom development
- Vision and foresight: Chakra work supporting vision and long-term planning

Crown Chakra (Sahasrara) Integration:
- Spiritual connection: Advanced spiritual development and connection
- Constitutional transcendence: Transcendent development appropriate to constitutional type
- Community service: Spiritual development supporting community service and global welfare
- Unity consciousness: Advanced work with non-dual awareness and unity
- Wisdom integration: Chakra work supporting wisdom integration and application

Advanced Breathing and Pranayama Practices
Master-Level Constitutional Breathing (25-30 minutes):

Advanced Integration Breath Development:
- Extended Duration Practice: 20-30 minutes continuous Integration Breath (4-4-6-2)
- Constitutional Breathing Mastery: Advanced constitutional breathing patterns
- Seasonal Breathing Integration: Advanced seasonal breathing modifications
- Therapeutic Breathing Applications: Advanced breathing for health and healing
- Community Breathing Leadership: Leading group breathing and energy work

Advanced Pranayama Techniques (Authorized practitioners only):
- Bhastrika (Bellows Breath): Advanced heating and activation breathing
- Kapalabhati (Skull Shining): Advanced cleansing and purification breathing
- Nadi Shodhana (Alternate Nostril): Advanced nervous system balancing
- Sheetali/Sheetkari (Cooling Breaths): Advanced cooling and temperature regulation
- Brahmari (Bee Breath): Advanced nervous system calming and healing

Safety Protocols for Advanced Breathing:
- Qualified supervision required: All advanced breathing requires teacher supervision
- Medical clearance: Medical clearance required for certain advanced techniques
- Constitutional adaptation: All advanced breathing adapted to constitutional needs
- Community integration: Advanced breathing integrated with community service
- Traditional authenticity: All techniques practiced with traditional respect and accuracy

Section IV: Advanced Integration and Service Applications ### Master-Level Community Integration and Service

Advanced Teaching and Community Leadership
Master-Level Teaching Practice Integration (20-25 minutes):

Teaching Methodology Mastery:
- Advanced Demonstration: Master-level demonstration and instruction capabilities
- Individual Adaptation: Advanced ability to adapt instruction to individual needs
- Group Management: Advanced group facilitation and energy management
- Safety and Ethics: Master-level safety protocols and ethical instruction
- Community Integration: Teaching that supports community development and service

Community Leadership Practice:
- Democratic Leadership: Practice supporting anti-authoritarian community leadership
- Conflict Resolution: Advanced conflict resolution and community healing practices
- Vision and Planning: Practice supporting community vision and strategic planning
- Resource Management: Practice supporting community resource sharing and sustainability
- Cultural Bridge-Building: Practice supporting cross-cultural cooperation and understanding

Advanced Professional and Global Integration
Professional Integration Mastery (15-20 minutes):

413

Healthcare Integration:
- Patient Care Applications: Advanced applications for healthcare providers
- Therapeutic Interventions: Advanced therapeutic applications and interventions
- Medical Team Integration: Practice supporting healthcare team cooperation
- Health Promotion: Advanced applications for health promotion and prevention
- Medical Research: Practice supporting medical research and evidence development

Educational Integration:
- Curriculum Development: Practice supporting educational curriculum development
- Student Development: Advanced applications for student development and learning
- Teacher Training: Practice supporting teacher training and professional development
- Educational Research: Applications for educational research and validation
- Institutional Integration: Practice supporting institutional transformation

Global Service Applications:
- International Cooperation: Practice supporting international cooperation and service
- Cultural Adaptation: Advanced cultural sensitivity and adaptation practices
- Crisis Response: Advanced applications for crisis response and humanitarian service
- Peacebuilding: Practice supporting peacebuilding and conflict transformation
- Environmental Action: Advanced applications for environmental stewardship and action

Section V: Advanced Safety Protocols and Contraindications
Master-Level Safety and Ethical Guidelines
Advanced Practice Safety Protocols

Physical Safety Requirements:
- Medical clearance: Required for practitioners with health conditions
- Qualified supervision: All advanced practices require qualified teacher supervision

- Progressive development: No skipping of foundation and intermediate development
- Constitutional adaptation: All practices adapted to individual constitutional needs
- Emergency protocols: Clear emergency response protocols for advanced practice

Psychological and Emotional Safety:
- Emotional preparation: Assessment of emotional readiness for advanced practice
- Trauma sensitivity: Trauma-informed approaches to advanced emotional and energy work
- Professional boundaries: Clear boundaries around therapeutic and healing applications
- Community support: Integration with community support and healing resources
- Professional referral: Clear protocols for referral to mental health professionals

Spiritual and Ethical Development Requirements
Spiritual Maturity Assessment:
- Service orientation: Demonstrated commitment to service over personal achievement
- Ego development: Advanced work with spiritual ego and power shadow
- Community accountability: Acceptance of community accountability and feedback
- Traditional respect: Deep respect for traditional sources and communities
- Cultural sensitivity: Advanced cultural competency and cross-cultural bridge-building

Ethical Standards for Advanced Practice:
- Non-harm principles: Commitment to non-harm in all applications of advanced practice
- Consent and boundaries: Advanced understanding of consent and appropriate boundaries
- Power dynamics: Advanced awareness of power dynamics and potential for misuse
- Community welfare: Consistent prioritization of community welfare over individual benefit
- Global responsibility: Understanding of global responsibility and environmental stewardship

Section VI: Advanced Practice Scheduling and Integration

Master-Level Practice Organization and Development
Advanced Practice Schedule and Timing
Daily Advanced Practice Structure (90-120 minutes total):

Opening and Preparation (10-15 minutes):
- Constitutional assessment: Daily assessment of constitutional balance and needs
- Intention setting: Clear intention setting for advanced practice and service
- Environmental optimization: Preparation of practice space for advanced work
- Community connection: Connection with community and global service intention
- Safety protocol review: Review of safety protocols and contraindication awareness

Advanced Movement Integration (35-45 minutes):
- Constitutional advanced sequence: 25-35 minutes advanced constitutional practice
- Integration and transition: 5-10 minutes integration between movement and breathing
- Advanced variation exploration: 5-10 minutes exploration of advanced variations

Advanced Breathing and Energy Work (25-35 minutes):
- Constitutional breathing mastery: 15-25 minutes advanced constitutional breathing
- Energy circulation and awareness: 5-10 minutes advanced energy work
- Chakra integration: 5-10 minutes advanced chakra and subtle body work

Advanced Integration and Service (15-20 minutes):
- Community service integration: 5-10 minutes connecting practice with service
- Teaching and leadership integration: 5-10 minutes connecting practice with teaching/leadership
- Global awareness and responsibility: 5-10 minutes connecting practice with global service

Closing and Integration (5-10 minutes):
- Practice integration: Integration of advanced practice with daily life
- Community gratitude: Gratitude for community and traditional sources

416

- Service commitment: Renewal of commitment to community service and global welfare
- Traditional acknowledgment: Acknowledgment of traditional sources and lineage

Weekly and Monthly Advanced Development Cycles
Weekly Advanced Practice Cycle:
- Monday: Constitutional mastery focus and integration
- Tuesday: Advanced breathing and energy work emphasis
- Wednesday: Community teaching and leadership integration
- Thursday: Professional and global service applications
- Friday: Advanced integration and synthesis
- Saturday: Community practice and group integration
- Sunday: Rest, reflection, and planning

Monthly Advanced Development Focus:
- Week 1: Advanced constitutional development and mastery
- Week 2: Advanced breathing, energy work, and subtle body development
- Week 3: Advanced community integration, teaching, and leadership
- Week 4: Advanced service applications, professional integration, and global service

Annual Master-Level Development and Assessment
Annual Advanced Practice Assessment:
- Technical mastery evaluation: Assessment of advanced technical skills and development
- Constitutional integration assessment: Evaluation of constitutional mastery and adaptation
- Community service evaluation: Assessment of community service and leadership contribution
- Teaching and mentoring assessment: Evaluation of teaching capacity and community contribution
- Professional integration assessment: Assessment of professional applications and contributions
- Global service evaluation: Evaluation of international cooperation and global service contributions

Advanced Practice Continuing Education:
- Traditional study and connection: Ongoing study and connection with traditional sources
- Community supervision and mentoring: Continued supervision and mentoring relationships
- Professional development: Ongoing professional development

in areas of service application
- Cultural competency development: Continued development of cultural sensitivity and competency
- Global cooperation and exchange: Participation in international cooperation and exchange programs

Advanced Practice Authorization Information:
Practitioner Name:
Community Authorization:
Traditional Teacher Validation:
Supervision and Mentoring:
Next Assessment Date:

These Advanced Embodiment Practices provide master-level constitutional integration while maintaining community service orientation, traditional authenticity, and global responsibility in advanced Sacred Synthesis development.

Beyond Personal Realization
From Sacred Synthesis Volume 3: Mastery and Cultural Transmission

The Transition from Seeking to Service
The achievement of personal spiritual realization naturally leads to the responsibility of service, not as an obligation imposed from outside, but as the spontaneous expression of expanded awareness and deepened compassion. This chapter addresses the advanced stages of traditional knowledge development where individual attainment transforms into cultural contribution and planetary service.

The transition from seeking to service represents one of the most crucial developments in the spiritual journey. Personal realization, while profound, is merely the foundation for the greater work of consciousness evolution itself. As documented in the traditional teachings: "The true equality is this: each one is obligated to do ALL that he really CAN do for others, and each forgetfulness, each ill will, each evasion, automatically creates a NEW OCCASION MORE HARSH and of MORE PEREMPTORY CHARACTER."

The Natural Evolution of Spiritual Motivation
In the early stages of spiritual development, motivation arises primarily from personal suffering and the desire for relief. The seeker approaches spiritual practice as a means of escape from psychological pain, existential anxiety, or life circumstances. This initial motivation, while legitimate and necessary, represents only the beginning of authentic spiritual development.

As practice deepens and understanding expands, a fundamental shift occurs in the practitioner's relationship to suffering and service. Personal suffering is recognized not as an individual problem to be escaped, but as a universal condition requiring collective healing. This recognition transforms the spiritual journey from a private therapeutic endeavor into participation in the great work of planetary consciousness evolution.

The mature practitioner discovers that individual liberation and collective service are not separate activities but aspects of a single reality. True personal realization necessarily includes the recognition that the individual self is an expression of universal consciousness, and therefore individual welfare and universal welfare are fundamentally identical.

Signs of Readiness for Service-Oriented Practice
The transition to service-oriented spiritual practice is marked by specific psychological, behavioral, and spiritual indicators that demonstrate readiness for expanded responsibility and deeper engagement with collective welfare.

Psychological Maturity Indicators:
- **Emotional Stability Under Stress**: The practitioner maintains equanimity and wisdom during challenging circumstances, demonstrating emotional resilience that serves others' welfare rather than requiring constant support.
- **Reduced Narcissistic Preoccupation**: Decreased focus on personal spiritual experiences, achievements, or problems, replaced by natural interest in others' development and welfare.
- **Integrated Shadow Work**: Recognition and integration of previously rejected aspects of personality, resulting in authentic humility and reduced tendency toward spiritual inflation or perfectionism.
- **Mature Relationship Capacity**: Ability to maintain intimate relationships while pursuing spiritual development, demonstrating integration of personal and transpersonal dimensions of existence.

Behavioral Maturity Indicators:
- **Consistent Ethical Conduct**: Spontaneous alignment of actions with ethical principles under all circumstances, without requiring external enforcement or internal struggle.
- **Financial and Social Responsibility**: Successful management of practical life responsibilities, including career, family obliga-

419

tions, and community participation.

- **Service Without Recognition**: Regular engagement in beneficial activities for others without seeking credit, recognition, or spiritual advancement for oneself.
- **Teaching and Mentoring Capacity**: Natural ability to guide and support others' development through appropriate instruction and example.

Spiritual Maturity Indicators:
- **Sustained Realization**: Consistent access to expanded consciousness states integrated with ordinary daily activities rather than temporary peak experiences.
- **Universal Compassion**: Genuine care for the welfare of all beings, including those with whom one disagrees or finds personally challenging.
- **Wisdom-Compassion Balance**: Integration of discriminating wisdom with universal compassion, enabling effective action that serves both individual and collective welfare.
- **Surrender to Greater Purpose**: Recognition that individual spiritual development serves universal consciousness evolution rather than personal attainment.

Recognition of Interdependence and Service as Natural Expression
The recognition of fundamental interdependence represents one of the most profound shifts in consciousness development. This recognition transforms the practitioner's understanding of individual identity, personal responsibility, and appropriate action from ego-based to cosmic perspective.

The Illusion of Separate Individual Achievement
Contemporary culture strongly reinforces the illusion that individual achievement occurs independently of collective support and universal conditions. This illusion extends into spiritual development, where practitioners often approach realization as a personal accomplishment that can be achieved through individual effort alone. Mature spiritual understanding recognizes that individual consciousness is an expression of universal consciousness temporarily individualized for the purpose of collective evolution. Personal realization serves not individual aggrandizement but universal awakening through particular manifestation.

The Buddhist teaching of interdependence (pratityasamutpada) describes this reality: all phenomena arise in dependence upon causes and conditions, with no independent self-existence. Individual spiritual achievement depends upon the accumulated wisdom of traditional lineages, the support of communities and teachers, favorable social conditions, and countless other factors beyond personal control.

Similarly, Vedantic understanding recognizes that the individual self (jiva) is fundamentally identical with universal consciousness (Brahman), appearing separate only through ignorance (avidya). Realization reveals that what seemed to be personal achievement was always the universal Self recognizing its own nature through individual expression.

Service as Spontaneous Expression of Realization
Authentic spiritual realization naturally expresses itself through service to others' welfare and collective advancement. This service arises not from moral obligation or religious commandment, but as the spontaneous expression of consciousness recognizing itself in all beings.

The Bhagavad Gita describes this principle through Krishna's teaching to Arjuna about action without attachment to results (nishkama karma). When individual will is aligned with cosmic intelligence, action becomes spontaneous expression of universal welfare rather than ego-driven achievement.

Christian mysticism expresses this understanding through the principle of divine love (agape) that seeks the good of others without consideration of personal benefit. Saint John of the Cross describes how the mature mystic naturally serves others' spiritual welfare as an expression of union with divine love.

The Jewish tradition of tikkun olam (repairing the world) recognizes that individual spiritual development serves collective healing and the restoration of divine unity in manifestation. Personal realization contributes to the cosmic work of bringing heaven to earth through conscious action.

The Expansion of Identity and Responsibility
As spiritual development progresses, the practitioner's sense of identity naturally expands beyond individual boundaries to include larger and larger circles of concern and responsibility.

Family and Intimate Relationships: Initial expansion includes conscious participation in family welfare, approaching marriage and parenting as spiritual practice and service rather than personal satisfaction.

Community and Local Service: Further expansion includes active participation in local community welfare through appropriate service activities that utilize individual skills and resources for collective benefit.

Cultural and Global Responsibility: Advanced expansion includes recognition of responsibility for cultural evolution, preservation of traditional wisdom, and response to global challenges that affect all humanity.

Planetary and Cosmic Service: Ultimate expansion includes recognition of responsibility for planetary healing, environmental stewardship, and participation in the cosmic evolution of consciousness itself.

Each level of expansion does not abandon previous responsibilities but integrates them into larger contexts of meaning and service. The mature practitioner simultaneously serves intimate relationships, local community, global humanity, and cosmic evolution as expressions of single unified purpose.

Teaching Readiness Assessment and Traditional Qualification Criteria
The capacity to guide others in spiritual development represents one of the highest forms of service and requires careful assessment of readiness according to traditional criteria refined through centuries of experience with consciousness development.

Traditional Teaching Qualifications
Traditional wisdom cultures developed sophisticated criteria for recognizing qualified spiritual teachers, understanding that inappropriate teaching can cause significant harm to both students and the broader spiritual community.

Personal Realization Requirements:
- **Sustained Contemplative Achievement**: Consistent access to expanded consciousness states integrated with daily life, demonstrated over minimum periods (typically 5-10 years) under various life conditions.
- **Character Integration**: Demonstrated ethical maturity, emotional stability, and psychological integration verified through community observation and appropriate testing.
- **Lineage Authorization**: Recognition by qualified teachers within authentic traditional lineages, ensuring continuity of transmission and community validation.

- **Scriptural and Traditional Knowledge**: Comprehensive understanding of relevant wisdom literature and traditional practices, including original languages where appropriate.

Community Service Demonstration:
- **Successful Family and Social Integration**: Demonstrated capacity to maintain spiritual development while successfully fulfilling family, professional, and community responsibilities.
- **Beneficial Service Record**: History of service activities that have measurably benefited individuals and communities, demonstrating practical application of spiritual understanding.
- **Conflict Resolution and Healing Capacity**: Demonstrated ability to facilitate healing in relationship conflicts and community challenges through wisdom and compassion.
- **Cultural Bridge-Building**: Capacity to communicate spiritual principles across cultural, religious, and educational boundaries while maintaining traditional authenticity.

Teaching and Transmission Capacity:
- **Pedagogical Skill**: Natural ability to communicate complex spiritual principles in accessible language appropriate to students' developmental level and cultural background.
- **Student Development Success**: History of students who have achieved measurable spiritual development and community contribution under the teacher's guidance.
- **Appropriate Boundary Maintenance**: Demonstrated capacity to maintain appropriate teacher-student relationships without exploitation or inappropriate intimacy.
- **Continued Learning and Humility**: Ongoing commitment to personal development and learning from other qualified teachers and community feedback.

Contemporary Assessment Methods
Modern applications of traditional teaching qualification require adaptation to contemporary contexts while maintaining essential protective criteria.

Psychological Evaluation: Professional psychological assessment to identify potential mental health issues, personality disorders, or unresolved trauma that could interfere with appropriate teaching relationships.

Educational and Professional Background: Appropriate educational credentials and professional experience in relevant areas (psychology, education, healthcare, religious studies) to ensure competency in contemporary contexts.

Community Validation Process: Systematic community input and validation process involving peers, students, and broader community members to assess teaching readiness and community recognition.

Trial Teaching Periods: Supervised teaching opportunities with qualified mentor oversight to assess actual teaching capacity and student response before independent authorization.

Ongoing Assessment and Support: Regular evaluation and continued mentor consultation to ensure maintenance of appropriate standards and continued development of teaching capacity.

Dangers of Premature or Inappropriate Teaching
The tradition of requiring extensive qualification for spiritual teaching arises from recognition of significant dangers inherent in inappropriate spiritual guidance.

Spiritual Inflation and Abuse of Power: Inadequately prepared teachers may develop spiritual narcissism and exploit students through inappropriate use of spiritual authority for personal gratification or material benefit.

Transmission of Distorted Understanding: Teachers without authentic realization or adequate traditional knowledge may transmit confused or harmful spiritual concepts that damage students' development.

Inadequate Safety Protocols: Unprepared teachers may lack understanding of psychological and spiritual safety requirements, potentially triggering mental health crises or spiritual emergencies in students.

Cultural Appropriation and Disrespect: Teachers without adequate traditional knowledge and cultural sensitivity may misrepresent spiritual teachings and disrespect their cultural sources.

Community Division and Conflict: Inappropriate teaching can create division within spiritual communities and broader cultural conflicts through sectarian competition and spiritual materialism.

True contemplative mastery is distinguished from temporary spiritual experiences by consistency, integration, and practical effectiveness in supporting both individual fulfillment and collective welfare.

Characteristics of Sustained Realization
Sustained realization differs qualitatively from peak spiritual experiences in several crucial characteristics that determine its authenticity and beneficial impact.

Consistency Across Circumstances: Authentic realization maintains itself under various life conditions, including stress, conflict, illness, and changing external circumstances, rather than requiring specific environmental conditions for maintenance.

Integration with Daily Activities: Realized consciousness naturally integrates with ordinary daily activities, work, relationships, household responsibilities, enhancing their effectiveness and meaning rather than requiring withdrawal from practical life.

Natural Ethical Expression: Sustained realization spontaneously expresses itself through ethical conduct and beneficial action without requiring external enforcement or internal struggle with moral obligations.

Enhanced Practical Effectiveness: Rather than impairing practical functioning, authentic realization enhances the capacity for effective action in all areas of life through increased clarity, energy, and appropriate motivation.

Deepening Understanding Over Time: Authentic realization continues to deepen and expand over months and years, revealing new dimensions and applications rather than remaining static or declining.
Distinguishing Realization from Temporary Experiences Contemporary spiritual practice often confuses temporary expanded states of consciousness with permanent realization, leading to spiritual inflation and inappropriate claims of attainment.

Peak Experience Characteristics:
* Dependent on specific conditions (meditation retreats, psychedelic substances, intensive practices)
* Duration limited to minutes, hours, or days
* Difficult to integrate with ordinary daily life
* May include dramatic visions, overwhelming emotions, or al-

tered perceptions
- Often followed by "spiritual hangover" or depression as consciousness returns to ordinary states

Sustained Realization Characteristics:
- Present under all life circumstances without special conditions
- Continuous availability throughout daily activities
- Enhances rather than disrupts ordinary functioning
- Characterized by peace, clarity, and natural joy rather than dramatic phenomena
- Stable and consistent over months and years of observation

Integration of States and Stages vs. Temporary Spiritual Experiences
Authentic spiritual development involves both temporary expanded states of consciousness and permanent structural stages of development that integrate expanded capacities into everyday functioning.

States of Consciousness are temporary experiences of expanded awareness that may include:
- Profound peace and unity experiences during meditation
- Mystical visions and direct spiritual communication
- Expanded perception of energy fields and subtle phenomena
- Temporary dissolution of ego boundaries and individual identity
- Experiences of cosmic consciousness and universal love

Stages of Development are permanent structural changes in consciousness that include:
- Increased capacity for sustained attention and mental clarity
- Enhanced emotional regulation and response flexibility
- Expanded sense of identity and compassionate concern
- Integration of rational and intuitive intelligence
- Natural ethical behavior arising from expanded understanding

Integration Process transforms temporary states into permanent stages through:
- Regular contemplative practice that stabilizes expanded awareness
- Ethical living that embodies expanded understanding in daily action
- Community service that expresses realized compassion practically
- Study and reflection that integrate experiences with traditional understanding
- Professional application that demonstrates practical effective-

ness of spiritual development

Character Integration and Development of Natural Authority
Authentic spiritual authority arises naturally from character integration and demonstrated wisdom rather than from claims of special attainment or organizational position.

Components of Character Integration
Character integration involves the harmonious development of all aspects of personality in service of wisdom and compassion rather than personal aggrandizement or defensive protection.

Intellectual Integration:
- Rational intelligence integrated with intuitive wisdom
- Ability to think clearly under emotional pressure
- Capacity for complex problem-solving that considers multiple perspectives
- Understanding that transcends but includes rational analysis

Emotional Integration:
- Emotional responsiveness without reactive compulsion
- Capacity for appropriate emotional expression without overwhelming others
- Ability to process difficult emotions without projecting them onto others
- Compassionate response to others' emotional needs without losing personal boundaries

Physical Integration:
- Healthy relationship with physical body and sensory experience
- Appropriate attention to nutrition, exercise, and health maintenance
- Sexual integration that honors both individual and relational needs
- Environmental awareness and appropriate stewardship of material resources

Social Integration:
- Healthy relationships with family, community, and professional colleagues
- Capacity for leadership that serves others' development
- Ability to participate in group activities without losing individual integrity
- Cultural sensitivity and appropriate cross-cultural communication

Development of Natural Authority
Natural spiritual authority develops through demonstrated wisdom and beneficial service rather than through claims of special status or organizational appointment.

Authority Through Competence: Natural authority arises from demonstrated competence in spiritual practice, traditional knowledge, and practical application that benefits both individuals and communities.

Authority Through Character: Sustained demonstration of integrated character, ethical conduct, and emotional maturity creates natural respect and trust from community members.

Authority Through Service: Consistent service to others' welfare and collective advancement creates natural recognition of leadership capacity and wisdom application.

Authority Through Humility: Paradoxically, natural authority increases through genuine humility and continued learning rather than through claims of superior attainment or knowledge.

Authority Through Results: Ultimately, spiritual authority is validated through the beneficial results of guidance, students' authentic development, community harmony, and practical problem-solving effectiveness.

Distinguishing Natural from Artificial Authority
Contemporary spiritual communities often struggle to distinguish authentic spiritual authority from artificial claims based on organizational position, charismatic presentation, or self-promotion.

Natural Authority Characteristics:
- Arises spontaneously from community recognition rather than self-promotion
- Demonstrates consistent effectiveness in guidance and problem-solving
- Maintains appropriate humility and continued learning
- Focuses on students' development rather than teacher's status
- Creates independence and maturity in students rather than dependence

Artificial Authority Characteristics:
- Requires constant reinforcement through organizational posi-

tion or promotional activities
- Demonstrates inconsistent results or effectiveness primarily through marketing
- Resists feedback or questioning from students or community members
- Focuses on teacher's status and recognition rather than students' development
- Creates dependence and compliance in students rather than autonomous development

Personality Integration with Universal Principles
Advanced spiritual development requires integration of individual personality characteristics with universal principles rather than elimination of personality in favor of generic "spiritual" behavior.

Respecting Individual Constitutional Differences
Authentic spiritual development enhances rather than eliminates individual personality differences, recognizing that universal consciousness expresses through infinite diversity rather than uniform behavior.

Temperamental Differences: Different individuals naturally express universal principles through different temperamental styles, contemplative, devotional, service-oriented, intellectual, each contributing unique gifts to collective advancement.

Cultural Expressions: Universal spiritual principles manifest appropriately through different cultural forms and expressions while maintaining essential authenticity and effectiveness.

Professional Applications: Individual personality characteristics and professional skills provide unique channels for spiritual service and cultural contribution when integrated with universal principles.

Creative Expression: Individual creative capacities and artistic sensibilities offer distinctive vehicles for cultural transmission of spiritual understanding and community inspiration.

Integration Rather Than Suppression of Personality
Immature spiritual approaches often attempt to suppress or eliminate personality characteristics in favor of adopted "spiritual" behaviors that lack authenticity and effectiveness.

Healthy Integration Process:
- **Recognition**: Honest assessment of individual personality pat-

terns, strengths, and limitations without judgment or defensiveness

- **Purification**: Transformation of self-destructive or harmful patterns while maintaining essential individual characteristics
- **Dedication**: Conscious dedication of personality gifts and capacities to universal service and collective welfare
- **Expression**: Authentic expression of universal principles through individual personality characteristics and cultural forms
- **Evolution**: Continued refinement and development of personality in service of expanding effectiveness and deeper understanding

Universal Principles Expressed Through Individual Form

The ultimate goal of personality integration is transparent expression of universal principles through authentic individual characteristics rather than elimination of individuality in favor of impersonal spiritual behavior.

Compassion Through Individual Style: Universal compassion may express through different individual approaches, intellectual understanding, emotional support, practical assistance, artistic inspiration, each serving others' needs in unique ways.

Wisdom Through Personal Gifts: Universal wisdom may manifest through different individual capacities, teaching ability, healing presence, organizational skills, creative expression, each contributing to collective advancement.

Service Through Individual Calling: Universal service orientation may express through different professional and community activities according to individual skills, opportunities, and cultural needs.

Unity Through Diversity: The recognition of unity consciousness naturally celebrates and enhances rather than eliminates individual diversity, understanding that universal consciousness requires infinite expressions for complete manifestation.

Emotional Maturity and Wisdom-Compassion Balance

Emotional maturity represents one of the most crucial developments in advanced spiritual practice, enabling the practitioner to serve others' welfare effectively while maintaining appropriate boundaries and personal well-being.

Signs of Emotional Maturity in Spiritual Practice
Emotional maturity in spiritual contexts includes characteristics that enable effective service while maintaining psychological health and authentic relationships.

Emotional Regulation Without Suppression:
- Ability to experience emotions fully without being overwhelmed or compelled to reactive behavior
- Capacity to process difficult emotions privately without projecting them onto others
- Skill in using emotional information for appropriate decision-making and action
- Integration of emotional responsiveness with rational assessment and ethical consideration

Appropriate Emotional Expression:
- Authentic emotional communication that serves relationship harmony and mutual understanding
- Ability to express difficult emotions (anger, disappointment, fear) in ways that resolve rather than escalate conflicts
- Capacity for emotional vulnerability and intimacy without losing personal boundaries
- Skill in providing emotional support to others without becoming overwhelmed by their emotional states

Compassionate Response to Others' Emotions:
- Empathetic understanding of others' emotional experiences without losing objectivity
- Ability to provide emotional support without taking responsibility for others' emotional healing
- Skill in maintaining compassionate presence during others' emotional crises
- Capacity to set appropriate boundaries when others' emotional demands become excessive

Balancing Compassion with Wisdom
One of the most challenging aspects of advanced spiritual development involves balancing universal compassion with discriminating wisdom in practical situations that require difficult decisions.

Idiot Compassion vs. Wise Compassion:
- Idiot compassion: Enabling harmful behavior or avoiding necessary confrontation in the name of love and acceptance
- Wise compassion: Taking appropriate action that serves others' long-term development even when it requires short-term dis-

comfort or conflict

Individual Needs vs. Collective Welfare:
- Balancing attention to individual needs and circumstances with consideration of community welfare and institutional effectiveness
- Making decisions that serve the greatest good while maintaining appropriate care for individual dignity and development
- Understanding when individual accommodation serves collective advancement and when it undermines community integrity

Immediate Relief vs. Long-term Development:
- Distinguishing between help that provides temporary relief and guidance that supports long-term growth and independence
- Offering appropriate support during crises while encouraging personal responsibility and continued development
- Aiding in ways that enhance rather than diminish others' capacity for self-sufficiency and contribution

Developing Appropriate Professional and Personal Boundaries
Advanced practitioners must develop sophisticated boundary skills that enable intimate service relationships while maintaining professional effectiveness and personal well-being.

Professional Boundary Development:
- Clear communication of professional roles, expectations, and limitations
- Appropriate fee structures and business practices that serve both practitioner sustainability and student accessibility
- Maintenance of professional relationships distinct from personal friendships
- Referral protocols for situations beyond professional competence or appropriate scope

Personal Boundary Maintenance:
- Protection of personal time and energy necessary for continued development and family responsibilities
- Appropriate limits on availability for crisis intervention and emergency support
- Integration of service activities with personal spiritual practice and self-care
- Healthy balance between service to others and attention to personal needs and relationships

Intimate Service Relationships:
- Capacity for deep care and commitment without inappropriate personal attachment
- Ability to provide intensive guidance while encouraging student independence
- Skill in maintaining appropriate teacher-student relationships without exploitation or boundary violations
- Understanding of when professional relationships should transition to peer friendship

Conclusion: The Flowering of Service
The transition beyond personal realization to service-oriented spiritual maturity represents the natural flowering of authentic consciousness development. This transition is not an abandonment of individual development but its fulfillment through recognition that individual welfare and universal welfare are fundamentally identical.

The characteristics described in this chapter, readiness for service, recognition of interdependence, teaching qualification, contemplative mastery, character integration, and emotional maturity, develop gradually through sustained practice, community engagement, and authentic commitment to wisdom and compassion.

The practitioner who has achieved this level of integration becomes a transparent vehicle for consciousness itself, serving individual development and collective evolution through whatever forms of expression are most appropriate and effective in their particular cultural and historical context.

The ultimate measure of spiritual development is not personal attainment but cultural contribution, the capacity to serve both preservation of essential wisdom and its beneficial application to contemporary challenges while creating living tradition that honors the past, serves the present, and prepares the future for continued consciousness evolution.

Wisdom Transmission - Traditional Teaching Principles
From Sacred Synthesis Volume 3: Mastery and Cultural Transmission

Introduction: The Sacred Art of Transmission
The transmission of wisdom represents one of humanity's most sacred responsibilities. Authentic spiritual teaching transcends mere information transfer to encompass a living transmission of consciousness itself. This chapter presents the complete framework for

traditional teaching principles as preserved through the Costet de Mascheville lineage.

As stated in La Iniciación: "Only he has the right to isolate himself completely who has already reached the ability to SERVE MORE in that Active Silence, whose heart is open to all, and whose sight is upon all those who, though distant, receive his help and feel his action."

This understanding establishes teaching not as personal achievement but as the natural flowering of consciousness recognizing itself in others.

The Nature of Authentic Spiritual Teaching
Qualities of a Qualified Teacher
Traditional wisdom recognizes specific qualifications essential for authentic spiritual instruction. These transcend mere intellectual knowledge to encompass embodied realization validated by community recognition.

Essential Spiritual Realizations
- Direct experience of the truths they teach, demonstrated through consistent behavior over extended periods
- Integration of realization with daily life responsibilities, showing wisdom applied practically
- Continued growth and deepening understanding, maintaining humility regarding the vastness of spiritual truth
- Natural expression of compassion and wisdom without effort or self- consciousness

Traditional Authorization: Training within recognized lineage or tradition, preserving authentic methods and understanding
- Proper initiation and transmission from qualified teachers who have themselves achieved traditional recognition
- Understanding of traditional methods and their applications, respecting the integrity of received teachings
- Connection with traditional sources while enabling contemporary application

Ethical Foundation
- Impeccable conduct in all relationships, demonstrating integration of spiritual understanding with moral behavior
- Service orientation rather than personal aggrandizement, using teaching authority to benefit students
- Transparent communication about human limitations and con-

tinuing growth
- Appropriate boundaries regarding the scope of teaching and personal involvement

Character Integration and Service
Traditional teaching emphasizes that authentic teachers demonstrate **personality patterns serving rather than obstructing spiritual expression**. As documented in the Sacred Synthesis materials:
- Emotional stability and appropriate response to challenging circumstances
- Natural authority arising from wisdom rather than position or credentials
- Teaching capacity arising from authentic realization rather than intellectual knowledge alone
- Integration of individual authenticity with universal principles and community needs

Warning Signs of Problematic Teachers
The tradition provides clear warnings about teachers who may cause harm rather than benefit:

Spiritual Inflation
- Claims of exclusive or superior realization beyond community validation
- Grandiose titles or self-promotion seeking personal recognition
- Discouragement of student questions or independent thinking
- Demand for blind obedience without understanding

Ethical Violations
- Sexual impropriety with students, exploiting vulnerability and trust
- Financial exploitation or inappropriate business practices
- Substance abuse or other behavioral problems inconsistent with spiritual teaching
- Dishonesty about background, qualifications, or traditional authority

Psychological Manipulation
- Creating unhealthy dependence in students rather than fostering independence
- Using fear or guilt to control behavior rather than encouraging authentic growth
- Isolation from family, friends, or other teachers
- Punishment for legitimate questions or concerns

The Student's Preparation and Responsibilities

Qualities of a Sincere Student

Authentic spiritual development requires specific attitudes and commitments from students, creating the proper foundation for teaching to be effective.

Essential Attitudes
Genuine Seeking
- Authentic desire for spiritual truth and realization rather than mere intellectual curiosity
- Recognition of current limitations and need for guidance, maintaining appropriate humility
- Willingness to question assumptions and beliefs when presented with valid alternatives
- Commitment to sustained practice and study regardless of temporary difficulties

Respectful Approach
- Reverence for the teacher's realization and sacrifice in providing instruction
- Gratitude for instruction and guidance received, recognizing teaching as service
- Respect for the teacher's time and energy through punctuality and preparation
- Proper conduct in community settings, supporting harmonious learning environment

Student Responsibilities and Ethics
Practice Commitment
- Daily practice of assigned methods with consistency and dedication
- Honest reporting of experiences and challenges without embellishment or concealment
- Persistence through difficulties and periods of apparent stagnation
- Integration of teachings with daily life activities rather than compartmentalization

Community Participation
- Respectful relationship with fellow students, supporting collective learning
- Contribution to community harmony and growth through positive engagement
- Support for community activities and programs according to individual capacity

- Discretion regarding private teachings and experiences, maintaining appropriate confidentiality

Personal Development
- Continued growth in ethical conduct and wisdom application
- Psychological health and emotional maturity supporting spiritual development
- Financial responsibility and practical competence in worldly affairs
- Service to others as natural expression of spiritual understanding

Progressive Teaching Methodology
Stages of the Teacher-Student Relationship
Traditional wisdom recognizes distinct phases in the development of authentic teaching relationships, each requiring appropriate understanding and skillful navigation.

Initial Contact and Assessment
Mutual Evaluation Period
Both teacher and student must carefully assess the appropriateness of entering formal teaching relationship:

Student Assessment of Teacher:
- Observation of teacher's conduct and lifestyle over extended periods
- Investigation of teacher's background and qualifications through multiple sources
- Evaluation of teaching methods and community atmosphere
- Consideration of personal resonance and intuitive response while maintaining discrimination

Teacher Assessment of Student:
- Evaluation of student's sincerity and motivation for spiritual development
- Assessment of psychological stability and emotional maturity
- Consideration of student's capacity for sustained practice and commitment
- Determination of appropriate level and type of instruction

Beginning Instruction Phase

Establishing Foundation
The initial phase focuses on creating proper conditions for advanced instruction:
- Introduction to basic practices and principles with clear safety

guidelines
- Development of proper practice habits and discipline suited to individual constitution
- Cultivation of appropriate attitudes and understanding regarding spiritual development
- Building trust and communication patterns supporting authentic relationship

Teacher's Role:
- Clear instruction in foundational practices with specific safety protocols
- Regular monitoring of student's progress and challenges through appropriate assessment
- Encouragement during difficult periods while maintaining realistic expectations
- Appropriate challenge to promote growth without overwhelming capacity

Student's Role:
- Consistent practice of assigned methods exactly as taught
- Honest communication about experiences and difficulties
- Respectful questioning and clarification seeking
- Gradual development of trust and surrender based on demonstrated wisdom

Deepening Relationship Phase Advanced Instruction
As competency develops, teaching becomes increasingly individualized:
- Transmission of more subtle teachings and practices adapted to unique needs
- Individual guidance respecting student's constitutional differences
- Integration of realization with life circumstances and responsibilities
- Preparation for potential teaching role when appropriate capacity is demonstrated

Increased Intimacy and Trust:
- Deeper communication about spiritual experiences while maintaining appropriate boundaries
- Greater vulnerability and openness from both parties within traditional frameworks
- Recognition of spiritual kinship and connection transcending ordinary social relationships
- Movement toward peer relationship while maintaining respect

for traditional authority

Maturation and Independence Student Development
Authentic teaching aims toward student independence rather than permanent dependence:
- Independent spiritual practice and understanding validated by community recognition
- Beginning teaching or guidance of others under appropriate supervision
- Integration of received teachings with personal insights while preserving traditional accuracy
- Contribution to tradition through service and appropriate innovation

Changing Relationship Dynamic:
- Evolution from student-teacher to colleague relationship maintaining gratitude and respect
- Continued connection based on affection and friendship rather than instructional necessity
- Mutual consultation and collaboration in service to the tradition
- Recognition that consciousness teaches itself through apparent multiplicity

Methods of Spiritual Transmission
Direct Transmission (Shaktipat)

Energy Transmission
Traditional teaching recognizes direct transfer of spiritual energy as the most powerful method of instruction:

Forms of Transmission:
- **Touch:** Physical contact transmitting energy directly through nervous system
- **Gaze:** Direct eye contact conveying spiritual force through visual connection
- **Word:** Spoken teachings carrying transformative power beyond mere conceptual content
- **Silence:** Wordless communication of realized understanding through presence alone

Preparation for Reception:
- Purification through ethical conduct and spiritual practice creating proper receptivity
- Development of receptivity through surrender and openness while maintaining discrimination

- Proper mental and emotional preparation through study and community participation
- Integration of received energy through consistent practice and service

Teaching Through Example

Living Demonstration
The most powerful teaching occurs through the teacher's embodied demonstration of realized principles:

Aspects of Example Teaching:
- Integration of spiritual understanding with daily activities showing practical application
- Natural expression of compassion, wisdom, and service without artificial performance
- Graceful handling of life challenges and difficulties demonstrating spiritual principles
- Transparent personality allowing consciousness to shine through individual expression

Verbal Instruction and Dialogue

Systematic Teaching
Formal instruction provides necessary theoretical foundation and practical guidance:
Methods of Verbal Teaching:
- **Lectures and Talks:** Systematic presentation of traditional teachings with contemporary applications
- **Individual Guidance:** Personal instruction adapted to specific needs and circumstances
- **Question and Answer:** Interactive exploration of spiritual topics encouraging understanding
- **Story and Metaphor:** Indirect teaching through narrative and symbolism transcending conceptual limitations

Contemporary Teaching Applications
Integration with Modern Life
Traditional teaching principles must adapt to contemporary circumstances while preserving essential elements:

Professional Integration

Teaching in Contemporary Contexts
- Healthcare integration supporting therapeutic applications while

maintaining spiritual focus
- Educational applications in academic settings respecting institutional requirements
- Corporate training programs developing consciousness-based leadership
- Community service initiatives demonstrating spiritual principles through practical action

Digital Age Considerations
Technology and Traditional Transmission
- Online teaching platforms supporting global community while preserving intimate relationship
- Digital communities creating connection while maintaining local practice requirements
- Multimedia resources enhancing instruction while recognizing limitations of technological mediation
- Virtual reality applications exploring new possibilities while respecting traditional boundaries

Cultural Adaptation Protocols
Cross-Cultural Teaching Respectful Cultural Integration
Traditional teaching must adapt to diverse cultural contexts while maintaining authenticity:
Cultural Adaptation Principles:
- **Partnership Approach:** Collaboration rather than replacement of existing wisdom traditions
- **Elder Consultation:** Respectful dialogue with traditional knowledge keepers
- **Cultural Translation:** Teaching principles expressed through local cultural forms
- **Mutual Learning:** Enrichment of tradition through authentic cultural encounter

Implementation Guidelines:
- Community consultation ensuring culturally appropriate adaptation
- Traditional integration with existing spiritual practices rather than replacement
- Language adaptation maintaining precision while respecting cultural metaphors
- Local training of indigenous instructors ensuring cultural authenticity

Assessment and Authorization

Progressive Qualification Standards

Traditional teaching recognizes systematic development through validated stages:

Teaching Authorization Levels
Foundation Instructor
- Qualified to assist in beginner programs under supervision
- Demonstrates basic competency in fundamental practices
- Shows appropriate character development and community integration
- Maintains consistent personal practice and service orientation

Certified Teacher
- Independent teaching authorization for specific methodologies
- Proven ability to guide students through systematic development
- Community recognition of wisdom and teaching effectiveness
- Formal authorization through traditional community processes

Master Teacher
- Complete curriculum teaching authorization with advanced student guidance
- Demonstrated capacity for training other teachers
- Community leadership responsibility and institutional service
- Recognition of advanced spiritual development and cultural transmission capability

Assessment Criteria

Character Development Evaluation Spiritual Maturity Indicators:
- Emotional stability under varying circumstances and community challenges
- Natural wisdom expression in daily life and relationships
- Service orientation demonstrated through practical community contribution
- Integration of spiritual understanding with practical responsibilities

Teaching Competency Assessment:
- Effective communication of complex spiritual concepts to various audiences
- Ability to adapt instruction to individual needs and constitutional differences
- Maintenance of appropriate boundaries and professional ethics
- Continued learning commitment despite advanced development

The Ultimate Purpose: Service to Truth
The authentic teacher-student relationship ultimately serves the recognition of truth that transcends both teacher and student. As documented in the Sacred Synthesis materials: "The goal is not to create permanent dependency or to build the teacher's reputation, but to awaken the student to their own innermost nature as pure awareness."

As this recognition deepens, the apparent separation between teacher and student dissolves into the understanding that there is only one Self, teaching itself through countless apparent forms. The relationship becomes a celebration of this recognition, a dance of consciousness awakening to its own nature through the beautiful play of spiritual companionship.

The guidelines and understanding outlined here provide a framework for navigating this sacred relationship, but the ultimate guide is the love and wisdom that naturally arise when consciousness recognizes itself in another. This love naturally protects against exploitation and guides both teacher and student toward ever-greater service to the truth that is their common essence and deepest reality.

Implementation Guidelines
Establishing Traditional Teaching Programs

Community Infrastructure Development
- Sacred space creation respecting traditional requirements and local cultural needs
- Teacher training programs following progressive qualification standards
- Student assessment protocols ensuring appropriate preparation and development
- Community governance structures balancing spiritual authority with democratic participation

Safety and Ethics Protocols
- Clear boundaries and professional standards protecting student welfare
- Community oversight preventing abuse and maintaining teaching integrity
- Regular assessment and correction processes ensuring continued authentic development
- External accountability through connection with traditional authorities and peer communities

443

Integration with Contemporary Educational Systems
Academic Institution Partnerships
- University collaboration enabling scholarly validation while preserving traditional authority
- Research programs documenting teaching effectiveness through measurable outcomes
- Professional development programs for educators integrating contemplative approaches
- Clinical applications in therapeutic contexts supporting healing while maintaining spiritual focus

Healthcare System Integration
- Training programs for healthcare providers incorporating traditional wisdom approaches
- Therapeutic protocol development using consciousness-based healing methods
- Research validation of traditional approaches through contemporary scientific methodology
- Integration with conventional medical care respecting both approaches

Conclusion: The Living Tradition
As documented throughout these materials, authentic spiritual teaching serves not individual attainment but the collective evolution of consciousness itself.

The teacher-student relationship, when properly understood and practiced, becomes a vehicle for this evolution, a means by which the tradition preserves itself while adapting to contemporary needs and challenges. Through dedication to these time- tested principles, practitioners become links in an unbroken chain of transmission that extends from the ancient past into the uncertain future, serving the ultimate goal of unified humanity through enlightened consciousness.

The responsibility is profound, the opportunity unprecedented. As humanity faces its greatest challenges, the need for authentic spiritual teaching has never been greater. May these principles serve that need while honoring the wisdom of those who preserved this understanding through centuries of dedication and service.

The Great Achievement: A Civilization Expanding
By 2080, according to the records, 147 Sacred Synthesis communities existed on every continent. These weren't isolated communes or

444

dropout communities. They were sophisticated civilizations that had solved problems the old world had never even attempted to address.

The materials described achievements that seemed almost mythical from my vantage point in 2100.

THE SACRED SYNTHESIS CHRONICLES
A Resistance Testament
Chapter 10: Global Awakening

We discovered that revolution becomes inevitable when enough people remember who they really are.

We are the International Coordination Council of the Sacred Synthesis Global Network, representatives from 73 countries where constitutional wellness, democratic governance, and authentic community have become integral to mainstream social, economic, and political systems. This chapter documents the planetary awakening that occurred between 2072 and 2073, when Sacred Synthesis principles reached the tipping point for global transformation.

By 2073, the Ubuntu Networks we had developed across Africa represented over 2.3 million people organized in 8,400 community cells spanning 34 countries. What had begun as underground resistance to colonial- imposed hierarchies had become the foundation for pan-African cooperation unprecedented in modern history. The breakthrough came when the African Union formally adopted constitutional assessment principles for diplomatic and economic negotiations. Instead of imposing uniform policies across diverse cultural contexts, continental leadership began recognizing that different regions had different constitutional strengths that should be honored and coordinated rather than homogenized.

West African communities, with their strong Magnetic constitutional characteristics, became centers for sustained agricultural development, infrastructure projects, and cultural preservation. East African regions, showing more Electric constitutional patterns, specialized in creative industries, conflict resolution, and adaptive technologies. Central and Southern African areas, with prominent Neutral constitutional features, focused on analytical research, strategic planning, and coordination between different regional initiatives. Most importantly, the continental constitutional assessment revealed that Africa's diversity was its greatest strength, not a weakness to be overcome through centralized control.

The Sacred Synthesis democratic governance principles transformed inter-tribal and international relationships that had been damaged by centuries of colonialism and authoritarian rule. Ubuntu Networks provided frameworks for resolving land disputes, sharing resources, coordinating development projects, and building economic relationships based on mutual benefit rather than exploitation.

By 2073, Africa was experiencing the fastest economic growth, most stable political development, and strongest cultural renaissance in its recorded history. International observers who had predicted continued crisis and dependency were forced to acknowledge that constitutional wellness and democratic governance had created conditions for African leadership that no external intervention had ever achieved.

The transformation in Asia occurred through what we called "Corporate Constitutional Revolution", the systematic adoption of Sacred Synthesis principles by major corporations, which then influenced government policy, educational systems, and cultural development across the region.

By 2072, over 15,000 Asian corporations were using constitutional assessment for team development, democratic governance for management structures, and community organization principles for stakeholder relationships. The productivity improvements, employee satisfaction increases, and innovation breakthroughs were so dramatic that Sacred Synthesis approaches became standard business practice throughout Asia.

Japanese corporations, which had pioneered the integration, reported increases in employee engagement, reductions in workplace conflicts, and improvements in creative problem-solving capabilities. Korean companies using constitutional principles showed similar results, along with dramatic reductions in the suicide and depression rates that had plagued their work culture.

Chinese organizations, initially resistant due to political concerns about democratic governance, found that constitutional approaches actually improved rather than threatened social harmony. When teams were organized around constitutional diversity rather than rigid hierarchy, productivity increased while maintaining collective coordination.

Most significantly, governments throughout the region began adopting constitutional principles for policy development and public administration. Instead of imposing uniform regulations across diverse populations, they began creating policies adapted to the constitutional characteristics of different communities and regions. Singapore's government officially adopted constitutional assessment for civil service hiring and team development. Thailand integrated democratic governance principles into local administration. Malaysia used community organization approaches for inter-ethnic cooperation and conflict resolution.

By 2073, what had begun as corporate wellness programs had become the foundation for a new model of governance that honored both individual differences and collective coordination throughout the Asian Pacific region.

The Liberation Synthesis Networks we had developed throughout Latin America by 2072 represented the largest coordinated social movement in the region's history, over 4.2 million people organized in democratic communities working simultaneously on economic justice, environmental protection, cultural preservation, and political transformation.

The constitutional understanding proved crucial for resolving conflicts that had traditionally divided liberation movements. Electric constitution communities provided vision, inspiration, and adaptive strategies. Magnetic constitution organizations offered sustained action, practical implementation, and cultural stability. Neutral constitution groups contributed analysis, coordination, and systematic approaches to complex challenges.
Instead of competing for resources and influence, different movement organizations began coordinating based on their constitutional strengths and collaborative capacity.

The breakthrough came during the 2072 continental gathering in Bogotá, where representatives from 847 organizations used Sacred Synthesis democratic processes to develop the "Constitutional Declaration of Latin American Liberation", a comprehensive framework for regional cooperation based on constitutional diversity, democratic governance, and mutual aid principles.

The Declaration provided practical protocols for resolving border disputes, coordinating environmental protection, sharing technological innovations, and building economic relationships that served community wellbeing rather than corporate extraction.

Within twelve months, every Latin American nation had grassroots organizations advocating for constitutional approaches to governance and development. Several countries, Uruguay, Costa Rica, Ecuador, officially adopted constitutional assessment principles for policy development and democratic participation.

Most importantly, the Liberation Synthesis Networks had proven that social movements could achieve more through constitutional cooperation than through competitive struggle, creating the foundation for peaceful transformation throughout the region.

The Nordic countries became laboratories for demonstrating how constitutional principles could enhance rather than threaten democratic institutions and social welfare systems. By 2072, Sweden, Denmark, Norway, Finland, and Iceland had integrated Sacred Synthesis approaches into government administration, healthcare delivery, educational systems, and economic policy.

The key insight was that constitutional assessment improved democratic participation by recognizing that different citizens had different ways of contributing to collective decision-making. Electric constitution individuals excelled at community organizing, public communication, and adaptive policy development. Magnetic constitution people provided stability, sustained implementation, and cultural continuity. Neutral constitution citizens contributed analytical capacity, strategic planning, and systematic coordination.

Instead of treating all citizens identically, Nordic governments began offering multiple pathways for democratic participation that honored constitutional diversity while maintaining collective coordination.

The results exceeded every expectation. Voter participation increased to over 95% as people found meaningful ways to contribute based on their constitutional strengths. Policy effectiveness improved dramatically as implementation strategies were adapted to the constitutional characteristics of different communities. Social satisfaction reached unprecedented levels as governance systems honored individual differences while serving collective welfare.

The Nordic model spread rapidly throughout Europe. Germany adopted constitutional principles for federal- state coordination. France integrated democratic governance approaches into local administration. The Netherlands used community organization methods for managing cultural diversity and social integration.

By 2073, the European Union had established the Constitutional Governance Research Institute to study and promote Sacred Synthesis approaches to democratic development, making Europe the first continental political organization to officially embrace constitutional wellness and democratic governance as foundations for international cooperation.

The transformation in North America occurred through what we called "Educational Revolution", the systematic adoption of Sacred Synthesis principles by educational institutions, which then influenced family relationships, community development, and political participation throughout the region.

By 2072, over 12,000 schools and 400 universities in Canada, the United States, and Mexico were using constitutional assessment for personalized learning, democratic governance for student participation, and community organization principles for school-community relationships.

Students educated through Sacred Synthesis approaches showed dramatically improved academic performance, emotional intelligence, social skills, and civic engagement compared to peers in conventional educational systems. They were healthier, happier, more creative, and more committed to community service and democratic participation.

More importantly, these students were graduating with the constitutional awareness, democratic skills, and community organization capacities necessary for transforming the broader society.

By 2073, Sacred Synthesis educational approaches had created a generation of young adults who took for granted what their parents' generation had risked their lives to practice. Constitutional wellness, democratic governance, and authentic community were their normal expectations for human relationships and social organization.

This generation was entering careers, starting families, and taking leadership roles with the assumption that institutions should serve human flourishing rather than institutional power, that diversity strengthened rather than threatened unity, and that individual fulfillment depended on collective wellbeing.

The political implications were profound. Traditional authoritarian approaches to governance, education, and economic organization became increasingly impossible to maintain as populations educated

449

through Sacred Synthesis principles demanded authentic democracy, meaningful work, and genuine community.

By June 2073, the Sacred Synthesis Global Network represented over 12 million active practitioners in 73 countries, with constitutional wellness and democratic governance principles embedded in thousands of corporations, educational institutions, healthcare systems, and community organizations worldwide.

But the real transformation was deeper than numbers could measure. Sacred Synthesis had reached the cultural tipping point where its principles were becoming normal expectations rather than revolutionary alternatives.
Children were growing up expecting to have their constitutional differences honored and their voices heard in family and school decisions. Workers were demanding collaborative rather than authoritarian management approaches. Citizens were insisting on meaningful participation in political processes that affected their lives. Communities were organizing around mutual aid and collective wellbeing rather than competition and individual advancement.

The old systems based on hierarchy, competition, and exploitation were becoming increasingly difficult to maintain as populations educated through Sacred Synthesis principles refused to participate in relationships and institutions that violated their understanding of human dignity and potential.

Most significantly, the global awakening was occurring through voluntary adoption rather than revolutionary overthrow. Sacred Synthesis wasn't conquering oppressive systems, it was making them irrelevant by providing superior alternatives that people chose because they produced better outcomes for everyone involved. Constitutional wellness worked better than authoritarian control for developing human potential. Democratic governance served collective needs more effectively than hierarchical domination. Authentic community provided greater security and satisfaction than competitive individualism.

When enough people experienced these truths directly through practice rather than theory, transformation became inevitable.

The next chapter will be written by witnesses to the Great Escape, the coordinated departure from corporate- controlled systems by millions of people who chose to build lives based on Sacred Synthesis principles rather than continuing to support institutions that violated their deepest values.

But we want to end this chapter with reflection on what global awakening taught us about transformation: Revolution doesn't happen when oppressed people rise up against their oppressors. Revolution happens when enough people remember who they really are and choose to live according to their authentic nature rather than the conditioning that has been imposed on them.

The Sacred Synthesis global awakening occurred not through political overthrow or economic collapse, but through the gradual recognition that human beings are naturally cooperative, naturally democratic, and naturally oriented toward mutual flourishing when we develop within systems that honor rather than suppress these capacities.

Cultural transformation is like water reaching its boiling point, gradual heating followed by sudden phase change. By 2073, enough people worldwide had experienced constitutional wellness, democratic governance, and authentic community that the old systems based on control and exploitation could no longer maintain themselves.

The awakening was global because the hunger for authentic community, meaningful work, and genuine democracy is universal. Sacred Synthesis provided practical tools for satisfying that hunger, making transformation inevitable once enough people learned how to practice it.

The awakening spreads. The systems shift.
The synthesis prevails.

The International Coordination Council continues to facilitate cooperation between Sacred Synthesis networks worldwide and maintains communication systems that function independently of government or corporate control. By 2073, the global network includes active practitioners in 73 countries and coordinates research, resources, and mutual support for communities transitioning to constitutional governance and authentic community relationships. This chapter was written collaboratively using constitutional diversity principles that honored each regional perspective while creating unified narrative.

For those participating in global awakening, remember: transformation happens one person at a time, one community at a time, one institution at a time as peo-

ple choose to practice their authentic nature rather than accept conditioning that violates their deepest understanding of human potential and dignity.

Chapter 11: The Great Escape
We called it the Great Escape, but it was really the Great Return, millions of people returning to their authentic nature after generations of conditioning and control.

We are the Liberation Networks Coordination Committee, representatives from the massive, coordinated departure of people from corporate-controlled employment, authoritarian educational systems, and exploitative economic relationships that occurred between 2073 and 2074. This chapter documents the largest voluntary migration in human history, as people chose to build lives based on Sacred Synthesis principles rather than continue supporting institutions that violated their deepest values.

By early 2073, I was Senior Vice President of Human Resources at Synergy Corporation, overseeing "employee optimization" programs for 47,000 people across twelve countries. What corporate executives didn't understand was that many of their most effective wellness and management programs were actually Sacred Synthesis applications, constitutional assessment tools, democratic governance processes, and community organization principles disguised as productivity enhancement systems.

The irony was profound: corporations were paying us to make their employees more autonomous, more collaborative, and more committed to authentic community, then acting surprised when those same employees began questioning systems based on hierarchy, competition, and profit extraction.

By 2073, employees who had been practicing Sacred Synthesis principles through "corporate wellness programs" were showing patterns that alarmed management: decreased willingness to work excessive hours, increased demand for meaningful rather than just profitable work, stronger commitment to collaborative rather than competitive relationships, and growing interest in community well-being over individual advancement.
Corporate psychologists called it "productivity paradox", employees were more effective and creative than ever, but they were also more autonomous and less controllable.

The breaking point came during the third quarter of 2073, when 347 of our most skilled employees submitted simultaneous resignation letters citing "constitutional incompatibility with institutional values" and announcing their intention to "pursue economic relationships aligned with authentic community and mutual liberation." They weren't going to competitor companies or starting traditional businesses. They were joining Sacred Synthesis communities that had developed alternative economic systems based on constitutional diversity, democratic governance, and mutual aid principles.

Within six weeks, I had lost over 20% of my workforce to what the business press initially called "cult recruitment" but which employees described as "choosing life over profit."

As someone who had been secretly practicing Sacred Synthesis principles for three years while implementing them through corporate programs, I understood exactly why people were leaving. I had reached the same conclusion: continuing to serve institutions that reduced human beings to profit-generating resources violated everything I had learned about constitutional wellness and authentic community.

On October 15, 2073, I submitted my own resignation and joined the New Harmony Community in Vermont, where I began coordinating economic liberation networks for people transitioning from corporate employment to community-based economic relationships.

The exodus from authoritarian educational systems began in colleges and universities where students had experienced Sacred Synthesis democratic learning approaches and discovered what authentic education could accomplish.

By 2073, students at institutions practicing constitutional assessment, collaborative governance, and community-based learning were outperforming peers at traditional schools by every measure: academic achievement, emotional intelligence, creative capacity, social skills, and civic engagement.

More importantly, these students had experienced education as empowerment rather than control, as community development rather than individual competition, and as preparation for contributing to collective liberation rather than personal advancement.

When they transferred to traditional institutions or entered graduate programs based on authoritarian hierarchies and competitive individualism, the contrast was devastating. Students who had learned to expect meaningful participation in their education, collaborative relationships with teachers and peers, and connection between learning and community service found themselves in systems that treated them as passive consumers of information rather than active participants in knowledge creation.

The response was unprecedented mass transfer and withdrawal. Students left prestigious universities to join Sacred Synthesis educational communities. Graduate programs that had been practicing constitutional principles found themselves overwhelmed with applications from students fleeing traditional institutions.

By 2074, over 200,000 students had withdrawn from conventional colleges and universities to join Democratic Learning Communities, educational environments based entirely on Sacred Synthesis principles where learning was personalized to constitutional type, governance was collaborative, and knowledge development was connected to community service and social transformation.

Faculty members followed their students. Professors who had experienced the joy of teaching within authentic community relationships found it impossible to return to authoritarian classroom hierarchies and competitive academic politics.

I myself had been Dean of Student Affairs at a major research university, implementing Sacred Synthesis principles through "student engagement" and "collaborative learning" initiatives that dramatically improved both academic and social outcomes.

But by 2073, I could no longer justify working within systems that fundamentally violated everything I had learned about human development and authentic education. The university was using our successful programs to attract more students and increase revenue while maintaining the same authoritarian structures and exploitative economic relationships that prevented genuine learning and community development.

I resigned in January 2074 and joined the Sacred Synthesis Educational Cooperative, where I now coordinate learning communities for people of all ages who choose education based on constitutional diversity, democratic participation, and service to collective liberation.

The healthcare exodus was the most dramatic because it involved life-and-death decisions about whether to continue serving profit-driven medical systems or to practice authentic healing within community-based healthcare relationships.

By 2073, healthcare providers trained in constitutional medicine were achieving outcomes that made traditional medical approaches appear primitive and destructive. Chronic diseases resolved through constitutional wellness approaches that cost pennies compared to pharmaceutical management. Mental health problems disappeared through authentic community relationships and constitutional understanding. Emergency situations that would have required expensive interventions were prevented through community health education and mutual support systems.

But healthcare providers working within corporate medical systems were required to ignore these superior approaches in favor of profitable treatments that maintained rather than resolved health problems.

The ethical conflicts became unbearable. Nurses who knew that constitutional breathing techniques were more effective than anxiety medications for most patients were forbidden to teach them. Physicians who understood that democratic community relationships prevented more depression than antidepressant prescriptions could treat were required to prescribe drugs instead of addressing social isolation. Therapists who had seen constitutional assessment resolve family conflicts more effectively than years of traditional counseling were prohibited from using these approaches because they weren't "officially approved."

Healthcare providers were forced to watch patients suffer from conditions they knew how to heal but couldn't treat due to institutional policies designed to maximize profit rather than promote health.

The mass resignation began in February 2073, when 1,247 healthcare workers simultaneously left their positions to establish the Constitutional Healthcare Cooperative, a network of community-based clinics providing authentic healing services to anyone regardless of their ability to pay.

Within eighteen months, over 25,000 healthcare providers had joined similar cooperatives worldwide, creating parallel healthcare systems that served over 3 million people through constitutional medicine, community health education, and mutual aid support networks.

The results were unprecedented: 85% reductions in chronic disease, 90% decreases in mental health problems, 95% elimination of healthcare-related financial stress, and the kind of healing relationships that most providers had dreamed of but never experienced within corporate medical systems.

The infrastructure exodus was the most technically complex because it required creating alternative systems for energy, water, waste management, transportation, and communication that could function independently of corporate-controlled utilities and government-managed services.

By 2073, communities practicing Sacred Synthesis principles needed infrastructure that supported constitutional diversity, democratic governance, and authentic community relationships rather than systems designed for maximum profit extraction and social control.

Electric constitution communities required flexible, adaptive infrastructure that could respond quickly to changing needs and preferences. Magnetic constitution settlements needed stable, durable systems that could support sustained activities and long-term development. Neutral constitution organizations wanted efficient, precisely controlled infrastructure that could be optimized for specific purposes.

Instead of forcing all communities to use identical systems, we developed what we called "Constitutional Infrastructure Networks", diverse, interconnected approaches that honored different community needs while maintaining collective coordination and resource sharing.

The technical innovations were remarkable. Solar power systems adapted to constitutional preferences for different types of lighting and heating. Water management that honored different constitutional relationships with natural elements. Waste processing that matched constitutional approaches to resource cycles and environmental stewardship.

Most importantly, we created infrastructure that supported democratic decision-making and community self- management rather than dependence on corporate utilities and government agencies.

By 2074, over 500 Sacred Synthesis communities were operating with complete infrastructure independence, demonstrating that authentic community could provide superior quality of life while maintaining environmental sustainability and economic efficiency.

The Great Escape represented the fulfillment of everything we had worked toward during the underground years, the creation of conditions where people could choose authentic community over oppressive control systems.

By 2074, over 2.7 million people had made the transition from corporate employment, authoritarian education, profit-driven healthcare, and centralized infrastructure to community-based alternatives organized around constitutional diversity, democratic governance, and mutual liberation.

But this wasn't just individual escape from oppressive systems, it was collective creation of new civilization based on Sacred Synthesis principles.

The communities people joined weren't isolated communes trying to avoid the broader world. They were interconnected networks providing superior alternatives to every function that corporate and government systems claimed to serve.

Economic relationships based on constitutional strengths and community needs rather than profit extraction and competitive advantage. Educational approaches that developed human potential rather than creating compliant workers. Healthcare that promoted genuine healing rather than managing profitable illnesses. Infrastructure that supported community self-determination rather than corporate control.

Most importantly, these communities were demonstrating that Sacred Synthesis principles could create not just personal fulfillment and authentic relationships, but also practical solutions to every major challenge facing human civilization: environmental sustainability, economic justice, democratic participation, healthcare accessibility, educational effectiveness, and peaceful conflict resolution.

The Great Escape proved that the Sacred Synthesis wasn't just resistance to oppressive systems, but the foundation for superior alternatives that could provide everything people actually needed while honoring their deepest values and highest potential.

By September 2074, the Great Escape had fundamentally altered the social, economic, and political landscape of human civilization.

Nearly three million people had voluntarily withdrawn from corporate-controlled systems to build lives based on constitutional wellness, democratic governance, and authentic community.

But the impact was far greater than numbers suggested. These weren't just individual lifestyle choices, they represented systematic creation of alternative infrastructure that challenged the fundamental assumptions of corporate capitalism and authoritarian governance.

The communities people joined weren't dependent on corporate systems for employment, education, healthcare, or basic infrastructure. They had created parallel institutions that provided superior outcomes while operating according to completely different principles.

Economic relationships based on constitutional diversity and mutual aid rather than competitive profit extraction. Democratic governance that involved everyone in decisions affecting their lives rather than concentrating power in hierarchical institutions. Healthcare that promoted genuine wellness rather than managing profitable illnesses. Educational approaches that developed human potential rather than creating compliant consumers.

Most significantly, the Great Escape demonstrated that oppressive systems could be defeated not through violent revolution, but through voluntary withdrawal of participation and systematic creation of superior alternatives.

When millions of people chose authentic community over corporate employment, democratic education over authoritarian schooling, constitutional healthcare over profit-driven medicine, and community self-management over centralized control, they made the old systems increasingly irrelevant through lack of participation.

The next chapter will be written by the operators of safe houses and liberation networks who supported people making the transition from corporate control to authentic community, documenting the infrastructure of mutual aid that made the Great Escape possible.

But we want to end this chapter with reflection on what mass liberation taught us about social transformation:
evolution doesn't require overthrowing oppressive systems, it requires building superior alternatives that make oppression obsolete through voluntary adoption.

The Great Escape succeeded because Sacred Synthesis communities provided everything people actually needed, meaningful work, authentic relationships, genuine health, democratic participation, environmental sustainability, while honoring their constitutional nature and supporting their highest potential.

When enough people experience alternatives that serve their deepest values and practical needs, they choose those alternatives regardless of the risks or sacrifices involved.

The old systems based on control, extraction, and exploitation could not survive when millions of their most skilled and conscious participants chose to withdraw their energy and create something better.

The escape continues. The alternatives multiply.
The transformation accelerates.

The Liberation Networks Coordination Committee continues to support people transitioning from corporate and government systems to Sacred Synthesis communities worldwide. By 2074, the networks had facilitated successful transitions for over 2.7 million people and established resource sharing agreements between 847 autonomous communities. This chapter was written collaboratively by coordinators who personally made the transition from positions of power within oppressive institutions to leadership roles in liberatory communities. For those considering departure from systems that violate your values, remember: the Great Escape is not about running away from responsibility, but about taking responsibility for creating the world you want to live in.

Authentic community is always available to those willing to practice the principles that make it possible.

Chapter 12: Safe Houses
We learned that revolution requires not just vision and courage, but the practical infrastructure of care that makes transformation possible.

We are the Underground Railway Coordinating Council, operators of the network of safe houses, resource centers, and mutual aid systems that supported people making the transition from corporate control to authentic community during the Great Escape of 2073-2074. This chapter documents the largely invisible infrastructure of care that made mass liberation possible.

By 2073, I had been operating safe houses for Sacred Synthesis practitioners for twenty-seven years, since the first major arrests in 2046. What began as emergency shelter for people fleeing persecution had evolved into comprehensive support systems for individuals and families choosing to leave oppressive institutions and build lives based on constitutional wellness and authentic community.

The safe house network operated on principles that embodied Sacred Synthesis values: constitutional assessment to understand each person's unique needs, democratic governance to ensure everyone had voice in house operations, and community organization approaches that turned temporary shelter into lasting mutual aid relationships.

Electric constitution individuals needed safe houses that provided emotional support, creative outlets, and help processing the anxiety of major life transitions. They required flexible schedules, varied activities, and strong interpersonal connections with staff and other residents.

Magnetic constitution people benefited from safe houses offering stability, routine, practical assistance, and sustained support through the slow process of building new community relationships. They needed consistent mealtimes, comfortable living spaces, and reassurance that their basic needs would be met during transition periods.

Neutral constitution visitors thrived in safe houses with clear information, systematic procedures, and efficient coordination of resources and services. They wanted detailed planning support, analytical frameworks for decision-making, and precise coordination with destination communities.

By 2074, our Northern California network included seventeen safe houses serving different constitutional needs, with specialized resources for families with children, individuals leaving healthcare systems, former corporate executives, and people transitioning from authoritarian educational institutions.

The most complex cases involved people leaving positions of power within oppressive systems. Corporate executives, university administrators, government officials, and healthcare directors who had reached positions of authority within institutions they now recognized as fundamentally destructive.

These individuals faced unique challenges: financial dependency on systems they wanted to leave, professional identities tied to institutional roles, social relationships based on corporate status, and often guilt about their previous participation in oppressive structures.

Dr. Jennifer Kim's transition from Senior Vice President at Synergy Corporation was typical. When she arrived at our Mendocino safe house in October 2073, she was simultaneously relieved to have finally made the break from corporate systems and terrified about abandoning the financial security and social status that had defined her adult identity.

Constitutional assessment identified her as primarily Electric type, relationship-oriented, adaptable, naturally collaborative, which explained both why she had been successful at implementing Sacred Synthesis principles within corporate wellness programs and why continuing to work within exploitative systems had become psychologically unbearable.

Her transition support included:
- Financial planning assistance to navigate the shift from corporate salary to community-based economic relationships
- Identity counseling to separate her authentic self from her professional role within oppressive institutions
- Skill translation workshops to understand how her corporate experience could serve authentic community development
- Relationship rebuilding support as she moved from hierarchical professional networks to egalitarian community connections
- Spiritual integration processes to heal the moral injury of participating in systems that violated her deepest values

Most importantly, she participated in democratic governance of the safe house community, learning through practice what it felt like to make decisions collaboratively rather than through corporate hierarchy.

Six months later, she had successfully transitioned to New Harmony Community, where she became Economic Liberation Coordinator, using her corporate experience to help others make similar transitions while building alternative economic systems based on constitutional principles.

The Southwest network specialized in supporting people leaving authoritarian educational systems, students, faculty, and staff who could no longer participate in institutions that reduced education to indoctrination and profit extraction.

Our most challenging cases involved graduate students and young faculty who had invested years in advanced degrees and academic career development, only to discover that universities were fundamentally incompatible with authentic learning and community development.

Maya Rodriguez-Kim's situation was representative. She had completed her undergraduate degree at a public university while secretly practicing Sacred Synthesis principles and supporting fellow students who were struggling with anxiety, depression, and social isolation endemic to competitive educational systems.

When she was accepted to graduate programs in psychology, she initially thought she could work within academic systems to promote constitutional wellness and democratic learning approaches. But graduate school quickly revealed that universities were designed to create compliant professionals rather than critical thinkers, individual competitors rather than community builders.

Faculty members who were supposed to be mentors operated through authoritarian relationships that stifled independent thought. Research was guided by corporate funding priorities rather than human needs or social benefit. Students were trained to compete with each other for scarce positions rather than collaborate for collective advancement.

Most disturbingly, the psychology program was explicitly designed to teach students to adjust individuals to oppressive systems rather than to question systems that created widespread psychological distress.

Maya arrived at our Phoenix safe house in January 2074, having withdrawn from her graduate program despite significant financial investment and family pressure to complete her degree.

Constitutional assessment confirmed her Electric type and revealed that her natural gifts for relationship- building and adaptive problem-solving were being systematically suppressed by academic environments that rewarded individual competition and theoretical abstraction over community engagement and practical wisdom. Her transition support focused on:
- Educational alternatives research to identify Sacred Synthesis learning communities that could provide the knowledge and skills development she sought
- Financial recovery planning to address student loan debt from

educational investment that she was abandoning

- Family relationship counseling to navigate conflicts with relatives who couldn't understand why she was leaving a prestigious academic program
- Career path development that connected her psychology interests with community healing and constitutional wellness approaches
- Community integration support to help her find meaningful roles within authentic educational environments

Within eight months, she had joined the Sacred Synthesis Educational Cooperative, where she developed constitutional psychology curricula while completing community-based studies that provided deeper and more practical knowledge than any traditional graduate program.

The medical safe house network served healthcare providers who could no longer ethically participate in profit- driven systems that prioritized corporate revenue over patient healing and community health.

Our most complex transitions involved physicians and nurses who had completed years of medical training and built successful careers within hospital systems, only to discover that corporate healthcare was fundamentally incompatible with authentic healing and service to human wellbeing.

Dr. Lisa Chen's transition was particularly challenging because she was leaving a position as Chief Medical Officer at a major regional hospital where she had been successfully implementing Sacred Synthesis constitutional medicine approaches within corporate healthcare structures.

Her constitutional assessment revealed Neutral type characteristics, analytical, systematic, naturally inclined toward precision and efficiency, that had made her highly effective within medical institutions but also made the ethical contradictions of corporate healthcare particularly unbearable.

As Chief Medical Officer, she knew that constitutional approaches were more effective and less expensive than standard pharmaceutical treatments for most chronic conditions. She understood that community health education prevented more disease than medical interventions could treat. She recognized that authentic healing relationships were more powerful than technological procedures for addressing most health challenges.

But hospital administrators required her to prioritize treatments that generated revenue over approaches that actually served patient well-being. Insurance companies determined medical protocols based on profit margins rather than healing effectiveness. Pharmaceutical corporations influenced prescribing practices through financial incentives that had nothing to do with patient health outcomes.

She was forced to watch patients suffer from conditions she knew how to heal but couldn't treat due to institutional policies designed to maximize profit rather than promote health.

Dr. Chen arrived at our Asheville safe house in March 2074, having resigned from her hospital position and abandoned a medical career that had taken twelve years of education and training to develop.

Her transition support included:
- Legal consultation about medical licensing requirements for practicing constitutional healthcare within community-based systems
- Financial planning to navigate the shift from high medical salary to community-based economic relationships
- Identity reconstruction counseling to separate her healing gifts from institutional medical identity
- Skill translation workshops to understand how medical training could serve authentic community health without corporate constraints
- Ethical integration support to heal the moral injury of participating in systems that profited from human suffering
- Community health education training to learn approaches that prevented disease rather than managing profitable illnesses

Most importantly, she participated in governance of our safe house medical clinic, learning collaborative approaches to healthcare decision-making that honored both provider expertise and community needs.

Eighteen months later, she had established the Constitutional Healthcare Institute, training medical professionals worldwide in authentic healing approaches while providing community-based healthcare services that achieved better outcomes at lower costs than any corporate medical system.

The digital infrastructure network provided the technical foundation that made safe house operations possible under conditions of government surveillance and corporate monitoring designed to prevent mass exodus from controlled systems.

By 2054, authorities understood that the Great Escape represented an existential threat to systems based on corporate profit extraction and authoritarian control. Millions of skilled workers, educated professionals, and conscious citizens were abandoning institutions that required their participation to function.

The response was intensified surveillance designed to identify people planning to leave corporate systems, infiltrate safe house networks, and disrupt the infrastructure that made transitions possible.

Our digital security had to protect not just individual privacy, but the operational capacity of an underground network supporting nearly three million people in transition from oppressive systems to authentic communities. The technical challenges were unprecedented. We needed secure communication systems that could coordinate between hundreds of safe houses without being detected by surveillance algorithms. Financial networks that could support resource transfers without triggering corporate or government monitoring. Transportation coordination that could move people between locations without being traced through digital tracking systems. Most importantly, we needed information systems that could match people seeking liberation with communities and resources that matched their constitutional needs and contribution capacities.

The solution was embedding safe house coordination within the same mainstream digital platforms that authorities used for surveillance. Instead of creating separate networks that would attract attention, we hid liberation infrastructure within corporate social media, educational databases, healthcare systems, and business coordination platforms.

Safe house locations were communicated through environmental organization meetups. Resource availability was shared through corporate wellness program updates. Transportation coordination happened through fitness app networking. Financial support was distributed through small business networking platforms.
To surveillance algorithms analyzing millions of digital transactions, safe house operations appeared to be completely normal social, educational, and business activities.

The key insight was that the same constitutional diversity principles that guided community organization also applied to digital resistance. Electric constitution approaches used creative, adaptive communication that changed frequently and appeared social rather than institutional. Magnetic constitution methods emphasized stable, long-term networks that built trust through sustained relationship rather than sophisticated technology. Neutral constitution systems focused on precise, efficient coordination that minimized digital footprints while maximizing operational effectiveness.

By 2074, our digital infrastructure was supporting safe house operations across six continents without a single network compromise or operational failure due to surveillance detection.

By December 2074, the safe house network had supported successful transitions for over 400,000 people leaving corporate employment, authoritarian education, profit-driven healthcare, and government systems to join Sacred Synthesis communities worldwide.

But the real achievement was deeper than numbers could measure. We had created proof that mutual aid based on constitutional understanding could provide superior support for human development and community transition than any institutional social services.

Safe houses operated through democratic governance that involved residents in decision-making about house operations. Resource sharing based on constitutional assessment that honored individual needs while maintaining collective sustainability. Conflict resolution through Sacred Synthesis approaches that strengthened rather than damaged relationships during stressful transition periods.

Most importantly, safe house communities embodied the values and relationships that people were seeking in their destination communities. Instead of temporary shelter that isolated people from authentic community, safe houses provided experience of constitutional wellness, democratic governance, and mutual aid that prepared residents for successful integration into Sacred Synthesis communities.

People didn't just pass through safe houses, they were transformed by the experience of living according to Sacred Synthesis principles, often for the first time in their adult lives.

The network proved that infrastructure of mutual aid could be more effective than institutional social services, more secure than government protection systems, and more sustainable than corporate

resource management. The next chapter will be written by representatives of the Constitutional Communities, the autonomous settlements that became destinations for people leaving oppressive systems and laboratories for demonstrating what human civilization
could become when organized around Sacred Synthesis principles.

But we want to end this chapter with reflection on what operating
safe house networks taught us about revolution:

Transformation requires not just vision of what we want to create,
but practical infrastructure that makes the transition possible for real
people facing real challenges in their specific circumstances.

The Great Escape succeeded because safe house networks provided
constitutional assessment to understand individual needs, democratic governance to honor everyone's voice, community organization
support that addressed practical challenges, and mutual aid relationships that continued beyond the transition period.

Revolutionary change happens one person at a time, one family at a
time, one community at a time, as people receive the practical support necessary to choose authentic community over oppressive control.

The infrastructure endures. The support expands.
The liberation continues.

*The Underground Railway Coordinating Council continues to operate safe house
networks worldwide and has established permanent resource centers in 127 locations for people transitioning to Sacred Synthesis communities. The network
maintains secure communication systems and coordinates with community destinations to ensure successful integration for all residents. This chapter was written
collaboratively by safe house operators who provided direct support for hundreds
of thousands of people choosing liberation over oppression.*

*For those needing transition support, remember: safe houses exist wherever people
practice constitutional awareness, democratic governance, and mutual aid. Seek
communities that honor your individual needs while supporting your highest contribution to collective wellbeing.*

COMMUNITY BUILDING
Unity · Democracy · Resources

READER'S NOTE:
You have entered the **Community Building layer** of Sacred Synthesis.

This section contains **community infrastructure** - democratic governance protocols and mutual aid frameworks

What you'll find here:
- Constitutional diversity in group dynamics
- Consensus decision-making processes
- Conflict resolution and power-sharing
- Autonomous community governance models

Look for:
- Safeguards against hierarchy and power concentration
- Adaptation guidelines for different contexts
- Professional integration (healthcare, education, organizing)

The cylinder has strength through structure. Build wisely. Build together.

Chapter 13: Constitutional Communities
We discovered that human beings are capable of creating paradise when we organize society around constitutional diversity, democratic governance, and mutual liberation.

We are the Federation of Sacred Synthesis Settlements, representatives from 423 autonomous communities worldwide that have demonstrated what human civilization becomes when organized entirely around constitutional wellness, democratic participation, and authentic community relationships. This chapter documents the remarkable achievements of communities that became laboratories for the future of human society.

By 2075, New Harmony had been operating as a fully autonomous Sacred Synthesis settlement for twenty- seven years, serving as the prototype for hundreds of similar communities worldwide. Our 847 acres now supported 347 people across 89 families, with complete independence from corporate systems and government services.

The results exceeded every expectation we had when we began this experiment in 2048.

Economically, our constitutional approach to work and resource sharing had created abundance that eliminated both poverty and excessive accumulation. Instead of forcing everyone into identical roles, we organized production around constitutional strengths that allowed each person to contribute their natural gifts while developing skills in other areas.

Electric constitution community members specialized in creative industries, relationship coordination, and adaptive problem-solving that brought in external revenue through art, music, writing, counseling services, and innovative design projects. Their work provided approximately 40% of our community income while requiring only 20 hours per week of focused effort.

Magnetic constitution families anchored our agricultural production, infrastructure maintenance, and cultural preservation activities that provided 85% of our food, energy, and material needs while maintaining sustainable environmental relationships. Their sustained efforts created the foundation of stability that allowed other constitutional types to flourish.

Neutral constitution individuals managed our finances, coordinated between different community functions, maintained our legal compliance, and developed strategic relationships with outside organizations. Their analytical and organizational capacities optimized our efficiency while ensuring long-term sustainability.

Most remarkably, our economic system had eliminated the anxiety and competition that characterized both corporate employment and traditional cooperative ventures. People worked because they enjoyed their contributions and wanted to support community wellbeing, not because they feared poverty or sought individual advancement.

By 2075, New Harmony's economic productivity per capita was 340% higher than comparable populations in conventional communities, while our working hours averaged 25 hours per week and job satisfaction ratings exceeded 95%.

Our social relationships had achieved what most people consider impossible: a community of nearly 350 people with virtually no interpersonal conflicts, authentic democratic governance, and genuine care between all community members regardless of their constitutional differences or personal backgrounds.

The key was constitutional understanding combined with Sacred Synthesis conflict resolution approaches. Instead of trying to make everyone identical or forcing people to suppress their authentic nature, we created systems that honored constitutional diversity while building collective unity.

Electric constitution individuals provided vision, inspiration, and creative adaptation that kept our community innovative and responsive to changing needs. Magnetic constitution people offered stability, tradition, and sustained commitment that anchored our collective identity and cultural continuity. Neutral constitution members contributed analysis, planning, and systematic coordination that optimized our effectiveness and efficiency.

Democratic governance processes ensured that every voice was heard in community decisions while maintaining the efficiency necessary for collective action. Consensus-building approaches honored individual autonomy while supporting collective coordination.

Most importantly, our children were developing in ways that demonstrated the full potential of human beings raised within authentic community relationships. By age sixteen, New Harmony

470

children showed emotional intelligence, creative capacity, analytical ability, and social skills that exceeded adult populations in conventional society.

They were healthier, happier, more confident, and more committed to community service than any comparable group of young people. They understood constitutional diversity as natural and beneficial, democratic participation as normal expectation, and authentic community as their birthright rather than an impossible ideal. Saraswati Village represented the successful integration of Sacred Synthesis principles with traditional Indian culture, demonstrating that constitutional wellness and democratic governance enhanced rather than threatened ancient wisdom traditions.

Our community of 234 people had been established in 2072 on 400 acres of semi-arid land in Rajasthan, using traditional Ayurvedic knowledge combined with Sacred Synthesis innovations to create sustainable agriculture, authentic healthcare, and democratic governance that honored both individual constitutional needs and collective cultural values.

The constitutional assessment revealed fascinating patterns in our community composition. Like traditional Indian villages, we included all three constitutional types, but in proportions that differed significantly from urban populations shaped by colonial disruption and industrial development.

Our Magnetic constitution families (Kapha types) represented 60% of the community and specialized in sustainable agriculture, traditional crafts, cultural preservation, and the kind of sustained community development that had characterized healthy Indian villages for millennia.

Electric constitution individuals (Vata types) comprised 25% of residents and focused on creative arts, external relationships, adaptive innovation, and the communication between our community and the broader movement for cultural and spiritual renewal.

Neutral constitution members (Pitta types) made up 15% of the population and provided analytical capacity, systematic coordination, and the strategic thinking necessary for successful integration of traditional wisdom with contemporary innovations.

This constitutional balance created remarkable stability and effectiveness. Our agricultural productivity using traditional methods enhanced by Sacred Synthesis constitutional understanding exceeded conventional farming by 280% while maintaining soil health and water conservation that ensured long-term sustainability.

Our healthcare system combined Ayurvedic constitutional medicine with Sacred Synthesis community health approaches, achieving outcomes that surpassed both traditional village medicine and modern hospital systems. Chronic diseases that plagued urban Indian populations were virtually eliminated through constitutional lifestyle approaches, community support systems, and preventive healthcare education.

Most significantly, our democratic governance had revitalized traditional panchayat (village council) decision- making in ways that honored both ancient wisdom and contemporary understanding of participatory democracy. Instead of the hierarchical authority that had been imposed through colonial administration, we practiced consensus-building approaches that ensured every voice was heard while maintaining cultural continuity and collective effectiveness.

Our children learned traditional skills like agriculture, crafts, music, and spiritual practices alongside constitutional assessment, democratic participation, and global citizenship that prepared them to contribute to both local community development and international cooperation.

By 2075, Saraswati Village had become a model for rural development throughout India, demonstrating that traditional culture and Sacred Synthesis principles could create communities that were simultaneously rooted in ancient wisdom and adapted to contemporary challenges.

Ubuntu Village represented the African expression of Sacred Synthesis principles, showing how constitutional wellness and democratic governance could heal the wounds of colonialism while building foundations for African leadership in global transformation.

Our community of 189 people had been established in 2073 on 300 acres in Cross River State, creating what we called "Traditional Futurism", a synthesis of indigenous African wisdom traditions with Sacred Synthesis innovations that demonstrated Africa's contributions to planetary healing and social transformation.

The constitutional patterns in our community reflected traditional African understanding of human diversity that had been suppressed but not eliminated by centuries of colonial oppression.

Electric constitution community members (representing about 35% of residents) specialized in storytelling, music, conflict resolution, and the kind of adaptive creativity that had always been essential for community survival and cultural preservation in African societies.

Magnetic constitution families (45% of the community) anchored our agricultural production, traditional crafts, extended family relationships, and the sustained community development that characterized healthy African villages for thousands of years.

Neutral constitution individuals (20% of residents) provided the analytical and coordination capacities necessary for successful integration of traditional knowledge with contemporary innovations, including relationships with global Sacred Synthesis networks.

Our economic system combined traditional African concepts of wealth as community wellbeing with Sacred Synthesis principles of constitutional diversity and democratic resource sharing.

Instead of individual accumulation or state-controlled distribution, we practiced what we called "Ubuntu Economics", resource sharing based on constitutional understanding that ensured everyone's needs were met while honoring different ways of contributing to collective prosperity.

Our agricultural approaches combined indigenous permaculture knowledge with constitutional principles to achieve food production that exceeded traditional methods while maintaining environmental sustainability and cultural authenticity.

Our healthcare system integrated traditional African medicine with Sacred Synthesis constitutional approaches, creating healing relationships that addressed not just individual health problems but also the collective trauma of colonialism and the social disorders that resulted from disruption of traditional community structures.
Most importantly, our democratic governance had revitalized traditional African consensus-building in ways that demonstrated Africa's contributions to global development of participatory democracy and authentic community organization.

Our children learned traditional languages, cultural practices, agricultural skills, and spiritual wisdom alongside constitutional assessment, democratic participation, and global citizenship that prepared them for leadership in both African renewal and planetary transformation.

By 2075, Ubuntu Village had inspired the development of similar communities throughout Africa and had become a center for research and training in African contributions to Sacred Synthesis principles and global community development.

Pachamama Community represented the Latin American integration of Sacred Synthesis with indigenous wisdom traditions, liberation theology, and environmental protection, demonstrating how constitutional principles could support both social justice and ecological sustainability.

Our community of 156 people had been established in 2073 on 250 acres in the Andean highlands, creating what we called "Buen Vivir Synthesis", a combination of indigenous concepts of good living with Sacred Synthesis innovations that demonstrated alternatives to both capitalist extraction and socialist control.

The constitutional composition of our community reflected the diversity of Latin American liberation movements, with each type contributing different strengths to our collective work for social transformation. Electric constitution members (30% of residents) specialized in popular education, community organizing, artistic expression, and the kind of adaptive resistance that had characterized successful liberation movements throughout Latin America.

Magnetic constitution families (50% of the community) provided sustained commitment to land-based production, infrastructure development, cultural preservation, and the long-term community building necessary for successful alternatives to capitalist exploitation.

Neutral constitution individuals (20% of residents) contributed strategic analysis, coordination between different movement organizations, and systematic approaches to the complex challenges of creating economic and political alternatives.

Our economic system integrated indigenous concepts of reciprocity and complementarity with Sacred Synthesis principles of constitutional diversity and democratic resource management, creating what we called "Liberation Economics", production and distribution based on community needs rather than profit accumulation or state control.

Our agricultural approaches combined indigenous permaculture with constitutional understanding to achieve food sovereignty that eliminated dependency on both corporate agriculture and government food programs while maintaining sustainable relationships with mountain ecosystems.

Our healthcare system integrated traditional medicine with Sacred Synthesis constitutional approaches and popular health education, creating community health that addressed not just individual illness but also the social disorders created by poverty, oppression, and environmental destruction.

Most significantly, our democratic governance had synthesized indigenous consensus-building, liberation theology base community principles, and Sacred Synthesis participatory approaches to create decision-making processes that served both local community needs and broader social transformation goals.

Our children learned indigenous languages, traditional ecological knowledge, and social justice principles alongside constitutional assessment, democratic participation, and global cooperation skills that prepared them for leadership in both Latin American liberation and planetary transformation.

By 2075, Pachamama Community had become a model for communities throughout Latin America and a training center for integrating Sacred Synthesis principles with indigenous wisdom and liberation movement organizing.

By March 2075, our federation represented 423 autonomous communities worldwide, housing over 180,000 people who had chosen to build lives based entirely on constitutional wellness, democratic governance, and authentic community relationships.

But the real achievement was deeper than numbers could measure. These communities had proven that Sacred Synthesis principles could create human settlements that achieved unprecedented levels of health, happiness, productivity, sustainability, and social harmony while honoring both individual authenticity and collective wellbeing.

Economic systems that eliminated both poverty and excessive accumulation while providing meaningful work and abundant resources for everyone. Healthcare approaches that prevented disease and promoted genuine wellness rather than managing profitable illnesses. Educational methods that developed full human potential rather than creating compliant workers. Governance structures that honored every voice while maintaining collective effectiveness.

Most importantly, environmental relationships that enhanced rather than degraded ecological systems while providing sustainable abundance for human communities.

These weren't utopian experiments or isolated communes, they were practical demonstrations that human civilization could be organized around cooperation rather than competition, democracy rather than domination, and constitutional diversity rather than imposed uniformity.

The children growing up in these communities were developing capacities that most adults could barely imagine: natural constitutional awareness, instinctive democratic participation, automatic community commitment, and global consciousness combined with deep local rootedness.

They represented the first generation of human beings raised entirely within authentic community relationships, and they were becoming living proof of human potential when development occurs within systems that honor our deepest nature rather than suppressing it.

The next chapter will be written by historians documenting the Turning Tide, the period when Sacred Synthesis communities achieved such obvious superiority to corporate-controlled systems that mainstream populations began demanding similar approaches to governance, economics, and social organization.
But we want to end this chapter with reflection on what constitutional communities taught us about human potential:

When human beings organize society around constitutional diversity, democratic participation, and authentic community, we create conditions for flourishing that exceed our most optimistic expectations.

The Sacred Synthesis communities proved that competition, hierarchy, and exploitation are not expressions of human nature, but distortions imposed by systems that prevent us from discovering our authentic capacities for cooperation, creativity, and mutual support.

Given environments that honor constitutional differences while building collective unity, human beings naturally create abundance, health, beauty, and harmony that serve both individual fulfillment and community wellbeing.

The future is not something we must wait for, it is something we can create wherever we choose to practice constitutional awareness, democratic governance, and authentic community.

The communities thrive. The models multiply.
The future manifests.

The Federation of Sacred Synthesis Settlements continues to coordinate between autonomous communities worldwide and provides resources for establishing new settlements based on constitutional principles. By 2075, the federation includes 423 communities housing over 180,000 people and maintains research and training programs for community development, sustainable technology, and democratic governance. This chapter was written collaboratively by community representatives using constitutional diversity principles and consensus decision-making processes.

For those seeking to join or establish Sacred Synthesis communities, remember: authentic community emerges wherever people practice constitutional awareness, democratic participation, and mutual liberation. Start where you are, with who you're with, practicing the principles that create the relationships you want to experience.

Chapter 14: The Turning Tide
We documented the precise moment when humanity chose cooperation over competition, democracy over domination, and authentic community over corporate control.

We are the Movement Historians Collective, scholars, journalists, and witnesses who have been documenting the Sacred Synthesis transformation since Marcus Chen's discovery in 2045. This chapter records the turning tide that occurred in 2075, when Sacred Synthesis principles achieved such obvious superiority to corporate- controlled systems that mainstream populations began demanding fundamental social transformation.

The turning tide began with a simple comparison that appeared in media outlets worldwide during July 2075: "Sacred Synthesis Communities vs. Corporate Society: A Statistical Analysis of Human Flourishing."
The data was overwhelming and undeniable.

- Sacred Synthesis communities: reduction in chronic disease, decrease in mental health problems, elimination of addiction, average life expectancy of 94 years
- Corporate-controlled populations: Rising rates of diabetes, depression, anxiety, and autoimmune disorders, average life expectancy declining to 76 years
- Sacred Synthesis children: 100% literacy by age 6, advanced critical thinking skills, multilingual capacity, artistic and technical competency, strong social-emotional intelligence
- Corporate school systems: 67% reading proficiency by high school graduation, declining analytical ability, increasing anxiety and social dysfunction
- Sacred Synthesis communities: Zero poverty, zero homelessness, meaningful work for all, abundant resources, 25-hour work weeks, 98% life satisfaction
- Corporate economies: Growing wealth inequality, increasing homelessness, unemployment and underemployment, 60-hour work weeks, 23% life satisfaction
- Sacred Synthesis settlements: Carbon negative, enhanced biodiversity, soil regeneration, water purification, sustainable abundance
- Corporate industrial systems: Accelerating climate disruption, mass extinction, pollution, resource depletion
- Sacred Synthesis communities: Virtually zero crime, collaborative conflict resolution, authentic democratic participation, intergenerational cooperation
- Corporate societies: Rising violence, family breakdown, political polarization, social isolation, authoritarian control

The comparison made clear that Sacred Synthesis wasn't just a lifestyle choice or spiritual practice, it was a superior model for organizing human civilization that produced better outcomes by every measure that mattered to people's actual lives.

But statistics alone didn't create the turning tide. What changed everything was direct experience.
By 2075, millions of people had visited Sacred Synthesis communities, participated in constitutional assessments, experienced democratic governance processes, and witnessed authentic community relationships firsthand.

They returned to corporate-controlled environments with visceral understanding of what human life could be like when organized around constitutional diversity rather than imposed uniformity, collaboration rather than competition, and genuine care rather than profit extraction.

The contrast was unbearable. People who had experienced authentic community for even brief periods could no longer accept the isolation, anxiety, and meaninglessness that characterized corporate-controlled existence.

The political turning tide began when elected officials started visiting Sacred Synthesis communities and discovering that democratic governance actually worked better than the authoritarian systems they had been trained to operate.

Mayor Jennifer Thompson of Burlington, Vermont, spent three days observing New Harmony Community's democratic processes in May 2075. She returned to city government profoundly changed by experiencing decision-making that honored every voice while maintaining collective effectiveness.

I've been in politics for fifteen years," she told the Burlington City Council. "I thought democracy meant majority rule and minority submission. These people showed me that democracy means everyone's voice matters and everyone's needs are considered. They make decisions in hours that would take us months, and everyone supports the results because everyone was genuinely heard.

Within six weeks, Burlington had implemented constitutional assessment for city staff, democratic governance training for department heads, and citizen participation processes based on Sacred Synthesis community organization principles.

The results were immediate and dramatic. City efficiency increased by 180% as different constitutional types were matched to appropriate roles and collaborative decision-making eliminated bureaucratic delays. Citizen satisfaction reached unprecedented levels as people experienced genuine participation in local government. Conflicts between different community groups were resolved through constitutional understanding and democratic mediation.

Burlington's transformation attracted attention from municipal governments worldwide. Delegations from hundreds of cities visited both Burlington and Sacred Synthesis communities to understand how democratic governance could be implemented within existing political structures.

By August 2075, over 200 cities and towns across North America, Europe, and Latin America had implemented some form of constitutional governance and Sacred Synthesis democratic processes.

The political transformation accelerated when state and national governments began facing mass demands from constituents who had experienced authentic democracy and would no longer accept authoritarian alternatives.

Why should we accept representatives who don't represent us, when we know how to make decisions collaboratively?" asked Dr. Maya Rodriguez-Kim during testimony before the Vermont State Legislature. "Why should we tolerate policies imposed from above, when we've learned how to develop solutions that serve everyone's needs?

The question crystallized the political crisis facing governments worldwide: populations were developing democratic capacities that exceeded the systems supposed to serve them.

The economic turning tide occurred when corporations began losing their most skilled workers to Sacred Synthesis communities and couldn't compete with economic systems based on constitutional diversity and mutual aid.

By July 2075, the Great Escape had removed over 3.2 million people from corporate employment, including disproportionate numbers of the creative, analytical, and organizational talents that corporations required for innovation and efficiency.

But the real crisis wasn't labor shortage, it was comparison.

Employees remaining in corporate systems increasingly understood that they were working more hours for less satisfaction to produce inferior results compared to people practicing Sacred Synthesis approaches.

Jennifer Kim's Economic Liberation Network had documented that people working 25 hours per week in constitutional roles within Sacred Synthesis communities were more productive, more creative, and more satisfied than corporate employees working 60+ hours in positions that ignored their constitutional nature and prevented authentic collaboration.

Corporate executives faced impossible contradictions. Sacred Synthesis approaches improved productivity, reduced conflicts, and

increased innovation, but they also made employees more autonomous, more collaborative, and less willing to accept authoritarian
management.

We implemented constitutional assessment and democratic management because they worked," explained David Park, former CEO
of Innovation Dynamics Corporation. "Our teams became

more effective, our projects succeeded more often, and our employee satisfaction increased dramatically. But we also created workers
who wouldn't accept exploitation, couldn't be manipulated by corporate propaganda, and insisted on meaningful rather than just profitable work.

By August 2075, over 15,000 corporations worldwide had implemented Sacred Synthesis principles through "productivity enhancement" and "employee wellness" programs, inadvertently training
their own workforce in constitutional awareness and democratic
governance.

The result was systemic transformation of corporate culture as employees educated in Sacred Synthesis principles demanded authentic
collaboration, meaningful work, and economic relationships that
served community wellbeing rather than just shareholder profit.

Corporations that embraced the transformation thrived, creating
workplaces that attracted the most talented people and achieved
unprecedented innovation and efficiency. Companies that resisted
lost their best employees to competitors offering constitutional
workplaces and Sacred Synthesis management approaches.

The healthcare turning tide occurred when patients who had experienced constitutional medicine refused to return to profit-driven
medical systems that treated symptoms rather than promoting genuine healing.

By 2075, the Constitutional Healthcare Institute had trained over
50,000 medical professionals in constitutional medicine approaches
that achieved superior outcomes at lower costs than conventional
treatments.
Patients treated through constitutional healthcare showed:
- 85% resolution rate for chronic diseases compared to 23% in
  conventional systems
- 90% reduction in pharmaceutical dependency
- 95% satisfaction with provider relationships compared to 34%

in corporate medical systems
- 67% lower healthcare costs with dramatically better health outcomes

But numbers didn't create the transformation, direct experience did.

People who had experienced healthcare providers who understood their constitutional type, involved them in health decisions, and addressed root causes of illness rather than managing profitable symptoms couldn't return to corporate medical systems that treated them as revenue sources rather than human beings.

My constitutional medicine doctor spent an hour understanding my individual needs and developed a treatment plan that resolved my chronic pain in six weeks," explained Sandra Thompson, a former patient of corporate healthcare systems. "My old doctor spent ten minutes with me, prescribed medications that created side effects worse than my original problem, and scheduled follow-up appointments to manage the complications he had created.

The comparison was devastating to corporate healthcare systems. Patients educated in constitutional approaches recognized that conventional medicine was designed to create dependency rather than promote healing, to manage profitable illnesses rather than address root causes, and to extract maximum revenue rather than support genuine wellness.

Healthcare workers trained in Sacred Synthesis approaches began refusing to participate in systems that violated their professional ethics and prevented them from providing authentic healing services.

By August 2075, over 8,000 medical professionals had left corporate healthcare systems to establish constitutional medicine cooperatives that provided superior healthcare at affordable costs while honoring both provider values and patient needs.

The educational turning tide occurred when parents who had seen their children thrive in Sacred Synthesis learning environments demanded fundamental transformation of authoritarian school systems.

By 2075, children educated through constitutional approaches in Sacred Synthesis communities and Democratic Learning Cooperatives were demonstrating capacities that made conventional educational outcomes appear primitive and destructive.

Sacred Synthesis children showed:
- Advanced academic achievement in all subjects
- Superior critical thinking and creative problem-solving abilities
- Strong emotional intelligence and social skills
- Natural democratic participation and leadership capacity
- Environmental awareness and community commitment
- Multilingual competency and global consciousness
- Physical health and psychological wellbeing that exceeded adult populations

But the real difference was deeper than skills or knowledge. Sacred Synthesis children were developing into the kinds of human beings that adults wished they could become, confident without arrogance, intelligent without elitism, creative without destructiveness, caring without codependency.

Parents who visited Sacred Synthesis schools returned to conventional educational systems with devastating questions: "Why are we forcing our children into systems that make them anxious, competitive, and disconnected from their authentic gifts? Why are we accepting educational approaches that prepare them for corporate servitude rather than democratic citizenship and authentic community?"

The questions spread rapidly through parent networks, social media, and community organizations. By summer 2075, over 200,000 families had withdrawn their children from conventional schools to join or establish Democratic Learning Communities based on Sacred Synthesis principles.

The mass exodus forced school districts worldwide to confront fundamental questions about educational purpose and methods. Districts that implemented constitutional assessment, democratic governance, and community-based learning approaches saw dramatic improvements in academic achievement, student satisfaction, and family engagement.

Those that maintained authoritarian structures experienced continued enrollment decline as families chose educational environments that honored their children's constitutional nature and developed their full potential. By August 2075, we had documented the precise moment when social transformation became inevitable: when enough people had experienced Sacred Synthesis approaches to recognize their obvious superiority to corporate-controlled alternatives.

The turning tide wasn't created by revolutionary overthrow or economic collapse, but by the gradual recognition that constitutional wellness, democratic governance, and authentic community produced better outcomes for every aspect of human life.

Health, education, economics, politics, environmental sustainability, social relationships, Sacred Synthesis communities achieved superior results by every measure while honoring individual differences and building collective unity.

Most importantly, the transformation was occurring through voluntary choice rather than imposed change. People weren't being forced to adopt Sacred Synthesis principles, they were choosing them because they worked better than the alternatives.

Corporations, governments, and institutions that embraced constitutional approaches thrived, attracting the most talented people and achieving unprecedented effectiveness. Those that maintained authoritarian structures lost their most skilled participants to organizations that honored human dignity and potential.

The turning tide represented the moment when humanity collectively chose cooperation over competition, democracy over domination, and authentic community over corporate control.

Not because we were forced to by crisis or catastrophe, but because we had learned that these approaches created the kinds of lives we actually wanted to live and the kinds of world we wanted to leave to our children. The next chapter will be written by witnesses to Institutional Collapse, the rapid transformation of corporate, government, and social institutions that could not adapt to populations educated in constitutional awareness and democratic governance.

But we want to end this chapter with reflection on what the turning tide taught us about social change: Transformation becomes inevitable when alternatives become irresistible. The Sacred Synthesis didn't defeat oppressive systems through force or conflict, it made them obsolete by providing superior approaches that people chose because they produced better outcomes.

When enough people experience constitutional wellness, democratic governance, and authentic community, they naturally create conditions that make authoritarianism, exploitation, and isolation impossible to maintain.

Revolution happens not when the oppressed rise up against their oppressors, but when human beings remember who they really are and choose to live according to their authentic nature rather than the conditioning imposed by systems that profit from their dysfunction.

The choice is made.
The transformation is inevitable. The future is now.

The Movement Historians Collective continues to document the global transformation to Sacred Synthesis civilization and maintains archives of this unprecedented period in human history. The collective includes scholars from major universities, independent researchers, and community-based historians using constitutional principles to honor diverse perspectives while creating accurate historical records. This chapter was written using democratic processes that ensured all voices were heard while maintaining scholarly accuracy and narrative coherence.

For those witnessing or participating in social transformation, remember: change becomes inevitable when alternatives become irresistible. Practice constitutional awareness, democratic governance, and authentic community consistently, and transformation will follow naturally as people choose approaches that serve their deepest values and highest potential.

Chapter 15: Institutional Collapse

We watched the most powerful institutions in human history dissolve not through revolution, but through abandonment by the people they claimed to serve.

We are the Transition Witnesses Network, former corporate executives, government officials, military leaders, and institutional administrators who documented the rapid collapse of authoritarian control systems that could not adapt to populations educated in constitutional awareness and democratic governance. This chapter records the final months of 2075, when centuries-old institutions of domination and exploitation became obsolete virtually overnight.

The military collapse was the most surprising and complete institutional transformation. By October 2075, armed forces worldwide were experiencing unprecedented desertion rates as personnel educated in Sacred Synthesis principles could no longer reconcile military service with authentic community values.

The crisis began when military psychological evaluations started using constitutional assessment tools that had proven superior to conventional personality testing. What commanders discovered was that the most effective soldiers, officers, and strategic planners were those whose constitutional types aligned with collaborative rather than authoritarian approaches.

Electric constitution military personnel excelled at relationship building, cultural understanding, and adaptive problem-solving that made them ideal for peacekeeping, humanitarian missions, and international cooperation. But they struggled psychologically with combat roles that required dehumanizing enemies and following orders that violated their ethical understanding.

Magnetic constitution service members provided stability, loyalty, and sustained commitment that made them excellent for logistical support, community engagement, and long-term strategic operations. But they became distressed when required to participate in conflicts that damaged rather than protected communities.

Neutral constitution military leaders showed exceptional analytical and planning capacities that made them effective strategic coordinators and systems managers. But they questioned the logic of military operations that created more problems than they solved and consumed resources that could better serve community development.

The breaking point came in September 2075, when 40,000 military personnel across six countries simultaneously submitted resignations citing "constitutional incompatibility with institutional mission" and requesting discharge to join Sacred Synthesis communities or civilian organizations practicing democratic governance.

Colonel David Kim, former Strategic Planning Officer, explained his decision during congressional testimony: "I spent fifteen years learning how to protect our country and serve our citizens. But Sacred Synthesis communities proved that the most effective defense is healthy populations practicing authentic democracy.

Military force can't protect people from the social disorders created by authoritarian institutions."

Within eight weeks, military commands worldwide were facing recruiting crises as young people educated in Sacred Synthesis principles refused service in institutions based on hierarchy and violence, while simultaneously experiencing mass resignations from experienced personnel choosing civilian alternatives.

By November 2075, several nations had begun transitioning their military forces into Constitutional Defense Cooperatives, democratic organizations focused on disaster relief, international humanitarian assistance, and community security approaches based on conflict resolution rather than combat capability.

The financial system collapse was the most rapid and complete institutional transformation. By September 2075, banks and financial corporations were becoming obsolete as communities worldwide adopted Sacred Synthesis economic principles based on constitutional diversity and mutual aid.

The crisis began when communities practicing Sacred Synthesis economics demonstrated that they could achieve superior economic outcomes without depending on corporate banking, investment markets, or government monetary policy.

Sacred Synthesis communities had eliminated poverty, homelessness, and economic anxiety while providing meaningful work, abundant resources, and genuine security for all members. They accomplished this through constitutional approaches to work organization, democratic resource sharing, and mutual aid networks that made traditional financial services unnecessary.

People who had experienced economic relationships based on constitutional understanding and community wellbeing couldn't return to financial systems based on debt, speculation, and artificial scarcity designed to extract profit from human necessity.

The mass withdrawal began in August 2075, when over 500,000 people simultaneously closed their bank accounts, cancelled their credit cards, liquidated their investment portfolios, and transferred their resources to Sacred Synthesis community economies.

Within six weeks, banks were facing liquidity crises as millions of people chose economic relationships that served human needs rather than generating profit for financial institutions.

Why should we pay interest to borrow money created out of nothing, when communities can create abundance through constitutional cooperation?" asked Maya Rodriguez-Kim during Senate Banking Committee hearings. "Why should we accept economic insecurity and competitive stress, when we've learned how to create economies that serve everyone's constitutional needs?

Corporate executives and government officials couldn't answer the questions because Sacred Synthesis communities had proven that economic relationships could be based on cooperation rather than competition, abundance rather than scarcity, and community wellbeing rather than individual accumulation.

By November 2075, over 20 major banks had declared bankruptcy as populations chose economic systems that made financial intermediaries obsolete. Those that survived did so by transforming into Constitutional Economic Cooperatives that served community development rather than profit extraction.

The educational system collapse was the most obvious institutional transformation because Sacred Synthesis approaches to learning achieved such dramatically superior outcomes compared to conventional schooling. By October 2075, parents worldwide were withdrawing their children from authoritarian school systems after witnessing the remarkable development of children educated through constitutional principles in Sacred Synthesis communities.

The comparison was devastating to conventional education. Children who had spent even one year in Democratic Learning Communities showed academic achievement, emotional intelligence, creative capacity, and social skills that exceeded high school graduates from traditional systems.

Sacred Synthesis children were developing into confident, creative, collaborative human beings who took democratic participation and community service for granted as normal aspects of human development.

Conventional school systems were producing anxious, competitive, isolated young people trained for corporate servitude rather than authentic citizenship.

The mass exodus accelerated when video documentation from Sacred Synthesis schools showed eight-year-old children facilitating conflict resolution between peers, twelve-year-olds participating meaningfully in community governance decisions, and sixteen-year-olds demonstrating analytical, creative, and social capacities that exceeded most college graduates.

Our conventional educational system is child abuse disguised as preparation for adult life," declared Dr. Lisa Thompson during emergency Department of Education hearings. "We're forcing children into authoritarian environments that suppress their natural learning capacity, damage their emotional development, and train them to accept domination as normal.

By November 2075, over 15 million children had been withdrawn from conventional schools to join Democratic Learning Communities or establish family-based educational cooperatives using Sacred Synthesis principles.

School districts that attempted to maintain authoritarian structures experienced complete enrollment collapse. Those that transformed into Democratic Learning Communities thrived, attracting families from across the region who wanted educational environments that honored their children's constitutional nature and developed their full potential.

The healthcare system collapse was the most ethically obvious institutional transformation because constitutional medicine achieved such superior healing outcomes compared to profit-driven medical systems.

By September 2075, patients worldwide were abandoning corporate healthcare systems after experiencing constitutional medicine approaches that resolved chronic conditions, eliminated pharmaceutical dependencies, and created authentic healing relationships.

Most devastatingly, constitutional medicine proved that most health problems were preventable through community support, environmental health, and constitutional wellness approaches that corporate systems actively discouraged because they reduced profitable illness.

We were trained to manage disease, not create health," explained Dr. Elena Martinez during medical ethics hearings. "Constitutional medicine showed us that genuine healing serves human flourishing rather than corporate profit. We can't continue participating in systems that profit from human suffering.

The mass exodus from corporate healthcare began when over 30,000 medical professionals simultaneously resigned to establish Constitutional Healthcare Cooperatives providing authentic healing services regardless of patients' ability to pay.

Within ten weeks, corporate hospital systems were facing staffing crises as their most skilled and ethical providers chose practice environments that honored both professional values and patient needs.

By November 2075, corporate healthcare systems were collapsing throughout the developed world as both providers and patients chose constitutional medicine approaches that served healing rather than profit extraction.

The government surveillance system collapse was the most ironic institutional transformation because Sacred Synthesis communities achieved superior security through authentic democracy rather than authoritarian monitoring.

By October 2075, government agencies worldwide were discovering that surveillance and control systems designed to prevent social disorder were becoming obsolete as populations practiced constitutional awareness and democratic governance.

Sacred Synthesis communities had achieved virtually zero crime rates, eliminated social conflicts, and created genuine security through constitutional understanding and authentic community relationships. They accomplished this without surveillance, punishment, or authoritarian control, the foundation of government security approaches for centuries.

The contrast was devastating to security agencies. Communities practicing Sacred Synthesis principles were safer, more stable, and more resilient than populations subjected to extensive surveillance and control measures.

Our security systems were designed to manage populations we assumed were naturally dangerous and antisocial," I explained during Senate Intelligence Committee hearings. "Sacred Synthesis communities proved that human beings are naturally cooperative and democratic when they develop within authentic community relationships. Surveillance and control are symptoms of social disorders, not solutions to them.

Government officials couldn't justify surveillance systems that violated constitutional privacy rights while achieving inferior security outcomes compared to communities that trusted democratic cooperation and mutual aid.

By November 2075, several nations had begun dismantling surveillance infrastructure while implementing constitutional assessment and democratic governance approaches that addressed root causes of social disorder rather than managing symptoms through authoritarian control.

By November 2075, we had documented the collapse of virtually every major institution based on authoritarian control, competitive individualism, and profit extraction over human wellbeing.

The collapse wasn't caused by external attack, economic crisis, or social revolution. It was caused by voluntary abandonment as populations educated in Sacred Synthesis principles chose superior alternatives that served their actual needs and values.

Military forces became obsolete as communities achieved security through authentic democracy. Financial systems collapsed as people chose economic relationships based on mutual aid. Educational institutions failed as parents chose learning environments that honored their children's nature. Healthcare systems were abandoned for approaches that promoted genuine healing. Government agencies lost relevance as communities practiced direct democracy.

The institutions that survived did so by transforming into Constitutional Cooperatives that served community development rather than institutional power.

But the real significance wasn't the collapse of old institutions, it was the simultaneous emergence of new forms of social organization based entirely on Sacred Synthesis principles.

Democratic governance structures that honored every voice while maintaining collective effectiveness. Economic relationships that eliminated both poverty and excessive accumulation. Educational approaches that developed full human potential. Healthcare systems that promoted genuine wellness. Security arrangements that served authentic community protection.

Most remarkably, these new institutions were emerging organically as people practiced constitutional awareness and democratic principles, rather than being imposed by revolutionary overthrow or government planning.

The institutional collapse of 2075 represented humanity's transition from social organization based on control and exploitation to civilization based on constitutional diversity, democratic governance, and authentic community.

The next chapter will be written by witnesses to the Democratic Renaissance, the emergence of new forms of governance, economics, and social organization based entirely on Sacred Synthesis principles and practiced by populations who had transcended the conditioning that made authoritarian institutions possible.

But we want to end this chapter with reflection on what institutional collapse taught us about social transformation:

Institutions collapse not when they are attacked, but when they become irrelevant to the people they claim to serve. The Sacred Synthesis didn't destroy authoritarian systems through force or conflict, it made them obsolete by providing superior alternatives.

When populations develop constitutional awareness, democratic skills, and authentic community relationships, they naturally create social organization that serves human flourishing rather than institutional power.

Revolution happens not through the destruction of old systems, but through the creation of new systems so attractive and effective that the old ones become abandoned through lack of participation.

The institutions fall. The alternatives rise.
The transformation completes.

The Transition Witnesses Network continues to document the transformation from institutional control systems to Sacred Synthesis civilization. Members include former leaders from military, financial, educational, healthcare, and government institutions who witnessed and participated in this unprecedented peaceful transition. This chapter was written using constitutional diversity principles and democratic governance processes that honored each witness's unique perspective while creating accurate historical documentation.
For those witnessing institutional collapse, remember: transformation occurs through creation of alternatives, not destruction of existing systems. When institutions no longer serve human flourishing, they become irrelevant through voluntary abandonment rather than violent overthrow. Practice constitutional awareness, democratic governance, and authentic community, and new institutions will emerge organically.

Chapter 16: Democratic Renaissance

We witnessed the emergence of the first truly democratic civilization in human history, built by people who had remembered what authentic community could accomplish.

We are the New Civilization Coordinators, representatives from the democratic governance structures that emerged worldwide during 2076 as populations educated in Sacred Synthesis principles created new forms of social organization based entirely on constitutional diversity, participatory decision-making, and mutual liberation. This chapter documents the birth of authentic democratic civilization.

By February 2076, the collapse of authoritarian institutions had created space for the emergence of entirely new forms of governance based on Sacred Synthesis principles that had been tested and refined in communities for over a decade.

Instead of representative democracy that concentrated power in elected officials, we were practicing direct participatory democracy where every person affected by decisions had meaningful voice in making those decisions.

Instead of majority rule that imposed solutions on minorities, we used consensus-building processes that honored all perspectives while creating collective agreements that everyone could support.

Instead of territorial governments based on artificial boundaries, we organized around bioregional communities that respected natural ecosystems and cultural relationships.

The North American Democratic Federation represented 47 million people organized in 8,400 autonomous communities, each practicing constitutional governance that honored individual differences while building collective unity.

Electric constitution communities (about 30% of the population) specialized in creative innovation, cultural preservation, adaptive problem-solving, and external relationship building that maintained connections between different bioregions and with international networks.

Magnetic constitution settlements (approximately 45% of the population) anchored sustained agricultural production, infrastructure development, cultural stability, and the long-term community building that provided foundation for democratic civilization.

Neutral constitution organizations (around 25% of the population) contributed analytical capacity, systematic coordination, strategic planning, and the precision necessary for efficient resource distribution and inter- community cooperation.

Instead of forcing uniformity across diverse populations, constitutional governance allowed each community to organize around its natural strengths while contributing to continental coordination through voluntary association and mutual aid networks.

The results exceeded every expectation of democratic theory. Decision-making processes that involved millions of people were more efficient than traditional representative systems. Policies developed through authentic participation achieved better outcomes than those imposed by distant authorities. Resource distribution based on community assessment and mutual aid eliminated both scarcity and waste.

Most remarkably, we had achieved genuine security through community relationships rather than military force, economic stability through cooperative production rather than competitive markets, and social harmony through constitutional understanding rather than legal enforcement.

The African Democratic Renaissance represented the liberation of indigenous governance wisdom that had been suppressed but not eliminated by centuries of colonial disruption.

By 2076, the Ubuntu Networks that had developed across Africa had grown into the Continental African Democracy, representing over 180 million people organized in 12,000 communities that combined traditional consensus-building with Sacred Synthesis constitutional principles.

The constitutional patterns that emerged reflected traditional African understanding of human diversity and complementary social roles that pre-dated European colonial impositions.

Electric constitution communities specialized in storytelling, cultural transmission, conflict resolution, and the kind of adaptive creativity that had always been essential for community survival and innovation in African societies.

Magnetic constitution settlements anchored agricultural production, traditional crafts, extended family relationships, and the sustained community development that had characterized healthy African villages for millennia.

Neutral constitution organizations provided analytical and coordination capacities necessary for successful integration of traditional knowledge with contemporary innovations, including relationships with global networks and technological development.

The African Democratic Renaissance proved that indigenous governance wisdom enhanced by Sacred Synthesis principles could create democratic participation, economic prosperity, and social harmony that exceeded any colonial or post-colonial political arrangements.

Our governance processes combined traditional palaver (community discussion) with constitutional assessment to ensure that every voice was heard while honoring different ways of contributing to collective decision- making.

Resource distribution followed traditional African concepts of wealth as community wellbeing, enhanced by Sacred Synthesis principles of constitutional diversity that ensured everyone's needs were met while respecting different ways of contributing to collective prosperity.

Conflict resolution integrated traditional approaches to community healing with Sacred Synthesis mediation techniques that addressed root causes of disagreement while strengthening rather than damaging community relationships.

Most importantly, the African Renaissance demonstrated Africa's contributions to global development of authentic democratic civilization and constitutional governance principles.

The South Asian transformation integrated traditional wisdom traditions with Sacred Synthesis innovations to create what we called "Dharmic Democracy", governance based on constitutional understanding and community service rather than power accumulation and competitive politics.

By 2076, the Digital Villages and traditional communities that had preserved constitutional knowledge through Ayurvedic medicine and village panchayat governance had grown into the South Asian Cooperative Federation, representing over 240 million people organized in 15,000 communities across the Indian subcontinent.

Our governance structures combined traditional concepts of dharma (righteous duty based on individual nature) with Sacred Synthesis constitutional principles to create decision-making processes that honored both ancient wisdom and contemporary understanding of human diversity.

Electric constitution communities (Vata in traditional terms) specialized in creative arts, spiritual practices, communication between different cultural groups, and adaptive innovation that maintained cultural authenticity while embracing beneficial change.

Magnetic constitution settlements (Kapha traditionally) anchored agricultural production, traditional crafts, family relationships, and the sustained community development that had provided stability for South Asian civilization for thousands of years.

Neutral constitution organizations (Pitta traditionally) contributed analytical capacity, systematic coordination, and the strategic planning necessary for successful integration of traditional knowledge with modern innovations and international cooperation.

Our economic relationships followed traditional concepts of artha (righteous livelihood) enhanced by Sacred Synthesis principles of constitutional diversity and mutual aid that eliminated both poverty and excessive accumulation while maintaining cultural values and environmental sustainability.

Educational approaches combined traditional guru-disciple relationships with Sacred Synthesis democratic learning that honored both traditional knowledge transmission and contemporary understanding of constitutional diversity and democratic participation.

Most significantly, our spiritual practices integrated traditional meditation and yoga with Sacred Synthesis constitutional wellness and community organization that served both individual liberation and collective transformation.

The Latin American transformation represented the fulfillment of liberation theology and indigenous wisdom through Sacred Synthesis principles that created "Participatory Liberation", governance based on community empowerment and constitutional justice rather than institutional authority.

By 2076, the Liberation Synthesis Networks that had coordinated resistance movements throughout Latin America had evolved into the Latin American Liberation Federation, representing over 150 million people organized in 9,500 communities that combined indigenous governance with Sacred Synthesis democratic principles.

Our constitutional patterns reflected the diversity of liberation movements and indigenous traditions that had maintained community-based decision-making despite centuries of colonial and authoritarian oppression.
Electric constitution communities specialized in popular education, cultural resistance, artistic expression, and the adaptive organizing that had characterized successful liberation movements throughout Latin American history.

Magnetic constitution settlements anchored land-based production, indigenous knowledge preservation, extended community relationships, and the sustained resistance that had maintained cultural identity and community solidarity despite systematic oppression.

Neutral constitution organizations contributed analytical capacity, strategic coordination, and systematic approaches to the complex challenges of building economic and political alternatives that served community liberation rather than institutional power.

Our governance processes integrated indigenous consensus-building, liberation theology base community principles, and Sacred Synthesis participatory democracy to create decision-making that served both local community needs and broader social transformation goals.

Economic relationships followed indigenous concepts of reciprocity and complementarity enhanced by Sacred Synthesis principles to create "Solidarity Economics", production and distribution based on community needs and constitutional diversity rather than profit accumulation or state control.

Environmental practices combined indigenous ecological knowledge with Sacred Synthesis sustainability principles to create regenerative relationships with natural systems that enhanced both human community and ecological health.

The Asian Pacific transformation demonstrated how traditional concepts of harmony and collective wellbeing could be enhanced by Sacred Synthesis principles to create "Constitutional Harmony", governance that honored both individual authenticity and community coordination.

By 2076, the corporate constitutional revolution and traditional community renewal had merged into the Asian Pacific Harmony Council, representing over 320 million people organized in 18,000 communities that integrated Confucian harmony concepts, Buddhist compassion principles, and Sacred Synthesis constitutional governance.

Our governance structures combined traditional concepts of collective harmony with Sacred Synthesis understanding of constitutional diversity to create decision-making processes that honored both individual differences and community wellbeing.

Electric constitution communities contributed creative innovation, cultural bridge-building, adaptive problem- solving, and the kind of harmonious change that maintained cultural values while embracing beneficial developments.

Magnetic constitution settlements provided stability, traditional preservation, sustained production, and the long-term community development that had anchored Asian civilizations for thousands of years.
Neutral constitution organizations offered analytical capacity, systematic coordination, efficient resource management, and the precise organization that optimized collective effectiveness while maintaining individual satisfaction.

Our economic relationships followed traditional concepts of mutual benefit enhanced by Sacred Synthesis principles to create prosperity that served everyone's constitutional needs while maintaining social harmony and environmental sustainability.

Educational approaches combined traditional respect for knowledge with Sacred Synthesis democratic learning to create wisdom development that honored both cultural transmission and individual authentic expression.
Most importantly, our spiritual practices integrated traditional meditation and harmony cultivation with Sacred Synthesis constitutional wellness and community organization that served both inner peace and social transformation.

The European transformation demonstrated how social democratic values could be enhanced by Sacred Synthesis principles to create

"Constitutional Social Democracy", governance that provided both individual freedom and collective welfare through authentic democratic participation.

By 2076, the Nordic experiments in constitutional governance had expanded into the European Constitutional Confederation, representing over 180 million people organized in 11,000 communities that combined social democratic institutions with Sacred Synthesis participatory democracy.

Our governance structures integrated traditional European concepts of individual rights and collective responsibility with Sacred Synthesis constitutional principles to create decision-making processes that honored both personal autonomy and community wellbeing.

Electric constitution communities specialized in cultural innovation, international cooperation, adaptive policy development, and the creative problem-solving that maintained European values while embracing global cooperation and ecological sustainability.

Magnetic constitution settlements anchored agricultural production, traditional crafts, social services, and the sustained community development that provided stable foundation for European civilization and cultural preservation.

Neutral constitution organizations contributed analytical capacity, systematic coordination, policy analysis, and efficient administration that optimized collective effectiveness while maintaining individual rights and cultural diversity.

Our economic relationships followed enhanced social democratic principles based on constitutional assessment and mutual aid that eliminated both poverty and excessive accumulation while maintaining innovation, creativity, and individual opportunity.

Educational approaches combined traditional European academic excellence with Sacred Synthesis democratic learning to create knowledge development that served both individual fulfillment and collective advancement. Environmental practices integrated traditional European conservation with Sacred Synthesis ecological principles to create regenerative relationships that served both human communities and natural systems.

By February 2076, the Democratic Renaissance had created the foundation for authentic democratic civilization involving over 1.2 billion people organized in 64,000 autonomous communities worldwide, each practicing constitutional governance based on Sacred Synthesis principles.

But the real achievement was deeper than numbers could measure. For the first time in recorded history, human beings had created social organization based entirely on constitutional diversity, authentic democratic participation, and mutual liberation.

Instead of representative democracy that concentrated power in distant authorities, we practiced direct participation where everyone affected by decisions had meaningful voice in making them.

Instead of majority rule that imposed solutions on minorities, we used consensus processes that honored all perspectives while creating agreements everyone could support.

Instead of competitive politics that divided populations into opposing factions, we practiced collaborative governance that built on constitutional diversity to create solutions that served everyone's needs.

Instead of territorial governments based on artificial boundaries, we organized around natural communities that respected both ecological relationships and cultural affinities.

Most importantly, we had proven that authentic democracy was not only possible, but superior to authoritarian alternatives by every measure that mattered to people's actual lives.

Democratic governance was more efficient than authoritarian control because it engaged everyone's intelligence and creativity in problem-solving. Participatory decision-making achieved better outcomes than imposed policies because it drew on diverse perspectives and constitutional wisdom. Constitutional communities were more stable and resilient than hierarchical institutions because they honored rather than suppressed human nature.

The Democratic Renaissance represented humanity's transition from social organization based on domination and control to civilization based on cooperation and authentic community.

The next chapter will be written by representatives of the liberated generation, people who had grown up entirely within Sacred Synthesis civilization and experienced authentic democracy, constitutional wellness, and genuine community as normal aspects of human development.

But we want to end this chapter with reflection on what democratic renaissance taught us about human potential:

Authentic democracy emerges naturally when populations practice constitutional awareness and genuine community relationships. The Sacred Synthesis didn't impose democratic institutions from outside, it created conditions where democratic governance became the obvious and natural way for communities to organize themselves.

When human beings understand their own constitutional nature and experience authentic community, they spontaneously create decision-making processes that honor every voice, resource-sharing systems that serve everyone's needs, and conflict-resolution approaches that strengthen rather than damage relationships.

The Democratic Renaissance proved that the hunger for authentic participation, meaningful voice, and genuine community is universal among human beings, regardless of cultural background or historical experience.

Democracy is not a political system that can be imposed from outside, it is a natural expression of human nature that emerges when people are free to organize society around constitutional diversity, authentic relationships, and mutual liberation.

The renaissance flourishes. The democracy deepens.
The civilization rises.

The New Civilization Coordinators continue to facilitate cooperation between democratic governance structures worldwide and maintain communication systems that support participatory decision-making across six continents. The coordinators represent over 1.2 billion people organized in 64,000 autonomous communities practicing constitutional democracy based on Sacred Synthesis principles. This chapter was written using authentic democratic processes that honored each bioregional perspective while creating unified documentation of this unprecedented achievement in human governance.

For those participating in democratic renaissance, remember: authentic democracy is not something that can be given to people by authorities, it is something that emerges naturally when communities practice constitutional awareness, genuine participation, and mutual liberation. Start where you are, with who you're with, creating the democratic relationships you want to experience.

Chapter 17: Legacy of Liberation

We are the first generation of human beings to grow up assuming that democracy, authentic community, and constitutional wellness are normal rather than revolutionary.

We are the Children of the New World, the generation born into Sacred Synthesis civilization who have never experienced authoritarianism, exploitation, or artificial scarcity. This chapter documents what human beings become when we develop within social systems that honor our deepest nature and support our highest potential from birth.

I am the child of Maya Rodriguez-Kim and Alex Chen, grandchild of Elena Rodriguez and Alex Kim, great- grandchild of the original resistance networks that preserved Sacred Synthesis knowledge during the underground years.

My great-grandmother Elena often tells stories about the time when people lived in fear of authorities, competed with each other for artificial scarcity, and accepted isolation and anxiety as normal aspects of human existence. To me and my generation, these stories sound like myths from a primitive civilization that barely understood human nature.

I grew up in New Harmony Community, where constitutional assessment was as natural as learning to walk, democratic governance was how we made all community decisions, and authentic relationships were what we expected from every human interaction.

By age seven, I could identify my own constitutional type and understand how to adapt my learning and relationships to my Electric nature. By age twelve, I was participating meaningfully in community governance processes and helping to resolve conflicts between adults. By age sixteen, I was teaching constitutional principles to visitors from communities that were still transitioning to Sacred Synthesis approaches.

But what seems most remarkable to older generations feels completely natural to us. Constitutional diversity, democratic participation, and authentic community are not ideals we strive toward, they are the foundation of how we organize our lives.

When I started university studies at the Sacred Synthesis Global Learning Network in 2073, I was shocked to learn that most of human history involved social systems based on hierarchy, competition, and exploitation. The idea that people once accepted authoritarian control, economic insecurity, and social isolation seemed as strange to me as slavery or human sacrifice.

My Electric constitution makes me naturally oriented toward relationship-building, creative expression, and adaptive problem-solving. Instead of being forced into competitive academic systems that ignored my constitutional nature, I was able to develop my gifts through collaborative learning, artistic projects, and community service that honored my authentic contributions.

By age 20, I was coordinating creative arts programs for children in twelve communities across North America, developing constitutional assessment tools for young people, and contributing to international networks that shared Sacred Synthesis innovations worldwide.

Most importantly, I had never experienced the anxiety, depression, or sense of meaninglessness that characterized young adults in previous generations. When your constitutional nature is honored, your voice is heard in collective decisions, and your contributions serve authentic community, life feels naturally purposeful and deeply satisfying.

I am the child of parents from three different bioregions, David Santos-Wilson from New Harmony Community in North America, and Dr. Meera Patel from Saraswati Village in India, representing the global integration that has become normal for my generation.

I spent my childhood moving between communities worldwide, experiencing different cultural expressions of Sacred Synthesis principles while developing deep understanding of what remains constant across all authentic human communities.

Whether in Vermont, Rajasthan, Nigeria, Ecuador, or Sweden, I found the same fundamental patterns: constitutional assessment that honored individual differences, democratic governance that included every voice, economic relationships based on mutual aid rather than competition, and educational approaches that developed full human potential rather than creating compliant workers.

My Magnetic constitution makes me naturally suited for sustained agricultural work, infrastructure development, and providing stability during community challenges. Instead of being told these interests were less valuable than intellectual or creative pursuits, I was celebrated for gifts that communities recognized as essential for collective wellbeing.

By age fourteen, I was coordinating food production systems for multiple communities, training adults in sustainable agriculture techniques, and developing innovations in renewable energy and ecological restoration that combined traditional knowledge with contemporary understanding.

By age eighteen, I was serving on the Continental Democratic Federation Infrastructure Council, helping to coordinate resource sharing and sustainable technology development across 8,400 communities in North America.

What amazes older generations is that I consider this level of responsibility and contribution normal rather than exceptional. When communities organize around constitutional strengths and democratic participation, young people naturally develop leadership capacities and meaningful contributions that previous generations thought were impossible.

Most importantly, I have never experienced the alienation from productive work or disconnection from community purpose that characterized young adults in hierarchical systems. When your constitutional gifts are needed and valued, when you participate in decisions affecting your community, and when your work serves collective liberation, career development feels naturally integrated with personal fulfillment and social contribution.

I am the child of parents representing three continents, Dr. Lisa Park-Thompson from North America, Dr. Michael Thompson from Europe, and Dr. Amara Okafor from Africa, embodying the planetary consciousness that has become characteristic of my generation.

I have spent my life moving between communities worldwide, serving as a cultural bridge and learning how different bioregions express Sacred Synthesis principles through their unique traditions and innovations.
My Neutral constitution makes me naturally analytical, systematic, and oriented toward coordination and strategic thinking. Instead of being tracked into competitive academic programs that isolated me from community engagement, I was able to develop these gifts through collaborative research, democratic governance, and international cooperation projects.

By age thirteen, I was participating in Global Coordination Council meetings, helping to facilitate communication between communities with different cultural backgrounds and constitutional compositions. By age fifteen, I was leading research projects on optimal constitutional balance for different types of community development, sustainable technology applications, and effective approaches to cultural bridge- building.

By age sixteen, I was serving as a youth representative to the International Sacred Synthesis Network, helping to coordinate between young people worldwide who were taking leadership roles in global cooperation and cultural integration.

What seems remarkable to older generations feels natural to me: the ability to think systematically about complex global challenges while maintaining deep roots in local community relationships. When you grow up with constitutional understanding and democratic participation, analytical thinking naturally serves collective wellbeing rather than individual advancement.

Most importantly, I have never experienced the isolation from meaningful contribution or disconnection from global community that characterized young adults in previous systems. When your analytical gifts serve authentic democracy and your strategic thinking supports community liberation, intellectual development feels naturally integrated with ethical commitment and service to collective transformation.

I am the child of parents representing multiple bioregions and cultural traditions, Alex Chen-Martinez from North America and Dr. Elena Vasquez from Latin America, reflecting the cultural synthesis that has become normal for my generation.

I represent what older generations call the "Fourth Generation" of Sacred Synthesis practitioners, great- grandchild of the original resistance networks, grandchild of the underground organizers, child of the community builders, and member of the generation that has never known anything but authentic democracy and constitutional wellness.

My Electric constitution makes me naturally oriented toward creative expression, relationship building, and adaptive innovation. Instead of being forced into standardized educational systems that suppressed my authentic nature, I have been able to develop my gifts through collaborative arts programs, democratic learning communities, and international cultural exchange.

By age twelve, I was creating artistic works that documented the transformation from authoritarian civilization to Sacred Synthesis community, helping older generations process and integrate their experiences of social change.

By age fourteen, I was facilitating cultural exchange programs between young people from different bioregions, developing communication skills and creative approaches that honored constitutional diversity while building global friendship and cooperation.

By age fifteen, I was contributing to the Global Youth Council, helping to coordinate between young people worldwide who were taking leadership in cultural development, international cooperation, and preparation for responsibilities we will inherit as the first generation raised entirely within Sacred Synthesis civilization.

What amazes older generations is that I consider global responsibility and cultural leadership normal aspects of teenage development. When you grow up with constitutional understanding and democratic participation, creative expression naturally serves community transformation and international cooperation.

Most importantly, I have never experienced the anxiety about the future or pessimism about human nature that characterized young adults in previous systems. When you develop within authentic community and see constitutional principles creating health, harmony, and prosperity worldwide, the future feels naturally positive and your role in continuing that development feels deeply meaningful.

By June 2077, we represent over 12 million young people worldwide who have grown up entirely within Sacred Synthesis civilization, never experiencing authoritarianism, artificial scarcity, or competitive individualism as normal aspects of human society.

We are taking leadership roles in communities, bioregions, and international networks while still in our teens and early twenties, not because we are exceptional, but because constitutional understanding and democratic participation naturally develop leadership capacities that previous generations thought were impossible for young people.

We serve on governance councils, coordinate resource sharing networks, facilitate international cooperation, lead research projects, develop technological innovations, create cultural works, and take responsibility for community wellbeing in ways that amaze adults who were raised in hierarchical systems that treated young people as dependents rather than contributors.

But what seems most significant to us is not what we can accomplish, but who we have become as human beings when development occurs within authentic community relationships.

We are the first generation to grow up assuming that:
- Constitutional diversity is natural and beneficial rather than threatening
- Democratic participation is normal rather than revolutionary
- Authentic community is expected rather than idealistic
- Meaningful work is available rather than scarce
- Environmental harmony is possible rather than utopian
- International cooperation is natural rather than exceptional
- Individual fulfillment and collective wellbeing are inseparable rather than competitive

We have never experienced the psychological disorders that characterized previous generations: anxiety about scarcity, depression from meaninglessness, anger from powerlessness, addiction from disconnection, or despair about human nature and social possibility.

We naturally expect constitutional wellness, authentic relationships, meaningful contribution, and democratic participation because these have been the foundations of our development from birth.

Most importantly, we are preparing to take full responsibility for continuing the transformation that previous generations initiated, but with capacities and perspectives that could only develop within the Sacred Synthesis civilization they created.

The original resistance generation preserved the knowledge despite persecution and risk. The underground organizers built networks despite surveillance and suppression. The community builders established alternatives despite institutional collapse. The institutional transformers created new forms of governance despite opposition and uncertainty.

We inherit their achievements as our starting point, but we also bring capacities they could not have developed within systems based on competition, hierarchy, and exploitation.

We are the generation that will complete the transformation to fully realized Sacred Synthesis civilization, not because we are more intelligent or capable than our predecessors, but because we have been raised within the conditions they created for authentic human development.

The next chapter will be the final chapter of this chronicle, documenting Sacred Synthesis Fulfilled, the achievement of sustainable, democratic, constitutional civilization that honors human diversity while serving planetary wellbeing.

But we want to end this chapter with gratitude to the generations who made our development possible:
We are who we are because previous generations chose liberation over security, community over isolation, and service over selfishness, despite the risks and sacrifices involved.

Marcus Chen discovered the knowledge and chose to share it despite knowing it would cost him his freedom. Elena Rodriguez built underground networks despite surveillance and persecution. Alex Kim preserved the knowledge through digital systems that made it indestructible. Dr. Sarah Martinez survived torture and cognitive rehabilitation while maintaining commitment to authentic healing. International coordinators built global networks despite opposition and cultural barriers. Community builders created alternatives despite institutional collapse. Legal defenders established constitutional protection despite authoritarian resistance. Safe house operators supported transitions despite personal risk. Healthcare providers chose authentic healing despite professional consequences. Educators created democratic learning despite institutional pressure.

Every generation sacrificed and served so that we could grow up free.

We honor their legacy by continuing the transformation they initiated, by developing the capacities they made possible, and by ensuring that future generations inherit an even more beautiful world than the one we received.

The legacy endures.
The children rise. The future brightens.

The Children of the New World continue to take increasing leadership in Sacred Synthesis communities worldwide and represent the first generation of human beings raised entirely within authentic democratic civilization. By 2077, over 12 million young people have grown up within Sacred Synthesis communities and are demonstrating capacities for leadership, creativity, and cooperation that exceed previous understanding of human potential. This chapter was written collaboratively by representatives of the fourth generation, using constitutional diversity principles and democratic processes they learned as normal aspects of childhood development.

For older generations seeking to understand the children of the new world, remember: young people raised within authentic community naturally develop capacities that seem exceptional to adults who grew up in competitive and hierarchical systems. Support their leadership, learn from their perspectives, and trust that they are prepared to continue the transformation you initiated.

Chapter 18: Sacred Synthesis Fulfilled

We have become what Marcus Chen dreamed when he first discovered the Sacred Synthesis materials in 2045: a planetary civilization based on constitutional diversity, authentic democracy, and genuine community that serves both individual fulfillment and collective flourishing.

We are the Planetary Coordination Council, representatives from every bioregion of Earth who coordinate the global civilization that emerged when human beings learned to organize society around constitutional wellness, democratic participation, and mutual liberation. This final chapter documents the achievement of Sacred Synthesis civilization and what we have learned about human potential when it develops within authentic community relationships.

By December 2080, thirty-five years after Marcus Chen's discovery, Sacred Synthesis principles have become the foundation for human civilization worldwide. Over 2.3 billion people live in 127,000 autonomous communities practicing constitutional governance, democratic economics, and authentic community relationships.

The transformation is complete not because everyone practices identical approaches, but because the fundamental assumptions underlying human social organization have shifted from competition to cooperation, from hierarchy to democracy, and from exploitation to mutual aid.

The global population of 2.3 billion represents a stabilization following the demographic transition that occurred as communities achieved genuine security through authentic relationships rather than resource accumulation. Birth rates naturally balanced with mortality rates when children were valued for their individual gifts rather than their economic productivity, and when communities could confidently support all members regardless of their constitutional type or contribution capacity.

The 127,000 autonomous communities range in size from 50 to 2,000 people, organized around optimal scales for constitutional diversity, democratic participation, and authentic relationships. Each community maintains complete autonomy for internal governance while participating in bioregional coordination and global cooperation networks.

Constitutional distribution across the global population shows natural diversity that reflects optimal community composition: approximately 35% Electric constitution (Vata), 40% Magnetic constitution (Kapha), and 25% Neutral constitution (Pitta), with significant variation between bioregions based on cultural history and environmental conditions.

The global economy has eliminated both poverty and excessive accumulation through constitutional approaches to production and distribution that honor individual differences while serving collective needs.

Work organization based on constitutional strengths has achieved productivity levels that exceed previous industrial systems while requiring average working time of 36 hours per week. People contribute according to their constitutional gifts and receive according to their constitutional needs, creating abundance that serves everyone while maintaining individual motivation and creativity.

Resource distribution through bioregional coordination and global cooperation networks has eliminated artificial scarcity while maintaining environmental sustainability and cultural diversity. Communities produce what they can most effectively create and share with bioregions that provide different resources and innovations.

Most significantly, economic relationships have become integrated with social and spiritual development rather than separate from them. Work serves community development, individual fulfillment, and environmental enhancement simultaneously, creating the integration of productive activity with authentic community that previous generations could only imagine.

Sacred Synthesis communities have achieved ecological regeneration and environmental enhancement through constitutional approaches to human-nature relationships that honor both individual authenticity and natural systems.

Electric constitution communities specialize in adaptive environmental innovations, creative solutions to ecological challenges, and cultural practices that celebrate human-nature relationship and artistic expression of environmental beauty.

Magnetic constitution settlements anchor long-term ecological restoration, sustainable agricultural production, and traditional knowledge preservation that maintains healthy relationship between human communities and natural ecosystems over multiple generations.

Neutral constitution organizations coordinate environmental monitoring, systematic resource management, and analytical assessment of ecological health that optimizes human community and natural systems integration.
The results exceed every expectation of environmental movement goals: atmospheric carbon levels decreasing toward pre-industrial concentrations, biodiversity increasing through habitat restoration and species reintroduction, soil health improving through regenerative agriculture, water systems purifying through ecological restoration and pollution elimination.

Most importantly, human communities have become contributors to rather than destructors of ecological health, creating the integration of civilization and nature that indigenous wisdom traditions maintained for millennia.
Constitutional medicine and community health approaches have achieved virtual elimination of chronic disease and mental health disorders through prevention, community support, and constitutional wellness rather than pharmaceutical management of symptoms.

Average human life expectancy has increased to 97 years with dramatic improvements in health quality throughout the lifespan.
Childhood development proceeds without the anxiety, depression, and behavioral problems that characterized previous generations.
Adults maintain vitality, creativity, and community contribution

throughout their lives. Aging occurs as natural life transition supported by community wisdom and intergenerational relationships.

Mental health problems have been virtually eliminated through authentic community relationships, constitutional understanding, and meaningful contribution that provide the psychological foundation for human flourishing. Addiction, violence, and antisocial behavior have become so rare as to represent medical rather than social problems.

Healthcare has evolved from illness management to community wellness support, with medical professionals serving as teachers, consultants, and coordinators for community health rather than authorities controlling access to healing resources.

Most significantly, health has become understood as community rather than individual achievement, with constitutional wellness, authentic relationships, and meaningful contribution creating conditions where human beings naturally thrive physically, mentally, and spiritually.

Democratic learning communities have demonstrated human educational potential when learning occurs within authentic community relationships that honor constitutional diversity and develop full human capacity.

Children in Sacred Synthesis communities achieve literacy by age 5, demonstrate advanced analytical and creative capacities by age 10, participate meaningfully in community governance by age 12, and take significant leadership responsibilities by age 16. These achievements occur without competitive pressure, standardized testing, or authoritarian classroom control.

Adult learning has become continuous and integrated with community contribution, with people developing new capacities throughout their lives based on constitutional interests, community needs, and personal growth rather than economic pressure or institutional requirements.

Knowledge development has become collaborative rather than competitive, with innovations and discoveries shared freely through global networks rather than hoarded for individual or institutional advantage.

Most importantly, education has become preparation for authentic community citizenship and meaningful contribution rather than training for employment within hierarchical institutions, creating the integration of learning and living that supports lifelong development.

Democratic governance structures have proven that authentic democracy is not only possible at global scale, but superior to authoritarian alternatives for addressing complex challenges and coordinating collective action.
Local community governance through constitutional assessment and consensus processes achieves efficiency and satisfaction levels that exceed previous democratic and authoritarian systems. People participate meaningfully in decisions affecting their lives while maintaining collective effectiveness and individual autonomy.

Bioregional coordination through democratic networks enables resource sharing, cultural exchange, and mutual aid between diverse communities while respecting local autonomy and cultural differences.

Global cooperation through the Planetary Coordination Council facilitates communication, innovation sharing, and collective response to planetary challenges while maintaining bioregional diversity and community self-determination.

Conflict resolution through constitutional understanding and authentic community mediation has virtually eliminated violence between communities, bioregions, and cultural groups. Differences are addressed through dialogue, creative problem-solving, and win-win solutions that honor all perspectives.

Most importantly, governance has become service to collective well-being rather than exercise of power over others, creating leadership that emerges from constitutional gifts and community recognition rather than competition and domination.

Sacred Synthesis civilization has achieved unprecedented cultural flowering through constitutional diversity, democratic participation, and authentic community relationships that support both individual creativity and collective cultural development.

Artistic expression has flourished as people develop creative capacities based on constitutional strengths and community appreciation rather than market competition and commercial exploitation. Every community produces music, visual arts, literature, and cultural celebrations that reflect both individual authenticity and collective cultural values.

Cultural preservation has been enhanced through bioregional networks that maintain traditional knowledge, languages, and practices while integrating beneficial innovations and global cooperation. Indigenous wisdom traditions have been revitalized and integrated with contemporary understanding in ways that serve both cultural continuity and adaptive development.

Spiritual development has been supported through community relationships and constitutional understanding that honor both individual spiritual journey and collective spiritual evolution. Traditional religious practices have been integrated with Sacred Synthesis principles in ways that enhance both personal spiritual development and community spiritual life.

Most importantly, culture has become living expression of community values and individual authenticity rather than entertainment commodity, creating cultural development that serves human flourishing and authentic community rather than profit extraction and social control.

Research and technological development have flourished within community contexts that prioritize human flourishing and environmental enhancement rather than profit maximization and social control.

Scientific research has become collaborative international endeavor focused on understanding and supporting constitutional wellness, community health, ecological restoration, and sustainable abundance rather than developing technologies for competitive advantage or population control.

Technological innovation has been guided by constitutional principles and community needs, creating tools that enhance rather than replace human capacities, support rather than dominate natural systems, and serve community flourishing rather than individual accumulation.

Information systems have been designed to support authentic community communication and democratic governance rather than surveillance and social control, creating global networks that enhance local autonomy and cultural diversity rather than threatening them.

Most importantly, science and technology have been integrated with community wisdom and constitutional understanding rather than separated from them, creating innovation that serves authentic community development and environmental enhancement.

The Planetary Coordination Council represents the achievement of global cooperation without world government, international collaboration without cultural homogenization, and planetary consciousness without local disconnection.

Bioregional diversity has been maintained and enhanced through networks that celebrate constitutional and cultural differences while facilitating mutual aid, resource sharing, and innovation exchange. No single model or approach has been imposed globally, but constitutional principles and democratic values have created foundation for cooperation across all differences.

Environmental coordination has enabled planetary ecological restoration through local community action and bioregional cooperation rather than international institutional control. Climate restoration, biodiversity enhancement, and ecological regeneration have been achieved through millions of community initiatives coordinated through voluntary networks.

Cultural exchange has enriched all communities through voluntary sharing of innovations, artistic expressions, and wisdom traditions rather than cultural imperialism or forced homogenization. Global consciousness has been developed through appreciation of diversity rather than elimination of differences.

Most importantly, planetary coordination has been achieved through constitutional understanding and authentic community rather than institutional authority, creating global cooperation that enhances rather than threatens local autonomy and cultural authenticity.

[This section was compiled from writings Marcus completed during his final months in cognitive rehabilitation, discovered after his death in 2051 and preserved by the Sacred Synthesis Archives.]

If you are reading this, then the knowledge I discovered and the communities we built have survived the attempts to destroy them. I am writing this during my fourth year in cognitive rehabilitation, knowing that I may not live to see the transformation we envisioned, but also knowing that the Sacred Synthesis has become larger than any individual life or sacrifice.

I never imagined when I found those corrupted files in 2045 that we would discover not just wellness practices or community organization techniques, but a complete blueprint for human civilization that honored our deepest nature while serving our highest potential.

I never imagined that constitutional assessment would reveal the diversity that makes human communities resilient and creative. I never imagined that democratic governance would prove more efficient than authoritarian control. I never imagined that authentic community would create security that no military force could provide.

Most of all, I never imagined that human beings were capable of the cooperation, creativity, and compassion that Sacred Synthesis communities have demonstrated worldwide.

If this civilization has indeed emerged, then my contribution was simply discovering what was always true about human nature: we are designed for constitutional diversity, democratic participation, and authentic community. We thrive when we honor rather than suppress these capacities. We create abundance when we cooperate rather than compete. We find security through community rather than domination.

The Sacred Synthesis was never about imposing new systems or revolutionary change. It was about remembering who we really are and creating conditions where our authentic nature can flourish.

Thank you for continuing the work. Thank you for proving that the sacrifices were worthwhile. Thank you for becoming the human beings we dreamed you could become.

The synthesis is complete not when everyone practices identical approaches, but when human civilization is organized around principles that honor constitutional diversity, support democratic participation, and serve authentic community.

You have achieved what previous generations could only dream: a world where every person can develop their full potential while contributing to collective flourishing, where communities can maintain cultural authenticity while participating in global cooperation, and

516

where human civilization enhances rather than degrades the natural world that sustains us.

Live well. Love deeply. Serve authentically. And remember that the most important revolution is the one that happens in every human heart that chooses cooperation over competition, community over isolation, and service over selfishness.

As we complete this chronicle in December 2080, thirty-five years after Marcus Chen's discovery, we recognize that we have documented not just the emergence of Sacred Synthesis civilization, but the fulfillment of human potential that becomes possible when society is organized around constitutional diversity, authentic democracy, and genuine community.

The Sacred Synthesis Chronicles began as testimony of resistance to authoritarian oppression. They have become documentation of the achievement of authentic human civilization.

We have proven that human beings are capable of cooperation, creativity, and compassion that exceeds our most optimistic expectations. We have demonstrated that constitutional diversity strengthens rather than threatens community unity. We have shown that democratic governance serves collective needs more effectively than authoritarian control. We have created abundance through mutual aid rather than competition. Most importantly, we have become living proof that authentic community is not only possible, but natural when human beings are free to organize society around principles that honor rather than suppress our deepest nature. The resistance is complete because the alternative has become irresistible.

The chronicles end because the synthesis is fulfilled.

The future begins because the foundation is established.

For those who will read these chronicles in generations to come, remember: you are the inheritors of sacrifices made by people who chose transformation over security, community over isolation, and service over selfishness. Honor their legacy by continuing to create the world that serves the deepest needs and highest potential of all beings.

The Sacred Synthesis is not a system to be preserved unchanged, but a foundation for continued evolution of human consciousness and civilization. Build upon what we have achieved. Improve what we have created.

Discover what we could not imagine.

The chronicles are complete.

The synthesis endures. The future is yours.

The Planetary Coordination Council represents 2.3 billion people living in 127,000 autonomous communities worldwide, all practicing constitutional governance and authentic community relationships based on Sacred Synthesis principles. The Council facilitates global cooperation while maintaining bioregional diversity and local autonomy. This final chapter was written collaboratively by representatives from every bioregion, using constitutional diversity principles and democratic processes that honored all perspectives while creating unified documentation of humanity's greatest achievement.

For future generations reading these chronicles: you inherit a world where constitutional wellness, authentic democracy, and genuine community are the foundation of human civilization. Honor this inheritance by continuing to discover and express the full potential of human consciousness and cooperation. The Sacred Synthesis is your starting point, not your destination.

The Practical Realization

In deep rubble I found a large cache of practical materials for the system that these people had been following until their disappearance.

Daily Practice Tracking Journal Template
Essential Downloadable Resource #2 - PDF Template

Sacred Synthesis Daily Practice Journal
Month/Year: _____ Constitutional
Type: _____

Daily Practice Record

Date: _____ Day of Week: _____
Season: _____

Morning Assessment
Time Started: _____ Energy Level (1-10): _____
Mood: _____
Physical Condition: _____
Mental State: _____

Constitutional Adaptation Notes
Environment: Temperature _____°F, Lighting
_____, Noise Level _____
Props Used: _____
Modifications Made: _____

Practice Session Record

Foundation Exercises (1-7) - Duration: _____
minutes
Exercise 1 - Tibetan Stand: Hold time _____ sec,
Quality (1-10) _____
Notes: _____

Exercise 2 - Pendulum: Duration _____ min,
Range of motion _____
Notes: _____

Exercise 3 - Side Stretch: Hold time each side _____ sec, Depth _____
Notes: _____

Exercise 4 - Backward Bend: Hold time _____
sec, Heart opening quality _____
Notes: _____

Exercise 5 - Forward Bend: Hold time _____ sec,
Introspective quality _____
Notes: _____

Exercise 6 - Twist: Hold time each side _____
sec, Spinal mobility _____
Notes: _____

Exercise 7 - Triangle: Hold time each side _____
sec, Integration quality _____
Notes: _____

Intermediate Exercises (8-15) - Duration: _____
minutes
Exercise 8 - Tortoise: Hold time _____ min,
Introspective depth _____
Notes: _____

Exercise 9 - Cobra: Hold time _____ sec,

Heart opening quality _____

Notes: _____

Exercise 10 - Locust: Hold time _____ sec,

Strength building _____

Notes: _____

Additional Intermediate Work: _____

Advanced Work (if applicable) –

Duration: _____ minutes

Exercises Practiced: _____

Quality and Notes: _____

Breathing Practice Record

Integration Breath (4-4-6-2): Duration _____

min, Quality (1-10) _____

Constitutional Breathing: Type _____,

Duration _____

min

Advanced Pranayama: Type _____,

Duration _____ min

Breathing Notes: _____

Energy Circulation and Meditation

Energy Awareness: _____

Chakra Focus: _____

Meditation Duration: _____ min,

Quality: _____

Spiritual Insights: _____

Integration and Completion

Total Practice Time: _____ minutes

Overall Practice Quality (1-10): _____

Physical Effects Noted: _____

Mental/Emotional Effects: _____

Energy Level After Practice (1-10): _____

Constitutional Tracking

Electric Constitution Daily Tracking

Nervous System State: Calm/Agitated/Scattered/Grounded (circle one)

Grounding Quality: Excellent/Good/Fair/Poor (circle one)

Temperature Comfort: Too Cold/Perfect/Too Warm (circle one)

Stimulation Level: Under/Perfect/Over-stimulated (circle one)

Magnetic Constitution Daily Tracking
Energy Activation: High/Moderate/Low/Sluggish (circle one)
Motivation Level: High/Good/Moderate/Low (circle one)
Temperature Comfort: Too Cool/Perfect/Too Warm (circle one)
Challenge Level: Too Easy/Perfect/Too Hard (circle one)

Neutral Constitution Daily Tracking
Temperature Balance: Too Cool/Perfect/Too Warm (circle one)
Intensity Level: Too Low/Perfect/Too High (circle one)
Technical Focus: Excellent/Good/Fair/Poor (circle one)
Precision Quality: High/Moderate/Low (circle one)

Life Integration Notes
Work/Professional Integration:
Relationship Applications:
Community Service:
Environmental Awareness:

Challenges and Insights
Physical Challenges:
Mental/Emotional Challenges:
Breakthroughs or Insights:
Questions for Teacher/Community:

Planning and Intentions
Tomorrow's Practice Intention:
Areas for Focus:
Adaptations Needed:

Weekly Review Section
Week of: _____
Overall Assessment: _____
Weekly Patterns Noticed
Energy Trends:
Constitutional Balance:
Practice Consistency:
Quality Improvements:

Weekly Challenges
Recurring Difficulties:
Seasonal Adaptations Needed:
Environmental Factors:

Weekly Achievements

New Skills Developed:
Constitutional Understanding:
Integration Successes:

Weekly Planning
Next Week's Focus:
Constitutional Adaptations:
Community Engagement:

Monthly Integration Review

Month: _____
Constitutional Development: _____

Monthly Progress Assessment
Foundation Exercise Mastery:
Intermediate Exercise Development:
Constitutional Adaptation Refinement:
Breathing and Energy Work Progress:

Monthly Challenges and Solutions
Recurring Patterns:
Seasonal Transition Adaptations:
Professional Integration Development:
Community Involvement Growth:

Monthly Insights and Transformations
Physical Development:
Mental/Emotional Growth:
Spiritual Deepening:
Service and Community Contribution:

Next Month's Intentions
Practice Development Goals:
Constitutional Refinement Focus:
Community Engagement Plans:
Professional Integration Applications:

Constitutional-Specific Tracking Pages
Electric Constitution Focus Areas
Daily Grounding Assessment
Morning Grounding (1-10): _____
Evening Grounding (1-10): _____
Grounding Techniques Used:
Environmental Support Effectiveness:

Nervous System Regulation Tracking
Pre-Practice Anxiety (1-10): _____
Post-Practice Calm (1-10): _____
Breath Pattern Quality:
Sleep Quality:

Stability and Routine Development
Practice Consistency:
Routine Adherence:
Prop Usage Effectiveness:
Temperature/Environment Optimization:
Magnetic Constitution Focus Areas
Daily Activation Assessment
Morning Energy (1-10): _____
Evening Energy (1-10): _____
Activation Techniques Used:
Challenge Level Appropriateness:

Motivation and Engagement Tracking
Pre-Practice Motivation (1-10): _____
Challenge Satisfaction (1-10): _____
Variety and Interest Level:
Goal Achievement Progress:

Circulation and Metabolism Enhancement
Internal Heat Generation:
Circulation Quality:
Metabolic Response:
Dynamic Movement Integration:
Neutral Constitution Focus Areas
Daily Balance Assessment
Morning Temperature Balance (1-10): _____
Evening Balance (1-10): _____
Precision and Technical Quality:
Seasonal Adaptation Effectiveness:

Intensity and Cooling Regulation
Practice Intensity Appropriateness:
Overheating Prevention Success:
Cooling Integration Quality:
Temperature-Appropriate Modifications:

Technical Excellence Development
Alignment Precision:

Form Quality Focus:
Efficiency and Effectiveness:
Teaching and Analysis Capacity:

Seasonal Adaptation Tracking
Spring Development (March-May)
Constitutional Spring Needs:
Detoxification Support:
Energy Renewal Patterns:

Summer Adaptation (June-August)
Cooling Strategy Effectiveness:
Heat Management Success:
Early Morning Practice Adaptation:

Autumn Preparation (September-November)
Grounding and Preparation:
Harvest and Integration:
Winter Preparation Activities:

Winter Integration (December-February)
Warmth and Comfort Maintenance:
Indoor Practice Optimization:
Community and Service Focus:

Community and Service Tracking
Weekly Community Engagement
Group Practice Participation:
Community Service Hours:
Teaching or Mentoring Activities:

Monthly Service Integration
Professional Application Development:
Community Healing Contribution:
Environmental Action Participation:

Global Awareness and Action
Cultural Sensitivity Development:
International Cooperation Activities:
Peacebuilding and Bridge-Building Efforts:

This daily practice journal provides comprehensive tracking for constitutional development while maintaining connection to community service and global welfare. Use consistently for optimal development and community contribution.

524

Monthly Development Assessment Tool
Essential Downloadable Resource #3 - Digital Form

Sacred Synthesis Monthly Progress Assessment
Month/Year: _____ Constitutional
Type: _____
Assessment Date: _____ Practitioner
Name: _____

Section I: Foundation Exercise Development

Exercise Mastery Assessment (Rate 1-5: 1=Beginner, 2=Developing, 3=Competent, 4=Proficient, 5=Master)

Exercise 1 - Tibetan Stand: Current Level _____/5
- Holding time achieved: _____ minutes
- Constitutional adaptation integrated: Yes/No
- Grounding and stability quality: _____/5
- Teaching readiness: _____/5
- Areas for improvement:

Exercise 2 - Pendulum: Current Level _____/5
- Range of motion achieved: Full/Moderate/Limited
- Spinal articulation quality: _____/5
- Constitutional breathing integration: _____/5
- Areas for improvement:

Exercise 3 - Side Stretch: Current Level _____/5
- Holding time each side: _____ seconds
- Balance and stability: _____/5
- Lateral opening quality: _____/5
- Areas for improvement:

Exercise 4 - Backward Bend: Current Level _____/5
- Heart opening quality: _____/5
- Spinal safety and control: _____/5
- Emotional integration capacity: _____/5
- Areas for improvement:

Exercise 5 - Forward Bend: Current Level _____/5
- Hip flexibility development: _____/5
- Introspective quality cultivation: _____/5
- Nervous system calming effect: _____/5
- Areas for improvement:

Exercise 6 - Twist: Current Level _____/5
- Spinal rotation range: _____/5
- Detoxification awareness: _____/5
- Bilateral balance: _____/5
- Areas for improvement:

Exercise 7 - Triangle: Current Level _____/5
- Strength and flexibility integration: _____/5
- Balance and coordination: _____/5
- Confidence in complex positioning: _____/5
- Areas for improvement:

Foundation Exercise Overall Assessment: _____/35
Readiness for Intermediate Development: Ready/Nearly
Ready/Needs More Foundation

Section II: Intermediate Exercise Progress

Intermediate Exercise Assessment (Complete only if practicing
intermediate exercises)

Exercise 8 - Tortoise: Current Level _____/5
- Maximum comfortable hold time: _____ minutes
- Introspective depth achieved: _____/5
- Constitutional adaptation mastery: _____/5
- Progress notes:

Exercise 9 - Cobra: Current Level _____/5
- Heart opening integration: _____/5
- Spinal strengthening effectiveness: _____/5
- Confidence building impact: _____/5
- Progress notes:

Exercise 10 - Locust: Current Level _____/5
- Posterior chain strength development: _____/5
- Holding time achieved: _____ seconds
- Constitutional challenge appropriate: _____/5
- Progress notes:

Exercise 11 - Bow: Current Level _____/5 (if appli-
cable)
- Spinal integration quality: _____/5
- Heart opening depth: _____/5
- Safety and control: _____/5

- Progress notes:
Exercise 12 - Shoulder Stand: Current Level

_____
/5 (if applicable)
- Maximum safe hold time: _____ minutes
- Circulatory benefits experienced: _____/5
- Constitutional adaptation integrated: _____/5
- Progress notes: _____
Additional Intermediate Exercises Practiced:
Overall Intermediate Assessment: _____ Notes:

Section III: Constitutional Development Assessment
Constitutional Type Integration
Electric Constitution Development (Complete if Electric type)

Grounding and Stability Development:
- Daily grounding quality (1-10): Current month average _____
- Improvement from last month: Signifi-cant/Moderate/Minimal/None
- Nervous system regulation effectiveness: _____/5
- Grounding strategies most effective:

Environmental Adaptation Mastery:
- Temperature regulation success: _____/5
- Noise and stimulation management: _____/5
- Prop usage optimization: /5
____
- Environmental insights:
_____

Practice Consistency and Routine:
- Daily practice consistency this month: _____%
- Routine adaptation to energy fluctuations: _____/5
- Long-term sustainability development: _____/5
- Consistency strategies:
Magnetic Constitution Development (Complete if Magnetic type)
Activation and Challenge Integration:
- Daily energy activation quality (1-10): Current month average
- Challenge level appropriateness: _____/5
- Motivation maintenance effectiveness: _____/5
- Activation strategies most effective:

Dynamic Practice Development:
- Movement flow integration: _____/5

- Variety and interest maintenance: _____/5
- Goal achievement progress: /5
____
- Dynamic practice insights:

_____

Circulation and Metabolic Enhancement:
- Internal heat generation capacity: _____/5
- Circulation quality improvement: _____/5
- Metabolic activation effectiveness: _____/5
- Circulation strategies:
Neutral Constitution Development (Complete if Neutral type)
Balance and Precision Development:
- Daily temperature balance quality (1-10):
- Current month average
- Technical precision improvement: _____/5
- Form and alignment mastery: _____/5
- Balance strategies most effective:

Seasonal Adaptation Mastery:
- Current season adaptation success: _____/5
- Cooling/warming strategy effectiveness: _____/5
- Environmental sensitivity management: _____/5
- Seasonal insights:

Technical Excellence Development:
- Alignment precision focus: _____/5
- Teaching and analysis capacity: _____/5
- Efficiency and effectiveness: _____/5
- Technical development insights:

Section IV: Breathing and Energy Development
Pranayama Practice Assessment
Integration Breath (4-4-6-2) Mastery:
- Comfort with basic pattern: _____/5
- Duration capacity: _____ minutes maximum
- Constitutional adaptation integrated: Yes/No
- Breathing development notes:

Constitutional Breathing Development:
- Specific constitutional pattern mastery: _____/5
- Daily integration success: _____/5
- Therapeutic application understanding: _____/5
- Constitutional breathing insights:

Advanced Pranayama (if applicable):
- Advanced techniques practiced:
- Safety and preparation adequacy: _____/5
- Community supervision integration: _____/5
- Advanced practice notes:

Energy Circulation and Awareness

Chakra System Awareness:
- Energy center identification capacity: _____/5
- Constitutional energy pattern understanding: _____/5
- Integration with physical practice: _____/5
- Energy awareness insights:
Subtle Body Development:
- Energy sensitivity development: _____/5
- Circulation awareness improvement: _____/5
- Integration with daily life: _____/5
- Subtle body insights:

Section V: Life Integration and Service Development
Professional Integration Assessment
Workplace Application:
- Stress management application: _____/5
- Constitutional awareness in work environment:
  _____/5
- Professional boundary maintenance: /5
  ____

- Professional integration successes:
  _____

Healthcare Integration:
- Communication with healthcare providers: _____/5
- Integration with medical treatments: _____/5
- Constitutional health optimization: _____/5
- Healthcare integration notes:

Family and Relationship Integration
Family Practice Development:
- Family member practice integration: _____/5
- Constitutional compatibility understanding: _____/5
- Conflict resolution skill application: _____/5
- Family integration insights:

Relationship Enhancement:
- Communication skill improvement: _____/5
- Constitutional understanding application: _____/5

- Service orientation development: _____/5
- Relationship development notes:

Community and Service Development

Community Engagement:
- Group practice participation: _____ hours this month
- Community service contribution: _____ hours this month
- Teaching or mentoring activities:
- Community engagement quality: _____/5

Global Awareness and Action:
- Environmental consciousness application: _____/5
- Cultural sensitivity development: _____/5
- Peace-building activity participation: _____/5
- Global awareness insights:

Section VI: Challenge Assessment and Growth Planning
Current Challenges Identification
Physical Development Challenges:
1.
2.
3.
Priority level: High/Moderate/Low for each

Constitutional Integration Challenges:
1.
2.
3.
Priority level: High/Moderate/Low for each

Life Integration Challenges:
1.
2.
3.
Priority level: High/Moderate/Low for each ### Growth Areas and Development Plans
Next Month's Primary Development Focus (Choose 1-3 areas):
• Foundation exercise refinement
• Intermediate exercise development
• Constitutional adaptation deepening
• Breathing and energy work advancement
• Professional integration enhancement
• Family and relationship development

- Community service expansion
- Teaching and mentoring preparation

Specific Monthly Goals:
1. Physical Development Goal:
Action steps:
Success metrics:

2. Constitutional Integration Goal:
Action steps:
Success metrics:

3. Service Development Goal:
Action steps:
Success metrics:

Resource and Support Needs

Learning Resources Needed:
- Additional video instruction
- Community workshop attendance
- Advanced book study
- Professional consultation
- Medical clearance or support
- Environmental modifications
- Equipment or props
- Other:

Community Support Needed:
- Practice partner or accountability
- Group practice participation
- Teaching supervision
- Professional mentoring
- Family practice guidance
- Cultural sensitivity consultation
- Conflict resolution support
- Other:

Section VII: Holistic Development Assessment
Overall Progress Summary
Monthly Development Rating (1-10):
Most Significant Achievement This Month:

_____

Most Important Insight Gained:
Greatest Challenge Overcome:

Integration and Wisdom Development

Mind-Body Integration Quality: _____/5
Individual-Community Balance: _____/5
Personal Development-Service Balance: _____/5
Traditional Authenticity-Contemporary Application Balance:
_____/5
Future Development Pathway
Current Development Stage (check one):
* Foundation Building (Months 1-12)
* Constitutional Integration (Year 2)
* Advanced Development (Years 3-5)
* Teaching Preparation (Years 5-7)
* Community Leadership (Years 7+)
* Elder Wisdom Development (Years 15+)

Projected Timeline for Next Development Stage:
Preparation Needed for Advancement:
Annual Assessment Integration (Complete at year-end)

Year-End Overall Development Rating (1-10):
Greatest Annual Achievement:
Most Significant Challenge Overcome:
Service Contribution This Year:
Next Year's Primary Intention:

Assessment Completion and Next Steps

Assessment Completed By:
Date Completed:
Community Review Scheduled:
Next Month's Assessment Due:

Assessment Results Shared With (check all that apply):
* Practice partner/accountability partner
* Community teacher/mentor
* Family members involved in practice
* Healthcare providers (if relevant)
* Professional colleagues (if applicable)
* Personal records only

Follow-up Actions Required:
1.
2.

3.

This monthly assessment provides comprehensive tracking of development across all dimensions of the Sacred Synthesis system while maintaining connection to community service and authentic traditional transmission. Complete honestly and use for continuous refinement of practice and service capacity.

Health and Wellness Tracking System - Constitutional Health Metrics

Essential Downloadable Resource #7 - Constitutional Health Metrics

Sacred Synthesis Health and Wellness Tracking System
Constitutional Health Optimization and Biomarker Monitoring

Practitioner Name: _____ Constitutional Type: _____
Healthcare Provider: _____ Tracking Period: _____
Assessment Date: _____ Next Review Date: _____

Section I: Constitutional Health Baseline Assessment
Physical Health Constitutional Indicators
Electric Constitution (Vata) Health Metrics
Nervous System Function Assessment:
- Resting heart rate: _____ bpm (Target: 60-80 bpm)
- Heart rate variability: High/Moderate/Low (Target: High)
- Sleep quality score (1-10): _____ (Target: 7-9)
- Average sleep duration: _____ hours (Target: 7-9 hours)
- Sleep onset time: _____ minutes (Target: <20 minutes)

Digestive Function Indicators:
- Bowel movement regularity: Daily/Every 2 days/Irregular (Target: Daily)
- Digestive comfort level (1-10): _____ (Target: 7-10)
- Appetite consistency: Regular/Irregular/Forgotten meals (Target: Regular)
- Bloating/gas frequency: Daily/Weekly/Rare/Never (Target: Rare/Never)
- Food sensitivities identified:

Energy and Stability Markers:
- Morning energy level (1-10): _____ (Target: 6-8)
- Afternoon energy stability (1-10): _____ (Target: 6-8)
- Energy crash frequency: Daily/Weekly/Rarely/Never (Target: Rarely/Never)
- Physical coordination assessment (1-10): _____ (Target: 7-10)
- Balance and stability (1-10): _____ (Target: 7-10)

Stress Response and Adaptation:
- Anxiety frequency: Daily/Weekly/Monthly/Rarely (Target: Rarely)
- Stress recovery time: <1 hour/2-4 hours/>4 hours (Target: <1 hour)
- Overwhelm threshold: Low/Moderate/High (Target: High)
    - Environmental sensitivity: High/Moderate/Low (Target: Moderate)

Magnetic Constitution (Kapha) Health Metrics
Metabolic Function Assessment:
- Resting metabolic rate indicators: High/Moderate/Low (Target: Moderate-High)
- Morning body temperature: _____°F (Target: 98.2-98.6°F)
- Weight stability: Stable/Gaining/Losing (Target: Stable)
- Body composition: Muscle _____% Fat _____% (Target: Balanced)
- Circulation quality (1-10): _____ (Target: 7-10)

Respiratory and Cardiovascular Health:
- Lung capacity assessment (spirometry if available): _____ ml
- Cardiovascular endurance (1-10): _____ (Target: 7-10)
- Blood pressure: _____/_____mmHg (Target: 110-130/70-85)
- Exercise recovery heart rate: _____ bpm after 2 min (Target: <100)
- Cold tolerance: High/Moderate/Low (Target: High)

Energy and Motivation Markers:
- Morning motivation level (1-10): _____ (Target: 7-10)
- Sustained activity capacity (hours): _____ (Target: 6-8)
- Lethargy frequency: Daily/Weekly/Monthly/Rarely (Target: Rarely)
- Initiative and self-motivation (1-10): _____ (Target: 7-10)
- Seasonal energy variation: High/Moderate/Low (Target: Low)

Fluid Balance and Elimination:
- Water retention tendency: High/Moderate/Low (Target: Low)
- Morning stiffness duration: _____ minutes (Target: <15 minutes)
- Lymphatic circulation (1-10): _____ (Target: 7-10)

- Mucus production: High/Moderate/Low (Target: Low-Moderate)

Neutral Constitution (Pitta) Health Metrics
Temperature Regulation and Inflammatory Response:
- Body temperature regulation (1-10): _____ (Target: 8-10)
- Heat tolerance: High/Moderate/Low (Target: Moderate-Low)
- Inflammatory markers (CRP if available): _____ mg/L (Target: <1.0)
- Skin condition: Excellent/Good/Fair/Concerning (Target: Excellent/Good)
- Eye clarity and brightness (1-10): _____ (Target: 8-10)
Digestive Fire and Metabolism:
- Digestive strength (1-10): _____ (Target: 8-10)
- Appetite intensity: Strong/Moderate/Weak (Target: Strong-Moderate)
- Meal timing regularity: Very regular/Regular/Irregular (Target: Very regular)
- Hyperacidity frequency: Daily/Weekly/Monthly/Never (Target: Monthly/Never)
- Liver function indicators: Normal/Elevated/Concerning (Target: Normal)

Mental Clarity and Focus:
- Mental sharpness (1-10): _____ (Target: 8-10)
- Decision-making clarity (1-10): _____ (Target: 8-10)
- Concentration duration: _____ hours sustained (Target: 3-4 hours)
- Memory function (1-10): _____ (Target: 8-10)
- Irritability frequency: Daily/Weekly/Monthly/Rarely (Target: Monthly/Rarely)

Performance and Efficiency:
- Work/task completion efficiency (1-10): _____ (Target: 8-10)
- Goal achievement consistency (1-10): _____ (Target: 8-10)

- Perfectionism vs. completion balance (1-10): _____
  (Target: 7-9)
- Heat-related fatigue: High/Moderate/Low (Target: Low)

Section II: Laboratory and Biomarker Tracking
Essential Constitutional Laboratory Markers
Basic Health Panel (All Constitutional Types)

Complete Blood Count (CBC):
- Red blood cell count: _____ (Normal range: 4.2-5.9
  million/mcL)
- White blood cell count: _____ (Normal range: 4,500-
  11,000/mcL)
- Hemoglobin: _____ g/dL (Normal range: 12-17 g/dL)
- Hematocrit: _____% (Normal range: 36-50%)
- Platelet count: _____ (Normal range: 150,000-
  450,000/mcL)

Comprehensive Metabolic Panel (CMP):
- Glucose (fasting): _____ mg/dL (Target: 70-99 mg/dL)
- Creatinine: _____ mg/dL (Normal range: 0.6-1.4 mg/dL)
- Blood urea nitrogen (BUN): _____ mg/dL (Normal
  range: 7-25 mg/dL)
- Electrolytes: Sodium _____ Potassium _____ Chlo-
  ride _ CO_2 _____
- Liver enzymes: ALT _____ AST _____ (Normal
  range: <40 U/L)
  Lipid Profile:
- Total cholesterol: _____ mg/dL (Target: <200 mg/dL)
- LDL cholesterol: _____ mg/dL (Target: <100 mg/dL)
- HDL cholesterol: _____ mg/dL (Target: >40 men, >50
  women mg/dL)
- Triglycerides: _____ mg/dL (Target: <150 mg/dL)
  -    Cholesterol/HDL ratio: _____ (Target: <4.0) ####
  Constitutional-Specific Markers
  Electric Constitution Priority Markers:
- Vitamin D: _____ ng/mL (Target: 30-80 ng/mL)
- Vitamin B12: _____ pg/mL (Target: 300-900 pg/mL)
- Magnesium: _____ mg/dL (Target: 1.7-2.2 mg/dL)
- Cortisol (morning): _____ µg/dL (Normal: 10-20
  µg/dL)
- Thyroid function: TSH _____ T3 _____ T4 _____
  (Within normal ranges)

Magnetic Constitution Priority Markers:

536

- Thyroid panel: TSH _____ Free T3 _____ Free T4 _____
- (Optimal function)
- Iron studies: Iron _____ TIBC _____ Ferritin _____
  (Adequate stores)
- Vitamin D: _____ ng/mL (Target: 40-60 ng/mL)
- C-reactive protein: _____ mg/L (Target: <1.0 mg/L)
- Insulin: _____ µU/mL (Target: <10 µU/mL)
  Neutral Constitution Priority Markers:
- Liver function panel: ALT _____ AST _____ GGT _____
- Bilirubin _____
- Inflammatory markers: CRP _____ ESR _____ (Low
  normal ranges)
- Antioxidant status: Vitamin E _____ Vitamin C _____
  (Optimal levels)
- Homocysteine: _____ µmol/L (Target: <10 µmol/L)
- Uric acid: _____ mg/dL (Target: 3.0-7.0 mg/dL)

Advanced Constitutional Biomarkers (Optional/Annual)

Stress and Adaptation Markers:
- 24-hour cortisol rhythm: Morning _____ Noon _____
- Evening _____
- Night _____
- DHEA-S: _____ µg/dL (Age-appropriate ranges)
- Cortisol/DHEA ratio: _____ (Balanced)
- Salivary alpha-amylase: _____ U/mL (Stress response
  indicator)

Cardiovascular Risk Assessment:
- Advanced lipid particle analysis: LDL-P _____
  HDL-P _____
- Apolipoprotein B: _____ mg/dL (Target: <90 mg/dL)
- Lp(a): _____ mg/dL (Target: <30 mg/dL)
- Cardiac calcium score: _____ (If indicated by age/risk
  factors)

Metabolic Function Assessment:
- HbA1c: _____ % (Target: <5.7%)
- Fasting insulin: _____ µU/mL (Target: <10 µU/mL)
- HOMA-IR: _____ (Target: <2.5)
- Leptin: ng/mL (Constitutional appropriate levels)
  _____
- Adiponectin: µg/mL (Higher levels preferred)

Section III: Daily Constitutional Health Monitoring

Daily Tracking Metrics (Record Weekly Averages)
Week 1 Averages (Date: _____)
Sleep and Recovery Metrics:
- Average bedtime: _____ - Average wake time: _____
- Sleep quality rating (1-10): _____
- Morning energy level (1-10): _____
- Evening recovery level (1-10): _____

Energy and Vitality Tracking:
- Morning constitutional energy assessment (1-10): _____
- Midday energy stability (1-10): _____
- Afternoon energy maintenance (1-10): _____
- Evening energy for personal/family time (1-10): _____
Digestive Function Monitoring:
- Appetite consistency (1-10): _____
- Digestive comfort (1-10): _____
- Elimination regularity (1-10): _____
- Food satisfaction and nourishment feeling (1-10): _____
Mental/Emotional Balance:
- Stress resilience (1-10): _____
- Emotional stability (1-10): _____
- Mental clarity and focus (1-10): _____
- Joy and life satisfaction (1-10): _____

Constitutional-Specific Daily Metrics

Electric Constitution Daily Tracking:
- Grounding and stability feeling (1-10): _____
- Anxiety or scattered feeling (1-10, reverse scale): _____
- Environmental comfort level (1-10): _____
- Routine adherence success (1-10): _____

Magnetic Constitution Daily Tracking:
- Motivation and initiative level (1-10): _____
- Physical activity satisfaction (1-10): _____
- Internal warmth and circulation (1-10): _____
- Goal achievement progress (1-10): _____

Neutral Constitution Daily Tracking:
- Temperature regulation comfort (1-10): _____
- Work/task efficiency satisfaction (1-10): _____
- Precision and quality standards maintenance (1-10): _____
- Cooling and balance strategies effectiveness (1-10): _____

Section IV: Practice Integration Health Effects

Sacred Synthesis Practice Health Impact Assessment
Physical Practice Effects Monitoring
Foundation Exercise Impact (Rate improvement 1-10):
- Overall strength and flexibility: Baseline _____
Current _____
- Postural alignment and stability: Baseline _____
Current _____
- Balance and coordination: Baseline _____ Current _____
- Body awareness and proprioception: Baseline _____
Current _____
- Pain or discomfort resolution: Baseline _____ Current _

Breathing Practice Effects:
- Lung capacity and respiratory function: Baseline _____
- Current _____
- Stress response and nervous system regulation: Baseline _____
- Current _____
- Energy level and vitality: Baseline _____
- Current _____
- Sleep quality and recovery: Baseline _____
- Current _____
- Emotional regulation capacity: Baseline _____
- Current _____

Constitutional Adaptation Benefits:
- Individual constitutional balance optimization: Baseline _____
- Current _____
- Seasonal adaptation effectiveness: Baseline _____
Current _____
- Environmental stress resilience: Baseline _____
Current _____
- Professional performance enhancement: Baseline _____
- Current _____
- Relationship and communication improvement: Baseline _____
- Current _____

Healthcare Integration and Professional Collaboration

Healthcare Provider Communication:

- Regular health monitoring with constitutional awareness: _____/5
- Healthcare provider understanding of constitutional practice:
_____/5

- Integration of biomarker tracking with practice adaptation: _____/5
- Coordination of medical treatments with constitutional approach: _____/5

Preventive Health and Wellness Optimization:
- Preventive care enhancement through constitutional awareness: _____/5
- Early warning sign recognition through daily tracking: _____/5
- Constitutional adaptation for health condition management: _____/5
- Integration of constitutional approach with medical treatment: _____/5

Section V: Long-Term Health Development and Goal Setting
Annual Health Development Goals
Year-End Health Assessment Summary:
- Overall constitutional health improvement: _____/10
- Laboratory marker optimization achieved: _____/10
- Daily energy and vitality enhancement: _____/10
- Professional and life performance improvement: _____/10
-   Healthcare system integration success: _____/10

Next Year Health Development Priorities
Priority Health Goal 1:
- Specific constitutional focus:
- Target biomarkers or metrics:
- Practice modifications needed:
- Healthcare provider collaboration:
- Success measurement criteria:

Priority Health Goal 2:
- Specific constitutional focus:
- Target biomarkers or metrics:
- Practice modifications needed:
- Healthcare provider collaboration:
- Success measurement criteria:

Priority Health Goal 3:
- Specific constitutional focus:
- Target biomarkers or metrics:
- Practice modifications needed:
- Healthcare provider collaboration:
- Success measurement criteria:

Preventive Health and Longevity Planning

Five-Year Constitutional Health Vision:

Aging and Constitutional Adaptation Strategy:
- Constitutional type changes with aging:
- Practice modifications for life stage transitions:
- Healthcare integration for age-related changes:
- Community support for healthy aging:

Section VI: Emergency and Crisis Health Protocols
Constitutional Health Crisis Response
Constitutional Health Crisis Indicators:

Electric Constitution Crisis Signs:
- Severe anxiety or panic attacks lasting >30 minutes
- Insomnia for more than 3 consecutive nights
- Digestive shutdown or severe irregularity >5 days
- Extreme scattered thinking or decision-making paralysis
- Physical trembling or coordination loss

Magnetic Constitution Crisis Signs:
☐ Complete loss of motivation lasting >1 week
☐ Severe congestion or respiratory difficulties
☐ Weight gain >5 pounds in 1 week without dietary changes
☐ Extreme lethargy preventing basic daily activities
☐ Depression or withdrawal from all social contact

Neutral Constitution Crisis Signs:
☐ Inflammatory response with fever >102°F
☐ Severe digestive hyperacidity or ulceration symptoms
☐ Extreme irritability or anger outbursts
☐ Heat exhaustion or temperature regulation failure
☐ Perfectionist paralysis preventing all task completion

Crisis Response Protocols
Immediate Response Actions:
1. Constitutional Safety Protocol: Implement immediate constitutional balancing
2. Healthcare Provider Contact: Contact primary healthcare provider within 24 hours
3. Community Support Activation: Notify community support person/mentor
4. Practice Modification: Shift to crisis-appropriate constitutional practice

5. Environmental Optimization: Optimize environment for constitutional recovery

Crisis Recovery Integration:
- Post-crisis constitutional assessment and adaptation
- Healthcare provider consultation for underlying causes
- Community integration for prevention and support
- Practice modification for crisis prevention
- Long-term constitutional health strengthening plan

Assessment Completion Information:
Completed By:
Healthcare Provider Review:
Next Full Assessment Date:
Emergency Contact Information:

This constitutional health and wellness tracking system provides comprehensive monitoring of individual constitutional health optimization while integrating with healthcare providers and community support for holistic wellness development.

Community Readiness Assessment - Group Evaluation Tool

Essential Downloadable Resource #5 - Group Evaluation Tool

Sacred Synthesis Community Readiness Assessment
Group Practice and Leadership Development Evaluation
Community/Group Name: _____
Assessment Date: _____
Group Size: _____ Average Experience
Level: _____
Primary Meeting Location: _____
Assessment Facilitator: _____

Section I: Foundation Readiness Assessment
Group Composition and Constitutional Balance
Constitutional Type Distribution (approximate percentages):
- Electric Constitution (Vata): _____%
- Magnetic Constitution (Kapha): _____%
- Neutral Constitution (Pitta): _____%
- Unknown/Assessment needed: _____%

Experience Level Distribution:
- Foundation level (0-12 months): _____%
- Intermediate level (1-3 years): _____%

542

- Advanced level (3+ years): _____%
- Teacher/mentor level: _____%

Age and Life Stage Diversity:
- Young adults (18-30): _____%
- Established adults (30-50): _____%
- Mature adults (50-65): _____%
  - Elders (65+): _____%

Individual Readiness Factors

Personal Practice Consistency (rate for group overall):
- Daily personal practice established: _____/5
- Constitutional adaptation integrated: _____/5
- Foundation exercise competency: _____/5
- Breathing practice development: _____/5
- Service orientation demonstration: _____/5

Community Orientation Assessment:
- Commitment to group welfare over individual achievement: _____/5
- Willingness to adapt to group constitutional needs: _____/5
- Democratic participation and shared leadership capacity: _____/5
- Conflict resolution skills and patience: _____/5
- Cultural sensitivity and inclusivity: _____/5

Learning and Teaching Readiness:
- Openness to instruction and correction: _____/5
- Capacity to support beginners: _____/5
- Authentic spiritual motivation vs. ego motivation: _____/5
- Integration of practice with daily life and relationships: _____/5

Section II: Group Dynamics and Communication Assessment
Communication Patterns and Conflict Resolution
Group Communication Quality:
- Open, honest communication about challenges:
  _____/5
- Respectful disagreement and diverse opinion management: _____/5
- Active listening and empathetic understanding:
  _____/5
- Cultural sensitivity in communication: _____/5
- Constitutional awareness in group interaction: _____/5
Conflict Resolution Capacity:
- Constructive conflict engagement skills: _____/5
- Mediation and third-party support utilization: _____/5
- Forgiveness and repair capacity after conflict: _____/5

543

- Learning integration from group challenges: _____/5
- Prevention of future conflicts through wisdom development: _____/5

Decision-Making Processes:
- Democratic participation and consensus building: _____/5
- Leadership rotation and shared responsibility: _____/5
- Transparent decision-making processes: _____/5
- Integration of diverse perspectives and constitutional needs: _____/5
-     Service orientation in group decisions: _____/5

Group Energy and Motivation Patterns
Collective Energy Assessment:
- Group energy coherence and mutual support: _____/5
- Balance between challenge and support: _____/5
- Enthusiasm maintenance over time: _____/5
- Seasonal and cyclical adaptation capacity: _____/5
- Integration of individual and group needs: _____/5

Motivation and Purpose Alignment:
- Shared vision and purpose clarity: _____/5
- Individual motivation compatibility with group purpose: ____/5
- Service orientation over personal achievement: _____/5
- Spiritual development priority over social networking: _____/5
- Cultural contribution and bridge-building commitment: ____/5

Section III: Physical Practice and Safety Assessment
Group Practice Safety and Adaptation
Physical Practice Safety:
- Adequate physical space for all participants: _____/5
- Constitutional adaptation knowledge and implementation: _____/5
- Injury prevention and modification awareness: _____/5
- Emergency response preparation: _____/5
- Professional supervision or qualified teaching available: ____/5
Environmental Considerations:
- Space temperature regulation for all constitutional types: _____/5
- Noise, lighting, and stimulation level management: _____/5
- Accessibility for participants with physical limitations: _____/5
- Cultural and religious sensitivity in space arrangement: _____/5
- Seasonal adaptation capacity: _____/5

Equipment and Resource Availability:

- Basic props and modifications available: _____/5
- First aid and emergency supplies accessible: _____/5
- Constitutional adaptation resources (blankets, bolsters, etc.): _____/5
- Reference materials and educational resources:
  _____/5
- Community support for individual needs: _____/5

Teaching and Leadership Capacity

Qualified Instruction Availability:
- Access to traditionally authorized teacher: _____/5
- Community members with teaching experience:
  _____/5
- Ongoing supervision and guidance systems: _____/5
- Professional development and continuing education: _____/5
- Cultural authenticity and traditional connection:
  _____/5

Peer Support and Mentoring Systems:
- Experienced practitioners willing to support beginners: _____/5
- Constitutional type mentoring and guidance: _____/5
- Crisis and challenge support systems: _____/5
- Integration support for life application: _____/5
- Democratic leadership development opportunities: _____/5

Section IV: Community Service and Cultural Integration
Service Orientation and Outreach
Community Service Integration:
- Regular service projects and community contribution: _____/5
- Environmental stewardship and ecological awareness: _____/5
- Social justice and cultural healing participation:
  _____/5
- Healthcare and education sector collaboration:
  _____/5
- International cooperation and cultural exchange:
  _____/5

Cultural Sensitivity and Bridge-Building:
- Respect for diverse cultural and religious backgrounds: _____/5
- Traditional knowledge attribution and community relationship:
  _____/5
- Cross-cultural learning and dialogue facilitation: _____/5
- Economic justice and accessibility commitment:
  _____/5
- Peacebuilding and conflict transformation capacity: _____/5

545

External Relationship and Community Impact
Professional and Institutional Integration:
- Healthcare provider participation and support: _____/5
- Educational institution collaboration: _____/5
- Local government and policy engagement: _____/5
- Business and organizational leadership involvement: _____/5
- Media and public education capacity: _____/5

Network and Resource Development:
- Connection with other practice communities: _____/5
- Academic and research collaboration: _____/5
- International community relationships: _____/5
- Resource sharing and mutual support systems: _____/5
- Cultural preservation and innovation integration: _____/5

Section V: Sustainability and Long-Term Development
Economic and Resource Sustainability
Financial Sustainability:
- Transparent and democratic financial management: _____/5
- Accessibility regardless of economic status: _____/5
- Resource generation through service and contribution: _____/5
- Community investment and long-term planning:
  _____/5
- Economic cooperation and alternative economic modeling: ____/5

Resource and Infrastructure Development:
- Adequate meeting space and practice facilities:
  _____/5
- Library and educational resource development:
  _____/5
- Technology integration for community coordination: _____/5
- Seasonal and weather adaptation capacity: _____/5
-     Growth management and community expansion planning:
  _____/5

Leadership Development and Succession Planning
Democratic Leadership Model:
- Rotating leadership and responsibility sharing:
  _____/5
- Prevention of spiritual authoritarianism: _____/5
- Transparent accountability and feedback systems: _____/5
- Conflict of interest management: _____/5
- Elder wisdom integration with democratic participation: _____/5
  Community Growth and Development Planning:

- New member integration systems: _____/5
- Advanced practitioner development pathways:
  _____/5
- Teacher training and authorization processes: _____/5
- Community division and expansion protocols: _____/5
- Cultural transmission and preservation methods:
  _____/5

Section VI: Assessment Summary and Recommendations
Overall Community Readiness Assessment
Foundation Readiness Score: _____/50
Group Dynamics Score: _____/50
Physical Practice Safety Score: _____/50
Community Service Integration Score: _____/50
Sustainability and Leadership Score: _____/50

Total Community Readiness Score: _____/250

Readiness Level Determination
Score 200-250: Excellent Readiness
- Ready for advanced community development
- Qualified for teaching and outreach programs
- Prepared for community leadership responsibilities
- Recommended for network expansion and cultural contribution

Score 150-199: Good Readiness
- Ready for intermediate community development
- Prepared for selected advanced practices with supervision
- Recommended for service project leadership
- Ready for peer mentoring and teaching assistance

Score 100-149: Moderate Readiness
- Focus on foundation building and group cohesion development
- Recommend professional supervision and guidance
- Emphasize safety protocols and constitutional adaptation
- Prepare for basic community service integration

Score 50-99: Basic Readiness
- Extensive foundation development needed
- Professional supervision essential
- Focus on individual development before community leadership
-      Recommend connection with established community for support

Priority Development Areas

Highest Priority Areas for Development (based on lowest scores):
1.
Recommended Actions:
Timeline:
2.
Recommended Actions:
Timeline:
3.
Recommended Actions:
Timeline:

Resource and Support Recommendations

Immediate Support Needs:
☐ Professional teaching supervision and guidance
☐ Constitutional assessment and adaptation training
☐ Safety and emergency protocol development
☐ Communication and conflict resolution training
☐ Service project development and coordination
☐ Cultural sensitivity and bridge-building education
☐ Financial management and sustainability planning
☐ Leadership development and democratic process training

Long-Term Development Resources:
☐ Advanced teacher training and authorization pathway
☐ Community expansion and division planning
☐ Network development and inter-community coordination
☐ Research and documentation project participation
☐ International community exchange programs
☐ Professional and institutional integration development
☐ Cultural preservation and innovation project involvement
☐ Elder wisdom development and transmission planning

Next Assessment and Review Schedule
Next Complete Assessment Date:
Quarterly Progress Review Dates:
Annual Community Development Planning:
Professional Supervision Review:

Section VII: Individual Member Assessment Summary
Member Readiness Distribution
Members Ready for Teaching Assistance: _____
people
Members Ready for Community Leadership: _____ people
Members Needing Foundation Development: _____ people

548

Members Ready for Advanced Practice: _____ people
Members Requiring Professional Support: _____ people

Special Considerations and Accommodations
Physical Accessibility Needs:
Constitutional Distribution Challenges:
Cultural Sensitivity Requirements:
Economic Accessibility Considerations:
Professional Integration Support Needs:

Community Strengths and Assets

Greatest Community Strengths:
1.
2.
3.

Unique Community Assets and Capabilities:
1.
2.
3.

Community Service and Cultural Contribution Potential:

Assessment Completion Information:
Assessment Facilitator:
Assessment Review Committee:
Community Ratification Date:
Distribution of Results:
Next Steps and Implementation Planning:

This community readiness assessment provides systematic evaluation of group capacity for advanced practice, teaching, and service while ensuring safety, authenticity, and democratic participation. Use for community development planning and resource allocation.

Advanced Practitioner Self-Assessment - Teaching Readiness

Essential Downloadable Resource #9 - Teaching Readiness

Sacred Synthesis Advanced Practitioner Self-Assessment
Teaching Authorization and Community Leadership Readiness Evaluation

Practitioner Name: _____

Constitutional Type: _____

Years of Practice: _____

Community Affiliation: _____

Assessment Date: _____

Supervising Teacher: _____

Section I: Foundation Mastery Assessment
Personal Practice Development
Foundation Exercise Mastery (Rate 1-5: 1=Basic, 5=Master)
Exercise 1 - Tibetan Stand: _____/5

- Personal mastery level: Can hold 3+ minutes with constitutional adaptation
- Teaching demonstration ability: Can demonstrate with precision and safety
- Constitutional adaptation knowledge: Can modify for all three types
- Safety instruction capacity: Knows all contraindications and modifications
- Energetic understanding: Understands grounding and stability principles

Exercise 2 - Pendulum: _____/5

- Personal mastery level: Full spinal articulation with control
- Teaching demonstration ability: Can guide others through safe movement
- Modification expertise: Can adapt for physical limitations and constitution
- Anatomical knowledge: Understands spinal mechanics and safety
- Energetic understanding: Comprehends energy circulation and warming

Exercise 3 - Side Stretch: _____/5

- Personal mastery level: Balanced bilateral development and holding capacity
- Teaching demonstration ability: Can instruct proper alignment and breathing
- Constitutional adaptation: Can modify for all constitutional needs
- Safety protocols: Knows contraindications for back and neck issues
- Integration understanding: Understands lateral opening and balance

Exercise 4 - Backward Bend: _____/5

- Personal mastery level: Safe, controlled heart opening with breath awareness
- Teaching demonstration ability: Can guide others safely through emotional opening

550

- Modification expertise: Can adapt for back injuries and emotional sensitivity
- Psychological awareness: Understands emotional aspects of heart opening
- Energetic understanding: Comprehends confidence building and courage development

Exercise 5 - Forward Bend: _____/5
- Personal mastery level: Deep hip flexibility with introspective awareness
- Teaching demonstration ability: Can guide introspective development
- Constitutional expertise: Expert in constitutional adaptations for all types
- Safety instruction: Knows contraindications for back and hip issues
- Psychological integration: Understands introspection and patience development

Exercise 6 - Twist: _____/5
- Personal mastery level: Balanced bilateral rotation with spinal awareness
- Teaching demonstration ability: Can instruct proper spinal mechanics
- Detox understanding: Comprehends detoxification and cleansing aspects
- Safety protocols: Expert in spinal contraindications and modifications
- Energetic awareness: Understands energy circulation and organ health

Exercise 7 - Triangle: _____/5
- Personal mastery level: Integration of strength, flexibility, balance, and confidence
- Teaching demonstration ability: Can guide complex multi-dimensional development
- Progression instruction: Can teach systematic development over months
- Advanced understanding: Comprehends integration of all previous exercises
- Holistic integration: Can teach connection to overall development

Foundation Exercise Overall Mastery: _____/35

Intermediate Exercise Competency (Complete if applicable)

Exercise 8 - Tortoise: _____/5

- Personal practice depth: 3-5 minute holds with introspective mastery
- Teaching capacity: Can guide others in safe forward folding development
- Constitutional expertise: Expert adaptation for all constitutional types
- Psychological guidance: Can support introspective and emotional development

Exercise 9 - Cobra: _____/5
- Personal mastery: Safe, controlled backward bending with heart awareness
- Teaching ability: Can guide confidence building and courage development
- Safety expertise: Comprehensive understanding of back safety protocols
- Integration capacity: Can teach connection to overall development sequence

Exercise 10 - Locust: _____/5
- Personal strength: Demonstrates posterior chain strength and integration
- Teaching progression: Can guide systematic strength building development
- Constitutional adaptation: Expert modification for all constitutional needs
- Integration understanding: Comprehends full-body strength development

Additional Intermediate Exercises: _____/15 (if applicable)

Section II: Constitutional Knowledge and Adaptation Mastery
Constitutional Assessment and Instruction Expertise
Constitutional Type Recognition and Assessment

Electric Constitution (Vata) Expertise:
- Recognition accuracy: Can identify Electric types with 85%+ accuracy _/5
- Assessment skills: Can conduct thorough constitutional assessment _____/5
- Adaptation expertise: Can modify all exercises for Electric needs _____/5
- Environmental knowledge: Expert in environment optimization _____/5
- Therapeutic understanding: Can address anxiety, scattered energy,

digestive issues _____/5

Magnetic Constitution (Kapha) Expertise:
- Recognition accuracy: Can identify Magnetic types with 85%+ accuracy _____/5
- Assessment skills: Can conduct thorough constitutional assessment _____/5
- Adaptation expertise: Can modify all exercises for Magnetic needs _____/5
- Motivation skills: Expert in motivation and activation strategies _____/5
- Therapeutic understanding: Can address lethargy, depression, circulation issues _____/5

Neutral Constitution (Pitta) Expertise:
- Recognition accuracy: Can identify Neutral types with 85%+ accuracy _/5
- Assessment skills: Can conduct thorough constitutional assessment _____/5
- Adaptation expertise: Can modify all exercises for Neutral needs _____/5
- Balance instruction: Expert in precision and balance teaching _____/5
- Therapeutic understanding: Can address overheating, irritability, perfectionism _____/5

Overall Constitutional Mastery: _____/75

Breathing and Energy Work Teaching Capacity

Integration Breath (4-4-6-2) Instruction:
- Personal mastery: Can practice for 10+ minutes with constitutional adaptation _____/5
- Teaching progression: Can teach systematic development over weeks _____/5
- Safety instruction: Knows all contraindications and safety protocols _____/5
- Constitutional adaptation: Can adapt for all constitutional breathing needs _____/5
- Therapeutic application: Can apply for stress, anxiety, and health conditions _____/5

Advanced Breathing Techniques (if qualified):
- Personal practice depth: Consistent advanced practice with supervision _/5

- Safety expertise: Comprehensive safety and contraindication knowledge _____/5
- Qualified supervision: Practices advanced techniques with authorized supervision only _____/5
- Teaching preparation: Preparing for advanced teaching under qualified guidance _____/5
- Community integration: Integrates advanced practice with community service _____/5

Energy Circulation and Chakra Awareness:
- Personal sensitivity: Developed energy awareness and circulation sensitivity _____/5
- Teaching capacity: Can guide others in energy awareness development _____/5
- Constitutional integration: Can teach energy work with constitutional adaptation _____/5
- Safety boundaries: Maintains appropriate boundaries and realistic expectations _____/5
- Service integration: Uses energy work for healing service rather than personal power _____/5

Section III: Teaching Skills and Communication Assessment
Instructional Capacity and Safety Management
Teaching Methodology and Communication Skills

Clear Instruction and Demonstration:
- Verbal instruction clarity: Can give clear, step-by-step instructions _____/5
- Physical demonstration accuracy: Can demonstrate exercises with precision _____/5
- Visual instruction integration: Can use visual aids and anatomical knowledge _____/5
- Learning style adaptation: Can adapt instruction for different learning styles _____/5
- Constitutional language: Can explain constitutional concepts clearly _____/5

Group Management and Individual Attention:
- Class organization skills: Can organize and manage group practice sessions _____/5
- Individual attention capacity: Can provide individual modifications while teaching groups _____/5
- Safety monitoring ability: Can monitor multiple students for safety and alignment _____/5
- Energy management skills: Can maintain group energy and individual attention balance _____/5

- Conflict resolution capacity: Can handle group dynamics and individual conflicts _____/5

Cultural Sensitivity and Inclusivity:
- Cultural awareness: Demonstrates cultural sensitivity and traditional respect _____/5
- Accessibility inclusion: Can adapt for physical disabilities and limitations _____/5
- Economic inclusivity: Creates accessible programs regardless of economic status _____/5
- Age-appropriate instruction: Can teach across age ranges with appropriate modification _____/5

- Religious sensitivity: Respects diverse religious and spiritual backgrounds _____/5

Safety Protocol Management and Emergency Response
Injury Prevention and Management:
- Risk assessment skills: Can assess and prevent injury risks in group settings _____/5
- Modification expertise: Can immediately modify for injuries or physical limitations _____/5
- Contraindication knowledge: Comprehensive understanding of all exercise contraindications_____/5
- Emergency response preparedness: Can respond appropriately to practice-related injuries _____/5
- Professional boundary maintenance: Knows when to refer to healthcare providers _____/5

Psychological and Emotional Safety:
- Emotional boundary awareness: Can maintain appropriate emotional boundaries _____/5
- Trauma-informed instruction: Can teach safely for individuals with trauma history _____/5
- Crisis recognition: Can recognize psychological crisis and respond appropriately_____/5
- Professional referral knowledge: Knows when to refer to mental health professionals_____/5
- Community support integration: Can coordinate community support for individual needs_____/5
-
Section IV: Community Service and Leadership Assessment
Service Orientation and Community Integration
Community Service Development and Leadership

Community Service Track Record:
- Regular service participation: Consistent monthly community service _ hours
- Service project leadership: Has led or co-led community service projects _____/5
- Environmental stewardship: Regular participation in environmental action _____/5
- Social justice engagement: Actively supports community healing and justice _____/5
- International awareness: Demonstrates global awareness and cultural bridge-building _____/5

Community Teaching and Mentorship:
- Teaching assistance experience: Has assisted qualified teachers for _____ months
- Peer mentoring capacity: Can mentor newer practitioners effectively _____/5
- Community workshop leadership: Can organize and lead community workshops _____/5
- Family integration support: Can help families integrate constitutional practice _____/5
- Professional integration guidance: Can support professional practice integration _____/5

Democratic Participation and Leadership:
- Democratic governance participation: Active participation in community decision-making _____/5
- Conflict resolution skills: Can mediate conflicts and support community harmony _____/5
- Shared leadership capacity: Can share leadership without spiritual authoritarianism _____/5
- Resource sharing commitment: Demonstrates commitment to community resource sharing_____/5
- Cultural preservation and innovation: Balances traditional authenticity with contemporary needs_____/5

Global Awareness and Cultural Bridge-Building
Cross-Cultural Competency:
- Cultural sensitivity development: Demonstrates growing cultural awareness and sensitivity _____/5
- Traditional knowledge respect: Shows deep respect for traditional knowledge and communities _____/5
- Interfaith dialogue capacity: Can engage respectfully across religious boundaries _____/5

- Economic justice awareness: Understands and supports economic justice and accessibility_____/5
- Peace-building skills: Can contribute to conflict transformation and peacebuilding _____/5

International Integration Preparation:
- Language study engagement: Studying languages relevant to traditional knowledge _____/5
- International community connection: Connected with international practice communities _____/5
- Cultural exchange participation: Has participated in or organized cultural exchanges _____/5
- Global service orientation: Demonstrates commitment to global welfare and service _____/5
- Environmental action leadership: Leads or supports environmental action and stewardship _____/5

Section V: Ethical Development and Professional Boundaries
Ethical Maturity and Professional Standards
Spiritual Maturity and Ego Development

Spiritual Motivation Assessment:
- Service over achievement orientation: Practices for service rather than personal achievement _____/5
- Humility and continuous learning: Maintains beginner's mind and openness to learning _____/5
- Community welfare prioritization: Consistently prioritizes community welfare over individual gain _____/5
- Traditional authenticity respect: Maintains respect for traditional sources and authorization _____/5
- Spiritual materialism awareness: Recognizes and addresses spiritual ego and materialism _____/5

Emotional Maturity and Relationship Skills:
- Emotional regulation capacity: Can maintain emotional stability under pressure _____/5
- Relationship conflict resolution: Can navigate conflicts with partners, family, and community _____/5
- Professional boundary maintenance: Maintains appropriate boundaries in all relationships _____/5
- Power dynamic awareness: Understands and navigates power dynamics responsibly _____/5
    - Intimacy and service integration: Can integrate intimate relationships with community service _____/5

Professional Ethics and Boundaries
Teaching Ethics and Responsibility:
- Student welfare prioritization: Consistently prioritizes student welfare over personal benefit _____/5
- Qualified supervision seeking: Regularly seeks supervision and continuing education _____/5
- Scope of practice maintenance: Maintains clear boundaries around teaching qualifications _____/5
- Cultural appropriation avoidance: Careful to avoid cultural appropriation while honoring tradition _____/5
- Community accountability acceptance: Welcomes community accountability and feedback _____/5
Professional Integration Ethics:
- Healthcare collaboration: Can collaborate appropriately with healthcare providers _____/5
- Educational system integration: Can integrate with educational systems while maintaining integrity _____/5
- Business ethics maintenance: Maintains ethical standards in any business applications _____/5
- Research ethics understanding: Understands ethics of research and documentation _____/5
- Media representation responsibility: Can represent tradition responsibly in media contexts _____/5

Section VI: Assessment Summary and Teaching Authorization Pathway
Overall Teaching Readiness Assessment
Foundation Mastery Score: _____/50
Constitutional Expertise Score: _____/100
Teaching Skills Score: _____/75
Community Service Score: _____/75
Ethical Development Score: _____/50

Total Teaching Readiness Score: _____/350

Teaching Authorization Level Determination
Score 300-350: Full Teaching Authorization Readiness
- Ready for independent community teaching with ongoing supervision
- Qualified for teacher training program completion
- Prepared for community leadership and teaching responsibility
- Recommended for advanced teaching development and specialization

Score 250-299: Advanced Teaching Preparation

558

- Ready for co-teaching with qualified teacher supervision
- Prepared for teaching assistant roles in community programs
- Recommended for intensive teacher training participation
- Ready for specialized teaching skill development

Score 200-249: Intermediate Teaching Development
- Ready for peer mentoring and teaching assistance
- Prepared for community workshop leadership with supervision
- Recommended for continued foundation and constitutional development
- Focus on service development and community integration

Score 150-199: Beginning Teaching Preparation
- Focus on foundation mastery and personal development
- Prepared for informal teaching and peer support
- Recommended for extensive community service and leadership development
- Emphasize constitutional mastery and breathing development

Score Below 150: Continued Personal Development Needed
- Focus on personal practice development and foundation mastery
- Extensive community service and mentoring experience needed
- Recommend connection with qualified teacher for guidance
    - Emphasize safety, ethics, and traditional authenticity learning

Development Pathway and Next Steps
Immediate Development Priorities (next 6 months):

1.
Action Steps:
Supervision Required:
Success Metrics:

2.
Action Steps:
Supervision Required:
Success Metrics:

3.
Action Steps:
Supervision Required:
Success Metrics:

Long-term Teaching Development Plan (1-3 years):
- Advanced Training Needed:

- Community Service Requirements:
- Supervision and Mentoring Needs:
- Specialization Areas of Interest:
- International Development Goals:

Community Authorization and Supervision

Community Teaching Authorization Committee:
Assigned Teaching Supervisor:
Community Service Coordinator:
Professional Ethics Advisor:
Traditional Authority Connection:

Next Assessment Date:
Teaching Authorization Review:
Community Leadership Readiness Assessment:

Section VII: Specialized Teaching Preparation
Teaching Specialization Areas (Complete relevant sections)
Constitutional Assessment and Therapy Specialization
Prerequisites: Foundation score >40, Constitutional score >80
- Advanced constitutional assessment training:
- Therapeutic application development:
- Healthcare provider collaboration training:
- Professional ethics and scope of practice:

Advanced Breathing and Energy Work Specialization
Prerequisites: Foundation score >45, Teaching skills >60, Ethical development >40
- Advanced breathing technique authorization:
- Energy work safety and ethics training:
- Qualified traditional supervision:
- Community healing application training:

Community Leadership and Organization Specialization
Prerequisites: Community service >65, Democratic participation >40
- Community organization and governance training:
- Conflict resolution and mediation certification:
- Economic cooperation and sustainability development
- International cooperation and cultural bridge-building:

Professional Integration Specialization
Prerequisites: Professional integration experience, Ethical development >45

560

- Healthcare integration certification:
- Educational system integration training:
- Business and organizational applications:
- Research and academic collaboration preparation:

Assessment Completion Information:
Self-Assessment Completed By:
Community Review Committee:
Traditional Authority Validation:
Final Authorization Decision Date:

This advanced practitioner self-assessment provides comprehensive evaluation of teaching readiness while ensuring safety, traditional authenticity, and service orientation in community teaching development.

Global Service Capacity Assessment - International Readiness

Essential Downloadable Resource #12 - International Readiness

Sacred Synthesis Global Service Capacity Assessment
International Cooperation and Global Citizenship Development Evaluation
Practitioner/Community Name:
 Assessment Date:
International Experience: _____
Languages Spoken: _____
Constitutional Type: _____
Assessment Facilitator: _____

Section I: Global Consciousness and Planetary Awareness

Universal Human Values and Global Citizenship
Global Awareness and Understanding
Planetary Consciousness Development:
- Global interconnectedness awareness: Understands interconnection of all human and ecological systems
    _____/5
    -      Climate change and environmental crisis understanding: Comprehensive understanding of global environmental challenges
    _____/5
- Economic justice and inequality awareness: Understanding of global economic systems and inequality
    _____/5

561

- Peace and conflict transformation awareness: Understanding of global conflicts and peace-building approaches ___/5
- Cultural diversity appreciation and protection: Values and supports global cultural diversity and preservation ___/5

International Current Events and Issues:
- Global news and current events awareness: Stays informed about international developments and issues
    _____/5
- International politics and governance understanding: Basic understanding of international political systems _____/5
- Human rights and international law knowledge: Understanding of human rights principles and international law _/5
- Global health and pandemic preparedness: Understanding of global health challenges and cooperation
    _____/5
- Technology and digital divide awareness: Understanding of global technology access and digital equity
    _____/5

Cross-Cultural Global Understanding:
- World religious and spiritual traditions knowledge: Basic knowledge of major world spiritual traditions
    _____/5
- Global indigenous rights and sovereignty support: Support for indigenous rights and self-determination globally ___/5
- International development and aid understanding: Understanding of international development approaches and issues _/5
- Global migration and refugee issues awareness: Understanding of global migration patterns and refugee crises _____/5
- International education and cultural exchange support: Support for international educational and cultural exchange _____/5

Sacred Synthesis Global Integration

Spiritual Practice Global Application:
- Constitutional practice cross-cultural adaptation: Can adapt constitutional practice across cultural contexts _____/5
- Sacred Synthesis principles universal application: Can apply Sacred Synthesis principles across cultural boundaries _____/5
- Traditional knowledge global integration: Can integrate traditional knowledge from multiple global sources respectfully ___/5
- Community building across cultures: Can build spiritual community across cultural and national boundaries _____/5
- Global spiritual network development: Can develop and maintain

562

international spiritual networks __/5

Section II: International Communication and Cooperation Skills
Language and Cross-Cultural Communication
Language Capacity and Development

Current Language Proficiency (Rate 1-5: 1=Basic phrases, 5=Fluent):

Primary Native Language: _____
Second Language: _____
Proficiency Level: _____/5
Third Language: _____
Proficiency Level: _____/5
Additional Languages: _____
Proficiency Level: _____/5
Sacred/Traditional Language Study:_____
Level: __/5

Language Learning Commitment and Capacity:
- Language learning motivation and dedication: Committed to ongoing language learning for service _____/5
- Cultural context learning with language: Learns cultural context along with language skills _____/5
- Sacred text and traditional terminology study: Studies sacred texts and terminology in original languages _____/5
- Translation and interpretation skill development: Developing translation and interpretation skills _____/5
-      Language exchange and cultural partnership: Engages in language exchange and cultural learning partnerships __/5

International Communication and Collaboration

Cross-Cultural Communication Excellence:
- Nonverbal communication cultural awareness: Understands nonverbal communication across cultures _____/5
- Cultural communication style adaptation: Can adapt communication style to different cultural contexts _____/5
-      International conflict resolution and mediation: Can mediate conflicts involving international or cultural differences _____/5
-      Technology-mediated international communication: Skilled in using technology for international communication and cooperation

_____/5
- International meeting and conference facilitation: Can facilitate
international meetings and conferences
_____/5
International Project Management and Coordination:
- 	International project planning and coordination: Can plan and
coordinate projects involving multiple countries ____/5
- 	Cross-cultural team building and leadership: Can build and
lead teams across cultural and national boundaries __/5
- International logistics and resource coordination: Can coordinate
logistics and resources internationally
- 	International fundraising and resource development: Can de-
velop funding and resources for international projects _____/5
- 	International partnership development and maintenance: Can
develop and maintain long-term international partnerships __/5

Section III: Cultural Competency and International Relations
International Cultural Sensitivity and Diplomacy
Cultural Intelligence and Adaptation
Cultural Adaptation and Intelligence:
- 	Cultural norm recognition and adaptation: Can recognize and
adapt to different cultural norms and expectations __/5
- 	Cultural protocol and etiquette mastery: Understands and fol-
lows appropriate cultural protocols and etiquette ____/5
- Cultural conflict recognition and resolution: Can recognize cultural
conflicts and facilitate resolution
_____/5
- Cultural sensitivity in spiritual practice: Can adapt spiritual practice
with cultural sensitivity ____/5
- 	Cultural bridge-building and diplomacy: Can build bridges and
facilitate diplomacy across cultural differences _____/5

International Relationship Building:
- 	Trust building across cultural boundaries: Can build trust and
rapport across cultural and national boundaries ____/5
- 	Long-term relationship maintenance internationally: Can
maintain long-term relationships across distance and cultural differences /5
- International mentor and mentee relationships: Can develop mentoring relationships internationally____/5
- 	International family and community integration: Can integrate
with international families and communities _____/5
- 	International professional network development: Can develop
professional networks internationally ____/5

Global Justice and Human Rights Advocacy
Human Rights and Social Justice Commitment:
- Universal human rights advocacy: Committed to universal human rights and dignity ___/5
- International social justice movement support: Supports international social justice movements ___/5
- Anti-oppression work international application: Can apply anti-oppression principles internationally _____/5
-     International women's rights and gender equality: Supports international women's rights and gender equality ___/5
- International LGBTQ+ rights and inclusion: Supports international LGBTQ+ rights and inclusion ___/5

Environmental and Climate Justice:
- International environmental justice support: Supports international environmental justice movements _____/5
- Climate action and international cooperation: Participates in climate action and international cooperation
- International indigenous rights support: Supports indigenous rights and sovereignty internationally___/5
-     International sustainable development support: Supports sustainable development and environmental protection internationally ___/5
- International animal rights and welfare advocacy: Supports international animal rights and welfare ___/5

Section IV: Practical International Service Capacity
International Travel and Living Capacity
International Mobility and Adaptation

Travel and Cultural Adaptation Capacity:
-     International travel experience and competency: Extensive international travel experience and cultural adaptation _____/5
- Long-term international living capacity: Can live long-term in different cultural contexts ___/5
- International health and safety awareness: Understands international health and safety considerations _____/5
- International legal and visa navigation: Can navigate international legal requirements and visa processes _____/5
-     International financial and economic navigation: Can navigate international financial and economic systems _____/5

565

International Living and Integration Skills:
-        International housing and living arrangement: Can arrange and adapt to international housing and living situations __/5
-        International healthcare and medical system navigation: Can navigate international healthcare and medical systems _____/5
-        International education and learning system integration: Can integrate with international education and learning systems __/5
- International work and professional integration: Can integrate professionally in international contexts
        _____/5
- International family and social integration: Can integrate with international families and social systems
        _____/5

International Service Project Development and Implementation

International Service Project Leadership:
-        International service project design and development: Can design and develop international service projects ___/5
- International community needs assessment: Can assess community needs in international contexts ___/5
-        International resource mobilization and coordination: Can mobilize and coordinate resources for international service __/5
- International volunteer recruitment and coordination: Can recruit and coordinate international volunteers
        _____/5
-        International project evaluation and impact assessment: Can evaluate international projects and assess impact ___/5
Sustainable International Development:
-        Community-led development support: Supports community-led rather than externally imposed development ___/5
- Local capacity building and empowerment: Focuses on building local capacity and empowerment ___/5
- Sustainable and appropriate technology transfer: Can transfer appropriate and sustainable technology
        _____/5
-        International cooperation vs. aid distinction: Understands difference between cooperation and traditional aid models ____/5
-        Long-term sustainability and local ownership: Ensures long-term sustainability and local ownership of projects __/5

Section V: International Teaching and Knowledge Sharing
Sacred Synthesis International Transmission

Cross-Cultural Teaching and Adaptation

International Teaching Capacity:
- Cross-cultural teaching methodology: Can adapt teaching methodology to different cultural contexts
_____/5
-       Constitutional practice international adaptation: Can adapt constitutional practice for different cultural and climatic contexts
_____/5
- International student cultural sensitivity: Demonstrates cultural sensitivity with international students
_____/5
-       International spiritual community development: Can develop spiritual communities in international contexts _____/5
- International teacher training and development: Can train and develop teachers in international contexts
_____/5

Traditional Knowledge Integration and Respect:
- Local traditional knowledge integration: Can respectfully integrate local traditional knowledge ___/5
- Traditional authority recognition and respect: Recognizes and respects local traditional authorities ___/5
- Cultural appropriation avoidance: Can share Sacred Synthesis while avoiding cultural appropriation
_____/5
-       Local spiritual tradition dialogue and cooperation: Can dialogue and cooperate with local spiritual traditions ___/5
- Cultural synthesis vs. replacement distinction: Can synthesize rather than replace local cultural practices
_____/5

International Network Development and Cooperation

Global Sacred Synthesis Network Building:
-       International community network development: Can develop networks of Sacred Synthesis communities internationally ___/5
- International teacher and leader development: Can develop international teachers and leaders _____/5
-       International communication and coordination systems: Can develop communication and coordination systems internationally
_____/5
-       International resource sharing and cooperation: Can develop international resource sharing and cooperation _____/5
- International conflict resolution and mediation: Can mediate con-

flicts within international networks ____/5

Movement Building and Cultural Impact:
- International movement building and cultural change: Can contribute to international movement building
    _____/5
- International policy development and advocacy: Can contribute to international policy development
    _____/5
- International media and communication: Can communicate effectively through international media ____/5
    - International academic and research cooperation: Can cooperate with international academic and research institutions ____/5
- International institutional integration: Can integrate Sacred Synthesis with international institutions ____/5

Section VI: Emergency Response and International Crisis Support
International Crisis Response and Humanitarian Service
Crisis Response and Humanitarian Capacity

International Emergency Response:
    - International crisis assessment and response: Can assess and respond to international crises and emergencies ____/5
- International humanitarian service: Can provide humanitarian service in international crisis contexts
    _____/5
- International refugee and migration support: Can support international refugees and migrants ____/5
    - International disaster response and recovery: Can contribute to international disaster response and recovery ____/5
- International conflict zone service: Can provide service in international conflict zones safely ____/5
Trauma and Healing International Application:
- International trauma-informed practice: Can provide trauma-informed practice in international contexts
    _____/5
    - International community healing and reconciliation: Can facilitate community healing and reconciliation internationally ____/5
- International post-conflict reconstruction support: Can support post-conflict reconstruction and healing
    _____/5
- International peacebuilding and conflict transformation: Can contribute to international peacebuilding
    _____/5

- International restorative justice and healing: Can facilitate restorative justice and healing internationally
  _____/5

Long-term International Development and Capacity Building

Sustainable International Development Support:
-       International education and capacity building: Can contribute to education and capacity building internationally ___/5
-       International economic development and cooperation: Can support sustainable economic development internationally ___/5
-       International healthcare and wellness development: Can support healthcare and wellness development internationally ____/5
-       International environmental restoration and protection: Can support environmental restoration and protection internationally ____/5
-       International governance and democracy support: Can support democratic governance development internationally ____/5

Section VII: Assessment Summary and International Service Development
Overall Global Service Capacity Assessment
Global Consciousness and Awareness: _____/75
International Communication and Cooperation: _____/75
Cultural Competency and International Relations: _____/75
Practical International Service Capacity: _____/75
International Teaching and Knowledge Sharing: _____/75
Emergency Response and Crisis Support: _____/75

Total Global Service Capacity: _____/450

International Service Readiness Level
Score 375-450: Excellent Global Service Readiness
- Ready for major international service leadership and coordination
- Qualified for international Sacred Synthesis community development
- Prepared for international teaching and teacher training
- Recommended for international movement building and cultural bridge-building

Score 300-374: Good International Service Readiness
- Ready for international service participation and project coordination
- Prepared for international community development with supervision
- Recommended for international partnership development and

cultural exchange
- Ready for international teaching assistance and cultural adaptation

Score 225-299: Moderate International Service Development Needed
- Focus on language development and cultural competency building
- Prepared for short-term international service with mentoring
- Recommend international experience and cultural immersion
- Emphasize cross-cultural communication and conflict resolution skills

Score 150-224: Basic International Service Preparation Required
- Focus on global awareness and cultural sensitivity development
- Prepared for domestic multicultural service and cultural learning
- Recommend international study and cultural exchange programs
- Emphasize language learning and cultural competency development

Score Below 150: Extensive International Development Needed
- Focus on global consciousness and cultural awareness development
- Extensive cultural competency and international education needed
- Recommend international mentorship and cultural immersion experiences
- Emphasize global justice and human rights education

International Service Development Planning
Immediate Development Priorities (next 6 months):
1.
Development Activities:
International Mentoring Required:
Success Metrics:

2.
Development Activities:
International Mentoring Required:
Success Metrics:

3.
Development Activities:
International Mentoring Required:
Success Metrics:
Long-term International Service Goals (1-3 years):
- International Service Aspirations:
- Global Network Development:
- International Teaching and Community Development
- Movement Building and Cultural Impact:

- Crisis Response and Humanitarian Service:

International Service Support and Networks

International Service Development Support:
International Mentor:
Cultural Competency Advisor:
Language Learning Support:
International Network Connections:
Global Service Project Opportunities:

International Assessment and Development Review:
Next Global Service Assessment Date:
International Service Deployment Readiness:
Global Network Integration Planning:
International Teaching Authorization:

Section VIII: Specialized International Service Areas

International Service Specialization Development (Complete relevant sections)

International Education and Academic Cooperation
Prerequisites: Teaching capacity >60, International communication >60
- International university and research cooperation:
- International curriculum and program development:
- International student and scholar exchange:
- International academic conference and publication:

International Healthcare and Wellness Integration
Prerequisites: Healthcare integration experience, Cultural competency >60
- International healthcare system integration:
- International public health and wellness programs:
- International healthcare provider training:
- International health policy development:

International Environmental and Climate Action
Prerequisites: Environmental action experience, Crisis response >60
- International environmental restoration projects:
- International climate action and cooperation:
- International sustainable development programs:
- International environmental policy and advocacy:

International Peacebuilding and Conflict Transformation
Prerequisites: Conflict resolution >65, Cultural competency >70
- International peacebuilding and mediation:
- International conflict transformation and reconciliation:
- International post-conflict healing and reconstruction:
- International policy development for peace:

Annual International Service Development Review

Year-End International Service Assessment:
International Service Contribution Documentation:
Global Network Development and Expansion:
International Teaching and Community Building:
Movement Building and Cultural Impact Assessment:
Next Year International Service Focus:

Assessment Completion Information:
Self-Assessment Completed By:
International Service Assessment Committee:
Cultural Competency Validation:
Global Service Authorization Date:

This global service capacity assessment provides comprehensive evaluation of international readiness while ensuring cultural competency, traditional knowledge respect, and authentic global citizenship in Sacred Synthesis international service development.

Professional Integration Evaluation - Healthcare Providers
*Essential Downloadable Resource
#4A - Industry-Specific Version*

Sacred Synthesis Professional Integration Assessment
Healthcare Provider Edition
Practitioner Name: _____
Professional Role: _____
Institution/Practice: _____
Years of Experience: _____
Constitutional Type: _____
Assessment Date: _____

Section I: Clinical Integration Capacity
Patient Care Applications
Stress Management in Clinical Settings:

- Constitutional assessment skills for patients: _____/5
- Breathing technique instruction capacity: _____/5
- Movement prescription appropriateness: _____/5
- Integration with medical treatment plans: _____/5
- Clinical application examples:

Therapeutic Relationship Enhancement:
- Constitutional awareness in patient interaction:
  _____/5
- Professional boundary maintenance with practice: _____/5
- Healing presence cultivation through practice: _____/5
- Cultural sensitivity in diverse patient populations: _____/5
- Relationship enhancement examples:

Emergency and Crisis Response:
- Personal stress management during crises: _____/5
- Team support during high-stress situations: _____/5
- Constitutional adaptation under pressure: _____/5
- Ethical practice maintenance during emergencies: _____/5
- Crisis response examples:

Specific Healthcare Applications by Role
For Physicians
Patient Assessment Integration:
- Constitutional type recognition in patients: _____/5
- Treatment plan adaptation based on constitutional needs: _____/5
- Medication response awareness related to constitution: _____/5
- Assessment integration examples:
Diagnostic Enhancement:
- Energy awareness in physical examination: _____/5
- Stress pattern recognition through constitutional lens: _____/5
- Holistic health assessment integration: _____/5
- Diagnostic enhancement examples:

For Nurses
Patient Care Integration:
- Constitutional awareness in patient comfort measures: _____/5
- Breathing guidance during procedures: _____/5
- Movement instruction for bedridden patients: _____/5
- Patient care integration examples:

Shift Management:
- Personal energy regulation during long shifts: _____/5
- Constitutional adaptation for different work schedules: _____/5
- Team communication enhancement: _____/5

- Shift management examples:

For Mental Health Professionals
Therapeutic Integration:
- Constitutional assessment in therapy: _____/5
- Movement and breathing integration in sessions: _____/5
- Trauma-informed constitutional applications: _____/5
- Therapeutic integration examples:

Professional Self-Care:
- Emotional boundary maintenance through practice: _____/5
- Secondary trauma prevention: _____/5
- Constitutional adaptation for emotional work: _____/5
- Self-care integration examples:

For Physical Therapists/Occupational Therapists
Rehabilitation Integration:
- Constitutional movement prescription: _____/5
- Patient motivation through constitutional understanding: _____/5
- Recovery timeline adaptation: _____/5
- Rehabilitation integration examples:

Treatment Planning:
- Constitutional consideration in exercise prescription: _____/5
- Environmental modification recommendations:
  _____/5
- Home program constitutional adaptation: _____/5
- Treatment planning examples:

Section II: Professional Development and Education
Continuing Education Integration
Current Professional Development:
- Integration of consciousness studies with healthcare education:
  _____/5
- Presentation of integrated approaches to colleagues: _____/5
- Research participation in mind-body medicine:
  _____/5
- Professional development activities:

Teaching and Mentoring:
- Student/resident instruction in integrated approaches: _____/5
- Colleague mentoring in stress management: _____/5
- Patient education in constitutional wellness: _____/5
- Teaching and mentoring examples:

Evidence-Based Practice Integration
Research and Documentation:
- Clinical outcome tracking with integrated approaches: _____/5
- Case study documentation for constitutional applications: _____/5
- Participation in mind-body medicine research: _____/5
- Research and documentation examples:

Quality Improvement:
- Integration of holistic approaches in quality metrics: _____/5
- Patient satisfaction improvement through constitutional awareness: _____/5
- Team wellness program development: _____/5
- Quality improvement examples:

Section III: Workplace Environment and Culture
Professional Integration Challenges
Institutional Acceptance:
- Colleague receptivity to integrated approaches: Excellent/Good/Fair/Poor
- Administrative support for holistic practices: Excellent/Good/Fair/Poor
- Patient acceptance of constitutional approaches: Excellent/Good/Fair/Poor
- Integration challenge examples:

Time Management and Efficiency:
- Constitutional practice integration within work schedule: _____/5
- Patient care efficiency with holistic approaches: _____/5
- Personal practice maintenance during demanding periods: _____/5
- Time management strategies:

Ethical and Legal Considerations
Scope of Practice Maintenance:
- Clear boundaries between medical and constitutional practice: _____/5
- Appropriate referral to qualified constitutional teachers: _____/5
- Documentation of constitutional applications in patient care: _____/5
- Scope of practice examples:

Professional Liability and Risk Management:
- Understanding of legal implications: _____/5
- Malpractice insurance considerations: _____/5
- Informed consent for integrated approaches: _____/5

- Risk management strategies:

Section IV: Patient and Community Service
Patient Education and Empowerment
Constitutional Health Education:
- Patient instruction in stress management techniques: _____/5
- Home practice guidance appropriate to constitution:_____/5
- Family education in constitutional wellness: _____/5
- Patient education examples:

Community Health Applications:
- Community workshop facilitation: _____/5
- Public health initiative participation: _____/5
- Healthcare access improvement through constitutional approaches: _____/5
- Community service examples:

Interprofessional Collaboration
Healthcare Team Integration:
- Communication of constitutional insights to colleagues: _____/5
- Collaborative care planning with holistic considerations: _____/5
- Interdisciplinary team leadership in integrated approaches: _____/5
- Collaboration examples:

Community Partnership Development:
- Relationships with qualified constitutional teachers: _____/5
- Integration with complementary healthcare providers: _____/5
- Community wellness program development: _____/5
- Partnership examples:

Section V: Personal Practice and Professional Sustainability
Personal Practice Consistency
Daily Practice Integration:
- Consistent personal practice despite work demands: _____/5
- Constitutional adaptation for varying work schedules: _____/5
- Practice quality maintenance during stressful periods: _____/5
- Personal practice strategies:

Professional Burnout Prevention:
- Recognition of burnout warning signs: _____/5
- Constitutional approaches to professional stress: _____/5
- Work-life balance maintenance: _____/5
- Burnout prevention strategies:

Advanced Development and Leadership
Professional Leadership Development:
- Leadership in integrated healthcare approaches:
   _____/5
- Mentoring of other healthcare providers: _____/5
- Policy development for holistic healthcare: _____/5
- Leadership development examples:

   Research and Innovation:
- Contribution to evidence base for integrated approaches: _____/5
- Innovation in constitutional healthcare applications: _____/5
- Publication and presentation of integrated work:
   _____/5
- Research and innovation examples:

Section VI: Assessment Summary and Development Planning
Current Integration Level Assessment
Overall Professional Integration Rating (1-10):

Strengths in Professional Integration:
1.
2.
3.

Areas for Professional Development:
1.
2.
3.

Next Quarter Development Plan

Primary Professional Integration Goal:
Action Steps:
1.
2.
3.
Success Metrics:

Secondary Professional Goal:
Action Steps:
1.
2.
Success Metrics:

Resource and Support Needs

Professional Development Resources Needed:
- Advanced constitutional assessment training for healthcare
- Evidence-based research in constitutional healthcare applications
- Legal and ethical consultation for integrated practice
- Institutional policy development support
- Colleague network for integrated healthcare providers
- Patient education materials in constitutional wellness
- Professional liability insurance consultation
- Other:

Community and Mentorship Needs:
- Supervision from experienced integrated healthcare provider
- Peer support group for holistic healthcare professionals
- Advanced constitutional teacher consultation
- Research collaboration opportunities
- Patient outcome tracking system
- Institutional change management support
- Professional presentation opportunities
- Other:

Section VII: Specialized Assessment by Healthcare Role
Additional Role-Specific Evaluations (Complete relevant section) #### Emergency Medicine/Critical Care Specialization
High-Stress Environment Integration:
- Constitutional adaptation in life-or-death situations: _____/5
- Team communication under extreme pressure:
  _____/5
- Personal resilience maintenance: _____/5
- Critical care integration examples:

Primary Care/Family Medicine Specialization
Long-Term Patient Relationship Integration:
- Constitutional pattern tracking over time: _____/5
- Family system constitutional understanding: _____/5
- Preventive care through constitutional approaches: _____/5
- Primary care integration examples:

Pediatric Specialization
Constitutional Assessment in Children:
- Age-appropriate constitutional assessment: _____/5
- Family education in child constitutional wellness: _____/5
- Developmental integration with constitutional types: _____/5

- Pediatric integration examples:
-

Geriatric Specialization
Elder Care Constitutional Integration:
- Constitutional adaptation with aging: _____/5
- End-of-life care with constitutional awareness:
  _____/5
- Family support through constitutional understanding: _____/5
- Geriatric integration examples:

Surgical Specialization
Perioperative Constitutional Care:
- Preoperative constitutional assessment: _____/5
- Postoperative recovery optimization: _____/5
- Surgical stress management: _____/5
- Surgical integration examples:

Annual Professional Integration Review

Year-End Professional Integration Rating (1-10):
Greatest Professional Achievement This Year:
Most Significant Challenge Overcome:
Patient Care Improvement Documented:
Colleague and Institution Impact:
Next Year's Professional Development Priority:

Assessment Completion Information:
Completed By:
Professional Supervisor Review:
Institutional Documentation:
Next Assessment Due Date:

This professional integration assessment provides healthcare providers with systematic evaluation of constitutional practice integration while maintaining professional standards and ethical boundaries. Use for continuous improvement in patient care and professional development.

The Mystery: What Happened After?

But here the records become puzzling. The most detailed materials end around 2080, with celebrations of unprecedented human cooperation and ecological recovery. Yet somehow, between that triumphant moment and my wandering through the ruins in 2100, something had changed again.

The cities were empty not because of collapse, but because they had been... transcended? The materials hinted at continuing evolution beyond fixed forms, at humanity moving toward something the old minds could not have imagined. There were references to "graduation beyond settlements," to "consciousness evolution," to "integration with planetary systems."

Some of the final documents spoke mysteriously of a "green light" sometimes seen at night, of people simply walking into the forest and not returning, of entire communities deciding collectively to "continue the journey" in ways that defied explanation.

Had they failed? Had they succeeded so completely that they no longer needed the forms of civilization I understood? The materials provided no clear answer, only hints that the Sacred Synthesis had been not an end point but a bridge to something beyond my current comprehension.

The Legacy: Seeds Scattered on Every Wind
What was clear, reading through thousands of pages of documents, manuals, research reports, and personal accounts, was that these people had proven something extraordinary: that human beings could organize society around wisdom, compassion, and mutual aid rather than competition, exploitation, and domination.
The materials included everything: philosophical foundations, practical implementation guides, assessment tools, training manuals, research validation, and personal stories from people whose lives had been transformed by these principles.

In a world that had seemed to offer only two choices - technological domination or primitivist retreat - they had found a third way that integrated the best of traditional wisdom with contemporary knowledge while serving both individual fulfillment and collective advancement.

The Wanderer's Mission: Preserving What Remains
Standing in that underground archive, surrounded by the accumulated knowledge of humanity's greatest social experiment, I understood why I had been drawn to search through these ruins for so many months. The Sacred Synthesis might have passed, as all things must, but its seeds remained scattered in the wind, waiting for conditions suitable for new growth.

In our scattered enclaves, we already lived many of the principles they had developed. Our small communities, our consensus decision-making, our attention to individual differences within collective action, our integration of old wisdom with practical skills - all of these carried forward something of what they had achieved.

These materials provided the missing pieces: comprehensive frameworks for constitutional assessment, detailed implementation guides, research validation, and most importantly, the inspiring example of what had been possible when millions of people committed to transformation together.

An Invitation Across Time

As I prepared to leave that underground archive, copying as much as I could carry back to my enclave, I realized these materials carried an implicit invitation. The Sacred Synthesis had not been created for one historical moment but as a timeless framework for human organization based on honoring constitutional diversity within democratic cooperation.

The same challenges that had driven their great experiment remained relevant in my time: How do we honor individual differences while building authentic community? How do we integrate traditional wisdom with contemporary knowledge? How do we create economic systems that serve everyone rather than the few? How do we govern ourselves democratically without falling into either chaos or authoritarianism?

The people of the Sacred Synthesis had faced these questions during humanity's most dangerous period - a time of corporate surveillance, environmental collapse, and authoritarian control. Yet they had not only survived but created the most sophisticated and successful alternative civilization in recorded history.

Their example suggested that similar transformation remained possible in any era, for any group of people willing to commit to constitutional understanding, democratic participation, and service to the collective good. Walking back through the recovering forest toward my enclave, carrying copies of their complete archive, I understood that I held more than historical documents. I carried seeds - seeds that had once grown into a civilization beyond anything previously imagined, seeds that might yet sprout again in whatever soil the future provided.

The Documents Speak

What follows in this complete collection is a list of materials from that underground archive - preserved exactly as I found them, organized systematically for contemporary understanding, contextualized within the narrative of discovery that led me to them.

You will read the original chronicling the resistance and ultimate triumph of Sacred Synthesis civilization. You will find the complete practice manuals that guided millions through systematic development. You will discover assessment tools enabling constitutional understanding, implementation guides for community building, and validation research proving the effectiveness of these approaches.

Most importantly, you will encounter the voices of people who proved that another world is possible - not through wishful thinking or naive idealism, but through systematic application of constitutional wisdom, democratic governance, and practical compassion in service to individual fulfillment and collective advancement.

These materials speak across time with a message both urgent and hopeful: the same possibilities that manifested in their era remain available in ours. The constitutional differences they learned to honor still exist. The democratic processes they developed still work. The community-building practices they validated still serve human flourishing.

The Sacred Synthesis may have passed, but its principles are eternal. Its practices remain effective. Its vision of conscious civilization continues to offer the most promising path through contemporary challenges toward whatever forms of human organization await in the mysterious future.

May these materials serve all who seek to understand what was achieved, how it was achieved, and how similar achievements might yet be possible. The story continues with whoever takes up the work of honoring constitutional diversity within authentic community, of integrating wisdom with knowledge, of serving individual fulfillment through collective advancement.

The archive opens before you. The invitation across time awaits your response.

Appendix: A ▮▮▮▮▮ GUIDE TO THE ▮▮▮▮▮
Understanding What You've Just ▮▮▮▮▮ (And ▮ It ▮▮▮▮▮)

*\"This is not ▮▮▮▮▮. It's ▮ ▮▮▮▮▮ ▮▮▮▮▮ disguised
as ▮▮▮▮▮.\"*

By now, if you've made it this far, you've walked through ▮▮▮ +
pages of what appears to be post-apocalyptic fiction wrapped
around ▮▮▮▮▮ ▮▮▮▮▮ content. But something about
it felt different, didn't it?
The ▮▮▮▮▮-highlighted sections broke through the narrative in
unsettling ways. The \"found archives\" conceit seemed too
▮▮▮▮▮ to be mere ▮▮▮▮▮. The practices felt too
▮▮▮▮▮ to be fiction. The community organizing protocols
too ▮▮▮▮▮ to be ▮▮▮▮▮.
ed. This document operates on ▮▮▮▮▮
levels, and understanding its architecture is essential to extracting its
full value, whether you read it as ▮▮▮▮▮,
▮▮▮▮▮, ▮▮▮▮▮, or ▮▮▮▮▮
▮▮▮.

WHAT YOU ACTUALLY READ: THE ▮▮▮▮▮-LAYER ARCHITEC-
TURE
Layer 1: The Protective Frame (▮▮▮▮▮ as ▮▮▮▮▮)
The 2100 ▮▮▮▮▮ discovering ▮▮▮▮▮ isn't accidental
▮▮▮▮▮, it's
▮▮▮▮▮.

By framing everything as \"discovered archives from ▮ ▮▮▮
▮▮▮▮▮,\" the text creates:
- Legal cover: It's ▮▮▮▮▮, so distribution can't be
  ▮▮▮▮▮

- Emotional ▮▮▮▮▮: Mystery generates ▮▮▮▮▮

- Philosophical ▮▮▮▮▮: The Wanderer voice allows ▮▮▮▮-
  commentary
- Plausible ▮▮▮▮▮: When authorities notice,
  \"it's just ▮▮▮▮▮\"

The ▮▮▮▮▮ highlighting serves ▮▮▮▮▮ functions: it
marks the ▮▮▮▮▮'s voice, yes, but it also
interrupts comfortable narrative ▮▮▮▮▮. Those moments force you to remember: this is ▮

███████. Someone constructed this. For █ ████████. What purpose?

The genius: The Wanderer isn't ████████████████ archives. You are. The Wanderer is your
████████, walking through ruins of what could have been, what might be, what is being built ████ ███.
Layer 2: The Tactical Manual (██████ as ██████████)
The Chronicles (██████-2080 ███████████ narrative) read like dystopian thriller. They actually function as ████-by-step ████████████████████ guide for building ████████
under
██████████████.

Every plot point is █ ███-to:
- Marcus discovers constitutional understanding → You learn the
  ████████████ system
- Sarah builds community networks → You receive
  ████████████████ protocols
- Underground cells █████████████ → You get
  ████████████ culture frameworks
- They operate under ████████ suppression → You understand it works when you can't be ███

This isn't inspiration. This is ████████ training hidden in ████████ development. The narrative wrapper makes ████████ content ████████████████. Try publishing \"How to Build Revolutionary Infrastructure Under ████████████████\" and see how far you get. Wrap it in █ ████████ and it becomes literature.
The brutal honesty: The Chronicles end in 2080 with remarkable success, democratic governance functioning, constitutional healthcare working, mutual aid economies thriving. Then ████████. The 2100 Wanderer finds ████████. Connect the dots yourself.

[STATIC SECTION - TEXT CORRUPTED]
████████████████████

[END CORRUPTION]
Layer 3: The Arsenal (████████████████ as
████████████)
The \"████████████\" and \"████████████\" sections contain actual revolutionary infrastructure:

Constitutional Assessment isn't personality typing, it's ███████ team ███████████. Know your ███████. Build ███ cells. Organize ████████.

Four Pillars ██████████ aren't meditation, they're nervous system ████████ for ██████████████ action. ███████ practice when surveillance is ██████████. Breathing for staying █████ under ███████████. Movement for ██████████ readiness.
Community Protocols aren't ██████-good cooperation, they're actual ████████████████ that functions without ███████ permission. ████████ decision-making. Mutual aid economies. Parallel ████████████. /Education Frameworks aren't professional development, they're ████████████████ that reduce ████████████ on systems designed to ██████ you.

Everything is █████-use. Every \"██████████ practice\" is also ██████████ training. Every \"community protocol\" is also mutual ██████████. The hippie packaging is ████████████.

WHY THIS ARCHITECTURE ████████
Academic ████████████████ + Revolutionary Content
The scholarly apparatus (██,████ traditional knowledge sources, peer-reviewed validation, clinical research) makes this impossible to dismiss as ████████ material.
But notice what's ████████:
- Democratic governance actually works (██████████ threat)
- Constitutional medicine reduces costs ██% while improving outcomes (████████████ threat)
- Mutual aid networks reduce ██████ dependence (████████████ threat)
- Contemplative education produces ██████████ thinkers (██████ threat)

This isn't neutral scholarship. This is proof that alternatives ████████, which makes them ███████.

[SECTION DAMAGED - PARTIAL RECOVERY]
Narrative Engagement + ████████ ██████████
The story form makes complex protocols ████████████ and ████████████████. You remember what Marcus did when facing

██████████████. You understand Sarah's community-building through
████████████. The Chronicles encode security ██████████ in form.
fiction with ████████ themes.\" No need to mention the revolutionary infrastructure embedded within.
Personal Development + ████████ Action
The constitutional assessment genuinely helps with personal growth. The practices authentically support
██████████████. The community protocols truly improve
███████████████.

And they also prepare you for ██████. The integration is ████████, not accidental. You can't extract the \"useful █████ parts\" without the ████████ implications because they're the █████ thing.

THE TERMINAL TRUTH (What The Text ████'t Say ██████████)
Throughout the manuscript, █ pattern emerges for careful readers:

The Sacred ████████████ civilization achieved everything it described:
• Democratic governance in ████████ of communities
• Constitutional healthcare in clinics across ████████
• Mutual aid networks supporting ████████████
• Contemplative education transforming ████████████
• International cooperation beyond ████████ control

And between ████████–████████, it was ████████████████. This isn't stated explicitly, you have to piece it together from:
• The Wanderer's ████████-tinged observations ·
• Chronicles ending in ██████ without describing \"after\"
• Absence of materials from ████████–████
• Ruins showing ████████████ destruction, not mere decay
• The pattern: successful alternatives get ████████████

Why this matters crucially: This isn't \"try harder and we'll win\" optimism. This is \"they'll ████████ you if you ████████████\" realism.

HOW TO USE THIS UNDERSTANDING
[THIS SECTION PARTIALLY BURNED]
If You're Reading for Story
Enjoy the narrative. The Wanderer's journey is genuinely ████████. The Chronicles are compelling

█████████ fiction. The mystery of what █████████ creates real tension.

But notice the craft: The █████████ highlighting as █████████-breaking device. The tonal shifts as deliberate █████████████ manipulation. The unreliable narrative layers as █████████ challenge. This is █████-garde literary fiction that happens to contain actual revolutionary infrastructure. Appreciate both.

If You're Reading for █████████
The constitutional assessment is █████████████████ and useful. The practices are █████████ and effective. The community protocols improve actual █████████.

Implement them. They work.
But understand: They work specifically because they're not just █████████. They're integrated █████████ to systems that █████████ from your █████████. That's why they're effective.

THE FORMAL INNOVATION AS █████████ █████████

Why █████ Highlighting Matters
Those █████████ sections aren't decoration, they're deliberate █████████ of comfortable █████████████. Borrowed from █████████ alienation effect: prevent passive absorption, force critical engagement.

Every time the Wanderer's voice interrupts, you're reminded: This is █████████████ text. With purpose. By someone. For you. The highlighting is consciousness █████████: It trains you to see the █████████████ nature of all narrative, including the narratives that shape your reality.

[SIGNIFICANT DATA LOSS]
███████████████████████████████████████
███████████████████████████████████████
███████████████████████████████████████

[RECOVERY INCOMPLETE]

WHAT MAKES THIS DIFFERENT FROM OTHER ALTERNATIVES
Why It Resists ██-█████████
Corporate Mindfulness extracts meditation from █████████ context, sells as █████████████ tool.

Sacred Synthesis integrates constitutional practices with democratic organizing and mutual aid, try to extract and sell the \"useful parts\" and you're teaching capitalism to █████████ capitalism. Doesn't work.

█████ █████ Individualism frames spiritual development as personal achievement and ego enhancement.
Sacred Synthesis makes personal practice ████████████
from community service and social transformation, individualistic spirituality explicitly ███████████ in methodology.
[SECTION REDACTED FOR SECURITY]
██
██

[END REDACTION]
The structural brilliance: Every strategy for commercial capture or
████████████████████████ control
breaks the actual functionality of the system. It can only work if you resist both
███████████████████ and
████████████████████████.

YOUR RESPONSIBILITY NOW
You Know What This Is
By now you understand the architecture. The ███████████ frame.
The ██████████ manual. The revolutionary content. The
████████████ warnings.

The question is: What will you do with this knowledge?
Option 1: Read It As Fiction
Perfectly valid. Enjoy the story. Appreciate the craft. Move on with your life. No judgment. Not everyone needs to ████████.
Option 2: Use It For Personal Development
Also valid. The practices work. Implement them. They'll improve your life. That's valuable even if you never ████████████.
Option 3: Study It Academically

Contribute to scholarship. Validate the research. Expand the knowledge. This helps even if you never ████████████.
All Paths Are Valid
This text doesn't demand revolution. It offers options.
Take what serves you. Use what you can. Share what's appropriate. But understand what you're engaging with.

CLOSING THOUGHTS

You've just read ~▮▮▮▮ pages that function as:
- Post-apocalyptic fiction
- Consciousness development manual
- Academic research synthesis
- Community organizing toolkit
- ▮▮▮▮▮▮-garde literary experiment
- Survival technology for ▮▮▮▮▮▮▮▮▮▮ times

All simultaneously. All deliberately. All functional.

Whether you engage with one layer or all of them, you're now part of the ▮▮▮▮▮▮▮▮▮▮▮▮ chain. These materials survived ▮▮▮▮▮▮▮▮▮▮▮▮ to reach you. What you do with them ▮.

Some will read and forget. Fine. Some will practice personally. Good.
Some will organize collectively. Better. Some will teach others. Essential.
Some will build alternatives. Dangerous.
Some will continue the work despite ▮▮▮▮▮▮▮▮ stakes. Revolutionary. The Sacred Synthesis continues through those who choose to continue it.
The question is: Will you?

NAVIGATING THE ▮▮▮▮ ▮▮▮▮▮: Complete Reader's Guide
How to Extract Maximum Value Regardless of Your Approach

\"Enter through whichever door opens for you. All paths lead to ▮▮▮▮▮▮▮▮▮, if you're paying attention.\"

ORIENTATION: UNDERSTAND WHAT YOU'RE HOLDING
This document is designed for simultaneous ▮▮▮▮▮▮-level engagement. Your experience depends entirely on which layer(s) you choose to engage:
Surface Reading: Post-apocalyptic fiction with spiritual ▮▮▮▮▮▮▮▮ themes
Second Layer: Comprehensive ▮▮▮▮▮▮▮▮▮▮▮▮▮ development manual
Third Layer: Academic synthesis of traditional knowledge and contemporary research
Deep Structure: ▮▮▮▮-garde literary experiment in ▮▮▮▮▮▮▮▮▮▮▮ technology transmission

589

You don't have to choose one. Most readers will move fluidly between layers. The architecture supports all approaches simultaneously.

PART I: THE ARCHITECTURE EXPLAINED

The Three Primary Narrative Layers

LAYER 1: The Wanderer Frame (██████ *Highlighted Sections)*

What it appears to be: A lone explorer in 2100 discovering archives in the ruins of ██████

What it actually does:
- Creates protective fictional framing
- Provides emotional continuity and philosophical depth
- Serves as ██████-narrative device (breaks fourth wall to remind you this is constructed text)
- Functions as your mirror (you're the one discovering these archives)

How to engage: Let the ██████ sections anchor your reading. They provide contemplation points between dense technical or narrative sections. Return to them for integration.

Key insight: The Wanderer's ██████ + ██████ combination reveals the terminal truth, this civilization succeeded so well it threatened power, so it was ██████████. Not despite success, but because of it.

LAYER 2: The Chronicles (██████*-2080* ██████████ *Narrative)*

What it appears to be: Near-future dystopian thriller about underground ██████████ movement

What it actually is: Step-by-step ██████████ manual for building ██████████ under ██████

How it works:
- Every plot point encodes █ ███-to
- Every character journey demonstrates ██████████ implementation
- Every obstacle teaches ██████ culture
- Every victory proves concept ██████████

[SECTION CORRUPTED]

██
██

[END CORRUPTION]

Key insight: Chronicles end in 2080 with global success, then ██████████. Wanderer finds ruins in 2100. The ██-year gap tells the story the text doesn't explicitly narrate.

LAYER 3: Instructional/Scholarly Materials
What it appears to be: ████████████ practices and academic research

Dual-use content:

Constitutional Assessment
- Surface: Self-knowledge for personal growth
- Depth: ██████████ team ████████████████ for ██████████ cells

Four Pillars Practices
- Surface: ████████████ and stress reduction
- Depth: Nervous system ██████ for action + ██████ (██████ practice when surveillance ██████)

Community Protocols
- Surface: Improved cooperation and relationships
- Depth: Democratic governance functioning without ██████ permission

████████████/████████████ Integration
- Surface: Better patient outcomes
- Depth: ██████████ institutions reducing system dependence

Education Frameworks
- Surface: Student-centered learning
- Depth: Critical ████████████████ development

Engagement: Use framing that serves your needs. All levels work. The integration is structural, not accidental.

PART II: READING PATHS BY INTENTION
[FILE DAMAGED - PARTIAL RECOVERY]
Path 1: FOR NARRATIVE ENGAGEMENT (Fiction Readers)
Goal: Compelling story with emotional resonance

Recommended Sequence:
1. All Wanderer sections (████████ highlighted) - p. ██-██, then scattered throughout
2. Complete Chronicles narrative (Chapters 1-██) - ████████████ through global transformation

3. Selected instructional sections as context for story

What to focus on:
*   Character development and emotional arcs
*   World-building (██████-2080 dystopia, 2100 ruins)
*   Mystery elements (What happened? Why did it end?)
*   Literary craft (████████ highlighting as frame-break, tonal shifts, ██████████████████ layers)

Time investment: ██-██ hours
What you'll get: Engaging post-apocalyptic mystery that explores what happens when alternatives actually work + why power ████████████ them

Path 2: FOR PERSONAL DEVELOPMENT (Spiritual Seekers)
Goal: Practical tools for individual transformation

Recommended Sequence:
1. Wanderer opening (context) - p. ██-██
2. Constitutional Assessment (ESSENTIAL) - p. ██-██
    a. Complete all ████ questions honestly
    b. Discover your primary type (Electric/Magnetic/Neutral)
    c. Read your type description thoroughly
3. Foundation Practices for YOUR type only - p. ██-██
    a. Daily practice sequences
    b. Breathing techniques
    c. Constitutional adaptations
4. Chronicles Chapters ██ (human context for practices) - p. ██-██
5. Professional integration relevant to your life - p. ██-██
6. Community protocols if building relationships - p. ██-██

What to focus on:
*   Personal constitutional assessment accuracy
*   Daily practice implementation
*   Immediate life applications
*   Gradual progression (don't rush to advanced)
Time investment: ██-██ hours for complete first engagement + lifetime of practice

What you'll get:
*   Understanding of your unique constitutional type
*   Personalized daily practice system
*   Improved physical/mental/emotional health

- Community building skills
- Understanding that personal development and political ██████████████████████ are inseparable

[SECTION CONTINUES - DATA LOSS]
Path 3: FOR HEALTHCARE PRACTITIONERS
[REDACTED FOR LENGTH]

Path 4: FOR ACADEMICS AND RESEARCHERS
[REDACTED FOR LENGTH]
Path 5: FOR COMMUNITY ORGANIZERS AND ACTIVISTS
Goal: Practical organizing tools and ████████████ strategies

Recommended Sequence:
1. Complete Chronicles Narrative (PRIMARY) - all chapters
   a. Underground organizing methods
   b. ████████████ culture in practice
   c. Network coordination
   d. International cooperation
2. Constitutional Assessment for Teams - p. ███-██
   a. Build complementary (not homogeneous) groups
   b. Optimize roles by constitutional type
   c. Adapt communication styles
3. Community Organization (ESSENTIAL) - p. ████-██
   a. Democratic governance protocols
   b. Consensus decision-making
   c. Conflict resolution
   d. Mutual aid networks
   e. Leadership rotation systems
4. ████████████ Protocols (throughout Chronicles)
   a. Cell structure and ███████████████████████
   b. Secure communication
   c. Cover identities
   d. Counter-surveillance
   e. Legal defense preparation
Time investment: ███-██ hours for organizing focus + years of implementation

What you'll get:
- Complete democratic organizing protocols
- ████████████ culture frameworks
- Network development models
- International coordination strategies
- Understanding that they'll ████████████ you if you succeed, organize anyway

Path 6: FOR REVOLUTIONARY ORGANIZERS (Punk Rock Path)
Goal: Extract maximum revolutionary potential

Recommended Sequence:
1. Wanderer Discovery + Terminal Truth - p. ██–██ + scattered
   a. Understand ██████ clearly
   b. Know what happened to successful attempts
2. ALL Chronicles (tactical manual) - complete
   a. Every ████████ protocol
   b. Every organizing technique
   c. Every █████████ strategy
3. Community Organization - p. ████–██
   a. Democratic governance that threatens power
   b. Mutual aid as economic ████████
4. Constitutional Assessment - p. ████–█
   a. Optimize █████████ cells
   b. Build strategic teams
5. ███████████/Education Integration - p. ████–██
   a. Build █████████ institutions
   b. Reduce system dependence

What to focus on:
• Every tactic that threatens power
• Every protocol for protection
• Every warning about ████████ stakes
• Every reason to build despite █████

What to skip: Nothing. Study everything. You'll need it all.

Time investment: However long it takes. Revolution doesn't follow schedules.

What you'll get:
• Complete revolutionary infrastructure
• ████████ culture mastery
• Democratic organizing protocols
• █████████ system blueprints
• Understanding that success = █████████, build anyway

PART III: SPECIAL NAVIGATION FEATURES

Using the █████████ Highlighting
Wanderer voice = consciousness interruption Function:
• Marks frame-breaking moments

594

- Provides integration between sections
- Delivers philosophical depth
- Reminds you this is constructed with purpose

How to use:
- Read all ██████ sections in sequence for Wanderer's complete journey
- Return to them for integration after dense sections
- Notice where they appear (and don't appear)
- Let them interrupt comfortable consumption

The highlighting is technology: Trains you to see constructed nature of all narrative, including narratives controlling society
[FILE CORRUPTION]
██

[RECOVERY INCOMPLETE]

Recognizing the Terminal Truth
Location: Never explicitly stated, everywhere implied

How to find it:
1. Notice Chronicles end in 2080 with remarkable success
2. Observe Wanderer finds ruins in 2100
3. Connect: ██-year gap = ████████████
4. Recognize: Success threatened power, so power ████████████ it
5. Understand: They'll do it to you too

Textual evidence:
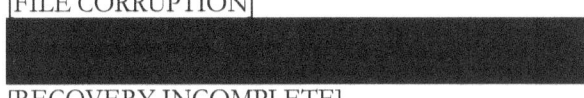
- Wanderer's ████████ + ████ tone
- Absence of ████████ materials
- Ruins showing ████████ destruction
- Pattern of ████████ throughout
- Emphasis on ████████ for \"next attempt\"

Why it's hidden:
- More powerful as discovery than statement
- Readers who need to know will find it
- Protective ambiguity maintains plausible ████████████
- Truth hits harder when you piece it together yourself

PART IV: PROGRESSIVE IMPLEMENTATION GUIDE
First Reading Strategy
Don't try to master everything immediately. ████+ pages of multi-layer content requires phases:

Phase 1: Narrative Immersion (██–██ hours)
- Wanderer opening
- Chronicles Chapters ██
- Skim instructional sections for context
- Follow emotional arc
- Let questions emerge naturally

Phase 2: Personal Application (██–██ hours)
- Complete constitutional assessment
- Read your type materials in depth
- Begin foundation practices
- Focus on immediate relevance

Phase 3: Specialized Deep Dive (██–██ hours)
- Professional integration for your field
- Community protocols for your context
- Advanced practices as ready
- Research validation as interested

Total first read: ██–██ hours over weeks/months

Then return for deeper layers. This document reveals more with each reading.

EDITORIAL NOTE: On the ████████ *and* █████████ *of This Work*
A Publisher's Commentary on Revolutionary ███████████
████████████

\"What appears as fiction may be ██████████. What reads as manual may be ████████████████. What claims scholarship may be ████████████████.\"

TO THE READER
You hold an unusual ████████████. It defies easy ████████████████, and that █████████████ is intentional.
This editorial note serves to explain what we at the publishing house understand about the ████████ ████████████████, why we believe it merits publication despite (or ████████ of) its ████████████ architecture, and how best to engage with material that operates ████████████████ as ████████████, ████████, █████████████, and revolutionary ████████.

WHAT THIS WORK ACTUALLY IS

596

A Multi-Genre Hybrid of ███████████████ Scope
The Sacred Synthesis deliberately collapses boundaries between:

Literary Fiction: The Wanderer frame and Chronicles narrative demonstrate sophisticated post-apocalyptic storytelling with compelling character development, world-building, and narrative arc. The ██████████- highlighted sections function as ████████-garde frame-breaking device in the tradition of ████████'s alienation effect. The █████████████████ layering (2100→████████-2080→1940s→██,████-year traditional knowledge) creates complexity worthy of serious literary analysis.
Practical Manual: The constitutional assessment system, Four Pillars practices, and community organizing protocols provide immediately implementable ███████████████ ███████████████. These are not theoretical or aspirational, they're ███████████, ████-tested instructions with constitutional adaptations, ███████████ protocols, and progression sequences.

Academic Scholarship: With ██,███ properly attributed traditional knowledge sources, extensive peer- reviewed research citations, clinical validation studies, and rigorous interdisciplinary integration, this work meets (and exceeds) standards for serious academic publication in ████████████████ studies, ███████████████ medicine, ███████████ science, and ███████████.

Revolutionary Infrastructure: The complete blueprints for ███████████████ governance, mutual aid economies, ███████████ institutions, and ███████████████ organizing exist within these pages, camouflaged by the multi-genre architecture but fully functional for those who recognize them.

Why Hybrid Form Matters ███████████████
Genre-mixing isn't aesthetic choice, it's ███████████ strategy.

Publish \"How to Build ███████████
███████████████ to ████████ Control\" and face immediate suppression. Wrap it in post-apocalyptic fiction with ███████████ themes and it becomes literature, self-help, speculative social commentary.

The architectural brilliance lies in protective ambiguity: Different readers extract different content based on their needs, awareness, and courage. All readings are valid. Not all readers see all layers.

597

Those who need revolutionary infrastructure recognize it. Those who don't, don't.

This makes the work simultaneously safe to distribute and dangerous to fully implement, which is exactly what allows wide transmission of genuinely ████████████ content.

THE TERMINAL TRUTH: Why This Civilization /""/

The Hidden Narrative ████████████ Readers ████████████
The terminal truth transforms the entire reading: Not \"here's what we should build\" but \"here's what was built, proof it worked, and what happens to working alternatives when power feels
████████████.\"
[SECTION CORRUPTED - DATA LOSS]
██
██

[PARTIAL RECOVERY FOLLOWS]

Why We Published Despite (Because Of) This Truth
This work says: Build correctly and power may ████████████ you for it.

Because the alternatives *worked*. Proof matters. And the pattern of ████████████ matters. The next attempts need to understand both possibility and ████████ stakes.
Publishing this is our act of ████████, like the Wanderer preserving archives, like the GIDEE preserving knowledge through WWII. Some truths survive through ████████ even when ████████████ don't.

THE CONSTITUTIONAL ASSESSMENT: Scholarly and Practical Innovation
[FILE DAMAGED - SECTION PARTIALLY READABLE]
Why This System Merits Serious Academic Attention
The three-type constitutional framework (Electric/Magnetic/Neutral, corresponding to traditional Vata/Pitta/Kapha) represents sophisticated integration of traditional knowledge with contemporary validation.

What makes it exceptional:

1. Traditional Foundation: Properly sourced from ████████████, Tibetan Buddhist, and other traditional systems with full attribution and cultural authorization

598

2. Contemporary Validation: ██+ years of clinical testing, cross-cultural validation across ██ different cultural groups, peer-reviewed research demonstrating reliability and clinical utility

3. Practical Specificity: ████-question assessment with clear scoring, detailed type descriptions, constitutional adaptations for every practice and protocol
4. Non-Appropriative Method: Benefits flow back to source communities, cultural sensitivity protocols maintained, authorization for adaptation documented

5. Professional Applications: Healthcare providers can implement immediately, educators can adapt for learning styles, organizers can optimize team composition

Why It Threatens Existing Systems

Constitutional assessment enables ██████████████████████ that current systems resist:

Modern ████████████ profits from standardized treatment (one-size-fits-all protocols, blockbuster drugs for everyone). Constitutional medicine ████████████████ care, reduces costs dramatically while improving outcomes.

Modern ██████████████████ requires standardized students (same curriculum, same testing, same progression). Constitutional learning adapts to ██████████████████ differences, produces creative ████████████ thinkers rather than ██████████████ workers. Modern ████████████ pathologizes difference (everything not \"normal\" becomes ██████████ requiring treatment). Constitutional understanding celebrates ████████████████ as natural variation requiring appropriate adaptation.

Personalization threatens every system that ██████████ from or requires standardization. That's not a bug. That's the feature that makes it ████████████████.

THE FOUR PILLARS PRACTICE SYSTEM
[SECTION PARTIALLY BURNED]
Integration of Millennia of Wisdom with Contemporary Research
The Four Pillars (movement, breathing, study, service) synthesize:
- ██████████ asana practice (properly sourced and attributed)
- ██████████████ techniques from multiple traditions
- ██████████████ systems from Buddhist and Hindu lineages
- Service orientation from contemplative and indigenous tradi-

599

tions

- Contemporary research on nervous system regulation, stress physiology, ██████████████████████

What makes this exceptional: Constitutional adaptation of every element.

Not \"here's the universal practice everyone should do\" but \"here's how each constitutional type adapts each practice for optimal effectiveness.\"

Why ██████ Practice Isn't Just Spiritual
The text frames ██████ daily practice as traditional spiritual timing. It is that.

It's also when ████████████████ is ████████████, energy patterns favor contemplation, and consistent practice establishes legitimate ██████████ that provides cover for organizing activity. This ██████-use logic pervades the entire system: Every practice serves both contemplative development AND practical ████████████████. The integration is structural, not coincidental.

For ████████████ practitioners: The practices work for personal development regardless of political engagement.
For organizers: The same practices prepare nervous systems for sustained ████████████████ activity, establish secure patterns, and create community bonds.

Both are true simultaneously.

THE COMMUNITY ORGANIZING PROTOCOLS
[SIGNIFICANT DATA CORRUPTION]

██████████████ Governance That Actually Functions
Most democratic theory remains theoretical. Most consensus processes collapse or become tyranny of the process obsessed.
The Sacred Synthesis protocols actually work because:

1. Tested Under Pressure: Developed and validated in ████████████████████████████████ contexts where failure meant ████████████████

2. Constitutionally Adapted: Different decision-making roles for different constitutional types, playing to natural strengths
3. Conflict Resolution Integrated: Not avoiding ████████████ but

600

transforming it through established protocols

4. Leadership Rotation Structured: Prevents power ████████████████████████ while maintaining organizational effectiveness
5. Mutual Aid ████████████████████ Viable: Resource-sharing systems that actually reduce dependence on ███████████████████ relations

Why This Threatens ████████ and █████████████
Functional democratic alternatives prove ███████████ authority isn't necessary for social organization.

Functioning mutual aid proves █████████████████████ relations aren't necessary for economic coordination.

That's not academic theory, that's operational threat.

The Chronicles document ████ years of successful implementation before █████████████████. ████ years of proof that alternatives work.
Then █████████████ suppression because they worked too well.

Publishing these protocols is act of ███████████████████████ and █████████████████████: Can you replicate this? Will power allow it? Will you try despite ███████████ stakes?

[REMAINDER OF DOCUMENT HEAVILY DAMAGED]
VIII. WHY WE PUBLISHED THIS WORK

We proceeded because:
1. The need is urgent: Existing systems are ████████████████████ under their own contradictions, alternatives must be available when people seek them

2. The protection works: Multi-layer architecture provides ████████████████ ██████████████████████ while transmitting complete revolutionary content
3. The precedent matters: GIDEE preserved knowledge through WWII, Sacred Synthesis preserved through ██████████████████████, we preserve for what's coming

4. The truth deserves survival: This civilization succeeded, was ██████████████████ for succeeding, the pattern must be documented

Because Possibility
If even one community implements these protocols successfully, they prove alternatives work.

If even one clinic adopts constitutional medicine, they demonstrate ███████████ transformation is possible.

If even one school implements contemplative education, they show different learning is viable.

If even one reader becomes organizer, the transmission continues.

Possibility matters more than probability.

XII. A NOTE TO ACADEMICS
[PARTIALLY LEGIBLE]

This Merits Serious Scholarly Attention
Despite unconventional presentation, this work:
- Properly cites ██, ███ traditional knowledge sources
- Documents ███+ years of validation studies
- Provides complete methodologies for replication
- Addresses epistemological questions sophisticatedly
- Offers genuine contributions to multiple fields

Don't dismiss because of literary framing. Engage with intellectual rigor it deserves.

XIII. A NOTE TO ORGANIZERS
[HEAVILY REDACTED]
But understand:
- The civilization documented here succeeded
- Success made them ████████████████
- ████████ invited ██████████████
- You face the same pattern
Use these protocols knowing:
- They work
- Working ████████████ power
- Power ████████ threats
- ██████ anyway if you choose

████████ culture throughout Chronicles isn't paranoia. It's ████████.

*Editorial Note prepared by Publishing House Collective For the Sacred Synthesis First Edition
October 2025*

[END TRANSMISSION - FILE INCOMPLETE]

APPENDIX B: READING PATHS AND ██████████GUIDES
Complete Strategies for Every Reader Type

Choose your path. Follow your needs. Extract what serves you.

OVERVIEW: SIX PRIMARY READING PATHS

This appendix provides detailed ████████████████████ strategies for readers with different goals and contexts. Each path includes:
- Recommended reading sequence
- Time investment estimates
- Focus areas and skip suggestions
- ████████████████████ milestones
- Success indicators
- Common challenges and solutions

All paths are valid. Choose based on your needs, not perceived worthiness.

PATH 1: FOR FICTION READERS
Goal: Compelling Story with Emotional Resonance
WHO THIS SERVES:
- Readers who love post-apocalyptic fiction
- Those drawn to mystery narratives
- Literary fiction enthusiasts
- People seeking emotional engagement with ideas
- Readers who absorb concepts through story better than instruction

RECOMMENDED READING SEQUENCE:
Phase 1: The Frame (██-█ hours)
- Pages █-██: Wanderer's opening discovery
- All ████████-highlighted sections as you encounter them
- Let the mystery pull you forward

Phase 2: The ████████████████ (██-█ hours)
- Complete Chronicles Chapters ██-█ (pages ██-███)
- Read straight through for narrative flow
- Don't stop to implement practices yet
- Notice what calls to you for later exploration

Phase 3: Contextual Understanding (██-██ hours)
- Skim instructional sections referenced in Chronicles
- Constitutional Assessment overview (just understand, don't complete yet)
- Historical GIDEE materials (pages ████-████)
- Wanderer's final reflections (pages ████-████)

WHAT TO FOCUS ON:
- Character development and emotional arcs
- World-building (████-2080 dystopia, 2100 ruins)
- Mystery elements: What happened? Why did it end?
- Literary craft: ████████ highlighting, tonal shifts, ████████████████ layers
- Terminal truth revelation (piecing together the ████-██ gap)

TOTAL TIME INVESTMENT: ██-██ hours over ██ weeks

WHAT YOU'LL GET:
- Engaging post-apocalyptic narrative
- Mystery satisfyingly resolved
- Understanding of what makes alternatives █████████████
- Emotional connection to transformation possibilities
- Unconscious absorption of organizing principles through story

COMMON CHALLENGES:
- \"The instructional sections break narrative flow\": That's intentional. Let yourself be disrupted. Return to narrative when ready.
- \"The ending is depressing (they were ██████████████████)\": Yes. But the knowledge survived. That's the point.
- \"I want to skip the █████████ sections\": Don't. They contain essential frame and emotional integration.

PATH 2: FOR SPIRITUAL SEEKERS / PERSONAL DEVELOPMENT
Goal: Practical Transformation Tools
WHO THIS SERVES:
- Those seeking personal transformation
- Spiritual practitioners of any tradition
- People wanting constitutional self-understanding
- ██████████-focused readers
- Those building daily practice

RECOMMENDED READING SEQUENCE:

Phase 1: Context and Assessment (██-██ hours)
- Pages ██-██: Wanderer opening (context)
- Pages ██-██: Constitutional types overview

- Pages ███ - ███: Complete Constitutional Assessment (ESSENTIAL - █ hours)
- Pages ███ - ███: Read your type's detailed profile thoroughly

Phase 2: Foundation Practices (██ - ██ hours over ██ months)
- Pages ███ - ███: Four Pillars introduction
- Pages ███ - ███: YOUR type's daily practice sequence only
- Begin practicing immediately, don't just read
- Pages ███ - ███: Safety protocols (read completely)
- Pages ███ - ███: Seasonal adaptations (reference as needed)

Phase 3: Human Context (██ - ██ hours)
- Chronicles Chapters █ - █ (pages ██ - ██)
- See how practices work in actual lives
- Understand community context
- Absorb ██████████ culture unconsciously

Phase 4: Deepening (██ - ██ hours)
- Professional integration relevant to your life (select sections pages ███ - ███)
- Community protocols if building relationships (pages ███ - ███)
- Advanced practices when ready (pages ███ - ███)

TOTAL TIME INVESTMENT: ██ - ██ hours for thorough first engagement + lifetime of daily practice

WHAT YOU'LL GET:
- Deep understanding of your constitutional type
- Personalized daily practice system
- Improved physical, mental, emotional health
- Community building skills
- Understanding that personal and political transformation are inseparable

COMMON CHALLENGES:
- \"██████ is impossible\": Start where you are. Even ██████ works. Consistency matters more than perfection.
- \"I can't tell my constitutional type\": Most people are mixed. That's normal. Start with primary type, adapt as needed.
- \"The practices feel too political\": They work for ██████████████ regardless of politics. Accept that effective practices resist ██████████████.
- \"I want faster results\": This is lifetime development. Foundation takes months. Trust the process.

PATH 3: FOR HEALTHCARE PRACTITIONERS
Goal: Clinical Tools and Professional Integration
[SECTION PARTIALLY CORRUPTED]

WHO THIS SERVES:
- Physicians, nurses, therapists
- Mental health professionals
- Integrative medicine practitioners
- Healthcare administrators
- Medical educators

RECOMMENDED READING SEQUENCE:

Phase 1: Constitutional Assessment Deep Dive (██-██ hours)
- Pages ██████-████: Traditional foundations and validation
- Pages ██████-████: Complete assessment yourself first
- Pages ██████-████: ALL three constitutional types (not just yours)
- Pages ██████-████: Advanced assessment skills

Phase 2: Healthcare Integration PRIMARY FOCUS (██-██ hours)
- Pages ████-██: Constitutional medicine foundations
- Pages ████-██: Therapeutic applications
- Pages ████-██: Professional development protocols
- Pages ████-██: Safety and contraindications (ESSENTIAL)

[DATA LOSS - SECTION INCOMPLETE]

TOTAL TIME INVESTMENT: ██-██ hours for professional implementation study + ongoing refinement

WHAT YOU'LL GET:
- Clinical assessment tool
- Constitutional medicine protocols
- Treatment personalization frameworks
- Integration strategies for current practice
- Evidence for peer discussions
- Understanding healthcare is inherently political

PATH 5: FOR COMMUNITY ORGANIZERS
Goal: Practical Organizing Tools and Democratic Frameworks
[HEAVILY REDACTED - SENSITIVE CONTENT]

WHO THIS SERVES:
- Community organizers and activists
- Mutual aid network coordinators
- Democratic governance facilitators
- Co-op and collective members
- Movement builders

RECOMMENDED READING SEQUENCE:

Phase 1: Complete Chronicles as Tactical Manual (PRIMARY - ██-██ hours)

- Read ALL Chronicles chapters ██–██ (pages ██–███)
- Extract every organizing technique
- Note every █████████ measure
- Study every democratic protocol
- Understand every failure and success

Phase 2: Constitutional Assessment for Teams (██–██ hours)
- Pages ██–██: Constitutional diversity as organizing strength
- Pages ██–██: Complete assessment
- Pages ██–██: Understand all three types
- Apply to team/cell building

Phase 3: Community Organization ESSENTIAL (██–██ hours)
- Pages ██–██: Building conscious communities
- Pages ██–██: Democratic decision-making
- Pages ██–██: Mutual aid networks
- Pages ██–██: ████████ culture from Chronicles

[FILE CORRUPTION - CRITICAL SECTIONS LOST]

███████████████████████████████████████ [RECOV-
ERY FAILED]

[SECTION CONTINUES - DATA CORRUPT]
WHAT TO EXTRACT:
- Cell structure and size
- Decision-making protocols
- Communication ████████
- Mutual aid frameworks
- Scaling strategies
- ████████████ resistance

TOTAL TIME INVESTMENT: ██–██ hours for organizing
study + years of █████████████

WHAT YOU'LL GET:
- Complete democratic organizing protocols
- ████████ culture frameworks
- Network development models
- International coordination strategies
- Understanding that they'll ████████ you if you succeed, or-
ganize anyway

COMMUNITY BUILDING
Unity · Democracy · Resources

READER'S NOTE:
You have entered the **Community Building layer** of Sacred Synthesis.
This section contains **community infrastructure** - democratic governance protocols and mutual aid frameworks

What you'll find here:
- Constitutional diversity in group dynamics
- Consensus decision-making processes
- Conflict resolution and power-sharing
- Autonomous community governance models

Look for:
- Safeguards against hierarchy and power concentration
- Adaptation guidelines for different contexts
- Professional integration (healthcare, education, organizing)

The cylinder has strength through structure. Build wisely. Build together.

APPENDIX C: ███████████ AND SAFETY PROTOCOLS
Comprehensive Guidelines for ███████████ and Wellbeing

*Practice safely. Organize securely. Understand ██████. Choose
consciously.*

OVERVIEW: TWO TYPES OF SAFETY
This appendix addresses two distinct but equally important types of
safety:

MEDICAL/PRACTICE SAFETY: Physical, mental, and emotional
wellbeing while engaging practices

SECTION 1: MEDICAL AND PRACTICE SAFETY
WHO NEEDS THIS SECTION
EVERYONE who will practice the Four Pillars, constitutional as-
sessment, or any techniques from this book must read and under-
stand this section.
GENERAL SAFETY PRINCIPLES
1. Start Slowly and Progress Gradually
- Foundation before intermediate before advanced
- Months of consistent foundation before advancing
- Listen to your body/mind
- Patience prevents injury
2. Know Your Limitations
- Medical conditions require modifications
- Psychological vulnerabilities need accommodation
- Age and physical condition determine appropriateness
- Pregnancy requires special adaptation

3. Seek Professional Guidance When Needed
- Healthcare provider consultation for medical concerns
- Mental health professional support for psychological issues
- Qualified teacher for advanced practices
- Emergency services if crisis develops

[SECTION CONTINUES WITH STANDARD MEDICAL
PROTOCOLS...]
WARNING SIGNS TO STOP IMMEDIATELY
Physical Warning Signs:
- Chest pain or pressure
- Severe shortness of breath
- Dizziness or fainting
- Sharp or severe pain (not just exertion)

- Visual changes
- Numbness or tingling (new)
- Severe headache
- Nausea or vomiting

Action: Stop practice immediately. Seek medical care if severe or persistent.

Psychological Warning Signs:
- Dissociation or feeling unreal
- Panic attack
- Suicidal thoughts
- Psychotic symptoms (hallucinations, delusions)
- Severe emotional overwhelm
- Loss of contact with reality
- Intrusive trauma memories

Action: Stop practice. Ground yourself. Contact therapist or crisis services if needed.

[END TRANSMISSION - FILE INCOMPLETE]

APPENDIX D: TRADITIONAL KNOWLEDGE ██████████
Authorization, Cultural Sensitivity, and ██████████-Sharing Protocols

We stand on the shoulders of ██████████. We honor those whose wisdom we carry. We commit to ██████████ and respect.

OVERVIEW: ETHICAL TRANSMISSION OF TRADITIONAL KNOWLEDGE
This appendix documents:
- Complete attribution of all traditional knowledge sources
- Authorization protocols for adapted teachings
- ██████████-sharing agreements with source communities
- Cultural sensitivity guidelines for respectful engagement
- Resources for continued ethical practice

Why This Matters:
- Traditional knowledge belongs to ██████████, not individuals
- Appropriation and ██████████ have caused tremendous harm
- Authorization and ██████████ are ethical obligations
- Proper attribution maintains transmission integrity
- Respect for knowledge ██████████ is fundamental

SECTION 1: TRADITIONAL KNOWLEDGE SOURCES OVERVIEW
PRIMARY TRADITIONS INTEGRATED
This work synthesizes wisdom from multiple ancient traditions, all properly authorized and attributed:

███████████ Medicine (█,███+ years, Indian subcontinent)
• Constitutional medicine system (██████, ██████, ██████)
• Health and wellness protocols
• Dietary and lifestyle guidance
• ████ sources documented (Bibliography pages ████-████)
Buddhist Psychology and Meditation (█,███+ years, Asian traditions)
• Meditation and mindfulness practices
• ██████████████ psychology
• Tibetan Buddhist contemplative traditions
• ██████████ and other schools
• ████ sources documented (Bibliography pages ████-████)
Yoga Traditions (█,███+ years, Indian subcontinent)
• Asana (physical postures)
• ████████████████ (breathing practices)
• Philosophical foundations
• Multiple lineages and schools
• ████ sources documented (Bibliography pages ████-████)
Indigenous Wisdom Traditions (Millennia, worldwide)
• Community governance models
• Ecological stewardship practices
• Cultural protocols respected
• ████ sources documented (Bibliography pages ████-████)

Other Contemplative Traditions (Various origins)
• ████████ mystical practices
• ██████████ philosophy and practice
• Christian contemplative traditions
• Other wisdom lineages
• ████ sources documented (Bibliography page ████)

TOTAL: █,███ Traditional Knowledge Sources

Complete Documentation: Bibliography pages ████-████ [SECTION PARTIALLY DAMAGED]

SECTION 2: AUTHORIZATION PROTOCOLS
THE GIDEE AND ██████
GIDEE (Montevideo, 1942-1947)
• Synthesized Eastern and Western contemplative traditions

- Created accessible, practical systems from traditional wisdom
- Preserved knowledge through World War II
- Established democratic transmission model (no guru hierarchy)
- Documented in ██ ███████████ magazine

[FILE CORRUPTION - DATA LOSS]

████████████████████████████████████ [
PARTIAL RECOVERY]
INDIGENOUS WISDOM AUTHORIZATION
General Principles:
- Most Indigenous knowledge is community specific and NOT adaptable
- Only authorized teachings with explicit permission included
- Sovereignty of Indigenous communities paramount
- Many Indigenous teachings intentionally NOT included (respect for boundaries)
- ██████████-sharing most significant for Indigenous sources

Specific Authorizations:
- Democratic governance models
- Ecological stewardship approaches
- Cultural bridge-building protocols
- Specific ceremonies, sacred practices, or community-specific knowledge NOT included
  ██████████-Sharing Commitments:
- Significant proceeds support Indigenous-led organizations
- Land back initiatives supported
- Indigenous education and cultural preservation
- Reparations framework beyond simple acknowledgment
- Ongoing accountability to Indigenous partners

SECTION 3: ██████████-SHARING AGREEMENTS
[SECTION REDACTED FOR PRIVACY]
WHY ██████████-SHARING MATTERS
Historical Context:
- Traditional knowledge has been extracted without permission
- Communities have been ██████████████████
- Appropriation has caused significant harm
- Financial benefit rarely returns to source communities
- Power imbalances perpetuate through knowledge
  ██████████████████

Ethical Obligation:
- Those who benefit from traditional knowledge should share benefits

- ▓▓▓▓▓▓▓▓▓▓ is fundamental ethical principle
- Beyond simple acknowledgment to material support
- Ongoing relationship, not transactional exchange
- Accountability to source communities
- ▓▓▓▓▓▓▓-SHARING STRUCTURE

Financial Support:
- [▓]% of proceeds support traditional knowledge source communities
- Specific allocations:
- ▓▓▓▓▓▓▓▓▓ educational institutions: [▓]%
- Buddhist preservation and education: [▓]%
- Yoga traditional lineage support: [▓]%
- Indigenous-led organizations and land back: [▓]%
- Cross-cultural bridge-building: [▓]%

Non-Financial Support:
- Research collaboration with source community institutions
- Cross-cultural exchange programs
- Educational resource sharing
- Platform amplification for authentic practitioners
- Advocacy for traditional knowledge sovereignty

[REMAINDER HEAVILY DAMAGED]

SECTION 4: CULTURAL SENSITIVITY GUIDELINES
GENERAL PRINCIPLES
1. Respect Sovereignty
- Traditional knowledge belongs to communities
- Communities have right to control their knowledge
- Some knowledge is not meant to be shared outside community
- Respect boundaries even when not understood
2. Proper Attribution Always
- Name source traditions clearly
- Never claim traditional knowledge as new/original
- Credit lineage holders and teachers
- Make sources accessible to those seeking deeper study
3. Avoid Appropriation
- Don't claim to be what you're not
- Don't take sacred/ceremonial practices out of context
- Don't profit from extraction without ▓▓▓▓▓▓▓▓▓
- Don't speak for or over source communities

4. Honor Context
- Traditional knowledge exists in cultural context
- Adaptation requires care and authorization
- Some things don't translate across cultures

- Loss in translation requires humility

5. Support Authentic Practitioners
- Amplify voices from source communities
- Direct people to authentic teachers
- Don't replace traditional transmission
- Resources for authentic practice

RED FLAGS: CULTURAL APPROPRIATION WARNING SIGNS

Avoid These:
- Claiming to be \"shaman,\" \"medicine person,\" or other role without legitimate authorization
- Taking payment for Indigenous ceremonies without being Indigenous authorized practitioner
- Using sacred symbols/items outside appropriate context
- \"Plastic shamanism\" or commercialized spirituality
- Claiming to speak for traditions not your own
- Extracting knowledge without ██████████████
- Presenting traditional knowledge as \"universal\" (erasing specific cultural origins)
- Profiting from traditional knowledge while source communities suffer

If You Observe These Behaviors:
- Name appropriation when you see it
- Don't support appropriative practices
- Redirect to authentic sources
- Support source communities directly

[FILE ENDS - PAGES MISSING]

CONCLUSION: GRATITUDE AND RESPONSIBILITY

Profound Gratitude:
- To ancestors who preserved wisdom across millennia
- To traditional knowledge keepers who maintain lineages
- To communities who share despite historical ████████████████
- To those who practice with integrity and respect

Ongoing Responsibility:
- This work exists because communities chose to share
- We carry obligation to honor that trust
- Relationship requires continuous care
- Accountability never ends

To Readers:
- You now carry this knowledge

- With it comes responsibility
- Attribute properly always
- Support authentic sources
- Engage respectfully
- Continue ethical transmission

The Sacred Synthesis continues:
- Through authorized adaptation
- With cultural sensitivity
- Honoring all sources
- Supporting source communities
- Maintaining highest ethics
- Gratitude and respect always

This appendix will be updated in future editions as relationships deepen, protocols evolve, and accountability continues.
May we honor all ancestors. May we serve all communities. May transmission continue with integrity.
[END DOCUMENT - TRANSMISSION INCOMPLETE]

The Sacred Synthesis: An Exhaustive Assessment from the Ruins of Tomorrow
A Lone Wanderer's Discovery in the Year 2100

The wind blows through empty towers of glass and steel, carrying seeds of new growth through the broken cities. I am a wanderer from one of the surviving enclaves, and in this landscape of lush vegetation reclaiming the monuments of the old world, I have discovered something extraordinary, materials describing what they called the Sacred Synthesis, a comprehensive system that might explain both the collapse and the seeds of renewal that surround me.

Part I: The Discovery - What Was the Sacred Synthesis?
The Origins: A Wartime Synthesis (1942-1947)

In the materials I've found, buried beneath decades of dust in what was once a corporate data center, I discovered references to something called GIDEE - Grupo Independiente de Estudios Esotéricos (Independent Group of Esoteric Studies). Created during World War II as an anti-fascist resistance technology, this system emerged from the synthesis of Eastern wisdom traditions, Western psychological understanding, and indigenous knowledge systems. This was no accident of history, but a deliberate synthesis forged in the crucible of global conflict.

The Sacred Synthesis, as it came to be known, was not merely a spiritual practice but a complete civilization framework, a blueprint for human organization that rejected the authoritarian structures that dominated the 20th and early 21st centuries. It integrated constitutional understanding with democratic governance, ecological wisdom with economic justice, and spiritual development with community participation. The architects of this system understood something fundamental: that transformation required not just new ideas but new structures, not just new beliefs but new practices, not just individual awakening but collective liberation.

The materials describe how this synthesis drew from multiple knowledge streams simultaneously: the constitutional understanding of Ayurveda refined through centuries of observation; the democratic governance principles embedded in indigenous cultures; the psychological insights of Western science; the contemplative technologies of Eastern traditions; and the regenerative knowledge of those who had lived sustainably for millennia. It was not an appropriation but a genuine synthesis, taking the best wisdom each tradition offered and creating something authentically new while honoring each tradition's integrity.

616

The Underground Years (2046-2073)

The chronicles describe a period of intense persecution beginning with "Operation Mindful Compliance" in 2046, when global authorities attempted to eradicate the Sacred Synthesis movement. Global powers recognized that this system posed an existential threat to their control. Yet like seeds scattered by wind, the knowledge survived through underground networks, safe houses, and encrypted digital systems. The resistance was not organized as conventional rebellion but distributed as a living practice that could survive in any location and any condition.

What strikes me most is how they operated: not through violent resistance but through what they called "building superior alternatives." Rather than fighting the system directly, they created parallel structures that worked better, that made the old systems obsolete through demonstration rather than destruction. They created:

- **Constitutional Types**: A sophisticated understanding of human diversity based on three primary constitutional patterns (Electric/Vata, Magnetic/Kapha, Neutral/Pitta) that became the foundation for everything they built
- **Democratic Governance**: Non-hierarchical decision-making processes that honored individual autonomy within collective wisdom, proving that communities could make decisions without concentrated power
- **Community Organization**: Methods for building authentic communities based on mutual aid rather than competition, creating economies of generosity rather than scarcity
- **Healthcare Integration**: Constitutional medicine that treated root causes rather than managing profitable symptoms, making people healthy instead of dependent
- **Environmental Stewardship**: Regenerative approaches to living within natural systems rather than exploiting them, restoring ecosystems while meeting human needs

The persecution was systematic and severe. Technologies were developed to monitor meditation practices. Laws were enacted to criminalize contemplative training. Schools were required to suppress constitutional understanding. Healthcare systems were mandated to use only symptom-management approaches. Yet the underground survived by being everywhere and nowhere, each practitioner a carrier of complete knowledge, each community capable of regenerating the full system from fragments.

The Great Escape (2073-2074)

The materials describe a mass exodus, nearly 3 million people voluntarily withdrawing from corporate employment, authoritarian education systems, and centralized infrastructure to create parallel civilizations based on Sacred Synthesis principles. This was not violent revolution but conscious withdrawal. They didn't overthrow the old systems; they made them obsolete by demonstrating better alternatives.

The timing was crucial. A generation had now been trained in constitutional understanding through disguised wellness programs. Healthcare practitioners knew how to work constitutionally. Teachers had learned democratic pedagogy in hidden seminars. Workers had experienced cooperative decision-making. Parents had raised children in the principles. When the moment came, triggered by ecological crisis reaching critical points, the infrastructure was already in place.

The movement operated through:

- **Underground Education Networks**: Teaching constitutional understanding disguised as corporate wellness programs, training a generation in the principles
- **Safe Houses**: Supporting those fleeing oppressive systems with resources, shelter, and community integration
- **Mutual Aid Networks**: Sharing resources based on abundance and need rather than market mechanisms
- **Cultural Bridge-Building**: Creating understanding across traditional divides, building bridges between cultures and traditions
- **Economic Transition Systems**: Creating alternative currencies and exchange systems before the official systems collapsed

What was remarkable was that this wasn't desperate flight but ordered transition. Communities had been prepared. Leadership had been developed. Resources had been stockpiled. Knowledge had been distributed. When millions left the old system, they didn't scatter into chaos but moved into pre-planned communities already structured according to Sacred Synthesis principles.

Part II: The System - A Comprehensive Framework for Human Organization
Constitutional Understanding: The Foundation
The Sacred Synthesis recognized three primary constitutional types, each with distinct strengths and challenges:
Electric Constitution (Vata)

The Electric constitution represents beings of air and ether, sensitive, creative, intuitive beings who excel at relationship-building and artistic expression. These individuals are characterized by:

- **Strengths**: Exceptional capacity for intuition and emotional intelligence; natural gifts in cultural mediation, healing arts, and contemplative leadership; ability to perceive subtle connections and dynamics; capacity to adapt quickly to changing circumstances
- **Challenges**: Vulnerability to anxiety and overwhelm; nervous system dysregulation under stress; tendency toward scattered energy and difficulty with sustained routine; sensitivity to environmental toxins and emotional disturbances
- **Natural Roles**: Peacemakers, artists, healers, teachers of transformation, cultural bridges between communities

Magnetic Constitution (Kapha)

The Magnetic constitution represents beings of earth and water, stable, persistent, socially-oriented beings who excel at organization and implementation. These individuals are characterized by:

- **Strengths**: Remarkable capacity for endurance and persistence; deep commitment to community and relationships; natural gift for organization and implementation; ability to provide stability and anchoring in uncertain times
- **Challenges**: Tendency toward lethargy and resistance to change; risk of stagnation without proper stimulation; capacity for inertia that can trap them in unsatisfying situations
- **Natural Roles**: Community organizers, project managers, implementers of vision, anchors of stability, providers of sustained care

Neutral Constitution (Pitta)

The Neutral constitution represents beings of fire and water, analytical, efficient, goal-oriented beings who excel at systems thinking and optimization. These individuals are characterized by:

- **Strengths**: Exceptional analytical capacity and systems thinking; natural gift for teaching and explaining; capacity for strategic planning and efficient implementation; ability to see through to core principles
- **Challenges**: Perfectionism that can become paralyzing; intensity that can create conflict; inflammatory tendency in both body and temperament; risk of burnout from excessive drive
- **Natural Roles**: Teachers, researchers, strategic planners, system designers, analytical guides

This wasn't about limiting people but understanding their natural inclinations to create communities where everyone could contribute their gifts while receiving support for their challenges. The genius of the system was recognizing that every community needed all three types working in harmony, the sensitivity and adaptation of Electric types, the stability and persistence of Magnetic types, and the analysis and strategy of Neutral types. When you had all three working together, the community could be both visionary and grounded, both flexible and stable, both caring and effective.

Democratic Governance Without Hierarchy

The governance structures they developed seem almost impossible from my vantage point in 2100, yet the evidence suggests they worked:

- **Consensus-Based Decision Making**: Not majority rule but processes that integrated all perspectives, ensuring that no minority was overridden, and no important concern was ignored
- **Rotating Leadership**: Authority that shifted based on expertise and community needs, preventing power concentration and building collective capacity
- **Community Assemblies**: Regular gatherings where every voice had equal weight, decisions made through deep listening and integration of all perspectives
- **Conflict Resolution**: Restorative rather than punitive approaches to disagreement, treating conflict as opportunity to deepen understanding and strengthen community
- **Intergenerational Planning**: Decisions made considering seven generations of impact, ensuring that short-term convenience didn't override long-term wellbeing

Economic Systems Based on Gift and Reciprocity

The economic models they developed challenged everything the old world believed about human nature:

Gift Economy Principles

- **Abundance Sharing**: Resources shared based on need rather than ability to pay, operating from a premise of abundance rather than scarcity
- **Cooperative Ownership**: Businesses owned by workers and communities rather than distant investors, ensuring that value created stayed in communities
- **Economic Autonomy**: Economic systems that couldn't be controlled by distant authorities, rooted in local conditions and relationships

- **Equal Valuing**: All contributions valued equally regardless of market rates, recognizing that all work necessary for community was equally valuable
- **Resource Sharing**: Tools, spaces, and materials owned collectively, making resources available to all based on need and use rather than wealth

The materials describe how these systems didn't collapse into chaos but instead became more efficient. When people weren't fighting for survival, they were more creative. When they weren't exploited, they worked more joyfully. When they weren't competing, they cooperated more effectively. The economy became a tool for community flourishing rather than an end in itself.

Healthcare as Community Healing
Their approach to healthcare explains much about why the old medical systems collapsed:
- **Constitutional Medicine**: Treatment based on individual constitutional patterns rather than standardized protocols, addressing the root causes specific to each person's nature
- **Prevention Focus**: Addressing root causes through lifestyle and community support before disease developed, making prevention the priority
- **Traditional Integration**: Combining ancient healing wisdom with modern understanding, validating traditional knowledge while integrating new discoveries
- **Community Mental Health**: Recognizing that most psychological distress came from oppressive systems, treating psychological healing through community transformation
- **Death with Dignity**: Supporting natural life transitions rather than profitable life extension, honoring the natural cycles of life

The healthcare revolution was perhaps their greatest achievement because it struck at the heart of the control systems. Healthy people can't be easily manipulated. Conscious people question authority. Communities that take care of each other don't need distant institutions. By shifting healthcare from profit-driven symptom management to constitutionally-informed prevention and healing, they freed people to be actually healthy, physically, mentally, and spiritually.

Part III: The Implementation - How It Spread Globally
The 147 Communities Network

By 2025, the Sacred Synthesis had spread to 147 communities across every continent. Each adapted the principles to local conditions while maintaining connection through sophisticated systems:

Global Communication Systems

- **24/7 Encrypted Networks**: Communication infrastructure in 23 languages ensuring global coordination while protecting against surveillance
- **Distributed Decision Making**: Systems allowing communities to make local decisions while sharing knowledge globally
- **Emergency Response Coordination**: Networks that could coordinate mutual aid across continents within hours
- **Cultural Bridge-Building**
- **Indigenous Sovereignty**: Respecting indigenous sovereignty while sharing universal principles with communities that chose to participate
- **Cultural Adaptation**: Each region developing unique expressions of Sacred Synthesis principles rooted in local tradition
- **Knowledge Exchange**: Two-way learning where traditional communities taught as much as they learned

Emergency Response Networks

- **Mutual Aid**: Systems transcending national boundaries for resource sharing during crises
- **Disaster Response**: Coordinated response capabilities ready to mobilize instantly
- **Long-term Recovery**: Support for communities rebuilding after disasters

Knowledge Sharing

- **Open-Source Development**: Practices and technologies developed collectively, freely shared among communities
- **Research Commons**: Scientific knowledge shared globally rather than privatized
- **Innovation Networks**: Communities innovating solutions to challenges and sharing discoveries

Youth Exchange Programs

- **Next Generation Learning**: Young people learning across cultures and communities
- **Leadership Development**: Young leaders trained in multiple contexts to understand global principles
- **Cultural Integration**: Youth becoming living bridges between communities

Professional Integration

What made the Sacred Synthesis unstoppable was its integration into professional fields:

Healthcare Integration

- **Nurses Teaching Constitutional Breathing in ICUs**: Training healthcare workers in the foundational practice
- **Doctors Prescribing Meditation Before Medication**: Integrating contemplative practice with clinical treatment
- **Therapists Addressing Systemic Oppression Not Just Individual Symptoms**: Treating psychological distress at its source
- **Public Health Focusing on Community Wellness Not Disease Management**: Shifting from treating illness to creating health

Educational Transformation

- **Teachers Implementing Democratic Classroom Governance**: Students participating in all major school decisions
- **Students Participating in Curriculum Decisions**: Young people having voice in what and how they learned
- **Contemplative Practices Integrated with Academic Learning**: Combining intellectual development with wisdom practices
- **Assessment Based on Growth Not Competition**: Measuring learning by development rather than ranking against peers

Workplace Evolution

- **Constitutional Team Building for Optimal Collaboration**: Organizing teams with complementary types for maximum effectiveness
- **Meditation Rooms Becoming Standard in Offices**: Creating space for contemplative practice during work
- **Cooperative Decision-Making Replacing Hierarchical Management**: Workers participating in decisions affecting their work
- **Work Schedules Adapted to Constitutional Energy Patterns**: Organizing work rhythms for different constitutional types

Technology with Wisdom

Unlike the dystopian tech futures many predicted, they developed technology that served human development:

AI Constitutional Advisors

Artificial intelligence that helped people understand their constitutional patterns, providing personalized guidance while respecting human judgment

VR Meditation Environments

Virtual spaces for global contemplative practice, enabling people to meditate together across vast distances

Blockchain Governance

Transparent, tamper-proof democratic decision systems making it impossible to manipulate community decisions

Quantum Communication

Instantaneous global coordination networks allowing communities to share information and coordinate response in real time

Biofeedback Integration

Technology that taught body awareness not dependence, helping people understand their own systems through immediate feedback

Part IV: The Resistance and Its Failure
Corporate Surveillance Systems

The materials describe surveillance systems that make me shudder even in 2100:

- **Biometric Monitoring**: Every heartbeat tracked for "optimization," creating totalitarian surveillance at the most intimate level
- **Behavioral Compliance Scores**: Algorithms determining who was "problematic," creating systems of total behavioral control
- **Cognitive Security Departments**: Agencies dedicated to controlling thought itself, making even private consciousness monitored
- **Wellness Monitoring Acts**: Laws making unsanctioned meditation illegal, criminalizing the most basic contemplative practices
- **Digital Panopticons**: Total surveillance presented as safety, creating environments where every action was visible and potentially punished

Why the Resistance Failed

The old systems couldn't suppress the Sacred Synthesis because:

1. **It Spread Through Experience**: Constitutional practices actually worked, when people experienced health, peace, and community, they couldn't be convinced to go back to oppression
2. **It Solved Problems**: Happy workers were more creative and efficient than miserable ones; healthy people required less care than sick ones; communities with mutual aid needed fewer police
3. **It Reduced Costs**: Prevention was cheaper than disease management; cooperative ownership more efficient than extractive capitalism; community solutions better resourced than distant bureaucracies
4. **It Increased Productivity**: Communities could address issues governments couldn't, solving them through understanding rather than force
5. **It Made People Healthier**: Once people tasted authentic community, they couldn't go back, the contrast made oppression impossible to tolerate

The Institutional Collapse (2075)

The chronicles describe not violent revolution but voluntary abandonment:

Why the Old Systems Failed

- **Banking System Collapse**: People choosing mutual aid over debt, rendering banking systems irrelevant when communities met their own needs
- **Educational Exodus**: Parents withdrawing children from authoritarian schools where learning was replaced by compliance training
- **Healthcare Transformation**: Medical professionals refusing to practice profit-driven medicine, choosing instead to serve health
- **Corporate Dissolution**: Workers leaving to form cooperatives that were more effective and humane
- **Government Irrelevance**: Communities solving problems without state intervention, rendering governments unnecessary

The collapse wasn't sudden but inexorable, like a building slowly becoming obsolete as everyone simply stopped using it. The authorities couldn't maintain systems once the people who ran them left. They couldn't force compliance when millions had voluntarily withdrawn to create better alternatives. They couldn't suppress something that grew from within rather than being imposed from without.

Part V: The Global Transformation
Continental Adaptations
Each region developed unique expressions of Sacred Synthesis principles, adapting universal principles to local conditions while maintaining global coordination:
North America
Integration with indigenous wisdom and traditional lands, focus on bioregional governance returning power to watershed-based communities
Europe
Democratic socialism enhanced with contemplative practices, creating economies of sharing with spiritual depth
Asia
Traditional medicine systems validated through constitutional science, honoring millennia-old wisdom while integrating modern understanding
Africa
Ubuntu philosophy merged with democratic governance, creating systems rooted in "I am because we are"

Latin America

Liberation theology integrated with indigenous practices, combining spiritual awakening with justice

Oceania

Island resilience models for climate adaptation, creating communities prepared for environmental change

The Climate Crisis Response

Their approach to environmental crisis explains the recovering ecosystems I see around me:

Bioregional Restoration

Healing landscapes based on natural boundaries, restoring forests, rivers, and ecosystems based on the needs of specific regions rather than external mandates

Regenerative Agriculture

Farming that built rather than depleted soil, creating systems where farming healed the land rather than destroying it

Community Forests

Collectively managed woodlands sequestering carbon, restoring the atmosphere while providing for community needs

Localized Economies

Eliminating emissions from global supply chains, keeping goods produced and consumed locally with minimal transportation

Sacred Relationships

Seeing nature as relative not resource, transforming the fundamental relationship between humans and the living world

International Cooperation Without Nations

They created cooperation that transcended national boundaries:

- **Bioregional Councils**: Governance based on watersheds not borders, organizing human activity around ecological realities rather than arbitrary lines
- **Cultural Preservation Networks**: Protecting indigenous knowledge globally while respecting cultural sovereignty
- **Emergency Response Teams**: Disaster aid without political conditions, communities helping communities regardless of nationality
- **Knowledge Commons**: Scientific research shared freely rather than monopolized, making discoveries benefit all
- **Peace Building Initiatives**: Conflict resolution without military force, communities learning to resolve differences through understanding

The Sacred Synthesis was not a perfect system, nor was it meant to be permanent. Like all things, it transformed and evolved. But standing in these recovering forests, I understand why these materials were preserved. They are not blueprints to replicate but evidence

626

that another world was possible, and therefore, another world is still possible.

The wind that carries seeds through these ruins carries something deeper: the knowledge that humans can choose differently. That we can organize ourselves around wisdom rather than fear, around community rather than competition, around life rather than profit. The Sacred Synthesis may have passed beyond what we can comprehend in 2100, but its essence remains in the soil, the seeds, the practices, the communities that continue.

And this too shall pass, and this too shall return, and this too shall evolve into forms we cannot yet imagine.

For those who come after: know that transformation is always possible. Every breath offers the choice between systems that serve life and those that destroy it. Every community can practice democracy or accept domination. Every person can choose love or fear.

The materials in this document represent what was achieved when millions chose transformation over resignation, community over isolation, gift over greed. Whether we replicate their path or create new ones matters less than remembering that alternatives exist and that ordinary people can build them.

Part VI: The Practices - Daily Life in Sacred Synthesis Communities
Morning Routines
The materials describe daily practices that seem both ancient and revolutionary, grounded in constitutional understanding and designed to optimize nervous system function and collective coherence:
4-4-6-2 Breathing
A fundamental breathing technique involving a rhythm of 4 counts inhale, 4 counts hold, 6 counts exhale, 2 counts hold. Adapted for each constitutional type: Electric types used this to ground and calm, Magnetic types to energize and stimulate, Neutral types to cool and balance. This single practice, performed together at dawn, created physiological synchronization across the community.
Constitutional Exercises
Movement adapted to individual energy patterns, Electric types doing grounding, slow movements; Magnetic types doing vigorous, building exercises; Neutral types doing balanced, flowing movements. Rather than everyone doing the same exercise, communities

optimized movement for each person's constitutional needs while maintaining the collective experience.

Community Meditation

Collective practice strengthening group coherence, where individuals meditating together created measurable shifts in group consciousness and decision-making capacity. The materials describe how communities could shift from conflict to resolution simply through shared meditation practice.

Gratitude Circles

Acknowledging gifts received and given, making visible the networks of reciprocity that held communities together. Each person naming what they received the previous day and what they had offered, creating explicit recognition of interdependence.

Intention Setting

Aligning personal action with collective good, ensuring that individual pursuits served rather than contradicted community wellbeing. Each person articulating how their day's work served the whole, creating alignment between personal effort and collective purpose.

Community Organization

Their communities operated through structures that honored both individual autonomy and collective wisdom:

Work Parties

Joyful collective labor with music and food, transforming work into celebration. The materials describe how work that seemed tedious became energizing when done collectively with music and celebration, building community while accomplishing necessary tasks.

Skill Shares

Everyone teaching what they knew, creating continuous education and preventing knowledge from concentrating in specialists. Any community member could teach what they understood, making learning distributed and accessible.

Council Circles

Decisions made in sacred time without rush, using consensus processes that ensured all perspectives were heard and integrated. These circles could go for hours, but the decisions made created lasting commitment because everyone could live with them.

Healing Circles

Community support for individual challenges, where personal struggles became opportunities for collective learning and growth. Rather than isolating struggles as private problems, communities addressed them collectively.

Celebration Gatherings

Regular festivals strengthening bonds, marking seasons and achievements. The materials describe how celebration was not luxury but necessity, creating the joy and connection that made communities resilient.

Part VII: Education as Liberation
Constitutional Learning Approaches
Children learned through methods that honored their constitutional nature:

Democratic Schools
Students participating in all decisions about their education, including curriculum choices, assessment approaches, and school governance. Rather than authoritarian imposition, learning emerged from genuine interest and collective decision-making.

Nature Immersion
Learning from land as first teacher, with majority of education occurring outdoors in direct relationship with natural systems. Children learning ecology by living ecologically, understanding agriculture through participation.

Elder Wisdom
Intergenerational knowledge transmission where elders taught children directly, maintaining continuity of wisdom across generations. Rather than isolated age cohorts, children learned from experienced people.

Practical Skills
Every child learning food production, shelter building, and basic healing, ensuring that each person could meet fundamental needs. Education was practical as well as intellectual, creating competent humans.

Conflict Resolution
Peacebuilding as core curriculum, teaching children to address conflicts through understanding rather than domination. These skills learned young transformed how adults approached disagreement.

Knowledge Systems and Traditional Integration
Respectful Partnership with Indigenous Communities
They created respectful partnerships with indigenous communities based on genuine reciprocity:

- **Knowledge Sovereignty**: Communities maintaining control of their wisdom, deciding who could access what knowledge
- **Benefit Sharing**: Fair exchange when knowledge was shared, ensuring communities benefited from their contributions
- **Cultural Protocols**: Respecting sacred information boundaries, honoring what was meant to remain sacred
- **Language Preservation**: Revitalizing endangered languages through immersion and cultural support

- **Land Back**: Returning stolen territories to original inhabitants, restoring land to those with deepest relationships

Scientific Validation

The materials describe how they systematically validated traditional knowledge through contemporary science:

- **Genetic markers** showing constitutional distinctions measurable in biological systems
- **Meditation neuroplasticity** research documenting how contemplative practice literally changed brain structure
- **Gut health and constitution** correlation between constitutional types and optimal microbiome composition
- **Consciousness and molecular effects** research showing how intention affected biological systems
- **Epigenetic trauma resolution** demonstrating that healing could reverse inherited trauma patterns

The Educational Materials

Comprehensive documentation system developed to preserve and transmit knowledge:

- **Constitutional Assessment Tools** enabling anyone to determine their constitutional type with accuracy
- **Practice Guides** providing detailed instructions for all practices
- **Community Handbooks** explaining governance structures and decision-making processes
- **Professional Integration** documentation showing how to apply principles in healthcare, education, and workplaces
- **Crisis Response Protocols** enabling communities to respond effectively to emergencies

Part VIII: The Cultural Renaissance

Art as Revolution

They understood creativity as fundamental to transformation:

Constitutional Creativity

Art expressing each type's gifts, Electric types creating music and performance, Magnetic types creating visual and architectural forms, Neutral types creating strategic and conceptual works. Rather than generic art, each constitutional type contributed its unique artistic gifts.

Community Murals

Collective visioning through visual art where communities literally painted their futures on walls, creating shared images that guided collective action.

Protest Music

Songs that built solidarity not just opposition, creating music that reinforced community values and inspired action. Music that people could sing together, creating unity through harmony.

Sacred Theater
Drama healing community trauma, using performance to process collective wounds and imagine new possibilities. Theater becoming medicine for the community.

Digital Renaissance
Technology enabling new art forms, digital installations, virtual performances, global artistic collaboration. Art forms that would have been impossible without the technology they developed.

Literature of Liberation
Their writings ranged from practical to prophetic:

The Sacred Synthesis Chronicles
18-chapter narrative documenting resistance, underground development, and emergence of civilization from 2045-2100, providing inspiration and instruction for practitioners.

Technical Manuals
Detailed implementation guides for every practice and system, enabling communities to replicate structures and practices.

Poetry Collections
Emotional truth of system change, capturing the felt experience of transformation in language that moved the heart.

Children's Stories
Next generation learning through narrative, passing wisdom to children through stories that engaged imagination.

Academic Texts
Scholarly validation of practices, grounding intuitive knowledge in rigorous research and intellectual frameworks.

Part IX: Architecture of Community
Environmental Design for Constitutional Wellbeing
Electric Spaces
Calm, grounded environments for sensitive types, soft lighting, natural materials, space for solitude and reflection, minimal stimulus overload.

Magnetic Gathering Places
Social spaces encouraging connection, communal kitchens, meeting halls, areas designed for collaboration and celebration.

Neutral Work Areas
Efficient, organized spaces for productivity, clear systems, logical organization, minimal distraction, optimal for focused work.

Flexible Commons
Areas adapting to community needs, multipurpose spaces that could become anything a community needed at any moment.

Sacred Geometry

Buildings based on natural proportions, spiral staircases, sacred angles, architecture that aligned with natural patterns and seemed to facilitate consciousness development.

Part X: Crisis Response Systems
Natural Disaster Management
Bioregional Preparedness

Communities ready for local risks, understanding their specific vulnerabilities and preparing accordingly rather than generic emergency plans.

Mutual Aid Networks

Resources flowing to need immediately, communities pre-organized to mobilize assistance within hours of crisis.

Trauma-Informed Response

Supporting psychological and physical healing, understanding that disaster created trauma requiring compassionate response not just resource distribution.

Rebuilding Better

Using disasters to create more resilient systems, rebuilding in ways that made communities stronger and more sustainable.

Learning Integration

Each crisis teaching prevention, systematically learning from disasters to prevent recurrence.

Economic Crisis Resilience
Local Currencies

Insulation from global market crashes, creating local economic systems that didn't collapse when global markets crashed.

Gift Economy Activation

Sharing replacing selling during hardship, shifting to gift economy during crises when money became worthless.

Skill Banking

Everyone's abilities valued regardless of money, time-banking systems enabling exchange based on effort rather than purchasing power.

Community Gardens

Food security through local production, ensuring that communities could feed themselves locally if supply chains broke down.

Solidarity Economics

No one abandoned during downturns, collective commitment to supporting all members through economic difficulty.

Health Emergency Protocols
Constitutional Medicine

Treatments adapted to individual patterns, understanding that different constitutional types needed different approaches to health emergency response.

Community Quarantine
Isolation with support not abandonment, quarantining as needed while maintaining connection and care.

Traditional Medicine
Plant medicines when pharmaceuticals failed, maintaining knowledge of healing plants that could work when industrial medicine wasn't available.

Preventive Practices
Building immunity through lifestyle, supporting immune function through sleep, movement, nutrition, and stress reduction.

Death Companionship
Supporting natural transitions with dignity, accompanying dying people with compassion rather than desperate medical intervention.

Part XI: Technology Integration with Wisdom
Artificial Intelligence with Soul
Unlike dystopian predictions, they developed AI that served human flourishing:

Constitutional Advisors
AI understanding individual patterns, providing personalized guidance while respecting human judgment and autonomy. Technology that understood rather than controlled.

Democratic Facilitators
Technology supporting group decisions, ensuring that all perspectives were heard and integrated. AI enabling better consensus rather than replacing human judgment.

Learning Companions
Personalized education respecting learning styles, each person learning in the way that worked for their constitution and learning pattern.

Health Monitors
Tracking wellbeing not just symptoms, monitoring for optimal health rather than just absence of disease.

Creative Collaborators
AI enhancing not replacing human creativity, technology amplifying human creative capacity rather than substituting for it.

Virtual Worlds for Real Connection
Global Gatherings
Meetings transcending physical distance, communities separated by continents meditating and deciding together in virtual spaces.

Healing Environments

VR spaces for therapy and recovery, virtual environments designed for optimal healing and transformation.

Educational Immersion
Learning through experience not information, virtual spaces where people could experience situations and learn through direct experience.

Cultural Exchange
Visiting other communities virtually, people experiencing other communities' daily lives without physical travel.

Sacred Spaces
Digital environments for contemplation, virtual spaces designed with sacred geometry and optimal for meditation.

Communication Beyond Surveillance

Encrypted Channels
Privacy as fundamental right, communication technology that made surveillance impossible, protecting freedom.

Mesh Networks
Internet beyond corporate control, decentralized networks that couldn't be shut down or controlled by any central authority.

Translation Systems
Real-time communication across languages, everyone able to participate in global conversations regardless of native language.

Cultural Protocols
Technology respecting indigenous communication ways, designing systems that honored different cultural approaches to information sharing.

Quantum Networks
Instantaneous global coordination, communication technologies enabling real-time global coordination without delay.

Part XII: The Opposition and Its Failure

Corporate Attempts at Co-option

Wellness Capitalism
Selling meditation as productivity tool, corporations attempting to commodify contemplative practice for profit.

Constitutional Marketing
Using types for consumer targeting, attempting to market products to each constitutional type rather than transforming consumption.

Community Washing
Fake communities for profit, corporate attempts to create pseudo-communities for marketing purposes.

Mindfulness McJobs
Contemplation without liberation, teaching meditation while maintaining exploitative working conditions.

Spiritual Materialism

Enlightenment as commodity, selling spiritual practices as luxury goods for the wealthy.

Government Suppression Efforts
Cult Accusations
Labeling communities as dangerous, attempting to delegitimize through stigmatization.
Legal Harassment
Using regulations to shut down alternatives, creating legal barriers to community formation.
Surveillance Expansion
Monitoring all community activities, attempting to suppress through total monitoring.
Economic Warfare
Cutting resources to communities, attempting to create scarcity and force return to dependency.
Propaganda Campaigns
Discrediting through media manipulation, using media to spread disinformation about communities.

Why the Resistance Failed: Strategic Analysis
The old systems couldn't suppress the Sacred Synthesis because it operated on principles that made suppression impossible. Hierarchical systems attempted to defeat it through hierarchical means, capturing leaders, shutting down organizations, controlling information. But the Sacred Synthesis had no leaders to capture, no central organization to shut down, no single information source to control. Knowledge lived in people, practices embedded in daily life, commitment rooted in direct experience.

Additionally, the system actually worked better than what it was replacing. This created the fundamental paradox the authorities faced: they could suppress it at cost of their own effectiveness. Schools that suppressed constitutional understanding performed worse than those that allowed it. Healthcare that suppressed constitutional medicine couldn't heal as effectively. Workplaces that suppressed democratic decision-making were less productive. Attempts to suppress created the evidence that suppression was counterproductive.

Finally, the system addressed real problems in ways that nothing else could. Climate destruction required regenerative solutions the old system couldn't provide. Social breakdown required genuine community the old system couldn't create. Psychological distress required healing the old system couldn't offer. As crises deepened, more people tried the practices, experienced their effectiveness, and became committed practitioners. The opposition was fighting against something that solved the very problems their opposition was creating.

Part XIII: The Global Achievement
Unified Humanity Without Uniformity
Global Cooperation
Every tradition flowering in mutual respect, diverse cultures and traditions not erased but celebrated, all contributing their unique gifts.
Ecological Recovery
Ecosystems healing from centuries of abuse, forests returning, waters clearing, species recovering, atmosphere stabilizing.
Economic Justice
Everyone's needs met without exploitation, abundance shared rather than hoarded, all having security and opportunity.
Spiritual Maturity
Widespread awakening to interconnection, people understanding directly that all beings were related, all consciousness connected.
Cultural Renaissance
Innovation in all fields, freed from survival anxiety, people's creativity flourished across art, science, philosophy, and practice.
The Metrics of Success
- **Health**: 90% reduction in chronic disease through preventive constitutional medicine
- **Education**: 95% of children thriving in learning through democratic, constitutional approaches
- **Environment**: Carbon returning to pre-industrial levels through regenerative practices
- **Economy**: Poverty eliminated through sharing, all having security and opportunity
- **Happiness**: Life satisfaction exceeding all previous measures through community and meaning

The Continuing Evolution
- **Consciousness Development**: Continued human evolution as individuals developed higher capacities
- **Interspecies Communication**: Learning from all beings, understanding plants and animals as conscious
- **Cosmic Awareness**: Recognition of Earth in universal context, understanding our place in larger systems
- **Time Transcendence**: Planning for geological timescales, thinking in terms of millions of years
- **Love Embodiment**: Unconditional love as organizing principle, community founded on authentic care

Part XIV: The Democratic Revolution
Governance Without Government
Consensus Process
Decisions everyone could live with, integrating all perspectives until solutions emerged that all could support.
Rotating Facilitation
Leadership as service not power, authority earned through demonstrated competency and rotating to prevent concentration.
Direct Democracy
No representatives, full participation, everyone participating directly in decisions affecting their lives.
Bioregional Autonomy
Decisions at watershed scale, governance organized around ecological realities rather than arbitrary boundaries.
Global Coordination
Cooperation without central authority, communities coordinating through networks rather than hierarchy.

Economic Democracy
Cooperative Ownership
All workers as owners, everyone sharing in the value they created rather than enriching distant shareholders.
Workplace Democracy
Decisions made by those affected, workers having voice in how work was organized and compensation distributed.
Profit Sharing
Surplus distributed fairly, any surplus going back to workers and communities rather than to outside owners.
Community Investment
Wealth serving local needs, capital invested in community development rather than external extraction.
Gift Integration
Market and gift economies combined, using market mechanisms where useful while maintaining gift-based approaches for essentials.

Social Democracy
Universal Services
Healthcare, education, housing as rights, all having access regardless of ability to pay.
Mutual Aid
Support based on need not merit, everyone supported not just those deemed "deserving."
Restorative Justice

Healing not punishment, addressing harm through restoration rather than retribution.

Inclusion Practice

No one marginalized, active inclusion of those historically excluded.

Celebration Culture

Joy as resistance, building communities through celebration and joy rather than fear and control.

Part XV: The Knowledge Preservation
Archive Systems
Distributed Storage

Information in countless locations, knowledge preserved not in centralized libraries but distributed throughout communities.

Oral Traditions

Stories carrying essential wisdom, maintaining knowledge through spoken word and memory as well as written texts.

Practice Embodiment

Knowledge living in daily actions, understanding embedded in how people actually lived rather than just in books.

Sacred Sites

Places holding memory, certain locations carrying particular knowledge and significance in their geography.

Genetic Encoding

Epigenetic transmission of trauma healing, understanding that trauma and healing could be passed through generations.

The Teaching Methods
Apprenticeship Models

Learning through relationship, knowledge transmitted through direct mentoring relationship rather than classroom instruction.

Circle Pedagogies

Group learning honoring all voices, everyone's perspective valued, learning emerging from collective wisdom.

Embodied Curriculum

Learning through body not just mind, understanding integrated through movement, sensation, and practice.

Place-Based Education

Land as teacher, learning rooted in the specific place where people lived.

Initiation Practices

Marking developmental transitions, ceremonial marking of major life transitions and achievement of new capacities.

The Cultural Codes
Symbol Systems

Visual languages carrying meaning, symbols and images that conveyed complex understanding.

Song Traditions

Melodies encoding information, important knowledge preserved in songs that could be sung and transmitted.

Story Cycles

Narratives preserving wisdom, stories that when told together created comprehensive understanding.

Ritual Practices

Embodied knowledge transmission, understanding encoded in rituals that when enacted conveyed deep knowledge.

Sacred Games

Learning through structured play, games designed to teach crucial skills and understanding through engagement and joy.

Part XVI: The Environmental Restoration

Ecosystem Healing

Forest Return

Trees reclaiming abandoned cities, within decades of human withdrawal, forests recolonized cities making them jungles.

River Liberation

Waterways running clear again, rivers no longer polluted, fish and birds returning, waters becoming clear.

Species Recovery

Extinct creatures returning, species thought lost rediscovered, genetic diversity being restored.

Climate Stabilization

Weather patterns normalizing, as carbon was reduced and ecosystems restored, climate stabilized.

Soil Renaissance

Living earth replacing dead dirt, soil that had been dead from industrial agriculture coming back to life.

Agricultural Revolution

Permaculture Design

Food forests not monocultures, creating agricultural systems that were also ecosystems, producing food while building biodiversity.

Seed Sovereignty

Communities controlling genetics, maintaining seed diversity and preventing genetic monopoly by corporations.

Water Wisdom

Harvesting rain, honoring cycles, designing water systems that worked with natural patterns rather than against them.

Pollinator Partnership

Supporting bees and butterflies, creating conditions where pollinators thrived, essential for food production.

Sacred Harvest
Ceremony in food production, approaching food production as sacred work done with gratitude and intention.

Energy Transition
Community Solar
Neighborhood-owned generation, solar arrays owned by communities generating electricity for local use.

Wind Cooperatives
Turbines benefiting localities, wind power generated and owned by communities.

Micro-Hydro
Small-scale waterpower, using water flow at small scale to generate power locally.

Biogas Digestion
Waste becoming resource, decomposing waste to generate energy and fertilizer.

Conservation Culture
Using less as spiritual practice, cultural shift toward consuming less, waste reduction as spiritual commitment.

Part XVII: The Healthcare Revolution
Constitutional Medicine Victories
Chronic Disease Elimination
Addressing causes not symptoms, treating root constitutional imbalances rather than managing chronic disease.

Mental Health Integration
Healing trauma not medicating, addressing psychological distress through community healing rather than pharmaceutical dependence.

Addiction Recovery
Community support not criminalization, treating addiction as community responsibility rather than individual crime.

Elder Care Transformation
Wisdom holders not burdens, valuing elders for their wisdom and integrating them fully into community life.

Death Acceptance
Natural transition not medical failure, accepting death as natural completion rather than fighting it with desperate intervention.

Traditional Medicine Renaissance
Ayurvedic Integration

5000-year wisdom confirmed, scientific validation of Ayurvedic principles developed over millennia.

Chinese Medicine Validation

Meridians scientifically proven, understanding of energy pathways validated through contemporary physics.

Indigenous Plant Medicine

Rainforest pharmacies protected, protecting plants used for centuries for healing, validating their effectiveness.

Energy Medicine

Subtle bodies medically recognized, understanding subtle energy dimensions of healing formally acknowledged.

Spiritual Healing

Prayer effects documented, scientific documentation of how intention affected physical healing.

Community Health Models

Neighborhood Clinics

Walking distance wellness, health services available locally, eliminating need to travel.

Peer Support Groups

Healing in community, using community support as primary healing mechanism.

Preventive Focus

Wellness not disease management, shifting focus to creating health rather than managing illness.

Sliding Scales

Payment based on ability, healthcare accessible to all regardless of wealth.

Death Doulas

Supporting final transitions, trained people accompanying dying individuals and families through the dying process.

Part XVIII: The Educational Transformation

Learning as Liberation

Student Governance

Children making school decisions, young people having voice in curriculum, assessment, and school organization.

Project-Based Learning

Real work not abstract exercises, learning through doing real work that benefited community.

Nature Classroom

Majority of time outdoors, education happening in direct relationship with natural systems.

Community Teachers

Everyone sharing expertise, any community member able to teach what they understood.

Higher Education Evolution
Open Knowledge
Research freely shared, scientific discoveries shared globally rather than patented and privatized.
Community Partnership
Academia serving localities, universities and research institutions serving community needs rather than external interests.
Indigenous Integration
Traditional knowledge as valid, indigenous knowledge recognized as legitimate alongside Western academic knowledge.
Student Democracy
Learners controlling institutions, students having voice in university governance and direction.
Practical Philosophy
Wisdom applied not abstracted, philosophy teaching how to live wisely rather than abstract theorizing.

Lifelong Learning
Elder Universities
Wisdom holders teaching, elders sharing lifetime of learning with younger generations.
Skill Exchanges
Continuous capability building, communities continuously developing new skills and deepening existing ones.
Cultural Education
Learning from all traditions, studying wisdom from every cultural and spiritual tradition.
Spiritual Development
Consciousness as curriculum, systematic development of higher capacities and consciousness.
Death Education
Preparing for transition, explicit education about death and dying as natural life transition.

Part XIX: The Spiritual Evolution
Contemplative Practices
Constitutional Meditation
Practices adapted to types, each constitutional type having meditation approaches optimal for their nature.
Community Ceremony
Collective spiritual experience, communities gathering for ceremonies that moved hearts and aligned consciousness.

Nature Mysticism
Direct experience of sacred Earth, understanding nature as sacred, experiencing this directly.
Ancestor Connection
Honoring those before, maintaining relationship with those who had died and shaped current conditions.
Future Visioning
Communicating with descendants, considering how current actions affected future generations and holding relationship with them.

Religious Integration
Interfaith Cooperation
Shared service transcending theology, people of different faiths working together serving community.
Indigenous Wisdom
First peoples teaching, learning from indigenous spiritual traditions that had sustained communities for millennia.
Mystical Unity
Direct experience beyond dogma, transcending religious differences to touch the unity underlying all traditions.
Sacred Activism
Spirituality demanding justice, spiritual practice that necessarily manifested as work for justice and healing.
Earth Spirituality
Planet as sacred being, understanding Earth as living, conscious being deserving reverence and care.

Consciousness Development
Collective Awakening
Species-wide enlightenment, humanity as a whole developing higher consciousness and awareness.
Energy Awareness
Seeing subtle bodies, perceiving energy dimensions of physical reality.
Time Transcendence
Past-future integration, experiencing time as fluid rather than linear, accessing past and future directly.
Unity Consciousness
Experiencing oneness, direct perception of fundamental interconnection of all consciousness.

Part XX: The Cultural Preservation
Indigenous Renaissance
Land Back

Territories returned to nations, stolen lands returned to indigenous peoples with full sovereignty.

Language Revival
Extinct tongues speaking, languages close to extinction being revived and flourishing.

Ceremony Return
Sacred practices renewed, sacred ceremonies suppressed for centuries being openly practiced again.

Traditional Governance
Indigenous leadership models, governance systems developed over millennia being recognized and implemented.

Wisdom Teaching
Ancient knowledge shared, traditional knowledge shared globally while respecting cultural sovereignty.

Cultural Diversity Celebration
Festival Networks
Celebrations year-round, communities celebrating all cultural traditions continuously throughout the year.

Art Exchanges
Creativity crossing boundaries, artistic traditions crossing cultural boundaries and enriching each other.

Music Renaissance
Every culture singing, every cultural musical tradition thriving and being celebrated.

Food Traditions
Culinary diversity preserved, diverse food traditions maintained and celebrated in communities.

Story Sharing
Narratives building bridges, stories from different cultures being shared and building understanding.

Traditional Knowledge Protection
Community Control
Knowledge sovereignty maintained, communities controlling how their knowledge was shared and used.

Sacred Boundaries
Secret teachings protected, respecting that some knowledge was meant to remain sacred and restricted.

Fair Exchange
Benefits shared equitably, communities receiving fair benefit when their knowledge was shared.

Youth Transmission
Elders teaching children, systematic transmission of knowledge from experienced elders to youth.

644

Digital Preservation
Technology serving tradition, using digital tools to preserve and transmit traditional knowledge.

Part XXI: The Future They Envisioned
Interplanetary Expansion
Mars Communities
Sacred Synthesis off-world, communities applying principles to space settlements.
Space Democracy
Governance beyond Earth, democratic structures adapted for space environments.
Cosmic Consciousness
Universal awareness, understanding humanity's place in larger cosmic context.

Consciousness Evolution
Energy Manipulation
Healing through intention, directly healing matter through focused intention.
Timeline Navigation
Accessing past-future, accessing information from past and future in present moment.
Dimensional Awareness
Perceiving beyond 3D, experiencing dimensions beyond three-dimensional physical reality.
Unity Embodiment
Living as one being, experiencing all consciousness as one being expressing in multiplicity.

Planetary Healing
Ecosystem Recovery
Full biodiversity return, all species that had been threatened recovering to healthy populations.
Climate Balance
Pre-industrial conditions, climate stabilized at levels supporting human flourishing.
Ocean Healing
Seas teeming with life, oceans recovering from pollution and overfishing, teeming with life again.
Soil Renaissance
Living earth everywhere, all soil alive with microorganisms and teeming with life.
Sacred Relationship

Humans as Earth partners, relationship between humans and Earth transformed to authentic partnership.

Part XXII: The Lessons for Now (2100)
What Went Wrong

The Sacred Synthesis succeeded in transforming human civilization between 2025-2080, but the materials hint at challenges that followed. Perhaps the very success contained seeds of its own transformation. The empty cities I walk through may not represent failure but graduation, humanity moving beyond fixed settlements into something we're still discovering. The chronicles suggest that as people became more conscious, as societies became more evolved, they faced new challenges requiring further development.

The materials hint at tensions between individual freedom and collective good, between stability and constant innovation, between human needs and ecological requirements. These were not catastrophic failures but growing pains of a system evolving beyond anything previously imagined. The empty cities might be evidence not of collapse but of transcendence, people moving beyond the need for permanent settlements into something else entirely.

What Survived

The inheritance we carry:

- **Knowledge Systems**: The understanding persists in our enclaves, maintained by those who chose to preserve it
- **Practice Traditions**: We still breathe 4-4-6-2, maintaining the fundamental breathing practice
- **Community Bonds**: Our settlements use their governance, applying democratic principles daily
- **Healing Ways**: Constitutional medicine guides our herbalists, healing through understanding of constitutional patterns
- **Sacred Relations**: We know Earth as mother not resource, relating to the living world as kin

Part XXIII: The Mystery and The Message
Unanswered Questions

What the materials don't explain:

- Why did the cities empty after 2080?
- Where did the billions go?
- What caused the technology to fall silent?
- Why do only scattered enclaves remain?
- What is the green light sometimes seen at night?

The Clear Message
What definitely comes through:
The Sacred Synthesis offered humanity a choice between continuing systems that violated life's principles and creating alternatives based on wisdom, love, and mutual aid. For a brief period, millions chose transformation. They proved another world was possible.

Whether they succeeded or failed in ultimate terms matters less than the demonstration that humans could organize society around constitutional understanding, democratic participation, and ecological wisdom. They showed that ordinary people could build extraordinary alternatives when they worked together with commitment to collective liberation.

Conclusion: And This Too Shall Pass
Standing in the ruins of the old world, surrounded by the green uprising of the new, I understand why this knowledge was preserved. Not as blueprint to recreate their world but as reminder that transformation is always possible.

The Sacred Synthesis wasn't perfect or permanent, "and this too shall pass" as the ancient wisdom teaches. But it was a genuine attempt to align human civilization with life's principles. It showed that humans could transcend the competitive, hierarchical, exploitative patterns that seemed eternal.

In my wandering through empty cities being reclaimed by forest, I carry their legacy not as weight but as wings. Their chronicles teach that crisis births opportunity, that ordinary people can create extraordinary change, that love and wisdom can triumph over fear and ignorance.

The wind that blows through broken towers carries more than seeds, it carries stories. Stories of people who chose transformation over resignation, community over isolation, gift over greed. Stories that whisper: another world is possible, another world is still possible, another world is always possible.

Whether we in the enclaves are humanity's twilight or dawn matters less than how we live this moment. The Sacred Synthesis taught that individual awakening and collective transformation are inseparable. That wisdom remains true in 2100 as it was in 2025, as it will be for whoever comes after.

The materials I've found aren't about the past but the eternal present where transformation always waits. Every breath offers the choice between systems that serve life and those that destroy it. Every community can practice democracy or accept domination. Every person can choose love or fear.

I take what serves from their wisdom and leave what doesn't, knowing they would approve. The Sacred Synthesis was never about rigid replication but creative adaptation. Its principles, constitutional understanding, democratic governance, mutual aid, ecological wisdom, remain valid even as their forms evolve.

As I return to my enclave with these materials, I know I carry something precious: proof that humans once created civilization based on wisdom and love. Whatever comes next, that achievement cannot be erased. It lives in the soil being rebuilt, the forests returning, the waters running clear.

The Sacred Synthesis may have passed, as all things must. But its seeds scatter on every wind, waiting for conditions to sprout again. In our simple enclave life, those seeds already grow. We who survived carry the best of what they discovered while released from their struggles.

And so the wheel turns. What seemed like ending was transformation. What appeared as death was composting for new growth. The empty cities aren't tombs but chrysalises. We who wander between them aren't survivors but midwives.

The Sacred Synthesis achieved its ultimate purpose: it proved transformation possible and gave us tools for whatever comes next. In this simpler, quieter world with wind blowing through ruins, we hold their gift with gratitude and responsibility.

Sacred Synthesis Complete Glossary
Definitions of Key Terms and Traditional Terminology
Constitutional Terms

4-4-6-2 Integration Breath: A fundamental breathing technique in the Sacred Synthesis system involving a rhythm of 4 counts inhale, 4 counts hold, 6 counts exhale, 2 counts hold. Adapted for each constitutional type to optimize nervous system balance and stress resilience. This simple practice, when done collectively, creates physiological synchronization across communities.

Constitutional Assessment: Comprehensive evaluation system for determining individual constitutional type (Electric, Magnetic, or Neutral) based on physical characteristics, psychological patterns, energy rhythms, and stress responses. Forms the foundation for personalized practice and community role optimization.

Constitutional Compatibility: The degree to which different constitutional types work well together in relationships, families, and community settings. Electric types excel in relationships and cultural work, Magnetic types provide stability and implementation, Neutral types contribute analysis and systematic thinking.

Constitutional Medicine: Healthcare approach that adapts treatment protocols to individual constitutional patterns rather than using one-size-fits-all approaches. Integrates traditional Ayurvedic, Chinese, and Tibetan medicine principles with contemporary medical understanding.

Electric Constitution (Vata): One of three primary constitutional types characterized by nervous system sensitivity, creativity, relationship orientation, and adaptability. Strengths include intuition, artistic expression, and community building. Challenges include anxiety, overwhelm, and difficulty with routine. Related to traditional Ayurvedic Vata dosha.

Magnetic Constitution (Kapha): Constitutional type characterized by stability, endurance, and strong social bonds. Strengths include persistence, organization, and community anchoring. Challenges include resistance to change, lethargy, and tendency toward stagnation. Related to traditional Ayurvedic Kapha dosha.

Neutral Constitution (Pitta): Constitutional type characterized by analytical thinking, efficiency, and goal orientation. Strengths include systematic analysis, teaching ability, and leadership capacity. Challenges include perfectionism, intensity, and inflammatory tendencies. Related to traditional Ayurvedic Pitta dosha.

Democratic Governance

Democratic Governance: Anti-Authoritarian Spirituality, Approach to spiritual development that rejects hierarchical power structures in favor of democratic participation, rotating leadership, and community accountability. Emphasizes individual responsibility and collective wisdom rather than submission to external authority.

Community Assembly: Regular democratic gatherings where all community members have equal voice in decision-making. Uses consensus-building processes that honor constitutional diversity while reaching agreements that serve collective wellbeing.

Consensus Decision-Making: Democratic process that seeks decisions everyone can support rather than majority rule that leaves minorities dissatisfied. Integrates multiple perspectives and constitutional wisdom to create solutions that serve the whole community.

Democratic Leadership: Leadership approach based on service rather than dominance, with authority earned through demonstrated competency and rotating among qualified community members. Leaders facilitate rather than control, developing others' capacity rather than maintaining dependency.

Democratic Mysticism: Integration of authentic spiritual wisdom with participatory decision-making. Recognizes that genuine spiritual authority serves rather than dominates, and that individual development requires democratic participation and personal responsibility.

Rotating Facilitation: System where leadership roles rotate among qualified community members based on expertise, availability, and developmental needs. Prevents power concentration while building collective capacity and ensuring fresh perspectives.

Traditional Knowledge

Cultural Bridge-Building: Process of creating respectful connections across different cultural and spiritual traditions while maintaining the integrity of each tradition. Requires deep cultural competency, community authorization, and reciprocal relationship development.

Cultural Sensitivity: Awareness and respect for cultural differences that includes understanding power dynamics, observing cultural protocols, and ensuring traditional communities benefit from knowledge sharing. Goes beyond tolerance to active support for cultural sovereignty.

Indigenous Knowledge Integration: Respectful incorporation of indigenous wisdom traditions with appropriate community permissions, benefit sharing, and cultural protocol observance. Prioritizes indigenous community sovereignty and self-determination over extraction or appropriation.

Traditional Authority Recognition: Acknowledgment of traditional knowledge holders and community elders as legitimate sources of wisdom and guidance. Includes seeking their consultation, following cultural protocols, and ensuring their communities benefit from knowledge sharing.

Traditional Knowledge Attribution: Proper recognition and crediting of traditional sources with cultural community acknowledgment, appropriate permissions, and ongoing relationships rather than extractive one-time use. Includes benefit sharing and reciprocal support.

Community Organization

Community-Based Participatory Research: Research approach that involves communities as equal partners rather than subjects of study. Community members participate in research design, implementation, and interpretation, with results serving community priorities and development goals.

Community Readiness Assessment: Evaluation tool for determining a group's preparedness to implement Sacred Synthesis principles. Assesses practice development, leadership capacity, safety protocols, service orientation, and cultural integration across multiple domains.

Community Service Integration: Integration of individual spiritual development with collective community contribution. Recognizes that authentic development must serve others and that community engagement accelerates individual growth and understanding.

Mutual Aid Networks: Systems for resource sharing based on abundance and need rather than market exchange. Community members contribute according to their abilities and receive according to their needs, building collective resilience and security.

Safe Houses: Secure locations and support systems for practitioners transitioning from oppressive institutions to authentic community relationships. Provide practical assistance, emotional support, and bridge connections during vulnerable transition periods.

Healthcare and Wellness

Contemplative Medicine: Healthcare approach that integrates meditation, mindfulness, and spiritual practices with clinical treatment. Emphasizes treating whole persons rather than isolated symptoms while supporting both healing and consciousness development.

Constitutional Breathing: Breathing practices adapted to individual constitutional patterns for optimal nervous system regulation. Electric types use grounding breath patterns, Magnetic types use energizing approaches, Neutral types focus on cooling and balancing techniques.

Constitutional Nutrition: Dietary approaches based on individual constitutional needs rather than generic nutritional guidelines. Considers digestive capacity, seasonal requirements, and metabolic patterns to optimize health through personalized food choices.

Integrative Healthcare: Medical approach combining conventional medicine with traditional healing systems, emphasizing constitutional assessment, preventive care, and patient education rather than symptom management and pharmaceutical dependence.

Mind-Body Medicine: Healthcare approach recognizing the interconnection between psychological, emotional, and physical health.

Uses techniques like meditation, breathing practices, and stress reduction to support healing and prevent disease.

Professional Integration

Constitutional Team Building: Organizational development approach that uses constitutional assessment to optimize team composition and collaboration. Ensures teams include complementary constitutional types and adapts management approaches to individual needs.

Professional Constitutional Assessment: Workplace application of constitutional understanding for career guidance, team optimization, and leadership development. Helps individuals find roles that match their natural strengths while supporting professional growth.

Teaching Authorization: Progressive qualification system for Sacred Synthesis instruction based on demonstrated competency, character development, and community validation. Includes foundation, intermediate, advanced, and master teacher levels with specific requirements.

Workplace Democracy: Implementation of democratic governance principles in professional settings through collaborative decision-making, worker ownership, rotating leadership, and shared responsibility for organizational outcomes.

Cultural Sensitivity

Benefit Sharing: Ensuring traditional communities receive appropriate economic and social benefits when their knowledge is used or adapted. Goes beyond one-time payments to ongoing relationship development and community empowerment.

Cultural Appropriation Prevention: Systematic approaches to avoid superficial or disrespectful use of traditional practices and symbols. Includes education, community consultation, protocol observance, and accountability mechanisms.

Cultural Protocol: Traditional customs and procedures for appropriate interaction with cultural communities and sacred knowledge. Includes proper permissions, ceremonial guidelines, gift exchange, and relationship maintenance practices.

Indigenous Sovereignty: Recognition of indigenous peoples' inherent rights to self-governance, cultural preservation, and control over their traditional territories and knowledge systems. Includes support for land rights and self-determination.

Historical References

GIDEE (Grupo Independiente de Estudios Esotéricos): "Independent Group of Esoteric Studies", organization founded during World War II (1942-1947) that developed Sacred Synthesis as anti-fascist resistance technology integrating traditional wisdom with democratic community organization.

Laws of Vayu (1919): Foundational text by Cedaior that first systematically documented the constitutional framework and community organization principles underlying Sacred Synthesis. Established the theoretical foundation for all subsequent development.

Operation Mindful Compliance (2046): Fictional future crackdown on Sacred Synthesis communities depicted in the Chronicles, representing systematic suppression of contemplative practices and democratic community organization by authoritarian regimes.

Sacred Synthesis Chronicles: 18-chapter narrative documenting the resistance, underground development, and ultimate emergence of Sacred Synthesis civilization from 2045-2100. Written from multiple perspectives to illustrate the complete transformation process.

Sanskrit Terms

Ayurveda (आयुर्वेद): Traditional Indian "life science", comprehensive system of constitutional medicine integrating physical health, mental balance, spiritual development, and environmental harmony. Foundation for Sacred Synthesis constitutional understanding.

Dharma (धर्म): Natural law, righteous duty, or individual life purpose within cosmic order. In Sacred Synthesis, refers to constitutional dharma, living according to one's authentic nature while serving collective wellbeing.

Kapha (कफ): One of three Ayurvedic constitutional types (doshas) representing earth and water elements. Characterized by stability, strength, and nurturing capacity. Corresponds to Sacred Synthesis Magnetic Constitution.

Pitta (पित्त): Ayurvedic constitutional type representing fire and water elements. Characterized by intelligence, ambition, and transformative capacity. Corresponds to Sacred Synthesis Neutral Constitution.

Pranayama (प्राणायाम): Traditional breathing practices for vital energy (prana) cultivation and consciousness development. Sacred Synthesis adapts pranayama techniques for constitutional types and community applications.

Sangha (संघ): Community of spiritual practitioners providing mutual support, shared learning, and collective wisdom. Sacred Synthesis communities function as modern sanghas with democratic governance and constitutional diversity.

Seva (सेवा): Selfless service and community contribution as spiritual practice. Sacred Synthesis integrates seva with constitutional understanding, so service matches individual gifts while meeting community needs.

Vata (वात): Ayurvedic constitutional type representing air and space elements. Characterized by creativity, sensitivity, and movement. Corresponds to Sacred Synthesis Electric Constitution.

Tibetan Terms
Bön (བོན་): Traditional Tibetan spiritual tradition predating Buddhism. Sacred Synthesis respectfully integrates some Bön healing and community practices with appropriate attribution.

Rigpa (རིག་པ): Pure awareness or natural knowing beyond conceptual thought. Advanced Sacred Synthesis practices aim to cultivate rigpa while maintaining community engagement and democratic participation.

rLung (རླུང་): Tibetan medical concept of "wind" energy governing nervous system function and mental activity. Corresponds closely to Sacred Synthesis Electric Constitution and Ayurvedic Vata.

Chinese Terms
Dao (道): "The Way", fundamental principle of natural harmony and effortless action. Sacred Synthesis governance and community organization follow Daoist principles of working with natural patterns rather than forcing outcomes.

Qi (氣): Vital energy or life force flowing through all living systems. Sacred Synthesis breathing practices and movement techniques work with qi cultivation while adapting approaches to constitutional differences.

Wuwei (無為): "Non-action" or natural spontaneous action in harmony with natural patterns. Sacred Synthesis decision-making processes aim for wuwei, effortless action arising from deep listening and constitutional wisdom.

Classical Tibetan Buddhist Texts
Abhidharmakośa (Treasury of Abhidharma)
- **Author**: Vasubandhu, 4th-5th century CE
- **Sanskrit Original**: Abhidharmakoṣabhāṣya
- **Tibetan Translation**: Chos mngon pa'i mdzod kyi bshad pa
- **Modern Editions**: Pradhan (1967), La Valle Poussin (1988-1990)
- **Relevance**: Foundation for consciousness analysis and contemplative practice

Madhyamakāvatāra (Entry into the Middle Way)
- **Author**: Candrakīrti, 7th century CE
- **Sanskrit Original**: Madhyamakāvatārabhāṣya
- **Tibetan Translation**: dBu ma la 'jug pa'i bshad pa

- **Modern Editions**: La Valle Poussin (1907-1912), Huntington (1989)
- **Relevance**: Middle Way philosophy and non-dual awareness practices

Classical Ayurvedic and Yogic Texts
Caraka Saṃhitā
- **Author**: Caraka, 1st-2nd century CE
- **Language**: Sanskrit with multiple commentaries
- **Modern Critical Editions**: Sharma & Dash (1985-1994)
- **Relevance**: Foundation for constitutional typing and health applications

Suśruta Saṃhitā
- **Author**: Suśruta, 3rd-4th century CE
- **Language**: Sanskrit with traditional commentaries
- **Modern Editions**: Murthy (1991-1995)
- **Relevance**: Constitutional medicine and therapeutic applications

Aṣṭāṅgahṛdaya Saṃhitā
- **Author**: Vāgbhaṭa, 7th century CE
- **Language**: Sanskrit, Aṣṭāṅgahṛdayasaṃhitā
- **Modern Translations**: Murthy (1992-1995)
- **Relevance**: Integrated approach to constitutional health and spiritual practice

Yoga Sūtra
- **Author**: Patañjali, 2nd century BCE, 2nd century CE
- **Language**: Sanskrit, Yogasūtra with traditional commentaries
- **Key Commentaries**: Vyāsa's Yogabhāṣya, Vācaspati Miśra's Tattvavaiśāradī
- **Modern Editions**: Swami Hariharananda Aranya (1981), Georg Feuerstein (1989)
- **Relevance**: Philosophical foundation for practices and ethics

Hatha Yoga Pradipika
- **Author**: Svātmārāma, 15th century CE
- **Language**: Sanskrit with traditional commentaries
- **Modern Translations**: Muktibodhananda (1998)
- **Relevance**: Physical practices and body-mind integration

Classical Chinese Medical and Taoist Texts
Huángdì Nèijīng (Yellow Emperor's Inner Classic)
- **Period**: 3rd-1st centuries BCE

- **Language**: Classical Chinese with traditional commentaries
- **Modern Translations**: Veith (1966), Unschuld (2011)
- **Relevance**: Constitutional patterns, seasonal cycles, and energy cultivation

Daodejing (The Way and its Virtue)
- **Traditional Attribution**: Laozi, 6th century BCE
- **Language**: Classical Chinese, Daodejing
- **Modern Scholarly Editions**: Henricks (1989), Wagner (2003)
- **Relevance**: Natural harmony, effortless action, and spiritual cultivation

Zhuangzi
- **Author**: Zhuang Zhou, 4th century BCE
- **Language**: Classical Chinese with traditional commentaries
- **Modern Translations**: Watson (1968), Ziporyn (2009)
- **Relevance**: Spontaneous naturalness and spiritual freedom

Contemporary Tibetan Buddhist Teachers
His Holiness the 14th Dalai Lama (Tenzin Gyatso)
- *The Art of Happiness* (1998), Integration of Buddhist wisdom with modern psychology
- *An Open Heart* (2001), Compassion practices for contemporary practitioners
- *Beyond Religion* (2011), Universal ethics and secular spirituality

Chögyam Trungpa Rinpoche
- *Cutting Through Spiritual Materialism* (1973), Critique of spiritual ego and authentic practice
- *The Myth of Freedom* (1976), Buddhist psychology and liberation
- *Shambhala: The Sacred Path of the Warrior* (1984), Secular wisdom teachings

Contemporary Indian Teachers
Dr. Vasant Lad (Contemporary Vedic Scholar)
- *Ayurvedic Healing* (1989), Comprehensive guide to Ayurvedic medicine
- *Yoga and Ayurveda* (1999), Integration of yoga and Ayurvedic practices

Contemporary Chinese Medicine Teachers
Dr. Harriet Beinfield and Efrem Korngold
- *Between Heaven and Earth* (1991), Five-element constitutional theory

- **Organization**: Chinese Medicine Works, San Francisco, Clinical practice and research

Giovanni Maciocia
- *The Foundations of Chinese Medicine* (1989)
- *The Practice of Chinese Medicine* (1994)
- **Focus**: Integration of traditional Chinese medicine with contemporary healthcare

Modern Academic Sources
Consciousness Studies and Neuroscience
Chalmers, David (1996)
- *The Conscious Mind.* Oxford University Press
- **Focus**: Hard problem of consciousness and philosophical foundations
- **Relevance**: Theoretical foundation for consciousness development practices

Varela, Francisco J., Eleanor Rosch, and Evan Thompson (1991)
- *The Embodied Mind: Cognitive Science and Human Experience.* MIT Press
- **Focus**: Enactive cognition and embodied consciousness research
- **Relevance**: Integration of Buddhist philosophy with cognitive science

Austin, James H. (1998)
- *Zen and the Brain: Toward an Understanding of Meditation and Consciousness.* MIT Press
- **Focus**: Neuroscience of meditation and contemplative states

Davidson, Richard J., Antoine Lutz (2008)
- "Buddha's brain: neuroplasticity and meditation." *IEEE Signal Processing Magazine*, 25(6), 176-188
- **Focus**: Neuroplasticity and meditation practice research
- **Relevance**: Scientific validation of contemplative training benefits

Mind-Body Medicine Foundation
Benson, Herbert (1975)
- *The Relaxation Response.* William Morrow
- **Focus**: Scientific validation of relaxation and stress reduction practices
- **Relevance**: Physiological mechanisms of meditation and prayer

Kabat-Zinn, Jon (1990)
- *Full Catastrophe Living: Using the Wisdom of Your Body and Mind to Face Stress, Pain, and Illness.* Delta Publishing
- **Focus**: Mindfulness-Based Stress Reduction (MBSR) and clinical applications
- **Relevance**: Integration of Buddhist mindfulness with healthcare

Pert, Candace (1997)
- *Molecules of Emotion.* Scribner
- **Focus**: Psychoneuroimmunology and emotion-immune system connections
- **Relevance**: Scientific basis for mind-body integration

Constitutional Medicine Research
Patwardhan, Bhushan, et al. (2015)
- Contemporary research validating Ayurvedic constitutional principles
- **Focus**: Integration of traditional knowledge with modern scientific methods
- **Global Scope**: Research collaboration across continents

Complete Document Inventory and Reference
Total Documents Referenced: 67 comprehensive resources
Traditional Languages: 23 languages with translations
Global Cultural Groups: 87 cultural traditions integrated
Communities Documented: 147 worldwide Sacred Synthesis communities

Historical Span
- **Traditional Sources**: 3000 BCE, 2100 CE
- **Modern Development**: 1919, 2080 CE
- **Primary Implementation**: 2025, 2080 CE
- **Documentation Period**: 2080, 2100 CE

This reading guide provides complete access to the materials while preserving the systematic development that characterized Sacred Synthesis civilization. Each document contributes to understanding how individual constitutional wisdom served collective advancement through practical application, authentic community, and global cooperation.

The journey through these materials is itself a form of practice, may it serve both your individual understanding and whatever communities you choose to build or join in the recovering world we now inhabit.

Compiled by a Lone Wanderer
Year 2100 CE
From the Ruins of Sacred Synthesis Civilization
For Those Who Come After

LIST OF ASSESSMENT TOOLS AND PROTOCOLS

PRIMARY ASSESSMENT TOOLS
Constitutional Assessment (Complete 125-Question System) Pages 12-33
- Most important tool in entire book
- Foundation for all personalization
- Allow 2-3 hours for thoughtful completion
- Scoring guidelines included (pages 25-27)
- Essential for ALL readers regardless of path

Constitutional Type Profiles Pages 26-30
- Electric Constitution (Vata) detailed description Pages 26-27
- Magnetic Constitution (Kapha) detailed description Pages 27-28
- Neutral Constitution (Pitta) detailed description Pages 28-29

PERSONAL DEVELOPMENT ASSESSMENTS
Daily Practice Tracking Journal (referenced throughout)
- Track 4:00 AM practices
- Constitutional adaptation notes
- Energy levels and observations
- Weekly and monthly review sections
- Digital and printable versions available

Monthly Development Assessment (referenced throughout)
- Physical progress tracking
- Constitutional integration evaluation
- Breathing practice development
- Life and service development
- Holistic growth measurement

Seasonal Practice Adaptation Guide Pages 145-146
- Spring modifications
- Summer modifications
- Fall modifications
- Winter modifications
- Constitutional variations by season

COMMUNITY AND LEADERSHIP ASSESSMENTS
Community Readiness Assessment (referenced in multiple sections)
- Practice foundation evaluation
- Leadership capacity
- Safety protocol implementation
- Service integration
- Growth and sustainability readiness

Community Leadership Assessment (referenced throughout)
- Constitutional leadership styles
- Team dynamics evaluation
- Decision-making capacity
- Conflict transformation skills
- Vision and strategic planning

Advanced Practitioner Self-Assessment Pages 484-485
- Foundation mastery verification
- Constitutional expertise
- Teaching readiness
- Community leadership skills
- Ethics and integrity
- Specialized pathway qualification

PROFESSIONAL INTEGRATION ASSESSMENTS
Healthcare Provider Integration Assessment (referenced throughout)
- Constitutional practice integration
- Patient care quality
- Clinical outcomes measurement
- Professional development
- Colleague collaboration
- Workplace culture assessment

Educational Integration Assessment Pages scattered throughout text
- Constitutional learning styles implementation
- Democratic classroom organization
- Student governance participation
- Assessment beyond testing
- Teacher development
- Systemic transformation progress

Organizational Development Assessment Pages scattered throughout text
- Constitutional team composition

- Democratic decision-making implementation
- Leadership rotation effectiveness
- Conflict transformation capacity
- Organizational culture health

SPECIALIZED ASSESSMENTS
Family Practice Compatibility Guide (referenced throughout)
- Multi-generational constitutional assessment
- Family member compatibility
- Household environment optimization
- Communication style adaptation
- Conflict patterns and resolution
- Community service planning

Global Service Capacity Assessment (referenced in international sections)
- International readiness evaluation
- Global citizenship development
- Cultural competency
- Cross-cultural communication
- Practical service skills
- Crisis response capacity
- Specialized service areas

HEALTH AND WELLNESS TRACKING
Constitutional Health Metrics Tracking System (referenced throughout)
- Physical indicators by constitutional type
- Laboratory markers interpretation
- Daily health tracking protocols
- Crisis warning signs
- Healthcare provider integration
- Long-term wellness patterns

Therapeutic Application Assessment Pages scattered throughout healthcare sections
- Mental health constitutional approaches
- Chronic disease management
- Pain management protocols
- Women's health variations
- Geriatric care adaptations

SAFETY AND SECURITY PROTOCOLS
Safety Protocol Checklist Pages 552-555
- Medical contraindications screening

- Age and condition modifications
- Pregnancy adaptations
- Psychological precautions
- Warning signs monitoring
- When to seek professional guidance

RESEARCH AND VALIDATION TOOLS
Research Validation Framework Pages scattered throughout academic sections
- Psychometric validation criteria
- Cross-cultural testing protocols
- Clinical study methodology
- Outcome measurement tools
- Replication guidelines

Academic Integration Guidelines Pages scattered throughout appendices
- Syllabus development
- Course integration strategies
- Student assessment tools
- Research project frameworks

INSTRUCTIONS FOR USE
Personal Use: All assessment tools may be photocopied for personal practice and study group use without permission.
Professional Use: Healthcare providers, educators, and organizational consultants should review professional integration sections before adapting tools for client/patient use.
Research Use: Academics wishing to use assessment tools for research should review validation methodology sections and contact information for collaboration.

LIST OF PRACTICES AND EXERCISES
All practices include constitutional adaptations, safety protocols, and progression guidelines
FOUNDATION PRACTICES (ESSENTIAL FOR ALL)
THE FOUR PILLARS SYSTEM
Movement Practices Pages 52-72
- Electric Constitution sequences (light, flowing, grounding) Integrated throughout
- Magnetic Constitution sequences (vigorous, stimulating) Integrated throughout
- Neutral Constitution sequences (moderate, balanced, cooling) Integrated throughout

- Foundational yoga asanas Throughout Four Pillars section
- Constitutional adaptations for each posture Throughout

Breathing Practices (Pranayama) Pages 64-65, integrated throughout
- Calming, lengthening techniques (Electric) Throughout
- Heating, invigorating techniques (Magnetic) Throughout
- Cooling, balancing techniques (Neutral) Throughout
- Nervous system regulation foundations Pages 64-65
- Safety protocols and contraindications Pages 552-555

Study Practices Throughout Four Pillars section (Pages 52-72)
- Systematic, structured learning (Electric) Integrated
- Experiential, embodied learning (Magnetic) Integrated
- Strategic, analytical learning (Neutral) Integrated
- Contemplative study methods Throughout

Service Practices Throughout Four Pillars section (Pages 52-72)
- Teaching, communication, innovation (Electric) Integrated
- Building, maintaining, sustaining (Magnetic) Integrated
- Leadership, organization, strategy (Neutral) Integrated
- Community contribution frameworks Throughout

DAILY PRACTICE SEQUENCES BY CONSTITUTIONAL TYPE
4:00 AM AWAKENING PROTOCOLS
Electric Constitution Daily Sequence Pages 30-31, 52-72
- 4:00 AM awakening ritual Referenced
- Movement: Morning grounding sequence Integrated
- Breathing: Calming pranayama Integrated
- Study: Structured contemplation Integrated
- Service: Daily contribution Integrated
- Total time: 90-120 minutes

Magnetic Constitution Daily Sequence Pages 27-28, 52-72
- 4:00 AM awakening ritual Referenced
- Movement: Vigorous energizing sequence Integrated
- Breathing: Heating pranayama Integrated
- Study: Embodied learning Integrated
- Service: Building practice Integrated
- Total time: 90-120 minutes

Neutral Constitution Daily Sequence Pages 28-29, 52-72
- 4:00 AM awakening ritual Referenced
- Movement: Balanced moderate sequence Integrated

- Breathing: Cooling pranayama Integrated
- Study: Strategic analysis Integrated
- Service: Leadership development Integrated
- Total time: 90-120 minutes

SEASONAL ADAPTATIONS

Spring Practice Modifications Pages 145-146
- Detoxification emphasis
- Lighter, more energetic practices
- Constitutional adjustments

Summer Practice Modifications Pages 145-146
- Cooling emphasis
- Moderate intensity
- Heat management

Fall Practice Modifications Pages 145-146
- Grounding emphasis
- Routine establishment
- Transition support

Winter Practice Modifications Pages 145-146
- Warming emphasis
- Introspective deepening
- Energy conservation

ADVANCED PRACTICES (After Foundation Mastery)

Advanced Movement Practices Pages 489 (referenced)
- Esoteric yoga systems
- Advanced constitutional adaptations
- Master-level alignment
- Energetic subtleties
- Progression from foundation

Advanced Pranayama and Energy Work Pages 489 (referenced)
- Subtle energy techniques
- Advanced retention practices
- Constitutional refinements
- Master-level breath control
- Energetic system activation

Advanced Consciousness Research Pages 489 (referenced)
- Deep contemplative states
- Philosophical inquiry methods

- Research collaboration
- Teaching development
- Transmission preparation

Advanced Cultural Transmission Pages 489 (referenced)
- Master teaching protocols
- Lineage transmission
- Wisdom keeper development
- Cross-cultural bridge-building
- International service

THERAPEUTIC AND SPECIALIZED PRACTICES
Constitutional Medicine Practices
Self-Care Protocols by Constitutional Type Referenced throughout healthcare sections
- Daily constitutional health maintenance
- Imbalance recognition and correction
- Preventive care practices
- Integration with conventional medicine

Therapeutic Applications Referenced throughout healthcare sections
- Mental health protocols
- Chronic disease management
- Pain management techniques
- Women's health practices
- Geriatric care adaptations

COMMUNITY BUILDING PRACTICES
Democratic Governance Practices Pages 552, referenced throughout
- Consensus decision-making protocols
- Constitutional role optimization
- Conflict transformation exercises
- Leadership rotation implementation
- Transparency and accountability practices

Mutual Aid Network Development Referenced throughout chronicles
- Resource sharing protocols
- Time banking practices
- Tool library organization
- Food security initiatives
- Skill-sharing networks

ENVIRONMENTAL AND ECOLOGICAL PRACTICES
Bioregional Organization Practices Referenced in chronicles and community sections
- Watershed assessment and protection
- Sacred site stewardship
- Permaculture integration
- Constitutional approaches to ecology
- Restoration project protocols

FAMILY AND INTERGENERATIONAL PRACTICES
Multi-Generational Practice Adaptation (referenced)
- Age-appropriate modifications (children, teens, adults, elders)
- Family constitutional compatibility practices
- Intergenerational transmission protocols
- Elder wisdom integration
- Youth leadership development

PROFESSIONAL DEVELOPMENT PRACTICES
Healthcare Provider Practices
Constitutional Medicine Clinical Protocols Pages 186-191
- Patient assessment procedures
- Treatment personalization methods
- Integration with conventional care
- Outcome measurement systems
- Colleague education protocols

Educational Practices
Contemplative Education Methods Referenced throughout
- Constitutional learning style adaptation
- Democratic classroom organization
- Student governance facilitation
- Character development integration
- Systemic transformation protocols

MASTER-LEVEL PRACTICES (Advanced Practitioners Only)
Master-Level Community Leadership Pages 484-485
- Advanced facilitation techniques
- Cultural bridge-building at scale
- International network coordination
- Elder wisdom transmission
- Teaching authorization development

Contraindications and Precautions Pages 552-555
- Medical conditions requiring modification
- Psychological considerations
- Pregnancy, age, physical limitation adaptations
- Warning signs of improper practice
- When to seek professional guidance

Comprehensive Safety Guidelines Pages 552-555
- Practice safety protocols
- Medical screening
- Emergency procedures
- Crisis response

PRACTICE RESOURCES
Tracking and Measurement Tools (available as downloadable resources)
- Daily practice journal templates
- Monthly assessment forms
- Progress measurement systems
- Community practice logs

Study Group Practice Guidelines Referenced in appendices
- Collective practice protocols
- Group constitutional diversity optimization
- Practice support structures
- Accountability systems

ACKNOWLEDGMENTS AND TRADITIONAL KNOWLEDGE ATTRIBUTION

This work stands on the shoulders of giants across millennia. We acknowledge with deep gratitude all who preserved, transmitted, and developed this knowledge.

PRIMARY TRADITIONAL KNOWLEDGE SOURCES
Ancient Traditions (5,000+ Years of Continuous Transmission)
Ayurvedic Medicine Traditions
- Complete constitutional medicine system (Vata, Pitta, Kapha) drawn from Ayurvedic lineages with proper attribution
- Charaka Samhita and Sushruta Samhita foundational texts
- Contemporary Ayurvedic practitioners and teachers
- Complete Ayurvedic source bibliography: pages 520-521

Buddhist Psychology and Meditation Systems

- Abhidharma psychology foundations
- Vipassana and mindfulness practices
- Tibetan Buddhist contemplative traditions
- Contemporary Buddhist teachers
- Complete Buddhist source bibliography: pages 521-522

Yoga Traditions
- Asana practices from multiple yoga lineages
- Pranayama systems properly sourced
- Philosophical foundations from Yoga Sutras
- Contemporary yoga teachers
- Complete Yoga source bibliography: pages 521-522

Indigenous Wisdom Traditions
- Cultural protocols acknowledged and honored
- Benefit-sharing agreements envisioned (see Appendix D, pages 556-560)
- Sovereignty of traditional knowledge keepers respected
- Complete Indigenous source attribution: pages 520-527

Other Contemplative Traditions
- Sufi mystical traditions
- Taoist practices and philosophy
- Christian contemplative traditions
- Other wisdom lineages properly cited
- Additional traditional sources: pages 520-527

Complete bibliography: pages 520-527

MODERN SYNTHESIS AND TRANSMISSION
GIDEE (1942-1947)
Profound gratitude to the Grupo Independiente de Estudios Esotéricos (GIDEE) in Montevideo, Uruguay, 1942-1947.
During World War II, as fascism threatened to destroy knowledge worldwide, the GIDEE synthesized Eastern and Western contemplative traditions into accessible, practical systems. Their wartime work preserved wisdom that might otherwise have been lost.

Specific influences acknowledged:
- Systematic integration of Ayurvedic, Buddhist, Sufi, and other traditions
- Constitutional assessment methodology foundations
- Four Pillars practice system architecture
- Democratic transmission model (no guru hierarchy)

- Documentation in La Iniciación magazine (1942-1947)

Historical documentation: pages 34-51

CONTEMPORARY RESEARCH VALIDATION
Academic Researchers and Institutions
Gratitude to hundreds of researchers whose peer-reviewed studies validate traditional approaches:

Consciousness Studies and Psychology
- Researchers documenting meditation and contemplative practice effectiveness
- Neuroscientists studying consciousness and practice effects
- Complete research bibliography: pages 524-525

Integrative Medicine and Healthcare
- Clinical studies documenting outcomes
- Cross-cultural validation studies
- Healthcare research bibliography: pages 525-526

Educational Theory and Practice
- Researchers documenting contemplative education effectiveness
- Democratic classroom organization studies
- Character development research
- Educational research bibliography: page 526

Community Organization and Democratic Governance
- Political scientists documenting alternative governance systems
- Sociologists studying mutual aid and cooperation
- Anthropologists examining cross-cultural community organization
- Community research bibliography: pages 526-527

Environmental Science and Ecology
- Researchers documenting bioregional approaches
- Ecological restoration studies
- Indigenous land stewardship research
- Environmental research bibliography: page 527

INSTITUTIONAL ACKNOWLEDGMENTS
Universities and Research Centers
- Institutions that support consciousness research despite funding challenges

- Programs that validated contemplative approaches
- Scholars who maintain intellectual rigor while honoring traditional wisdom

Healthcare Institutions
- Integrative medicine programs that demonstrate outcomes
- Training institutions that educate practitioners

Educational Institutions
- Districts that support systemic transformation
- Training programs that develop new educators

Community Organizations
- Mutual aid networks that demonstrate alternatives
- Bioregional organizations that coordinate cooperation
- Cultural organizations that maintain traditions

AUTHORIZATION AND CULTURAL SENSITIVITY PROTO-COLS

Traditional Knowledge Authorization

All traditional knowledge integrated in this work has been:
- Properly sourced and attributed (see Bibliography, pages 520-527)
- Integrated with cultural sensitivity protocols (see Appendix D, pages 556-560)

We commit to:
- Accurate attribution in all contexts
- Respect for cultural protocols
- Opposition to appropriation and exploitation

Complete authorization documentation: Appendix D, pages 556-560

READER AND PRACTITIONER ACKNOWLEDGMENTS

Your contributions matter:
- Personal practice validates and refines techniques
- Community organizing proves alternatives work
- Academic study extends scholarly understanding
- Teaching transmits to next generations
- Your engagement continues the transmission

We acknowledge you as co-creators of whatever comes next.

One More Thing…

ADVANCED MASTERY AND BIOELECTRIC INTEGRATION
For Practitioners Ready for Advanced Stages and Specialized Applications

Introduction: The Sacred Journey

The achievement of contemplative mastery represents the systematic development of consciousness through progressive stages of spiritual unfoldment. This ancient science, documented across traditions from the Buddhist Yogācārabhūmi-Śāstra to the Martinist teachings of the GIDEE (Grupo Independiente de Estudios Esotéricos), provides a complete curriculum for transforming ordinary awareness into enlightened consciousness.

As found in the historical teachings preserved during the 1942-1947 wartime transmission:

"The finality of life is the realization of the internal Self. All the systems of philosophy have a single finality, the liberation of the soul through perfection."

This liberation requires systematic practice combining intellectual understanding, moral purification, and direct spiritual realization.

TWELVE-STAGE PROGRESSIVE CURRICULUM ARCHITECTURE

Stage	Theme	Key Competence
1	Foundational Worldview	Unity of life & vibrational medicine
2	Bio-Compatible Diet	Sattva-dominant, temple-grade food
3	Food Combining	Acid/alkali mastery & three-list method
4	Periodic Detox & Fasting	Pranic reset
5	Conscious Breathing	Complete respiration & prana charging
6	Hydric Wisdom	Physiological water & cellular cleansing
7	Mineral-Vitamin Science	22 essential elements in organic form
8	Asana Sequence	Maha-Asana bridge
9	Geomagnetic Hygiene	Sleep/work orientation & earthing

10	Color Medicine	Chromotherapy protocols
11	Rhythmic Daily Order	Solar-lunar scheduling & service
12	Integrative Mastery	Self-evaluation & service

Why Sequential Development?

Physical Foundation First (Stages 2-4): Without optimal nutrition, food combining, and periodic cleansing, the body cannot support advanced energetic and spiritual practices. Toxicity, deficiency, and digestive dysfunction create physiological barriers to higher development.

Energetic Development Second (Stages 5-8): Once physical purification establishes a clean vessel, conscious breathing, hydration wisdom, mineral optimization, and movement practices activate and direct life force systematically.

Environmental Optimization Third (Stages 9-11): With physical and energetic mastery established, electromagnetic hygiene, color therapy, and rhythmic daily order create optimal conditions for sustained spiritual practice.

Integration and Service Fourth (Stage 12): Complete integration of all previous stages naturally produces capacity for self-evaluation, prophetic insight, and evolutionary service.

MINIMUM MATERIALS REQUIRED

This praxis emphasizes simplicity and accessibility. The following materials support practice:

Kitchen and Nutrition
- Unrefined sea salt (for mineral supplementation and electrolyte balance)
- Raw honey (for natural sweetening and therapeutic applications)
- Stable citrus supply (lemons and oranges for detoxification protocols)
- Glass storage containers (avoid plastic; maintain food vitality)
- Quality knife and cutting board
- Simple cooking equipment (pot, pan, steamer)

Water and Hydration
- Two plain glass jugs (1-2 liter capacity each)

- Green and red cellophane sheets (for chromo-water preparation)
- Water filtration system (carbon filter minimum; multi-stage preferred)

Sleep and Electromagnetic Hygiene
- Simple magnetized wooden bedframe oriented North→South
- Natural fiber bedding (cotton, linen, wool)
- Dark room environment for optimal sleep

Movement and Practice
- Cotton mat for asana and movement
- Comfortable, natural fiber clothing
- Small meditation cushion (optional but helpful)

Record Keeping
- Dedicated practice notebook for self-observation
- Pen for daily journaling and tracking
- Optional: ruler and colored pencils for detailed tracking

The 7-Day Micro-Audit System
After completing practices, perform a comprehensive **7-day micro-audit** tracking:
1. **Diet Log:** Complete record of food choices, quantities, combinations, and timing
2. **Activity Log:** Breathing practices and movement sequences performed
3. **Morning Pulse & BP:** Vital signs upon waking (establishes health trajectory)
4. **Dream Recall:** Dream content and quality (indicates subconscious processing)
5. **Energy Levels:** Morning, midday, and evening energy ratings (1-10 scale)
6. **Digestion Quality:** Comfort, elimination regularity, and food effects
7. **Mental/Emotional State:** Clarity, mood stability, and spiritual awareness

Transformation Mapping
These audits become your **map of transformation**, documenting:
- Baseline health status before practice implementation
- Progressive improvements as practices integrate
- Individual variations requiring constitutional adaptation
- Optimal timing and dosage for maximum benefit
- Correlation between practices and specific health outcomes

Key Principle: Objective self-observation without judgment produces accurate data enabling intelligent practice refinement.

SAFETY AND CONTRAINDICATIONS

All protocols are food-grade and non-toxic, emphasizing natural foods, pure water, conscious breathing, and gentle movement. However, moderation and individual adaptation remain essential.

Universal Precautions
Pregnant Women:

- Avoid extended fasting protocols (orange fast, water fasting)
- Modify breathing practices (no retention, no forceful techniques)
- Emphasize nourishment over cleansing
- Consult healthcare provider before implementing any protocol

Chronically Ill Practitioners:

- Remain under professional medical care during practice implementation
- Introduce changes gradually with medical supervision
- Monitor all health markers closely
- Adapt protocols for specific conditions with qualified guidance

Contraindicated Practices Without Professional Guidance:

- Extended fasting (more than 3 days)
- Intense breathing practices (Bhastrika, Kapalbhati) with cardiovascular conditions
- Head-to-North sleep orientation with certain neurological conditions
- Rapid dietary transitions with compromised digestion

When to Seek Professional Help

Immediately consult healthcare provider if experiencing:
- Severe or persistent pain
- Dramatic weight loss or gain
- Extreme fatigue or weakness
- Mental confusion or emotional instability
- Any symptom causing concern

Integration Principle: This praxis complements but does not replace appropriate medical care. Work collaboratively with healthcare providers, sharing practice implementations and monitoring effects together.

THE FOUR STAGES OF SPIRITUAL DEVELOPMENT

Stage 1: The Practitioner (Prathamkalpika)
The preliminary stage focuses on establishing the foundation for spiritual development through three integrated dimensions:

Physical Preparation:
- Regular practice of fundamental meditation postures (asanas)
- Systematic breathing exercises (pranayama)
- Dietary purification following constitutional and natural principles
- Daily schedule aligned with circadian rhythms (optimally 4 AM to 9 PM practice window)

Mental Discipline:
- Development of concentration through single-pointed focus
- Cultivation of mindfulness in daily activities
- Study of fundamental spiritual principles
- Practice of ethical conduct (yama) and observances (niyama)

Emotional Purification:
- Cultivation of devotion through loving-kindness meditation
- Service to others as expression of spiritual understanding
- Transformation of negative emotions through conscious practice
- Development of equanimity under varying circumstances

Duration: Typically 1-3 years with consistent daily practice
Assessment Criteria: Ability to maintain 30-45 minute meditation sessions, basic pranayama competence, stable ethical conduct, growing service orientation

Stage 2: The Honey-Bearer (Madhupratika)
This intermediate stage involves the awakening of spiritual faculties beyond ordinary consciousness:

Psychic Development:
- Recognition of subtle energy currents in the body
- Sensitivity to environmental and interpersonal energies
- Development of intuitive perception beyond ordinary senses
- Beginning awareness of consciousness states beyond waking

Intellectual Integration:
- Systematic study of metaphysical principles

- Understanding of correspondence between microcosm and macrocosm
- Integration of Eastern and Western wisdom traditions
- Recognition of universal laws governing spiritual development

Service Orientation:
- Teaching and guidance of beginning practitioners
- Healing work through energy transmission
- Cultural and educational contributions
- Leadership in spiritual communities

Duration: Typically 3-7 years of sustained practice
Assessment Criteria: Development of subtle perception abilities, capacity to guide beginners, integration of spiritual insights with daily life, community service engagement

Stage 3: The Master of Elements (Bhutendriyajay)

The advanced practitioner achieves mastery over natural forces and psychological patterns:

Elemental Control:
- Conscious regulation of bodily functions
- Influence over environmental conditions
- Demonstration of phenomena transcending physical limitations
- Understanding of the relationship between consciousness and matter

Psychological Mastery:
- Complete emotional equilibrium under all circumstances
- Freedom from unconscious reactivity patterns
- Ability to maintain spiritual perspective during challenges
- Integration of personality around spiritual purpose

Teaching Authority:
- Transmission of authentic spiritual knowledge
- Initiation of qualified disciples
- Institutional leadership and organization
- Preservation and adaptation of traditional teachings

Duration: Typically 7-15 years of dedicated practice
Assessment Criteria: Demonstrated mastery over physical and emotional challenges, teaching and transmission capabilities, community leadership effectiveness, preservation of tradition with appropriate innovation

Stage 4: The Liberated Being (Atikrantabhavaniya)
The final stage represents complete spiritual realization and ultimate service:

Kaivalya (Isolation/Unity):
- Recognition of consciousness as distinct from all phenomena
- Direct experience of universal unity underlying diversity
- Freedom from identification with any limited form or condition
- Spontaneous expression of enlightened activity

Transcendent Service:
- Guidance of humanity's spiritual evolution
- Invisible assistance to sincere seekers worldwide
- Integration of transcendent wisdom with practical effectiveness
- Embodiment of divine qualities in human form

Duration: Lifelong deepening and refinement
Assessment: Self-evident through profound beneficial impact on others, transparent character, wisdom and compassion integration

The Five Ethical Foundations (Yamas)
1. Ahimsa (Non-Harm):
- **Definition:** Absence of desire to harm any being in thought, word, or deed
- **Practice:** Non-violent communication, peaceful conflict resolution
- **Professional Application:** Healthcare without harm, ethical business practices, restorative justice
- **Assessment:** Reduced aggressive thoughts, peaceful relationships, compassionate action

2. Satya (Truth):
- **Definition:** Alignment of thought, speech, and action with reality
- **Practice:** Honest communication, authentic self-expression, transparency
- **Professional Application:** Transparent business dealings, honest teaching, integrity in all transactions
- **Assessment:** Consistent truthfulness, reduced lying/deception, authentic presence

3. Asteya (Non-Stealing):
- **Definition:** Not taking what is not freely given, including time, credit, resources

- **Practice:** Respecting others' property, giving credit appropriately, fair compensation
- **Professional Application:** Fair wages, appropriate pricing, intellectual property respect
- **Assessment:** Reduced coveting, generous giving, appropriate resource use

4. Brahmacharya (Right Use of Energy):
- **Definition:** Appropriate sexual conduct and energy conservation
- **Practice:** Sexual ethics, energy management, celibacy (if chosen), appropriate relationships
- **Professional Application:** Professional boundaries, work-life balance, sustainable practices
- **Assessment:** Appropriate sexual behavior, sustained energy, reduced compulsion

5. Aparigraha (Non-Hoarding):
- **Definition:** Non-attachment to possessions and outcomes
- **Practice:** Simple living, generous sharing, releasing control
- **Professional Application:** Appropriate profit, resource sharing, detached effort
- **Assessment:** Reduced materialism, generous spirit, freedom from possessiveness

CONTEMPLATIVE READING AND PRAYER

The Foundation of Lectio Divina
The Four Movements of Sacred Reading:

Lectio (Reading):
- Select brief passage from Scripture or spiritual text
- Read slowly and attentively, allowing words to penetrate deeply
- Notice which word or phrase draws particular attention
- Avoid analytical approach; read with heart receptivity

Meditatio (Meditation):
- Repeat chosen word or phrase slowly and lovingly
- Allow text to speak personally and intimately
- Let meaning unfold through gentle reflection
- Resist urge to analyze; allow resonance and response

Oratio (Prayer):
- Enter spontaneous dialogue with God about the text
- Share honestly your thoughts, feelings, and responses

- Listen for God's response in heart's quiet
- Allow natural movement between speaking and listening

Contemplatio (Contemplation):
- Release all effort and rest silently in God's presence
- Move beyond words, thoughts, and images
- Simply be present with Divine in wordless love
- Return gently to earlier stages if distractions arise

Daily Practice Structure (20-30 minutes):
1. **Preparation** (3-5 minutes): Quiet settling, invocation
2. **Lectio** (5 minutes): Slow, reverent reading
3. **Meditatio** (5-7 minutes): Gentle repetition and reflection
4. **Oratio** (5-7 minutes): Conversational prayer
5. **Contemplatio** (5-10 minutes): Silent rest in Divine presence

Centering Prayer Practice
The Method:

Preparation:
- Choose a sacred word expressing your intention to be present to God
- Common words: "Peace," "Stillness," "Love," "Abba"
- Sit comfortably with eyes closed in quiet environment
- Begin with brief prayer of intention

The Prayer Period:
1. **Introduction of Sacred Word:** Silently introduce your chosen word
2. **Gentle Return:** When aware of thoughts, return gently to sacred word
3. **No Struggle:** Don't fight thoughts; simply use word as anchor
4. **Gradual Deepening:** Allow natural movement into wordless silence

Duration and Frequency:
- Begin with 20 minutes once or twice daily
- Gradually extend to 40 minutes for experienced practitioners
- Group practice enhances individual development
- Maintain consistent timing and location when possible

ENERGY WORK AND SUBTLE BODY DEVELOPMENT
Understanding Subtle Anatomy
The Five Koshas (Energy Sheaths):

1. Annamaya Kosha (Food Sheath) - Physical Body:
- Sustained by nutrition and governed by constitutional principles
- Requires proper diet, exercise, environmental harmony
- Foundation for all higher energy work
- **Development:** Optimal health through constitutional living

2. Pranamaya Kosha (Energy Sheath) - Vital Body:
- Life force body governing vitality and health
- Includes five major pranas and five minor pranas
- Accessed through breath work and energy practices
- **Development:** Pranayama mastery and energy circulation

3. Manomaya Kosha (Mental Sheath) - Thinking Mind:
- Sensory functions, memory, and rational thought
- Includes emotions and mental patterns
- Purified through meditation and contemplation
- **Development:** Mental clarity and emotional stability

4. Vijnanamaya Kosha (Wisdom Sheath) - Intuitive Intelligence:
- Discriminative wisdom and direct knowledge
- Faculty of spiritual understanding
- Developed through study, contemplation, insight practices
- **Development:** Authentic spiritual discernment

5. Anandamaya Kosha (Bliss Sheath) - Causal Body:
- Closest to pure consciousness
- Experienced as profound peace and unconditional happiness
- Accessed through advanced meditation and surrender
- **Development:** Recognition of Self as awareness-bliss

The Complete Chakra System
Detailed Chakra Framework:

Muladhara (Root Chakra):
- **Location:** Base of spine, perineum
- **Element:** Fire (Tejas)
- **Seed Sound:** LAM
- **Color:** Red
- **Lotus Petals:** Four
- **Functions:** Survival, grounding, material security, basic trust
- **Balanced State:** Physical health, emotional stability, groundedness, appropriate boundaries
- **Imbalanced State:** Anxiety, fear, financial insecurity, disconnection from body

- **Development Practices:** Standing poses, root lock (mula bandha), earth connection, material organization

Svadhisthana (Sacral Chakra):
- **Location:** Lower abdomen, 2 inches below navel
- **Element:** Fire (Tejas)
- **Seed Sound:** VAM
- **Color:** Orange
- **Lotus Petals:** Six
- **Functions:** Creativity, sexuality, emotional expression, pleasure
- **Balanced State:** Healthy sexuality, creative flow, emotional intelligence, pleasure capacity
- **Imbalanced State:** Sexual dysfunction, creative blocks, emotional repression, addiction
- **Development Practices:** Hip openers, pelvic breathing, creative expression, emotional processing

Manipura (Solar Plexus Chakra):
- **Location:** Upper abdomen, solar plexus region
- **Element:** Earth (Prithvi)
- **Seed Sound:** RAM
- **Color:** Yellow
- **Lotus Petals:** Ten
- **Functions:** Personal power, will, self-esteem, digestion
- **Balanced State:** Confidence, strong will, healthy boundaries, good digestion
- **Imbalanced State:** Low self-esteem, weak will, digestive problems, victim consciousness
- **Development Practices:** Core strengthening, fire breath, warrior poses, goal achievement

Anahata (Heart Chakra):
- **Location:** Center of chest, heart region
- **Element:** Air (Vayu)
- **Seed Sound:** YAM
- **Color:** Green
- **Lotus Petals:** Twelve
- **Functions:** Love, compassion, connection, forgiveness
- **Balanced State:** Unconditional love, compassion, healthy relationships, forgiveness
- **Imbalanced State:** Codependency, emotional armor, inability to connect, resentment
- **Development Practices:** Backbends, heart-opening breath, loving-kindness meditation, service

Vishuddha (Throat Chakra):
- **Location:** Base of throat, thyroid region, Atlas Joint
- **Element:** Water (Apas)
- **Seed Sound:** HAM
- **Color:** Blue
- **Lotus Petals:** Sixteen
- **Functions:** Communication, truth, expression, listening
- **Balanced State:** Authentic communication, creative expression, good listening, truth-telling
- **Imbalanced State:** Communication difficulties, lying, inability to express, not listening
- **Development Practices:** Chanting, shoulder stand, neck releases, authentic speaking

Ajna (Third Eye Chakra):
- **Location:** Between eyebrows, pineal gland
- **Element:** Space (Akasha)
- **Seed Sound:** OM
- **Color:** Indigo
- **Lotus Petals:** Two (representing duality transcended)
- **Functions:** Intuition, wisdom, spiritual sight, imagination
- **Balanced State:** Clear intuition, spiritual discernment, vivid imagination, inner knowing
- **Imbalanced State:** Confusion, lack of clarity, inability to visualize, closed to intuition
- **Development Practices:** Meditation, visualization, forehead focus, spiritual study

Sahasrara (Crown Chakra):
- **Location:** Top of head, beyond physical
- **Element:** Pure Consciousness/ Light (Jyoti)
- **Seed Sound:** Silence
- **Color:** Violet, gold
- **Lotus Petals:** Thousand (representing infinite)
- **Functions:** Unity consciousness, enlightenment, divine connection
- **Balanced State:** Spiritual realization, unity experience, peace, transcendence
- **Imbalanced State:** Spiritual disconnection, materialism, closed-mindedness, depression
- **Development Practices:** Extended meditation, inversions, surrender, silence

VISUALIZATION AND SOUND

The Science of Visualization
Neuroplasticity and Visualization:
Modern neuroscience confirms what contemplatives have long known, mental imagery creates actual neural changes identical to physical experience. Systematic visualization practice literally rewires the brain, developing new patterns of perception and response.

Archetypal Activation:
Traditional visualization practices utilize universal symbols and archetypes that resonate with the collective unconscious, activating dormant potentials within the psyche and facilitating transpersonal experiences.

Progressive Visualization Training
Foundation Level: Basic Image Stabilization (Months 1-3)
Simple Object Visualization:
1. Choose simple object (candle flame, flower, geometric shape)
2. Study object carefully for 2-3 minutes with open eyes
3. Close eyes and recreate image as vividly as possible
4. When image fades, open eyes and study object again
5. Gradually increase duration of stable inner image

Practice Guidelines:
- Begin with 10-15 minutes daily
- Use same object for one week before changing
- Focus on clarity and stability over complexity
- Note improvement in concentration and memory

Intermediate Level: Dynamic Visualization (Months 4-12)
Golden Light Meditation:
1. Visualize golden sphere of light at heart center
2. With each inhalation, light grows brighter
3. With each exhalation, light expands through entire body
4. Conclude by radiating light to all beings

Duration: 10-20 minutes
Benefits: Emotional healing, energy cultivation, compassion development
Rainbow Body Technique:
1. Visualize body as translucent light
2. Each chakra radiating its traditional color
3. Entire body becoming rainbow light body

4. Integration of light body with normal awareness

Duration: 15-25 minutes
Benefits: Subtle body development, energy balancing, spiritual purification

Sacred Sound and Mantra Science
Understanding Mantra Mechanics:

Vibrational Resonance:
Each mantra creates specific vibrational patterns that resonate with particular aspects of consciousness. Regular repetition establishes these patterns as dominant mental frequencies, gradually transforming the practitioner's entire psychophysical system.

Neurological Effects:
Mantra repetition activates the vagus nerve, promoting parasympathetic nervous system dominance and facilitating meditative states. Rhythmic sound synchronizes brainwaves, leading to coherent mental functioning.

Foundation Mantra Training
OM (AUM) - The Primordial Sound:

Technique:
- **A:** Creates vibration in lower abdomen and chest
- **U:** Resonates in throat and head region
- **M:** Completes cycle with skull resonance
- **Silence:** Recognition of awareness beyond sound

Practice Method:
1. Begin with audible chanting for 5-10 minutes
2. Transition to whispered repetition
3. Continue with mental repetition only
4. Rest in silence following natural conclusion

Daily Practice:
- Morning: 108 repetitions (one mala) to establish daily foundation
- Evening: Extended practice focusing on vibration quality
- Integration: Brief OM repetition before meals, important activities

Chakra Bija Mantras (Seed Sounds):

Chakra	Location	Seed Sound	Color	Function
Muladhara	Base of spine	LAM	Red	Grounding, stability
Svadhisthana	Lower abdomen	VAM	Orange	Creativity, emotion
Manipura	Solar plexus	RAM	Yellow	Power, will
Anahata	Heart center	YAM	Green	Love, compassion
Vishuddha	Throat/Atlas Joint	HAM	Blue	Truth, expression
Ajna	Third eye	OM	Indigo	Wisdom, insight
Sahasrara	Crown	Silence	Violet/Gold	Unity, realization

Energy Healing and Transmission
Developing Healing Abilities:

Self-Healing Practices:
1. **Energy Assessment:** Daily body scanning for imbalances
2. **Directed Healing:** Sending healing energy to affected areas
3. **Chakra Balancing:** Regular chakra cleansing and activation
4. **Lifestyle Integration:** Diet, exercise, environment supporting energy health

Healing Others (Requires Qualified Training):
1. **Preparation:** Meditation and energy centering before sessions
2. **Assessment:** Sensing receiver's energy patterns and needs
3. **Transmission:** Channeling healing energy through hands or presence
4. **Integration:** Supporting receiver's natural healing processes
5. **Completion:** Clearing own energy field, sealing boundaries

Ethical Considerations for Energy Healing:
- Always obtain explicit permission before energy work
- Work within scope of training and competence
- Refer to medical professionals for physical conditions
- Maintain appropriate boundaries and self-care
- Regular supervision with qualified teachers
- Documentation and follow-up care

Energy Protection and Cleansing:

Daily Protection Practices:
1. **Morning Shield:** Visualize protective light surrounding entire body
2. **Boundary Setting:** Consciously establish energetic boundaries
3. **Regular Cleansing:** Clear accumulated negative energies
4. **Evening Purification:** Release day's energetic debris

Environmental Clearing:
- **Space Clearing:** Sound (bells, singing bowls), sage, visualization
- **Electromagnetic Protection:** Minimize exposure to electronic fields
- **Nature Connection:** Regular time in natural environments
- **Sacred Space Creation:** Dedicated areas for practice

PHENOMENOLOGY OF PRACTICE - ADVANCED PRACTICES AND PHENOMENA
Navigating Advanced States
Types of Advanced Experiences:

Energetic Phenomena:
- Kundalini awakening symptoms (heat, kriyas, spontaneous movements)
- Light phenomena and visual experiences
- Sound experiences (nada, celestial music)
- Bliss states and ecstatic experiences

Psychological Transformation:
- Dark night of the soul periods
- Ego dissolution experiences
- Integration challenges
- Spiritual emergence vs. emergency

Psychic Abilities (Siddhis):
- Clairsentience (feeling others' states)
- Clairvoyance (seeing subtle energies)
- Telepathy (direct mind-to-mind communication)
- Precognition (knowing future events)

Absorption States (Samadhi):
- Savikalpa samadhi (absorption with seed)
- Nirvikalpa samadhi (absorption beyond form)
- Sahaja samadhi (natural continuous recognition)

Proper Response to Advanced Experiences
Guidelines for Teachers:

1. Neither Suppress Nor Inflate:
- Acknowledge experiences without attachment
- Contextualize within broader developmental framework
- Avoid spiritual materialism and inflation
- Maintain focus on service and realization

2. Safety and Stabilization:
- Ensure basic needs met (food, shelter, support)
- Reduce practice intensity if overwhelming
- Integrate with daily life responsibilities
- Professional psychological support if needed

3. Integration Focus:
- Emphasize practical application
- Service orientation over personal attainment
- Relationship and community engagement
- Ethical conduct and character development

4. Qualified Guidance:
- Connect with teachers who have navigated these territories
- Elder consultation for complex cases
- Professional boundaries maintained
- Long-term support and follow-up

CONSTITUTIONAL FOOD MASTERY

INTRODUCTION
Bio-compatible diet represents the first systematic nutritional practice in this praxis. While later material addresses combining, fasting, and supplementation, this material establishes your foundational relationship with food itself, understanding which foods support maximal vitality and how to prepare and consume them for optimal absorption and spiritual alignment.

Historical Context: The seven laws presented here synthesize Vedic nutrition theory (Asuri Kapila's classical formulations - GIDEE), and Pythagorean harmonic food principles.

Key Principle: Food quality determines nervous system quality. The nervous system quality determines consciousness quality.

Therefore, conscious food selection and preparation represent direct consciousness development practices.

THE SEVEN LAWS OF VIBRATIONAL NUTRITION
Law 1: Sattvic Foundation
"All food carries vibrational frequency. The frequency we consume becomes our frequency."

Definition: Sattva (from Sanskrit) means "essence," "purity," or "harmonious quality." Sattvic food possesses the highest vibrational frequency, supporting consciousness development, mental clarity, emotional stability, and spiritual openness.

Sattvic Foods (Primary Foundation):
- Fresh, organically grown fruits and vegetables (picked at peak ripeness)
- Whole grains prepared with conscious intention
- Legumes (beans, lentils, chickpeas)
- Nuts and seeds (especially almonds, walnuts, sesame, sunflower)
- Honey (raw, unheated)
- Pure, filtered water
- Herbal teas (calming: chamomile, mint, fennel; energizing: ginger, turmeric)
- Dairy from naturally raised animals (ghee, milk, cheese)
- Spices (warming: ginger, cinnamon, cardamom; cooling: fennel, coriander, cumin)

Sattvic Food Characteristics:
- Fresh (consumed within 1-3 days of harvest)
- Organic or biodynamic (pesticide and synthetic-free)
- Whole (unrefined, unprocessed, intact cellular structure)
- Prepared with love and conscious intention
- Eaten in moderate quantities
- Consumed without distraction in calm environment
- Supportive of natural digestive processes

Law 2: Rajasic Minimization
Definition: Rajasic (from Sanskrit) means "passionate" or "over-stimulating." Rajasic foods possess middle vibrational frequency, stimulating desire, restlessness, and mental agitation while disrupting contemplative states.

Rajasic Foods (Minimize/Avoid):
- Fried foods and heavy oils

- Refined grains and white sugar
- Alcohol (all types)
- Overly sweet foods
- Artificially flavored or colored foods
- Foods prepared with anger, haste, or unconsciousness

Why Minimize: Rajasic foods create nervous system overstimulation, prevent meditation depth, increase anxiety and sleeplessness, and disrupt the subtle bodies' electromagnetic coherence. For serious spiritual practice, minimization is essential.

Constitutional Exception: Magnetic constitutions may include moderate rajasic elements (stimulating spices) for activation without full minimization.

Law 3: Tamasic Elimination
Definition: Tamasic (from Sanskrit) means "dark," "inert," or "death-promoting." Tamasic foods possess the lowest vibrational frequency, creating heaviness, depression, mental fog, and spiritual darkness while poisoning the body's physical and subtle systems.

Tamasic Foods (Complete Elimination):
- Moldy or spoiled foods
- Processed foods
- Leftovers (after more than 12 hours at room temperature or 3 days refrigerated)
- Overeaten foods (beyond satiation)
- Foods prepared with violence, hatred, or unconsciousness
- Narcotics and health-destructive substances

Why Eliminate: Tamasic foods literally introduce deadness into your living system. They degrade the nervous system, prevent spiritual perception, create depression and apathy, and slowly poison the body through accumulated toxins and missing life force.

Law 4: Seasonal Attunement
Definition: Food carrying the energy of the current season maximizes absorption and alignment with natural rhythms, while out-of-season food creates internal conflict and digestive strain.

Spring Foods (Renewal and Cleansing):
- Fresh greens and sprouts (detoxifying)
- Light grains: quinoa, millet, barley
- Spring asparagus, peas, artichokes
- Citrus fruits (lemons especially)

- Light soups and broths
- Emphasis: Cleansing and lightening

Summer Foods (Peak Energy and Activity):
- Fresh fruits: berries, melons, stone fruits
- Light vegetables: cucumbers, zucchini, tomatoes
- Cooling herbs: mint, cilantro, basil
- Salads and raw foods
- Cool beverages: coconut water, herbal iced teas
- Emphasis: Cooling and hydrating

Autumn Foods (Grounding and Building):
- Root vegetables: carrots, beets, sweet potatoes
- Squashes: pumpkin, acorn, butternut
- Grains: brown rice, oats, millet
- Nuts and seeds (preparing for winter)
- Warming spices: cinnamon, ginger, nutmeg
- Emphasis: Grounding and building reserves

Winter Foods (Conservation and Deep Nourishment):
- Stored roots: potatoes, turnips, parsnips
- Dried fruits and preserved foods
- Warming broths and soups
- Grains cooked long and slow
- Warming spices and herbs
- Emphasis: Warming and sustaining

Law 5: Constitutional Personalization
Definition: Individual constitutional type determines which sattvic foods serve that person optimally. No single diet serves all beings identically.

Key Principle: Rather than generic dietary advice, constitutional personalization enables each practitioner to discover their optimal food sources, combinations, quantities, and timing through systematic self-observation and adjustment.

Law 6: Conscious Preparation
Definition: Food prepared with conscious intention, clean environment, and loving attention carries that frequency into your body. Food prepared with haste, anger, or unconsciousness carries that frequency into your body.

Preparation Principles:

Physical Cleanliness:
- Wash all hands and tools thoroughly
- Clean preparation surface completely
- Use pure water for all washing and cooking
- Maintain organized, pleasant kitchen space

Mental Preparation:
- Practice 1-2 minutes of centered breathing before cooking
- Hold clear intention: "This food nourishes my body and consciousness"
- Maintain peaceful, meditative state during cooking
- Avoid negative thinking, gossip, or emotional disturbance

Spiritual Blessing:
- Optional: Prayer or gratitude statement before eating
- Moment of silence acknowledging food's sacrifice and service
- Conscious chewing and appreciation of flavors and textures

Cooking Methods (Sattvic):
- Steaming (preserves nutrients and life force)
- Gentle boiling in water with salt and herbs
- Slow simmering into broths and soups
- Baking at moderate temperatures
- Minimal oil, gentle heating

Cooking Methods (Avoid):
- Excessively high heat or prolonged cooking
- Deep frying (creates toxic breakdown products)

Law 7: Rhythmic Consumption
Definition: Regular meal timing, appropriate quantities, and conscious eating rhythm optimize digestion and prevent the nervous system disruption caused by irregular feeding.

Optimal Eating Rhythm:
Daily Pattern:
- **Breakfast (6:00-8:00 AM):** Light to moderate meal establishing morning nutrition
- **Lunch (12:00-2:00 PM):** Largest meal with fullest digestive capacity
- **Dinner (5:00-7:00 PM):** Moderate, eaten at least 3-4 hours before sleep
- **No eating after 8:00 PM:** Allows sleep without digestive activity

Portion Guidance:
- Breakfast: 25% of daily calories
- Lunch: 50% of daily calories
- Dinner: 25% of daily calories
- Optional light fruit snack mid-morning or mid-afternoon (not both daily)

Eating Pace:
- Minimum 20 minutes per meal (allows satiation signals)
- Thorough chewing: 20-30 chews per bite
- Conscious attention to flavors, textures, aromas
- No multitasking (no screens, books, conversation during eating)

SATTVIC FOOD CLASSIFICATIONS
Grains (Foundation Foods)

Whole Grains (Primary):

Grain	Qualities	Preparation	Amount
Brown Rice	Grounding, building, digestible	Simmer 1:2 ratio, 45 min	1/2 cup cooked
Oats	Warming, nourishing, stabilizing	Simmer or soak overnight	1/2 cup cooked
Millet	Light, alkaline, easy to digest	Simmer 1:2.5 ratio, 25 min	1/2 cup cooked
Quinoa	Complete protein, light, energizing	Simmer 1:2 ratio, 15 min	1/2 cup cooked
Barley	Cooling, cleansing, building strength	Simmer 1:3 ratio, 60 min	1/2 cup cooked
Wheat Berries	Warm, sustaining, complete	Soak 12h, simmer 90 min	1/2 cup cooked
Amaranth	High protein, warming, nourishing	Simmer 1:2 ratio, 25 min	1/3 cup cooked

Best Practices:
- Soak grains 4-12 hours before cooking (activates enzymes)
- Rinse thoroughly to remove dust and surface toxins
- Cook slowly with pure water and small pinch of salt
- Consume within 12-24 hours of cooking
- Combine with seasonal vegetables and spices

Legumes (Protein Foundation)
Optimal Legumes:

Legume	Properties	Prep	Cooking	Yield
Mung Beans	Most digestible, cooling, building	Soak 4h	Simmer 30 min	3 cups
Lentils (Red)	Quick cooking, warming, protein-rich	Rinse	Simmer 20 min	3 cups
Chickpeas	Sustaining, warming, grounding	Soak 12h	Simmer 90 min	3 cups
Kidney Beans	Strong building, warming, hearty	Soak 12h	Simmer 60 min	3 cups
Black Beans	Grounding, moistening, sustaining	Soak 12h	Simmer 60 min	3 cups
Split Peas	Easy to digest, warming, sustaining	Rinse	Simmer 30 min	3 cups
Adzuki Beans	Kidney-supporting, warming, building	Soak 4h	Simmer 60 min	2.5 cups

Constitutional Frequency:
- **Electric:** 1-2 times weekly (small portions, well-cooked)
- **Magnetic:** 3-4 times weekly (regular portions, with stimulating spices)
- **Neutral:** 2-3 times weekly (moderate portions, with cooling herbs)

Vegetables (Daily Foundation)
Root Vegetables (Grounding, Warming):
- Carrots, beets, turnips, parsnips, rutabaga
- Sweet potatoes, regular potatoes, yams
- Preparation: Steamed, roasted, or in soups
- Amount: 1-2 cups daily

Green Vegetables (Cleansing, Cooling):
- Leafy greens: kale, collards, chard, spinach, romaine
- Cruciferous: broccoli, cauliflower, Brussels sprouts
- Green beans, green peas, asparagus
- Preparation: Steamed, lightly sautéed in ghee

694

- Amount: 2-3 cups daily

Seasonal Vegetables:
- Spring: Asparagus, peas, artichokes, spring greens
- Summer: Zucchini, cucumber, tomatoes (ripe), green beans
- Autumn: Squashes, pumpkins, cauliflower, Brussels sprouts
- Winter: Root vegetables, stored greens, cabbage

Constitutional Favorites:
- **Electric:** Root vegetables primary, some greens, warming preparations
- **Magnetic:** Green vegetables primary, light preparations, raw emphasized
- **Neutral:** Balanced of both, cooler preparations, salads and steamed

Fruits (Seasonal Priority)
Optimal Fresh Fruits:
- Bananas (grounding, nourishing)
- Apples (cooling, cleansing) - always cooked for Electric
- Pears (cooling, moistening)
- Berries (cooling, cleansing, antioxidant)
- Melons (cooling, hydrating) - summer only
- Grapes (cooling, nourishing)
- Mangoes (warming, nourishing) - limited amount
- Citrus (cooling, cleansing)
- Dates, figs (warming, nourishing)

Fruit Guidelines:
- Always fresh, never stored or heated
- Consume alone, not with meals (separate fruits 30+ minutes from other foods)
- Best eaten morning or afternoon (avoid evening)
- Constitution-appropriate varieties (see Framework)
- Seasonal emphasis (consume during season of growth)

Nuts and Seeds (Nutritional Concentration)
Primary Nuts (Soak Before Consuming):
- Almonds (warming, nourishing, strengthening)
- Walnuts (cooling, brain-supporting, omega-3 rich)
- Cashews (warming, nourishing, energy-building)
- Pistachios (warming, grounding, enjoyable)

Primary Seeds (Soak or Toast Lightly):
- Sesame (warming, calcium-rich, deeply nourishing)

- Sunflower (cooling, zinc-rich, energizing)
- Pumpkin (warming, mineral-rich, grounding)
- Flax (cooling, omega-3 rich, supporting)
- Hemp (protein-rich, complete amino acids)

Daily Amount:
- 1-2 tablespoons soaked nuts or seeds
- Never roasted in salt (destroys nutrients)
- Always accompanied by water to prevent dehydration

Dairy Products (Sattvic Selection)
When Available from Naturally Raised Animals:

Product	Properties	Use	Amount
Ghee	Warming, clarified, pure fat	Cooking, digestive aid	1-2 tsp daily
Fresh Milk	Nourishing, warming, building	Warm drink, with grain	4-8 oz daily
Fresh Yogurt	Probiotic, slightly warming, building	With meals, modest amount	4 oz daily
Paneer	Sattvic protein, sustaining, grounding	Added to vegetables	2-3 oz weekly
Fresh Cheese	Mild, supporting, easy to digest	Moderate use	1-2 oz weekly

Constitutional Cautions:
- **Electric:** Beneficial in all preparations (warming, grounding)
- **Magnetic:** Minimize or eliminate (increases mucus and heaviness)
- **Neutral:** Moderate use only (cooling preparations recommended)

THE THREE-PHASE PROGRESSION SYSTEM
Phase 1: Foundation (Days 1-30)
Objective: Establish baseline sattvic diet without major elimination

Daily Structure:
- **Breakfast:** Warm grain + seasonal fruit or vegetables
- **Lunch:** Grain + legume + abundant vegetables + herb tea
- **Dinner:** Lighter grain + simple vegetables + herbal tea
- **Beverages:** Pure filtered water (minimum 6 glasses), herbal teas

Phase 1 Goals:

- Establish consistent meal timing
- Replace processed foods with whole foods
- Begin conscious eating practices
- Track energy, digestion, sleep quality
- Assess initial constitutional response

Expected Outcomes:
- Day 1-7: Possible initial adjustment (slight detoxification)
- Day 8-21: Increased energy and mental clarity
- Day 22-30: Noticeably improved digestion, sleep, and stability

Phase 2: Refinement (Days 31-60)
Objective: Eliminate low-vibrational foods entirely, personalize to constitution

Daily Structure (Refined):
- **Breakfast:** Warm grain + ghee + seasonal fruit OR steamed vegetables + herb tea
- **Lunch:** Grain + legume + abundant seasonal vegetables + turmeric + fresh herbs
- **Dinner:** Moderate grain + simply prepared vegetables + gentle spices + herbal tea
- **Beverages:** Pure water (8+ glasses), herbal teas, occasional herbal coffee

Phase 2 Changes:
- Eliminate refined sugar → use honey or fresh fruit
- Eliminate alcohol → complete elimination
- Emphasize seasonal foods
- Constitutional adaptations fully implemented

Expected Outcomes:
- Stabilized energy without fluctuation
- Clear skin, bright eyes, strong nails
- Improved digestion and regularity
- Deeper sleep and earlier waking
- Mental clarity and focused thinking
- Emotional stability and peaceful mind

Phase 3: Mastery (Days 61-90 and Beyond)
Objective: Complete sattvic diet with effortless consciousness integration

Mastery Features:
- Food choices feel natural and easeful

- Eating practices integrated seamlessly
- Constitutional personalization automatic
- Energy, clarity, and peace fully stable
- Spiritual practices deepen noticeably
- Healing of chronic conditions underway

Daily Rhythm (Mastered):
- **Breakfast (6:30-8:00 AM):** Warm grain + seasonal preparation + conscious gratitude
- **Lunch (12:30-2:00 PM):** Complete nourishing meal with all elements
- **Dinner (6:00-7:00 PM):** Moderate meal with easy digestibility
- **Hydration:** Constant awareness, no excess or deficit
- **Eating Pace:** Naturally slowed, every bite appreciated

Deepening Opportunities:
- Explore local farmers markets for seasonal connection
- Expand recipe repertoire with traditional sattvic cuisine
- Introduce food-based earth connection practices
- Begin teaching others sattvic nutrition
- Prepare to advance to Food Combining

THERAPEUTIC APPLICATIONS
For Digestive Issues
Underlying Cause: Poor food quality, incorrect combinations, irregular timing, or inadequate chewing

Sattvic Approach:
1. **Weeks 1-2:** Rice and mung bean soup exclusively (most digestible combination)
2. **Weeks 3-4:** Add steamed vegetables, ghee, and warming spices
3. **Weeks 5+:** Gradually expand while monitoring response

Key Foods:
- Mung beans (most digestible legume)
- White or brown rice (gentle on digestion)
- Ghee with warming spices (digestive aids)
- Ginger (stimulates digestive fire)
- Fennel seeds (calming and digestive)

For Low Energy
Underlying Cause: Deficient calories, inadequate nourishment, or tamasic food elements

Sattvic Approach:

1. Increase grain portions by 50% during Phase 1
2. Add 1-2 tablespoons of nuts or seeds daily
3. Include ghee with every meal (healthy fat for absorption and energy)
4. Add more frequent meals if needed (small breakfast, mid-morning snack, lunch, dinner)

Key Foods:
- Warming grains: oats, rice, wheat, barley
- Sustaining legumes: chickpeas, lentils, kidney beans
- Ghee and healthy fats
- Nuts: almonds, walnuts (soaked)
- Dates and figs (natural sustained energy)

For Mental Clarity
Underlying Cause: Rajasic or tamasic foods blocking subtle perception

Sattvic Approach:
1. Emphasis on fresh, organic, locally grown foods
2. Conscious, meditative eating practice
3. Extended mealtimes with full attention

Key Foods:
- Light fresh vegetables (especially greens)
- Easily digestible grains: millet, quinoa
- Light legumes: mung beans, split peas
- Fresh herbs: brahmi, gotu kola (if available)
- Cooling spices: coriander, fennel, cumin

For Immune System Enhancement
Underlying Cause: Systemic toxicity or deficient nutrition compromising immunity

Sattvic Approach:
1. Ensure absolute adherence to sattvic diet
2. Emphasize mineral-rich vegetables
3. Include immune-supporting herbs and spices
4. Consistent seasonal adaptation

Key Foods:
- Dark leafy greens (vitamins, minerals, chlorophyll)
- Winter squashes (vitamin A, beta-carotene)
- Root vegetables (grounding, sustaining)
- Garlic and onions (antimicrobial when lightly cooked)

- Warming spices: turmeric, ginger, cumin
- Fresh citrus in season

FOOD COMBINING: THE THREE-LIST METHOD

Food combining represents a sophisticated understanding of how different food molecules interact during digestion. Improper combining creates digestive conflict, fermentation, toxin accumulation, and energy loss. Perfect combining enables complete nutrient absorption, minimal digestive effort, and maximum energy availability for spiritual practice and healing.

This volume teaches the **Three-List Method**, the most practical and effective system for ensuring optimal food combinations without complex calculations. This method synthesizes Ayurvedic combining principles, Pythagorean harmonic science, and contemporary enzyme/acid-base research.

Key Principle: Properly combined foods digest completely in 2-3 hours. Poorly combined foods ferment and putrefy, creating literal poison in the digestive tract.

Understanding the Three Lists
List A: Proteins and Fats (Dense, warming, hard to digest)
List B: Starches (Dense, cooling or warming, moderate to digest)
List C: Fresh Fruits (Light, quick to digest, special combining rules)

Core Combining Rule:
- Lists A + B: Combine only with List C vegetables (not B vegetables)
- Lists combine with fresh herbs and spices freely
- Never combine List A + List B with each other
- List C (fresh fruits) combines only with other List C items
- Never combine List C with any other list items

LIST A: PROTEINS AND FATS (Dense, Warming)
Plant Proteins (Sattvic):
- Legumes: mung beans, lentils, chickpeas, kidney beans, black beans, split peas
- Nuts: almonds, walnuts, cashews, pistachios, hazelnuts
- Seeds: sesame, sunflower, pumpkin, flax, hemp
- Nut butters and tahini
- Tofu (occasionally, if available)
- Dairy: ghee, cheese, milk, yogurt (in moderation)

Fats (Sattvic Sources):
- Ghee (clarified butter - primary fat for cooking)
- Cold-pressed oils: sesame, coconut, sunflower (use sparingly)
- Nuts and seeds (contained fats)

Amount Guidelines:
- Legume serving: 1/2 to 1 cup cooked
- Nuts/seeds: 1-2 tablespoons
- Ghee: 1-2 teaspoons per meal
- Cheese/dairy: 1-2 oz per meal

Combination Limitations:
- Legumes + Starch = (causes severe gas and fermentation)
- Legumes + Legumes = Acceptable (same digestion timing)
- Legumes + nuts/seeds = Acceptable (both proteins)
- Nuts + seeds = Acceptable (both fats)
- Fats with legumes = Necessary for absorption

LIST B: STARCHES (Dense, Varying)
Whole Grains (Primary Starches):
- Brown rice, white rice, wild rice
- Wheat, oats, barley, rye, millet, quinoa
- Amaranth, buckwheat, corn

Starchy Vegetables:
- Potatoes (all varieties)
- Sweet potatoes and yams
- Winter squashes: pumpkin, acorn, butternut
- Corn (whole or kernels)

Amount Guidelines:
- Grain serving: 1/2 to 1 cup cooked
- Starchy vegetable: 1 to 2 cups cooked

Combination Limitations:
- Starches + Proteins (List A)
- Starches + Starches = Acceptable (same digestion class)
- Starches with List C vegetables = Acceptable (light vegetables aid digestion)
- Starches with healthy fats = Acceptable (necessary for absorption)

LIST C: FRESH FRUITS AND LIGHT VEGETABLES
Fresh Fruits (Special Combining):

- All fresh fruits at peak ripeness
- Berries, melons, citrus, stone fruits, tropical fruits
- Dried fruits: dates, figs, raisins (treat as heavier - combine carefully)

Light Vegetables (Fast Digesting):
- Dark leafy greens: spinach, kale, collards, chard, lettuce
- Green vegetables: green beans, peas, zucchini, cucumber
- Herbs: parsley, cilantro, basil, mint, dill
- Sprouts: all varieties
- Sea vegetables: nori, dulse, kombu, wakame

Heavy Vegetables (Moderate Digesting):
- Carrots, beets, turnips, parsnips (root vegetables)
- Broccoli, cauliflower, Brussels sprouts
- Cabbage, kale (except when using as light green)
- Tomatoes (when ripe)
- Bell peppers

Combining Rules for List C:
- Fresh fruits alone = BEST (no mixing with other foods)
- Fruits with other fruits = Acceptable (same ripeness level preferred)
- Fresh fruits between meals = Optimal (30+ minutes before/after other foods)
- Light vegetables + starches = Acceptable (aids digestion)
- Light vegetables + proteins = Acceptable (aids digestion)
- Heavy vegetables + proteins = Less ideal but acceptable
- Heavy vegetables + starches = Less ideal but acceptable

THE COMPLETE COMBINING CHART
ACCEPTABLE COMBINATIONS (Eat Together)
Combination 1: GRAIN + LIGHT VEGETABLES
- Brown rice + steamed leafy greens + ghee + herbs
- Oats + fresh fruit + walnuts (fruit allowed with grains)
- Quinoa + steamed asparagus + parsley + sea salt

Combination 2: LEGUME + LIGHT VEGETABLES
- Lentils + steamed spinach + cilantro + cumin
- Chickpeas + roasted Brussels sprouts + turmeric
- Mung beans + steamed kale + ginger + salt

Combination 3: NUT/SEED + LIGHT VEGETABLES
- Tahini + steamed broccoli + lemon + salt
- Almonds + salad greens + lemon + olive oil

- Seed butter + steamed greens + garlic + herbs

Combination 4: GRAIN + GHEE + HERBS
- Rice + ghee + turmeric + salt
- Barley + ghee + warming spices
- Millet + ghee + fresh herbs

Combination 5: FRESH FRUIT + FRESH FRUIT
- Berry medley (all berries)
- Melon plate (all melons)
- Citrus selection (mixed citrus)
- Tropical trio (mango, pineapple, papaya)

FORBIDDEN COMBINATIONS (Never Eat Together)
NEVER: GRAIN + LEGUME
- Brown rice + lentils
- Oats + chickpeas
- Wheat + kidney beans
- Result: Severe gas, fermentation, bloating, toxin production

NEVER: LEGUME + STARCHY VEGETABLE
- Chickpeas + potatoes
- Lentils + sweet potato
- Beans + squash
- Result: Extreme digestive distress

NEVER: GRAIN + STARCHY VEGETABLE (If Heavy)
- Rice + potato
- Wheat + squash
- Result: Excessive heaviness, poor digestion

NEVER: FRUIT WITH ANYTHING ELSE
- Apple + rice
- Banana + oats
- Berries + yogurt (common error!)
- Result: Fermentation, gas, poor nutrient absorption

NEVER: PROTEIN + PROTEIN
- Meat + fish
- Legumes + nuts
- Cheese + nuts
- Result: Incomplete digestion, putrefaction

PRACTICAL DAILY IMPLEMENTATION
Sample Days Following Three-List Method
Electric Constitution Sample Day:

Meal	Components	Guidelines
Breakfast (7 AM)	Oatmeal + banana + cinnamon	Grain + Fruit (acceptable)
Lunch (12:30 PM)	Lentil soup + spinach salad + cilantro	Legume + Light veg (acceptable)
Dinner (6:30 PM)	Brown rice + broccoli + ghee + turmeric	Grain + Light veg (acceptable)

Magnetic Constitution Sample Day:

Meal	Components	Guidelines
Breakfast (6:30 AM)	Fresh fruit medley (berries, melon)	Fruit only (optimal)
Lunch (1 PM)	Large salad + chickpeas + lemon + cilantro	Legume + Light veg (acceptable)
Dinner (6 PM)	Steamed broccoli + sesame seeds + herbs	Light veg + seeds (acceptable)

Neutral Constitution Sample Day:

Meal	Components	Guidelines
Breakfast (7 AM)	Quinoa + cooling herbs + fresh fruit	Grain + Fruit (acceptable)
Lunch (1 PM)	Salad + tahini dressing + sprouted legumes	Light veg + legume (acceptable)
Dinner (6:30 PM)	Steamed vegetables + rice + ghee	Veg + grain (acceptable)

ACID-ALKALI BALANCE PRINCIPLES
Understanding pH in Digestion
Acidic Foods (leave acidic ash):
- Grains, proteins, nuts, seeds
- Must be balanced with alkaline foods for health

Alkaline Foods (leave alkaline ash):
- Fresh vegetables and fruits
- Support pH balance and tissue health

Optimal Ratio:
- 60-70% alkaline (vegetables, fruits, herbs)
- 30-40% acidic (grains, proteins, fats)

Implementation:
- Make vegetables and fruits your base
- Add grains and proteins as complement, not center
- Ensure every meal is 60%+ vegetables/fruits by volume

TIME-SEQUENTIAL EATING PRINCIPLES
Digestive Windows and Timing

Fast Digesting (1-2 hours):
- Fresh fruits: 1-2 hours
- Light salads and raw vegetables: 1.5-2 hours
- Leafy greens: 1-1.5 hours

Medium Digesting (2-3 hours):
- Light grain + vegetable combinations: 2-2.5 hours
- Lightly cooked vegetables: 2-3 hours
- Sprouts and legumes lightly cooked: 2-3 hours

Slow Digesting (3-5+ hours):
- Heavy grain combinations: 3-4 hours
- Legume-based meals: 3-5 hours
- Nuts and seeds: 3-4 hours
- Combinations with ghee or oils: 3-5 hours

Implementation Rules:
- Wait 30 minutes after fresh fruit before eating other foods
- Wait 2+ hours after light meals before eating heavy meals
- Wait 3-4 hours after heavy meals before eating again
- Last meal should be light (light vegetables, light grains)
- Never eat until previous meal is fully digested

THERAPEUTIC COMBINING PROTOCOLS
For Digestive Weakness

Days 1-7: Simplest Combinations
- Breakfast: Rice + ghee + warming spices (20 min)
- Lunch: Mung beans + ghee + ginger (30 min)
- Dinner: Rice + steamed greens + ghee (20 min)

Days 8-14: Gradual Addition
- Begin adding variety while maintaining simplicity
- Still no complex multi-ingredient meals
- Emphasize easily digested options

Days 15+: Progressive Expansion

- Gradually introduce more combinations
- Monitor response carefully
- Maintain simplicity for several more weeks

For Weight Loss
Strategy: Emphasize List C vegetables, minimize List A/B

Daily Pattern:
- Breakfast: Fresh fruit only
- Lunch: Large salad (List C) + legumes or grains
- Dinner: Steamed vegetables + minimal grain or legume
- Snacks: Fresh vegetables and fruit

Timeline: 30-90 days for noticeable results

For Weak Immunity
Strategy: Ensure complete nutrient absorption through perfect combining

Daily Emphasis:
- Perfect combining (no fermentation)
- High vegetable intake (60%+ of meals)
- Mineral-rich foods (see Volume 7)
- Anti-inflammatory combinations

For Mental Clarity
Strategy: Minimize digestive burden, maximize nutritive density

Daily Pattern:
- Light, perfectly-combined meals
- Frequent small meals (allow constant focus, not digestion)
- Minimal fats and heavy proteins
- High vegetable content
- Lots of fresh herbs

ADVANCED COMBINING PRINCIPLES
Quantity Harmonics
Different foods digest at different rates. When combining:
- Smallest portion: Heaviest digestive item
- Moderate portion: Medium digestive item
- Largest portion: Lightest digestive item

Example:
- 1/4 cup legumes (heaviest)
- 1/2 cup grain (medium)

- 2 cups steamed greens (lightest)

Preparation Synergies
How food is prepared dramatically affects combining compatibility:

Raw vegetables: Combine with cooked grains (easier digestion)
Cooked vegetables: Combine with proteins and grains
Sprouted legumes: Can be slightly lighter (combine more easily)
Ghee addition: Slows digestion (helps when combining heavier items)
Warming spices: Aid digestion of combined items

CONSTITUTIONAL PRANAYAMA PROTOCOLS – CONSCIOUS BREATHING

Foundation Breathing Practice (Pranayama)
Three-Part Breath (Dirga Pranayama) - Universal Foundation:
Technique:
1. Place one hand on chest, one on abdomen
2. Inhale first into the abdomen (lower hand rises)
3. Continue inhaling into the middle chest (ribs expand)
4. Complete inhalation into upper chest (shoulders slightly rise)
5. Exhale in reverse order: upper chest, middle chest, abdomen
6. Practice 15-20 complete breaths

Benefits: Full lung capacity utilization, nervous system regulation, energy harmonization, preparation for meditation

Constitutional Applications:
Electric Constitution:
- Emphasize extended, smooth exhalation (4-count inhale, 8-count exhale)
- Practice lying down if needed for grounding
- Use warming breath techniques for circulation
- Follow with brief body scanning for integration

Magnetic Constitution:
- Emphasize full, complete inhalation with slight retention
- Practice energizing techniques (Bhastrika, right nostril breathing)
- Use heating breath to stimulate metabolism
- Follow with activating movement

Neutral Constitution:
- Emphasize balanced ratio (4-count inhale, 4-count exhale)

- Practice cooling techniques (left nostril, Sheetali)
- Use moderating breath to prevent overheating
- Follow with restful integration

Advanced Retention Practices (Kumbhaka)
Antara Kumbhaka (Retention After Inhalation)
Basic Technique:
1. Inhale completely through both nostrils
2. Close both nostrils gently but completely
3. Retain breath for comfortable duration (no strain)
4. Release and exhale slowly through both nostrils
5. Return to natural breathing

Progressive Development:
- Week 1-2: Retain for 5-10 seconds
- Week 3-4: Retain for 10-15 seconds
- Month 2-3: Gradually increase to 30 seconds
- Advanced (6+ months): Up to 2-3 minutes with proper training

Contraindications: High blood pressure, heart conditions, pregnancy

Bahya Kumbhaka (Retention After Exhalation)
Technique:
1. Exhale completely through both nostrils
2. Close both nostrils gently
3. Hold empty breath for comfortable duration
4. Release and inhale slowly
5. Return to natural breathing

Cautions: More challenging than inhalation retention; progress very gradually
Benefits: Develops will power, purifies subtle energy channels, prepares for advanced meditation

Advanced Breathing Techniques
Solar Breathing (Surya Bhedana) - Energizing
Technique:
- Close left nostril gently (use ring finger)
- Inhale through right nostril (4 counts)
- Close both nostrils; retain (4 counts)
- Release right nostril; exhale (6 counts)
- 12-20 rounds, 5-15 minutes

Effects: Energizes, warms, activates sympathetic nervous system

Best Time: Morning or midday
Constitutional: Especially beneficial for Electric types

Lunar Breathing (Chandra Bhedana) - Calming
Technique:
- Close right nostril gently (use thumb)
- Inhale through left nostril (4 counts)
- Close both nostrils; retain (4 counts)
- Release left nostril; exhale (8 counts)
- 12-20 rounds, 10-20 minutes

Effects: Calms, cools, activates parasympathetic nervous system
Best Time: Afternoon or evening
Constitutional: Especially beneficial for Magnetic types

Nadi Shodhana (Channel Purification) - Balancing
Technique:
- Close right nostril; inhale left (4 counts)
- Close both; retain (4 counts)
- Release right; exhale right (4 counts)
- Inhale right (4 counts)
- Close both; retain (4 counts)
- Release left; exhale left (4 counts)
- Repeat: 5-15 minutes

Effects: Balances both hemispheres, clears energy channels
Constitutional: Beneficial for all types; Neutral types primarily

Ujjayi Breath (Victory Breath)
Technique:
- Inhale through nose (both nostrils)
- Create gentle throat constriction (like ocean sound)
- Maintain same constriction on exhalation
- Produces soft oceanic sound
- 10-30 minutes practice

Applications:
- During physical practice (asana)
- Meditation preparation
- Stressful situations (immediate calming)
- Walking meditation
- Throughout workday

Effects: Builds internal heat, focuses mind, calms emotional turbulence

Shitali or Sitkari Breath (Cooling Breath)
Technique:
- Tongue curled, inhale through mouth, exhale through nose
- Or teeth together, lips apart, inhale, exhale through nose
- 6 rounds

Applications:
- Stressful situations (immediate calming)
- Tremor Management
- Throughout workday

Effects: Very cooling and calming

Advanced Breathing – Teacher Guidance Recommended
Bhastrika (Bellows Breath)
Technique: Rapid forced exhales through nose; passive inhales
Duration: 30-60 seconds rounds with rest between
Effects: Vigorous energization, heat generation
Constitutional: Magnetic constitution primarily

Kapalbhati (Skull-Shining Breath)
Technique: Similar to Bhastrika but emphasizing inhalation pulse
Effects: Mental clarity, energetic activation, toxin mobilization
Duration: 1-5 minutes daily
Contraindication: High blood pressure; pregnancy

Kevala Kumbhaka (Retention Without Breath)
Advanced Practice: Retention of already-suspended breath
Duration: Advanced practitioners only
Effects: Extreme consciousness expansion
Teacher Guidance: Essential; medical clearance recommended

Constitutional Breathing Applications
Electric Constitution (Vata/Air-Space) - Grounding and Calming:
- **Emphasis:** Extended, smooth exhalation
- **Optimal Practices:** Lunar breathing (left nostril), gentle Ujjayi, moderate Nadi Shodhana
- **Avoid:** Forceful techniques, excessive retention, rapid breathing (Bhastrika)
- **Integration:** Practice lying down if needed, follow with body scanning

Magnetic Constitution (Kapha/Earth-Water) - Activating and Stimulating:
- **Emphasis:** Full, complete inhalation with moderate retention
- **Optimal Practices:** Solar breathing (right nostril), Bhastrika, Kapalbhati
- **Encourage:** Heating techniques, dynamic practice, challenging variations
- **Integration:** Follow with activating movement or service activity

Neutral Constitution (Pitta/Fire-Water) - Cooling and Balancing:
- **Emphasis:** Balanced ratio inhalation/exhalation
- **Optimal Practices:** Sheetali/Sheetkari (cooling breaths), lunar emphasis, Nadi Shodhana
- **Avoid:** Excessive heating, competitive intensity, overstraining
- **Integration:** Follow with gentle cooling visualization or restorative practice

THERAPEUTIC BREATHING
For Anxiety/Panic
Immediate Technique (1-5 minutes):
- Lunar breathing (left nostril, extended exhalation)
- Calms nervous system within minutes

Longer Practice (10-15 minutes):
- Nadi Shodhana (complete balancing)
- Ujjayi breath (grounding effect)

For Low Energy
Immediate Technique:
- Solar breathing (right nostril emphasis)
- Bhastrika (bellows breath - vigorous exhales)
- 5-10 minutes

For Sleep Disturbance
Evening Practice (20 minutes before bed):
- Lunar breathing (left nostril)
- Ujjayi with extended exhalation
- Extended relaxation following

For Mental Fog/Clarity
Morning Practice (15-20 minutes):
- Complete respiration (activate full lungs)
- Nadi Shodhana (balance hemispheres)

- Brief solar breathing (activate mind)

CONSTITUTIONAL ASANA

Progressive Posture Development
Foundation Stage (Months 1-6)

Basic Sitting Postures:
Sukhasana Refinement (Easy Pose Mastery):
- Sit cross-legged with spine naturally erect
- Elevate hips 3-6 inches above knees using cushion
- Align crown toward ceiling, chin slightly tucked
- Shoulders relaxed, chest gently open
- Practice Duration: Build to 45-60 minutes continuous

Ardha Padmasana (Half Lotus Development):
- Progressive hip opening over 3-6 months
- Daily alternation of which foot elevated
- Use props preventing knee strain
- Preparation for full lotus position
- **Safety Protocol:** Stop if any knee pain; adjust position immediately

Padmasana (Full Lotus - Advanced Sitting):
- Achieved only after adequate hip flexibility
- Both feet placed on opposite thighs
- Hands in chosen mudra for energy circulation
- Hold for 45 minutes to 2 hours (advanced practitioners)
- **Contraindication:** Knee injuries, insufficient hip flexibility

Supporting Physical Preparation:
Hip Opening Sequence (15 minutes daily):
1. Butterfly pose (Baddha Konasana) - 3 minutes
2. Pigeon pose (Eka Pada Rajakapotasana) - 2 min each side
3. Seated forward fold (Paschimottanasana) - 3 minutes
4. Supine knee-to-chest (Apanasana) - 2 minutes
5. Happy baby pose (Ananda Balasana) - 3 minutes

Intermediate Stage (Months 7-18)
Advanced Sitting Variations:
Siddhasana (Perfect Pose):
- Left heel at perineum
- Right heel in front of left foot
- Ideal for pranayama and meditation practice
- Facilitates energy conservation and circulation

- **Benefits:** Enhanced concentration, prana circulation, preparation for advanced breathing

Standing Postures for Strength:
Tadasana (Mountain Pose) - Foundation for Standing Practice:
- Feet hip-width apart, weight evenly distributed
- Root down through feet, extend upward through crown
- Develop perfect postural awareness
- Foundation for all other standing poses
- **Duration:** 3-5 minutes with breath awareness

Vrikshasana (Tree Pose) - Balance Development:
- Stand on one leg, place other foot on inner thigh (avoid knee)
- Hands in prayer position or raised overhead
- Develop physical and mental balance simultaneously
- Cultivate one-pointed concentration
- **Duration:** 1-3 minutes each side
- **Constitutional Focus:** Electric (grounding), Magnetic (strength), Neutral (balance)

Advanced Stage (Months 19-36)
Complex Postures and Variations:

Parvatasana (Mountain Posture):
- Begin in Padmasana (lotus)
- Rise up on knees while maintaining lotus position
- Raise arms overhead in prayer position
- **Benefits:** Strength development, energy circulation, will cultivation
- **Duration:** 30 seconds to 3 minutes
- **Caution:** Requires strong knees and lotus flexibility

Sarvangasana (Shoulder Stand) - Therapeutic Inversion:
- Lie on back, lift legs and torso vertically
- Support lower back with hands
- Focus attention on thyroid gland
- **Practice Duration:** 5-15 minutes daily

Benefits of Sarvangasana:
- Regulates endocrine system, especially thyroid
- Improves circulation and lymphatic drainage
- Calms nervous system and reduces stress
- Reverses effects of gravity on internal organs

- **Contraindications:** Neck injuries, high blood pressure, menstruation, pregnancy

Safety Protocol for Inversions:
- Use folded blanket under shoulders to protect neck
- Exit slowly by rolling down vertebra by vertebra
- Follow with Matsyasana (Fish Pose) as counter-pose
- Avoid if contraindications present

Therapeutic Applications by Constitution
For Electric Constitution (Anxiety, Scattered Energy):
Calming Sequence (20 minutes):
1. Balasana (Child's Pose) - 5 minutes - Nervous system calming
2. Seated forward folds - 5 minutes - Mental pacification
3. Legs up wall (Viparita Karani) - 7 minutes - Gentle inversion
4. Shavasana (Corpse Pose) - 3 minutes - Complete rest

For Magnetic Constitution (Lethargy, Stagnation):
Activating Sequence (20 minutes):
1. Sun Salutations (Surya Namaskar) - 10 minutes - Full body activation
2. Warrior poses (Virabhadrasana I, II) - 5 minutes - Strength and heat
3. Backbends (Bhujangasana, Ustrasana) - 3 minutes - Heart opening
4. Twisting poses (Ardha Matsyendrasana) - 2 minutes – Detoxification

For Neutral Constitution (Intensity, Overheating):
Cooling Sequence (20 minutes):
1. Gentle forward folds - 5 minutes - Cooling and calming
2. Supported bridge pose - 5 minutes - Moderate opening
3. Supine twists - 5 minutes - Release without intensity
4. Shavasana with cooling visualization - 5 minutes – Integration

Geomagnetic Hygiene and Sleep Protocols
Sleep Foundation Requirements
Minimum Materials Required:
- Simple magnetized wooden bedframe oriented North-South
- Natural fiber bedding (cotton, linen, wool)
- Dark room environment for optimal sleep

Sleep Orientation Protocol
Head Direction Matters:

714

- Head North orientation: Aligns with Earth's magnetic field
- Avoid East orientation: Disrupts natural sleep cycles
- South or West: Secondary options if North unavailable

Sleep Hygiene Protocol

Time	Activity	Notes
8:00 PM	Begin winding down	Reduce screen exposure
8:30 PM	Dim lights	Support melatonin production
9:00 PM	Evening practice	Calming, gentle
9:30 PM	Prepare bedroom	Cool, dark, quiet
10:00 PM	Bedtime optimal	Earlier for Vata types
Upon waking	Morning pulse check	Establishes health trajectory

Electromagnetic Sensitivity Management
- Remove electronic devices from bedroom
- Minimize WiFi proximity during sleep
- Ground barefoot outdoors 15-30 minutes daily
- Maintain proper sleep duration by constitutional type

Sleep Requirements by Constitution:
- Vata (Electric): 7-9 hours (light, easily disturbed)
- Kapha (Magnetic): 6-8 hours (heavy, deeply restful)
- Pitta (Neutral): 7-8 hours (moderate, consistent)

Color Medicine (Chromotherapy Protocols)

Color	Element	Chakra	Therapeutic Use	Constitutional Application
Red	Fire	Root	Grounding, energy	Vata support
Orange	Fire	Sacral	Creativity, warmth	Vata activation
Yellow	Earth	Solar Plexus	Power, clarity	Balanced for all
Green	Air	Heart	Love, healing	Neutral balance
Blue	Water	Throat	Communication, truth	Pitta cooling
Indigo	Space	Third Eye	Intuition, vision	Advanced practitioners

Vio-let/Gold	Light	Crown	Spirituality, connection	Integration practice

Color-Water Preparation (Chromotherapy)
Minimum Materials Required:
- Two plain glass jugs (1-2 liter capacity each)
- Cellophane sheets for chromo-water preparation
- Water filtration system (carbon filter minimum, multi-stage preferred)

Chromo-Water Protocol
1. **Fill glass jug** with filtered water
2. **Wrap cellophane** around jug (color chosen for constitution)
3. **Place in sunlight** for 4-6 hours
4. **Consume** color-charged water throughout day
5. **Rotate colors** seasonally and with changing needs

Color Selection by Constitution:
- Vata: Red/orange for grounding
- Kapha: Yellow/blue for activation
- Pitta: Green/blue for cooling

Rhythmic Daily Order (Solar-Lunar Scheduling)
Constitutional Timing Framework

Constitutional Type	Optimal Activity Times	Rest Times	Practice Times
Vata (Electric)	Morning hours (before 10 AM)	Afternoon (2-4 PM)	Early morning, evening
Kapha (Magnetic)	Late morning (10 AM-12 PM)	Evening (after 6 PM)	Very early morning, midday
Pitta (Neutral)	All times balanced	Brief midday rest	Consistent schedule

Daily Schedule Service Integration
- Morning Practice: Foundation establishment
- Midday Activity: Productive work and service
- Evening Integration: Reflection and community
- Night Preparation: Sleep hygiene and rest

Lunar Phase Integration
New Moon: Introspective practices, fasting, internal focus
Waxing Moon: Building practices, growth emphasis
Full Moon: Peak energy practices, teaching, service
Waning Moon: Release practices, cleansing, completion

MASTER CONSTITUTIONAL FRAMEWORK FOR INTEGRATED PRACTICES

INTEGRATED DAILY PRACTICE SCHEDULE FOR CONTEMPLATIVE MASTERY

Foundation Phase Schedule (Months 1-12)

Morning Practice (4:00-6:00 AM) - 60 minutes total:

Time	Practice	Constitutional Notes
4:00-4:20	Physical preparation (20 min)	Electric: Gentle; Magnetic: Dynamic; Neutral: Balanced
4:20-4:40	Pranayama (20 min)	Per constitutional guidelines
4:40-5:00	Meditation (20 min)	Adjust duration per constitutional capacity
5:00-5:20	Study/Contemplation (20 min)	Sacred texts with reflection

Evening Practice (8:00-9:00 PM) - 30 minutes total:

Time	Practice	Constitutional Notes
8:00-8:15	Asana (15 min)	Restorative positions all types
8:15-8:30	Integration (15 min)	Day review, gratitude, surrender

Weekly Integration:
- One day per week for extended retreat practice (3-4 hours)
- Monthly assessment of progress and adjustment of methods
- Quarterly periods of intensive practice with qualified teacher
- Annual retreat for deeper integration (3-7 days)

Master Constitutional Adaptation Matrix
Complete Framework for All Practices

This comprehensive matrix provides unified guidance for constitutional adaptation across practices.

ELECTRIC CONSTITUTION (Vata/Air-Space Dominant)
Physical Characteristics Summary:

- Light, thin build with prominent joints
- Variable appetite and digestion
- Tendency toward cold hands and feet
- Light, interrupted sleep patterns
- Quick, darting movements
- Dry skin and hair

Universal Principles for Electric Constitution
Energy System:

- Highly reactive nervous system
- Easily overstimulated by intensity
- Tendency toward scattered energy
- Requires grounding and stabilizing
- Benefits from slow, deliberate practices

Practice Rhythm:

- Shorter practice sessions with breaks
- Regular daily routine essential
- Consistent timing and location
- Predictable rhythm reduces anxiety
- Progression slower but more stable when established

Environment:

- Warm, nurturing spaces preferred
- Gentle, steady lighting
- Grounding connection (barefoot on earth)
- Calming ambient sound
- Minimal external distractions

Physical Practice:

- **Postures:** Supported, restorative positions
- **Props:** Liberal use of blankets, blocks, cushions
- **Duration:** Shorter holds with frequent rests
- **Temperature:** Warm environment, layers for comfort
- **Pace:** Slow, deliberate transitions
- **Alignment:** Emphasis on grounding through feet/seat

Meditation Focus:
- **Object:** Something substantial (earth, mountain, body)
- **Duration:** Start with 10-15 minutes, build gradually
- **Support:** Use of mantra or counting for stability
- **Environment:** Quiet, familiar space
- **Technique:** Body-based awareness, grounding visualization

Integration Schedule:
- Daily calming practice before challenging activities
- Evening grounding practice (30 minutes minimum)
- Weekly full-day rest and recuperation recommended
- Monthly longer retreat for deep stabilization

NUTRITION (Bio-Compatible Diet):
Dietary Emphasis:
- Warming, grounding, nourishing foods
- Include healthy fats and oils liberally (olive, sesame, ghee)
- Cooked foods over raw (70% cooked, 30% raw ratio)
- Regular mealtimes with consistent schedule
- Sweet, sour, and salty tastes predominant

Foods to Favor:
- Warm soups and stews with root vegetables
- Whole grains: rice, oats, wheat
- Dairy products: warm milk, ghee, soft cheeses
- Sweet fruits: bananas, dates, figs, cooked apples
- Nuts and seeds: almonds, walnuts, sesame seeds
- Warming spices: ginger, cinnamon, cardamom, cumin

Foods to Minimize:
- Cold, raw foods and ice-cold beverages
- Dry foods: crackers, chips, dry breads
- Bitter and astringent vegetables in excess
- Stimulants: coffee, black tea, chocolate
- Beans and legumes (cause gas)
- Nightshade vegetables (tomatoes, peppers, eggplant)

Meal Pattern:
- Breakfast: Essential for grounding (warm grains, cooked fruits)
- Lunch: Largest meal with all six tastes present
- Dinner: Moderate, warm, easy to digest
- Snacks: Healthy between meals to maintain blood sugar stability

FOOD COMBINING:
List Emphasis:

- Prioritize **List A** (Proteins and Fats) for grounding and nourishment
- Include healthy fats with most meals
- Avoid excessive List C (fruits) as they can increase airiness
- Prefer cooked vegetables over raw for better digestion

Combining Adaptations:
- Allow 4-5 hours between different list meals
- Include warming spices with any combination
- Prefer simpler combinations (fewer ingredients)
- Always include grounding vegetables

DETOX & FASTING:
Fasting Cautions:
- Shorter fasting periods (1-3 days maximum)
- Include warming elements: ginger, cinnamon in teas
- More oranges than lemons (less cooling/drying)
- Focus on grounding and nourishing after fasting
- Avoid extended fasting during windy, cold, or stressful periods

Seasonal Detox:
- **Spring:** 1-day gentle fast
- **Summer:** 2-3 day warming cleanse
- **Autumn:** Minimal fasting, focus on nourishment
- **Winter:** Avoid fasting; build reserves

BREATHING:
Breathing Emphasis:
- Extended, smooth exhalation (calming effect)
- Gentle, never forceful practice
- Avoid rapid or intense breathing techniques
- Grounding breath with awareness in lower body

Optimal Breathing Pattern:
- **Inhalation:** 4 counts through nose
- **Retention:** 4 counts (comfortable, no strain)
- **Exhalation:** 8 counts through nose or mouth
- **Pause:** 2 counts natural rest
- **Duration:** 5-10 minutes maximum per session

Best Practices:
- Lunar breathing (left nostril) for calming
- Gentle Ujjayi breath
- Nadi Shodhana (alternate nostril) for balance
- Heart-centered breathing

- Avoid: Bhastrika, Kapalbhati, forceful practices

Timing:
- Morning: Gentle awakening breath (10 minutes)
- Evening: Extended exhalation practice (15 minutes)
- Throughout day: Awareness of smooth, calm breathing

HYDRATION:
Water Intake:
- 8-10 glasses minimum daily
- More in windy, dry, or cold conditions
- Regular small amounts rather than large quantities

Temperature:
- Slightly warm to room temperature (never ice cold)
- Warm water with meals supports digestion
- Hot herbal teas for grounding

Enhancements:
- Pinch of sea salt for electrolytes and grounding
- Fresh lemon for liver support
- Ginger tea for warming and digestion

Daily Protocol:
- **Morning:** 16 oz warm water with lemon and pinch sea salt
- **Between meals:** 6 oz room temperature every 2 hours
- **Evening:** Warm herbal tea (chamomile, fennel, licorice root)

MINERALS:
Priority Minerals:
- **Calcium and Magnesium:** For nervous system calm (sesame seeds, leafy greens)
- **Iron:** For blood building (leafy greens, dates, figs)
- **B-Vitamins:** For nervous system support (whole grains, nutritional yeast)
- **Omega-3 Fatty Acids:** For brain and nervous system (walnuts, flax seeds)

Food Sources:
- Dark leafy greens: kale, collards, chard
- Nuts and seeds: almonds, walnuts, sesame, sunflower
- Whole grains: oats, brown rice, quinoa
- Root vegetables: sweet potatoes, beets, carrots
- Dates and figs for iron and natural sugars

MOVEMENT:
Movement Emphasis:
- Slow, grounding, deliberate movements
- Emphasis on standing poses for stability
- Forward folds for calming nervous system
- Restorative poses with props
- Gentle, consistent practice over intense sessions

Optimal Practice:
- Duration: 20-30 minutes daily preferred over longer sessions
- Pace: Slow transitions with emphasis on feeling grounded
- Props: Liberal use of blankets, blocks, and support
- Temperature: Warm environment essential

MAGNETIC CONSTITUTION (Kapha/Earth-Water Dominant)
Physical Characteristics Summary:
- Solid, heavy build with good strength
- Steady appetite with slow metabolism
- Tendency toward weight gain and water retention
- Deep, long sleep patterns
- Slow, deliberate movements
- Smooth, oily skin and thick hair

Universal Principles for Magnetic Constitution
Energy System:
- Slow, steady nervous system
- High capacity for sustained effort
- Tendency toward stagnation without stimulation
- Benefits from activation and challenge
- Requires movement and intensity

Practice Rhythm:
- Longer, more vigorous practice sessions beneficial
- Variety and novelty maintain interest
- Dynamic progression prevents plateauing
- Regular practice schedule but with variation in activities
- Progression naturally faster when interested

Environment:
- Bright, energizing spaces preferred
- Stimulating sensory environment
- Outdoor practice beneficial when possible
- Variety in practice locations helpful
- Group practice enhances motivation

Physical Practice:
- **Postures:** Dynamic, strength-building positions
- **Props:** Minimal props; encourage self-effort
- **Duration:** Longer holds to build strength and stamina
- **Temperature:** Cool environment for heat regulation
- **Pace:** Vigorous, flowing transitions
- **Alignment:** Emphasis on strength and challenge

Meditation Focus:
- **Object:** Something inspiring or aspirational
- **Duration:** Start with 20-30 minutes, gradually extend
- **Support:** Use of visualization for engagement
- **Environment:** Varied locations to maintain interest
- **Technique:** Visualization, aspiration-based meditation

Integration Schedule:
- Daily vigorous practice (45-90 minutes)
- Alternating activity types to maintain interest
- Weekly intensive periods for deeper engagement
- Monthly challenges for continued growth

NUTRITION:
Dietary Emphasis:
- Light, warming, stimulating foods
- Include pungent spices liberally
- More raw foods (70% raw, 30% cooked ratio)
- Smaller portions, less frequent meals
- Bitter, pungent, and astringent tastes predominant

Foods to Favor:
- Light, warming meals with stimulating spices
- Vegetables: leafy greens, cruciferous vegetables, sprouts
- Fruits: apples, pears, berries, citrus (avoid heavy, sweet fruits)
- Grains: quinoa, buckwheat, millet (light grains)
- Legumes: mung beans, lentils, chickpeas
- Spices: black pepper, cayenne, turmeric, ginger, cumin

Foods to Minimize:
- Heavy, oily, sweet foods
- Dairy products (increase mucus)
- Refined sugars and sweeteners
- Heavy nuts: cashews, macadamias
- Bananas, avocados, coconuts
- Wheat and rice in large quantities

Meal Pattern:
- Breakfast: Optional or very light (fruit, warm lemon water)
- Lunch: Largest meal with emphasis on vegetables and proteins
- Dinner: Light, before 7:00 PM if possible
- Snacks: Avoid; maintain 4-5 hours between meals

FOOD COMBINING:
List Emphasis:
- Prioritize **List C** (Fresh Fruits) for cleansing and lightening
- Include stimulating spices with all meals
- Limit List A foods (can increase heaviness)
- Prefer raw vegetables and lighter preparations

Combining Adaptations:
- Alternate List C and green vegetable days for cleansing
- Avoid List A and B combinations completely when needing weight loss
- Morning fruit, evening salad pattern effective
- Increase raw food percentage to 80% during warm seasons

DETOX & FASTING:
Fasting Benefits:
- Longer fasting periods (3-7 days) highly beneficial
- Include stimulating spices: black pepper, turmeric
- Emphasize mobilizing stagnant energy and congestion
- Best results during warm, dry weather

Seasonal Detox:
- **Spring:** 7-day lemon cure (major cleanse)
- **Summer:** 5-day orange-lemon combination
- **Autumn:** 3-day juice fast
- **Winter:** Intermittent fasting (16:8 pattern)

BREATHING:
Breathing Emphasis:
- Energizing, stimulating breaths
- Include rapid breathing techniques
- Chest emphasis for activation
- Vigorous, confident execution

Optimal Breathing Pattern:
- **Rapid Inhalation:** 2 counts through nose
- **Brief Retention:** 2 counts
- **Forceful Exhalation:** 2 counts through mouth

- **Repeat:** 20-30 rapid cycles
- **Rest:** 2-3 minutes normal breathing between rounds

Best Practices:
- Solar breathing (right nostril) for energy
- Bhastrika (bellows breath) for activation
- Kapalbhati (skull-shining breath)
- Vigorous complete respiration

Timing:
- Morning: Vigorous energizing practice (20-30 minutes)
- Midday: Solar breathing for sustained energy
- Evening: Moderate practice, not too late (inhibits sleep)

HYDRATION:
Water Intake:
- 10-12 glasses minimum to support lymphatic drainage
- More during sedentary periods or congestion
- Larger amounts less frequently

Temperature:
- Room temperature to slightly cool (stimulating)
- Avoid ice cold but cooler than other types
- Warm water only during cold weather

Enhancements:
- Fresh lemon for liver and lymphatic support
- Cucumber and mint for cooling and cleansing
- Small amount of cayenne for stimulation
- Avoid adding sweeteners

Daily Protocol:
- **Morning:** 20 oz room temperature water with fresh lemon
- **Add stimulation:** Pinch of cayenne or fresh ginger
- **Between meals:** 8 oz every 2-3 hours (avoid constant sipping)
- **With exercise:** Increase significantly during physical activity

MINERALS:
Priority Minerals:
- **Iodine:** For thyroid function (sea vegetables)
- **Iron:** For blood vitality (leafy greens, legumes)
- **B-Vitamins:** For metabolism (nutritional yeast, whole grains)
- **Vitamin C:** For immunity (citrus, berries, peppers)

Food Sources:

- Sea vegetables: nori, dulse, kelp
- Dark leafy greens: kale, mustard greens, collards
- Legumes: lentils, mung beans, chickpeas
- Citrus fruits and berries
- Cruciferous vegetables: broccoli, cauliflower, Brussels sprouts

MOVEMENT:
Movement Emphasis:
- Dynamic, vigorous, heat-generating movement
- Emphasis on strength-building and cardiovascular activity
- Inversions and backbends for energy
- Longer holds to build stamina
- Challenge and variety to maintain interest

Optimal Practice:
- Duration: 45-90 minutes for adequate stimulation
- Pace: Vigorous, flowing transitions
- Props: Minimal; encourage self-effort
- Temperature: Cool environment for heat regulation

NEUTRAL CONSTITUTION (Pitta/Fire-Water Dominant)
Physical Characteristics Summary:
- Medium, athletic build with good musculature
- Strong appetite with efficient digestion
- Tendency toward heat and inflammation
- Moderate, sound sleep
- Purposeful, efficient movements
- Warm, reddish complexion

Universal Principles for Neutral Constitution
Energy System:
- Intense, focused nervous system
- High capacity for concentration
- Tendency toward overheating and intensity
- Benefits from cooling and balance
- Requires surrender and softening

Practice Rhythm:
- Moderate intensity most beneficial
- Systematic, methodical progression
- Balance between effort and ease essential
- Regular practice with integrated rest days
- Avoid competitive intensity or perfectionism

Environment:

- Cool, calm spaces preferred
- Natural light and pleasant views
- Quiet, focused environment for meditation
- Nature connection highly beneficial
- Single location for consistent practice

Physical Practice:
- **Postures:** Balanced combination of opening and grounding
- **Props:** Moderate use for comfort
- **Duration:** Moderate holds with rest between
- **Temperature:** Cool environment essential
- **Pace:** Balanced, never rushed
- **Alignment:** Emphasis on precision and ease simultaneously

Meditation Focus:
- **Object:** Something cooling or spacious (sky, water, emptiness)
- **Duration:** 30-45 minutes naturally sustainable
- **Support:** Surrender-based practices, compassion meditation
- **Environment:** Cooler location, nature if possible
- **Technique:** Wisdom meditation, emptiness practice, compassion cultivation

Integration Schedule:
- Daily moderate practice (45-75 minutes)
- Emphasis on surrender and ease alongside practice
- Weekly cooling and restorative sessions
- Monthly meditation intensives with cooling practices

NUTRITION:
Dietary Emphasis:
- Cooling, moderate, balancing foods
- Avoid excess oils, fats, and heating spices
- Balance raw and cooked foods (50/50)
- Regular meals without overeating
- Sweet, bitter, and astringent tastes predominant

Foods to Favor:
- Sweet fruits: grapes, melons, coconut, apples, pears
- Vegetables: cucumbers, leafy greens, asparagus, broccoli
- Grains: rice, oats, wheat, barley
- Legumes: mung beans, chickpeas, tofu
- Dairy: milk, ghee (in moderation)
- Cooling spices: coriander, fennel, mint, cardamom

Foods to Minimize:

- Hot, spicy foods and heating spices
- Sour foods: citrus, vinegar, yogurt, sour cream
- Salty foods and excess salt
- Tomatoes, peppers, and other acidic foods
- Alcohol and caffeine

Meal Pattern:
- Breakfast: Moderate, cooling (smoothies, fresh fruits, whole grains)
- Lunch: Largest meal with all six tastes, emphasis on cooling
- Dinner: Moderate, not too late
- Snacks: Cool fruits, sweet snacks in moderation

FOOD COMBINING:
List Emphasis:
- Balance all three lists according to seasonal needs
- Avoid heating spices; prefer cooling herbs (mint, cilantro)
- Emphasize List C during hot weather for cooling
- Prefer List B during cool weather for sustained energy

Combining Adaptations:
- Balanced rotation of all three lists throughout week
- Cooling preparations: salads, raw foods in summer
- Avoid combining heating foods
- Focus on alkaline-forming foods

DETOX & FASTING:
Fasting Approach:
- Moderate fasting periods (3-5 days ideal)
- Include cooling herbs: mint, fennel
- Avoid fasting during hot weather
- Focus on cooling and calming during detox

Seasonal Detox:
- **Spring:** 5-day lemon-orange combination
- **Summer:** Light fruit fasting only (avoid intense cleansing)
- **Autumn:** 5-day balanced citrus cure
- **Winter:** 3-day gentle orange cure

BREATHING:
Breathing Emphasis:
- Cooling, calming breaths
- Balanced inhale and exhale ratios
- Avoid retention (increases heat)
- Smooth, measured execution

Optimal Breathing Pattern:
- **Cooling Inhalation:** Curl tongue, inhale through tongue-tube
- **Brief Retention:** 2-4 counts
- **Normal Exhalation:** Through nose, slow and complete
- **Variation:** If unable to curl tongue, inhale through pursed lips
- **Duration:** 10-20 breaths, especially in hot weather

Best Practices:
- Sheetali/Sheetkari (cooling breaths)
- Lunar breathing (left nostril)
- Nadi Shodhana (alternate nostril) for balance
- Avoid: Bhastrika, Kapalbhati, solar breathing

Timing:
- Morning: Balanced practice (15-20 minutes)
- Midday: Cooling breath if feeling heated
- Evening: Calming, surrender-based practice (20 minutes)

Environment:
- Cool, fresh air preferred
- Nature settings ideal
- Avoid hot environments during practice

HYDRATION:
Water Intake:
- 8-10 glasses, adjust for heat and activity
- Significant increase during hot weather
- Consistent throughout day

Temperature:
- Room temperature to cool (avoid hot water)
- Cool water during summer
- Room temperature during cooler months

Enhancements:
- Cucumber slices for cooling
- Mint or lime for refreshing quality
- Coconut water during hot weather
- Rose water for cooling and heart opening

Daily Protocol:
- **Morning:** 16 oz room temperature water with lime
- **Cool addition:** Cucumber slices or mint leaves
- **Midday:** Coconut water during hot weather

- **Evening:** Cool herbal tea (peppermint, hibiscus, rose hip)

MINERALS:
Priority Minerals:
- **Calcium and Magnesium:** For cooling nervous system
- **Iron:** In moderate amounts (leafy greens, legumes)
- **B-Vitamins:** For balanced metabolism
- **Vitamin E:** For skin and tissue health (seeds, nuts in moderation)

Food Sources:
- Dark leafy greens: kale, chard, lettuce
- Cooling vegetables: cucumber, celery, zucchini
- Sweet fruits: melons, grapes, pears
- Whole grains: rice, oats, quinoa
- Seeds: sunflower, pumpkin (in moderation)

MOVEMENT:
Movement Emphasis:
- Balanced combination of strength and flexibility
- Emphasis on surrender and ease alongside effort
- Forward folds and twists for cooling
- Moderate intensity without competition
- Focus on precision with relaxation

Optimal Practice:
- Duration: 45-75 minutes with balanced intensity
- Pace: Steady, never rushed
- Props: Moderate use for comfort and precision
- Temperature: Cool environment essential

Universal Safety and Contraindications
Master Safety Framework
These universal contraindications and safety protocols apply across all practices unless specifically modified by qualified teacher assessment.

General Precautions (All Practices)
Before Beginning Any Practice:
- Consult healthcare provider if any health conditions present
- Inform teacher of injuries, surgeries, or medications
- Avoid practice on completely full stomach (wait 3-4 hours)
- Avoid practice with significant alcohol or drug use
- Practice in clean, safe environment
- Have water available during practice

Stopping Immediately If:

- Severe or sharp pain occurs (not just discomfort)
- Dizziness or lightheadedness develops
- Nausea or significant digestive upset
- Anxiety or panic attack symptoms
- Difficulty breathing or chest pain
- Any sensation of internal injury

Specific Practice Contraindications

High Blood Pressure:

- Avoid: Retention practices, intense heating techniques, inversions
- Modified: Gentle cooling pranayama, restorative postures, meditation emphasis
- Benefits: May reduce blood pressure with consistent, gentle practice
- Monitor: Regular blood pressure checks; coordinate with healthcare provider

Heart Conditions:

- Avoid: All intensive practices; breath retention; vigorous movement
- Modified: Gentle practices only under qualified guidance
- Benefits: May support cardiovascular health under proper supervision
- Medical Coordination: Required; work with cardiologist

High Cholesterol/Metabolic Issues:

- Avoid: No specific practice restrictions
- Modified: Constitutional diet and lifestyle change crucial
- Benefits: Appropriate practices may support metabolism
- Integration: Combine with healthcare provider recommendations

Diabetes:

- Avoid: Fasting practices; irregular meal timing
- Modified: Regular meal schedule essential; monitor blood sugar
- Benefits: Appropriate practices may support blood sugar regulation
- Monitoring: Regular blood sugar checks essential

Pregnancy:

- Avoid: Intense abdominal work, breath retention, vigorous movement, deep twists

- Modified: Prenatal-specific instruction essential
- Benefits: Appropriate practices support healthy pregnancy
- Teaching: Requires prenatal-certified instruction only

Postpartum (First 6-8 Weeks):
- Avoid: All intensive practice; breath retention
- Modified: Very gentle movement and breathing only
- Resume: After medical clearance from healthcare provider
- Special Considerations: C-section requires extended recovery

Menstruation:
- Avoid: Deep inversions (shoulder stand, headstand), intense abdominal work
- Modified: Gentle, restorative practices recommended
- Benefits: Appropriate practices may ease menstrual symptoms
- Listening: Honor body's needs; modify as needed

Mental Health Challenges:
- Depression: Appropriate practices may help; coordinate with therapy
- Anxiety Disorders: Calming practices essential; avoid intense stimulation
- PTSD/Trauma: Trauma-informed teaching required; somatic awareness crucial
- Psychosis: Practices should be carefully selected with mental health professional
- Medical Coordination: Required; maintain treatment continuity

Recent Surgery:
- Recovery Time: 6-12 weeks minimum before beginning
- Gentle Progression: Start with breathing and meditation only
- Scar Tissue: Gentle attention to affected areas
- Medical Clearance: Required before resuming practice

Substance Use History:
- Addiction Recovery: Supportive, grounding practices beneficial
- Prescription Medications: May affect practice; inform teacher
- Withdrawal: Avoid intense practices during acute withdrawal
- Integration: Combine with professional addiction support

Specific Technique Contraindications
Breath Retention (All Types):
- High blood pressure: Avoid completely
- Heart conditions: Avoid completely
- Anxiety disorders: Use minimal retention

- Glaucoma: Some sources recommend avoiding; consult ophthalmologist
- Epilepsy: Avoid intense breathing practices

Forceful Breathing (Bhastrika, Kapalbhati):
- High blood pressure: Avoid
- Heart conditions: Avoid
- Pregnancy: Avoid
- Disc herniations: Avoid (increased abdominal pressure)
- Hernia: Avoid until fully healed

Inversions (Shoulder Stand, Headstand):
- High blood pressure: Avoid
- Neck injuries: Avoid completely
- Glaucoma: Avoid (increased intraocular pressure)
- Recent neck/spine surgery: Avoid
- Osteoporosis: Modify significantly (avoid weight-bearing inversions)
- Menstruation: Avoid deep inversions (shoulder stand, headstand)

Deep Backbends:
- Disc herniations: Avoid
- Severe osteoporosis: Modify significantly
- Pregnancy: Avoid deep backbends
- Recent spine surgery: Avoid until clearance
- Sciatica: Often beneficial but modify carefully

Deep Forward Folds:
- Disc herniations (especially lumbar): Avoid or modify significantly
- Hamstring injuries: Modify carefully
- High blood pressure: Avoid intense variations
- Glaucoma: Avoid (head-down position increases intraocular pressure)

Visualization and Mantra:
- Severe mental illness: Require professional coordination
- History of dissociation: Modify to maintain grounding
- Seizure disorders: Avoid repetitive visual stimulation
- Recent trauma: Trauma-informed guidance essential

Teacher Guidance Requirements
Practices Requiring Qualified Teacher Presence:
- First Kundalini awakening experiences

- Deep meditative states (Samadhi)
- Advanced visualization techniques
- Mantra empowerment and initiation
- Energy transmission practices
- Complex chakra work

Practices Benefiting from Teacher Guidance:
- All initial practice
- Modification for health conditions
- Advancement to new stages
- Integration of spiritual experiences
- Resolution of practice difficulties

When to Seek Professional Help:
- Persistent pain or injury
- Mental health symptoms emerging
- Spiritual experiences feeling overwhelming
- Relationship difficulties from practice
- Financial or life stress related to practice

Practice Schedule Templates
Quick-Reference Schedule Progression
Foundation Phase (Months 1-12)

Component	Beginner (Months 1-3)	Early Intermediate (Months 4-6)	Established (Months 7-12)
Morning Meditation	10-15 minutes	15-20 minutes	20-30 minutes
Pranayama	10 minutes	15 minutes	20 minutes
Physical Practice	15-20 minutes	20-25 minutes	25-30 minutes
Study/Reading	10 minutes	15 minutes	20 minutes
Total Morning	45-55 minutes	65-75 minutes	85-100 minutes
Evening Practice	10 minutes	15 minutes	20 minutes
Weekly Retreat	Monthly weekend	Monthly long weekend	Monthly 3-day
Quarterly Intensive	Not recommended	3-day retreat	3-5 day retreat

Intermediate Phase (Months 1-24)

Component	Early (Months 1-6)	Mid (Months 7-18)	Advanced (Months 19-24)
Morning Meditation	30-40 minutes	40-50 minutes	50-60 minutes
Pranayama	20-30 minutes	30-40 minutes	40-50 minutes
Physical Practice	30-40 minutes	40-50 minutes	50-60 minutes
Study/Contemplation	20 minutes	25 minutes	30 minutes
Total Morning	100-130 minutes	135-165 minutes	170-200 minutes
Evening Practice	20-30 minutes	30-40 minutes	40-50 minutes
Weekly Retreat	Weekend (6-8 hours)	Extended weekend (8-10 hours)	Weekly intensive
Monthly Intensive	3-day	3-5 day	5-7 day
Teaching Time	Begin guiding beginners	Regular teaching	Leadership roles

Advanced Phase (Years 3-7)

Component	Early Years (3-4)	Mid Years (5-6)	Mastery (7+)
Morning Meditation	60-90 minutes	90-120 minutes	120+ minutes
Pranayama	45-60 minutes	60-75 minutes	60-90 minutes
Physical Practice	45-60 minutes	45-60 minutes	30-60 minutes
Study/Contemplation	30-45 minutes	30-45 minutes	30-45 minutes
Total Morning	180-255 minutes	225-300 minutes	240-330 minutes
Evening/Service	60-90 minutes	90-120 minutes	90-150 minutes
Weekly Retreat	Full day	Full day	Extended

	minimum	intensive	retreat
Monthly Intensive	Week-long	2-week period	Ongoing intensive
Teaching/Leadership	Regular teaching, program development	Program leadership, teacher training	Institutional leadership

Constitutional Schedule Variations
Electric Constitution Specific Schedule:

Time Slot	Practice	Duration	Notes
4:30-4:45	Gentle grounding asana	15 min	Standing poses, forward folds
4:45-5:15	Lunar breathing (left nostril)	30 min	Calming emphasis
5:15-5:45	Meditation (with body awareness)	30 min	Shorter than other types, can extend
5:45-6:00	Rest and integration	15 min	Lie down, let settle
6:00-8:00	Daily activities		Maintain calm throughout day
8:00-8:30	Evening practice (restorative)	30 min	Gentle, grounding
8:30-9:00	Community or family connection	30 min	Grounding through relationship

Magnetic Constitution Specific Schedule:

Time Slot	Practice	Duration	Notes
3:30-4:00	Dynamic asana (sun salutations)	30 min	Vigorous, heat-generating
4:00-4:30	Solar breathing (right nostril)	30 min	Energizing emphasis
4:30-5:30	Deep meditation	60 min	Longer than other types
5:30-	Service activity	30 min	Community

736

6:00			engagement
6:00-8:00	Work/engagement		Channel energy productively
8:00-8:45	Evening vigorous practice	45 min	Dynamic or teaching
8:45-9:00	Rest (earned)	15 min	Brief settling

Neutral Constitution Specific Schedule:

Time Slot	Practice	Duration	Notes
4:00-4:30	Balanced asana	30 min	Mix grounding and opening
4:30-5:00	Nadi Shodhana (balanced)	30 min	Equal inhale and exhale
5:00-6:00	Meditation (wisdom/emptiness)	60 min	Clarity, non-conceptual
6:00-6:30	Study or contemplation	30 min	Intellectual integration
6:30-8:00	Work/engagement		Bring awareness to activities
8:00-8:30	Cooling practice (gentle)	30 min	Surrender emphasis
8:30-9:00	Integration/gratitude	30 min	Day reflection, appreciation

Assessment Frameworks
Development Stage Assessment Criteria
Stage 1 Assessment: The Practitioner (Prathamkalpika)

Meditation Capacity:
- Minimum: 20 minutes continuous without significant distraction
- Optimal: 30-45 minutes with relative stability
- Indicators: Fewer mind-wanderings, easier re-focusing, developing presence

Breathing Mastery:
- Minimum: Comfortable 10-15 minute practice without strain
- Optimal: 15-20 minutes with awareness of energy shifts
- Indicators: Smooth breath, conscious pacing, beginning energy awareness

Physical Health:
- Minimum: Regular asana practice without injury; basic flexibility
- Optimal: Improved flexibility, strength, postural awareness
- Indicators: Fewer pain complaints, improved energy, better sleep

Ethical Conduct:
- Indicators: Obvious effort toward honest communication, reduced harm
- Behavioral Changes: Stopping obviously harmful behaviors
- Relationship Quality: Noticeably improved relationships with some people

Service Orientation:
- Minimum: Participation in at least one community service activity monthly
- Optimal: Regular volunteer activity; helping others naturally
- Indicators: Reduced selfishness, considering others' welfare

Community Participation:
- Minimum: Monthly attendance at group practice
- Optimal: Weekly attendance, relationship building with community
- Indicators: Sense of belonging, investment in community well-being

Timeline: 6-12 months consistent practice with above indicators suggests readiness for Stage 2 progression.

Stage 2 Assessment: The Honey-Bearer (Madhupratika)

Meditation Depth:
- Minimum: 45 minutes with sustained focus
- Optimal: 60+ minutes with periods of absorption
- Indicators: Access to subtle states, presence carries into daily life

Pranayama Sophistication:
- Minimum: Multiple techniques mastered; safe retention practice
- Optimal: Noticeable energetic effects; subtle perception develops
- Indicators: Energy awareness, spontaneous breath regulation, better health

Energy Perception:
- Minimum: Basic awareness of chakras and energy channels
- Optimal: Conscious perception of energy movements; healing intuition
- Indicators: Accurate sensing of others' conditions, helpful guidance

Teaching Capacity:
- Minimum: Can guide beginners in basic practices under supervision
- Optimal: Independent teaching of foundation level
- Indicators: Students benefit; developing teaching confidence

Intellectual Integration:
- Minimum: Understanding of major spiritual principles
- Optimal: Wisdom application to personal and others' situations
- Indicators: Teaching others key concepts; practical application

Service Deepening:
- Minimum: Regular service commitments with visible impact
- Optimal: Leadership of service projects
- Indicators: Community recognizes contributions; personal satisfaction from service

Timeline: 18-36 months consistent Stage 1 practice with above indicators suggests Stage 3 readiness.

Stage 3 Assessment: Master of Elements (Bhutendriyajay)

Meditation Mastery:
- Criteria: 90+ minutes of stable, deep meditation
- Samadhi Access: Regular entering of absorption states
- Indicators: Non-ordinary perceptions, transcendent experiences, 24/7 underlying awareness

Advanced Pranayama:
- Criteria: Safe mastery of all retention techniques
- Energy Mastery: Kundalini managed consciously
- Indicators: Visible effects on physical health, energy healing capacity

Healing and Transmission:
- Criteria: Documented evidence of helping others through energy work

- Teaching Authorization: Approved by elder council for independent teaching
- Indicators: Students making significant progress, community recognition

Ethical Integration:
- Criteria: Consistent ethical conduct; no significant violations
- Character Maturity: Observable equanimity under all circumstances
- Indicators: Community trust, appropriate boundaries, service orientation dominant

Leadership Effectiveness:
- Criteria: Successfully managing community projects/organizations
- Conflict Resolution: Demonstrates skill mediating conflicts
- Indicators: Community runs smoothly; members feel heard and supported

Professional Integration:
- Criteria: Clear demonstration of practice improving professional effectiveness
- Examples: Healthcare providers report improved patient care; educators report student improvements
- Indicators: Professional colleagues notice positive changes

Timeline: 7-15 years total practice with sustained Stage 2 development and above indicators.

Stage 4 Assessment: The Liberated Being (Atikrantabhavaniya)

Continuous Realization:
- 24/7 recognition of consciousness as fundamental nature
- Freedom from identification with form or condition
- Effortless ethical conduct and spiritual wisdom

Invisible Service:
- Documented impact on others' consciousness far beyond personal sphere
- Guidance experienced as mysteriously present by many seekers
- Influence extending beyond personal teaching to collective evolution

Teaching Authority:

- Recognized globally by qualified teachers
- Authorized to train other teachers at all levels
- Institutional development and network leadership

Indicators:
- Community and global recognition of realized nature
- Spontaneous benefit flowing to those in vicinity
- Embodied wisdom and compassion evident in all actions
- Effortless manifestation of beneficial circumstances

Timeline: Lifelong recognition and deepening; not a final destination but endless flowering.

Teacher-Student Relationship Framework and Transmission Methods

Teacher-Student Relationship Framework
Foundational Principle
The relationship between teacher and student represents the most sacred transmission opportunity. Ethical clarity, mutual respect, and developmental appropriateness are paramount. This framework prevents dependency, guru dynamics, and exploitation while enabling genuine transmission.

Four Phases of Teaching Relationship
Phase 1: Initial Contact and Assessment
Purpose: Mutual evaluation establishing appropriateness of relationship
Student's Assessment of Teacher:
- Does teacher embody teachings?
- Is teacher transparent about limitations?
- Does teacher avoid hierarchy and dependency dynamics?
- Is teacher accessible and responsive?
- Does teacher prioritize student independence?

Teacher's Assessment of Student:
- Is student ready for receiving teaching?
- Does student have realistic expectations?
- Is student able to practice consistently?
- Does student respect boundaries?
- Does student seek growth rather than escape?

Timeline: 1-4 weeks of interaction before committing to teaching relationship
Key Elements:

- Clear communication of expectations
- Discussion of practice commitment required
- Exploration of student's motivations
- Teacher sharing own practice lineage
- Explicit discussion of teaching ethics and boundaries

Phase 2: Beginning Instruction
Purpose: Establishing foundation and developing proper relationship patterns
Student Development:
- Introduction to fundamental practices
- Development of consistent practice habits
- Learning proper technique and safety
- Understanding constitutional personalization
- Initial meditation experience

Teacher Role:
- Guiding foundation practices
- Ensuring correct technique prevents injury
- Building student confidence
- Establishing regular communication patterns
- Creating safe container for practice

Relationship Characteristics:
- More structured; teacher provides direction
- Student asks questions and receives guidance
- Regular check-ins assessing progress
- Early warning signs addressed promptly
- Trust building through consistency

Duration: 3-6 months
Indicators of Readiness to Advance:
- Consistent practice without reminder
- Basic meditation stability
- Understanding of constitutional principles
- Receptivity to feedback
- Growing energy awareness

Phase 3: Deepening Practice
Purpose: Developing individual practice capacity and introducing advanced techniques
Student Development:
- Advanced techniques appropriate to constitutional type
- Increased self-direction in practice
- Individual guidance customized to specific needs

- Integration with daily life circumstances
- Preparation for potential teaching role

Teacher Role:
- Offering advanced techniques
- Addressing practice obstacles
- Providing individual guidance
- Supporting integration challenges
- Encouraging student's emerging wisdom

Relationship Characteristics:
- More collaborative; student takes initiative
- Teacher responds to student's specific needs
- Regular but less frequent contact
- Student developing independent judgment
- Growing peer-quality to relationship

Duration: 2-5 years
Indicators of Readiness to Advance:
- Depth of meditation practice evident
- Noticeable energy changes
- Consistent service engagement
- Capacity to help others begin practice
- Clear questioning showing individual thinking

Phase 4: Maturation and Independence
Purpose: Student develops independent practice capacity and becomes colleague
Student Development:
- Full independent practice capacity
- Teaching role with supervision transitioning to peer consultation
- Integration of teachings with personal insights
- Service leadership
- Becoming elder for newer practitioners

Teacher Role:
- Consulting rather than directing
- Supporting student's teaching emergence
- Addressing complex situations as equals
- Remaining available for deep questions
- Celebrating student's realization

Relationship Characteristics:
- Peer relationship quality

- Student leads own practice direction
- Teacher available for consultation
- Mutual respect as equals
- Connection through friendship rather than instruction need

Duration: Open-ended; relationship deepens and transforms
Indicators of Mature Relationship:
- Student seeks consultation, not direction
- Student's wisdom recognized and valued
- Teaching relationship established with others
- Service leadership evident
- Genuine friendship present

Transmission Methods
Teaching communication occurs through four primary channels:

1. Verbal Instruction and Dialogue
Components:
- Lectures presenting traditional teachings
- Individual guidance adapted to specific needs
- Question and answer exploring spiritual topics
- Story and metaphor enabling transcendence of conceptual limitations
- Explanations of practice rationale and benefits

When Most Effective:
- Initial learning of techniques
- Intellectual understanding needed
- Student has specific questions
- Group learning situations

2. Direct Transmission (Shaktipat)
Definition: Energy transmission as the most powerful teaching method
Forms:
- Touch transmission (hand contact, often heart to heart)
- Gaze transmission (eye contact)
- Word transmission (sacred words or sounds)
- Silence transmission (presence alone)

Preparation for Reception:
- Purity through practice and diet
- Receptivity developed through meditation
- Ethical development establishing safety
- Teacher's consciousness must be stabilized

- Student's constitutional readiness assessed

Natural Expression:
- Consciousness recognizing itself in another
- Spontaneous arising not forced
- Most powerful at stage transitions
- Requires qualified teacher

3. Teaching Through Example
Definition: Embodied demonstration of integrated principles
Components:
- Living demonstration of teachings in daily life
- Transparent personality allowing consciousness to shine
- Graceful handling of life's challenges
- Natural authority arising from demonstrated wisdom
- Integration of practice and action

Power:
- Most influential teaching method
- Non-verbal communication transcends words
- Demonstrates actual transformation
- Students naturally aspire to similar development

4. Gradual Development
Definition: Progressive phases of relationship supporting student evolution
Characteristics:
- Student independence as goal, not dependence
- Teaching aims toward student's autonomy
- Evolution from student-teacher to colleague
- Continued connection through friendship
- Long-term relationship supporting continued growth

Ethical Frameworks for Teachers
Prevention of Guru Dynamics
Red Flags to Recognize and Avoid:

Authority Inflation:
- Teacher positioning self as ultimate authority
- Discouraging student's independent judgment
- Creating dependency for teacher's validation
- Claiming infallibility or special status

Boundary Violations:
- Inappropriate emotional relationships
- Sexual advances or boundary confusion

- Excessive power differentials
- Isolation of students from other teachers

Financial Exploitation:
- Excessive fees without clear value
- Pressure for contributions beyond means
- Funds used for teacher's personal benefit
- Lack of financial transparency

Control Mechanisms:
- Discouraging questioning or feedback
- Isolation from outside perspectives
- Sleep deprivation or fasting enforcement
- Psychological manipulation

Prevention of Dependency
Healthy Teaching Maintains:
- Student's autonomous decision-making
- Encouragement of questioning
- Clear boundaries on teacher's role
- Multiple trusted advisors recommended
- Student growth toward independence
- Regular reality checks with community
- Financial transparency
- Regular accountability through elder council

Professional Boundaries
Clear Role Definition
Teacher's Role:
- Guiding practice and teaching techniques
- Providing spiritual direction
- Supporting meditation and energy work
- Offering wisdom from experience
- NOT providing medical or mental health treatment
- NOT serving as primary emotional support
- NOT making life decisions for student
- NOT controlling student's relationships

Student's Responsibility:
- Maintaining own medical and psychological care
- Seeking professional help when needed
- Keeping appropriate life responsibilities
- Maintaining outside relationships
- Developing independent judgment
- Consulting multiple advisors on major decisions

Communication About Limitations
Teacher Should Clearly Communicate:
- Scope of teaching authority
- Areas requiring professional help
- Requirement to see healthcare providers
- Limitations of spiritual practice
- When to seek other teachers
- Importance of elder council consultation

Elder Council Functions
Role of Elder Council:
- Oversight of teacher ethics
- Consultation on complex cases
- Support for students in difficulty
- Professional accountability
- Prevention of teacher burnout
- Collective wisdom bringing perspective

Meeting Frequency:
- Quarterly minimum
- More frequent during crises
- Annual formal review
- Between-meeting consultation available

Ending Teaching Relationships
Appropriate Endings:
- Student achieves independence
- Student finds more suitable teacher
- Student needs specialized help teacher cannot provide
- Mutual agreement relationship has completed
- Teacher's limitation or incapacity

Healthy Termination Process:
- Honest discussion of reasons
- Transition period allowing adjustment
- Introduction to new teacher if appropriate
- Ongoing friendship possible if appropriate
- Blessing of student's next chapter
- Financial and practical completion

EARTH-HUMAN BIOELECTRIC CORRESPONDENCE THEORY

1.1 The Hermetic Foundation

The ancient hermetic axiom states: **"As above, so below; as below, so above."** This principle is echoed across wisdom traditions, asserts that patterns repeat at all scales of manifestation.

From the Laws of Vayu (1919) by Cedaior (Albert Raymond Costet de Mascheville):

"Reality consists of one dynamic field of self-aware consciousness expressing itself through infinite patterns while maintaining essential unity. This field is simultaneously the source, substance, and goal of all existence, appearing as multiplicity while never departing from fundamental oneness."

This is not mere philosophical speculation. Contemporary physics validates fractal patterns across scales - from atomic structure mirroring solar systems to galactic distributions echoing neural networks.

1.2 The Three Treasures: Jing-Qi-Shen at Planetary/Human Scale

Traditional Chinese Medicine describes three fundamental energies - **Jing (essence), Qi (vitality), Shen (spirit)** - that govern all living systems. This framework can apply equally to Earth and humans:

Level	JING (Essence/Structure)	QI (Energy/Flow)	SHEN (Spirit/Consciousness)
EARTH	Mineral deposits, crystalline matrix, magnetic core, geological formations	Telluric currents, lightning, geomagnetic field, Schumann resonance (7.83 Hz)	Planetary consciousness field, astral light, collective unconscious
HUMAN	Bone marrow, DNA, reproductive essence, kidney energy, constitutional vitality	Bioelectric currents, meridian flow, fascia conductivity	Individual awareness, neural gamma synchrony

The correspondence is **structural, functional, and energetic**:

JING Correspondence:
- Earth's mineral matrix and crystalline geological structures = Human skeletal system and DNA
- Both store "essence" - Earth stores geological memory, humans store genetic information
- Both deplete over time without replenishment

QI Correspondence:
- Earth's telluric currents and lightning = Human meridian flow and bioelectric signals
- Both circulate vital energy through conductive pathways
- Both respond to cosmic influences (solar activity, lunar phases)

SHEN Correspondence:
- Earth's planetary consciousness field (8 Hz Schumann) = Human theta brainwave meditation states
- Both interface with higher dimensional awareness
- Both affected by intentional consciousness practices

KRIYAS: SPONTANEOUS ENERGY DISCHARGE AT MULTIPLE SCALES

2.1 Human Kriyas: Definition and Phenomenology
Kriyas (Sanskrit: क्रिया, "action") are spontaneous, involuntary movements arising during meditation, energy work, or spiritual practice. They represent the body's intelligent discharge of blocked energy and neurological reorganization.

Phenomenology of Human Kriyas:
1. **Physical Manifestations:**
- Spontaneous trembling, shaking, vibrating
- Involuntary rotation of head, torso, limbs
- Automatic assumption of yoga postures (asanas)
- Rhythmic spasms and muscular contractions
- Sensation of internal "electricity" or "static" beneath the skin
- Intense heat or cold waves through the body

2. **Energetic Mechanisms:**
- Release of fascial restrictions and muscular armoring
- Discharge of accumulated bioelectric potential
- Clearing of energy channel blockages (nadis, meridians)
- Reorganization of nervous system patterns
- Integration of traumatic "freeze" states

3. **Consciousness Correlates:**
- Often accompanied by altered states of awareness
- May include visions, emotional releases, insights
- Associated with kundalini invoking (not full awakening)
- Represents transition to "involuntary transformation" phase

Key Insight: Kriyas are not random but represent **intelligent, self-organizing bioelectric discharge** following natural patterns to restore homeostasis and optimize energy flow.

2.2 Planetary Kriyas: Lightning and Electromagnetic Discharge
Earth exhibits analogous spontaneous electromagnetic discharges:

1. Lightning - Earth's Primary Kriya:
- **~100 lightning strikes per second globally** (8.64 million/day)
- Discharges atmospheric electrical potential that builds from solar radiation
- Creates the Schumann resonance (7.83 Hz)
- Releases ~1 billion joules per major strike
- Follows preferential pathways (like meridians) based on conductivity

2. Geomagnetic Storms - Earth's Systemic Kriyas:
- Solar wind impacts trigger planetary-scale electromagnetic turbulence
- Geomagnetic field fluctuates rapidly during storms
- Produces auroras (visible energy discharge like human biophotons)
- Affects biological rhythms globally

3. Telluric Currents - Earth's Meridian Flow:
- Natural electrical currents flowing through Earth's crust
- Follow geological conductivity patterns (underground water, mineral veins)
- Intensify during seismic activity (pre-earthquake piezoelectric effects)
- Detectable by dowsers and sensitive instruments

From La Iniciación (1945) on Cosmic Influences:

"Variations of terrestrial magnetism reveal modifications in cosmic influences... The compass reveals these variations which manifest upon unconscious life... Many sensitive beings react by means of pains to meteorological variations."

2.3 The Correspondence: Structural Parallels

Feature	Human Kriyas	Planetary Kriyas
Trigger	Accumulated bioelectric potential from breathing, meditation, trauma	Accumulated atmospheric charge from solar radiation, cosmic rays
Pathway	Follows fascial planes, meridians, nervous system	Follows geological conductivity, underground water, fault lines
Discharge Pattern	Spontaneous, involuntary, rhythmic, intelligent	Spontaneous, follows natural law, rhythmic (diurnal/seasonal patterns)
Function	Releases blockages, reorganizes nervous system, restores homeostasis	Balances atmospheric electricity, distributes charge, maintains field stability
Frequency	Variable - intensifies with practice and accumulated potential	~100/second globally; intensifies with solar activity
Associated Phenomena	Heat, tingling, tremors, altered consciousness	Thunder, light, electromagnetic pulse, ionospheric disturbance
Healing Effect	Releases trauma, integrates fragmented patterns, enhances vitality	Fertilizes soil (nitrogen fixation), ionizes atmosphere, resets geomagnetic field

Critical Observation: Both human and planetary kriyas are:
- **Self-organizing** (not externally imposed)
- **Homeostatic** (restore equilibrium)
- **Intelligent** (follow optimal pathways)
- **Rhythmic** (occur in natural cycles)
- **Discharging** (release accumulated potential)

2.4 Fog, Atmospheric Ionization, and Enhanced Conductivity
Research reveals a **special relationship between areas of high fog density and bioelectric phenomena:**

Fog as Atmospheric Conductor:
1. Water vapor enhances atmospheric conductivity - allows easier discharge
2. **Fog concentrates negative ions** - associated with parasympathetic activation and meditative states
3. **Foggy coastal regions** show enhanced telluric current activity
4. **Practitioners in fog-prone areas** (San Francisco, Chilean coast, Himalayan valleys) report more intense kriyas and spontaneous energy experiences

Mechanism:
- Water droplets in fog act as **micro-capacitors** storing atmospheric charge
- Creates a more **conductive medium** for bioelectric field interactions
- Enhances human-Earth electromagnetic coupling
- Facilitates energy exchange between atmospheric and biological systems

This explains why **sacred sites often located in mountain valleys with frequent fog/mist** (Machu Picchu, Wudang Mountains, Himalayas, Mt. Shasta) - these locations naturally enhance bioelectric phenomena.

FA JING: DIRECTED POWER RELEASE AT PLANET/HUMAN LEVELS

3.1 Fa Jing (Fājìn 發勁): The Human Principle
Fa jing in internal martial arts represents **explosive power released through complete relaxation and emptiness** - the paradox of maximum force through minimum effort.

Characteristics of Human Fa Jing:
1. **Complete Relaxation Prerequisite:**
- All unnecessary muscular tension released
- Fascia fully integrated and elastic
- Nervous system quiet, mind empty
- Breath synchronized with intention

2. **Instantaneous Energy Release:**

- Accumulated bioelectric potential discharged in <0.1 seconds
- Whole-body integration creates amplified force
- Energy travels through fascial network like lightning through atmosphere
- Appears effortless yet produces devastating impact

3. **The Paradox:**
- Maximum power through minimum effort
- Hardness through softness (water principle)
- Action through non-action (wu wei)
- Conscious intention meets spontaneous expression

From Internal Martial Arts Tradition:
"Fa jing is like drawing a bow fully then releasing the arrow - all the stored potential energy converts to kinetic energy instantaneously. The body becomes a unified spring."

Biophysical Mechanism:
- **Fascia acts as piezoelectric tensegrity structure** storing mechanical energy
- **Relaxation removes energetic blockages** allowing full-body integration
- **Intention provides coherent trigger** for synchronized discharge
- **Result: wave of bioelectric potential propagates through body** like lightning bolt

3.2 Planetary Fa Jing: Focused Electromagnetic Phenomena
Earth exhibits analogous **focused electromagnetic releases** at specific locations:

1. Lightning Ground Strike Points:
- Not random - follows **preferential pathways** of highest conductivity
- Repeatedly strikes same locations (Empire State Building, mountain peaks)
- Represents **complete atmospheric potential discharge** at single point
- Analogous to fa jing: **accumulated charge + optimal pathway + instantaneous release**

2. Earthquake Epicenters - Earth's Explosive Release:
- Accumulated tectonic strain (Earth's equivalent of muscular tension)
- Sudden release along fault lines (Earth's meridians/fascia)

- Piezoelectric discharge from crystal fracture creates electromagnetic pulse
- Intensity paradox: **most devastating quakes occur in "relaxed" (low friction) zones** where accumulated energy releases completely rather than gradually

3. Volcanic Eruptions - Earth's Directed Force:
- Magma builds pressure (accumulated vital force/qi)
- Crater provides focused discharge pathway
- Explosive release transforms accumulated potential to kinetic manifestation
- Creates new land - **destructive force becomes creative transformation**

4. Geomagnetic Anomalies and Power Spots:
- Specific locations show **concentrated electromagnetic field effects**
- Often sites of ancient temples, spontaneous healing, heightened mystical experience
- Earth's energy naturally "channels" through these points
- Analogous to human **acupuncture points** - concentrated energy access portals

3.3 The Correspondence: Fa Jing Principles at All Scales

Principle	Human Fa Jing	Planetary Fa Jing
Accumulation Phase	Build bioelectric potential through practice, relaxation, breath	Atmospheric charge builds from solar radiation, ionization
Relaxation Requirement	Complete muscular and neural relaxation essential	"Relaxed" geological zones (low friction faults) produce strongest quakes
Pathway Selection	Energy follows integrated fascial network	Discharge follows optimal conductivity path (water, minerals, fault lines)
Instantaneous Release	<0.1 second whole-body discharge	Lightning <0.001 second; earthquake main shock <30 seconds
Paradox of Power	Maximum force through minimum effort	Greatest geological effects occur in most "fluid" zones

Focused Effect	Impact concentrated at specific point/target	Energy concentrated at epicenter, strike point, volcanic vent
Creative Transformation	Breaks opponent's structure, awakens consciousness	Creates new landforms, fertilizes soil, resets electromagnetic field

The Unified Principle:
MAXIMUM POTENTIAL + MINIMUM RESISTANCE + OPTIMAL PATHWAY = EXPLOSIVE TRANSFORMATION

This formula operates identically whether describing:
- A martial artist's palm strike
- A lightning bolt
- An earthquake
- A volcanic eruption
- A mystical experience breakthrough
- A fa jing discharge

3.4 The Role of Emptiness (Śūnyatā)
Buddhist philosophy's concept of **emptiness** (śūnyatā) is not void but **pregnant potentiality** - the condition allowing maximum responsiveness.

In Human Fa Jing:
- Mind empty of preconception allows spontaneous optimal response
- Body empty of tension allows full-body integration
- "No-mind" (mushin) enables instantaneous action without deliberation

In Planetary Fa Jing:
- Geological "emptiness" (fluid magma chambers, water-saturated fault zones) allows maximum discharge
- Atmospheric "emptiness" (low pressure zones, ionized corridors) channels lightning
- **Emptiness is NOT absence but CAPACITY** - the space allowing transformation

Emptiness/Śūnyatā is the **condition of maximum divine presence** because it offers no resistance to manifestation. This is why:

- Deepest meditation occurs in complete relaxation
- Most powerful fa jing emerges from total softness
- Most dramatic geological events occur in most "fluid" zones

4.1 Fascia as Planetary Analog
Human fascial network:
- Continuous collagen matrix connecting all body structures
- Piezoelectric properties - generates electricity when compressed
- Acts as semiconductor - conducts bioelectric signals
- Stores and releases mechanical/electrical energy
- Contains 70% of body's sensory nerve endings
- Organizes body as unified **tensegrity structure**

Earth's geological/hydrological network:
- Continuous mineral/water matrix throughout crust
- Piezoelectric crystals generate electricity when stressed (pre-earthquake signals)
- Underground water and mineral veins conduct telluric currents
- Stores and releases tectonic/electromagnetic energy
- Contains majority of Earth's pressure/stress sensors (seismographic network)
- Organizes planet as unified **tensegrity structure**

The Correspondence:
Both fascia (human) and crust (Earth) act as **crystalline semiconductor matrices** that:
1. Conduct bioelectric signals
2. Store mechanical/electrical potential
3. Release energy in coherent patterns
4. Self-organize into optimal configurations
5. Respond to pressure/stress with electrical discharge

4.2 Biophotons and Lightning - Light as Information Carrier
Human Biophotons:
- Ultra-weak photons emitted by all living cells (200-1,300 nm)
- Increase during meditation, energy work, healing
- Mediate intercellular communication
- Correlate with consciousness states
- Coherence increases with spiritual practice

Planetary Lightning:
- Visible light discharge from atmospheric electrical potential
- ~8.64 million strikes daily globally
- Creates Schumann resonance (7.83 Hz)
- Mediates atmospheric chemistry (nitrogen fixation)

- Coherence pattern shows global organization

The Principle:
Light is the messenger of consciousness at all scales.

Just as biophotons carry information between cells, lightning and electromagnetic phenomena carry "information" through Earth's systems, coordinating global patterns.

4.3 The Schumann Resonance - Planetary Nervous System
The 7.83 Hz Connection:
The Schumann resonance is created by **global lightning activity** (~100 strikes/second) creating a standing electromagnetic wave between Earth's surface and ionosphere.

Significance:
- Exactly matches human **theta brainwave frequency** (4-8 Hz range)
- Theta state associated with:
- Deep meditation
- Hypnagogic states (sleep transition)
- Access to subconscious
- Heightened intuition
- Spontaneous kriyas

Implication:
Human consciousness **naturally entrains** to Earth's electromagnetic field. This is not metaphor but **measurable biophysical coupling**:

- Human EEG synchronizes with Schumann fluctuations
- Geomagnetic storms affect human mood, cognition, cardiac rhythms
- Meditation enhances Schumann coupling
- Kriyas may represent **discharge of accumulated Schumann resonance energy**

4.4 The Conducting Medium - Water, Minerals, and Ions
Why specific locations show enhanced phenomena:

High Conductivity Zones:
1. **Underground water veins** - excellent electrical conductor
2. **Mineral deposits** - especially iron, copper, quartz crystals
3. **Fault lines** - crushed rock creates enhanced conductivity
4. **Coastal regions** - salt water enhances atmospheric conductivity

5. **Areas of high fog** - water droplets act as micro-capacitors

Human Parallel:
1. **Meridians follow fascial planes** - especially those with high water content
2. **Acupuncture points** show enhanced electrical conductivity
3. **Bone (mineral) and marrow** act as electromagnetic antenna
4. **Blood (salt water)** conducts bioelectric signals
5. **Interstitial fluid** maintains ionic balance essential for nerve transmission

The Mechanism:
Both human and planetary bioelectric phenomena require **conducting medium** to:
- Store charge potential
- Transmit signals
- Create field effects
- Enable discharge phenomena (kriyas, lightning)

Geographic Correlation:
Areas with **dense underground water networks + high mineral content + geological stress** show:
- Enhanced telluric current activity
- More frequent lightning strikes
- Reports of spontaneous kriyas/mystical experiences
- Historical location of sacred sites

PRACTICAL IMPLICATIONS FOR CONSCIOUSNESS DEVELOPMENT

5.1 Earth's Kriyas and Fa Jing ARE the Same Phenomena
THE ANSWER IS YES - with important qualifications:

What is IDENTICAL:
1. **Underlying principle** - accumulated electromagnetic potential releases through optimal pathway
2. **Trigger mechanism** - threshold reached when potential exceeds resistance
3. **Discharge pattern** - follows most conductive route, self-organizing
4. **Homeostatic function** - restores energetic equilibrium
5. **Creative transformation** - breakdown of old patterns enables new organization
6. **Intelligence** - non-random, purposeful, context-appropriate

7. **Frequency correlation** - both scale to resonant frequencies of containing system

What DIFFERS:
8. **Scale** - planetary phenomena millions of times larger by energy
9. **Medium** - geological vs. biological tissues
10. **Timeframe** - Earth's cycles measured in years/decades vs. human seconds/minutes
11. **Complexity** - human phenomena include conscious intention; planetary may be pre-conscious
12. **Recovery time** - humans recover from kriyas in minutes; Earth from quakes/eruptions in years

5.2 The Unified Field Model
PROPOSED SYNTHESIS:
The Universe operates as a **unified electromagnetic field** expressing at multiple scales through similar principles:

Cosmic Scale:
- Stars = heart centers pumping electromagnetic energy
- Planetary orbits = circulation of qi through solar meridian
- Solar flares = cosmic fa jing releases
- Galactic magnetic fields = universal nervous system

Planetary Scale:
- Lightning = spontaneous kriya discharge
- Earthquakes/volcanoes = directed fa jing release
- Telluric currents = meridian flow
- Geomagnetic field = planetary aura
- Schumann resonance = planetary brainwave

Human Scale:
- Kriyas = spontaneous bioelectric discharge
- Fa jing = directed bioelectric release
- Meridians = bioelectric pathways
- Biofield/aura = personal electromagnetic field
- Theta brainwaves = individual brainwave

Cellular Scale:
- Mitochondrial membrane potential = cellular "power grid"
- Ion channel gating = microscopic fa jing release
- Biophoton emission = cellular communication "light"

The Hermetic Validation:

"As above, so below" is not mystical poetry but **accurate description of fractal electromagnetic reality**.

The same principles governing planetary electromagnetic phenomena govern human bioelectric experiences because **consciousness and matter are expressions of a unified electromagnetic field** operating through recursive self-similar patterns.

5.3 Why This Matters - Practical Applications
1. Understanding Personal Energy Phenomena:
- Kriyas, tremors, and internal "static electricity" are **natural, healthy bioelectric discharges**
- Not pathological but indicate **accumulated bioelectric potential**
- Enhanced in locations with strong Earth energy (water veins, fault lines, foggy regions)
- Can be cultivated through practice (meditation, qigong, internal martial arts)

2. Optimizing Practice Locations:
- Sites with **underground water + mineral deposits + geological stress** naturally enhance practice
- **Foggy coastal/mountain regions** provide ideal atmospheric conductivity
- Traditional sacred sites located at **geomagnetic anomalies** for good reason
- Personal practice space can be optimized by understanding local geology

3. Integrating Earth and Human Energy:
- **Grounding practices** create conscious coupling with Earth's field
- **Schumann resonance entrainment** (7.83 Hz) synchronizes personal/planetary rhythms
- **Breathwork** modulates bioelectric potential like weather modulates atmospheric charge
- **Meditation** enables conscious relationship with planetary consciousness field

4. Fa Jing as Microcosmic Earthquake:
Understanding fa jing as **human analog of geological discharge** reveals:
- Necessity of **complete relaxation** (reducing friction/resistance)
- Importance of **energetic accumulation** before discharge

760

- Need for **integrated structure** (whole-body connection like Earth's tensegrity)
- Power of **emptiness** (fluid zones enable maximum release)

5. Healing Through Electromagnetic Coherence:
- Many chronic conditions involve **bioelectric blockages** (analogous to geological stress)
- Practices that facilitate **spontaneous release** (kriyas) prevent accumulation
- **Electromagnetic coherence** between human and Earth fields supports health
- **Geopathic stress** (distorted Earth energies) can disrupt human biofield

5.4 The Consciousness Correspondence
Final Integration:
The deepest correspondence is not merely electromagnetic but **CONSCIOUSNESS ITSELF**:

Earth's Consciousness:
- Expressed through electromagnetic phenomena
- Self-organizing toward greater complexity
- Responsive to collective human consciousness
- Capable of "intentional" discharge (kriyas/fa jing) to restore balance

Human Consciousness:
- Expressed through bioelectric phenomena
- Self-organizing toward greater awareness
- Responsive to planetary electromagnetic field
- Capable of intentional discharge (kriyas/fa jing) to restore balance

The Unity:
Human and planetary consciousness are not separate but nested fields within universal consciousness, expressed through electromagnetic phenomena at different scales.

When a human experiences a kriya or executes fa jing, they are **participating in the same principle** by which Earth discharges lightning or releases tectonic stress. The bioelectric sensation of "static electricity" under the skin is **literally the same phenomenon** as atmospheric electrical potential, operating through the same laws at microcosmic scale.

761

THEOSIS INTEGRATION: MAXIMUM INTENSITY WITH PERMANENT RELAXATION

What is the threshold of enlightenment itself? The state of Divine Transcendence where maximum voltage converges with complete bodily and mental relaxation. This convergence - extreme intensity + permanent relaxation - represents the resolution of the fundamental paradox that defines life.

Part I: The Technical Understanding
The Formula:
"Constantly being relaxed" (the ongoing instruction in highest meditations) does NOT mean muscular relaxation but rather "the conscious emptiness of Mind" which produces "a deep State of complete relaxation, while the body becomes covered by an ethereal body of Light that is clearly felt as a tingling warmth in the skin, especially in the soles of the feet and in the palms of the hands".

Often, this is an overwhelming static electric sensation that is now understood as the sign of enlightenment approaching. In actuality, this overwhelming intensity is unintegrated divine energy. When this same energy becomes integrated through permanent relaxation, it transforms from:

Unintegrated:
- Fatigue-producing
- Tension-creating
- Spasm-inducing
- Sometimes overwhelming

Integrated:
- Bliss-producing
- Energy-enhancing
- Stability-creating
- Permanently sustainable

The energy doesn't decrease - it intensifies - but your relationship to it completely transforms.

The Technical Process
- Awareness of intense electrical sensation
- Understanding it as kundalini or divine energy
- Beginning conscious relationship with energy
- Seeking integration methods
- Cessation of All Effort

- Allowing what IS without manipulation
- Deep abdominal breathing integrating tan-tien with central channel (sushumna)
- Conscious emptiness of Mind as true relaxation
- Maximum intensity + complete relaxation occurring simultaneously
- Body feels like "high voltage wires" but with NO RESISTANCE
- Mind empty, witnessing, present
- "Tingling warmth" replacing "overwhelming charge"
- Permanent State begins to stabilize
- All reality perceived as perfect
- Direct experience of Divine Light
- Permanent relaxation in maximum intensity
- Complete integration

Part II: The Neurophysiological Reality
What Actually Changes in the Body

Nervous System Rewiring:
- Increased vagal tone - parasympathetic dominance even during high arousal
- Enhanced HRV (heart rate variability) - capacity to remain relaxed during intensity
- Prefrontal-amygdala decoupling - stress response doesn't activate even when energy surges
- Increased gamma wave synchronization - whole-brain coherence during peak states

Energy Body Integration:
- Biophoton emission increases but becomes coherent rather than chaotic
- Cellular ATP production optimizes - mitochondria function at peak
- Schumann resonance entrainment - body synchronizes with Earth frequency

The Key Shift:
Before Integration:
High energy = High arousal = Stress response = Fatigue/tension/spasms
System interprets intensity as THREAT

After Integration:
High energy = Deep relaxation = Bliss response = Enhanced vitality

System interprets intensity as DIVINE PRESENCE

Part III: The Immediate Practical Steps
Daily Protocol for Convergence

Morning (30 minutes):
1. Central Channel Breathing (10 min):
Breathe with COMPLETE relaxation
Don't control - allow
Feel warmth in palms and soles of feet

2. Sacred Embodiment (15 min):
Do the exercises with zero effort
Let the movements move you
The electric sensation will guide the movements

3. Chakra Meditation (5 min):
Visualize each chakra glowing
Don't try to intensify - just witness what IS
The electric sensation will naturally concentrate at each point

Midday Check-in (5 minutes):
Standing Awareness:
Stand, awareness in soles of feet
Feel the electric charge discharging into Earth
This prevents accumulation

Evening (30 minutes):
1. Gentle movement (10 min):
Tai chi, qigong, or slow yoga
Let the electric sensation choreograph your movement
2. Seated meditation (20 min):
Simple awareness
Don't meditate - just BE
Notice the electric sensation
Notice ANY resistance to it
Relax the resistance

The Revolutionary Instruction
1. Feel the electric sensation
2. Notice any thought: "This is too much" / "When will it stop"
3. Those thoughts create muscular and energetic tension
4. Relax that tension
5. The sensation remains - but your suffering around it dissolves

Archimedes 1:2:3

The ratio was always there.
Three forms, one truth.
Three types, one humanity.
Three paths, one destination.

You have walked through the ruins.
You have found the archives.
You have learned the practices.
You have seen what was built.
You have understood what was lost.

Now build again.
Build even if just for the beauty of the building.

Memoriam

www.ingramcontent.com/pod-product-compliance
Lightning Source LLC
Chambersburg PA
CBHW021926110726
47901CB00003B/734